Y0-BDH-790

THE EMPIRE CITY

THE EMPIRE CITY

PAUL GOODMAN

VINTAGE BOOKS
A DIVISION OF RANDOM HOUSE
NEW YORK

FIRST VINTAGE BOOKS EDITION, April 1977

Published in the United States by Random House, Inc., New York, and simultaneously in Canada by Random House of Canada Limited, Toronto. Originally published by The Bobbs-Merrill Company, Inc., in 1959.

Library of Congress Cataloging in Publication Data

Goodman, Paul, 1911–1972 The empire city.

Reprint of the ed. published by Bobbs-Merrill, Indianapolis.
I. Title.
[PZ3.G6235Em5] [PS3513.0527] 813'.5'2 76-41277
ISBN 0-394-72277-9

Manufactured in the United States of America

Cover painting: Robert Rauschenberg, *Estate,* from the Philadelphia Museum of Art; given by the Friends of the Philadelphia Museum of Art.

In the original edition of *The Empire City* there appeared a single chapter of a proposed Book 5, entitled "Here Begins." Chapter 25 of Book 4, "Spoiling for a Fight," was shifted into Book 5, to give the volume its strong ending. Later Goodman regretted having been talked into this conclusion. Although he wrote one more chapter of Book 5, he never found the action he had predicted would be necessary for him to resume Horatio's adventures. In this edition, the final intent of the author, so far as can be determined, has been followed.

Taylor Stoehr
September, 1976

Preface

"I love you—it's nothing personal."

The Empire City is a teaching of our times in New York City by one for whom the city itself, not its classrooms, is both the source of learning and its object. The project is a tremendous one. Especially if one begins, as Goodman does, not with the etiquette of a social class, or under the enchantment of social ambition or snobbery, but as a sidewalk primitive, one of André Gide's impudent illegitimates, with no obligations to ancestors, with an animal's shrewdness and all data to pick from. "What he really wants is to use the City as a school. Back to Socrates." Not a school for the paltry picturesque, street-scene violence or newcomers' schmaltz of the usual Big City narrative, but for the large idea of man and nature. For to Goodman, the metropolis is the city-dweller's "nature"; the rocky skin and bones of the Empire City belong to Mother Earth herself, the same female he sees stretched out up the Hudson in her original voluptuousness in the sunset. She is to be studied by touching, and the relearning of her body by the city man is Goodman's *scienza nuova.*

Horatio Alger, protagonist of *The Empire City,* starts his education by quitting school. His street-corner curriculum corresponds to the ruses of reality. "He knew the physics of the bounds and rebounds of the Spaulding High-Bouncer from a wooden wall and a cement floor. He knew the chemistry of substitute and preserved foods, which could be read directly on the labels by Federal law. He knew the biology of washrooms . . . In linguistics he knew how to pretend that he came from Brooklyn or the Bronx." These things are only learned in being told—until he started to explain, "he [Horatio] never realized what a lot he knew." It is upon the communication of such knowledge that a city culture must be built. The first merit of Goodman as a writer is his totally unself-conscious acceptance of the facts of our time and place, any of them—a rusting machine standing in an empty lot, a Jewish boys' camp—as ranking with those of all times and places as objects of intellectual and esthetic interest. He was the citizen of his historical situation; in this lay his patriotism.

The Empire City, three of whose four parts were published as separate fictions over a period of twenty years, is an abstract autobiography. In it events that happened to the author and his friends in New York City during the Depression, the war and the postwar years have been converted into parables of their successive ideas and cults.

Horatio's instruction opens in the Depression, when everyone was the ward of Eliphaz, the capitalist, who "wanted to change all use value into exchange value." "The Grand Piano," book of the paupers' luxury, is followed by "The State of Nature," in which Eliphaz becomes a memory, and his dependents are "weeded in" to the War either as soldiers or as pacifists. The setting loose of the beasts gives way to the postwar blues of "The Dead of Spring," which interprets the poisoned atmosphere of New York in those days as an emanation of the forgotten corpses of the War. Finally comes "The Holy Terror," the present "sociolatry" in which success cannot be escaped even by the radical critic—"I felt I had something to contribute and I got up to speak. To my amazement I was met by a round of unanimous applause instead of the scattering I had hitherto always encountered." In this period Horatio attends PTA meetings. Obviously, this history is thoroughly relevant to the 1970's.

The Empire City could have been subtitled "The Memoirs of an Ideologist." Not only is his hero a street urchin, the novel itself is, among other things, a tract on behalf of urchinism. Unlike naïve conceptualists and joiners, Goodman takes in ideas in order to get rid of them—"back to Socrates," indeed! In this "education" in reverse, the characters learn (or unlearn) by teaching. In every episode they scent a lesson to be passed on to others. Conversations consist of revelations of unique experiences, or at least hints; occasionally, summaries of the points are drawn up; when necessary a mass meeting is held. At times the author cannot help but step out of character and add his bit; who can blame him?—if he held on to his notion instead of passing it on, it might impede his development. While other intellectuals like to talk about "putting things into question," with Goodman questions and answers keep turning into each other to form a kind of biological increment.

Of the four books, the one I like best is Number Three, "The Dead of Spring," perhaps because the intangible processes of ideological liquidation characteristic of America in the postwar years responded to Goodman's idea-burying passion; here, longer, more narrative chapters draw the reader in, while the rhetoric broods instead of buttonholing—the anguished passage on "dark fire" has the eloquence of a Shakespearean clown.

Goodman as teacher does not merely show facts; what he shows is an example. The exemplary tale turns toward allegory—it contends that this is the way things are at bottom. But for allegory the master must be convinced that he knows the answer. Goodman has no answer, though he is loaded with answers. Like a good student of Aristotle and medieval logic, he conceives life as a problem; like a proper child of the present century, he sees all solutions stamped with the Indian sign of inevitable failure. *The Empire City* has the look of allegory, with the non-natural ways of its happenings and its cast of personifications. Horatio, the sharp-eyed street Arab; Mr. Moneybags Eliphaz; Mynheer Duyck Duyvendak, rationalistic Father Knickerbocker; Lothair, the romantic radical. But New York is the city neither of God nor of Karl Marx; and having recited his parable, our sage must invent another tale of foxes and grapes with which to take it back. Here, in the real world, Goodman knows (as some vanguard novelists of the seventies do not) you can't even depend on it that things will be lousy.

The Empire City is not an allegory but a fabulous adventure amid the commonplace, thus a true descendent of the Horatio Alger tales. A psychiatrist and social scientist as well as a storyteller, Goodman makes everything—the way people sit at lunch counters, why one takes the trouble to make a million—the business of his speculation, and a drama out of speculating his way out of his speculations.

To risk the cold cash of experience for the profits of theory does not, of course, always pay off. Parts of *The Empire City* are definitely under water; yet even in these waters appear the markers of Goodman's lobster pots. "She looked grander than life size, like a queen of Memphis. When she kneeled with her child, playing with toys, they seemed to be two giants, a greater and a smaller, and the toys no toys at all but our towns. Our ranch houses and cars and cannon were the size of toys, but the mother and child were flesh and blood larger than a cathedral."

Goodman knows what is hidden from other ideologists: that the secret of the ideological age is a hunger for miracles. Mass belief and action aim at evocation—as Sartre has pointed out, a Communist demonstration, though it be devoid of practical results, has the function of a testamentary ritual. To Goodman every doing is a sacrament or ought to be. What did not change in him over the years was his belief that man ought to pour out his energies as an oblation to the opening of the heavens.

The most accessible miracle, the old reliable, is sex, but there are others. Sex in *The Empire City* is therapeutic, sociological, political, philanthropic—in a word, the sex of sex-reform, of "outspokenness" and "healthy relations," as much as of the wonder of creation. Horatio is Eros, Eros is a therapist and the therapist is Paul Goodman. As impulse and reflection "become one feeling of faith" in the gift to be received, art and thinking become ways of praying for it, that is, ways of evoking and seducing, which are the same thing. In Goodman's esthetic, writing a novel is an exercise in calling up intentional dreams that will act as a love charm to entice the world, with a second intimate spell to affect the close ones.

As a priest of enthusiasms Goodman centers his teaching on what follows from attempts to work natural magic in public. On the streets of the Empire City a visible sacrament may bring down shame or even trouble with the police. Perhaps this is as it should be, but Goodman has a classicist's revulsion to hiding in hotel rooms. Let the whole city become a sacred grove "and over it all an exulting community spirit." Only the public presence can make the magic real.

The celebrant thus turns into a philosopher of the reconstituted community. And his outlook contains a principle that is beyond modern ideologies: that "a community occasion takes place under God's providence." Yet God's oversight only emphasizes that community ecstasies occur at the expense of privacy. Goodman is thoroughly aware of this, and approves. Other utopians keep their shared excitements for the end, when the phalansteries are set up and in working order. Goodman menaces privacy at every step. Indeed, for him, it is the hiding that is "dirty," not anything done under human impulse or appetite. In that it demands this basic revision of the individual's attitude toward himself and of his sentiment toward others, his revolution is total.

Happily, however, Goodman's threat to privacy remains a private one. For as an ideologist in retreat from ideologies—in one of his essays he even questions whether freedom is not weakened by the ideal of freedom—Goodman is never a mere agitator. He does not wish to organize a force for his desire, having so deep a belief in desire as a force. By testing in actual and imagined situations how far this belief in the efficacy of desires is to be trusted, the celebrant passes through the ideologist into the sage. Goodman's description of Eliphaz's mind is evidence of his adeptness in a duality of outlook that is the opposite of fanaticism. "As a wise man, he had the same thoughts by impulse as by reflection, in the dead of night as by daylight. The difference was that by impulse and at night he thrilled with delight at the prospect of an abyss; by day and on reflection, he was prudent. It is as these feelings gradually become one feeling of faith that a wise man grows into a sage."

With its "acting out" amid frustrations of the wonder-working fulfillment of desire, Goodman's fable of ideologies is also an epic of infantilism, including in this term its New Testament meaning as a synonym for resurrection. Children and animals snuggle against the tireless debates of this "romance of spontaneous joy, freedom and fraternity"—I am reminded of a photo in The Lion House in Salt Lake City of Brigham Young, also a miracle maker through fecundity, lost in a mob of his offspring and his wives. *The Empire City* is written in the perspective of nature's newcomers who take nothing for granted and to whom the race of adults is simply a breed of larger animals that behave like lunatics. The chapter "On The Shore" in Book Three, in which a baby girl plays in the surf, is the high point of writing in the work; its low is Horatio's comic-book argut—"ourn," "gee you're green," "'cause"—as the boy philosopher of Book One.

Dramatically speaking, the sage runs the risk of being a bore—Dostoyevsky, for example, recognized this risk in creating Prince Myshkin and other enlighteners, and strove consciously to overcome it. Whether as American scout leader or sanctified messenger from Moscow, Rome or the Dark Mothers, the sage can draw lessons from events only at the price of emptying them of interest. Most novelists try to reduce this price through devices for "letting the facts speak for themselves"; Goodman multiplies it by making every character into a personification of his own brand of wisdom. Above his metropolis hovers the Buddha, Christ, Zarathustra, in a ring of disciples. This basic image draws Goodman into traditional scriptural conceits; it leads to phrases such as "they drew back from him . . . his eyes flooded with tears and he got up and went." The Knower, with his Reichean pantomime of eroticism, suffering, fury, defiance, supplies—for example, in Chapter Three of Book Four, entitled "Dancing,"—a reverse kind of farce in *The Empire City*.

The novelist is a different kind of writer from the fabulist—his talent includes listening to his audience while it listens to him, and yielding to it for the sake of the story. The novelist is the most compliant among artists; no meaning in his tale stands higher for him than its power to catch him hearers. Goodman is eager to be listened to too, but on his own terms, not at any cost. It is not from the novelists that he has derived the measure of his ingratiation. His affinities are with philosophers and poets, particularly the seekers of the absolute and of intoxication: Rilke, Kafka, Cocteau, Mallarmé.

By the end of *The Empire City*, Goodman has almost succeeded in getting rid of ideas. Thus his fable has, finally, the quality of a true novel, in that by living through its incidents a development of character has taken place and an outcome has been reached: the catharsis of concepts. But however one judges *The Empire City* as a novel, there is no doubt that it is a great book—as one might say of Melville's *Mardi* that it is a great book though it does not maintain a continuous narrative grip on the reader. Goodman has the humor, high and low, of a never-failing contradictory intelligence, plus the exuberance of one who has been visited by the animal faith—with which Horatio's education is concluded—that there are weapons "that do not weigh one down" and that the lover of life has also on his side "the force that is in the heart of matter, that, as if stubbornly, makes things exist rather than be mere dreams or wishes."

Harold Rosenberg

New York

THE EMPIRE CITY

CONTENTS

BOOK 1 THE GRAND PIANO

Before a War

for Alice

Whoever makes an idol for others, although he is punished with stripes, is nevertheless allowed remuneration for his labors. The reason is that an idol does not become forbidden till it is completed; and the last tap of the hammer is worth less than a *perutah*.

—MAIMONIDES, *Mishneh Torah*

Chapter 1 ▪ CONVERSATIONS BETWEEN MYNHEER AND HORATIO

1.

"Boy, do you want to make a quarter?"

"Budge Only for Folding Money," said Horatio sententiously, and he continued to spell out headlines on the newsstand. It was his morning lesson in reading.

"See here—

THERE'S PLENTY OF TROUBLE

—that's 'count of Eliphaz." Eliphaz was a magnate who fished in troubled waters and also stirred them up. The boy pointed to another column of no good news: "Informed quarters say this is Eliphaz too. 'Informed quarters,' that's good, ain't it?" As with many other active and amorous boys his fingernails were neatly bitten to the quick. "And I personally happen to know that *this* is!" Turning over the paper he pointed triumphantly to an item at the bottom:

VICE SQUAD
ROUND-UP
MME. VANETSKA
NEW CZARINA

"Come around tomorrow, we provide chairs," said the owner of the stationery store.

"Shall I buy you the paper?"

"Naw, that'll do for this A.M.," said Horatio. "That's some Eliphaz!" His face glowed with pleasure as he was able to talk about his model hero. But although he had a strong slogan that, One Thing Leads to Another, he little realized that through Mynheer Duyck Colijn, this young man who had accosted him on the corner, he would soon come face to face with Eliphaz himself.

No fool, little Horatio had already seen Mynheer half a dozen times before, but Dyck, who had no eyes in his head, had never seen him. "He wants me to make a date for him with Sis upstairs, but he don't even know she's my sis. There he's got the envelope stickin' outta his pocket. Maybe I will an' then again maybe I won't. Will for what I can get."

This envelope contained an invitation to a performance of *The Mastersingers* on Friday at the Imperial Opera.

Now Horatio was jealous of anyone who wanted to have sexual relations with his sister. He had understood this clearly two years ago, but by now he had forgotten it. His animosity now took the form of resentment that such a fool should aspire so high; of shame that she, betrayed no doubt by lust, should sink to the gutter.

The Dutchman seemed to be rich—on such a point Horatio distrusted appearances; he had a wonderful pearl runabout of European make, parked round the corner to preserve his anonymity. "Does he think people are idiots?" thought the boy vindictively. "This idiot walks along and never notices who's on the other side o' the street, then he lays his plans accordingly. . . . I'll write it down!" he resolved, for like Hamlet he kept a notebook, but unlike Hamlet's, his were maxims of action, not to stall action. *"I hate the Dutchman. Why? I don't know. 'Cause I hate him, I see he's a fool. I hate him 'count of L."* From this discovery began the end of his hatred for the Dutchman.

From a certain point of view Horatio's family was poor; they were on the relief rolls twice one-and-a-half, or three times: Sis and her dependent Horatio, brother Lothario and his dependent Horatio. But this was solid money, the interest of the wealth of the empire itself. Did Mynheer have as good?

The small boy was lonely. Perhaps he could come to like Mynheer as much as he hated his brother Lothario.

He said: "Here—this paper hates Eliphaz!" It was a radical paper.

"It does and it doesn't," said Dyck surprisingly, as if he knew something about politics. *"Why aren't you in school?"*

"What do you mean it does an' it doesn't! If you'd read it instead o' shootin' your mouth off, you'd know they hate him like poison."

"When you get older, you'll understand about these things. Look here, *why aren't you in school?"*

"When I get older I'll be a fool too," cried Horace. Now he was beating around desperately to avoid that question a third time, so that he violated one of his strongest slogans, Never Make an Offer. "I'll carry that there letter for a dollar."

If a question gets to be asked three times, it is too obvious that you are avoiding it, just as if an Angel calls your name thrice, you had better answer him.

"Oh? Do you know Miss Sis Alger?"

"Yeah, I know her. 'Partment 44C." Betrayed by fear, he violated another rule, Never Let On.

Dyck gave him the letter and the dollar and said, "There's an answer. I'll wait right here."

"Wait up——" said Horace, and was lost. "Do you mean that this paper tells *lies?*"

"No-o-o, not lies. There is such a thing as a party line, an official story. By the way, *why aren't you in school?*"

In a flash—his face went white—the small boy grasped the idea that not only speech could be deceptive, but even *printing.* This he had never thought of—it was because he didn't understand the process of setting type and making the impression, that these things are also done by men, and he had therefore thought of them as ultimate data.

In a flash—his face went white—he realized that the question had been thrice repeated and suspicion was rife. "Miss Stillwagon sent me out to buy stamps," he said.

"Oh, if you're on an errand for your teacher, of course you can't run an errand for me." And Dyck took both the letter and the dollar bill from his nerveless fingers.

The boy looked away and the tears flooded his eyes. Unlike his serious picture of himself, he was merry and subject to fits of tears.

Though he had already forgotten many things, at the age of eleven going on twelve Horatio was at the acme of the human powers, close enough to original desire (and that desire stormily reviving) not to be befuddled by associations of associations of ideas, not to be resigned to second-best choices, to painful substitutes for satisfaction that get you into even hotter water than if you stuck to what you really wanted. All over his notebook he now scribbled, *"Lies Lies Literature is Lies."*

But handsome Sir Dyck, Mynheer Duyck Duyvendak of Zeebrugge, was also not such a fool as Horace thought. In the general war in the Indies his wealth was in escrow; but he, taking advantage of the lag of the perhaps bygone structure of the world (nobody knew for sure), was living on credit unlimited.

The clock in the barbershop touched ten and the long bell from the tiled hall of Public School 46 jangled up the avenue three blocks. Now was the hour to avoid truant officers! Sometimes Horatio went among the concrete arches of the viaduct to make running comments to the engineers; sometimes he searched for epigraphical remains on older walls and in tunnels; or he sharpened his knife to whittle homunculi; or he went fishing for the finless eels.

Turning his tear-stained face to the other, he sobbed, "Now you'll watch if I go back to that school an' I'll have to run an awful risk. Why the fuck don't you mind your own business?"

He had resolved to confess to this tall fellow his secret, the first of anyone in the entire world! But if Dyck was now going to let him down and go away, he'd sit on the ground and bawl for loneliness.

"I was goin' to take my wheel apart an' fix the brake," he sobbed, "but now I can't an' I'll be killed. Lot you care."

"What's the matter, boy?" ("I don't think it's the dollar," thought Dyck.) "Here is the dollar back."

"You can keep your lousy dollar! Thanks," he said, pocketing it.

Horatio made up his mind to be now almost perfectly truthful, for he knew better than anyone how far astray you can go if you start with an ambiguity or even a flat lie.

"What's your name? My name's Roger," said Dyck, holding out his hand to shake.

"My name's Tony," said Horatio.

"What! Is he making a pass at me?" he thought, for he had come across this handshake come-on before. But this notion struck him so brightly that his tears dried up in the sun of it and a burst of amusement lit his face. This likelihood, of which he was confident, suddenly assuaged all his resentment of the relation of Dyck and Laura. Yet he was *still* resolved to confide in him, for he liked him sex or no sex. They shook hands and Dyck pressed his hand comfortingly. "Worse an' worse," thought little Horace, "next he'll ask if I'm a Boy Scout. He'll shake my hand in the scout shake an' tickle my palm."

"Why don't we take a drive in your Mercedes parked round the corner?" said Horace. "But first buy me an ice-cream cone. Come along, Danton!" And his little dog leaped up on him in ecstasy and trotted ahead.

Dyck let himself be conducted.

2. A Nonregistration

"I was never to school one day in my life," said Horace. "My muvver—she's post-mort'm now—took me to register when I was six, just like everybody else; but I looked sharp an' I stole the records."

"*Did* you?" said Dyck with lively interest.

"Woman there with red hair wrote it all down on a card how I'll come back next day an' be put in a *class,* but I sneak back and watch till she went to the toilet, an' I stole it!"

"How did you know which was yours? Weren't all the cards in a box?"

"Naw—it was still on the table. Anyway, I can read my name printed since I was two months old.

"If you don't steal it *then* when it's first new," cried Horatio Alger, "then you're *sunk!* Then they copy it an' they have all kinds o' *records.* I know all about that. They send *copies* of it to all the departments o' the whole empire. It says whether you're white or black or yellow an' which diseases you got an' whether you're married or single." This was the questionnaire for military conscripts which he had seen in a newspaper. "They send it to a *teacher* an' you're clapped into a *class!* Says who's dumb an' who's smart, an' who screws his sister an' who hates his brother. Then all the teachers have a *list,* an' they make copies o' these lists too, so soon there are *thousands* o' copies. It has your address on so they can always *find* you. An' they clap 'em all into iron boxes like you said. I seen them there, I been around. Then there are also *report* cards! Says who's good an' who's *bad*—that's deportment."

"Yes, that's deportment."

"But if you catch them at the neat minute," said Horace in a loud voice, while they flew through space in the powerful car, on the rolling world, in our solar system bound for Hercules, *"there is no record in the whole world!* They don't even *start* to look for you."

The Dutchman laughed for joy, and the tears started into his eyes because of his own wasted childhood.

"It's no joke," cried the boy, " 'cause if they once start to look for you, they'll surely always find you. I've seen it. I *know.* My friend Timmy was caught by the troo'nt officer——" This was a big boy picked up by the police for robbing a grocer with a toy gun. "Now they even got a *picture* o' him. Thumbprints. He's sunk."

"Yes, you've got to catch them at the neat minute——" said Dyck.

"Not a minute too soon—not a minute too late!" cried the boy.

"But then you're free forever!"

"Oh, no, *oh,* no, what do you think? Are you nuts? You *still* got to watch your step!"

"Why are you telling this to me? Supposing this minute I took you to a school and put your name down; eh, Tony?"

"Oh, you're safe," said Horace, " 'cause you're scared I could tell the cops you made a pass at me."

Mynheer jammed the screaming brakes—amid the outcries of horns, there was almost a pile-up on the highway.

"Nix, nix," said Horace through clenched teeth. "When there's accidents they make you show your license an' One Thing Leads to Another. You better let me out."

A motorcycle pulled alongside at once, with its looming policeman. The boy went white again. But as soon as Mynheer exhibited his license with its mysterious consular privileges, the officer touched his cap respectfully. "Try to be more cautious on this new drive, sir," he said gently. "We haven't had a bad one yet and we're trying to keep the record clean."

A hand raised in wonder, the boy stared at the little license case dangling from the key.

"The system is not so perfect as you believe," said Mynheer as they drove on. "You see, he is merely preserving us all from destruction."

He himself had no precise idea how far he was privileged; the law has loopholes. But with a perfect confidence, with an affectation of perfect confidence, he took for granted, tentatively, his freedom in each situation as it arose.

"It's only the Creator of the heavens and the earth you *have* to respect," he said.

"Do you think it's fair?" said Horatio. "I can't even ride my new wheel safe any more 'cause they're goin' to make 'em have licenses. I seen it in the papers yesterday. Do you think they let me roll on a highway like this? Not much. I ride on the back streets an' up an' down the alleys."

3.

"Do you always say the teacher sent you to buy stamps?"

"Only on that corner where I know who's who. Sometimes I say that my family had a moider. If it's an old woman, I say I'm just gettin' over polio; that's great. Other times I tell 'em my mother—who's really post-mort'm—is a schoolteacher an' won't send me 'cause it stinks. A good one is: when a lady asks you say, I'm ashamed to tell, it's dirty, and burst out laughing or crying, depending. Or the Boy Scouts are goin' to call on the Mayor. I can make these up by the million—I'm good at it. You tell tramps you're playin' hooky an' they say, That's the right spirit! an' give you a roll-your-own cigarette that you can stick up a pig's ass."

Best of all was to say—nothing. But it was better to tell a flat lie than an ambiguity such as, Don't have school today, because this led to *more* questions. You must plan a conversation like a game of checkers with the object that the other person should have no next move. Thus, the following was wrong:

A.: "Why aren't you in school?"

B.: "Teacher sent me for stamps."

A.: "She's got her crust, on the taxpayer's money! Does she always send *you* out. . . . You must be teacher's pet. . . . I'll walk you back that way, etc."

But the following was right:

A. (a lady): "Why, etc."

B.: "I'm shamed to tell, it's dirty" with a wild laugh. Then, either she stops or she's safe. A two-move game. But even so, the more definite the stop, the more curiosity, resentment, inquiry, later. She tells her neighbor, grills her little boy; this leads to a general investigation and all the unsolved misdemeanors are attributed to you. You get a bad reputation. Therefore, this gambit was absolutely only for transient neighborhoods; yet how could one tell which neighborhood is transient, for the interesting and the desirable always live round the strange corner? Therefore–never. It's great, but the time to use it is–never.

Regarding the case in a somewhat exterior way–for no one can comprehend that another person is really in earnest–Mynheer asked, "Don't you want to see what it's like in school?"

With silence, with disgust and agony, the small boy stared in front with eyes preternaturally wide. His hairs rose on his head. The entrails within him violently contracted so that he urinated, and his heart was visibly pounding. His breath came short. He was like a man who sees on a platter before him a bleeding slice of his totem animal.

Once, to escape an officious accompanist, he found himself in the school. There was infernal noise. In a stone court many were clumsily tramping in a circle, rhythmically shouting,

Oafy bees!
barley boes!
oafy bees!
barley boes!

while a great woman rang on a piano that had not been tuned since 1905. *"You,"* a woman shouted, advancing on him like an avalanche, *"which is your class?"* He ran down a hall where some of the doors were open and the little boys, he could see, had their hands chained to the tables. Some of the teachers had pointed sticks. *Aw Glay Dan Zing!* The Incantation! An earsplitting bell jangled. And now chaos involved him, for the rooms poured out their thousands, some freely, some marching and tramping. He was caught between converging groups, like the traffic coming at you when you mistakenly turn your bicycle up a down-way street. There was an iron cage with ringing stairs; the legs were swallowed up as the children ascended. He backed defensively into this stairway, and fell. . . . Next he was running rapidly down a corridor while great angry women appeared in the doorway, but they were too clumsy to pursue the nimble boy; from the rooms there were shouts and cheers of the prisoners, and these gave him heart. But now

Mrs. T (he never thought that *she* would be there, that large lady who took him into the movies), appeared serenely sailing, like a ship up New York Harbor. "Good morning, Horatio," she said, and sailed on. There was then silence everywhere. After long wandering in this maze he emerged more dead than alive on Amsterdam Avenue.

"Horatio! Horatio, is it? You said your name was Tony, you little liar. Why should I believe any of the rest of it?"

"Then don't."

"Horatio–Alger!" said the well-read Dutchman, heartlessly smiling at his literary allusion.

"Found out!" thought Horace, but he didn't care if he was. Surely he was looking for someone to find him out. "Joker," he said.

"What?" cried Mynheer. "Don't the American boys read this author any more? In Zeebrugge he was considered a fine genre realist. He was a kind of humanitarian and idealist who wrote in 1890 as if it were 1840. He colonized New York newsboys in the West."

4.

They were now across the Hudson River, that has no peer in Europe or the East.

"This is the time o' day I gen'lly feed the dog," hinted Horatio.

They were passing Luis Mendoza's roadhouse.

"I can't eat in *this* place," said Dyck indignantly.

"Looks great to me. What's wrong with it?"

"His neon sign! It's a blot on the Palisades. When first I came to the Empire City," said Mynheer, "because of the descriptions in certain old letters in my family, I looked across the river with anticipation–and there was this sign, like a slap across the eyes."

Nevertheless, they drove in. With a kind of paralysis of will, Dyck fatuously confronted himself with the thought that his heroic little friend did not know what was fitting and proper, the same boy who was to be the most courtly warrior ever taught on the streets of our Empire City. Dyck, like all who attach their energy to the forms of things, could not see causes and effects, that the contrary comes from its contrary, that we are educated for what we are not educated for.

Horatio ordered everything he had never before eaten and waited anxiously for it to appear. Danton sat at the table with a napkin, just like the dogs in Amsterdam.

Now in his lapel the waiter had a little sign of a fiery hand.

"What do you want to be when you grow up?" said Dyck, making conversation. It was the wrong note.

"I am grown-up," said Horace ominously.

"Well, you've won your one-move game. Enjoy it." And on a sunny place on the cloth Dyck began meticulously to build sugar cubes into a white art object, manner of De Stijl. He paid the boy no more attention.

"I want to be Eliphaz," said Horace finally.

"Another Eliphaz? Isn't one enough?" said Mynheer, but he went on with his tableware sculpture because it was taking shape.

"There's room for *only* one," said Horace laconically.

"Wouldn't you like to be a sailor, boy?" asked Dyck, who had been a naval lieutenant in Java and Bali.

"Never guv it a thought. Maybe I would, and then again maybe I wouldn't."

While he halved a cube diagonally with the precision of the diamond cutter, his maternal great-grandfather, Mynheer described the sea and its ships and the storms in the islands.

"Who owns those ships?" said Horace.

"Must you own them too?" Mynheer was hurt. With strong formal violence he added a twist of tinfoil to his sculpture, another texture, almost another color. "If you want to be a boss-man why don't you become a policeman?"

"Don't make me laugh. The cops are scared o' even you."

Yet maybe at the sound of that word policeman, he lost his appetite and the tears rose to his eyes. "Don't wanta boss *anybody,*" he said. "Want 'em to leave me alone so I don't have to hide. I don't wanta *be* anybody else either. I don't wanta *have* to do what nobody else ever tells me about anythin'. Is that clear?"

"What are you crying about?"

"I go with you an' you insult me an' tell me I'm not grown-up an' don't understand an'—I could say somethin' about you too if I wanted."

"Cry, cry, man—it makes no difference who sees."

"Ain't it bad enough that the minutes are flying by like a snowstorm?"

From his tumbler Dyck fished out a piece of ice and rested it, glistening, among the cubes and the foil. "Do you like it?" he asked.

"What! Do you like that shit too?" said the boy scornfully.

"Too!" said Dyck, and his nostrils flared. "What do you mean, 'too'?"

"What do you mean what do I mean?"

"You said 'too.' Who's 'too'?"

"It's the little brother!" realized Mynheer, astounded. "The name is really Alger! Am I a moron!" He was trembling with longing, now fortified by pride and love for Sis's little brother *too*. He thought it was the "too" that had put him on the track. But it was that the boy had ordered oyster stew; it was the gesture of disdain with the left pinkie; the tilt of the nose that went with the sharp contradiction. Now the situation was crowded with references; and he took the small gold ring from his own little finger and balanced it precariously on the angle of a cube.

"At least when I make these," he said, "nobody decides *for* me what to put here or there."

"That's what you think," said Horace; for preparatory to serving the salad, the waiter swept everything off the table onto his tray—but not the deathless proportions.

"Give me my ring, please," said Mynheer Duyck Duyvendak imperturbably. "Bring me a lemon, a clove of garlic, and some paprika. We'll mix the dressing ourselves. . . . Do you have any brothers or sisters, Horatio?" he asked quietly.

"If newspapers tell *lies*," cried Horatio passionately, "maybe there ain't any Eliphaz after all."

"He exists, don't worry."

"I know that, you dope. I seen him when they launched the S.S. *Tuscaloosa*, heavy cruiser, twelve thousand tons. (Cruisers is named for cities.) His daughter Emily broke a bottle on it."

"I was there."

"You bet you were. Only you wasn't on the program as no Roger. You leave my sister alone, Duyvendak," said Horace hotly.

Dyck had failed to make the least amorous gesture toward him, and his resentment against his sister's beau began to flare up again.

"Now don't you believe everything you read in the papers, Horatio Alger, that's just what I've been telling you," said Dyck, for he imagined that Horace's heat was in reference to the repeated false announcements that he and Emily Eliphaz were to be married; which was *her* idea, but it wasn't his idea at all. "Why don't you read a book sometimes instead of newspapers? Do you belong to the library?"

"No!" cried the boy in terror. The library was almost as bad as the school; it was worse, because there the silence fell without a command.

"What's the matter now?"

"What's the use? You yourself said that what's printed is a lie just as bad as when you talk." Horace had thought that if he could stay out of school; if he could avoid the officers; if he could range the streets of our Empire City for social studies, and learn the geography of catastrophe from the newspaper maps—this would give him an advantage, an advantage. But in one instant he saw that he was in the prison of maya as far off as China.

"Look, boy," said the Dutchman compassionately, and took his hands across the table. Horace brightened up and assumed a sly expression. "Their system isn't perfect. You see how even you have been able to get away with murder. I'm stoned with admiration. It's not perfect, it's too big to be perfect. From a certain point of view the loopholes are even part of such perfection as it has. There are books—" he said sententiously—"*there are books in which every sentence is true.*"

"*Are* there? Which one? So help me, I'll look it up."

"Hm. For instance—the *Paradoxes of Zeno.*"

"What's that?" said Horace dully.

"You'll know about that too when you get a little older."

"God help my sis—if she ever marries a dope like you!" said Horace in a white fury, because what he wanted above all was *not* to grow up, judging by the results. "But I'll queer it. Maybe you think, you dope, that she's as rich as Emily Eliphaz. She's on the relief, that's where she is! . . . Maybe you're right! From now on I won't try any more not to be a dope. I won't read nothin' except books. I'll get a *modus vivendi.* I'll spend the whole day makin' wooden homunculi. What do I care if they train me up to be a soldier an' fight in the Philippine Islands an' Java? My sis will be ashamed of me when I wear a uniform instead of my faded red jersey, but I'll laugh behind their backs. Cops an' soldiers all around me, but I'll just laugh up my sleeve. Teachers—let 'em catch me, I don't care—'cause I'm just laughin' up my sleeve. Ha, ha!"

Dyck looked at him at a loss. Like a well-read person, he no longer remembered how simple cogent arguments can awaken infinite dismay. But again like those well-read persons, he was especially susceptible to the contagion of any real display of feeling, and his iron tentative confidence was disturbed. He did not know, since every spot was sore, where to begin to offer consolation.

5. A View of New York

But when they came back to New York and parked and climbed out in the underparts of the city, in these haunts Horatio was at home; at ease and well informed. It was his advantage, given to few, to begin his education from under the ground up.

There was a concrete viaduct through the arches of which Horatius conducted the nobleman to study the writings on the walls: declarations of mutual love made either before, or after, or in the place of the acts of desire; statements of vaguer aspiration expressed in random monosyllables; of longing, accompanied by telephone numbers and the dates of prospective rendezvous. Political convictions; racial opinions. So many *names,* some graven into the very concrete when it was still moist; lists of boys and girls together and in their *confréries* and sororities.

"Under the places where some people drive, you see," said the guide, "all kinds o' things get written by other people." He pointed to a series of hearts in various alcoves:

"A great lover," he explained. In another place was the angry invective: LOUSE IS A HOOR & DOES IT FOR MONY. THE GREEN HORNIT. "She stood him up; he was mad; I had 'em both." Elsewhere in an ornate oblong border was the whole list, which the police would like to know, of those dangerous lads called

RED DEVILS

It was not a random scatter. Some galleries were quite blank; others were decorated with dozens of diagrams and pictures, even nearer than writing to the original dreams.

"It's 'cause they copy. Only the first is made up," explained Horatius. "The others just copy. If it's initials they write initials. If it's pictures they try to draw pitchers."

"That's because this writing isn't really intentional; they don't know what they're doing," explained Dyck.

"Correct! See, this wall here for instance. It was empty till I wrote that word on it, and now look at it. Some queers come here at night and write in the pitch dark. They're scairt o' their own shadows. In spring this place is a center of activity, you wouldn't believe it.

"You see the same copyin' worse in other places—I don't need to tell you 'bout that," he said modestly, referring to public toilets. He pointed to a legend:

DANNY LOVES BETTY

"She wrote that herself to put the idea in his mind."

Everywhere were also *dates,* the dates of the inscription, sometimes nothing but the date of the preoccupation:

1939 1939 1939 1939

"This is where I see I was gettin' old an' soon be dead like my mom," said Horatius. "I'm half as old as my brother already." (Lothario was in fact 27.)

"What, is *he* dead?" asked Dyck shrewdly.

Horace looked up quickly; what had been found out now? "Let me show you a thing or two this way," he said, and led him to a distant gallery where barely visible was the legend:

I HAT MY BRUDER LIK POSN

"Some dope wrote that ten years ago," said Horace.

Another wall proclaimed:

SUAZO TROEL AMURA

"What's this mean? Are they three names or one? Is it a sentence?"

Horatio answered nothing.

"What *is* this strange message? Don't you know?"

"I'm not sayin' I don't know. Then again, I'm not sayin' I do know."

"It's just the teaser of an advertising campaign."

"Is that what you think? You better think again. . . . I know everybody whose names an' initials is on the walls!" cried Horatius proudly. "See this ball team—GINTS—that's my team." He pointed out a name, JERY, 3B—"that's me. My gang, we hook cigars an' candy. This is me: TIMMY."

"How do you keep it all straight?"

"Easy. I got a notebook o' the past an' future."

"But what do you tell them about yourself."

"Different lies."

Enthusiasm for himself, for his role, for his beautiful friends, made him sublime; his head struck the stars; his eyes shone in the demidark. "Him, me, her—I know 'em one an' all."

Down here even the presumptuous posters, with their injunctions to pay out money for despicable commodities, were not allowed to shine in their insolence, but were darkened by mustaches and the accentuation of what all men desired.

In the round apertures the sunlight cast the blackest shadows cut by arcs of brilliant white. The ground was hilly, and where the arcade was low it seemed to leap swiftly from pier to pier; where high, the arches seemed to stand under a strain of the weight; where it was mean, the arcade stood in architectural repose, very light and easy. Here on the riverside was a beautiful urban atmosphere, for the massy structures and the hurrying thousands had all about them a large free space, so that there seemed to be the conditions of an almost possible existence. Among these arches the two human beings and the dog were tiny. The river

was flowing at its own sweet will.

A large boy was leaning over the balustrade and disconsolately staring at the water.

"That's Eaghan on the hook again," explained Horace. "He's a feature o' the place."

"Doesn't he ever go to school?"

"He can't keep up with the work," explained Horace. "Most o' them play the hook 'cause they can't keep up with the work."

"Don't any of them get bored just because they're too smart and it's nicer outside?" Such was Mynheer's romantic self-projection.

"I have heard o' them on the hook because they can't keep up with the work; I have not heard of anyone playin' the hook 'cause he was too smart."

"But if he stays away it gets worse, doesn't it?"

"Worse and worse."

"Why doesn't he quit?"

"Ha! Gee, you're green. Then they get the police after 'm an he goes to jail school."

"What difference does it make to them whether or not he goes to school?"

"They can't let a single one get away," said Horace, "otherwise they don't land up in the army! Hiya, Eaghan!" he cried.

Eaghan's face brightened a thousandfold as he turned, with a start, to some object to occupy his vacant mind. "Hiya, Louie!" he said to Horatio.

Mynheer could see at a glance, from the scrofulous complexion and discolored eyes, the physical causes of Eaghan's deficiency.

Chapter 2 ▪ THE HOME OF HUGO ELIPHAZ

1. How Eliphaz's Home Was a Department Store

In the Empire City, the façades of the rich neighborhood were more anonymous than those of the poor. The poker face of Park Avenue told little, and threatened much. Here no Irish pennants hung out the windows to reveal that they still wore old-fashioned red drawers; nor was degeneration allowed to work its unequalizing changes, but everything was kept tiptop.

This orderly reticence was a symbol of stronger class agreement than the poor have, and it was a protection.

Hugo Eliphaz, however, could not bear these manners; he had nothing but contempt for their snobbery and timidity. "Please!" he used to say. "Are they ashamed that we were merchants? But we are still merchants." And his own place on 79th Street was a daily scandal of disorder that the Park Avenue Association tried to put a stop to in vain, because he was the Park Avenue Association. From early in the morning activity poured out on the sidewalk. Delivery trucks and moving vans blocked the traffic. And the doorman sometimes worked.

"In the old days," said Eliphaz, "we lived in the back of the shop. That was because we liked our work. The children too took their turns behind the counter and then we had something to talk about at the supper table. Do you think I could get my good-for-nothings to? For them it was the Lincoln School, to learn by doing. And what would Abe have thought about it all?"

But the business *had* expanded, and a visitor to his rooms upstairs was astounded. Apollo Leader of the Muses (in pawn from the Vatican) stood gently poised in the rotunda, where plasterers and electricians came and went making alterations. Eliphaz loved to make alterations and have new Rooms, a Georgian Room, a Queen Anne's Room, that he transferred from the Victoria and Albert Museum in London. From beautiful room to room the porters were carrying furniture in and out, lowering it through the windows from the roof, or dropping it with a crash to the sidewalk.

Harry and Larry, the chief porters, stuck their heads out adjoining windows to see what had happened. A crowd gathered below. Zeke, the doorman, shouted up questions.

Watching all this, the Winged Victory (reparations from Paris), stood armless in the foyer. And there was a shattered wall, frozen, "the moment after an accident had taken place," as Jean said of the painting of di Chirico.

For it was impossible, even at Eliphaz's, to dispose of the many treasures of the world in their proper places. Some rooms had become warehouses of heterogeneous contents gathering dust. And the bathtub was filled with Dutch paintings. Yet these items were still precisely catalogued and when a purchaser appeared, Harry or Larry could promptly show him to the spot, and Zeke knew how to sing out, "Tenth Floor, Old Building!" as at Macy's.

Sometimes in the radical alterations it was necessary to introduce new communicating dumbwaiters which were then abandoned; and old Eliphaz liked to think that in these loopholes were generating live animals, if only rats and mice. He refused to have them disturbed. These animals were called "Vortex" and "Apocalypse" and "Angry" and so forth, and there were tamer rabbits like "Southern Vanguard."

From most of his exchanges, he was able to turn a small profit—he liked to turn a small profit—yet there was no doubt that the alterations and the additions had long ago begun to eat up the profits, so that a greater net, if not gross, would have accrued from a rigorous retrenchment. His department store, like Wanamaker's before the fire, was on its last legs.

There is no doubt that during this period the merchant prince was becoming more than a little crazy. His family bored him to tears and he bought and sold the furniture for the excitement.

2. An Advocate of Retrenchment

The advocate of the policy of deflation was his daughter Emily, and a crisis developed in the household. Emily was careful, she belonged to a later century of the bourgeoisie than her father, and finally she could no longer put up with his Venetian irrationalities which she "absolutely could not comprehend"—it was a favorite expression of hers.

"I'm a businessman," he said sharply. "If I sold all these things from a warehouse, I could make more money out of them; even I know that. But then I'd have to have a home somewhere else, and what about *that* furniture?"

"A businessman!" she cried. "You mean you're in your second childhood. It's simply a matter of bookkeeping. This *costs* you more."

"Please! Some respect for my gray hairs if not for the truth. You remind me of this literary man who was here the other day who was telling us of the mistakes Goethe made in his life; *he* was telling us how Goethe should have lived in order to become Goethe. You seem to think I'm interested in saving money. I'm trying to make a profit, girl! But a profit not on the exchange of these commodities, but on their worth, even on their use; and maybe, for all you know, even on their *real* worth, maybe even on their *real* use. How can I do it unless they are *my* things and I know what it is that I am exchanging away?"

His mania was a simple one: to live with a piece long enough to appreciate its worth—he had a good sense of worth—and then as quickly as possible to exchange away that which he loved best.

"But *I* am tired of living in an auction room!" said Emily from the bottom of her heart. "I want to have an at least semipermanent establishment." She was thirty-one and still unmarried.

"Does it look to you like an auction room?" said the father, surprised. "I thought I had a shop. Have the times changed so much? Is it all old?" He looked about with bewilderment.

Harry and Larry came to carry away the sofa that she was sitting on.

"I refuse to budge!" she said. "Not even for folding money."

The porters lifted up the sofa and bore it and Emily smoothly away while she maintained a stony dignity. That she had. To the astonishment of the crowd always gathering below to watch the moving at Eliphaz's—it was better than a loan exhibition at the Metropolitan Museum—she allowed herself to be stowed onto the moving van (the moving company belonged to Eliphaz), and they went to Parke-Bernet.

She wrote a daily column for the *Times* which bore somewhat the same relation to her father's activity that Mrs. Roosevelt's writing used to have to her husband's: it expressed her own opinion, bolder, clearer than his, less compromising with the opposing social ideas; but when the moment of action came, her readers were never prepared for the crushing force of the catastrophe.

Returning from her ride on the van, Emily expressed her resentment by leaving each room as the porters entered it, and violently slamming the door.

The old man's heart sank. "*Now* what's the matter?" he asked himself.

3.

Arthur, her younger brother, who was twenty-two, had made a better adjustment to this flowing environment. He hid. He had a private apartment that even Samuel the detective did not dare to enter. This remarkable institution dated from his sixth birthday, the very day that his mother died. To be alone he locked his door with the key, and this arrangement became permanent. "May I come in, sonny?" asked Eliphaz on that day, to comfort him. "No," said the little boy, "you may not."

Arthur was one who could speak, uncannily, to the rats and mice, and he kept pets.

4. Transactions

Eliphaz did all his business at home; he had no other business office. He kept the account of his successes in a little black notebook whose contents consisted mainly of accumulating zeroes.

At work he was quiet and inconspicuous, and often when a visitor (a purchaser) came to see him in one of the rooms, it would be a long time before one noticed, with a start, that Eliphaz was sitting there: he fitted in so well, in a world where everything was in flux. Indeed, he used it as a test of a man's quick wit: how soon they could perceive that Eliphaz was there. So at this period I find no description of his person except that "he had merry black eyes that saw a good deal."

Père Grandet came with the war news. (In the room of The Night Watch.) Finally, after a long pause, the ambassador caught sight of him. "Ah, there you are!" he began.

Eliphaz listened to him somewhat impatiently, for he was accustomed to take his own interpretations of events from the articles of famous exiled statesmen who had nothing to do in the world except make correct technical comments, especially Trotsky.

"Don't fret so, young man," he said. "Do you think I want to go on this victorious way forever? To where? The Man," he said gravely, "is bent on a course that does not lead where he thought he had intended to go; he knows this but he cannot deviate from it. . . . You seem to be interested in that bowl," he insinuated.

Sensing he did not have the old man's attention, Grandet was nervously fingering a frightful little yellow bowl used as an ashtray. Eliphaz always kept such a thing handy, the way merchants carry beads to Africa.

"I? . . . It's lovely."

"Take it! Take it! Fair exchange, heh? Send me those sandals—" And he kicked Grandet's ankles under the desk so that the broker winced.

He made a phone call: "So I'm *sending* you the ambassador's sandals. You couldn't get them; *I* can get them. Copy them at fifteen dollars. . . . How should I lay out three hundred dollars this minute?" he asked Grandet.

"Buy more ashtrays," said the Frenchman bitterly.

"What? Don't you like the ashtray? I'll buy it back. Please! Don't be angry. Do you think *I* like to part with this bowl? Let me tell you something about this bowl. This is some little dish—ugly, eh?—but every item has its story. I got it in Truro. There is a Lucy Clarke there and she's cleaning out the attic before going abroad to see the famous cities of Europe. She finds this bowl and she tosses it out on the garbage dump. You know the Cape? Well, then you know Zeke's Junkyard, a quarter of a mile further up the town-dump road. (Yes, yes, Zeke downstairs.) So every Tuesday Zeke picks over the garbage and he sees this bowl and naturally he carries off this bowl. What's it worth? Five cents, ten cents. He sells it for a quarter to Mrs. Dora Peabody, Yankee Antiques, Chatham. *She* sells it to Hetty Abramowitz for nine seventy-five. Three months have passed, and Hetty gives this bowl as a gift welcome-home to Mrs. Clarke, who promptly tosses it on the garbage dump. That's when *I* picked it up. What a commodity! What a commodity is this bowl! Do *your* shoes have a history? But take the bowl! Take it! Business is business."

In a rage the ambassador kicked off his shoes then and there, and went downstairs in his socks.

A panel flew open disclosing a brilliantly lit whatnot in the wall, and Eliphaz smilingly put one of the sandals on the shelf as a souvenir—*out of circulation*. He marked the transaction in his little notebook in ink, but the war in the Indies only in pencil, as if he might choose to erase it. (We shall return to the treasures that he kept in that brilliant closet, and why he kept them there.)

"He went away angry——" The old man shrugged. *"Do* his shoes have a history? When I look at a commodity it has a history. And they call me commercial?"

Sam, the detective, brought in his report. His job was to shadow young Arthur and find where it was that he squandered his father's credit.

The report had two headings: 1. Looking for sex. 2. Sex.

"He always goes to the same club till it's closed by the police."

The policy was that if the young man's bill at a club ran above a certain figure, his father bought out the place to keep the money in the family. Eliphaz was always ready to swap one hole for another—in the course of a year it cost him hardly a penny.

"Is there still no girl?" said Eliphaz puzzled.

"Nothing but Mme. Vanetska's." This was a brothel owned by Eliphaz.

"You mean except when he gives you the slip."

Sam was no fool, yet invariably Arthur gave him the slip.

"You don't open your eyes!" said the old man. *"He's* not invisible—he's just doing the too obvious thing—but you don't open your eyes."

"It don't cost anything," protested Sam. "You can see there are no bills."

"That's just it," said Eliphaz tartly. "In principle everything legitimate costs money. There are too many loopholes."

The father was proud of his vanishing son, about whom he knew nothing, yet enough. He was sure that, like himself, if only you knew the clue everything that Arthur did would make perfect sense. But Emily!—he heard her angry voice in the hall—women were not transparent.

5. Father and Daughter

She came in slamming the door, and his heart sank another inch. From her adolescence on he had been bearing the impossible burden of a father trying to make a daughter happy.

He wanted to be friendly, and her resentment abated.

"I'm sorry about the sofa," he said humbly; "it was nothing personal." This was a favorite saying of his: "It's nothing personal, it's nothing personal." And nevertheless the other persons persisted in taking their injuries personally.

"Do you know why you get me so mad?" said Emily. "It's because up to a certain point I *feel with* everything you're doing; then when I'm all in inward motion with you, you suddenly cross me with something that doesn't follow. Like sitting next to somebody else driving; for Crissake, pass him! Or if you don't pass him, get in the other lane."

"There you have it, daughter. Always decisions. You never think of saying, Wait, who's honking me? You always have to shit or get off the pot. Why is this necessary? You can't write a column without making a prediction. Sit on it awhile!"

She nodded dumbly. She wanted to look up at him—but it was already too long ago—and say, *"Tell* me the indispensable secret!" But she was too big to look up at him because she was the same height; and *if* she asked, he would only reply, like a Jew, *"Is* there a secret?"

"Where's Mynheer today?" he asked, feigning interest, and, as always, evading dangerous ground by blundering into worse.

"He's with the reliefer again."

"Do you think—have you any expectations—?"

"Look, father," she said, trying to conceal her misery, "I have told you a hundred times that you're making a mistake here too. This Dutchman is without a penny. Every penny he has is frozen by five governments, including your own."

"Emily, please! This boy is a wonder! Look how he manages! What a worldwide basis in nothing! I tell you that he will grow up to be a philosopher." But he saw the tears start in her eyes, and he said, "The fact is, Emily, believe me—if I didn't think it was *only* he, I mean a person in just his situation, who has and who hasn't everything, who could make you happy——"

"What do you want me to do, stand on my head?" said the chaste woman and bit her lip to keep from crying. Knowing that she was failing him again.

Again he retreated from the danger zone; but with a father and daughter everything is a danger zone. "This Miss Alger——"

"Yes," cried Emily passionately, "and can you make *her* out? Not only she *has* nothing—this, after all, doesn't matter, it doesn't matter—but she *does* nothing, absolutely nothing!"

"I thought she was studying architecture."

"Architecture! Cooper Union!"

"What does *he* do but nothing? Maybe that's what they have in common," said the old man shrewdly.

"You see what he does all day. This morning he went riding off with a little vagrant he picked off the street."

"And what do you suppose *I* do? Do you think I do anything all day but nothing?" This was typical; it was impossible to talk to him because he kept egotistically succumbing to a mania to be everybody. Yet the course of the conversation was inevitable, for she wanted to fall into his arms wailing, "I love *you,* I love *you!*" because he was her great man, her father; and he, of course, uneasily felt the pressure and withdrew into bragging, shutting her out, both of them in full retreat and, instead, slugging it out.

"You're too old to be so clever," she said brutally.

"I was just about to remark," said Eliphaz, bending his brows, "how often you find yourself obliged to say you cannot understand something or that there is absolutely nothing to understand. But I never read this in your column. How do you conceal it from your readers?"

At this moment Harry and Larry entered and began to carry away the furnishings under their arms.

"You're not going to sell the rose vase!" wailed Emily blanching. "It's the only pretty thing we have." And she finally burst into tears.

"Rose?" Eliphaz started; the vase was green as the grass of Ireland. The father was at a loss, as he was each time he realized that the poor woman was color-blind (but who ever heard of a woman color-blind?).

Yet her attachment was deep and strong to these objects of whatever color, for they were the mementos of her second to her fifth years. She was not speaking vulgarly when she said the vase was pretty; she might even have said beautiful, for with her the beautiful was not, as with most, the promise of a future pleasure, but the secure memory of long possession. And it was this beauty that the father took out of her life.

She said bitterly, "You've brought up Arthur and me in an auction room with nothing to call our own; and now it seems I can't attract the one man I ever wanted. With what should I attract him? You know what Mama would have said about it."

"Why don't you set yourself up in privacy like your brother?"

"But he hasn't anything there either," she wailed.

"What! Have you been in his apartment?"

"Certainly. Arthur has no secrets from me."

This casual remark reversed the whole balance of forces. The old man was so deeply wounded that he spoke earnestly, in a more revealing style than he meant to. "My daughter," he said gravely, "we are to dwell as if in tents."

6. An Impulsive Gift

Dangling from the roof, a grand piano began to nudge its way through the window.

Through the doorway arrived Mynheer Duyck Duyvendak. Emily hastily fixed up her face.

"My daughter says she's going to move out," said Eliphaz sadly, attempting to rid himself of a nuisance by the same technique as he sold Grandet the bowl. "She wants a home of her own with permanent *objets d'art* and accretions like the chambered nautilus."

"I can understand that," said Mynheer. "But what's wrong with it here?"

"Father, will you be still! How do you do, Sir Dyck?" said Emily. "What are the cables?"

"From my point of view, marvelous!" said the Dutchman, bitterly. "We have at least three legal governments, and six permutations of hope and fear. Now we have also a Japanese flag. A smooth talker has plenty to go on. I have never been so rich in my life. Unfortunately, I am a Dutchman." He was in despair for his country, but he did not know, in his heart, whether it was Holland or Indonesia or the world.

The two porters came to ease the grand piano into the room.

It was at this moment that Eliphaz stuck his head out of the other window and shouted up to the roof. "Lower the piano down to the street! We don't need it here. Deliver it to 880 Audubon, Apartment 44C."

"To *where?*" cried Dyck.

"The name is Alger. Say it's with the compliments of the company."

"What are you sending a grand piano to her for?" cried Emily indignantly.

"You've been trailing me!" said Dyck.

"Make 'em take it, whether they want it or not!" shouted up Eliphaz.

"Why the fuck don't you make up your mind?" floated down a bass voice.

"Lower away! Lower away!" shouted the old man gleefully.

This was what he loved: a shot in the dark.

"He has gone completely out of his mind," thought Emily compassionately.

The three of them were now leaning out separate windows ten stories off the ground, while that enormous black animal poised on the long hawsers, legs thrust out and swinging from side to side, slowly descended. Harry and Larry also thrust their heads out the windows, one on either side of the three (the windows multiplied), and they began with unerring skill to throw down unlit matches in such a way that the heads struck the pavement and burst into flame. The porters had in their lapels little signs of a fiery hand.

A moderate crowd was collected below to watch, and passing motorists craned their necks.

"He's moving out the piano," said one man, "we'll crash sure."

"This means the war," said a stout fellow who, distrustful of rhetoric, put his faith in slips of the tongue and other natural signs.

Up above: "All my life," thought Eliphaz, "I am trying to recreate a certain situation; is this it?" Watching the piano descend while the porters threw down matches.

"Another man," shouted Emily across two windows, "would leave these matters to the servants, but to you every little nonsense is worth wasting your time on."

"Who knows? Maybe the rope will break. Is that what I want?" thought Eliphaz.

Down below this thought seemed to occur also, for they drew back in a wide circle. Policemen appeared.

The piano came to a pause on its feet and its dignity descended on it like the robe of a judge.

Hugo was red with pleasure.

"Wasn't that great?" he said.

"Yes, you collectors—" said Mynheer, who was the corresponding secretary of the Psychoanalytic Institute of The Hague—"you collectors are always flushed when you finally give something away."

Eliphaz leveled at him a glance, and the Dutchman discreetly withdrew with Emily to look at the Van Eycks in the bathtub.

7. The Problem

Alone, with enthusiasm still mounting, Eliphaz finally turned his mind to the family Alger. And first, thinking of Laura and Emily and Mynheer, he shrugged; for much as he wanted his disagreeable daughter to be content, he knew there was nothing he could do about it. He listened, but he could not hear any inspiration of the holy spirit. Sentimental considerations simply took the heart out of him; he liked fun. (As for the Indies—if there were going to be any Indies, which he doubted—he did not rely on sentiments to turn a profit, he was not a rigid moralist; though he liked to turn a profit on also these, for there they were.)

Was his daughter, after all, a petty bourgeoise? What! In his house? He could not repress a shudder of disgust, at the filth of five hundred years of home and furniture. But he loyally, and therefore truly, refused to believe it.

But now here was Laura Alger on the dole, she and the others *absolutely profiting from the Empire.* Everybody else was somehow engaged in producing surplus value; they had little ratios that could be altered (he liked to make alterations); but Laura did nothing but enjoy the day. What was to be done? If he had been evading this puzzle—and he had a qualm of conscience that told him that he had—there was no use in trying to do so any longer, for here were the Algers confronting him. He marveled to find again how one's small personal problems invariably bring one face to face, around a corner, with the great problems of the spirit. What then? Just to abolish the dole? This was mere campaign oratory, for what of the labor reserve, the army reserve and the open market for competitive distribution—in short, the prerequisites of empire and exchange—those who luxuriate at home, not without risk and glory, because of the situation overseas, and those who have money in their pockets in order to choose among the good things on the market? All this was familiar and not puzzling.

But the puzzle was that these people did not have the right attitude. There were *rentiers* of all levels of income, but Laura and her friends profited absolutely and they did not accumulate. The capital of the others was on the Exchange and could be fluctuated away; but this one group drew on the system itself and avoided the relativity in the system: its capital was solid, it was not on the Exchange, it was insured. And what *could* such a group accumulate? For of course he did not neglect to collect every cent back, from the moment she cashed her check: from whatever she bought, the space she occupied, there was not a penny left. But this very scrupulosity on *his* part gave *them* the wrong attitude. Indeed, there was an absolute conflict of interests: he himself was, of course, not even in the business of accumulation but of reinvestment, whereas they had nothing to do but consume. If he was going to attend to his proper business (it was his vocation), he had to pension a class of consumers!

But then, if you thought about it that way, it was not only she! Here was all this ultimate consumption going on apace, minute by minute, the breath drawn, the bread taken from its fungible package and finally eaten. He himself was as guilty of it as anybody else. Yet if people did not consume, they could not produce. You start out by saying "these people" do not have the right attitude, and you end by saying that *people* do not have the right attitude; yet they are all the people there are. "This is a radical evil in the universe," thought Eliphaz; "perhaps it is an original sin." He had a thrill of fear and a flush of excitement as he felt the power in the existence of things.

Eliphaz was at this period a wise man, almost a sage (though transiently more than a little crazy). As a wise man, he had the same thoughts by impulse as by reflection, in the dead of night as by daylight. The difference was that by impulse and at night he thrilled with delight at the prospect of an abyss; by day and on reflection he was prudent. It is as these feelings gradually become one feeling of faith that a wise man grows into a sage.

It was therefore with awe, as well as in ungrudging admiration, that he had impulsively sent that grand piano to Miss Alger with his compliments. "Let her take it! Let her take it over! I see that that is some grand piano!" said the financier shrewdly to himself. "I wonder whether she plays it better than I."

Likewise he thought spitefully: "It's always worth while to hurl large gifts toward your adversary. Where is she going to put such an animal? How is she going to explain it to the relief investigator I'll send around tomorrow?"

8. Toots

"What do I want?" he asked himself. "What I want is to change all the use value into exchange value. But what I want is impossible. Therefore, apparently I want nothing. . . . And what's wrong with that?"

He knocked at Arthur's. "May I come in?"

"Who is it? Papa?" said Arthur from within.

"It's your father."

"Certainly you may not come in."

There was a barking or bleating, or even growling, of some animal.

"You invite Emily in," said the father aggrieved. "I have lived almost half my life—" Eliphaz was about sixty-five— "and have not won the confidence of my own son."

"Ha! So I invite Emily in. That's what she thinks," said Arthur cryptically. "What do you want?"

"I have an important proposition to discuss with you. It's about getting married."

"Who, me?"

"Yes. It's time you got married and had some children. By your age I had had my first set." ("The first were better," muttered the father *sotto voce*.)

"I'll be right out, though I'm very busy just now."

There were vociferous yelps or shrieks or cries—Eliphaz could not make them out. Perhaps there was even whispering. Arthur came out and deftly closed the door without showing a crack.

"Was there somebody in there with you? I thought I heard voices."

"That? That was Toots," explained Arthur.

"Toots? . . . Your sister is in love," said the father, deciding that this was the best gambit. "Toots! A distinguished name!"

"I doubt it," said Arthur. "When *my* sister really loves the Dutchman, she will get him into bed." He said this with an odd pride.

"I see you know all about it, smart aleck. Well, there's an obstacle."

The yelping continued.

"What goes on here, anyway?" cried Eliphaz. "What is that thing?"

"Toots, hush up! . . . You call Laura Alger an obstacle? Ha! This I must tell her."

"How can I carry on a serious conversation with that noise going on? What? Do you know her too?"

"Do *I* know her! He asks if I know her! It was *I* who made the pickup in the park. I got her away from about a hundred sailors. *Hush,* Toots."

"What is this Toots anyway?" cried the magnate. "Well, so much the better."

"What's better? What's even good?"

"So much the better you know her, because I want you to think of marrying her."

At this Arthur began to laugh. He almost choked. And Toots fell silent.

"I just sent her a grand piano; that ought to facilitate the first steps."

"A grand piano!" cried Arthur. "What in hell will she do with a grand piano?"

"Hee hee, that's just it!" said Eliphaz, rubbing his hands.

"Well, the joke's on you; the big brother happens to be a composer."

"Ah."

"The big brother happens to be Lothar Alger."

"Ah. Ah." By now the poor miser began to suspect that there was a plot against him of bewildering ramifications, as was indeed the case.

But Arthur lapsed from laughter into deep melancholy, for the big joke was really on *him.* He had lost Laura by vainly—as it now turned out—trying to protect his cursed anonymity at certain critical moments. And it was typical that he—made the pickup.

"What I want," said Eliphaz briskly, "what is necessary," he corrected himself, "for it is not a personal matter, is more children. When we have to maintain each one of us so preciously, the price is too high. If there were replacements, we could amortize more quickly."

Toots began to whine behind the closed door.

Chapter 3 • FURTHER CONVERSATIONS BETWEEN MYNHEER AND HORATIO

1.

"'Leaping my shadow—'" sang Horatio,

> "'Leaping my shadow and Prick my dog
> I took to walk the park,
> the streets, the bars, the wooden dock,
> all a hot afternoon.
>
> "'My shadow had a merry run
> and long stretched out he came back home,
> but Prick had never a sniff or jump
> that twenty-first o June.'

Now accordin' to you the newspapers ain't reliable. Is *The Times* lies? But if it's gonna lie anyway, why is it so borin'? Answer me that."

"I didn't say they told lies, I said they were part of a system."

"Six o' one an' half a dozen o' the other. Now accordin' to you, *some* printed matter *ain't* part o' the system. Right? How? Which? Name it! An' don't gimme any more Greeks."

"You're so insistent, boy. I only meant it as a kind of possibility," said Dyck, embarrassed to think of the book.

"No, no, you can't weasel out of it. You said it, you did say it."

"Well, supposing *I* wrote a book——"

"You? What could *you* write a book about? To write a book you gotta have experiences of life."

"Good, you won that game. Then, supposing *you* wrote a book——"

"I have wrote a book—it's a diary," said Horace. "This notebook where I keep my names an' shit, it has political commentary too."

"*Has* it? Let me see it," said Dyck eagerly. "Maybe I'll get it printed."

"No!" cried Horace in terror, and clutched at his little book in his pocket with that repression of exhibition which keeps authors correcting their proofs.

"Oh, yes. Give it here! Give it here!"

"Whaddya gonna do?" said Horace.

"I'll get it printed and then they'll give it a *number* at the library and put a *card* in the *catalogue.* And besides, there are books which are nothing but catalogues of all the catalogues in all the libraries! And every book has a number and a date and a place of publication. That's how they know how to get their hands on any book! And that's what's going to happen to *your* book! What do you think of that?"

"So what! So what!" crowed Horace. "My little book will keep explodin' away like a grain o' radium, with a half life o' five thousand years!"

2.

But as high as he was one moment, he was mournful the next. "I can't belong to no lib'ary," he said, "cause I got no report card to show."

"Ah!"

Dyck said nothing, but he could not repress an itching smile.

"Laugh at me," said Horace in misery.

"I'm not laughing because it's you, Horatio. It's nothing personal. But because of the human comedy. Don't you see how we contradict ourselves? We try to live in the loopholes and then we also want to have the advantages of proper citizens. Don't you see that it's comic?"

"No. I don't have a sense of humor, an' when I mean business I take it personal."

"You want to keep them from getting your number, but then there are opportunities when it's an advantage to have a number, a report card on deportment, a certificate of vaccination, even a review in the *New York Times.* I knew a man who even got something out of being fingerprinted, when somebody left him a fortune in a will and he was able to prove that it wasn't he who did him in. This is because there are also places of privilege to work your way into."

"That's all bullshit," said Horace shortly. "I'm showin' you the plain facts o' life, an' you gimme exceptional cases. Nobody ain't gonna leave me nothin' in no will, but when they got your number, they come after you an' you're stuck. Period."

"I'm sorry, boy, I have to disagree. I've been around a little myself. Say, supposing you want to build a bridge—everybody wants to build a bridge—then you have to have a university diploma," said Mynheer, who had been a civil engineer in Curaçao.

"A diploma?" Horatio was momentarily confused, for he had always guessed that this word meant a kind of lesion or disease.

Dyck pressed his advantage. "I didn't mean to say it," he said, "but they've already got *you* down, in your birth certificate. They start right off by taking your name and footprint."

"Don't let *that* worry you," said Horatio Alger. "If you knew my ma and the man she sometimes used to say was my pa, you wouldn't let that worry you."

"Oh, but if they don't have your name, then you're an *alien*, and that's worse," said Mynheer, whose name was not absent from the chronicles of Burgundy. "They've got you coming and going. If there are any rewards of privilege and power, you don't think they're going to give them to an alien!" said Mynheer, who was tentatively making his way in the foreign land with an ambiguous visa, and living on the credit of a false supposition (as it turned out).

But in a loud voice, little Horatio said bravely: "No, no! I won't let 'em get near me! Even accordin' to you the system ain't perfect, an' they only *try* to get you comin' an' goin'. But I'll experiment on all the cracks an' see how far I can get away with murder. An' then," cried Horace, "when in spite of 'em all I'm grown up to be as strong as he is, I'll come to Eliphaz an' he'll *forge* me a birth certificate an' a report card an' a driver's license an' make it all official!" In the enthusiasm of his faith, his face flushed and his clear eyes shone, and he said: "An' he'll adopt me to be his son an' heir!" His voice rang out. "An' then he'll up an' die."

There was an embarrassing pause. Mynheer was simply shocked.

3. First Portrait of Eros

Mynheer was shocked; nevertheless—and we might of course write "therefore"—at this moment he felt impelled to take the boy's cheeks in his hands and bend down and kiss him on the brow.

"Would you like to go to a progressive school, little brother?" he asked.

"What's *that?*" wailed Horace.

"At last!" thought the wicked little boy, and with a quick glance roundabout, he groped at Mynheer with his left hand.

"For heaven's sake," said Dyck and pushed him brusquely away, "you mustn't do that! The people, the people."

Frozen on Horatio's face was a smile of hieratic amiability.

Mynheer was momentarily puzzled to identify this look, but then he knew it: it was the invitation on the face of the eighth-century Apollos.

"Don't you have any girl friends?" he faltered.

Horace stared at him a long time.

"I can't make it out," he said at last.

"Now what's the matter?"

"You're what's the matter. You keep astin' me questions an' leadin' the talk around like you was makin' a pass. First you shake my hand with a little extra; then you give me the sweet-uncle kiss on the forehead. One, two. Next you ast me if I got a girl friend. One, two, three. What's four? Suppose I say I *do* have, that's easy: 'How far do you get?' and et cetera. Suppose I say I don't, then 'What *do* you do for nooky?' You can't miss. O.K., O.K. So far I'm with you. But then when it comes to *doin'* anythin', suddenly you act like a non. A boy don't know whether he's comin' or goin'."

As he listened to this, the tears of joy streamed from Mynheer's eyes, and he laughed out loud. "I wasn't brought up in America," he said. "I don't know these games, that's why I play so bad. I'm really not a square. But tell me, what stops a body from saying what he's after directly, just like that?"

It was now Horace's turn to choke, at how could anybody be so green. To see the two of them, it was hard to tell whether they were laughing or crying.

"It's all right, little Eros, we'll get along fine," said the man, hugging him warmly but fraternally.

"Name's Horace," said Horace.

"I know, I know." For the first time Mynheer saw clearly who was before him, with concealed wings. And now for the first time the energy of his soul moved with its ancient strength and pleasure, so that Horace ceased to regard him as a dope and was momentarily satisfied for his sis.

Mynheer held him off, by the shoulders, at arm's length, and looked at him. It was the Eros of Anacreon, the same as comes out of the rain—

βρέφος ἐιμί, μὴ φόβησαι—

"just a child, don't fear: lost and wet in the moonless night." But when you unbolt the door and let him in, he dries his bow at the fire and shoots you painfully to the heart. And *then* what is to be done?

And looking at him, Mynheer learned something that he had not known (though Socrates had said it): that the child of Have and Lack is hard up for love himself, like those brats who watch the brave and the fair embrace in the bushes—small satisfaction. That's why he came buzzing around, stinging, rousing you up; touching, whispering, suggesting. But at last, if you take pity on *him,* or let yourself become aroused: you turn on *him,* perhaps seize him round the waist and say, "I'll screw you, little bastard. I think you're asking for it!" then he screams and struggles and insultingly wipes your kiss off on his knuckles; you let him go because your feelings are hurt; then he laughs in your face, not to speak of frisking you from behind and shouting, "Catch me!"

"What you thinkin' about, feller?" said Horatio, looking at him curiously. It felt good to him to have the big hands so firmly on his shoulders, keeping him in a place; but what was the faraway look in the man's eyes? "What you thinkin' about?"

"Do you really want to come up to my place for a half hour?" said Dyck compassionately.

"What for?"

"Oh? Nothing. Just like this."

"For nothing? Naw."

"We could have some fun."

"What do you call fun?"

"What do you mean what do I call fun?" said the Dutchman annoyed. "Damn it, you know what I mean by fun."

Horace threw back his head and roared for joy. "Jesus, you learn fast! How to keep from sayin' what you mean! I thought you wasn't born in America! . . . It's no use, feller. We're both too goddam smart and only opposites attract. But I like you all the same. You're really a grand guy."

"I like you, Horatio. I think we're going to be friends." And they solemnly shook hands.

"Come along, Danton!" said Horace, and the little dog leaped up on him in ecstasy and trotted ahead.

Chapter 4 ▪ THE POLITICS OF LOTHARIO

> I have not seen one well-bred man since I came to New York. At their entertainments there is no conversation that is agreeable; no modesty, no attention to one another. They talk very loud, very fast, and all together. If they ask you a question, before you can utter 3 words of your answer they will break out upon you again and talk away.
>
> —JOHN ADAMS, 1774

1. History of a Campaign Against War

When Lothario Alger was in college, he was a vigorous leader in a fight against war, to expel from the school every vestige of militarism, every uniform, every colonel, every student corps whether compulsory or voluntary. This fight was directed not against the possibility of war (at that time there was no such possibility), but against the idea of the possibility; and it was correlated with mighty international efforts along the same lines, led by governments that had just won the victory in a generally disastrous war, though one not so disastrous to the victors as to the vanquished.

It was the aftermath of a great war (1914-1918), and far from there being a new danger of war, it was above all necessary to remove all traces of that old awful war before it was even possible to think of waging a new war. The student agitators were glad to be of service to help clear the atmosphere, so that everywhere could shine bright peace. Even the professors recanted the lies that they had told in the interest of the old war. Whenever anyone died who had been connected with that war, such as a statesman, a commander or even a garrulous veteran of one's acquaintance, on all sides there was discreet satisfaction; but every such death might well have caused a pang of dread, for when they were *all* dead it would be easier to recommence.

Now was the era of peace, quite essential for international trade in the capital, raw materials, weapons, new inventions and the exchange through spies of strategic innovations in order to make possible an equitable new war. And Lothar and his friends, at the cost of being themselves expelled from school, succeeded in eliminating every vestige and idea of the old war.

Their plan was, along with this victory, to fight also against colonial imperialism; but at this time that institution was not popularly connected with the old war as such—it rather belonged to the fruits of victory—so that on this issue there was not the same popular support, and no international support, and here perhaps they did not succeed at all. Yet the enormous success that they did achieve, they summed up in the formula: "Comrades, we have made a dent!" And they felt that *if they carried through the struggle on any real issue, they would destroy the capitalist system.*

Soon new war clouds gathered thick and black, and the well-armed hostile powers were threatening to destroy the generally unprosperous order of civilization. Lothar and his friends, who were—because of their previous success—important youth leaders (though they *were* growing older), now resolved on measures of heroic resistance to the inevitable war. It was necessary, they argued, that at no point in the general peaceful order should a break occur, for if it did the entire order of civilization would at once be destroyed. (A lot of people didn't care much whether it was or not.) The formula of the friends was: "The peace is indivisible." It was true that several breaks had occurred already and indeed it seemed that the entire system was being destroyed.

Yet there were many arrangements and deals still possible under the old co-operative system; this form of commerce was internationally called the Appeasement. So the young people took a great oath: that in no circumstances whatsoever would they ever allow themselves to be drafted for any war whatsoever. That was flat, wasn't it? In the circumstances this resolve was revolutionary and would overturn the entire capitalist system, for since the system was now about to thrive on the carefully prepared breakdown of the system, the effort to carry through the conservation of the system would surely overturn the system itself. But of course, as it proved, there were still many profitable arrangements to be made under the peaceful system, though not exactly, from a certain point of view, according to the plan of those who took the great oath.

Finally, at the time of our history, the storm of war was modestly raging everywhere. In the Empire City preparations were being made, including the registration and draft of all the young men. And the youth leaders—by now they were rather old for youth leaders—seeing the opportunity to work among the masses on this important issue, proposed the following practical program: A raise in the soldiers' pay to $30; adequate furloughs for all draftees;

healthful conditions in the cantonments; democratic political representation for privates (through the youth leaders); and several other good and necessary immediate aims. They felt that by pushing through this program, they could eventually overturn the entire capitalist system.

2.

"Wait a minute, not so fast," said Lothar, a little troubled. "Our course of the last ten years is not altogether clear to me. First we pledged in no circumstances to allow ourselves to be drafted; now we are demanding adequate furloughs."

"True. But it is necessary to carry on the struggle on the issues actually confronting the people. If we can assure military democracy, we can easily change the nature of the war and eventually overturn the entire capitalist system."

"What do you mean 'true'?" cried another comrade, trained in the C.P. "What he says is a lie. He has no knowledge of history. He's a wrecker."

For the time being, Lothar disregarded this second fellow, and addressed himself to the reasoning: "You say the issues actually confronting the people, etc. But these issues have actually been presented to us by Eliphaz, haven't they?"

"Of course! If you choose to put it that way. They are presented to us by History, as our comrade says, by the dynamics of society."

"But why is the issue drawn exactly here?" cried Lothar. "Why not urge abstention from the registration and draft altogether, as we agreed?"

"That's illegal. The penalty is three years in jail and ten thousand dollars fine. Is it revolutionary to sit in jail? Who's got ten thousand dollars?"

"Ah! It seems," said Lothar bitterly, "that once we began to operate within the framework of *their* system, our program did not develop exactly according to *our* plan. All this comes originally from the fact that there is a registration of our date and place of birth. Why did I fail to take advantage of the fact that I was expelled from school?"

"You mustn't lose your head, Lothar! Remember that *that* agitation was successful and we made a dent. Your present attitude reminds me of the time when the I.W.W. expelled the lumbermen from the union because they *won* a strike, since winning meant signing a contract! You make me laugh."

"You think that was so absurd?" cried Lothar miserably. "If we hadn't been successful, in a certain sense, all along the line, we shouldn't now be asking for adequate furloughs. You're the ones who make *me* laugh. Ha!"

"What did I tell you?" said the comrade trained in the C.P. "He's an idealist, a wrecker."

3. Trying to Register

Because of the peculiar dynamics of his soul, Lothario tried to register for the draft nevertheless.

To his surprise he found that he could not fill out the registration questionnaire which bristled with personal, economic, political and ethical questions impossible for him to answer unambiguously. Every question, he now discovered, presupposes a theory of the nature of things: exclusive alternatives are proposed, of which you are to choose one, or say Yes or No; or a genus is given with a species to be filled in. But in the first case Lothar most often found that the middle was not excluded; and in the second case, when he found that the genus was nonexistent, he was at a loss for the species. These questions, for the most part, failed to correspond to anything in his experience.

The registrar was a helpful young chap named Cooley, a secretary of the Y.M.C.A.—for it was the Imperial policy to keep the draft entirely out of the hands of the military, whose methods were too crude for sociological accuracy.

Cooley was puzzled by Lothario's replies. "Let's see then," he began briskly: *"Are you married or single?"*

Lothario explained that he was no longer living with his legal wife—in fact she was now married to somebody else, though whether legally or not he didn't know because he didn't know whether the divorce ever went through. He himself still occasionally sent her money for support. He had, however, two children by another woman, who was in a sense his present wife, but this relationship didn't count for the purposes of the registration, he supposed, since she was able to support both herself and the children, and he didn't like her anyway. He resided with his sister and brother.

"I see—I see," said Cooley and wrote down: *Single. "Do you have any dependents?"*

Lothario's dependent for the purposes of the Imperial relief was Horatio, who was, however, Laura's dependent also. ("Was this quite honest?") The fact was that Lothar had many dependents for whom he felt responsible and therefore needed the money, since he belonged to a rather large organization many of whose members often had to come to him for assistance, despite the fact that they also were on relief. Besides, he partly supported his perhaps-wife, though since he was marked "single" this could hardly count.

"Yes, I see—I see," said Cooley and wrote down: *None. "Are you employed?"*

"Employed?" asked Lothar unbelievingly.

"That is, are you employed? Do you have your own business? Or are you out of work?"

"Oh. Now I dig you. What is involved here," explained Lothar, "is a theory of vocation and avocation, work and leisure, the ratio between a certain number of hours of labor time, a certain quantity of commodities produced or exchanged, or services rendered, a certain stipend and a quasi-political relationship between the entrepreneur and his aides."

"Precisely!" said Cooley enthusiastically.

"I don't believe in any of that," explained Lothar.

The facts were that he was a member of a fairly large organization run not for profit; a considerable amount of money passed through his hands; sometimes as need arose he appropriated some for his own use; at other times he scrounged from anywhere what he could for his friends: they kept no books.

"Ah, what is the name of this organization?"

"Unfortunately I can't tell you that," explained Lothar.

"But previously you said you were on the Imperial relief?"

"Yes."

"Fine," said Cooley, and wrote down: *Relief.*

"Oh, I must explain to you that I am by vocation a musician."

"A musician! Do you mean you are a professional musician?"

"A vocation is not a profession," said Lothar gravely.

He began to explain that he was the composer of a book of études for the piano, a concerto in no key——

But Cooley interrupted him and asked: "Is this secret organization of yours perhaps a kind of orchestra?"

"An orchestra? No. That is to say, yes. . . ." faltered Lothario. For now suddenly he saw the fallacy of this interrogation and he lost heart.

Once again! Once again his earnest effort to co-operate was thwarted.

"What is your education?" asked Cooley.

"I was expelled from school," said Lothar dully.

"Ah, I see—how unfortunate," said Cooley and wrote it down. *"Do you have any serious diseases?"*

"I am sick at heart," explained Lothar.

"That's bad," said Cooley, and wrote: *Heart disease (no document). "Do you have any conscientious objections to the war?"*

"Yes! Yes! I have the most serious objections!" cried Lothar so eagerly that Cooley looked up for the first time.

"According to the tenets of what religious group?" he dutifully continued.

At this intimate question Lothar became enraged. He snatched the paper from under Cooley's fingers and looked at it trembling.

"In what kind of world does the young man live who made these questions up!" he shouted. "What kind of witty ambiguities must I invent today in order to live a little longer in this Empire City?"

"I beg your pardon——" said Cooley.

"No! How would *you* know? I'll go down to the capital and confront him face to face, and I'll prove that it's he and not I who has perverted our dear English tongue! . . .

"Ah, here is a question of *fact* that I can answer unambiguously!" he said. "*When and where was I born?* I was born in the Empire City on such a day 19——. I see that this has assigned me a place and time to go astray on all the other points. But how could I go so far astray in a single generation?" And he tore up the questionnaire and rushed out of the room.

Once again! Once again his earnest effort to restore the original social peace of his early childhood—before the birth of Laura, before the coming of Horatio into a gypsy life—when the first child, the mother and father were a serene and regular constellation like those triplet suns which revolve around one another, around their epicenters, little perturbed by the crowds of heaven: it lay there shattered—once again!—his effort to belong. To have had a Golden Age is fatal to all the rest of one's life!

But he had no cause to be amazed that he had gone so far afield in a single generation, for any single alienating principle, such as honor or pleasure or common sense, operating continually, can achieve any degree of peculiarity you want.

4.

He decided, instead, to register under the Alien Registration Act, whereby all aliens must be registered and fingerprinted. Apparently he was not so certain of the "time and place" of which he had just boasted.

"Since you were born in this country," said the officer, a military man, "you must at some time have forsworn your allegiance or you would not be an alien. Precisely when and where did this occur?"

"It was not by any single act," said Lothar. "In a sense there has been a progressive alienation."

"A progressive alienation! I have not heard of this category."

"Maybe the critical moment occurred this morning in my own neighborhood."

"In your own neighborhood! This morning! What kind of garbage are you telling me here? To what flag do you imagine that you swore allegiance this morning?"

"To what flag? To what flag?"

"Yes, you heard me. To what flag do you adhere?"

"I—"

"Have you registered for the draft?" asked the officer bluntly. "You have to register *whether* you are a citizen or an alien."

"I am a citizen of Equity!" cried the young man sententiously. "I can bear arms only when I have a conviction which with regard to your present war I do not feel!"

"Of *Ecuador?*" cried the officer disbelievingly. "Show your passport," he said sternly.

"From a certain point of view I am a citizen of this country," said Lothar proudly, "and a better one than you are!"

And with this remark he stood up and walked out.

This sentiment was sometimes expressed by the slogan: "If Thomas Jefferson were alive today, he'd be a member of the C.P."

The officer promptly phoned the Bureau of Investigation to follow the case of Lothario Alger, presumably a draft dodger (penalty three years and $10,000 fine).

5. N.I.B.

Lothar came out of these interviews waving his hand in front of his eyes, as a man does coming out of an art gallery of surrealist pictures. Returning to the comparative reality of his own activities, he saw he had to hurry home to the meeting, at 880 Audubon, of his friends the National Industrial Boycott, to make final arrangements for the celebrated Candle Campaign, and indeed to begin distributing the candles that very afternoon.

Let me introduce the reader to this group by quoting the opening clauses of their charter:

1. We call ourselves N.I.B. because as yet we are tentatively nibbling at the present system. But if we find the right technique we'll take a good bite.

2. Our method is experimental but fundamental, because we do not aim at a mere political change, as if we were a bourgeois or Marxist party with the purpose of coming to power to choose the opposite alternative of questions proposed by the present structure

of institutions; nor do we aim at a mere economic change in the relations of capital and labor. But we affirm direct action in the matters of daily home economics and fastidiousness in industry.

3. Our method is possible and easy, because the present system depends on the voluntary co-operation of the people, and can be destroyed by the voluntary nonco-operation of the people. It is a system not of tyrannical exclusion but of tyrannical exploitation. Therefore, it is possible to temper slightly this involuntary-voluntary co-operation. In the distinction of an old philosopher: We affirm the direct action of the general rather than the sovereign will.

Besides these there was a fourth or secret clause, as follows:

(4. Failing economic boycott, there remains always the more profound voluntary possibility of the Sabotage of Personality, by fasting and excess and by abnormal virtues and vices. In such a case we propose to put into effect Mandeville's *Fable of the Bees* and/or to affiliate with the organization S.P.V.)

6.

The annals of N.I.B. were so far brief: they were entering their second campaign. I have elsewhere reported the first, the excessive proposal of Henry Faust's called *Doing Without*:

Let every one subsist on the minimum of necessities; then, since the economy is geared not to necessities but to superfluities, it will soon come to terms.

This proposal was too grandiose and the results were disappointing. They were, on the one hand, to free a certain few, with a deep emotion of relief, from the competitive strain after commodities obviously undesirable; on the other hand, the development in others of an inordinate craving for the same commodities (for as the Indian statesman has shown, nothing increases the relish like a fast).

Lothario was not in sympathy with Doing Without, although he loyally gave it his best energies. "Henry," he said, "makes an arbitrary distinction between necessities and luxuries. The cosmopolitan desires of the Empire City must, after all, be taken as elementary data."

"Certainly," jeered Henry, "we must conserve the toasters that cast their bread on high and ring the joyous bell! We must take as elementary data the six hundred films that Hollywood grinds out each year."

It was true that, unlike his sister Laura, Lothar was quite lacking in the immediate intuition of absolute nonsense, which in every case for him required demonstration.

7. The Candle Campaign

The so-called Candle Campaign was Lothario's own proposal and it swung, of course, to the opposite extreme:

Our aim is to boycott the monopoly price. We will determine the just profit of monopoly commodities and pay this just profit.

We try out the scheme on electric light. Let every consumer revise his monthly bill according to the criterion agreed on and honor this much of the debt and no more.

The company, controlled by Eliphaz, will then turn off the electricity; the consumers will then light candles.

It will be seen that this idea was a moderate one. It did not violate the mores by distinctions between necessities and luxuries. The aim was not even directly to do without electric lighting. It was not an attack on the capitalist system, but rather an attempt to conserve the system in a purer, unmonopolistic, form. (They felt that if this issue could be carried *through*, the entire system would collapse.)

8.

When Lothar finally arrived, the other eleven were already collected in the small front room.

"There you are! We'll commence at once," said Henry Faust, who was the chairman. "The problem before us is nothing but the Just Profit. I propose that it be Zero Percent. The investors can vote themselves wages of management commensurate with their attendance at board meetings."

"But, Henry——" said Lothar, trying to catch his breath.

"A token deficit would be more like it!" said a long lean person named Mario. "I propose Minus One Percent. This is to indicate that we remember a long past. Not that they can ever repay!"

"You're not serious!" protested Lothar.

"Never more so! If we can go to court on the issue at all, we can also argue a vested interest in the old exploitation."

"Don't be so sure," said the lawyer.

The rule was that debate was unlimited but restricted to brief propositions. You could argue all you wanted, but were not to make boring speeches.

The meeting was sitting in the larger room at 880 Audubon, Apartment 44C. At the beginning of the meeting they were all crowded at one end of the small room because Laura, who took all such functions upon herself, had so arranged the chairs that there would be a balance of people on one side against a pretty white canary named Chickadee on the other. But sometimes in anger a member picked up his chair and banged it down apart. This got the bird too excited.

The family of refugees below was outraged and knocked on the radiator.

"They keep knocking up," explained Lothar apologetically.

"What's *your* rate of interest?" asked the chairman.

"Six Percent, of course," said Lothario, betrayed by the catastrophic pleasures of his first to his fourth years. "If you want to propose some other strong campaign, I'm always with you, as you know. But the very point of the candles is that business goes on almost as usual."

"Six Percent!" cried several indignantly. "Where can you get Six Percent these days?"

"Four Percent is the maximum for new investments—I propose that," said the broker.

"The government pays Two Percent. This at least gives us a reasonable yardstick."

"The point is to give a *token* interest: I therefore propose One Percent."

"Excellent! First rate!" said Henry, who was a careful chairman and often summarized. "Now we have before us Minus One, Zero, One, Two, Four and Six Percent. Won't somebody say Three and Five so we can have a smooth series?"

"One minute please," said Peter Underwood, holding up his hand. "I am a medievalist and, as you know, in the Middle Ages there was no such thing as a legal rate of interest because there was no interest on money—but oh, *lucrum cessans, damnum emergens,* and so forth, a fabric of fictions to get around Deuteronomy xxiii. Now so far you are talking of this percent and that percent, but perhaps—correct me if I am wrong—you are lost beforehand if you talk about percentages at all."

On the floor, in several piled-up tin cracker boxes, were the candles. Round each one was stuck the label

N.I.B.

"Half of Six Percent is Three Percent," suggested a quiet old man with the irrelevance with which a person counts one, two, three and commits suicide.

There was a loud knocking at the door.

"It's downstairs," said Lothar apologetically. "He wants us to stop banging down the chairs."

When he went to open, it was a moving man in a striped denim apron, breathing fire.

"The grand piano's here," he said.

"What piano? There's some mistake," said Lothar impatiently and slammed the door.

"Something about a piano . . ." he began to say, but there was a thunderous knocking.

"Look here——" he said, opening the door.

The moving man, breathing smoke and fire, thrust him aside and pushed into the crowded room.

"We bring it in through the window," he explained cheerily.

He stuck his head out the window and shouted down, "Hokay! Right here!"

With a chisel he began to rip off the window frame.

The canary let out a piteous shriek.

"Look here! look here!" said Lothario.

"Whatsamatta?"

"The name here is *Alger*."

"Tha's right! 880 Audubon! Apartment 44C! The boss, he said bring it here."

"There's a mistake," said Lothar.

"No mistake!" bellowed the jocose mover, the chips flying. He drew on his pipe, which he kept lit in his pocket, and again expelled a cloud of sparks and smoke. He took the window from its frame. The glass rattled.

"Who sent it?" shouted Lothar.

"Who sent it? Who you think sent it?" cried the mover.

A second mover appeared, carrying the rollers. "Where you want it? There ain't much room," he said crisply. He pushed the table over under the birdcage, and began to pile the chairs on top. "Parron me."

"Am I in the way?" said the lawyer, getting up.

Chickadee hopped about wildly, speechless.

"Where'd you get it?" asked Henry Faust.

"It's from Eliphaz," said Lothar, turning white.

For it struck him that somebody might imagine—not only might somebody imagine it but in a certain sense it was so—that there was a connection between this gift of a grand piano and the fact that he was holding out for Six Percent on the investment. His mouth fell open—as the piano appeared in the window.

When the huge body of the grand piano appeared in the window, it completely blotted out the space, so that they were plunged in darkness. The mover turned the electric switch, but the company had already turned off the current for nonpayment, though it was not yet on precisely the same principle that the Algers hadn't paid. Thinking that it was now suppertime, the canary began to chirp plaintively.

"Whatsamatta, no lights?" said the mover.

Lothar lit one of the N.I.B. candles.

"I am sorry no one pays any attention to my objection, yet I must insist." So said the medievalist, standing square in the middle of the room and making no offer to budge. "If you once admit the idea of a per centum profit at all, you accept the entire economic structure of modern times. Our real enemy is the Arabic numerals."

There was a feeble tap at the door which the broker went to answer. It was the little man from downstairs.

"Are you having a piano too?" he asked in a shaking voice. "Just tell me—I am not making a complaint—I want I should have the facts before I know how to make up my mind."

When the piano advanced into the little room, everybody was pushed to the wall among the chairs and the boxes.

"Nib—nab!" said the big mover, reading the sticker on the candle. He extinguished the flame by swallowing it. He started to hammer back the windows.

"O.K. Let's agree on Five Percent," said Lothar in a shaking voice. "This indicates the direction of our next step."

"Very nice," said the moving man, in the doorway, looking at the beautiful assembled piano. "Looks very nice."

Chapter 5 ▪ AN AESTHETIC ROMANCE

1.

"*What* goes on here?" said Laura when, with Dyck, she opened the door and for one fantastic moment in the candlelight she thought there was a hippopotamus at midnight.

She touched the switch, there was no light. In the candlelight she brusquely found herself breast to breast with the grand piano.

"There's a grand piano in the house," she said to Dyck.

"So there is."

"But where are the boys going to sleep?" she said, with breath-taking practicality. "There's barely room for the cots, no more a grand piano!" She pushed it; it did not intend to move.

"Here, let me—where do you want it?"

"Oh, it's very convenient just where it is," said Laura. "By squeezing sideways I can get into the kitchen, and if we crawl under it we can get into my room. It's very well just where it is. Where would *you* put it, dear?"

She squeezed sideways and went into the kitchen which was dimly lit with a candle on a dish and the flaming faces of the brothers Alger at the deal table playing rummy. "There's a grand piano in this house!" announced Laura.

"Yes, so there is," said Lothar, and threw down the jack of hearts.

"*Rummy,* dope!" said Horace, and spread out his hand.

Laura *still* didn't take it as funny. Like Horace, she had no sense of humor in business; unlike Lothar, who had a thrilling sense of humor, like a file. At this moment Horace looked up and saw Mynheer's face in the doorway, lurid in the candlelight, and his own face flushed black. The rival intruding in his very house! *"Get out of my house!"* he did not say; "Out of my house before I break your fuckin' neck, but good!" he did not say; but in a split instant his complexion returned to that peculiar color men have when they make the best of it.

On the table, face up in the candlelight, lay the picture cards:

> *Le beau valet de coeur et la dame de pique*
> *causent sinistrement de leurs amours défunts*

—"the handsome jack of hearts and the queen of spades."

Laura shrugged her shoulders and said, "Well, if there is a piano,

I guess there's nothing to do but play on it"; and squeezing her way back into the other room, while the others rose, she struck a key.

The tone that Laura struck on the grand piano when first it was sent to their flat on an impulse by Eliphaz, was middle *E*. This living tone swelled to the edges of the room and made them tremble and float; and to it the white canary uttered a piercing sweet response, *E* an octave above high *E*.

She now arranged for the boys to sleep in layers, like a sandwich. "Sonny," she appointed, "will sleep on top of the piano; and try not to roll off and break your head. But Lothar will stretch his mattress under the piano and sleep among the legs."

So it came to pass. They obediently tried it out, and this arrangement of society was from then on seen to be reasonable.

2.

"Play us something, Mynheer, and try out the piano," she said.

He obediently sat down. "What do you want?"

"The Gavotte and Variations of Rameau."

"Oh, no—not on a *piano*," he said, pained.

"Yes, yes. We must take Rameau according to our own circumstances. *Here* they are!"

But he shook his head stubbornly and he wouldn't.

"Maybe our circumstances, as you call them," said Lothar, who was still on the floor under the piano, "would be less barbarous if we paid attention to the right style, and didn't take everything slipshod as it comes."

"Exactly!" Mynheer bent down to exchange a look of understanding with the big fellow who was trapped there; but it was too dark for either one to see the other.

"Another county heard from!" sang out Horace up above. "Dopo down there is tone-deaf, anyway. Where there's no sense there's no feeling."

Instead, Dyck played off a thunderous page of the "Paganini Variations" of Rachmaninoff. The room, the house, the whole neighborhood rang; the canary hid his head under his wing, and little Horace on top of the sounding board quaked.

"It's a good piano," said Dyck, breaking off. "It was made before the depression."

Lothario, under the piano, was stunned. The piano was, of course, out of tune.

"I can get more explosive noises than that out of that box," thought Horatio ominously.

Sis blew out the candles.

"Good night," she said; and she and Dyck crawled into her room.

"When am I gonna get lights again?" called out the boy, with spite and hate.

3.

Now Laura, who had dawn-blue eyes, was the glancing Day as it passes, and the omnicapable Mynheer was the intellect of Man. And the problem I pose myself in describing their loves is simply this: Can they be happy together, once they have met?

The Period of the Grand Piano was the honeymoon of Laura and Mynheer, when everybody else was bent on some task or duty (each down his own slope), and only they had nothing to do. In the love of Mynheer and Laura can be seen the apparently miraculous affinity of the archaic aristocracy (there is always an élite being left behind) and the lumpen proletariat (there are always those who are marginal). These groups are not social classes but are free as the wind. It is not that they have no function, but that their functioning makes no difference; it is idleness, philosophy; the passing of the day and the abiding underlying truth that people also do not notice.

They live on the work of the others; but unlike the strenuous bourgeoisie or the financiers, they assume no responsibility in continuing their happy exploitation, for they exert no social leverage. (Indeed, they must not try to, as in reactionary cabals, for then they are likely to get shot.)

And deep down, of course, there is not absent between them, in the forgotten childhood of each, that mutual envy and terror of the extreme classes which seems to be essential for the fascination of falling in love, as when the Jews and the Irish become infatuated with each other because each believes that the other is dirty and sexy.

4. Watching Water Boil

"Want tea?" asked Laura. They were at Dyck's.

"Certainly, let us have tea," said Dyck.

With a little explosion, the flame ran round the range, and the molecules in the kettle began at once to feel the uneasy desire to vibrate. And while the water was heating they talked, but they were fascinated by the water coming to a boil.

"Every time I come here," said Laura, "I've got to bring something new or throw something out, to disturb the set expression that seems to develop."

"If you had your way," said Dyck annoyed, "the whole city would be flowing in and out of here."

"Why not?"

"I get confused."

"*Rentier!* If you had your income, the way I do, from the working Empire, instead of from no longer existing estates in the Far East, you wouldn't get all mixed up."

"Why do you give me the money?"

"Who? Me? I don't have any money," said Laura smiling.

"*Your* Empire!"

"You've got me. Search me."

"It's because you don't dare forget your history or you wouldn't know where you are. For instance, your grammar: 'Who? Me?' Especially your little brother's grammar. If everybody talked like that, soon nobody would be able to understand anybody."

"Will you listen to the Dutchman taught in school teaching my baby how to talk New York! 'Certainly,' says he, 'let us have tea.' You mean, 'Sure, let's have tea.' "

So forth. This was a typical "argument," which she started by making a personal remark about his home, to which he retorted by making a personal remark about her speech.

But the roar in the kettle was followed by the little hiss, and the beads of gas were now rising from the hot water in the form that the Chinese call crab's-eyes.

Another conversation was mutual admiration:

"Let's not quarrel, honey. I'm crazy for the way you can blow smoke rings and make sculptures out of sugar cubes and do shadow plays with your fingers. And make Mondriaans too."

"Thank you. They're just the forms of pure nature," he said modestly. "But you have an astounding intuition for what's popular. You can always anticipate the new fashions and guess what radio programs will catch on."

"That's because I know they're a mess and don't bother. I just stick up my antennae." This was no metaphor, for when you looked at her when she was in the mood you could virtually see the pair of little waving antennae. "I go by feel. What I really enjoy is the feeling of the approaches of various cities, the way the highways are banked, and what they do with the public buildings."

"I like to analyze the kinds of campfire, and mountain music, and ecclesiastical ritual."

"If I were a painter," said Laura, "I'd paint with neon tubes."

"If I were a composer," said Mynheer sadly, "I'd only compose *Don Giovanni* all over again. I don't know how to invent anything new."

And the water was now bubbling full pigeon's eggs, and the steam was pouring from the spout. They brewed their tea and drank it, and it tasted good.

At the same moment each reached for the other's hand.

"I love you and am afraid of you, Dyck," said Laura, "because you're so heroically stubborn in judging everything as what it is and not another thing."

"Heroically?" he said, and flushed darkly.

"All my men are heroes," she said proudly, "Lothar and Horace *and* you."

"I am afraid *for* you, Laura," he said and his eyes clouded, "because you are so beautiful that, as the world is, the poison in the air, the war, you will not be able to live."

They were suffering from Romantic Love, and they never *did* get in touch with each other; yet at this stage it was still charming to consider them together, so lovely and busy with ideas. It was only later, as we shall see, that they learned that the ending of that kind of love is death.

5. Local Patriotism

A glittering morning they would be standing on a height overlooking New York—the old footbridge across the Harlem, the leaping arcade that used to serve as an aqueduct to the now unused reservoir—and she would praise the good features of the city ("my own neighborhood where I am inscribed on the rolls!"), and not mention the bad features. She would praise the dramatic juxtaposition of the heights and the rivers, and the concrete-and-steel engineering that bound them together.

But he would look at her dumb with love because she was praising her native neighborhood.

6. Love in the Woods

They used to spend nights in the near woods across the Hudson.

Dyck was a preservationist. He raised to a general theory his longing not to lose any bygone expression of the arrangements of life. He knew that it was impossible, when once the material circumstances of a function were altered, for its aesthetic expression to survive. And he knew that it was impossible to reproduce bygone circumstances.

He was on the Executive Council of the Netherlandish Boy Scouts and he belonged to that wing of scouting—led by Dr. Irving Houghton, as I have narrated elsewhere—which concentrated on recapturing as far as possible the moral and emotional meanings of forest and field, and of living with the machines at the period of their invention.

To Laura, who was so proudly patriotic of her own estate, he was the first to demonstrate the simple causality of the woods, where there were not so many steps between the work of one's hands and the finished satisfaction. You cut the wood and struck flint and steel, and there was fire!—a kind of relation almost unknown to Laura.

They lay by the fire, the branches crackled and the rising stars continually died upward into the night. The licking flames rioted, freed from their prison of sticks, and feeding on the food of the sticks. And the sticks at last—as Rilke said in those magnificent lines as he lay dying—*the sticks were burning in the fire that they fed.* Within the hypnotic sameness of looking at the warm fires, there were endless variations of form, fancy and thought. These endless pleasures often soon enough vanished as a whole into impulsive affectionate gestures. But the starlit night and the forest and the fire remained always there in the background.

They were experts at gestures of affection and terms of endearment, and they liked each other's style. But this style often soon enough gave way to strong lust. Yet it is this traditional play, at once forgotten, that recurs in memory.

Acts of lust are formal because they directly express the nature of the animal bodies involved, and each species has what possibilities it has. And soon enough they vanish into orgasm, and the sense of mutual dependence, and sleep.

7.

Dyck was also disastrously committed to the preservation of *objets d'art* and other specimens of culture. *Noblesse oblige,* he was the champion of all the other relics against vandalism. Against the whims and ways of ordinary individuals—to whom no doubt the Holy Spirit was an infrequent visitor—it was necessary to protect the little objects in which the Holy Spirit was congealed forever. This was the theory.

But in practice it was often hard to distinguish which was the spirit and which was the vandal. Thus, no doubt it was vandalism for the young excavator, eager for his Ph.D. at the University of Pennsylvania, to disturb the sempiternal rest of the desert. Once the pot was uncovered, however, it was vandalism in the dirty Arab, eager to get home for supper, to break it with a careless pickax. But once it was irrecoverably chipped, surely it was vandalism to attempt to "restore" it by a dubious guess, in order to have something to show in the museum. It was preservationist enough to keep the relic in the cellar of the museum if there was no room to put it on display, but what vandalism if it should perhaps be mislaid!

By virtue of his connections with the Rijksmuseum—he was the curator of the East India Department—Mynheer, who happened to be in Madrid during the Spanish War, was called to the Prado to help preserve the treasures, for that government was a famous friend of culture. During the evacuation he was fleeing in a taxi with a classical set of pictures about war. On all sides the torpedoes were exploding. The taxicab sped by pedestrian fugitives who would have dearly loved to ride. The airplanes came over in waves and machine-gunned them from overhead, so that one lay shot through the ear in a ditch and another sat down with his trousers filling with blood. Some of them were not quite dead, and Mynheer stopped the cab. But if he got them into the cab, what to do with the pictures, with that classical set of pictures about war? But fortunately soon enough a shell burst in the cab, destroyed the *objets d'art,* and Mynheer was on foot like all the rest.

Chapter 6 ▪ WALPURGISNACHT

Parturiunt montes, nascitur mus cum bubonico morbo.

1.

The general war was not yet raging. The courageous artists were already trying to pick up the pieces of the aftermath. It was a meeting of the Committee for Post-War Art. (We were in a sociable period when there were many committee meetings, and it was believed that love and family, art and a man's plain duty, could be promoted according to the rules of parliamentary procedure. This was expressed by the formula, "It's nothing personal; we don't mean to hurt *your* feelings.")

In this room where the doorbell sounded the notes *Dies Irae*—

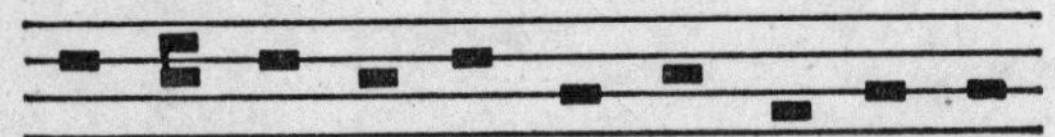

many a heartsick critic was gathered. Arthur Eliphaz and little Horatio were also there. Arthur was not an artist, he belonged to the practical kind, but he came as a spectator and he brought his small friend, hoping—not vainly—that Horace would be *his* bombshell. Horace did not know who his big friend was, but called him John Malaga and even imagined that this was his name; for so confusing was Arthur's diffidence, Horace could not see why he was so reticent if he was only going to tell a lie after all.

And Mynheer and Laura were there, huddled against the wall by the window. What made the lovers look so wan? It was that they had taken off their masks of ready awareness and were naked to no good future.

All these people were terribly well dressed, in shirts of acid-green or cerise.

The bell rang and new critics arrived. Roditi, Rosenberg, George Dennison and Raditsa.

What did these people want? They were preparing the Manifesto of Bombism.

Dressed in overalls, an old painter from the Midi arose to make an historical introduction. Now there is a concerted cheer, *Création du Monde*—it consists at first in random cries of an undistinguishable name from every throat in disunison, but then these cries cohere until at last the name itself is shouted thrice clear and loud. At this meeting the speakers were greeted by the *reverse* of that cheer: the name first sounded loud and clear, succeeded by raucous jeering and disintegrated catcalls, to whispers dying away—

to undo the work of the Creation,
returning from the Sixth to the First Day!

"At the end of the First War was Dada," said the artist quietly in the hush.

It was shattered by clamor as the window on the right flew into fragments: the ghost of Tzara.

The splinters of glass tinkled on the eyeglasses.

Attention called in that direction, Arthur suddenly noticed Sis and Dyck sitting in the breeze. "*Look* who it is," he said to Horace. "What are they doing in a place like this?"

"Don't know 'em," said Horace, who knew them both.

"Who would deny that Dada was complete?" thundered the orator graciously. "But item one: It is not the expression of the *Second* Post-War! We must be more practical!"

Several in the front row cringed, for he was looking at *them.*

"Item two: *Was not Dada betrayed?*"

In explication of this proposition—it was a rhetorical question—he embarked on a lengthy analysis of *surréalisme,* etc., which to Horace at least—and let us take him as the norm of our comprehension—was almost unintelligible. But the gist of it was simply that Dada, having begun in objective astonishment, was soon enough betrayed into a quasi-therapeutic probing of the repressed desires of the soul. Very few, and not even including the speaker, were willing to concede that this change was ruinous; but it was necessary to raise a voice for Classicism against Decadence, and for the purity of genres.

It was on this note that the orator concluded. "Over my shoulder," he cried, "I hear Apollo's whisper. There are Seven Arts but Nine Muses. Not a single inspiration to a single medium, but to each medium one and two-sevenths of a genius, as every family in America has two and a quarter children."

With the close possessiveness of a French peasant, he cannily withheld the rest of this hermetic doctrine from possible plagiarists.

"Sometimes you gotta push down the walls in order to see the street!" shouted Horatio from his place. In a general discussion he always found that he had something to say, which occurred to him by magic as he was carefully listening.

Arthur was ruby with pride in his protégé.

"Does the young architect want to incorporate this feature into the new clubhouse?" asked the shaggy architect who had perfected the Flying Stairway, the flight of stairs from whose top riser one walks boldly off into space.

Through the broken window the cold draft filled the chamber and people began to cough.

"It's Arthur and little Horace!" said Laura, covered with snow. "What's my brother doing in a place like this?" she said disapprovingly. "Do you think he's getting into bad company?"

But Bombism, or Practical Dada, the leonine critic who now took the podium was quick to point out, would be not so easy to pervert to angelic uses! At least, if it *could* be so perverted, the blessed alterations would redound to the endless benefit of mankind—and more in the same vein.

How was Bombism "practical dada"? Not in the sense of pragmatic or instrumental dada, god forbid—this would again be surrealism. But in the sense of *active* dada! The work of art that gets up on its hind legs and does something—for example, explodes in your face or exudes a poison gas.

"Not so easy to invent!" said the shaggy architect, who had invented it.

"I go further!" cried Horace. "Sometime you gotta push down the walls in order to see the countryside!"

"What did he say?" whispered a girl, the *couturière* of the Nessus shirt.

"He merely repeated what he said before."

"No, no! Now, don't you see, he's talking about the *city* walls. Like the walls of Jericho. Before he mentioned only a house. How rapidly he gets on. *Bravo!*" she shouted. "Good for you, Jericho Kid."

It was thus that Horace came to be known as the Jericho Kid, like a prize fighter.

A bombist work, it was unanimously adopted, was to be known as a *bomb-bomb*.

A bombist poem was a *bomb mot*.

Bomb jour, messieurs et mesdames.

Continually and everywhere there were random stenches and smoky fires on the floor, as a good deal of pre-post-war experimentalism was going on. (And it *was* cold.) The chairman shouted, "It's not by practical jokes that you're going to make Eliphaz look to his laurels."

"Right!" shouted another. "These unframed agonies of real life are nothing but Marinettism."

This hit the spot, for there was a general shriek: *Down with Marinetti!* and that name was subjected to the brutality of the locomotive cheer in which the name is dragged among the wheels.

But the doorbell rang its gruesome eschatology and in was wheeled a box.

"More secret weapons!" jeered one of the epigoni.

On the contrary! It was the Cyclotron of that physicist of Long Island which he was afraid to set in motion because it might initiate the disintegration of all the atoms of the universe; curiosity getting the better of him, he set it going anyway, but nothing happened. It was a failure in the laboratory, but what a specimen for the museum!

In its presence the wags stopped shooting fire crackers.

To Sis's amazement, Mynheer Duyck Colijn & Duyvendak was introduced—though he hardly spoke—as the corresponding secretary of the Society for the Annihilation of Cultural Relics.

There was now no one who was not coughing. The snow drifted in strongly and its pure odor penetrated the stenches.

"I am at a loss——" Duyck began.

When it became evident that this was his whole message, the enthusiasm knew no bounds.

I also, let me say, was at this meeting. I followed Mynheer and delivered my usual little homily on the Sublime, commenting on the passage in Immanuel Kant on the "mathematical sublime," the frustrated attempt to perceive an object too quantitatively extended for the senses to grasp all at once, even though the mind takes it as one whole. So, painfully I droned on, the attention shuttles back and forth between the overexerted senses and the understanding. "You may experience such a painful vibrato if you stand close under the tower of the suspension bridge at 178th Street," I pointed out. "My brother bombardiers!" I cried. "I submit to your technique the problem of transforming such objects to the proper proportions of restful beauty——" and more of the same kind, recommending several dynamitings. These remarks were greeted with the scattered applause which at that time seemed to be the judgment on all my efforts whether spoken or written (before the total silence set in).

And now, reducing to quiet the boisterous chamber, rose Raymond, the boy beloved of us all, our dancer, beloved for his gray-blond color and clear eyes and his gentle air; whom we used to address in the air of Handel:

Where'er you tread
the blushing flowers shall rise,
and all things flourish
where'er you turn your eyes.

He had a little painting to show, a "Baby Tank," that is, a tank meant to run down babies. He set the picture up on a chair. The tank had bristly zip guns.

To all nostrils the pure waft o' the snow penetrated, for the smokes of different densities either lifted to the ceiling or sank slowly to the floor, and opened a space between.

It was the dead of spring.

With a loud report, the picture recoiled; smoke curled from a gun mouth. And with a cry Raymond, who had been bending over his work, staggered backward and a bloodstain spread on his jacket.

He fell to the ground. All were frozen fast,

a leg half-lifted
a lifted hand about to grasp,

all save Mynheer, who was a physician; he rushed forward, but he could tell at once it was a dead man.

"It's no use," said Mynheer: "it is a dead man."

In the restrained hubbub of his dear friends about the fallen youth—and all were his dear friends—nevertheless, the critic, the big man with the tawny mane, was shaking his head from side to side and frowning.

"Now what's the matter?" I asked.

"Why should I cast an aspersion on this martyr?" he said. "But this episode was already in Cocteau's cinema. She said, *'Si vous n'avez pas l'as de coeur, mon cher, vous êtes un homme perdu'*—if you haven't the ace of hearts, you're a goner."

Raymond heard the words and opened his eyes. *"Oui! Ce cher Jean—cet aimable soleil d'Hiver,"* he said smiling—this lovely winter sun. And in this act of recognition—nor is there any activity more perfect in the busy soul—our friend died.

"No, listen to me! Listen to me!" said Horatio. "Sometime you gotta push aside the walls o' this body in order to see." And he began his bitter sobbing, the beginning of nearly twenty years of mourning, having lost in a single instant at the age of eleven his only love.

Indeed the minutes were flying by like a snowstorm.

The bell sounded; the police were at the door; and most of us vanished through the window, leaving it to the president and the leonine critic to explain to these cops that it was a meeting of aestheticians.

2. The True Theory of Our Friends

On the corner, before we scattered, we did look in our black coats like so many wizards and witches.

"Isn't it late, Horatio Alger?" said Laura tartly, to his mortification. "Shouldn't you be home in bed?" He was mortified especially by the fact that she called him by his right name.

"What are *you* doing here, Eliphaz?" Mynheer said to Arthur. "I thought you never left the sailor bars. You're leading a double life."

—But I spoke up and said: "No matter how much you all repel and avoid one another, you're all much more friends than you know. Allow me. I can explain it to you. We people are more personally engaged in what we do than the average folk, and therefore as we turn from one of our activities to another, we again find one another there. Because everything is of a piece. And likewise, unlike the ordinary folk, if two of us find we have one acquaintance in common, we will prove to have three hundred in common, for we have these activities in common. We have gone to the same marginal schools; we have praised to the skies the dancer whom the rest of New York has not yet heard of; and if one of us steals off to a secluded coast that seems to us promising, he will meet another one of us walking naked toward him up King's Beach."

"Oh, God, how true!" groaned Arthur, and without doubt they all glared at me with hatred for explaining to them the Theory of Our Friends.

"I'm not so overjoyed about it either, I assure you," I said, stung, "to come upon your same faces everywhere! Nevertheless, I'll write it down, the history of our friends."

3.

After passing along the black walls of streets ominously impending through the snowfall, the lovers were suddenly quite close under the tower of the suspension bridge. Laura was almost frightened at the height of it; she was shivering, being clad for a May night. This tower is only nine hundred feet high, but high enough when seen suddenly up close.

"It's true," she said in abject terror. "If you cannot take it in, the soul oscillates. My teeth hurt."

But Dyck found himself in the situation that he could not say anything, nothing whatever relevant at the same time to the situation and his feelings. He twisted and turned each way in his mind, but hardly came to voice a grunt in his throat. Perhaps if he explained *how* he was at a loss—no, no! This was fatal to say, for in principle it could lead nowhere else, and nothing to do but repeat it after a pause, in a more strangled voice. How long could such a conversation continue?

But perhaps it was not a set of fatal contradictions that he felt in his heart, but only confusion? Then he could say, he could begin to say, "I for my part have always found that conflicting opinions exist in my heart very well together; I believe them all pro tem; I'm confident that something will turn up——" But with these lies he did not get so far as the initial grunt. He began to say flatly: "There is nothing to say——" Now why say *that?*

An idea occurred to him: *"Try and find your deepest issue in every confusion, and abide by that."*

"What did you say?" asked Laura.

"Nothing. I was thinking of a slogan of D. H. Lawrence's, but it's not to the point." For that slogan was for *serious* persons; it was precisely this that he could not achieve, to be serious. He was almost always serious and meant just what he said (with a face as serious as an animal's); and he was only too willing to be practical about it, for he was infinitely resourceful in practical expedients; but nevertheless, he did not "mean" it, he was not engaged, and therefore his every judgment was categorically hypothetical. Up to a point he was always tentatively positive, positive as only an aesthetic or resourceful or philosophical person can be, for there is always an object of immediate perception as a basis of certain judgment; except just at the point where one is at a loss.

He was at a loss.

Why was he so? He didn't know and I don't know.

Was there some compensating advantage?

Yes! There was the compensating advantage of waiting, the strength of waiting: it is patience in anxiety.

All about them the silence was solidly empty. The snowflakes were rushing toward—sinking in—the black water,

flake after flake
dissolved in the dark and silent lake,

as Bryant saw it.

This radical waiting is accompanied by the most painful sensitivity; Mynheer Duyck at the same time powerless and susceptible, felt his heart sinking with strong pangs, as a person at a loss in a vengeful company turns to each one after he has struck. Now *nothing* has an aesthetic surface and everything is a menace to wound. He turned to each perception after it had struck.

Flake after flake
all lost in the dark and silent lake.

This avoidance, this nonavoidance, this agony of nonserious passivity, is a great compensating advantage. The silence of it is worse than empty; its feeling is the ennui suffered with fear and trembling. Patience in anxiety is a kind of ennui suffered with fear and trembling.

When every perception has no aesthetic surface and has a portentous meaning.

4.

When Horace returned home after midnight, he looked with unmixed hatred at the big brother snoring under the piano and at the grand piano itself. But he did not hate his sleeping brother so powerfully as he hated the huge machine. At worst he could think of only stilling Lothario's rough breathing, but in imagination he smashed the piano to smithereens, amid plangent chords and wiry cries. Already it was down, its chin on the floor, only one leg remaining. Some of the teeth were already extracted from the woeful keyboard. With an abrupt decision Horatio tore out also the wires, which were the soul of the machine.

Chapter 7 ▪ A NOCTURNAL VISIT

1.

It was the same snowy night as the meeting. Lothar, by candle-light, was patiently tuning the piano that had been much jarred. Tone by tone, *C″, C′, C, c, c′, c′-C″′; C-G; C-G-c.* He lovingly listened for the overtones as they whispered around the ceiling. It was a splendid piano, he was enchanted by its tone. It was rich and more interesting *out* of tune, full of ideas; but he was patiently, wire by wire, tightening it into tune for the others. *C–G–c–g:* suddenly he let loose the arpeggio into the heavenly commencement of Zarathustra's waltz. Smiling broadly with his great square teeth at that music. But he patiently went on tuning the piano, now *D; G–D–g–d; D″, D′, D–a,*

he could stretch that easily.

The doorbell rang (a kind of *a″* flat).

"*Come* in!" he sang. The door was always open.

A strange woman stood there. "Is Laura Alger home?"

"Out," he said, and paid no further attention. "You can sit down." His attention was all in his ears: *D–A–a–a′; A–bA, a–ba* . . . "Oh, I'm sorry," he cried, rising, for there was no place to sit. She had snow on her hat. "Name's Lothario Alger. I'm the brother. Can I do anything for you?"

"Oh!" she exclaimed. It was Emily Eliphaz. "Are you the notor—the famous Lothar Alger?"

"The notorious Lothar Alger?" He grinned at her with his big teeth.

She looked at him squarely for a full minute. "The *famous* Lothar Alger," she said firmly. "I am Emily Eliphaz."

He looked at her with confusion. It was hard for him to drag himself back from Zarathustra's waltz. "What the devil do you want this time of night?" he said sharply. "Oh, I'm sorry—there are no lights," he said with a helpless gesture roundabout. "Is it about the piano? Did you come about the piano?"

"No-o. I see you are tuning it. Is it good?"

He was surprised. How did the woman know that he was tuning a piano, though to be sure he had the wrench in his hand and was patently tuning a piano? But he did not have a high opinion of women. "Beautiful!" he replied. "The action's all right; the tone is simply lovely."

"Oh! Then I'm glad he sent you the piano!" she said impulsively and blushed. And she burst into tears.

"Do you want some coffee?" said Lothar.

"I'm sorry," she said, recovering. "I'm disturbing you. I'll go. Thanks."

"But please——" He touched her arm. "You're not disturbing me at all. Why did you come? Laura is off at some meeting; I really don't know when she'll be back. The boy is somewhere too. There's a little brother. We——"

"No, no, please let me go. I just came to see what your sister was like. You see, I–I have been frightfully jealous."

"Oh? . . . Oh. Yes, I understand. Then you'd better come back when she's here."

"There's no need to," said Emily brightly, "I've already seen what I came to see. I'm satisfied."

What did she mean by that? "Now *I* don't understand."

"May I look around here a moment?"

"Please."

She squeezed sideways into the kitchen.

"There's not much room," said Lothar apologetically.

"No, there's not."

This immensely annoyed him. Who in hell was this bourgeoise to tell him that there wasn't much room in his flat!

"How do you get in *there?*" asked Emily.

"How do you think? You crawl under, of course," he said brusquely. She caught the tone but she crawled under anyway, and she broke into a merry laugh.

"Where *do* you all sleep?" she cried. "It's just like Papa said! 'Where are they going to sleep with a grand piano in the house?' "

"My brother sleeps on *top* of the piano and I sleep *under* the piano. That's where we sleep. Any objections? Where do *you* sleep? What in hell do you mean you've seen what you came to see? *You're* satisfied, are you? What did you expect to see my sister was like? How did you expect to see she lives? 'I've been *frightfully* jealous!' Oh, Christ!"

She got up from her hands and knees and stood and faced him. "Lothario Alger! What in hell's the matter with *you*? First let me say, for you certainly have the right to ask. I came to see—and I have seen—that Laura has a home; the brother is tuning the piano; the brother is Lothar Alger—*I* cannot compete; certainly I am not insulted by losing out. That's what I've learned. She's pretty, isn't she?"

"Yes, Laura is very pretty. Everybody thinks so. Even I."

Emily paled a little and the tears rose to her eyes again. She recovered. "Why are you angry if I giggle at the way you people live. Do *you* think it's tiptop? . . . Or maybe—do you really think that Emily Eliphaz regards it with contempt? I don't believe it. You're too smart for that. There must be something else, and it's none of my business."

"No, it's not," he said. He liked her. She was direct like many of his friends. He was not especially surprised by this, for he thought her column was pretty good too, and nothing comes from nothing. What did surprise him was how she gave him the benefit of the doubt, which he deserved; he was not used to it. "I like you, Emily," he said.

"Thank you," she said, frankly pleased.

"You came on me tuning the piano—for the others——"

"For the others? I thought *you* were the musician."

"Yes, I am; but I don't use that scale. (It's a technical matter.) I—I expect to be arrested tomorrow or the next day. Eighteen months, maybe two years—— So you see I'm not tuning the piano for my own use."

"I expect that you'll get five years, Lothar Alger."

"As much as that?" he said mournfully, and tossed his head slightly, the way a child does when he has a headache, to see if it still hurts. He recovered. "My guess is that I blew up about your remarks about the furniture because of—this." He bent his head.

She touched a few keys on the piano. Then abruptly, "I love property, I love possessions!" she said.

"Do you?" he said, surprised, looking up. "I shouldn't have thought so. I should have thought you'd had it."

"Ah, man! But it must *be* property, it must be *possessed!* And do you know who has *that,* Lothar Alger? Only those who are just *about* to have it—what the hand is *closing* on——"

He looked away. "We're not interested in any of that. We do not intend to grab it. Maybe—no offense—you can't understand that. But thanks for trying to make me feel better. You're unusually generous."

"I am sorry you hate my father. You would like him."

"Are you mad?" he cried, astonished. "How would I hate him? I have the highest esteem for him. He is the Man. An absurd specimen but the only one. With what else would you compare him? With *my* friends? *These* days? *Might* is right. What else would be right? But of course it must, as you say, *be* might, it must operate and not just keep everything else from operating. I do think your father is more than a little crazy."

"Are you telling *me!*" she exclaimed. "Please! I *must* go now." And without another word, not so much as a good-by, she fled.

He was again astonished and followed her to the door, but she had vanished down the stairs.

He was disappointed, he felt the night was empty. But he sat down and patiently went on tuning the piano that had been much jarred.

2.

Emily fled in a tumult of emotions when the young man began to praise her father. The way the men had, even when they were enemies (or even especially when they were enemies), of being knightly just to one another, objectively admiring of one another: to Emily this was always unbearably poignant. And the thrilling and not brutal way in which he said, as a matter of course, that might is right. And her own incestuous wishes storming near the surface.

Chapter 8 ▪ HORATIO'S DIARY

I hate amachoors.

198 St. Ft.W./3:30 Mae—"Rudy" B+

[*An assignation on that corner with Mae after school, under the name of Rudy. Negligible if someone of higher rating turns up.*]

DOPO IS WEAK IN THE HEAD.

[*A reference to his brother.*]

Sez "even if we had the dow we wont turn on electric. Getting even with Eliphaz"*** this rings the bell 3 times

he cant be stupid or whats heredity?

some A.M. hes keen, but fresh air gets him.

The lift of the 1st sip of coffee in the morning, & you feel tird after you com off.

Dutch is even jerkier. how dos Sis take it? *answer*—THERES A SECRET i hav to wate til i get older, but its not sex like Marcia thinks. Dutch sez there is no secret, when you get older you lern theres no secret.

plot to ful us.

$$\frac{8642}{3} = 2880 \text{ \&} \qquad \begin{array}{r} 8 \\ 6 \\ 4 \\ \underline{2} \\ 20 \end{array} \qquad \frac{20}{3} = 6 \text{ \&}$$

[*Work in the theory of numbers on the experimental method. "&" means "there is a remainder."*]

F. drugstor NW 134/8:30 69B—

[*An old friend*]

the Ambassador giv me 2 clippings.

Editor *New York Herald Tribune*
Dear Sir:

I note with amusement the mounting fever to license the bicycles of little boys. This is necessary to prevent these bandits from fleeing the scenes of their crimes. But who is to secure us from the speeding kiddie-kar, whose license would be larger than the machine itself?

This ordinance would effectively keep the average manly boy off the road altogether. "License indeed!" he'll aver, and put his wheel to gather dust in the basement. The flying tricolor of blue jeans, red shirt, and silvery spokes will be seen no more.

No numbers for the free yeomen of the highway who imitate the motions of the heavens and perfect their endoskeletons with wheels!

TIMAEUS

hes a gret kidder, thinks this is simply howling**
he sez "al you need is put the mater in the rite atmosfer & pepl wil com around"
sez "fair play & ralery they never fail"   ful of shit
i ask "cd you get the H.T. to tak the CIO in the rite atmos.?" stumps him*

To the Editor of the *New York Herald Tribune*
Dear Sir:

As a Dutchman one of whose ancestors was with Hendrick Hudson when first white men cast eyes on the lordly Hudson and the Palisades in their glory, may I ask your paper to print a protest against an act of vandalism?

Across Hudson's River, not far from the Point at 178th Street, the sight is painfully wounded by a monstrous sign, advertising the roadhouse of one Luis Mendoza. At night this sign is illuminated a baleful red.

Perhaps Señor Mendoza y Pidal does not realize that he wins himself only ill-will by maintaining such an eyesore.

DUYCK PIET COLIJN & DUYVENDAK
VAN DER MEER

so what?

HUNCH CONFERMD***** IMPORTANT*

$$12\quad \begin{array}{r}1\\ \underline{2}\\ 3\end{array}\quad \frac{12}{3}=4 \qquad 18\quad \begin{array}{r}1\\ \underline{8}\\ 9/3=3\end{array}\quad \frac{18}{3}=6 \qquad 57\quad \begin{array}{r}5\\ \underline{7}\\ 12/3=4\end{array}\quad 57/3=19$$

i trid it out 50 tims at arch 5. NOT 1 MISS***
shd i let Dutch in on it if he tels me the secret?

[*the Rule of Three*]

im worrid about Dope.

sis & me we tak car of rselvs. but hes not strong upstars, they play him for a sucker. hes my broter. if i dont lok out for him who wil?
A.M. hes grand, fresh air gets him.
if El. gets him in the jal, sis wil jus die.

I hate dopo lik posn caus hes not proud of me. Means im conseted. is this rit atmos.?

M. stans me up again. fuck her* too good for her* "rudy" bad luck, dont use.

evenings venus is dragd down after the Sun. & outfeelders swing over to the rite when a lefty bater coms up.

Grade C means O.K. to pass time, nothing to look forard to. D means to kik out of bed.

"everybody is going to Mastersingers," sez Dutch. seems its all musik. they explane it to me, dutch sez "youll see Peece in Sciety, you wdnt believ it" you bet i wldnt.

hes cute. when he gets exsitd his hairs stand up.

sis has all the luck.

sis has all the luck, sis has all the fuck.

i told him bout my secret 3's, & he get teers, I cd see. 1st i jus drop a hint but he dru me rite out, hes keen, then i explane & he begun almos to cry. ??? what goes on? i dont catch, but its not dirty.

wors than posn i hate amachoors lik Dope*

he'll queer me with El.

tims I cd kil him when he lies ther blowing in his sleep.

The hook-up for the Piano is eesy*

[*This refers to a scheme of Horatio's to wire a certain key of the piano to an explosive.*]

thisll kil em at the Bombardeers***

malaga wil love it. i wish he was my broter. MALAGA IS YUNG EL.*

i dedikat my Art to raymon.

why dos evn my Sis hav to screw me up bout Mastersingers? i think they evn ful thrselvs, the poor 1s.

[*Horatio finds it hard to accept the explanation of* Die Meistersinger *as Peace in Society.*]

thursty. simplify to

145-155 stikbal
155-165 rawlee

165-175 hanbal
175-185 gallia
185-195 donalson

musnt hav to much on the mind.
[*A retrenchment of neighborhood amours and sports.*]

LIES LIES LIES LIES

dutch is rong bout what i rite. if i rite it its lies lies
i rite it jus caus i got so much on the mind
when i cn rite it i say Good-by to al that*

we luv dopo, sis & me bot. if they get him ill jus die.
if El tris to hurt r Dopo ill get evn.

Chapter 9 ▪ ELIPHAZ

1.

When Eliphaz looked at his son in the window, and saw him standing in the sunset light as if in a show window, like a model of careless college elegance, his heart sank. He felt affection for him; he had to sell him.

He wished he could slow up his headlong career. "What about our little Ultimate Consumer?" he said, going backward; harshly, because he felt affectionate.

Arthur pricked up his ears. Now what demand was going to be made? "Why do you ask?" he said.

"Just like that. To see more of her."

To Arthur these days, only one thing was important, to get rid of Samuel. He had begun to feel himself hounded. His own activities were becoming livelier and it was harder and harder to preserve the anonymity that he thought he wanted. "How could I ask her to come here?" he said to his father.

"Why not? I can accommodate everyone."

"There is no modern furniture!"

The old man was at a loss how to take this. There was an entire apartment of Mies van der Rohe, brought stick by stick from Myn-heer's seat and installed amid ruinous alterations. "If it's only that," said Eliphaz humbly, "I could make exchanges." By this time he could see the tag attached to Arthur's cuff. He edged nearer to see the price.

"You'll never understand," said Arthur in the manner of the younger generation. "It's no use having anything in the modern *style*. What Sis wants is the presentness of existence."

"Sis?"

"The formality of department stores!"

"A distinguished taste."

"As pure as a snowstorm."

"Don't get so heated, boy. You're just like Emily—you always take it for granted beforehand that Papa is stupid. Don't you see that there is no profit to be made from such popular commodities whose elegance has had no time to accumulate interest? What is popular becomes more worthless every time it is purchased and the mills are encouraged to produce another copy. The real money is in Old Masters."

He got a good look at the tag. The boy was worth eighty-four, ninety-five.

2.

Arthur said coldly, "You'll have to call off Sammy or I won't answer for the consequences."

"Ah."

By this cold remark, Arthur drove his father to the wall. Now Eliphaz was forced into the dilemma of Father Abraham, called on to sacrifice the boy on Mount Moriah. The tragedy was pressing closer on him day by day, almost to the point of destroying his peace of mind. The dearer Arthur became to him—and this was the inevitable result of his taking an interest in his life (this was his mistake! he should not have tried to enter his son's room in the first place)—the more he had to make a profit out of him. And the advantage of Sammy was that, that way, he could turn a penny on the innumerable details of Arthur's daily life, and so he was able to adjourn the fateful confrontation with Arthur himself, standing in the evening sunlight. Now no more Sammy. $84.95.

"If I order a drink," cried Arthur, "Sam must get to see the label on the bottle."

"Yes; then I purchase a share of the stock and can show a token profit."

"Is it the same with everything I use and wear?" said Arthur in a hoarse voice.

"With everything." The doting father knew the history of the hat and the shoes; he shared in a certain sense in every article of his boy's food and clothing.

Arthur's eyes clouded with tears.

"What's wrong with it, son? Do you think it's not interesting to follow the vagaries of somebody else's personal habits, to let *him* pose all the problems, not to intervene at any turn, and still make a profit at every turn? This is a way to learn the world and its values! And what do *you* lose?"

"What about Madame Vanetska's?" said Arthur quietly. This was the brothel.

"*I* am Madame Vanetska!" cried Eliphaz, clapping his hands.

"Oh, it's beautiful! Beautiful!" cried Arthur in anguish—as a thousand acts of polymorphous love were suddenly touched with the infection of incest. Like Phèdre, he felt that his clothes were a heavy burden to him. "How these vain ornaments weigh on me!" Indecisive where to begin tearing them off, he kicked off his right moccasin which flew across the room and hit the wall.

Here was another example of the merchant prince's ability to collect his guests' shoes and other personal belongings.

The other men of his class were only financiers, but Eliphaz was great not only in financial and industrial exchange, but in the little exchanges of individual commodities, like the keeper of a general store in a frontier town. This very fact exasperated his colleagues, so that willfully, like small children, they had tantrums and kicked off their shoes.

"You're smart," said the boy. "You've spoiled the satisfaction of our lives in order to make money out of your own children. I hope you choke."

"Please. Not so fast," said Eliphaz sternly. "When you talk about your own feelings, I respect you, because you know what you're talking about. But when you presume to judge somebody else's behavior, you speak generalities and you don't know what you're talking about.

"I also know that I can't eat and drink money, if this is what you mean by choking. I can't even make love to it directly like the ancients, because we're off the gold standard. You're not a new discoverer in this field of Roman comedy." The old man's voice was golden with sarcasm and his eyes were silvery with history. "Now God forbid," he said, "that I should seem to defend on moral grounds the behavior which is my vocation and springs spontaneously from my heart. But do you think that as a financier I lead a more corrupted life than your artists or lovers or politicians, if that's what you esteem (I wouldn't know)? The criterion of *my* behavior is objective and exact—I record my virtue in quantitative terms in this notebook——" And he laid his hand on the famous black-leather-covered book. "*I* have no place for personal envy or animosity, for backbiting, poisonous resentment or drunken illusions: *these* will not alter the figures. All is here pure and scrupulous. The friendship of everyone is to my advantage—it is the basis of a free market; even though every transaction is a battle and I have transactions with everyone. But there is nothing personal in it. Do you find that I cannot smile and eat without indigestion with the man who seems to be my enemy? In a moment we are allies again. The relations of business are limpid and flowing like water, like sweet water," said the owner of the Hawaiian Islands, land of the pineapple. "As the Scripture says, '*Money answers all things——*' "

But Arthur was regarding him with such a peculiar air that the father's smile grew wan and he broke off. His fatherly feelings were homicidal and sacrificial—he was rising to a dangerous pitch of exaltation.

The case was (but he had no way of knowing it) that Arthur's look was sympathy and appreciation for the profoundly reasonable things he was saying.

"Don't feel bad, Arthur," said his father.

Arthur was not feeling bad, but it was these tender words of his father that at once brought the tears to his eyes.

Suddenly Eliphaz recalled the imperious shouts, for a piece of cake or a cigar, of the small two-year-old, who had been a fiercely willful child. Emily was too.

"I'll surely disinherit them both for the first comer," he vowed.

All this time Arthur was standing with one shoe off and one shoe on. When they noticed it, they broke out laughing. But when the young man now made an effort to recover the shoe, Eliphaz said, "No, no, leave it to me as a memento of a sacrificial hour."

3. A Bargain

There was a hidden panel in the wall. Eliphaz touched a button and it flew open, disclosing a closet crammed with variegated commodities arranged in rows. There were as many as ten odd shoes, including the ambassador's sandal; a tennis sneaker from the center court at Wimbledon (before the bombardment); a ragged brogan got by a sharp trick. A fishing rod that he had picked up by way of business at the Pennsylvania Station; a crimson and silver velvet gown on a hanger; a brassy trumpet. Real odds and ends.

There were the contents of St. Francis' wallet as once before I have described them: a broken crucifix, a tape measure, a boy's top and a copy of the *Song of Songs*; yes, and the wallet itself.

The hostages that the young poet gave to Fate:

a sky-blue car, a cat, a daughter Susan,

these were also in the financier's closet. And the memorials of a trip to Lake George.

When that door flew open, a light lit within. And these various colored objects glittered in their rows.

He put Arthur's moccasin there and slid the panel shut.

"Please. Not so fast," cried Arthur. "I'll buy the whole lot for fifty dollars. It's just what we need for our collection."

"I beg your pardon," said Eliphas; "none of these is on the market. It's a mistake to regard them as commodities. They are my *objets trouvés.*"

"*Objets trouvés* indeed! Today there's a great trade in *objets trouvés.* Please. If there's a buyer there's a market. Do you think I couldn't dispose of that left-footed torn brogan? I know the very lady who would enjoy it."

"But these things are all I have in the world," said Eliphaz.

"I never thought," said Arthur, "I never thought that the merchant of whom we have been so proud—I see now why Emily is also a little exasperated—would turn out to be a hoarder."

"Make it sixty dollars," said Eliphaz.

"Bought for sixty dollars!"

"Sold for sixty dollars!"

Arthur set to heaping up his purchases in a blanket, to carry them off. He smiled as he recognized Mynheer's thinking cap. There were toys that Eliphaz had once cheated the children of, to teach them, little thinking that the boy would better the instruction. "But what's this?" said Arthur, blanching. It was the little cross bow of the Anacreontic Cupid, that had gone out of circulation about the time of Tom Moore.

There was a framed ten-dollar bill that was Eliphaz's first salary for his first job.

"Father," said Arthur sternly, "I don't mind these other things; but to take paper money itself out of circulation is too much. Everything is what it is and not another thing." (Everybody in this story seems to quote from Bishop Butler.) He broke the glass and pocketed the bill.

Eliphaz had no comment to make; the young man was right. As these symbols of sentimental attachment, so unlike the fluid pleasures of trade, went one by one into the blanket, he alternately blushed and blanched. Yet he had nothing to reproach himself with. It was really a remarkably shrewd stroke on his part to keep such a home depository of instincts and lusts—in a sense, nothing but a lot of junk—as a medicine against disastrous dreams on the Stock Exchange. To a young man such a safeguard is invaluable, but "at seventy," as Confucius says, "a sage can safely do as he likes."

And now to get rid of all this box of junk at once! He rubbed his hands: he had made a good deal after all. How easy it made the other business, to sell off the boy, which was now just an incident in the clearance sale! "Going out of Business, Must Move."

4.

In gratitude and admiration he put an arm round Arthur's shoulders. They were pleased with each other; both were radiantly smiling. To his father Arthur seemed larger and more manly. "I never thought you had it in you, man! To drive a deal through like that!"

"Oh, our group has nothing but a simple slogan," said Arthur modestly. *"Help each one down his own slope.* (It's from the Zen.)"

"Your group?"

Arthur drew out a card—

S.P.V.–S.V.P.

—the Society for the Propagation of Vice: S'il Vous Plaît.

"How interesting! And you bought this for *their* collection?"

Arthur nodded with a self-satisfied air.

Eliphaz looked younger, ageless. His rejuvenation was nothing but ceding more completely to his fixed desires, for such fixations occur in early years. Some old men, they say, achieve even a second childhood.

He made a phone call.

"Now I have turned all my capital into interest!" he said sententiously.

5.

"But you can't do that, you know," said Arthur, putting on his other shoe and stamping once or twice. "You get your interest on your investment."

"My investments are made with forthcoming interest."

"Please. There has to be something in the beginning."

"Don't be childish," said Eliphaz gaily. He felt there was a permanent crisis in his affairs, and if only he could keep on trusting to it! "We do it every day. Ponzi did it. I write a draft on the First National Bank; before it's cleared I've covered it with a draft on the Second National Bank; and so forth. After a while it's the credit structure of the country. The trouble is that the people are so wonderfully productive that they keep providing a basis for the credit. I'd like to keep it floating in the air. My ambition is to get along just pyramiding between the First and the Second National Banks, like a forger. To get rid of all this primary accumulation and rationalization of labor and the export of capital. Instead I have to bother about wars in China.

"I should like to found a Penny-of-the-Month Club, where for, say, a dollar a year dues, I guarantee to each subscriber on the first of every month a Typical Penny."

6.

"Do you know this notebook?" he asked.

It was the worn leather-bound book in which he kept his accounts.

"I've seen it around," said Arthur indifferently.

"There's no other record," said Eliphaz confidentially. "Maybe you think that whether or not I kept a record the quarterly dividends would arrive like clockwork? Let me tell you, those things pass *through* my hands. I never even see them. All I have is right here." And he tapped his little notebook.

Arthur shrugged, he couldn't be less interested.

His father was hurt. "Look into the book, please do, son. Don't feel so unkindly towards me."

"I don't mean to be cruel to you, papa. But I'm not interested in what I can't understand. If I were interested to begin with, I'd try to make something out of it——"

"Look into it, Artie! it's easy to understand."

"If you think I'm not ashamed," said the young man, "that at twenty-four years of age I hear my father ask me to feel a little kindly towards him!"

"Look, look! Look into the book."

Embossed in the leather cover of what Arthur expected to be a book of accounts–and it was only a book of accounts–was the slogan:

> To undo the work of the Creation,
> returning from the Sixth to the First Day!

"What! Do you belong to it too?" he said; although he had been suspecting it for half an hour. He broke open the book.

The pages contained nothing but ciphers, as follows:

0.000
00.000
000.000
0000.000

He turned a page and another page. There was nothing but lists, pyramids, of ciphers, for page after page:

000 000 000 000.000
0 000 000 000 000.000

"There's nothing here but zeros!" said Arthur.

"You see, I keep it scrupulously down to the mil part of a dollar," said Eliphaz.

"But it makes no difference, does it, how many zeros you put down? If there's no integer in front it still comes to nothing."

"It *makes* a difference! These are all the commodities that I have fixed in their exchange value and alienated from use forever."

000 000 000 000 000 000. 000

"Especially during times of war, you'd be surprised how many extra zeros you can slip in without anybody's noticing.

"Here you see it!" said Eliphaz. "Money answers all things—comforts and lusts, quiet memory and forgetfulness . . . violence, temptations to benevolence. . . . Possibilities, possibilities. . . ." He was turning the pages musingly. "Every item has its history."

"Alas for my sister Emily!" said Arthur mournfully. "For myself I am not far from seeing it your way. It makes a difference or it makes little difference whether my home or my native Empire City has been gorgeous and rich with irresistible attractions, or quite streamlined, as they say, to the mere symbols of strong pleasure in a period of hasty transition, exchangeable for money. The course *we* have adopted, my friends and I, has been designed to reduce the importance of all such alternatives. In our weakness they do not depend on us, anyway, but on you. I must have had a lucky childhood, and I passed my adolescence in hiding. But Emily needs an at least semi-permanent establishment; and apparently she hoped to find it in this house, with an amazing ignorance, I confess, of the historical role of our class."

"I shouldn't pity Emily for her naïve ignorance," said Eliphaz. "It's the cause of her success and has made her the Joan of Arc of the entire liberal middle class."

"Emily is one of those people—" said Arthur, "I don't know how it came about; I'm sure it's my fault; maybe Mama robbed her of love in order to give it to me—Emily has to have a long and proprietary acquaintanceship with things in order to be easy with them. She never takes anything for granted just for the sake of argument. Mind you, she's not stupid—that's why I say 'semi-permanent establishment' rather than 'permanent establishment.' But boring! Nevertheless! Just because her ideas are boring to you and me, that's no reason to treat her like a dog. Excuse me—but my poor sister has grown up in a home where the furniture was sold before we sat down to dinner, and they carried it off between salad and dessert. Not only the furniture but the house. Not only the house, my City. Here sits my sister in transit, simply bewildered—you think I'm speaking strongly, but you don't know her—bewildered by these flowing zeros without an integer. If she ever found out the truth, she'd faint."

7. A Homily

Eliphaz considered these remarks seriously for a few moments and then shrugged again; they didn't amount to much. "The earth is the *Lord's,* and the fulness thereof," said the patriarch tartly. He meant to say by his emphasis that it was not *his,* and certainly not *yours.*

"When I was born into this evil world," he said, "because of my happy childhood and my blessed first marriage—may she rest in peace!—I was able easily, but none too soon, to find out and enjoy the kinds of satisfaction that are here available, such as they are. I have been told that many persons suffer frustration—this is a strange thought to me—and it seems that because of their early misfortunes and deprivations they are never properly able to measure their desires, to make them precise, in terms of what this world has to offer. And when their pleasures do come (if they do) they are no longer fulfillments of desire; it is too late. They have forgotten what they want. Must be sad. This is why the rabbi says that poverty too early makes a man a beast, but when it comes after he has established himself, after, as we say, he knows the score, it makes him a saint.

"*I* was well established and I easily perceived that there was not much hereabout, a somewhat meager little creation at its best, and that my appetite was infinite in only a formal sense.

"I am speaking of things in general and *at their best.* But we are far from paradise, and what shall we say of things in concrete in the early imperial society of 1875-1910, when anything you could name was already incurably corrupted by the present system—no doubt corrupted for five thousand years or more? I mean when even the convivial Chablis and the sedative Havana tasted of the profits of a huckster. I mean, when the circumstances in which I could advance a useful and benevolent invention were *handled*—I am not exaggerating when I employ these disgusting words—by captains of industry. These are still dispensable commodities; but imagine my overpowering nausea and suffocation when I tasted this same infection in the vital necessities of food and saw it daily in the architecture of my native Empire City! Arthur my boy, I don't want to disturb your emotions with coprophilic imagery, for perhaps—you are not a financier—your desires are differently grounded from mine——"

"It's O.K., papa. I can take it any way," said the young man proudly.

"—But if I was ready to vomit in those earlier days, what dirty words must I employ to mention the decades of 1920-1940, the sabbath of publicity and advertising, and every word of it an insult to honor and intelligence? Even the conceivable perfections of life are trivial; but what a degrading, ruinous and wasted effort to try for a single one in this sink of corruption! Who could have a clean taste?

"Thank God I found another way, and I am a master at it.

"Blest art Thou, O Lord, who hast freed me from the enjoyment of these commodities. (Let us say, Amen.)

"By transforming every corrupted satisfaction—I am speaking of subsistence, of pleasures, of artworks and family relations—by transforming them into their values in exchange, I have alienated from myself not only the filth of 1940 but many of the human frailties that beset us even in the Golden Age. I'm not boasting; there is no step of the way that is not a creative act and does not need the help of the spirit. But God has been good to me and has put profitable transactions in my way. In a time when I could not eat or breathe for disgust and oppression, I became free and all I touch is pure and my own. Isn't this a miracle?

"*This* miracle, of salvation, I have been privileged to record day by day, and often minute by minute (for you must read also between the lines), in that little black notebook with its lists of endless zeros without an integer. These are the history of my liberation from the values of the evil world into which I was born, just like anybody else, in the year 1875."

8. A View of New York

"Come here, look out the window, Son, at our busy Empire City that I loved as a native son, and now love as a compassionate father, though I am no longer a New Yorker.* Those millions, what are they doing? You would not believe it possible that those millions would continue without interruption, even in the dead hours in low bars, the innumerable exchanges of value, in bewildering currency, with little immediate satisfaction for anyone. Yet so it is! Perhaps it is simply because people leap from bed at an appointed hour (why do they?) and after they have taken a train ride from their hearts the day is well lost. So many devoted lambs! Certainly they must be doing some penance, my little friends and co-workers.

"Look again, Arthur. Now it is evening, see the million lights. These are a million penitents in identical cells up three, five, fifteen stories. Many are having supper: we do not deny ourselves the simple needs of the flesh, but we pay a grace at every moment, when we

* I am baffled as to the meaning of Eliphaz's statement that he was no longer a New Yorker.

eat the bread in packages and drink the wine bottled in Brooklyn.

"Consider the packages. Have you noticed that the food becomes economically worthless once you open the airtight wrapper. *Nobody* wants it then—including the people who are going to eat it. You might as well throw the clothes away once you have taken them home from the store. For these things are not on the market any more, and you can see that all we are interested in is making money. Consider these packages, and the opening of these packages!

"I want you to take it in your hands and look at it and turn it this way and that like a beryl: this sacramental moment when the value departs from the commodity. It is not when you pay the money over the counter, but when you break the seal. And are you not thunderstruck, as I am, by the scavengers who mortify themselves by indulging in gross quantities in these profit-bearing delights?"

9.

"Listen to me closely," said the saintly old man confidentially, lowering his voice. "This is first theology, not usually spoken in a company of even two. But I am your father, and it is the duty of a father one time in his life to instruct his son in these things.

"The Lord created the heavens and the earth. The earth is the Lord's, and the fulness thereof. What is our part? Our part is to undo the work of the Creation, returning from the Sixth to the First Day. You seem to know the poem—I cannot imagine where you learned it, but each in his own way. One man, as the poem says,

> *"one man by 11 hours sleep*
> *and sexual intercourse with animals——"*

When he quoted this couplet, Arthur flushed.

"But this poet," cried Eliphaz excitedly, "did not understand finance! In the whole poem he does not once mention me. But I also have lent my hand in restoring the creation to that beginning where, as it is written, is hovering the spirit of the Lord.

"Now today almost anywhere, indeed everywhere, the bombs are 'bursting in air' as the song says, and also on the ground. There is a lot of crude destruction. But as for me, I am of a scrupulous and methodical disposition; and this kind of incendiary or explosive annihilation does not satisfy me—it does not exhaust the negative possibilities. At one blow it destroys a complex situation that I should patiently have undone element by element, with a great increment of nonbeing. Alas! I foresee clearly that this random destruction, bypassing so many unexplored satisfactions along the way, will not teach people anything. People imagine that they have been deprived of something. So they will turn away from that kind of destruction and take up their old rounds. But in my way people become disgusted with every aspect of existence and stay disgusted forever.

"Yet I am not so lacking in imagination but that I too can feel the worldwide thrill of joy when the cities are bombarded, and the historical landmarks, the man-eating factories and the institutional buildings tumble down. Up to a certain point, this popular kind of destruction gratifies the deepest needs of all mankind."

Chapter 10 ▪ S.P.V.–S.V.P.

1.

After the confessions of his father, Arthur went for his walk.

Often while his father was talking, he had been about to say, "Wait up! Not so fast! You think there's only one way, but there is another way." But since he agreed with him in the end, he was generous enough, or sure enough of himself (it comes to the same thing), not to quarrel with him along the way.

He stared over his shoulder; Sammy was no longer on his trail. He suffered a pang, as we do when we get what we wish for. His father had given him up.

He hesitated only a moment, and shrugged his shoulders, and plunged again into his beloved misery of looking for love in the face of self-imposed insurmountable obstacles.

2.

Changing his pace at a given instant, so that there was a perceptible pause-in-between, from the unconscious and the moderate to a wary nonchalance accompanied by darting glances, he entered the gate of the great park, looking for love where it can't be found. It was already late at night, and obviously he was looking for love where it couldn't be found. Looking where he was not likely to find anything, and if he found anything it was certainly not going to be love. He was looking for danger, to be held up and hit on the head around the next dark turning of the path. Around the next dark turning was no doubt love seated on a bench in the lamplight; in the light so as to be visible and easily surveyed in all the beauty belonging to such an object. There was no bench under the lamp. But a person seemed to be moving in the shadows. It is hard for a man walking rapidly along like Arthur not to mistake the parallax of objects in the different planes for the motion of a person in the shadows: this is a well-known phenomenon of looking for love where it can't be found. But *here* was a lighted lamp with a bench under it, and on this light-bathed bench sat no one at all.

Arthur sat down there and relaxed his tense awareness, and felt abased. This abasement is an incident of looking for danger where it may not be found, and then again it may.

It is also possible to wait for love where it will not come. This is easy when you have no appointment; and it is inevitable when your appointment is tending in another direction on the infinite plane than where you are. While Arthur was waiting for love where it would not come, his attention crowded into his ears; yet there wasn't any sound to fill his attention and his soul responding; so that the features of his face, while he waited in vain, were fixed, without order or composure, or even fixed in an agony of *dis*order.

Since, seated under the lamp, he was waiting for that which would not come, he had no need to pretend not to be waiting for what he was waiting for (as a person who is looking for something has to pretend that he is not looking for anything, since around the next turning he might or might not come on it). He did not dissemble his features; and the case was that this situation he was in, apparently so unpromising, yet well enough fulfilled the need of his soul to overflow and release his dammed-up tears. Supposing somebody came by now: would not that person fail to be greeted by a smile of indifference?

Arthur started up. For obviously love might at this very moment be found in some other corner of the midnight park; and if one is looking for love where it can't be found, one has to be up and about it. He had to go rapidly at least around the next turning, for surely he would never be fruitlessly looking if he stayed in one place, even though it was under a lamp easily visible to love when it would not come. He looked back to the place he had left, but it was not the case that another person had yet come to that solitary light-bathed bench, not even Sammy, yet he was loath to move out of its sight.

At a given instant changing his pace, so that there was a perceptible pause-in-between, Arthur plunged suddenly into the darkest grove in all the park, off any pathway, a place that he knew well, from long experience, to be the least likely, nor did it fail to disappoint him. There was no one there. He was standing in the lone blackness among the almost formless tree trunks. Here no one could know he was there, but he was lying in wait for danger in the enormous jungle of the Empire City, where far off on the lighted streets were passing the lovely boys and girls, and where along the river loomed the gigantic companies, Burns Coal and the United Electric Light and Power, beasts of impressive force who, having devoured their competitors, were smoking peacefully.

And, oh, fraught with crisis and indecision and decision, abrupt changes of gait, so that there is a perceptible pause-in-between, this boredom can go on and on for five or six hours till dawn. It is scarcely believable! But I am describing an athlete of desire in his power, fully satisfying the need of his dear soul. For there are athletes of lust, of love and of desire, and Arthur was an athlete of desire.

3.

At other times Arthur used to find love where he never looked. Where he so carefully neglected to look that one day in one neighborhood, he found not only Laura but little Horace as well.

When Arthur was, by chance, making love to somebody, he pastured his soul. (The expression is Gide's.) And then he was pleased and really handsome, whereas otherwise he looked harassed and gloomy.

He suffered from a common dilemma of young persons: that he was only handsome when he was happy and only happy when he was loved and only loved when he was handsome. Obviously for the most part he was doomed to be lonely, harassed and gloomy. But let a touch of wit ignite him, and he blazed like a Christmas tree, handsome, happy and loved all together.

In a doorway on the bright-lit avenue, he lay in wait; and youth and beauty were continually going by, so thickly that he smiled, and then he blazed like a bonfire made of Christmas trees, and he too was youthful beauty. The touch of wit, the invitation to love, igniting when it was not looked for, nor waited for; especially when he was lying in wait in a doorway on 181st Street and Broadway, near the brightly lit busses and the clanging trolley cars.

And soon he was pasturing his soul, on the touch of wit, the erotic smile, the easy success, the touch of wit. The acrobatics of athletes of desire. Igniting one another, they were all ablaze like Christmas trees, and quickly burned out like bonfires made of Christmas trees.

That is, often Arthur found love where he never looked and then he was pasturing his soul.

4.

In these loves it was necessary for him to preserve his anonymity.

At first he thought that this meant that he was to conceal his name. Like everyone else, then, he used a false name. But he soon found out that the new name also soon became his name and did not preserve his anonymity; though indeed it now had no (incestuous) relation to his father and sister.

He tried then to falsify his name by associating it with a false appearance. He dissembled his face and the cut of his clothes. He undid the information and the methodical habits of his careful education—with great loss of ease, for it is hard for well-educated persons to find a subject of conversation when they cannot draw on anything they know; nor is it easy to seem to be an idiot when one is by habit observant and reflective. (His social left-handedness was usually misconstrued as indicating this or that trait of his character, and usually the misconstruction hit off his real nature to a T; so he might as well have been frank to begin with.) Further, just the touches of contagious wit and quick gestures, which were calculated to wreathe his face in smiles and make him handsome and lucky, were beyond the influence of his careful forgetting, and they betrayed him.

And even if all his disguises were successful, impenetrable, they were useless in actually making love, but it was toward this that he was aiming. For in the acts of love, beneath all disguises and changes of voice, it was evident who Arthur was. He tried to falsify his practices of love, but it cannot be done, for one is soon embarrassed by uncontrollable revelations of both a positive and negative kind. For instance, you either get a hard-on or you don't.

5.

What Arthur wanted in the end was such a desire and satisfaction of desire as would be abstract from personality; to be able to say, "I love you—it's nothing personal." This was pure desire. He was happy until there was a question of names, identities, roles, classes, genders, species. And he was, surprisingly, able on a basis of pure desire to be a loyal and faithful friend and lover. But most often in so-called love affairs, after the first exciting encounters, they wanted to find him out, or worse he found himself out.

What he liked and often cleverly achieved was the marvelous exhilaration of chance meetings in hotel lobbies. But such meetings proved, alas, to lead only to the hotel rooms where we let our tired youth be thrown.

So perhaps best of all was the anxiety of looking out the window of a swift train: there he could see at the crossroads or in the thickets, or on hay wagons or sleeping on haystacks, or swimming naked from the rocks along the river, many a beauty. There was an inexhaustible plenty of objects of desire, more than any soul could cope with, all copied off by God from the angel-bodies of His acquaintance. Each one was already sped by the train window, before he could smile or ever an answering smile could form, and without the expense of spirit in a waste of shame.

6. S.P.V.

So, at the end of the interesting train trip, Arthur came to the weekly reunions of the Society for the Propagation of Vice, which were appropriately held in Nyack, N. Y.—population 5,000.

This powerful organization had—and has, for it has survived the years—a simple object: to disturb the social structure by earnest practice of the very vices which in their normal virulence are the bulwarks of commercial and political institutions.

They pushed their program especially in the military states where strong vices like fornication, sodomy and sadism were among the chief political virtues; in those nations, where so much satisfaction was to be got in the way of public duty and no one thought of freedom, it was the job of S.P.V. to aggravate private pleasures beyond public utility.

This organization cannot fail to triumph generally; it has every advantage to begin with, for temptations to vicious practice need only be suggested to be acted on; and then the act as well as the suggestion generates its own propaganda. As Jean has said, *Qui a fumé fumera, l'Opium sait attendre.*

And we may ask, What is the relation between S.P.V. and N.I.B., the National Industrial Boycott? For you remember we spoke of a secret affiliation. S.P.V. was a development and a refinement of N.I.B.; for whereas Lothar's friends made a frontal attack (pardon the expression) on the social behavior, S.P.V. went behind (pardon the expression) and undermined the impulses that prompt each one to get up at dawn and go to work. Further, some of those Nibblers, I suspect, wanted precisely to prevent the rebellion from getting out of hand (pardon the expression), but the friends of pleasure aimed at such a decay as was not reconstructible.

7. Seventy-One

The chairman was the septuagenarian, M. Léon Tarot, the only original inventor of the famous joke *Sacrebleu, Soixante-Onze.*

A wild red-headed adolescent, Miss Flora Sachs, was trying to force the discussion of a publicity campaign: to assign distinct vices to each one of the forty-eight states.

But the agenda called for the discussion of an ode commissioned for the society, and Miss Sachs was violently and periodically restrained.

"Do you want to read the poem all at once," they asked the poet, or have it discussed point by point?"

"Point by point!" someone shouted.

"New York: *Gum Chewing!*" shouted Miss Sachs.

"Point by point," agreed the little poet, who wore a goatee.

"You'll never get to the end," he was warned. "New Yorkers are bad listeners."

"It's too long anyway," said the docile fellow. He was a little academic from whom the ode had been commissioned for the sake of dryness. Indecisively he mounted the podium and began in a tentative voice:

"Lest we neglect to add
a little more confusion
and Chaos halfway come
harden to reaction——"

"*For-mi-dable!* Just the tone," cried Tarot.

"Do you call that a rime?"

"Some o' the rimes are off, others pat, depending on the context," said the goatee wagging.

"A 'little more'? A lot more! No compromises."

"You mean 'soften to reaction,' don't you? Harden to action, soften to inaction."

"No, sir. The metaphor is taken from plaster, not from erections; I am speaking of a good mouthful of plaster, at the dentist's—

"for the crunch o' the war already
weary is solidifying
in the Parises as yet
only dying."

"Plaster in the mouth—crunch o' the war, that's good!"

"It's from the Prime Minister of England," said the poet modestly. "He surpasses himself especially when they lose a battle."

"There was only one Paris, monsieur," said Tarot sadly.

"You picture these Parises as a kind of mannikins in the mouth of a Luna Park, is that the idea?"

"In the teeth of the Big Devil; but he's tired and they're not yet chewed up."

"Oh, horrible! Horrible! You're probably a *biter,* that's what you are!"

"Sir, my personal failings are not relevant; I never approached you——" cried the poet indignantly.

"Fat chance you'd have with those whiskers!"

"Messieurs, messieurs—*s'il vous plaît,*" said Tarot. "Continue."

"At least make these teeth chatter!"

This was surprising! Truly excellent! A hail of applause rang through the hall. More than one's neck flushed and hair crept. Many leaped to their feet; it was an ovation. "Massachusetts: *Biting!*" cried Miss Sachs, but was restrained. The applause rang louder. They approved of both the form and the content. "I move we adopt it as our slogan!" someone roared. "At least make these teeth chatter! Help each one down his own slope!"

"Means and end!"

"Make these teeth chatter!"

"For—mi—dable!"

In the height of the hubbub the gratified poet shouted in a terrifying voice:

"Pleasure is the rage
to set the sour
teeth on edge——"

Many wept for joy. The scene of rejoicing was indescribable.

There was a Marshall Ficino, a runty Italian tough with a Greek background who peddled narcotics outside of De Witt Clinton High School. He was in the S.P.V. only for business reasons, but, as we have seen, it was in the nature of the case that the Society could make use of even such hypocrites without risk, for the heart generates its own propaganda. Yet now, beside himself with enthusiasm, little Nicky set fire to a large envelope of heroin, crying out: "Po'try, dat's got de kick!"

The odor was overpowering, the effect paradisal.

"Please, please, don't overlook—" said the poet floating heavenward—"don't overlook that rime of 'rage' and 'edge'—rage-edge, eh?"

"Yes, yes! It's not by accident that one is wounded to the heart."

Even Miss Sachs was moved.

"I now commence the dedicatory couplets," announced the poet in the general atmosphere of peace and glory. He spoke slowly and the universe as a whole was in slow motion.

"Today a League for the Furtherance of Vice
we found: oh, to our thoughtful device
rally you explorers o' desire
and all technicians o' the learned fire."

"What does he mean by this?"

"It—is—Tarot—he means!" cried one slowly.

"Ta-rot! Ta-rot!"

For this old man was indeed the explorer of desire and the technician of the learned fire—whose *Art,* in abridgment but with the original photographs, will sell under the counter forever.

And in his honor—and never out of order—someone began to tell the joke *Sacrebleu, Soixante-Onze!* The atmosphere of mutual satisfaction and dreamy endlessness that had developed was a perfect setting, with infinite, and infinitely subdividing, divisions of time in which to elaborate each detail of the 70 positions of the build-up, not without practical illustrations.

"*Sacrebleu!* Sav-an-ty Wan!" sang out an enthusiast every other minute.

"*For—mi—dable!*"

A pair of young acrobats, with drunken indecision but acrobatic precision in the closes, miming the 69 and hitting off to a T the maliciously humorous illustrations of the Tarot Pack, had the center of the floor, while the rest made a ring and sang out. In the form in which they were telling the joke, after each incident the American interposes: "In America we just do it face to face," and the rest shout the refrain, "*Sacrebleu, Sav-an-ty Wan!*"

Some were already sleeping and others were saying in a faraway voice "*For-mi-dable.*" But the wild red-headed girl was mumbling along: "Wyoming—state flower Carnation—state motto Labor Omnia Vincit—*Sheeplovers.* Alabama—state flower Magnolia—Festina Lente—*Sleeplovers.* Pennsylvania—Phlox (pardon the expression——"

Little Remo was excitedly outlining his plan of the Joy Scouts of America. This organization was to do for country boys what the Boy Scouts does for city boys: to introduce them to the manners of urban life. Subway hikes to the dens in Harlem and exercises in rolling reefers. Tying of one's self in knots and signaling out the corner of the eye. Demerit badges. Etc.

No one was paying any attention whatever to the bespectacled poet with the goatee, but he sang on:

> *"No one can stay the chemical plague i' the blood*
> *nor the forgotten craving of childhood."*

"Sacrebleu!"

"For-mi-dable!"

"My name is Sachs, you should pardon the expression!"

"Sacrebleu, Soixante-Onze!"

> *"—who can tell? the dammed-up energies*
> *of war will trickle hereby into ease*
> *and Germany be by his victim del-*
> *icately devoured with vinegar and oil!*

—French dressing," explained the little poet.

"C'est formidable."

Chapter 11 ▪ THE MASTERSINGERS

1.

From their box at the opera house, Mynheer and Laura, and Lothario and Horatio, were looking at the play (it was only a play) of *The Mastersingers.*

It is a play when someone does something and someone else looks at it and does not intervene, for it is only a play. And in the opera house, from the floor and the horseshoe tiers, hundreds and hundreds of pairs of eyes were brightly reflecting the lighted stage. Most of the spectators, whether or not they were in boxes, were in separate boxes alone, but our quartet were looking on together and sharing their experiences.

The frame of the proscenium was in the form of a flattened ellipse, very closely imitating the total field of vision, in order to invite you to take the brightly lighted world of the stage as if it were the actual world. The rest of the theater was dark, leaving only that world for your eyes. That world *and* your eyes. If you raised your binoculars, then suddenly you were so close onto the stage and the persons there, that you might almost touch them and intervene before it was too late; or maybe, at the end of *The Mastersingers,* slip into that world of social peace on its red-letter day—before the curtain could fall in your face and bring back our war—but it was only a play.

The others were used to plays, but to little Horace it was really his first play, and he was thunderstruck at this relationship of the actor and the onlooker so enormously magnified at the opera house. He looked at what he was supposed to look at—one could not help but, because of the lighting and the architecture—but he also looked away at the onlookers looking. And he soon sized it up, that it was a play, in which one could lose one's feelings but not alter the events in that brightly lit universe not continuous with ours. "It's like a child," he thought shrewdly, "who watches the grownups doing it; but he's not supposed to, and they're not supposed to know he's watching." With what busy eyes they watched! And from time to time, he could see, there were tears of pleasure in the hundreds of pairs of eyes.

2. The Play, Act III, sc. 1

But vast, as vast as every corner of the sound-filled hall and moving in the colored figures on the stage, was the ghost of the dead poet. (Horatio did not know him yet; he was only beginning to make his acquaintance.) And his play was at the moment that:

The wild night of the Second Act, Midsummer's Eve, was over. That had been the night of errors inspired by the fairies through human agents. It was the night when even wise men like Hans Sachs have impossible delusions of what could make them happy. Night of slips of the tongue, wanton impulses, and masks. Elopements, brawls that spring from nothing and leave broken heads, and milk turned sour. The small and fatal accidents that you cannot account for, but which bring the honest people out of bed with inquiring lanterns rushing through the street, to get into trouble themselves, for the mania is epidemic. That erroneous night, *Polterabend,* the poet expressed by a wild chase, a brawl and a continual *fugato* among the strings.

But the serene orchestral prelude of Act III is tense with closes and agreements. It is the Dawn of St. John's Day itself. And Horatio, who had rather enjoyed the excitement of the night, now understood, from the small indicative behavior of his grownups, that now he was to pay special attention. Lothar touched his sleeve and raised a finger; it was the first evidence that Horatio had ever had that his brother knew of his existence, and he was so flabbergasted that he came near falling over the railing into the pit. And Mynheer smiled at him a slow sad smile of delight, as the curtain rose.

3.

Midsummer Morning, and first we are in the house, as if the poet meant to say (c.1850) that it is there that social peace and glory must begin. When there is love, renunciation and reconciliation in that so-called primary environment, we shall achieve art in all Nuremberg. On St. John's Day the master is kind to the apprentice: "He never was like this before, although he's a good fellow," says the youth deeply moved.

And now Hans Sachs is alone. *"Wahn! Wahn!"* he sings, *"Über-all Wahn!"*—"They're all mad!" They certainly are mad, for who can find a rational cause, in local or universal history, why they should quarrel and shed blood? Where is the use in it? They don't hear even the shriek of their own anguish; when they tear their flesh they are in the illusion that they're having a good time: explain *that,* says Hans Sachs, singing in the paradisal and somewhat ignorant dawn (for obviously many causes could be assigned)—

ein Kobold half wohl da!

—"Surely an imp had a hand in it!"

Our eyes are hypnotically fixed on the bright-lit scene, where the morning sun is streaming in on the philosophical cobbler, and we are well content to believe that surely an imp had a hand in it last night, but that today he has gone away and left us in peace.

Enters the lover, a radiant knight, a young nobleman who has sold his lands because he is destined on this very day and in this very Nuremberg to win the bourgeois bride and a wreath of the local laurel. Now last night he had a dream: in that dream the morning shone with rosy light, and beside him there was a wondrous woman like a bride, and on the laurel tree not fruit but a crown of stars.

Poetry, says Sachs, is true dream-interpretation. *Here* is the maiden, Eva herself!

(Haven't I skipped something? Beckmesser sneaked in and stole the song off the table. But he is an interruption; we do not want interruptions. One blink, and you would never know he was there. One convenient assumption, for instance, that there is such a thing as sublimation, and you need not remember that the fatherly old man is a deadly frustrated rival of the youth.)

Nay, here are both the young lovers together! They are splendidly arrayed, and are made to appear first in this simple interior in order that the angelic splendor of their garments may shine to the hundreds and hundreds of pairs of eyes. Their clothes are shining in the sunlight of the morning; and at sight of each other they are spellbound; and in this pause . . . there is the business of a shoe that now *fits,* as it did not fit last night.

As a man commits suicide or drowns in his woe, Hans Sachs gently frees the apprentice, renouncing all his claims and properties at once, in order to become, like the howling sacrifice built into the wall, the creator of harmonious social peace and glory. (Not like King Mark.)

So now when these five, Walther and Eva, David and Lena, and Hans Sachs alone, have all come together, they sing the Quintet of the end of the first scene of the last act of *The Mastersingers.* And, oh! it is a Red Letter Day. The sun of St. John's is streaming indoors; and Eva sings, "Joyous as the sun," Walther sings, "Thy pure love," David and Lena sing, "Am I awake or dreaming," but Hans Sachs sings, "It *was* a lovely dream of night."

We might say that, in this quintet, the bass voice is the basis wherefrom those others soar at last so freely, on the Red Letter Day of glory. Oh! On that Red Letter Day of lovely glory.

Tears are glistening here and there in the hundreds of pairs of eyes.

Red Letter Day of lovely glory, stay!

This quintet is not momentary or transitory; it lasts for sixty measures. This song does not slide suddenly to its destruction, like that music in King Mark's garden before the dawn; it ends on long notes, on cadences; on firm chords, on indestructible resolutions; it is even giving way to a forthright march. It is progressing into a broad march. It ends on firm chords; and progresses into a broad march, as the scene changes.

4.

"It's mighty pretty," said Mynheer, shaking his head contrariwise from side to side ruefully.

"It sure is our Red Letter Day!" said Lothar grimly.

"Whatsamatta with it—brother?" Horatio asked him. Awkwardly he did not call him Dopo.

"It's all ass-backwards," said Lothar, "but really very good, and you pay attention you'll learn something."

But Laura's eyes were shining; she believed; and Horatio did not know *what* he was to think, as the scene opened on the fair, on our Red Letter Day, that was all colors and shouts, banners, refreshments in booths on the side, and continual disembarking from little boats that came up a narrow stream "practicable in the foreground" (says the stage direction).

The groups of apprentices came on with their bumptious waltz, and then the ranks of the guildsmen: the contrasting entrances of youth and age. For that is the plot of the play; or, put otherwise, the acceptance of new art into tradition. And over it all an exulting community spirit.

5.

Now Dyck and Laura were experts at ceremonials of all kinds. Amid so much noise it was possible to speak freely and Mynheer pointed out the structure of it: "First the Entrance March, with its characteristic participants; then the Prayer; then the Business of the Day."

"Why not God's part first?"

"No, ma'am. A community occasion is under God's providence,

but first the occasion must be given. Aware of what we are and where we are, we become aware of our auspices. Therefore, the celebration of the occasion before the hymn, but the hymn before the business. Sometimes there is both a prayer and a national anthem, indicating the secular as well as the sacred auspices, and guaranteeing that nothing very interesting will occur."

"In this play, if I remember," says Laura, "he comes to mention the nation at the very end."

"Yes, the German Art. That was *his* problem, to make propaganda for himself by riding the tide of the new empire; but that's not patriotism."

With a mighty sound they broke into the Chorale, and Mynheer fell into a hush, for this sound was sublime.

"But it's not a prayer," persisted Laura, "it's a poem by Sachs."

"Yes, yes. Hush up, dear."

"But you said after the Entrance comes the Prayer."

He took her hand as if to say though they must not speak he was not without her. The heat of love communicated itself through their hands and the dull golden horseshoe flickered with the blinding bright stage.

They came to the end of it. "This *is* the prayer," said Mynheer softly.

Wach' auf, es nahet gen den Tag

"Wake up, the day draws nigh. I hear a nightingale upon the hawthorn. For the Providence of this day is the musician. *He* will be immortal, he deserves to be, since he has made the renunciation of any possible happiness for himself. This is a much better-made play than people think. Look at him there still alive and present among the people, in Nuremberg, on this very day."

And Lothar said, "It's a wonderful thing to hear the common people whistling your song."

"Anyway," said Mynheer, "the verses are symbolic of the reformed faith."

"But whatcha *upset* about, Dopo?" said Horace in alarm and, to his own astonishment, took his brother's enormous paw; for Lothar was certainly shaken by silent sobs. For the horns and the trombones of the march of the guildsmen, that would have been the proud moment of great Lothar's life. It *is,* alas, our proudest moment. He withdrew his paw.

But now all on the stage are laughing uproariously at the discomfiture of Beckmesser. In haste and shame the pedant flees and vanishes into the crowd. It's not a convincing scene. "Ha!" said little

Horace, on the alert, for he had an infallible sense for sleight-of-hand. "It's all to be paid for at his expense, is that it?"

"Hush," said Dyck.

"Hush up yourself. You can't shush me. Who's this Beckmesser? What's *his* problem? What's Wagner afraid of? Suppressed! Suppressed!"

"No, hush up, Horace," said Laura, who thought he might make a scene. "You can't have a comedy and a generally satisfactory ending without a scapegoat."

"I don't like it!" cried Horace stubbornly. "It's all spoilt by this little man spirited away."

"You're right, kid. Don't give in to them," said Lothar.

And now, being able to read correctly from the paper, Walther von der Stolzing proves himself indeed a master; he wins the laurel, the girl and the golden chain. And the triumph and pleasure are general.

"Oh, very nice, very nice," hissed Lothar. For he fancied himself a rival of Walther's.

But in the end it is to the philosophical shoemaker that the greatest honor falls, for the people cry out with one voice:

"Heil Sachs! Hans Sachs!
Heil Nürnbergs theurem Sachs."

—Hail to Nuremberg's darling Sachs!

"Very nice," hissed Horace, for he fancied himself the rival of Hans Sachs.

6.

Lothar waited for the curtain to fall, and burst out: "Really! And what hypocrisy! This young man—suppose he is less than thirty, like myself—has the gall to stand there with a crown on his head and a foolish face of acquiescence among that general public which is what it is. And that's why the Prize Song is what it is, a well-made academic piece at the moment when he is supposed to blow your head off. Do you know how *I* would do it?"

"How would *you* do it, brother?" asked Horace, with an eagerness and admiration that astonished himself.

"He would turn on them and give them what for; he'd give them a song they wouldn't like so much. Sold out! Shame! Shame, Richard! *'Nicht Meister! Nein! Will ohne Meister selig sein!'* That's what he *says*: 'No master for me; I'll do well enough without being a master!' But you see he takes the chain anyway! The crown, the girl and the chain. I don't begrudge him the girl; a fellow has the right to a lay even if he uses tricks. But the crown? Isn't he even suspicious? They've made a monkey out of him. Do you think Wagner believed it himself? Oh, yes, he did, that's just the pity of it."

"It's only a play," said Mynheer fatuously. "Surely the poet has the right to portray an ideal situation."

"Ideal!" cried Lothar with a scornful laugh. "What's ideal about it? Show me a *great* Prize Song! *That's* the test. You can't fool the music. (And what the devil makes you think that a work of art is a play?) Look, Mynheer," he said earnestly, "Here he is, say twenty-five years old, and apparently he is the composer of radical lyrics—he has even given away his property. Behold, the academic masters cry out, 'Noble singer!' Do *you* believe it? This is not ideal, this is a *joke!* At such a price you can find social peace and glory every day and not far from Times Square; you don't need to come to the Imperial Opera House."

"You're right," said Mynheer. "But the hero isn't Walther, it's Hans Sachs, the German poet."

"Oh, great," said Horace, giggling.

"What are you laughing at, toothpick?"

"Just when I see that fat fellow becomin' all of a sudden Nuremberg's dear Hans Sachs."

"What's so funny about that?"

The rounds of applause and the curtain calls were now dying down in the great house. The hundreds of pairs of eyes were eclipsed; and the footlights went out. There was now no longer a play, but only the inner disturbances that each man carried away after having seen the play.

"You—you tricked me," said the small boy with tears in his eyes. "You told me in this play I'd see peace and glory among the people at the Fair, where everybody would get what they need by sociable buying and selling. And what I see is little Beckmesser dressed in black slinking away into his hole. It's all at his expense. Anyway, his music wasn't so bad by comparison with the blond boy's, specially the serenade part, if that idiot woulda stopped hammering shoes. . . . What I think is this: how'd you like to live in a place where everything is just ducky, where you don't get a toothache an' nobody is a pain in the ass—but it's all because that little dope is left *out*. What about the feller who is a pain in the ass?" said Horace. "It's all paid for at the expense of one chap off-stage in continual envy and rage and no victory at all. I think that's a bad place. If you ask me," he said confidentially, "this Beckmesser is a poor relation of Wagner's that he's ashamed of."

"Lothar is right," said Laura sadly. "The Prize Song does make concessions to conventional taste. I see it every day. There *is* something fishy in this alliance between Sachs and von der Stolzing. If he wanted to show us the miracle, he should have had him *stun* the bourgeoisie, and bring them to a pause—and then, in this little pause, they suddenly hear the sweet secret of the Prize Song. Even though, afterwards, all hell breaks loose."

"Oh, good, good!" said Lothar deeply moved. "That would be simply beautiful." He was going to go off to jail and (maybe therefore) he realized how proud he was of his sister and his little brother.

Dyck shook his head. "This public," he said, "has already had all those shocks you mention. The First World War really did the business. It has developed an invulnerable defense against perception of any kind. You'd be surprised to study into what a perfect acquiescence the enormities of my friends Jean and Franz and Paul Klee were allowed to fall with a dull thud. I am not an artist, but I have studied the problem: there is only one way to make a dent."

"Is there a way?" asked Horace eagerly.

"Boredom!" said Mynheer Duyck Colijn. "This they cannot endure. Just keep hewing to the line. All that's required is honor and scruples and people die of anxiety."

"But what about *me,* meanwhile?" cried Horace pitiably.

Chapter 12 ▪ AN EDUCATIONAL ROMANCE

1. The Social Worker

It was well after dawn that Dyck left them off at home, all in a mellow mood of drunkenness tempered by breakfast, and little Horace fast asleep in Lothar's arms.

Fast asleep, Horatio was dreaming with a settled smile on his face of a situation, somewhat the opposite of the play, in which everybody was in horrible straits except one pony happy at their expense, yet by his brisk gait he gave hope to all.

It was the important day on which, as it turned out, he was going to meet Eliphaz.

But they were in a mood more amiable than was necessary, for when they came upstairs, Lothar carrying the sleeping boy, there grimly sitting on the steps was Miss Pitcher, the relief investigator.

"You've all been *out!*" she said, surprised. "I heard somebody inside and I thought you were afraid to open the door, so I was just going to sit down and wait, because you have to come out sometime. . . . Well. Good morning."

"Drop dead," said Lothar.

"I beg your pardon?"

"Oh, it's all right. I'm not offended. I just say it," explained Lothar matter-of-factly, "in order to save time. You say good morning. Good. Supposing *I* say good morning. Then you begin to ask questions—where have you been? Where did you get the money? You start to butt into my business. I try to answer the questions, but in the end I'll say, Drop dead. So I might as well say it right off and save time."

"Where *have* you all been?" asked Miss Pitcher, accusingly.

"Drop dead," said Lothar.

"Ah! *There's* the grand piano!" said Miss Pitcher, bruising her chin on it as she came through the door, for she was a tiny woman. "There's been a lot of talk. I'm to ask you about that. It's point three," she said, consulting her agenda.

Horatio was lodged in the berth under the piano, and as soon as he settled and turned over, "*Suazo,* there go the busses!" muttered the little sleeper hoarsely but loudly and distinctly. It was a dream about the demolition of the Elevated, and in that glorious transformation of the Empire City everybody was going to ride in omnibusses.

Miss Minetta Pitcher belonged to that curious class of persons that is interested in saving other people's money for them. On the face of it, what difference could it make to her how the Imperial income was distributed and whether a little more or less came to this family or that family? On the contrary, precisely the way in which this small cross-eyed woman was at home in the great society was to make sure that everybody had his station and its duties mathematically defined. You could not help but like her.

A somewhat deeper explanation of her behavior (though it came to the same thing) was that she was a revolutionary and she communicated to her cases her own resentment by showing how inflexible was the system as a whole: there was nothing to do, she said in effect, but struggle to the death. She would even explain this to you if you bothered to ask.

"There is a complaint from the Electric Light and Power Company, Mr. Alger, that you haven't been to have the lights turned on since they cut you off."

"You see," said Lothar, turning to Laura triumphantly, "we've got them guessing."

"We don't need lights," explained Laura; "we see in the dark."

"I don't believe you," said Miss Pitcher hastily. "That would be most unusual. If you have nocturnal vision, as you claim, we'll have to reclassify you and this will take about six weeks. (My advice, off the cuff, is to keep it under your hat.) The assumption in my case load—" she had a case load—"is that you have normal vision, burn lights till about midnight except when there is daylight saving, and read *Liberty* magazine. . . . Anyway—" she hesitated—"don't get in any of the abnormal categories—it's—it's not good. Except post-polio—post-polio is really good; they roll out the carpet because of Roosevelt."

"Thanks for the tip," said Laura.

"The fact is we burn candles," said Lothar bluntly.

"Oh, that's out of the question," she cried. "It's not only against the fire laws, but the whole schedule is planned for electrification. Look at it in the big way—you people are intelligent. In an urban area like this a certain percentage of the home relief comes from the power company; how are we to justify the outlay in *your* case? I'm sure that if you once consider the situation as a *whole,*" she said blushing, "we won't hear of it again. Now next——"

She became confused and was blushing furiously. I must explain that this was because from her girlhood certain sounds and certain words had become indissolubly associated with forbidden sexual or physiological ideas. And soon these were a formidable list: the word "whole" of course; everything connected with tubes, oil, lubrication; everything connected with sucking, suction, friction, pumping; words like "constitution" or "stay" or "support." Magnetism was taboo; the word "taboo" was taboo. Fruit, seed, planting, fertile were all concepts to be avoided in any context. You can see that this made communication pretty difficult for her. The word "communication" was absolutely taboo.

"Now next–" she stammered, "about–this piano."

But the fact was that the next item was not the piano at all; she realized with embarrassment that she had already said that that was Item 3. The second item was Dependents. But she found it impossible to talk about Dependents. Invariably a discussion on that subject led to mentioning either children or parents, and both these set before her an impassible psychological block. By association men, women, boys and girls were involved in the same complex, so that she could not discuss any of these either.

They had tried, without success, to check Horatio in the school records. But so long as Miss Pitcher remained the investigator, Horatio was safe; both Laura and Lothar were able to claim the one boy as a dependent of each, even though from an official point of view he didn't exist at all.

Naturally, the worse she lapsed on Dependents, the stricter she was on Furnishings.

It was referring particularly to Miss Pitcher that Sadler of Chicago generalized concerning all social workers: "The maladjusted take care of the maladjusted and they say it don't stink." But that amiable sociologist overlooked the advantages.

"Tro-el, zooosh!" cried the boy under the piano hoarsely. It was a dream that along the new streets of the New Heavens and New Earth they would erect mighty skyscrapers. But this idea of the erections going up was accompanied, in the speaker, by vague but unmistakable overt behavior. And this spectacle of the child under the piano quite perfected Miss Pitcher's disorientation. In reckless anxiety she stammered out: "You st-st-stole the piano!"

The siblings (they were siblings) roared with joy, at the idea of stealing a grand piano. And though still asleep, Horatio opened one eye wide as could be.

Miss Pitcher was offended and cried, "I'll call a policeman and I won't have to come here any more! Anyway, it's a man's job, to come to a house with children. Even if you didn't steal it you should sell it and be reclassified and I won't have to come here any more. Or supposing you actually play on this grand—this instrument—then you're musicians and should be on the music project."

Her condition was pitiable, for suddenly the word "piano" had got itself connected to "penis"; and when she veered away from it she fell flat on her face with "instrument," which was of course far, far worse. A succession of shameless associations, especially to the sentence she never came to utter, made her cross-eyes flash and straighten out. What she partly meant to say was that *she* should have such a piano to play on and be on the music project, for she was a competent performer and an expert on Poulenc, that childlike spirit.

"Why don't you mind your own business?" said Lothar indignantly.

But Laura knew, intuitively, what the trouble was, and she cried out tactfully, "Wake up, Horatio! Wa-aake up, little Horace!"

Horace opened his other eye and said, out of his dream, *"Amura,"* while Miss Pitcher gathered up her papers in confusion.

"What is ut?" muttered the sleepy boy.

"Ride your bicycle down to Eliphaz's," said Laura, "and bring back a certificate that *he* gave us the piano." She laid a stress on "he," with a familiar pride that perhaps only she, the liberal pensioner of the Imperial dole, only she of all the exploited millions on the globe, could legitimately feel for her patron prince.

"I had such a dream!" said Horatio in a somnolent voice. "The name of my dream was Suazo Troel Amura all in color." He spoke as if he were still catching hold of the tail of his vanishing dream, for indeed just by chance he had been asleep with one eye open and he had caught these deep dreams out of the corner of his eye, X-rayed with his waking fears, with the filtered light of the morning. "My friend Raymon riz rosy from the dead all in color an' he said, 'Horatio, don't be scared to jump! One day all our friends can fly. An' another day we'll all be eatin' men like cannibals.' Good mornin', Miss Pitcher! I hear my sis's voice an' she says to take a ride to Eliphaz."

With an effort he sat bolt upright and banged his head against the bottom of the piano. The piano hummed. And at this whirring sound, like the electric motor they used to live next to on 146th Street, Horatio, who was as cunning as a bourgeois in striking the most profitable spiritual bargain, crystallized his doubts into the following most agreeable maxim of waking life: *Agree to take a fatal loss and you'll get what you want.*

With this slogan ringing in and a lump on his head began *his* Red Letter Day.

2. Horatio's Bicycle Journey

As he rolled from Fort George Hill to Park Avenue midtown—

At each crossing the eastern sunlight burned in the spokes; was eclipsed by a block of houses; briefly burned; was eclipsed. The old fort had been on one of the twin heights (to enfilade the valley), so downslope was the prelude of his journey, and quicker and quicker flickered the stripes of sun and shadow; and the sunlight gleamed in the spokes as in a mirror. At 183rd Street, given to the wind, the boy cried out, "SUAZO! TROEL!" and so went the first half-mile.

STOP, said the red light on the corner of 181st Street which, with its clanging trolleys, was the first great crossing.

He did not stop but flew, for these rules did not apply to this cyclist. Although, approaching from opposite directions, two of those noisy trolley cars were rapidly closing up the rectangular space, the shouting wind flew through, amid the screaming of other people's brakes. Horatio stopped never, but saved his impetus for the flat, now pumping and swinging from side to side.

(Sometimes such a cyclist, with the beautiful advantage that he presumes in the law, can pass rapid motorcars continually caught short.)

So at 165th Street, he came onto Broadway, Route 9 of the United States.

Now if he followed another avenue, there were certain declivities that he might temporarily coast down with slavish ease. But the expert cyclist, lover of New York and of its routes and courses, did not succumb to the snare, for in this art above all it was a principle that *whatever coasts down must grind up.* Horatio was reckless only with respect to his life and the laws; but with respect to the art, in which he had a habit of freedom, he did not for a moment omit prudence, to be sure an aggressive prudence, for there were certain dips and rises which were advantageous if the rise could be taken on the impetus of the dip; but for this it was necessary not to hope but to know.

So he sailed through the red lights onto the great and famous thoroughfare starred with the proud shields: U.S. 9.

Now concerning these shields: It was an important day when first they shone forth on every lamppost to the eyes of startled New Yorkers. Then there was a strange division among the natives of the Empire City. On the one hand, were those—and this author was among them, for I am a regional novelist—who were shocked, humiliated and angered to see that "our" Broadway was, as we saw it, demoted from its unique position to become a section of the Albany

Post Road: significantly we thought in terms of this ancient coach-road. But others were charmed to find that they had bearings in the Empire: they were on the highway to Montreal! And of that highway, this Broadway was not a segment, but all that colossal stretch of highway was our Broadway! Therefore, to wear the proud shield was the apotheosis of Broadway:

Horatio, who was a new beginner, with everything to learn and nothing to lose, was among those who wept for joy.

On this broad avenue, whose blocks were not yet towering cliffs, the sunlight burned continually in his wheels, as he flew with the moving traffic and threaded between the traffic stalled. There were cars, with which he maintained a fabulous pace of twenty miles an hour, that had licenses from Montreal and Quebec.

As he was rolling with the friendly traffic, let us draw away a moment and see him. He was wearing a jersey of faded scarlet and denim jeans of washed-out blue, and the sun burned silver in his wheels. This pastel tricolor riding dangerously close was cursed by the drivers of sullen-hued cars, but blessed by the men and matronly women who love bold boys. His eyes were frank and seeing, but his tongue did not let on any more than was necessary. He much needed a haircut.

At 135th Street began the terrifying slope into the abyss down to Harlem. This descent was at that time paved with the cobblestones calamitous for bicycles. For an instant's hesitation, he was going to turn off onto the beautiful level viaduct along the river, along

our lordly Hudson hardly flowing,

to breathe the fresh wind and see the white excursion boat cut the water displaying its pennons. But it was untechnical, out of the way, and he plunged down——

With a subway train emerging from the underground roaring at his left hand, he plunged into the hole so ancient that it was paved with cobblestones, and teams of horses dragged loads of beerkegs from the breweries. His wheel bridled with fear and the handlebars were momentarily torn from his grasp—and he was in the lea of a gigantic moving-van and pursued by an evil omnibus. (Such had their armor outside, but he had only an endoskeleton and his wits.) Thick blue fumes poisoned the air. Here even the dragons from the subway world emerged and hurtled overhead, not silently dripping flaming sparks that singed his hair; and in this place of trade was only a thin natural light.

Here one *bounded* along, as on a horse, rather than rolled with the circular motion of the smooth and deathless planets.

Nevertheless, he regained control and leaped faster downhill. He shouted "AMURA!" and lost consciousnes, releasing every pressure on the restraint. "I oughtn't t'av did it!" he thought at the last moment as he saw the crack vanish between the thundering truck and the bus and the iron posts on which the electric train was screaming overhead.

There was a serial shriek of brakes along the line, vibrating like a siren. An odor of brakes burning. A car crashed into one in front, with a lovely tinkle of glass.

And onto a side street at the bottom of the hill deftly swerved our little tricolor and came to a stop for a breather, to observe from a safe distance the arguments and the damage.

The quiet street was Old Broadway, a street known to few; it was a spur left when many years ago they straightened our Broadway, long before there was any thought of Route 9.

On Old Broadway a hydrant was trickling at its own sweet will, and Horatio moistened his forehead. There was a pushcart of golden oranges, but it was not convenient to take one. Two boys were catching and throwing a rubber ball to each other from one sidewalk to the other.

"D'ye see that?" said Horatio amiably, pointing to the troubles.

"It happens every minute—we don't even go to look," said the boy.

"*I* did it," said Horatio Alger.

"Big deal!" said the boy.

A policeman with dandy white gloves was coming across the cobbled square.

"Uh-uh," said the boys, and Horace rolled.

Pleasantly rolling—for the way was now flat and there sure was no hurry with the time he made—the sunlight burned more mildly in the spokes—Horatio moved among the black people of Seventh and Lenox avenues.

He rode down Fifth Avenue.

He cut across to Madison Avenue.

And so he came to Eliphaz's house.

Zeke stopped him short, but without conviction, for to Eliphaz's came all sorts.

"Tell the man it's Horatio Alger," said the boy haughtily.

They rolled the bicycle into a storeroom.

"Give her some oil in the ass—I sure did punish her," said Horace.

—It was nearly ten minutes later (so fast had Horatio flown) that the little dog Danton loped panting up to the entrance, and lay down in the shade, with his heart thumping, to await his master's reappearance.

3.

Horatio stood perplexed, staring at the unusual routine of Eliphaz's. They were carting furniture out the doors, importing large pieces through the window and rolling up the rugs. Harry and Larry were not idle for a minute.

He was cruelly disappointed. He had imagined that the home of Eliphaz would resemble the display windows of certain department stores, but more grandiose and brilliant; instead, it resembled the shipping department of the same stores. Here was nothing but activity. He himself stood fast.

Now Eliphaz was at his desk (in the room of the Belvedere), looking into educational romances: *The Republic* and *King Henry the Fourth* and *Fifth, Democracy and Education* and *Julius the Street Boy, Gertrude and Leonard* and *The Boy Scouts of Westhampton.*

Horatio, I say, stood fast—with the shock of disappointment with which, because of their deceptive dreams, people miss the wonders before their eyes. But only for a minute or two, for he was not grown-up and so did not have to unmake his entire life every time he needed to revise his opinion. Very soon, still staring, he was walking from room to room.

Next, in a more directed way, he followed Harry and Larry at their tasks.

Coming into the Belvedere, he playfully groped the statue. He saw at a glance that that must be Eliphaz seated at the desk; he had no trouble at all in recognizing him; *he* had a quick wit. But he proceeded on his way, surveying the operations and beginning to have ideas of his own.

Meantime Eliphaz, observing the boy's businesslike behavior out the corner of his eye, was speculatively rearranging on different principles the contradictions of the various educational romances: Rousseau, Kant and Froebel, Xenophon, and *The Ethics Geometrically Demonstrated.*

Horace returned and courteously did not disturb the old man who seemed to be using his mind; but he leaned familiarly with his elbow against the pedestal of Apollo. Finally—

"I see you're in charge here," said Horace.

"Yes, sir. What can I do for you, sir?"

"How much is some good advice worth to you?"

"Ten cents is my regular rate."

"Budge Only for Folding Money," said Horatio Alger indignantly.

"No, sir! That's where you're wrong," said Eliphaz with strong disapproval. "Many a mickle makes a muckle. If those are your principles, you can keep your advice. What is it?"

"Am I wrong?" said Horatio, his face falling. "I'll have to think o' that. But I'll tell you my advice anyway, for free, 'cause you gave me *your* advice."

"Thank you, young man. Now let's hear it."

"Seems to me," said Horatio, "what you're runnin' here is a department store. Good stock too, I been lookin' around. I ain't a conysur, but I betcha it's the best. Leastways so the Dutchman says. Trouble is, you got no escalators. An' no pneumatic tubes, how d'ye make cash 'n' change? An' I seen a gimmick in Grand Central Station that oughta be right up your alley: it's a revolving floor; puts the Cadillac on display in various angles, if you get what I mean. Take this queer boy here now," he said, imitating the Leader of the Muses, "you oughta let him turn around, if you get what I mean. Like so." He spun himself slowly. "That way you can case him front an' back."

"Yes, I get what you mean," said Eliphaz.

"Gee! Wouldn' that be somethin'!" cried Horace, in love with his beautiful vision. "When everythin' is spinnin' an' the escalators goin' up an' down, an' you step onto that escalator an' slowly, slowly rise over the people's heads. *There's* interior decoratin'! My sis would go just crazy over it! Y'know, I got another sujjestion. It's about you."

"Yes?" said the prince apprehensively.

"Sure! You oughta have a pocketful of faces to put on. This way a body don't know how to take you. F'r instance now, *what* are you thinkin'? *I* don't know. You oughta have a buyer's mask an' a seller's mask, a conysur's mask, an' a mask for the artist who has to sell at any price. It's simply ridiculous when everything else is movin' in an' out for you to keep sittin' there like a wooden Indian. Say somethin'! D'ye like me?"

4. Horatio's First Trial

"Impudent snot-nose!" said Eliphaz. "Because they let you off the usual discipline, you think you're smart for your age. Wandering about the streets under no control, anybody can pick up a few tricks, a specious practicality that's always rushing to the extreme. But what good is it? Where does it get society? What's surprising if an outsider, an alien, should notice certain things that we sober citizens overlook because we are too busy keeping the system alive? You're like an eccentric I knew, a cross-country runner named Westover, who was able to tell the Highway Commission where to put the road because he did nothing all day but run along it. They gave him a bonus, but he at least put it in A. G. & E. debentures and had a stake in the general circulation (was that ever a goldbrick!) Oh I know all about you and your precious family living on the fat of the land. And now you expect me to give you the certificate of ownership of the Grand Piano as well! A certificate I'll give you! Thank God we still know how to take care of ourselves."

Eyes flashing, he threw open a roll-top desk and produced several blank forms of documents.

"Oh!" gasped the boy, and once again his eyes went wide and showed their whites, his hairs rose on his head, and he showed the signs of preternatural horror, not unlike a dog of the Society for Psychical Research.

"First, here's a birth certificate. Seems in your case there was an oversight but that's soon remedied. It makes no difference what plausible lies I write down here," he said, writing. "You were born, that's for sure. Hm. You came to me for a certificate for the Grand Piano, did you?"

He laughed briefly. "That's that. Next, I have school records. Suppose I enter you in the eighth grade: this will put you well ahead and they'll think you're a prodigy. A prodigy is the one who's allowed not to fit—it's our regular class of the unclassified. Miscellaneous. Then next year you'll be in high school where everybody starts out fresh anyway, and you won't be out of the way again."

With a flourish he forged the appropriate signatures. "Item, a library card.

"Next, as for your brother and your sis. I herewith make Lothar Alger a vice-president of the Utilities Workers International Union. This way we can deal with him according to the rules. (My rules.) He is an invaluable opponent, full of thought-provoking suggestions; *you,* of course, don't begin to appreciate his integrity and good nature."

He wrote.

"Laura, finally, will head the lecture bureau at the Museum of Modern Art on 53rd Street. By this institution we contrive to regulate the latest oracles of the Holy Spirit.

"Are these conditions hard? On the contrary, they are rigorous but tolerable; they flatter your talents; they bring out the second best in each. By these means we compel affection to be freely given."

Horace stood congealed with fright.

At first he was sure that it was all a hoax, because simple decency and American sportsmanship made it quite impossible for the other to take advantage in this way. But then he slowly thought (as was not usual with him) of the real world, the quick and slow death dealt in it, and the universal bondage with no questions asked. His blood froze and he expected no mercy.

And then he smiled. For himself, he had an absolute confidence in his own resources, and Eliphaz with his papers was really ridiculous. But—the tears began to roll down his cheeks—"I don't care about myself or even my sis," he said proudly. "So far as us, you can take your registration certificates an' you know what. It wouldn' even make any difference to me if I sat in ten schools an' sang the 'Star-Spangled Banner.' I might even pick up an item or two of information there. An' don't you rely on my sis, 'cause she can come late to work every day in the week, 'specially if it's in the morning.

"But it's my big brother Lothar. He ain't strong in the head. An' he mustn' be put where it's too confusin' for him. We'd just die if he turned out to be a labor-faker."

He was, as we know, quite mistaken about Lothar's fortitude. Nevertheless, it was brother love—energized, of course, by deep hatred—that now made the small boy inspired.

5.

In the rolled-up desk he spied the black-leather-covered account book. With a cry he snatched it up and ran over to the fire.

"Put that down!" said Eliphaz in anguish.

"Swell chance!" cried Horatio Alger triumphantly. "I know what *this* is—Arthur tells me everythin'. You ain't the only one who snoops in other people's business. But when I asted questions about you——" he said and his voice broke—"it was 'cause I loved an' admired you an' wanted to find out much as possible so I could do the same. But I see that Circumstances Alter Cases."

Keeping a wary eye out, he opened the book.

"Just like he said, all full of zeros! Trillions o' billions o' millions o' zeros! Oh! Oh! Nothin' but!"

Eliphaz jumped for him, but managed only to bark his knuckles on the fireplace.

"Not so fast," crowed Horace. "One more move outta you an' in she sails, an' then you'll never know where you are."

The prince subsided into an armchair and rolled his eyes from side to side. He was a proper villain.

Standing in front of the licking flames, Horace read off a choice page or two of this poetry, this history.

"What do you want?" asked Eliphaz finally.

"Would cost you that ten cents without any strings attached," said the boy, "but you couldn't give me that if you wanted to!"

"No, I couldn't," admitted Eliphaz. "Ask me for something possible."

"Yes, I know what I want. I know what I want you to give me," said little Horace, and his voice suddenly began to come from deep in his throat, from the bottom of his heart, "an' then I'll give you back your old book an' you can do whatever you want about *me*."

"What *do* you want, Horatio? I like you. I'll give it to you if I can."

"You let my brother Lothar off o' that jail, that's what I want. Call them off an' tell them not to arrest 'im. Will ye? Will ye?"

But to his profound disappointment, Eliphaz silently shook his head from side to side.

Horatio stared at him with unbelieving eyes, brimming with tears. "But y' *said* y'would! Y'said you would if y' could. Y'can't back out of it!"

"But I can't," said Eliphaz.

"Y'*can't!*" cried Horace frantically. "*Sure* y'can! Y' just pick up the phone. I seen how you do. Y' pick up the telephone an' you call the F.B.I., an' they *know* you 'cause you're a V.I.P., an' that's that. Whaddymean y'*can't?*"

"You don't understand, son," said Eliphaz with great kindness in his voice. "Don't you trust me?"

Horatio looked at him. And looked at him. "Yes, I trust you, father," he said. "What don't I understand?"

"I can't because your brother won't. Yes I could pick up the phone, but I can't tell them to change the whole system of the world, can I? Do you follow me? Our society is what it is and is doing what it's doing—and Lothar Alger doesn't like it, and he won't! He won't! Do you understand?"

"Yes, I understand. He's stubborn, ain't he?"

"Look, sonny, I'm older than you." That was for sure. "You have to learn that some people ain't easy to help. You learn to take care of yourself."

Horatio grinned at him with his beautiful small teeth, and Eliphaz smiled back at him with hardly any teeth at all.

Standing up, Eliphaz tore the documents into bits, the birth certificate, the school records, the union card; the passport and the visa of the passport; the certificate of commitment, the dossier of the court. All fluttering in snowlike bits of paper onto the maroon rug. But not the certificate of death, which he handed over to Horace; and Horace looked at it a long moment and tore it into snowlike bits flying like the minutes onto the maroon rug. "You're quick! That's a smart kid!" Eliphaz kept chuckling, half in flattery of his young friend and half to himself.

Horace gave him the account book.

Eliphaz glanced through it ironically. "D'ye know," he said—he was, astonishingly, rapidly picking up Horatio's accent—"except that it would be carrying coals to Newcastle, I'd tell you to take that book and shove it you know where. Let me tell you something about high finance." And he bent over and whispered a sentence in Horace's ear apropos of a financier's primitive erotic constitution (namely, that money is shit), and the boy, who for all his upbringing was quite clean-spoken, was properly shocked.

"I have learned," said Hugo Eliphaz with gravity, so that Horatio, who did not understand him, looked at him with awe, "that the Lord is so scrupulous of the least tithe, and the tithe of the tithe, that I for my part do not dare to be fastidious. The fact is—I no longer attach the least importance to this book," he said, and suiting the action to the words, he idly tossed the famous account book into the midst of the flames.

"Hey!" cried Horace.

8. Dissolution of an Anal Character

But now, belying the indifferent gesture, the old man, with the liveliest excitement and the most intense concentration, jumping up and down and yet fixed in his place, and as if going into a hypnotic trance, was gazing into the flames devouring the pages. All his life—all his life he had been waiting for this certain situation!

Horatio was himself fascinated at the sight of the burning book, but he was embarrassed by the excitement of the old man, so he tried to carry on a conversation and said, "I guess the figures don't make no difference, so long's you have the business."

"Oh, no! There're holding companies burning there, no relation to tangible assets!" His attention was concentrated on nothing but the curling leaves, the browning leaves. He spoke truly to say he took no account of the book; but oh, he took account of the book-in-the-flames!

"Ain't there stock in those holding companies all along the line?" said Horace. "Won't there be a panic?"

"I haven't been unloading that stock for many a year; it goes too slowly. There it all goes at once!" There was a puff of flame.

The ammoniac fumes of the burning leather suffused the room. The burst of flame blazed up the chimney. The old man faltered and near fell into the fire himself. All his life trying to recreate a certain situation! As if the Chinese War, cornering the market on January 4, the sending of the Grand Piano, the Trial of Horatio Alger, had no other end in view than this end result of the black-leather-covered account book going up in smoke in a puff of flame.

Quieter little flames were now more systematically eating the blackened pages. With a smile of satisfaction, and now more as if asleep than hypnotized, Eliphaz watched this more systematic conflagration. Half-dreaming—a generous gesture to adopt the small boy who had no father, as if he in his old age had had a new child. "Fact is, these days," he said to Horatio, "I have become interested in a new hobby. Child training. Education."

9. Horatio's Attainments

He questioned Horatio on his attainments.

"What do you want to know for?" said Horace cautiously.

"There's a Dutchman who's interested in making a school. But it's not exactly a school. You see, he's the Commissioner of Education of the League of Nations. (*Look* at the League of Nations!) So he don't have much to do and he's on the lookout for educational ideas. It seems he met some kid on the street who gave him a new idea."

"Kid on the street, is it!" thought Horace. "There's gratitude for you." . . . "What!" he cried, "do they put *that* one in charge of education?"

Poor Mynheer, his soul so rich with intellectual and visible forms, but without the responsibility of power nor the clog of strong passions, found himself endlessly idle, and was always undertaking—and carrying through—new enterprises in medicine, museums, pedagogy.

"Whaddymean not exactly a school?"

"A school where you never go into a school. There's no building, no special subjects to learn and no teacher. Ha, I knew you'd be interested! You see, if from the beginning they put you in a building and separate you from the world you're supposed to study, then they have to bring the things back inside again and that's the teacher; and since he can't bring it all in, he makes a convenient selection, and those are the subjects. Supposing you don't start out that way, says Mynheer. Therefore he has a slogan, We Must Push Down the Walls in Order to See the World!"

"Oh, no!" Horace corrected him. "He never gets *anythin'* straight! I didn't say it that way. I said, '*Often* we must push down the walls, etcetera.' Sometimes y'gotta come in outta the rain, don't ye?"

"O.K., O.K., you're right," said the old man. "What he really wants is to use the City as a school. Back to Socrates. You have a man who drags half-a-dozen ten-year-olds around the City: they learn to read from the headlines——"

"Yeah, I get the idea," Horace interrupted him. "This is old stuff. The kids fall in love with the teacher an' that's the end o' that."

"There are technical devices to prevent that," said the old man fatuously.

At the age of eleven going on twelve, Horatio knew the geography of military and economic warfare: the names of the frontier towns where rumors are born, and of capitals where smiling optimism prevails. He knew the sections of the United States as the headquarters of propaganda lobbies. He knew the local civics of the vice squad. He knew universal history according to the rhetorical analogies of editorial writers, whereby all antiquity is contemporaneous and no events, including the present ones, are understood in context and according to their real influence. He knew the spelling and punctuation of the *Herald Tribune* style book. He knew how to read the graphs of the Daily Average of 100 Stocks, and the Rails. All of this he knew according to the best precepts of progressive pedagogy, in precise and inaccurate functional relationships.

He knew Routes and Courses; how to mix cement and lay macadam; and how to regulate traffic and distribute population in order to produce confusion.

He knew the harmony and counterpoint of a Minute before the Dawn, to which ambulance sirens, police sirens and fire sirens lend their voices.

The pictorial techniques of joining the idea of certain commodities to the fear of loneliness and sexual failures. In architecture, how to make time bombs; in interpersonal relations, how to make zip guns.

He knew the physics of the bounds and rebounds of the Spaulding High-Bouncer from a wooden wall and a cement floor. He knew the chemistry of substitute and preserved foods, which could be read directly on the labels by Federal law. He knew the biology of washrooms, the sociology of Miss Pitcher. In linguistics he knew how to pretend that he came from Brooklyn or the Bronx.

In philosophy (for he made no distinction of lower and higher studies) he knew that the Future Lies Ahead of Us, yet—alas—One Thing Leads to Another.

He knew the poetry of desire as written on the walls of dim tunnels.

In general, he knew the basic jokes which can be found if you dig under the City.

10.

"This is good—excellent—knowledge," said Eliphaz admiringly. "It is neither all theoretical nor all practical. Not all intellectual, not all artistic. Not all for work, not all for play. Some of it is abstract, some concrete. Some requires independent research and initiative, some teaches you how to consult reference works. A reasonable amount is false, so you still have surprises in store; yet no important branches are omitted, so you will never feel grossly ignorant. Perhaps you might have a little astronomy—nothing about the tides? The phases of the moon? When to go fishing? What is it with the boys these days? . . . Yet really, I'm amazed. This is more than a foundation!" And the tears rolled down the old man's cheeks as he thought of his own wasted childhood.

Horatio's ears glowed with pleasure as he heard himself praised in this way, for what he wanted above all was to be well informed. He wanted Eliphaz to continue questioning him, to recall to him item by item his beautiful knowledge, to his joy; he never realized what a lot he knew.

"It's good," said Eliphaz, "but the commissioner won't be satisfied with it, and I'm not satisfied with it."

Horatio's heart sank; he was always being dashed down. "Whatsamatta with it?" he said sullenly.

"The matter with it is that this is just life; all you know is life. What we want for you, boy, is a life worth living, and that's Culture, that's Education. Education is a habit of the selection of life; in a pinch it's a protection *against* life. What we want to give you, boy, is the *Habit of Freedom.* (Mynheer tells me that he got that phrase from Immanuel Kant, but I look for it in vain. But Kant *did* say that we mustn't put infants in swaddling clothes, in order that they can learn to use their powers.)"

It was quite touching, the way the old man was beginning to talk about infants and swaddling clothes. But the boy looked at him in blank dismay.

"Do you believe any o' that?" said Horace. "Think! Think, man!" he said, tapping his head. "First you say, no school! Grand! Then you say there'll be a leader draggin' me around. Not so grand. Then you say we don't get life but a selection o' life. So you have a school after all! I seen 'em walkin' along the street two by two on the way to the Aquarium! An' you call it habit o' freedom in order to make it stick. *Oh,* no! Definitely! Include me out! Freedom is freedom—you don't need to teach me no freedom."

"Well, maybe I'm not explaining it right," said Eliphaz puzzled.

At this moment in walked Duyck Colijn himself. It was not surprising that he arrived so opportunely, for a person of many interests is always likely to arrive pat for something or other.

11.

"You're still here!" he said excitedly. "I know—I saw your dog downstairs. They're going to move the Grand Piano onto the street!"

The boy went white. "Sis will be mad as hell," he said. But what really alarmed him was that, for purposes of his own, he had wired the piano with a stick of dynamite. "He never giv me the certificate," he said defensively; "it ain't my fault."

"Just in time!" exclaimed Eliphaz. "Explain to him about the Sample Day! I've been trying to, but he makes such simple remarks that I get all confused."

"Please, not now; they're collecting a crowd. The idiot downstairs called the police."

Horace winced.

"Lothar thinks you were hit by a truck."

"Oh, he does, does he? Is that what he thinks?" cried Horace indignantly. "Thinks I was hit by a truck! *He* thinks that *I* was hit by a truck! Dopo thinks that Horatio Alger got himself hit by a truck! I think that's rich. Don't you think that's rich?"

"Sit down, sit down," said Eliphaz. "Have a drink. We're having a quiet discussion here. Shove the Grand Piano. I tell you what, I'll go with you myself in five minutes."

"He *wants* me to be hit by a truck!" cried Horace. "Well, I hope they all get blown up an' die! Anyway, there's no use in goin' till he gives us the paper or comes along hisself."

"Sit down! Sit down!" said Eliphaz, and stretched himself in the easy chair in front of the fire.

"What in hell have you been burning here?" said Dyck sniffing. "Leather!" He looked sharply at Eliphaz. "There's been a change of character in him," he concluded at once. "I wonder what's up."

"All right, five minutes," he said. "Give me a drink, what do you call that Calvados—applejack, neat?"

It was in order to create an art object for the Society of Bombardiers that Horatio had wired up the piano. The idea was as follows: you wired up a certain note, and you sat down to play, and you made music always calling for that tone as a resolution, but avoided touching it as long as you could. The tone was *B* Flat.

Chapter 13 ▪ AN EDUCATIONAL ROMANCE, II

1. Mynheer's Three Lectures on Pedagogy

"The aim of education," said Mynheer patiently, "is to make us at home in the Empire City. You shut up," he said to little Horace, who was about to protest his first proposition. "You let me expound this the way I please. This is a lecture. To make us feel at home, because we don't feel that way now."

"Ho-hum," said Horace and fell fast asleep.

"He's asleep, he's not being impudent," said Eliphaz, and nudged him. "Wake up, kid."

"I can't help it!" said Horace, starting awake. "I wasn't trained up to listen to no lectures if I can't talk back. An' they keep wakin' me up, didn't get enough sleep last night. An' I keep lookin' at that leapin' fire an' it puts me to sleep. It's not you, Dyck; you ain't specially boring. Anyway, I know just what you said: people don't feel at home. How the fuck can you feel at home if they keep wakin' you up?"

"Shall I go on?" said Mynheer.

"Go on, I'll try to pay 'tention."

"All right. Now the reason people don't feel at home is that they can't cope with the problems. They're too many, too big and too complicated; so we have to take them in the right doses. This I call Tempering Experience to Our Powers:

> *Make us at home again by tempering so*
> *experience to our powers that we may grow.*

You feel easy when you feel adequate. Is that clear? Any questions, class?"

"Yes, I have a question," said Eliphaz. "What if home's no good to begin with? What if the problems ain't worth coping with? Is *that* clear?"

"Good!" said Mynheer. "This is a damn better class than I ever had at Teachers College. Your point is: The aim of education is to make us feel at home, and who wants to feel at *home?* So we have to have a Counter Principle (and let's not forget it, either): I'll call it Detachment or Nonattachment. On the one hand, this City is the only one you'll ever have and you've got to make the best of it. On the other hand, if you want to *make* the best of it, you've got to be able to criticize it and change it and circumvent it. Are we agreed then on these three simple preliminaries: 1. learn to be at home with what we have; 2. temper experience to the growing powers; 3. cultivate nonattachment."

"Go ahead, we'll see," said Horace, who somehow had already developed a prodigious detachment.

"The rest is merely technical and I go back to antiquity. It seems to me *prima facie* to use the Empire City itself as our school. Instead of bringing imitation bits of the City into a school building, let's go at our own pace and get out among the real things. What I envisage is gangs of half a dozen, starting at nine or ten years old, roving the Empire City with a shepherd empowered to protect them, and accumulating experiences tempered to their powers. Questions?"

"Holy cats!" cried Horace, goggle-eyed to think of others carrying on the way he did. "Would they ever make trouble and stop traffic!"

"So much the worse for the traffic," said the professor flatly. "I'm talking about the primary function of social life, to educate a better generation, and people tell me that tradesmen mustn't be inconvenienced. I proceed."

2. Divisions of the Curriculum

"Lecture Two. Fundamentally our kids must learn two things: Skills and Sabotage. Let me explain.

"We have here a great City and a vast culture. It must be maintained as a whole; it can and must be improved piecemeal. It is relatively permanent. At the same time it is a vast corporate organization; its enterprise is bureaucratized, its arts are institutionalized, its mores are far from spontaneity: therefore, in order to prevent being swallowed up by it or stamped by it, in order to acquire and preserve a habit of freedom, a kid must learn to circumvent it and sabotage it at any needful point as occasion arises."

"Wait up! Wait up!" said Horace. "Ain't this a contradiction? You say we got to learn to be easy at home here, then you say we got to sabotage at every point. On the one hand, you gotta love an' serve 'em; on the other hand you gotta kick 'em in the shins. Does it make sense to you?"

"There's nothing in what you say, young man. In the Empire City these two attitudes come to the same thing: if you persist in honest service, you will soon be engaging in sabotage. *Do* you follow that?"

"Yes, I think *we* follow that," said Eliphaz quietly, "but I doubt that other people do."

"Let me illustrate," said Mynheer.

3. A Thousand and One Lesson Plans

"Lecture Three. The flesh and bones of any system of pedagogy is a Thousand and One Lesson Plans, in order that the teachers may have a storehouse of ideas to draw from. Now the way to get that is to experiment with a pilot group and I'll start on that next week. But here's a sample, to give you the taste."

He consulted some notes written on the back of an envelope:

"May Fifth. Going uptown we start out early with a game of Subway Tag."

Eliphaz interrupted him. "That wasn't the program you read to me yesterday. That started with breakfast in the automat."

"I lost that piece of paper. What difference does it make? This one's just as good.

"1. Subway Tag is a game where 3 try to catch 3 on the trains and stations. They can get off anywhere and ride 2 stations north or 1 south. (Special rules for express and local stops.) Let them find out by asking for information where they can cross over between northbound and southbound without paying another fare. The aim is to study the accuracy of such random informants. Who misleads you and why, do you think? How do the trainmen and the passengers put up with such a game when everybody is rather sleepy in the morning? This is the southbound rush hour: note the sentiment of going against the crowd: harder? easier? Size up the train schedules. Play about 1 hour and arrive at Columbia. Were there any attempted seductions or other interesting experiences? What did you do? What might you have done? Did you arrive? Why?

"2. A session of mathematics on the sidewalk outside the subway. Statistics of the passersby in different classifications; how many of what will come next? Which predictions were faulty and why? . . . A lesson in geometry expounded in chalk on the sidewalk. (Archimedes and the soldier.) Develop line, angle, straight angle, up to the theorem that vertical angles are equal. Keep at this for several days till there is a geometrical proof, as well as an intuitive one. Make them see the beauty of such proof. . . . Draw back from the figures (always draw back afterward) and notice how confused the total picture is, though we can remember why this line and that. . . . Add doodles, names, pictures; and draw back and look at the *tout ensemble* of geometrical figures, cartoons, dates.

"3. In that neighborhood, most of the tenements have elaborate cornices, a few do not. The latter are newer. Ask a passerby, a janitor, about these ancient curiosities. Association of the cornices with other ornament: in the lobbies, in the flats (paneling and moldings). Now find out the comparative rents. What are the varying relations of ornament, age and expense? Why these varying relations? What is modish? . . . Each one to describe and draw details of his own dwelling in these respects. . . . What is their prediction of the next change of style? Look for a house still being built; try to find someone from the architect's office, and check the prediction. Does this fellow know much about it? Start making a history of recent art to explain the latest-style building.

"4. Now to the playground and let them play a round-robin tournament of handball. This—do not let them know it—is in honor of the musician my friend R., *my* funeral service for him. But do explain something of these games, like handball, tennis and pelota, where the ball flies across the rectangles, as ritual astrological ceremonies. . . . As referee, be usually fair but sometimes outrageously arbitrary and let them cope with that. Forensic evidence to prove something. . . . Let 4 watch 2 play and have a session of criticism of form: form and success: canonic form and individual style. What is the factor of luck? Willful bad luck. Making the breaks. . . . In the name of God the Creator do not discourage the kids with gloomy reflections on these sad games, for after all it was not *their* friend who died.

"5. Time to eat. On the fifth of May let's have our soup, sandwich and tea in a clean bright restaurant. Make them confront the fact that some of this food comes from a dead animal, even at the risk of spoiling their appetites or getting them nauseous. (This is very important.) . . . We mix our own salad, buying the ingredients beforehand in a local store. 10 spices. Mix and try—try and mix. Different kinds of greens and different formulas of the dressing. Theory of cutting the oil with lemon and vinegar. Are there contraries among the spices? Sweet salt bitter sour. . . . Now compare our dressing with a popular bottled brand, with an expensive bottled brand. Why need those be so awful? (Another day, different breads.)

"Pause. Scatter. Meet again.

"6. Walking southward toward midtown and Queensboro bridge. Time the traffic lights. Advantages and disadv. of progressive lights. Theory and practice of jaywalking and of preventing jaywalking. Go up to the roof of a high building for a total view of the traffic as it moves and stops: where does it come from? Where is it going? Should there be red and green lights only, or red, green and yellow? What are the reasons for *these* colors? Proposal to control the colored neon lights and keep them off certain avenues: we compose a letter on this subject to the *Times*. Compose letters pro and con. Will such letters have any influence? In what circumstances?

"7. Across the bridge there is a strike at the B. factory, and it is being picketed. Look for Timmy: this old man is the inventor of the idea of igniting the phosphorus as it escapes from the chimney, a gas that would otherwise poison the community (this was in Indiana). Note that Timmy is still working in these factories and is out on strike with the others. Compose a letter to the *Times* on Timmy's case. Do the others deserve letters? Point out to the kids that I own stock in these works; I defend my own interests vigorously with the usual patter, and see how they cope with that. . . . Added question of finding a process for using the gases which are now burned up.

"8. Take the old man Timmy to tea with us. Since he happens to be interested in that kind of thing, try to get an argument going between us on the Methodical Doubt. Produce some powerful metaphysical saw, e.g. *Cogito.* At the same time, get the 6 kids involved in it, and nevertheless let the argument become as abstruse as it will, with plenty of big words that they cannot possibly understand. The argument must be like a balloon that comes down from time to time then bounces aloft again. But they must keep quiet even when they can't pay attention. . . . What's important is that they grasp that this is the same Timmy as before.

"9. Some are sleepy; it's four o'clock. What's sleepiness like? What's breathing like? How does the dog breathe? How does each of the kids walk? What does it express? Character of the panhandler. Character of the crowd outside the employment agency. Question an angry man. . . . The colors in the air toward dusk—talk about the Monets and awake an interest in seeing them soon. The rhythm of the day.

"Next day no school."

"Well, that's about it for May Fifth," said the commissioner. "We have to work it out for a Thousand and One Days."

"What do they do after dark?" said Horace.

"I haven't thought of that," said Mynheer thoughtfully.

"Hm," said Horatio thoughtfully.

"They go home to their families?" asked Eliphaz.

"Yes. Crazy, isn't it?"

"Hm, hm," said Horatio.

"What are you thinking about there so hard, boy?" asked Mynheer curiously.

"It could be done!" said Horatio, with surprising seriousness. "O' course it don't compare with the kind o' life an' activity that *I* go through every day, on my own; but it compares *favorable* with what those other kids 'v got, I mean the ones chained in a school *an'* the ones on the hook. I'm a special case an' you can't go by me, but I *like* it. Not for me."

4. A Quintet

At this interesting moment Emily and Arthur came in, happy but tired and uncommunicative. It was midday and they were still drunk. Nor was it surprising that they arrived so inopportunely, for persons who have been having a good time are always arriving out of touch with the world. They were embarrassed to find the others there.

"They've been kissing or——" saw Dyck, annoyed, at a glance. He suffered what was very like a pang of jealousy; but he interpreted his response as disapproval.

"You're just in time," cried Eliphaz, "for I have an important announcement to make. I am going to adopt Horatio Alger as one of my heirs."

"Why, that's just bully!" said Arthur with enthusiasm, and pumped the boy's hand.

Horatio was speechless.

And now these five, Eliphaz and Mynheer, Horatio, Arthur and Emily, momentarily paused, lost in thought—while the world and the other planets moved on their courses as usual.

Horace thought: "Why have I, who have always had the blessing——"; Arthur thought: "I could cry when I think of the hotel rooms——"; Mynheer thought: "Again again again and again——"; Emily thought: "My father had two children——"; and Eliphaz thought: "*Look* at the fire, licking at nothing——"

These five were in the extraordinary situation, every one, of having what they really wanted.

Horatio was saying to himself: "Why have I, who have always had the blessing of having no parents, and have not failed to take advantage of it, why then have I always wanted, as I have, this moment when Eliphaz would butt into my business? Now I have to call him father or some such other term; now I am allowed to do so. Oh, but in almost everything I have ever done I have been looking for some authority great enough to be neither possible nor obligatory to avoid. (So strong was my envy of the well-established boys!) *My* father is great enough to agree with anything that passes through my mind! So now I have what I most desire! Yet—it makes me uneasy. Up to now, when I went after any particular thing, I could do it with a light heart because this was never the solid thing I was after, the sure thing; I could even possess it with a light touch. But now whatever I go after with all my heart, and especially when I get it, I am stuck with it, for it is what I really want. The things

I want have now become three-dimensional, they cast shadows; I am responsible for them; how can I avoid being responsible for what I really want? It's intolerable to be so uneasy; how long should I let it go on?"

Said Arthur to himself: "I could cry when I think of the hotel rooms where I have let my tired youth be thrown. Yet they have always been the scenes of my best hours; how could they fail to be, since I landed there by following impulses strong enough to distract me from the sure pleasures I thought I was bound for; impulses strong enough to get me into trouble? If I had a composite photograph of the things that distract me on the avenue, this one's gait and that one's glance, perhaps I would discover something about myself. Certainly I would not for the world do that which I have been doing tonight; and now I have what I most desire! But I could cry when I think of the hotel rooms where I have let my tired youth be thrown."

Mynheer was saying to himself: "Again again again and again! My enterprises do not prove to be abortive. By an inspiration of the Holy Spirit again and again I succeed according to my expectation, so that I have even come to expect the inspiration. This is the sin against the Holy Spirit, and my punishment is that, after I have achieved what I set out to do, *I* am left just where I am (I cannot even imagine where else a person might be left). What then? Shall I rather explore among the things I by nature avoid, the acts of disgust, of death, failure and loathing? Of vice, of need, despair, disgrace? No, even though I guess that I would find, further on, myself there. Neither way. For I take comfort in this: that the Good is not itself good; although it gives luster to what we desire as the Good. So that it is by good and beautiful success, again and again, that a person like myself comes to no good; and now I have what I most desire!"

Emily was saying to herself: "My father had two children, a daughter and a son. Any one could observe that we were different in nature, yet both sprang from that great man. But he has now become a fool and destroys himself with new heirs; so much the better, he will no longer stand in our way with his hateful and dangerous existence. Now my duty is to preserve and restore this whole man by reunion with my brother Arthur, and now therefore I have what I most desire! I am beginning to remember that there was once another time, which I do not remember, in which I was not so incapable of understanding what it is that my father is doing and intends us to do."

But Eliphaz was not saying anything to himself, but was looking at the fire in the fireplace, and thinking: "*Look* at the fire, licking at nothing—it *riots,* freed from prison of the coal and the sticks. It is because of this wild spirit that I am content to remain at home. If you light even a burning match and look at the world through the flame, it is bright and warm. The identical destroyer of Chicago! So gentle and friendly. It is not tamed; is it tamed? . . . Let me found a movement to repopularize the open fireplace: it is founded herewith, the Committee for the Restoration of the Hearth!"

"Come along, Danton!" And the small dog leaped up on him in ecstasy and trotted ahead.

Chapter 14 ▪ THE LAST PAGE OF HORATIO'S DIARY

Blast Off**** 10* 9* 8* 7* 6* 5* 4* 3* 2* 1* zeeerooooooo thats potry, musik. i herd it on the radio.

som do it with any 1 at all. thats called promiskus it aint worth the trubl. others is choosy & it must be A+ A+ thats to tuf to mak out. best is in-between.

if you look 2 × as much, you dubl the chances. also if you cut yr stanards in ½ you dubl the chances. that maks 4 ×.
thats why i mak out so good.
[*Work in the theory of probability.*]

wen I explod it i wont hav any more ris caks frm the chink. Got to think o things lik that.
i watch lothar behind door. hes sad. El. is rit, stubrn lik an ox. strong lik an ox.

Abby D– * Ester D– * Chuckie D– * coms frm tryin to pruv therys insted o folowin my dik. snap out*

Yello sun shins out & the pepl sing lik brids. Cold day I hav hot soop & sudnly i sing lik a brid. must be the hot?
[*Observation in physiological psychology.*]

im to serus today. am i getn sik?
wen i explod it wont be troont ofs.
wen i explod it rthur wd miss me
[*Pros and cons of blowing up the piano.*]

DOPO IS THE LIMIT* he thinks 1 000 000s pepl think lik us. my ges is about 58.

met a man sez "the lordly hudson". grand** also h. hudson who 1st fond it got lost in ice in labador. thot hed go to China insted o just to albiny. weak upstars lik lothar. his ship stuk in ice.
im getn awfl sad. tim for a pees. donalson?

remem ast Dutch whats cornisses? why gren red & yello lits? dutch is grand to. most pepl o.k. but dul. tel kids ded animals r food, mak a fuckin lot o canibls*

IMPORTNT* r frens com akross. sis coms akross. dutch coms

akross. El. to. rthur 100%. horatio coms akross. good to hav a spec. mark = "come akross". ‡ super-plus*
[*Inventing a new symbol ‡ to mean "a person who comes across."*]

donalson muvd away. nuthin but lousy luk* dogs my ftsteps. good-by* good-by* thes days i look 3 × as far & just get tird ft. lousy thery.
[*His faith in probability is shaken.*]

wen i explod it good-by* good-by*

El.‡

"lordly hudson"‡

do rthur & emily?? **

good-by* my diry* wen i explod it.

Chapter 15 ▪ THE GRAND PIANO

1. A Carnival Spirit

At the tiptop of Fort George Hill they had the Grand Piano chained out on the sidewalk, and around it in a star extended a colorful crowd, including perambulators and wheelchairs.

In the stadium across the street there was a crack of the bat and the ball lifted high into the sunlight. The Imperial flag was flapping from its mast on the tower of the high school.

"This Grand Piano," said Sis, stamping her foot, "properly belongs to the one who can play it. I myself don't play, but both my brothers are artists and my fiancé knows all the music of the masters. Here he comes now! He'll show you."

Even before Dyck's car drew up and came to a stop, Horatio leaped from the running board and disconnected the explosive. He had, as they say, a whim of iron but he did not intend to injure anyone but himself.

The young adolescents out of school for lunch were swelling the crowd around the piano. Marshall Ficino was prejudicing their appetites by selling them narcotic candies at his stand.

"Listen, Dopo!" cried Horace wrathfully confronting Lothar. "I hear you thought I was hit by a truck. You *want* me to be hit by a truck, that's why you dream up I was hit by a truck. Did I ever wish *you* any hard luck that you go an' wish I was hit by a truck? Jeez."

"I don't wish you any hard luck, Horatio," said Lothar gravely, "and I'm glad to see you safe and sound." Lothar was handcuffed to a Federal agent, and they were waiting for the police wagon.

"Do you think," cried Miss Pitcher passionately to Laura, "that you Algers are the only ones that can play the piano? There are thousands of competent pianists. I myself studied with Poulenc."

"D'ye call that baby stuff music?" snorted Horatio. "I could play you music that'd blow your brains out!"

With a wild whistle a red car braked behind Mynheer's and the Spaniard, Luis Mendoza, leaped out, brandishing a copy of the *Herald Tribune*. "Listen, Dutchman," he hissed, "I gotta see you. What's your *game?*"

Eliphaz, meantime, had insisted on getting out at 181st Street and unloading the boy's bike from the rumble seat, and he could now be seen in the distance, slowly pedaling up the hill. As soon as he was pointed out, the crowd roared its approval.

"Hurry up, please, it's time," said one of the bailiffs who had come to take away the piano.

It was a time. The noon bells clanged from the high-school tower.

The sun passed behind a cloud.

This moment also was the end result of the long process of time—as the marijuana in the candy began to have its wonted effect.

"That's him!" they shouted downhill toward the sexagenarian cyclist.

"Break it up here," said one of the fifty cops.

All up and down the street the electricians were cutting off the power.

Mynheer turned sharply on the Spaniard and said:

"⸮?"

"!¡"

". . ."

"?"

Saying which Mendoza y Pidal backed Dyck into an alley, but instantly the Dutchman showed him a hold whereby, with a flick of his wrist, he had him over his shoulder and flat on his back, and he was wiping off his hands on a white handkerchief.

Some of the crowd ran downhill to be an escort and cheer Eliphaz on.

Some of the kids sucking on the lollipops began to dance in the street.

A class that was imprisoned in the high school pressed its noses to the window.

Lothario watched it all gloomily, and was already thinking of the contradictions between penal theory and penal practice.

And someone played the chord:

Surrounded by admirers Eliphaz was pedaling up from 185th Street; and now could be seen the application of two principles: the first belonging properly to the art of cycling, that when we have coasted down, we must pump up; the second belonging more generally to all arts of travel, that coming back we traverse all old places in reverse order.

"For God's sake, resolve that chord!" cried Miss Pitcher and sharply struck the *G*.

The *G*, the crack o' the bat, the flapping flag, the sun behind a cloud. The crack o' the bat. The silvery sphere, the cheering thousands. The noses pressed to the window. The noses pressed to the window. The noses pressed to the window, and the music that'd blow your brains out.

And 'mid rattling acclaim from every throat and tattered newspapers snowing from heaven, Eliphaz arrived at the Grand Piano and the crowd opened before him to hem him in from behind. Horatio looked to see whether he had favored the worn-out brake as he had warned him. Eliphaz climbed up on the piano stool and, as a hush fell over the crowd, he said in a loud voice: *"The Grand Piano belongs to Horatio Alger!"* "Oh, no," said Lothar, "don't trust him with it yet!" "Jerusalem!" whispered Mynheer, suddenly noticing an item in the Spaniard's paper that certified that he was bankrupt on an international scale. "Furthermore," said the old man on the piano stool, "I now publicly announce for the first time—is there a reporter in the crowd?—*Horatio Alger is my son and heir!*" Horatio was again appropriately speechless.

The reporter made the financier pose for a picture on the bicycle. He made the blushing and smiling boy pose on the bicycle to show that he was a regular boy. Horatio's modesty immediately won the affection of everybody. He posed at the piano in order to show that he could sit at a piano. Eliphaz posed giving a dime to an old woman in a wheelchair. Lothario posed handcuffed to the detective.

Finally Horatio found his voice and said: "The great honor bestowed on me, I shall try to be worthy of my father's choice of me as his heir, which I have always looked forward to keenly. But as to the disposition of the Grand Piano, I am afraid that I must contradict him and must second in this, as in everything else, the opinion of my dear sis when she says that the piano belongs to the one who can play it. Therefore, there ought to be a contest."

At this suggestion there was a buzz of excitement, for a contest always rouses keen anticipation.

"Who'll be the judge?"

"Let the people be the judge!"

"Can you win it, son?" Eliphaz asked the boy.

"I think so," answered Horatio quietly.

After a hasty poll, it was found that the contestants were to be:

Eliphaz
Miss Pitcher
Lothario
and Horatio Alger

2. The Magic Fire

A hush fell as Eliphaz took his place to play.

But to Horatio's horror he opened a panel under the keyboard, unwound an electric cable, and asked a woman looking out of a ground-floor window to plug it into her line. Horatio sank his head between his shoulders and held his hands over his ears: the current streamed through the wire and the field was magnetized, but instead of the disastrous explosion that he expected the keyboard rippled triumphantly into "Wotan's Farewell" and the "Magic Fire" by Wagner-Liszt-Paderewski. For it was a mechanical piano and could play, drawing on the power company, the library of the classics.

With astonishment Horatio watched the keys, fingered by the ghost, for he had never seen a mechanical piano.

"What strength, what bravura! . . ."

"Nobody's playin' it!" cried a small girl, and let out a shriek.

"Be quiet, silly," explained her mother.

Loge! Loge!

—"Loki! Loki!" proclaimed the song, and at these words the old man rose to his feet and said, "Ladies and Gentlemen:

"During this well-known and appropriate music allow me to make an appeal for a philanthropy in which I have lately become interested. I am not accustomed to come before the public in this way, so you may judge how near this matter is to my heart. I give you the Committee for the Restoration of the Hearth. Our slogan is *Keep the Home Fires Burning.*

"In these times of rapid change, you must often have felt, as I have, if only it were possible to have a personal, a living symbol that one could call one's very own! Here it is—the home fire. What a bulwark for a vital conservatism! Against such a standard as this we can measure every innovation and ask, 'Is it as warm as our fire? Is it as bright?'

"Now our engineers have perfected a handy brazier within the reach of every pocketbook, with a patent fuel modeled after genuine Irish peat and obtainable from Esso. (The kit, with fuel for ten days, sells for forty-six, fifty, and by special arrangement with the Board of Estimate tax-exempt.) By means of this ingenious kit, it is no longer necessary, no matter how much you move about on your jobs, even to Brooklyn, for any family to be without its own family hearth.

"Especially since in the near future," continued Eliphaz, "so many sons, husbands and fathers will be engaged in the dangerous business of war, and perhaps risking their lives in faroff lands: what a comfort it will be for each one of them to be able to visualize definitely the particular home fire that he is fighting to defend."

The phantom pianist was elaborating that tinkling and laughing figure:

with which Loki erects curtains of flame between the sleeping maiden and every interloper but Siegfried.

"And we at home——" said Eliphaz, but suddenly the electrician in the basement cut off the power of Apartment 1D for nonpayment, and the music stopped dead.

3. A World's Record

"I," precisely announced little Miss Pitcher, standing beside the piano stool that came up to her waist, "am going to play the Andantine of a sonatino by François Poulenc. I mean," she corrected herself precisely, "the Andantin*o* of a sonatin*uh.*"

She seated herself, played an attention chord and one rippling arpeggio.

Then very well indeed, she played this pastoral of the lambs rather than the shepherds.

She played these dances of good children, *des enfants sages;* this simple-mindedness in which some of us have taken refuge because our feelings are so deeply wounded these days.

During these decades some of the wounded sensitive people were stormy and insurrectionary; others were patiently adequate to all calamities; still others kept spitefully probing the sore spots as if in the expectation that something intolerable would turn up. But Miss Pitcher was among the small ones and she made an adjustment by simplifying the world.

Perhaps she laid a stress of pain on a repeated note in the triplets as if some of the lambs bounding over the fence broke a leg in the act.

As if the eyes of even a well-behaved child filled with tears.

During these decades (1920-1940) it was partly as a satire—and not because they did not understand their plight in and out—that several sensitive poets and musicians concerned themselves with small children.

It was partly just in order to be able to maneuver lightly in the strange and cumbrous world, which they did not understand and in which they were too weak; but it was partly as a satire, because in so far as they did understand it through and through, it did not seem to them that one could maneuver lightly there. Partly it was perversity.

It was partly in order that they could cry more unashamedly.

Miss Pitcher did not let herself think of these things. There was almost nothing in how she played to express her desperate anxiety. She found little difficulty in behaving sagely even yet. In her own round, for example, Miss Pitcher found that if she pushed a button, almost always a bell sounded thrillingly within, just as she expected; if there was a dispute of jurisdiction, it was arbitrated in a democratic committee by the district supervisor; if she returned home in the evening, the sofa was cowering against the wall. The sofa was cowering against the wall and the easy chair was crouching behind the door.

During these decades some of our artists concerned themselves with small children in order to astonish the bourgeoisie with the enormities of innocence.

Partly because, indeed, there is truth in these little mouths which right out the grownups are unable to speak. Also out of perversity.

And also that they might cry more unashamedly.

Yet if she idly ran over the multiplication table, she still came to the conclusion that $12 \times 12 = 122$. If she limited the agenda of her daily inquiries, she could adequately cover the ground except for those headings that were impossible for her to discuss. If she tried to explain honestly what she was about, the tears still did not fail to blind her eyes. And if she played a piece of music from memory——

"Surely something is wrong here! It's impossible that he could have written twelve *G*-major chords in a row——"

"Thirteen! Fourteen! Fifteen! Sixteen——"

"One hundred twenty-two!"

This was a world's record for successive *G*-major chords.

4. Invention of the Lorrainean Scales

The third competitor, as we saw, was handcuffed to a Federal detective.

"It's no great matter," said Lothario with his characteristic proud independence. "I'll improvise something for the left hand alone. Won't be so loud as if I had two hands but——"

But the crowd roared, "Two hands! Two hands! Fair play! We gotta right to two hands!" The detective had to loosen the cuffs, though he stood by with a drawn pistol.

Lothar played the piano like a composer, that is, badly; as if he were reading off or mumbling the other fellow's thoughts, or his own past thoughts, and commenting or criticizing as he went along, making corrections, and sometimes stopping in surprise, to try the phrase again; at the end he left you with nothing but the music.

When he improvised, however, he was like a boxer, with the instrument as his opponent or his partner (it comes to the same thing). He feinted and the piano would respond whatever it would respond, according to its nature, and there was Lothar on his toes, jabbing, feinting and after a while slugging. That is, he showed the same character as a musician and as a man; but how could he show a different character?

And this afternoon first, as if to blow off the sounding board the inhibitions of Miss Pitcher, he rang all the keys full pedal from top to bottom, with an electrifying effect. The meaning of it was: "I allow myself as yet this limited chaos in order to create a world." The chaos was limited because he had himself tuned the piano in tempered twelve-tone scales. And this much he speedily organized with a dozen staccato thumps.

Now the secret of Lothar as an artist, especially within the diatonic scale, was that whenever he happened to strike a false note, whether because of his broad fingers and heavy touch or by an inner compulsion—but it seemed to him that it was the piano that responded perversely (but it comes to the same thing)—he at once made the relatively unlimited possibilities of this false relation equipollent in harmony with everything that had gone before; and he matter-of-factly addressed himself to a grander resolution. Shall we not say, he *sought out* false relations; *they* were the medium in which he composed? But he doggedly and scrupulously, and often triumphantly, made the best of it. And some harmonies he had to play with his palms and forearms.

There is a parable that Buber tells and that I want to repeat here to do honor to Lothar: A Western sage is toiling up a mountain carrying on his back a heavy treasure chest, and making slow progress and sometimes no progress. And he meets an Eastern sage who has already been to the top and is lightly coming down. "Why don't you put down that box?" asks the Easterner. "And then you could easily go up." "But what," says the Westerner, "if I want to get to the top just with this box, and otherwise it is nothing to me?"

As you can imagine, by the time Lothar came to the climax of his progressions, that huge piano was at the limit of its resources. Or, when that huge piano was at the limit of its resources, then it was the climax Such a volume of packed sound that the piano bucked at the knees, and the audience looked at one another startled; but on the face of the musician began to gleam a smile,

> such a moist beam
> among the dark blue frowns
> as Ganymede
> knew how to win from Jove

—and he momentarily closed his eyes, as he perceived and planned to execute a most simple return.

Naturally at this moment, with equally loud clangs, arrived the police wagon, and the detective tapped Lothar on the shoulder.

"Presently," said Lothar. And with his wrench he deftly untuned here and there a dozen strings to quarter-tones and invented the Lotharingian scales. And when he had changed the possibilities of the tonal chord, he pressed his foot on the pedal and struck a chord.

The strange voices! They did not seem to come from the same sounding board as the others. Lothario was himself taken aback and ventured only lightly to touch the keys again. In this new world everything yet seemed possible; but one must proceed with caution. He struck another tone—it almost failed to sound; it would sound as strongly as any if he struck it with confidence. Strike again, musician! He struck the same keys firmly, and the whole, the whole world of the tired harmonies of so many rhapsodies and sonatas (but let me speak no evil of the master musicians of the past) faded from the memory of every ear.

5. The Breaking Out of the War

As soon as Horatio, the boy Bombardier, sat down to the Grand Piano, he reconnected his dynamite to the key

the middle of the piano, a tone below that, and also flat. Now all was ready for action. His face was white.

He planned to approach this tone gingerly, by playing first in the further octaves of the piano; and this would give him five variations to get to touch it. He started around

down in the regions of the last note of Tchaikowsky's last symphony, but a step below that note, for it is not on the last note, but after it, that we expect to hear the revolver shot.

When Horatio saw his brother arrested and driven away in the clanging vehicle, sadness unnerved him, and the sentiment, which had already begun to surprise him in his diary, that these things were flat and unprofitable. So on the keys that Lothar had dislocated—in the so-called Lorrainean scale—he played with one finger a sad monody for his brother Lothar; nor was it hard to play a strange and poignant melody with intervals that no one had ever heard before.

As if burnt, he withdrew the little finger of his right hand with which he had almost closed the song with a fatal resolution. He put this little finger in his mouth, as a very small child does when embarrassed by the presence of a stranger.

He shrugged, and now addressed himself to the bright and likely

In this variation he wished to tell a wonderful joke, such an elementary and eerie joke as, for instance (as if there were another instance!) that with which Christians begin the Gospel of their Lord. For it says (Matt. I:1-18):

1. The book of the generation of Jesus Christ, the son of David, the son of Abraham. . . .

16. And Jacob begat Joseph the husband of Mary, of whom was born Jesus, who is called Christ. . . .

18. Now the birth of Jesus Christ was on this wise: When as his mother Mary was espoused to Joseph, before they came together, she was found with child of the Holy Ghost.

Horatio played with it for a moment, and dismissed it, and turning to

he surrounded it with a clamorous variation in imitation of the manner of his brother Lothario; but such an imitation as if Lothar were finally to lose confidence. Insistent emphases that came to nothing. Sound and fury signifying nothing. This is what it meant to be grown-up; for they say that one is not yet an adult so long as he looks forward to the time when everything will be different because he'll know the secrets; but he *is* an adult when he comes to realize that there is no secret after all. And on this criterion even little Horace was grown-up, as he played in the third octave of the Grand Piano, when his brother Lothario had been arrested and carried away; and the time of life itself, he saw, was vanishing away with an unbelievable swiftness. . . .

His head sank between his shoulders and Laura became alarmed. "He is running a fever, I'm sure," she said to Dyck. "There's been too much excitement. I'll make him stop and go to bed——" And she moved forward to take him around the shoulders.

But his animal spirits returned in a flood as he addressed that indispensable and famous note,

for hundreds of our anthems and folksongs have come to be transposed in *F*. And he played:

He played the scrawlings on the walls of heavenly tunnels. And his motto theme–yes, especially when full joy and freedom possessed him and his animal spirits were at their flood–was just this phrase to which he now came:

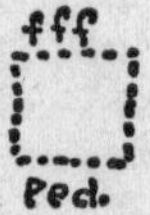

a fortissimo silence. The people spontaneously laughed; he had won it; the music was sublimely comic; for it deflated all these interests to absolutely nothing; these sadnesses to nothing; these jokes to absolutely nothing.

So, much refreshed and almost happy again, he turned his attention to the middle of the piano, where he had started, although his fingers were trembling.

And he said, "Come here, Danton, sit by me."

And the small dog leaped up on him in ecstasy.

BOOK 2 THE STATE OF NATURE

A War

to my brother and Naomi

PART 1 THE WEAKNESS OF THE EGO

The separation of the ego from the id seems justifiable, is indeed forced upon us by certain findings. Yet on the other hand the ego is identical with the id, is only a specially differentiated portion of it. If in our thinking we contrast this portion with the whole, or if an actual disjunction of the two has come about, then the weakness of this ego becomes apparent. If, however, the ego remains one with the id and indistinguishable from it, then it is its strength that is apparent.

—FREUD, *The Problem of Anxiety*

Chapter 1 ▪ A QUICK, FRANK GLANCE

1. How Our Society Was Organized

Our society had seemed to be organized as a factory and market, in which the majority of ultimate consumers worked hard and accumulated nothing but years, but a small number of enterprisers protected what they had and accumulated more and more money. So it had seemed to any quick, frank inspection; and in fact it *was* so. There was, of course, much that was done for other interests, interests of nature and friendship and even deep concern; but these interests were more or less influenced by the market, especially if they became social institutions. And of course happiness, if not misery, was always independent of the organization of society (except as it could organize its own little bands). Yet the most personal institutions, such as home and school, were likewise organized as we have said.

2. How Horatio Had a Quick, Frank Glance

Now Horatio, our boy liberally endowed by nature, happened to have no parents to set him the example of correct economic behavior and how to be anxious. He was brought up, in his dependency, as an equal by a brother and sister who lived on the dole, the relatively solid income of our Empire itself as a whole. And when it came time to go to school and be systematically retarded like the rest, he tore up the records, roamed the streets, and learned to read and write from the headlines in the newspapers. An escaped child, a lumpen aristocrat, our heir.

Further, he formed himself by lending a hand to the business that went on in the city: by lending a hand, but not giving a hand; surely not giving himself.

He, therefore, had the quick, frank glance to see what was going on. He was not organized into a role in this great organization, yet his experience consisted entirely in its business.

3. How Horatio Found It Hard to Take Them Seriously

Lend a Hand was one of Horatio's mottos—just as he had the motto, Budge only for Folding Money.

Not that the boy valued his hand very highly and wanted it back at all costs, but he got the idea by evaluating the business of everybody else. For it was impossible for a child to take seriously what all the adults seemed to be doing as a tedious joke; for instance, they worked hard for the acquisition of a piece of furniture, or they seemed to believe and obey propositions that were transparent lies, meant for fancy and not belief. Yes, even after people burst into tears of exhaustion and disappointment, he still could not believe that their hearts were in it. (But though their hearts were often not in it at the beginning, when they lent their hands, they were in it at the end when they didn't get them back.)

Nevertheless, there were some few persons whose intelligence Horatio did not question and who seemed to take these people seriously. Such was his brother Lothario, who persisted in trying to serve these people even when they didn't want to be served, and whom they took off to a jail when he declined to be drafted into their army. What was it—it was a puzzle to Horatio—that his big brother took seriously in these people?

4. How Horatio Adopted Eliphaz as His Father

By studying the news and the events in fact, Horatio was quick to see that Eliphaz the financier was a man of freedom, magnificence and power. He set him up as his model hero. And when his own inability to take seriously the things that went on began to oppress him and to engender in him wild moods, he decided to seek out this Eliphaz in person.

At the age of eleven, at the height of his boyish powers—the powers of the intellect fired by appetite but unclouded by confused desires—Horatio adopted the financier Eliphaz as his father, riding to him on shining wheels and avoiding death in the abyss of 125th Street.

Obviously there is an important difference between having a natural or foster father and adopting a father of one's own choice at a time when too much freedom turns toward emptiness. It was hard to say which one had the greater influence on the other.

Soon the father and the boy left Eliphaz's home, which was a great department store where all desire was a commodity, and they went to live in a loft without furniture.

5. Eliphaz's Purpose

This Eliphaz was a sage. No fool like the rest of the magnates who sold their time of life to the accumulation of money that made little difference to them in fact, Eliphaz made immediate use for his soul of the capital accumulation itself. Having gotten during youth such satisfactions as there were in our decaying society, he determined during maturity to purge himself of the contamination, for all these goods were contaminated by the profits of low people. Then he had hit on a method: to change all of his use value into exchange value, into money that has no stain! To purify pleasure and possession and memory, yes, and his relations with his natural children, Arthur and Emily.

He was pious in the theology that says that God is known by negation, and his purpose was to undo the work of the Creation, returning from the Sixth to the First Day.

The account of his progress he kept in a notebook of accumulating zeros with never an integer.

6. How Horatio Was a Psychopathic Personality

Now, what is the psychology of such a boy as Horatio, who, on the eve of adolescence, invited by deep feelings, has adopted for his father the model hero he himself has chosen by a frank inspection? This is a cheerful ego whose master is the social reality itself! Not some myth but the very reality; and no master but a respected friend.

Let us not make the mistake of thinking that such a boy would be subservient, would conform to society just because it was his very own. On the contrary! If out of the darkness of original desire should come to him a little hint, he would unrestrainedly blow the fabric of society to smithereens. And so one day Horatio, playing on The Grand Piano—for our society is like a grand piano and also like a mechanical piano—one day he had wired the key *B* Flat to a stick of dynamite; and he played a song leading to touch this key.

Ha! One would then think that Horatio would not be surprised by a disaster.

7. How with the Outbreak of War Horatio Was at a Loss

Nevertheless, with the outbreak of war—and caught in the endless drizzle of the continuing war—Horatio was at a loss.

He could still afford the luxury, in such a case, of being at a loss! Yet, indeed, our society was so rich that some persons were still able, in such a case, to consult their feelings.

Some felt that since so many others were involved in disaster, they also, in common humanity, ought to be. This feeling was so widespread that it became almost an article of national policy.

Others relied on disasters of the war to minimize their private misery.

But Horatio could no longer recognize his own reality.

To be baffled, to be at a loss, is perhaps a slight thing to you or me (slighter to you than to me); we are used to not having a clear idea, and we have conventions that work even better when one is a little confused. But to Horatio it was as if, a small child in a crowded park, he could not find his mother—if he had had a mother. (But the earth is our common mother.)

It was now impossible for him not to believe that most of the people were serious. Many, chosen by lot, were dying or becoming invalids and cripples; the ones who were not dying were close friends and lovers of the ones who were dying; all were wrenched from their dear habits into other habits. But *how?*

Puzzled, Horatio listened, externally and internally, to the sounds of society, and he could not detect any difference in rhythm and tone. (The meanings he had long ago learned to disregard.)

Was it for this nothing that Lothario sat in jail?

By what advertisement were they led, not to buy, but to die? Was it, after all, not an advertisement but a serious word? *Where* was it being said? *Who* was saying it?

When there is a war, both sides are far more essentially in agreement than they differ, being in agreement to have a war. *Why* did they want to?

Like all teen-agers, to ward off the confusion rising in themselves they hotly insist that other people make sense; they do not yet understand that this animal has a built-in disposition to go crazy.

8. Good-by to Many Readers

Yes, at this point let us, with Horatio, take leave of such readers as explain by political differences these enormous things concurred in by all; or who think that this universal noneconomy is economical for a few; or who think that people are persuaded by the usual means to action unlike what they ever knew. Such readers may be right—*are* partly right—but they won't find much of interest to them in what follows.

Chapter 2 ▪ THE DEATH OF ELIPHAZ

1. How It Was Drizzling

It was drizzling.

The cannon in the steeple proclaimed the war time, not the same as the time o' the sun. Two in the morning, when the soul is tenuously bound to the body. The first salvo shattered the windows in the neighborhood, but the second—for which all inanimate things had now braced themselves—aroused only echoes. Within the homes the alarm clocks were pointed dead at the sleepers' heads.

Even the pealing music of the bells of victory would turn to jangling (have we not heard it?), for it is in the shape of bells that their pealing turns to jangling. For if their tonic is tuned true and peals out clear, the overtones come jangling after.

The chronometric cannon in the steeple was pointed at the cloudy sky, and the alarm clocks were pointed at the heads of the sleepers.

At the first salvo the skylight of the loft of Eliphaz was shattered. But the harmless old dotard never noticed the inconvenience; he saw only with joy that now at last the drizzle was freely entering his house. He had a sharp awareness of only physical facts; to this extent he was a baby again, but as for expecting mother's comfort when he cried, he was free of it. The cold drizzle was the drizzle of the war, for in the middle the war is not like a noisy storm but a steady drizzle. He spread his supper with Horatio under the broken skylight where it could be well drizzled on, and the wine and the soup were preternaturally wet.

"Thanks, I'll eat in the dry corner," said the boy, crouching on the floor in the lee.

In his old age the financier was properly wet and cold. Babies, according to the old anthropology, are *wet* and *hot*: they exude hot moisture through the skin, run at the nose and ears, weep at the eyes and excrete incontinently; and their heat of lust and hunger keeps all this liquid at a boil. A youth is *hot* and *dry*: though his body fire is not so hot as a baby's, it is not diffused in water but burns intensely its hot breath of anger and hot oil of love and arid deserts of mirages. Middle age is *dry* and *cold*: impassive as stone, striking like steel, sometimes producing an electric fire, but its elements are not chemically active. But old age is *cold* and *wet*: wet because decay is wet; its solid elements are at last dissolving into liquids, teeth gone, eyes watery and chin rheumy.

Such old men like to sit by fires and lie abed with adolescent girls. But Eliphaz chose to sit wheezing and coughing in the drizzle, eating his supper diluted and sometimes darting a fiery glance.

The ticking of little bombs was minute by minute threatening the home front, while the noiseless points of little rain were drizzling endlessly on roofs and hats. One person in ten was absent from the streets. Airplanes were blooming into fires, and ships were sinking in the sea. "It will be worse before it's better (it may not get any better)." And "the duration will last longer than the war." Such were the drizzling remarks of the old man.

"Goyim Nachus!" said Eliphaz. "It means Gentile Pleasures."

2. How a Son Could Be Killed

The old man was continually freezing and cackling, wrapping a blanket around himself and sitting in the wet.

But the youth was speechless with fright. If he remained shut up with a lunatic, he certainly was not going to discover why the people were serious. More and more frequently the old man kept lapsing into his mother tongue, and Horatio Alger didn't know what he was talking about. How to get out of here! He had never thought, when he lent himself to the great merchant, that he would one day be longing for the world. *What* world?

Gone is the happy boy it used to be so delightful to describe. It is distasteful to write about an adolescent who wants always to be in a different place but, of course, doesn't know where.

But the old man had regressed completely to his earliest years before his father left the community; and now he fished up an ancient joke.

"Listen, Horace, did I tell you about my boy Arthur in the Army? They put him in the Army! So he *went* in the Army. So they gave him a uniform, so he *put on* the uniform.

"Then there was practice in shooting, and Arthur shot at the target, *Bang! Bang!* 'Stick the bayonet in the dummy!' So he *stuck* the bayonet in the dummy.

"Finally they were on the battlefield. Such a noise! Such bullets whizzing! Such cannonballs landing on your toes! Some men were coming on like madmen, with their bayonets not even in their cases.

" '*For heaven's sake!*' my boy cried, '*a man could be killed here!*'

"Goyim Nachus! Goyim Nachus!"

3. How Eliphaz Explained the War

"Gentile Pleasures!" said the bereaved father, for Arthur lay dead on a far-off field.

The field was so far off that a person could not seriously explain what he had been doing *there* but would have to go into strategy and politics for an explanation.

It would not be a serious explanation, for a man in the so-called enemy army also lay dead, and this would be explained by an opposite strategy and politics; and the fact was that both lay dead.

When you read the history of Florence or of old France or of Greece, you come always on this same circumstance: that the men lie dead on a far-off field. But most disheartening is it to read the same thing of the Greeks, that those inventors, the sons of the morning, could not improvise anything better than we.

"Look, Horace, here's *Goyim Nachus!*" cried the old man merrily. "They have a secret weapon, and the man who invented it for them is busy circulating this petition to have the use of it forbidden. What is it? What can it be? Boom! *Goyim Nachus!*" He began to sing:

> Blast *off!*
> Now everybody's talking war,
> talking *Goyim Nachus—*
> making *Goyim Nachus—*
> dying *Goyim Nachus.*

"It means, Gentile Pleasures.

"Believe me, the duration will last longer than the war!"

His eyes filled with tears, but it was hard to know what were tears and what was just the rain. He sucked at the wet bread for strength and drank the water wine for courage.

"As for me," he said, "there was a day—one day—I saw my son standing in the window with a price tag on his cuff, like a clothier's dummy. The price was eighty-four ninety-five. Seventy-five dollars cash? Good! Sold! Yes, I counted what he was worth. Did I love him any the less on this account? No, no! My Arthur and I, we stood outside these dirty transactions.

"He and I, we bid against each other, and for half a century note he bought my box of memories. Did he love me any the less on this account, my Arthur? No, no!"

"Papa!" Horatio tried to interrupt what he thought was his raving.

"Eh?"

"This war—is it possible that they are serious when they go off to die in the war?"

The old face took on a sly expression. "War? You want to hear about a war?"

The boy looked at him. With all his soul he wanted to know.

"Really?"

The boy froze in horror.

"You could have gone to the wrong person!" cried Hugo Eliphaz, rubbing his hands. "Instead, you came to the right person!"

And he leaned forward and whispered:

"Goyim Nachus."

4. Anecdotes of the Market

Like the youth David who sang to the mad king raving in the house, and sang him, no doubt, the chronicles and other news to win him back to the world (but Saul was mad and the world sane), Horace tried to divert the old merchant with the news of buying and selling.

The market also was out in the drizzle.

When, in the interests of having a war, they divided the lands into two exclusive parts—exclusive for every purpose except dying in the war—the trade between the camps stopped dead, and there was a fluctuation in the prices. The raw materials that fell to one coalition piled up in a mountain; the other countries exhausted their stock piles to the floor; the prices fluctuated in the opposite directions. Then certain industries ill supplied slowed down. Then strange uneconomical substitutes appeared, with quite a different standard of cost.

A little Chinese came to the market with his half dollar, but the price was quite different because of the fluctuation. "Flucked again!" cried he.

Meantime—continued Horace merrily—they were manufacturing nothing but weapons of war, and there was nothing for sale. And yet—here was the neat point—there were still advertisements in the papers. If you stood at the counter in the drizzle and watched the conversation between the customer and the salesgirl, you could see the man's features slowly contorted with frustration.

Furthermore, there was the following paradox: everyone who worked extra hours received extra wages, and if he worked even harder he received still more. But they were manufacturing nothing but weapons of war and there was nothing for sale.

And since there was nothing for sale, they invented a second kind of money and divided it equally among everybody; but people were so concerned about this second kind of money that it would have been possible (if there were anything for sale) to charge any kind of price in the real money.

With such anecdotes Horatio tried to divert the old man.

"A *second* kind of money?" said Eliphaz, narrowing his eyes.

But Horatio was so delighted with narrating these boyish paradoxes that he did not perceive that to the old merchant it was past a joke. But it was Hugo Eliphaz. "A second kind of money, is it?" he said, and his nostrils became pinched.

He stiffly rose to his feet and picked up the goblet overbrimming with drizzle, and he raised the cup to the level of his eyes. "I curse them if they have a second kind of money!" He sipped a sip of this poison.

With a mixed cry he dashed the cup on the floor.

5.

He cried out, "They have poisoned me! With their peace money and their war money! With their hard money and their soft money! I am sick.

"Please! In the system of finance capital, perfected (God willing) by myself, did they not have freedom, the possibility of purity and an arithmetical certitude in morals? Answer me, did we not keep scrupulous accounts?"

"Yes, father," said Horatio, "you kept them in the book of endless zeros."

"The freedom was the freedom of choice of a customer at the market. For before every customer who appeared at the counter were set a commodity in a white package and a commodity in a black package, and he was free to choose between them. What! And do you think it was a small matter, to make a choice of wrappings? I shall show you that by this freedom they exercised a tremendous social power, far greater than they could possibly know.

"Let me tell you a secret example, known to few. There was a manufacturer, one of the princes of the market, who happened to believe in the transmigration of souls, an unorthodox doctrine repugnant to the vast majority of the public. Now he thought that this doctrine was of the first importance to the salvation of mankind; yet he said nothing in order not to alienate a potential purchaser!

So every man who had thirty-five cents in his pocket dictated the public behavior of this man of wealth and power. Isn't that a remarkable story?"

"Yes, father, that is a remarkable story."

"This freedom, this little freedom of choice between the packages, reduced us all to a brotherhood of equality, determined in the end by the possession of a single penny. And who doesn't have a penny, at least in principle?

"Please, these were ignorant people who did not know their ass from their elbow; on what other matters would you have them free to choose, except between identical packages? Please, if like Spinoza our teacher I promise freedom and a mathematical certitude in morals, don't expect—in our times—something wonderful from it.

"But the Bourse is closed! The Bourse is closed! Gone are the good old days, when people had a way of measuring in dimes and cents the goods of friendship and of fatherhood, of pleasure, of health and of fatherhood. Then could not a father know clearly and distinctly what he was about? No images or emotions clouded his estimation; he had an arithmetical certitude of worth. Such a man could be made pure! He could be freed from desires that exist only in the imagination, for he would soon learn that he could exchange one for another, using the common measure.

"*'You drive a hard bargain!'* they used to tell me. Please! The hardship is in the business itself; am I the author of Nature? If a man would exchange bitter love for pleasures, must he not pay double of his money? And suppose he wants to exchange pleasures for bitter love, must he not pay fourfold of his money? This is called *paying* the penalty. The wages of sin is death.

"Well! I for my part turned the use into the exchange; and I converted the capital into credit; and I kept a book of zeros without an integer.

"And now?" he said with a sly and happy intonation, shrugging his shoulders to his ears and spreading wide his hands in the famous elegant and hieratic gesture of the absolute humility of absolute arrogance: "They have a second kind of money?"

6. How Eliphaz Catechized Horatio for the Last Time

"I'll tell you the war!" he shrieked, as if he had heard Horatio's question. "Let them start in violence and end in slavery! What is violence, Arthur?"

It was pitiful to see him; he had had a stroke. His sly smile had grown into a crescent in one cheek, his wrists and hands graceful as palm fronds were wildly shaking; and he thought that Horatio was his son Arthur.

"Arthur!" he said, peremptorily.

Controlling fear, Horace answered according to the old learning that *when something moves by its own nature, it is natural motion; when it is pushed it is violent motion.*

"Don't you want to sit down on the cot, father?" said Horatio, trying to lead him.

But the dying man fixed him with one glowing eye and said, "Presently. But first pay attention to what is important." For he was a teacher.

"The opposite of violence is bargaining. True bargaining is emptying the soul step by step according to the nature of the exchange. And the commercial contract is the form of the free soul in its purity. Violence has many shapes: freezing the price, forgiveness of debts, expropriation. These fall like so many blows. But the essence of them all is a *second kind of money*—would not a man cry out, 'For heaven's sake!'

"Let us rather ask about 'emptying the soul.' When the soul is empty, will it not finally be flooded by superabounding love, that makes the grass spring on the hillside and in the heart burn a new kind of courage? Arthur?

"Look out the window, Arthur, at our busy Empire City!" He was reconciled with his son, and he wanted to show him, in the dusk, the million lights, the million lights of the great Empire City at dusk in the winter. He dragged himself toward the window.

There was nothing but the drizzle. No Empire City at all, but only the world-wide war.

And through the ether—or by whatever other medium are transmitted the little extrasensory perceptions, the pulses and impulses and the pangs of death—were thronging from far-off fields the messages of blows both given and received.

The first salvo of three in the morning shattered the window, etc.

Momentarily the old merchant lost the faculty of speech, and for the first time he recognized his condition.

Horatio laid him on the mattress, and at once numbness invaded his feet and hands.

When Socrates drank the poison and died, we read that his extremities became numb, but it seems that the brain and especially the faculty of speech did not succumb till the end. Surely it is a symbol; for what if the poison worked in another way, and the young men would have seen, and would have had to report forever, the philosopher as an idiot for half an hour? This bitterer lesson has no part in that dialectic.

7. Augustulus

Dressed in black weeds of mourning for her brother Arthur, Emily Eliphaz appeared carrying a small child on her arm.

She towered, a black figure, by the mattress, while the little one, whose name was Augustus, pattered and slid across the wet floor. At first he stood motionless and speechless in a corner, with his finger in his mouth; then he darted from side to side shouting joy-laden physiological nonsense syllables. He ran to his grandfather, never noticing his tireless grimace, and urged him to get up.

He made a house under the table and set the dishes for supper and draped a towel for the door.

And pushed a shoe to be a train and made preparations for a trip, cramming a spoon, a magazine and his hat into a manila bag.

And with a piece of chalk he drew on the floor big rhomboids for the game of hopscotch; and soberly he tried to imitate the jumps, the hops and the *volte-faces* of the game that he was too young to understand—the dance in which each man traverses, by skill and chance, the houses of the zodiac across the sky.

With hilarious guiltiness he destroyed everything at once; he pulled the little table down and scattered the luggage across the floor and crossed out the hopscotch in endless spirals of smoke. Casting defiant happy glances. He laughed so uncontrolledly that he wet himself.

Then he wailed inconsolably, and his mother had to pick him up.

During the time, she had been towering there motionless, except that she took off her black coat and disclosed a party dress.

8. How Private Goldberg Became a Hero

Unconscious or hardly conscious of the presences in the room, the old man recovered the use of his childhood speech and in a stream of Yiddish he was telling the joke of the incompetent Private Goldberg.

"Mama, did you hear the joke of how Private Goldberg became a hero?

"He was a *schlemiel.* When they said right face, he did left face. And they said, 'Hit the target,' so he shot himself in the foot.

"He tried all his might to be a good soldier but he couldn't do it.

"At last the drill sergeant gave up and had Private Goldberg sent to the front lines. But here it was even worse. Listen, mama! Here he got everybody else in trouble, too; he put his head up out of the hole and the enemy knew where to shoot.

"Mama, don't stop listening; it's only a short joke!

"Suddenly Private Goldberg became the biggest hero in the whole war! They gave him a ribbon of many colors, a remnant of the original garment of many colors that Father Jacob gave to his boy to show that he was so dear to him! Ha! Now you're asking how it's possible? How was it possible that such a schlemiel became the biggest hero in the war?

"Well, I'll tell you.

"The sergeant called him and said, 'Artie, you're hopeless. I tried my best to make a soldier out of you, and you stick your head out of the hole so the enemy know where to shoot. So good-by and good luck. (Good-by, my boy; good-by, Emily, you strange woman; good-by, little Horace.) Here's food, here's a machine gun. Now you're in business on your own.' "

Chapter 3 ▪ A MOODY ADOLESCENT

1. A Jovial Proprietor

The old merchant was dead, and Horatio, walking wildly in the drizzle, was blinded by the tears in his eyes for that kindly man who had been his only teacher. Even so he did not yet comprehend his loss.

Rather, as he erratically wandered straight on across town and down toward the Hudson River, he unaccountably began to be hilarious. He forgot his grief and strutted, and began to feel like a young proprietor. Proprietor of the winds and the river—and the city itself for that matter—and he was out on his tour of inspection and was satisfied. His things were doing their jobs! The winds were *serviceably* shifting, north or south, as the case might be. He nodded to the sparrows and he saw that the oaks, good trees, had clung to a few sere leaves through the blizzards. (It was March.) Even the lousy weather had a use. The river was dragging its ice floe toward the sea. And all the ice was boiling into air.

"What goes on here?" he stopped and asked a peremptory question. For it seemed to him that while the main floe in the middle was drifting downstream, the slower ice inshore was moving upstream; but this was against the economy. "No, boss, it is only an optical illusion; *all* of the ice is drifting downstream, at different rates but fast as it can." Then the jovial proprietor smiled and continued his walk.

He was wet to the skin.

The city also, he saw, was industrious on schedule. The people on the streets were all moving as if bound some place; he liked that. Those not on the streets were presumably where they should be. No doubt there were dissensions going on, cross-purposes, bickering belowstairs, complaints and even this tiresome universal war. But these are the kind of troubles that a prudent owner overlooks; he does not officiously intervene in age-old quarrels, especially since the estate is entailed from generation to generation.

He passed a churchyard; this too was as it should be. Here the people were *un*industrious on schedule. In his daydream he did not think of his own dead.

During these five minutes—for such a mood lasts five minutes—the blissful harmony of his happy ego and its dominating ideas emerged in triumph at last; as if all his life he had been waiting for this certain situation. He had wanted to be free of the merchant; and now he *was* free. He was free, and he was the heir.

2. The Great Ship Capsized

At this moment, he noticed that on the shore a crowd of men and women were collected under what seemed to be an overhanging mountain. Something was wrong. How came there to be a mountain? The people's heads were hunched in their collars but they were spread over, as if by a sail, by hats. As he came closer, he could hear their rich silence teeming with thoughts; as he forced his way through, the crowd docilely gave way before him.

It was the great ship, the *Normandie,* capsized, lying on her side in the water, yet towering like a mountain and with half a pier dangling aloft in space. This was the mountain he saw looming there, for the *Normandie* was a giantess. And the effect of the sight—the first of such melancholy effects that I must describe in this book—was that among many men, each man's mind was stunned and did not think, but some common idea emerged and gripped them one and all.

At once Horatio became wary; in the presence of unconscious thoughts the old man had taught him to be wary. "Now supposing that were a small boat wrecked there——" he asked himself.

"If it were a small boat, a yawl, a schooner, a yacht, then we should feel sad, for the human activity bound up with the boat, the work or play, has foundered with the wreck.

"Now supposing it were a big ship——" So the old man had taught him to compare and measure. "The sight of such a wreck would be comic. For here is this complicated machine, really only accidentally related to the people aboard her, and now she's not functioning at all, she's only a machine after all. This would be comic: a dead machine that used to make a big show! So a big locomotive on its nose is pretty comic—the more it used to bluster like a dragon. And oh, if you see the liner actually dive into the sea, it is almost *very* comic.

"Good; but when the ship is not a liner but the *Normandie?* A quarter of a mile long and as high as a tenement house—I see it's past a joke."

She was lying on her side like a mountain and dangling half the dock in the air; and her funnel on its side contained a lake like the mouth of Christ in Bosch's picture, the "Descent to Hell." This was past a joke. The home of a big cityful had received a deadly wound, and the salvagers were crawling on the slope like lice. Looking at it, the people were stunned: and coming from below some deep feeling was about to emerge and grip them one and all.

3.

Horatio was not stunned, but suddenly he began to comprehend his loss.

"They can't do this to me!" he muttered. "Such as they, these big things were the subjects I was taught in our school; I have not been educated to anything else, nor have I heard that somebody has something else to offer.

"I never myself thought that these imperial masterpieces were very impressive; in a certain sense, I never took them seriously. But for heaven's sake, they are the monuments of the only city I ever had. I tried my best, roaming the streets, to learn this childish society; and I think I did learn to love it when I was eight or ten. Not such contemptible monuments. By becoming huge enough, they became simple again; you could take them in at a glance and say, That's that!—if you didn't get involved. *I* was not overwhelmed by the Empire City; I thought I could live there fine. But now, lay the *Normandie* on her side; blow up the bridge upstream; bombard the skyscrapers; and empty the glorious highways numbered One to One Hundred and Fifty—then I'll live my life in mourning without a single example of magnificence. . . . Yes, let the war last only a few years longer and the problems of architecture will be whether it's safer to live in the trees or the caves, and ought one to put up the cow in the kitchen—if there were a kitchen—if there were a cow?

"I should have been blown up with the piano myself in a childish fit, and never waited for the monuments of my beautiful Empire City to melt away in the rain.

"Meantime my brother Lothar is sitting in a jail idle—but at least it's dry there."

He fell silent to himself; and like the rest he hunched his head in his collar and took shelter from the drizzle under his hat, all of them as under one sail.

4. What the Crowd Felt

> As if, having spread a sail over many men, you should say there is one whole among the many.
>
> —*The Parmenides*

Recovering his spirits, Horatio curiously peeped out at the others in the crowd. On one of the faces staring at the wreck he saw the fright that he himself had felt; on another the loss; and on a third an answering glance of curiosity.

But now he noticed again the peculiar atmosphere that had put him on his guard: there was a difference between the crowd and the sum of its persons. This was something beyond his previous experience, and he didn't like it: for he was used to hearing each person speak out his mind, in conversation or in large committees run according to the rules of parliamentary procedure. But here the people had gathered at random and had been stunned, and what he noticed was the following: that each person was reacting in his own way to the spectacle of the giantess brought low, according to his own character or powers of intepretation or peculiar circumstances; but the people collectively were reacting in a different way altogether, with a unanimity in which no one seemed to take a part and with a passion of which no one was aware.

Noticing it, Horatio bridled with indignation. He wanted to hit them in their faces. This feeling of his own astonished him even more. "What's it to me? Am *I* in it too?" He took a couple of good breaths and calmed down. "No, I am not in it. But let me question them. Maybe this crowd can explain to me the war. Sir!"

Here was a man in a fedora hat whose face was a study in outraged citizenly sensibility, busily composing in his head his letter to the *Times* which pinned on the Navy the blame for the disaster; smiling as he came mentally to the phrase, "Heads must roll."

"Sir! Sir!"

A second gentleman in a derby hat was consulting only his feelings, and was unable to contain them but kept gasping: "Oh, my God! . . . Oh, Jesus! . . . What next?"

"Sir!"

An alcoholic philosopher in a woolen watch cap was smug about it, and he thought that it only went to show.

And a soldier in his cap was dubiously comparing, from his own point of view, the chances of having traveled to the far-off field on this fleet giantess that would have outrun both the convoy and the submarines, or now on a lesser ship that would loiter with the pack.

So every hat had its thoughts.

But from all collectively, individually stunned, collectively released, came a free-flooding, serene, complacent and almost gay excitement in the destruction of the monumental ship. "So *this* is what they are feeling!" thought Horatio Alger with scorn. And indeed, as he looked rapidly from face to face, their canine teeth were bared and you could hear their deep breathing hissing, as if the crowd felt that it was at that very moment destroying the ship.

5. Horatio's Funeral Oration for His Father

And his gorge rose, and this time he was beside himself, and with his back to the water he turned on them and shouted:

"How petty can you get, you resentful crowd! Because you couldn't make out in my father's city, now you're glad to destroy these magnificent monuments which are the only things we had, such as they were. You've already despoiled my Empire City where I learned to read and write, and the cars no longer run and the streets at night are black."

This outburst was the occasion, in the crowd, of an anti-shock that boded no good for Horatio.

"*I* destroyed?" shouted a man angrily. "You young fool—"

"Look, he is crying."

For Horatio, suddenly realizing the full extent of the disaster, burst into tears of surprise and loss.

"My father is dead," he sobbed, "and already the world he left me is passing away. I see that you're doing it because you hate him. You never even knew him. But which of you would have stood up against him when he was strong and he would have taken your credit away and you would have crashed?"

"It is the son of Eliphaz. I recognize him," said one in awe.

"He created the Empire City, whose like never was and never will be again. When else was there a city as grand as a department store? It was made for you and me (for you more than for me). You all traded here, didn't you? If you did anything, you traded. Tell me, strictly speaking, was anyone cheated?"

The question met a sullen silence, for each one felt that he had been cheated of everything, but not strictly speaking.

"Whose fault is that?" Horatio answered them. "No one asked you to *give* your hands, much less to give your*selves!* Why are you resentful against my father? But I understand, I understand—you couldn't get out of the market even though you seemed to have a free choice. What a pity! Oh, years from now—after we had learned to live and had abandoned New York City, I should have liked to come back here on a moonlit night and seen the buildings gleaming. Now it's too late! You have started these wars, one touching off another like dynamite."

Such was the Funeral Speech that Horatio delivered for Eliphaz on the pier where the *Normandie* was lying on her side.

6. How Horatio Dealt a Blow

Throughout this brief speech, there was dissatisfaction in the crowd. They were by no means willing to have him point out what they did not know they were feeling. When he abruptly ended, their restiveness turned to rage. "He's against the war!" someone cried out; and that was for sure; he was certainly not *for* the war. Since he didn't understand it, he was neither against it nor for it, but simply not *with* it. "He's an enemy agent!" shouted another and this crystallized everybody's opinion. Some tried to seize hold of him, some to beat him up, depending on whether reason or passion prevailed.

Actual enemy agents—for there were enemy agents everywhere—rushed to his defense.

There was a fellow in front of him, and Horatio felt himself deliver a blow—as yet, *he* did not deliver it—and this blow, even after it struck home, seemed to him to pause in the air: it seemed to be a creative act. The youth was so amazed by this curious metaphysical object that he stopped in his tracks and tried to see it better, but of course he had nothing to stare at but his fist. Then somebody gave him a clout in the ear and knocked him down.

With a shriek of whistles the police arrived and made arrests; and Horatio, seated on the ground and still staring at his little blow, came near to ending up in a jail next to his brother Lothar.

But a brisk gentleman, sensibly dressed for the weather in a yellow sou'wester, stepped up to the cops and showed his pass. They touched their caps and left their prisoner to him.

It was Mynheer.

"Are *you* out of your *mind?*" he said bitterly, before ever Horatio recognized him. "I never thought I would see the day that my little brother-in-law didn't know enough to come in out of the rain."

With a cry Horatio recognized him, and the two stood on the pier wrapped in a damp embrace.

7. Mynheer's Bitterness

The Dutchman looked at the scene well strewn with hats as though he would vomit. "What are you doing here?"

His bitterness was in part sorrow that the old man, his old friend, was dead. It was one less person in the world who knew what he was about and with whom one could exchange a reasonable word.

But it was even more the spectacle of little Horace grown up like a weed and seriously involving himself in the affairs of these people. He would have admitted in principle that a boy must become an adolescent and start all over to forget the good sense he has learned; but this did not make him any the less sad at the waste, nor feel any the less that he himself—he felt a thousand years old—was half a dozen years older. Everywhere, as Morris Raphael said, the lambs were becoming more sheepish.

"All the same—all the same," insisted Horace, "I dealt a blow and it stood in the air. Mynheer! Mynheer! *You* explain to me the war!"

But Mynheer was not able to appreciate that there was no sense in being *not* in it, in that collective feeling, if in fact one *was* in it. This reasoning did not convince him at all, not at all. He had a long memory.

"You'll get no answer from me," he said coldly. "Oh, how I hate this drizzle like poison! . . . Look rather at that! Doesn't *that* give you to think?"

Drawing away from the damaged pier, they had come into a full view up the river northward. And there could be observed a remarkable meteorological phenomenon. The city was shrouded thick in its fog and drizzle—you would have said that there was no Empire City at all. (It was camouflaged.) But the river and its millionfold ice floe was in the clear and indeed, as it stretched northward, there was a rift of blue sky and a flash of sunlight far off, where the Hudson made the bend among the first round hills (those round hills like the breasts of a mother where the river broadens into the Tappan Zee).

In between, at the northern end of the island, at the Spitting Devil, there was a violent storm played above by forks of lightning.

And even here, through the fog and the drizzle, sounded a voice of nature. A corner boy was shouting up to a girl in the window, "C'mon down." She was coy; she explained that her mother would be angry if she came back from the plant; it was raining; and she had other reasons. "F' Chrissake," said the boy, "don't you know there's a war on?" And literally in no time she was downstairs, as if there were no interval between her leaving the window and her appearing at the door.

As the fog momentarily thickened or thinned, the scene seemed to rush toward you or away from you.

8. The Committee for Constructive Bombardment

"Let me explain what I mean by taking something too seriously." Mynheer Duyck Piet Colijn van der Meer spoke to Horace like an elder brother. "You are so used to their social reality, which you take for what it's worth, that when suddenly you come across a fact, you take it seriously. But there are *plenty* of other facts besides the fact that everybody is resentful."

"But it's nothing but vindictiveness," protested Horace, still trembling with excitement. "To strike a blow out of vindictiveness—is that what they call being serious?"

"They are what they are. If you'd calm down, I'd tell you simply what's to be done."

"They implement it! They have armies of killers and even have a secret weapon. . . ." And then, right on, without connection, as if in a dream, he said, "See, it pauses in mid-air; it falls with the actuality of a creative act——" looking at his fist, as if this were the secret weapon.

"See here, young man," said Mynheer sharply—he had been the middleweight champion of Her Majesty's Navy—"if you imagine you're going to throw random punches around, just because you're seventeen years old, you can expect to get your nose pushed in. Stop looking at your fist."

Horace looked at his fist as though he were seeing it for the first time and, blushing, he stuffed it in his pocket. "What is to be done?"

"What is to be done?" said Mynheer. "Like a human being I belong to a committee. That's why I'm out in the rain. People are vindictive, destructive, call it what you will. Good! The problem is to make something of it. There'll be an end to this too, you know. Do you remember the Society for Post-war Art?"

"Do I remember the Society for Post-war Art!" cried Horace—and in a flash he saw again the dead dancer and heard the loud gunshot. "Yes, I remember," he said.

"These are the same people. In wartime we are reconstituted as the Committee for Constructive Bombardment. Our aim is simply to see that the right little items are razed to the ground. Not only the right ones, that would be hard, but at least the right ones. Since something must go, it might as well be South Hall at Columbia. Now *there's* a building of which not a line could be altered without improving the proportions.

"We are with the camoufleurs all over the world. The rest is easy. The others conceal what they want to preserve; we expose to constructive bombardment the slums that interest us. We have done wonders in London already. Shh—" he raised a warning finger—"it's a secret service."

Horatio stared at him blankly through the fog. "What do they use camouflage for in this weather?"

"Look." Mynheer pulled out a map of the city, already liberally scored with crosses. "We have a plan for reconstruction and are saving the trouble of court proceedings, condemnation and demolition. This is what I mean by accepting a fact and making the best of it."

Horatio hardly knew whether to laugh or to cry; or perhaps enthusiastically to offer his services, for he too knew a few little items.

He looked at his brother-in-law with love and with compassion, not for him but for them both. And he smiled.

From the alleyway near by rang out a cry of refusal, and he seized Mynheer by the arm. But in no time—so that there was no interval, etc.—it subsided into a throaty giggle.

"Without violence is accomplished no good thing," said Mynheer.

Horatio asked about his sister Laura. "I'm ashamed," he said. "I was living with the old man like a hermit. Study. Study. No word from Lothar; nothing from Mynheer. As if my sister and I were angry with each other. Only Arthur writes me—used to write me——"

"Laura is in Michigan with the two handy boys," said Mynheer stiffly. "I am living with Emily."

So? Something was wrong. But Horace said nothing, and they walked along a little in silence, out of earshot of the moans of nature.

"Laura is involved in personal difficulties," volunteered her husband dryly. "So involved that she is lending—how shall I say?—the wrong kind of co-operation to our war. This makes it difficult for me to go to Michigan."

But they talked of Eliphaz, while tears flowed down Horatio's face and he kept saying, "I'm sorry," because he could not control them. Mynheer told him anecdotes of the Eliphaz that Horace had never known, of the rich man, the secret patron of artists everywhere, of whosoever was making something that had no value in exchange. For Eliphaz used to distinguish sharply between those things that are made and sold and those things that, although made, by nature cannot be sold. And the first class, as we have seen, Eliphaz himself rapidly bought and sold, wherever there was a profit in the exchange, turning his home into a department store, but always improving the elegance and value; for it was the highest value that he wanted to convert into the exchange value. In this way he bartered admiration, learning, joy into money; and wit and novelty and beauty into money. Nevertheless, there were also secret voices, those symbols so close and necessary to the heart of such and such a man that to lose them was certain death—they were not commodities—or even so close to every man that soon they lived in every heart, and who could exchange for money what all eternally possessed? By his ruthless method of reduction, the old man would arrive at these, the things that are made and by nature are not sold, and he used to smile when he knew of them, for they are the elixir of life.

Chapter 4 ▪ STEPS AND BLOWS

1. First Step

But let us return to the time when the war broke out, and see if we can answer Horatio's question.

Everywhere small groups were listening close to radios to hear that the first blows were struck. Not family groups, but groups of friends were listening to this news of the most intimate semiprivate concern, hardly aware of one another, but listening as a group. Not a public crowd: for as yet people were still critical, and the public feeling was too crude to be appropriate to the grave news. Not the family: which was as yet too bound by its affections to listen with anything but fright.

One did not listen to such news alone. And soon the public crowds and families were also waging the world-wide intimate war.

Such a group of friends, huddled close to the radio, were the old associates of Lothair, the National Boycotters. (But Lothair himself was already in his cage.) These were keen political scientists, and moment by moment, as the mental blows fell, they saw that their convictions were affirmed and their predictions came true, for they had known and shown all along that everything was moving pace by pace toward waging the war, just as it turned out.

But what the devil were they doing *here,* huddled close to a radio and receiving so many mental blows, and anticipating iron blows, almost as if they were striking the blows, those predictors! If it concerned them so close—how could it not?—and if they had foreseen it step by step, did not so inventive a group have a more practical business to do than huddling passively, striking mental blows and waging the war?

But in fact all the human beings in the universal world were intelligent and foresaw it step by step; and they themselves were taking the steps. (As Kaplan has pointed out, they predicted everything exactly as it turned out, except "their own attitude"; but he should have said, "except that they themselves were taking the steps.") For the important thing to grasp is that people foresaw, or were told, or could have listened beforehand to, everything exactly as it turned out, and that they also took step by step. Or were taken step by step—it comes to the same thing. Can we say that they were not deliberately taking stride by stride? That they were tricked, or ill advised, or that some were and most weren't, or that, seizing at small advantages along the way, they neglected the grave consequences at the end? But this is absurd: they are *still* waging the war, from generation to generation.

On the faces, in the behavior, of our friendly group as they cringed under the mental blows (that they were also striking, those predictors), or as they got up and paced the room, or sipped tea during the August days, was a suppressed excitement: they were certainly being *taken* giant stride by stride. Their exclamations of despair contained a vital jangle: not that the despair was false, but that precisely the despair had vitality.

Various formulas occurred to them to relate this vitality to reasonable hopes, and all of them contained the words, "At last!" Thus one said: "At last! Better now before the situation gets any worse."

Another: "In the nature of the case, each succeeding issue on which a general war could have started has been less just than the one before, and this one—at last!—is almost perfectly dubious." This opinion was held by vast numbers in both camps.

Another: "At last! For how could they continue to take nothing seriously?" This opinion was held by renegade poets. But strangely, it was just *this* issue, of waging the war, that they were going to take seriously, whereas all the other beautiful issues were somehow able to languish on from generation to generation.

"Bah!" said a big fellow in disgust. "At last! This clears the atmosphere—of the last breath of air."

All of them uniformly, whatever opinion they held, were avidly waging the war.

"But where the devil is Lothar?" asked Henry Faust absentmindedly as in a dream.

The radio burst forth in its fury into a national anthem. And this particular friendly group at once shut the box off. But another friendly group listened through to the loud end. And still another group made the best of it and broke into song; for "what was the sense of being in it and acting as though you were not in it?"

2. Second Step

Some of our friends took a further step and soon they were in the Army. One was Arthur Eliphaz.

When he came to camp, Arthur looked about with excitement by no means suppressed. To him the situation of being put in danger of his life was an old story; he had cheerlessly done it a thousand times. But to be able to do so cheerfully, in the crowd of an army, was very different; when it was not necessary to think up on one's own initiative how to get into trouble. In armies, how to get into trouble is provided for one; they take care of that and food and clothing.

Getting into a war and getting into an army are two different things, and have different satisfactions; but they are ideally suited to each other.

This army, as he looked about at it, seemed to be constituted fundamentally of a crowd of men.

This crowd encouraged itself to be mentally stunned and have deep common feelings. There were so many, dressed alike, that personal follies easily found they had no place, and it was possible to concentrate seriously on the vital problem of getting into desperate trouble. These law-abiding young men had had little other desperate opportunity, especially as our society became more organized; and the Army did a great thing for them by formally organizing, in a way even stricter than they were used to, the outburst of the fury of the heart.

Boot training consisted in breaking their morale; and Arthur, who was an expert in the problems of the sabotage of personality, noticed with admiration the efficacy of age-old devices.

He became a sergeant and bore the full weight of the resentment of each individuality as it vanished away. So he was able to pry authoritatively into the personal machinery. For, of course, Arthur had work to do—that was not be interrupted just because there was a war—in order to learn how to channelize this colossal sabotage into a flood of safety.

But as yet he was simply delighted and excited by the endlessly repeated fact that all ended up in the Army, including himself. "They weed them in!" cried Arthur.

There was a middle-aged man who was physiologically secretive, so that he could not urinate in a public place, yet he had ended up in the Army fit to burst.

Another man, who had been deeply absorbed in his socially, morally and soul-satisfying work, and who flatly rejected conscription because he did not have the time, and he ended up in the Army at his wits' end.

A proud man, who could adjust to anything and take any punishment, but he would not, because he could not, obey a barking voice, and he ended up in the Army struck dumb.

And a queer man who used up in lust for the other fellows the energy that was supposed to potentiate among the banded brothers for the one blow against bad father in the other camp, and he ended up gaily in the Army.

And Arthur himself, who was ahead of the game. Yes, weed him in.

Weed him in! And weed *him* in!

Surely there was a stronger force than appeared that made them all end up in the Army!

And when all were weeded in, they soon conceived a strong *esprit de corps* consisting of hatred of civilians, the gang's contempt of women and defiant approval of such details of their regulations as did not immediately commend themselves to common reason.

This was grand! As he looked about with mounting excitement, Arthur quickly laid his plans to reorganize a committee of the Society for the Propagation of Vice to channelize in a reasonable way this colossal energy of self-destruction. He founded the Fellowship for Courting Disaster.

For he saw that there would always be a war until people found a better way to put themselves in jeopardy en masse.

Poor Arthur! He was really never in their army; he had too long been waging, not potentially but actually, his own war. It was only by accident that *he* came to die on the far-off field.

3. A Letter from Arthur to Horatio

> I've kicked out all the things I've been told I ought to think about, like it's good to kill Germans, and all the other things like "Thou shalt not kill." And when those things are kicked out, I find I don't think about anything at all.
>
> —REPORTED BY STEINBECK

"Dear Jericho Kid,

"There was a rumble again today. After a while it hushed up. The shells and the bombs were silently tearing holes in the field—afterward they fill up with rain to the brim and reflect the sky in yellow. So I sat me down in a hole with my pipe and I was watching this soldier boy. He must have stood there half an hour——

"He was alone with a blow that he had struck or received. He held his weapon far advanced, as if it, but not he, had struck; and blood was flowing from a flesh wound down the side of his face, but, so far as you could tell, that was equally distant from him. Maybe he shot himself; it made no difference. He was alone with the blow.

"He was like an artist simply fascinated by the work he has just finished; you'd say that that blow fell like a creative act."

When he read this much of the letter, Horatio broke into a sweat and began to tremble, for *he was understood*. He knew that Arthur would understand him, just as Mynheer would not. The next moment he remembered that Arthur was dead, and so he went on reading the letter.

"Of course I've talked seriously to this kid (you know me). And you must understand that between the battles he is in an impasse; he doesn't know what to think and he doesn't think at all. This can't go on indefinitely.

"He told me that he used to think there was an enemy. But they fought. And in the middle of the fight they both turned, and there, *opposite them both,* was the Blow. It happened to be the enemy that fell dead. 'D'ye get it?' He was very insistent. 'We're standing face to face—and then we turn—and there, standing in the air is this blow. I know it sounds crazy.' I'll let him hang around a couple of days more; he gets more comfort out of talking with me than he will from the medics; but then I'll have to send him back.

"But, little Horace, I'm mad for this abstracted blow, persisting in the space! It falls—and it persists—with the actuality of a creative act. For when the heart is emptied of its thoughts—and does not think—will not the creator spirit flood into there with superabounding meaning, the same as is the springing of the grass?

"That's what I think—as I sit here and the shells and the bombs fall silent as they tear their holes in the field; and my friendly and hostile brothers have left me in solitude.

"That God created the world at a blow—and made the grass spring on the hillside! He committed Himself.

"Such a blow, out of all the possibilities of being or not-being, is a commitment! And soon it is storming at every heart.

"For that lad there won't be any next blow. It's impossible for him to deal it, and if they try to make him, he'll throw up.

"I watched him—he dropped the weapon, he recognized that he was bleeding, and then he began to feel bad, like a child who suddenly notices that he is hurt.

"Well, let me end this letter on a more cheerful note. Our side is winning, no doubt of it. Soon it will be all over. And I want you to read up your history and notice how, often, a people after a terrible war has won a brilliant victory and could now with a little effort reap the spoils of it; but in fact they don't make the effort because of the nausea, and all they want to do is lie down and lick their wounds. That's what *I* hope.

"Don't be alarmed, but something tells me that this is the last letter you'll be getting from

"John Malaga."

4. How Many Blows Make a Losing Fight?

Horatio had read this letter with dry eyes but hot eyes. The author of it was dead. He reread it once. He held the pages of it first in his right hand, and then in his left hand. He thought, for the first time, that he understood something, a little bit, about the war.

"Best of all," he thought, with the kind of inspiration that never failed him in a crisis, *"best of all is to fight a drawn-out losing fight.* I must think about this carefully, or I will never understand how these people are serious."

And with the training he had got from the old man—Take it apart, and look at each part separately, and then put it together again if you can—he thought:

To fight a fight: it did not, certainly, mean to fight their fight; but it meant, certainly, to fight *in* their fight—for what was the use of being *not* in it, if one was *in* it? That is, a different fight in, or even against, their fight. The problem was to find a way, as some fellows were looking to go into the Air Force or the Navy, or jail, or hiding. The problem was, How to Put Oneself in Jeopardy. The people did it *en masse,* in order to be guiltless; he could do it alone or *en masse* or with a few, for he was guiltless.

Jeopardy: one put oneself in jeopardy in order to come very close to one's dear life, in order to *touch* it. That is, to feel, *Is* there anything there?

Very close: therefore, a *drawn-out* fight. For instance, a drawn-out fight was the following: First to hear about it in far-off places; and then step by stride to become involved; and giant stride by leap to be waging the war. And first to be waging it with strangers fighting strangers, and by means of complicated machines that one hardly touched with a finger; but then to be fighting with your friends and dear ones, and feel the violence in their bodies and in your own. This was searching, this was close; a youth had *plenty* of time to meditate what was befalling so many others on the way—and to see that many people are so unlucky that they are hit by a chance blow and never do get to close quarters at all.

But best of all was to fight a drawn-out *losing* fight. For victory is distracting. It senses itself coming and it gathers around itself a lively excitement, excited plans for getting in the finishing blow, and *after*—and all of this is irrelevant, it is not close. So that in the end the victor is not meditating at all on the Blow Abstracted. (It is even known for people, "scenting the victory," to become bored.) But defeat comes closer! And in the end, gasping for breath, weary in every limb and no longer able to lift another blow, one is meditating strictly, so to speak, on the Blow Abstracted.

Best of all was to fight a drawn-out losing fight.

5.

Who was fighting such a fight? His brother Lothair!

This answer (what he took to be the answer; but I suppose that each of us is fighting, according to his skill, a drawn-out losing fight), this answer came to him not without a flood of love, respect and admiration for his big brother, whom he had used to regard with only love and hate.

Surely it was a fight. With respect Horatio came to realize how Lothair had never alienated himself from our people, even when it was not yet clear to most people that they were waging a war. He had wondered what it was that made Lothario take these people seriously; and now he saw that it was because they were all in fact waging a war.

Surely a drawn-out fight. Not pace by pace, but inch by inch, percent by percent and mishap by mishap, Lothair and his friends took issue. And when his friends deviated into radical remedies, it was only Lothair who continually wearied his heart.

And surely a losing fight, as they joined issue not on the issues set by human nature or the nature of things (these would have been bad enough), but set by convention and by special interests that had all the history of the past to learn to pose issues in an ignorant and insoluble manner.

It was only where Lothair ended up that still puzzled Horatio: this did not seem to him to be *very* close; on the contrary, he thought that it must be rather quiet to sit in a jail eating out one's heart. He could not envisage clearly the economy of such a place. But he supposed, with pride, that big Lothair could get into trouble anywhere.

Chapter 5 ▪ TWO WOMEN: EMILY

1. How Emily Looked Grander Than Life-size

He visited Mynheer's, to ask Emily about the war. But when he saw her, he gazed at her with awe.

Everyone had changed, the merchant and his son, Lothar and Laura, and the Boycotters and the Propagators of Vice. They used to have a motto, "Help each one down his own slope!" And lately they had been getting toward the bottom.

But of them all, Emily was the most changed. Indeed, Horatio never before had looked at her, when he used to see in her the color-blind and frustrated, plain journalist, hopeless to compete with his sister Laura. Now, when the rest were rushing into the jaws of death, here was Emily placidly kneeling in her perfection. She was kneeling on the tiles in front of the fireplace, building blocks with the little boy Augustus. The child lost interest in the game and, screaming with delight, began to throw the blocks into the blaze. His mother did not reprove him—for there are plenty of blocks in the world—but laughed in a throaty way and said, "You're a ter'ble, ter'ble boy."

She looked grander than life size, like a queen of Memphis. When she kneeled with her child, playing with toys, they seemed to be two giants, a greater and a smaller, and the toys no toys at all but our towns. Our ranch houses and cars and cannon were the size of toys, but the mother and child were flesh and blood larger than a cathedral. And soon, when the onlookers in the room fell into the usual trance of watching only the child in the room, abdicating from their interest in one another and in the present, and remembering but never becoming conscious of the time oneself was a child among the grownups—then, when the mother rose and stooped and gathered him up, how large her motion was! And throwing her head back, Emilia laughed full-throated, not like a person who is mourning a husband and father.

Horatio could see that she was frantic at the loss, within a few days, of her father and her brother-husband. (But the dynasty was saved!) He had brought to show her Arthur's last letter, but he decided not to show it. Her relations with them had been enormously guilty. Nevertheless, or therefore (it comes to the same thing), he sensed in all her actions an enormous relief at their deaths, that chilled him with admiration. Or the simple triumph, already a year old, of every woman who *has* her child and succeeds in losing its father, especially such fool fathers as run away to die on far-off fields.

A kneeling queen of Egypt: her face was composed of regular geometrical shapes that you put together into a grand whole, and it was an occupation of a long time to scan her face; her profile succeeded her face with great suddenness as she turned.

2. How at Mynheer's Were Fire and Wine

At Mynheer's one was out of the drizzle. There was a rich warmth from the glorious fire on the hearth, which he fed from time to time with the furniture, but there was plenty of furniture, there was furniture to burn. And the host poured out his historic sherry. Everyone was changed—except Mynheer; for it was not the little irregularities of our twentieth-century universal war that would have any surprises for the heir of, say, 1625 in the Low Countries.

And the lovely laughing fire, feeding on the sticks of furniture, was bickering with two voices. Said one:

X. Freedom at last—eh, brother?—to riot!

Y. If I remember, our energy comes from the old forests.

X. Here's the gay and empty journey that Franz wrote about!

Y. Yah, it's easy to burn up the inherited wealth.

X. Endless pleasure, when one stick touches off another.

Y. Rat! Endless ashes.

X. Oh, you burn me up——

At this Augustulus began to throw the blocks in the fire, which the flames leaped on like wolves.

The sherry had stored in it the weather of an old year and a distant country; and it had burning in it many a better thought, not *second* thoughts but thoughts that were not even the first thought. So at Mynheer's were the cronies Fire and Wine.

It was a pleasure to get in out of the rain.

3. How Emilia Was in Jeopardy

Soon enough, however, they began to talk about the war. Emilia spoke disdainfully, but rather sensibly, of the men in camps and overseas.

Horatio listened carefully for her secret, for she, in the drizzle that wilted all life, was a-flower. He noticed that her nostrils tightened when she spoke of the army camps, partly in spite, but partly as if she did not intend to breathe that in.

"Seems to me," said Horace, "and that's what Arthur said too, that people want to put themselves in jeopardy, in order to feel something."

"Do you think so?" she said. She drank again—and it was no cup of drizzle—and she said, "*We* were in jeopardy four years ago, when this one was born!" And with a large motion she gathered the child into her arms.

She liked the idea, and—again with the analytic method that Horace now knew she had learned from her father—she compared the jeopardy of the woman in childbirth with that of the man in the war. In both, she said, there are danger, and fear, and pain, and action during pain, leading to a crisis of the self. But——

The man in the battle is in jeopardy, of course, she said. Each one crouching alone in his hole——

"They are *not* alone!" Mynheer interrupted her sharply. "On the cruiser *Willem* we were not alone!"

Then they are not even alone! She bared her teeth at him. But they're close to their dear lives. As the missiles burn by, there's plenty to fear.

If a man is lucky enough to get the right kind of wound, there's plenty of pain.

The patient hysteria of firing away, or maybe even having to get up and go in, there's action!

And no doubt from time to time in this chaos, there comes a crisis in which the soul can bear no more. *This* is the crisis that should lead to delivery. But——

She turned her profile with great suddenness: "*Nothing* is delivered. The man's mind clears again and there is nothing new born in the world to love, nothing to reattach the wandering soul. And the poor fellow is too disturbed to be himself again."

(As she spoke, and spoke so well, Mynheer was making his own interpretation of what she was saying: "She thinks she is describing the man in the war, but she is describing how the *child,* no doubt a man-child, comes into the strange world." He did not speak this out.) He said gruffly, "You are wrong, Emily; the men do not want to reattach. They are not so willing, nor able—it comes to the same thing—to readjust to civilian life."

"Exactly. That's just what I'm saying. They're shocked out of themselves, and nothing to turn to. They drift around afterwards in the city like lost animals. They have lost one mind and never found another. Next step, they form armed Fascist bands spoiling for violence at a time when violence has become so universally nauseating that one could vomit. . . . But the woman—has given birth to something."

Dyck looked at her with tragic eyes, and Horatio, who took it that he was worsted in the argument, was awestruck anew.

"I don't mean to jeer, really I don't," she said, "but I can't help it. You do what you can. Yes, that's excellent how you say it, Horace: Everybody has to be put in jeopardy—at least we can agree on that. To put himself or herself in jeopardy. To plunge into it. But with women it's a matter of course; we don't think about it beforehand. Men have to work it up as a song and dance, with politics and armies. You are justified to take comfort in one another in armed camps. But what about afterwards? Here *we* are; and where are you?"

There was a pause, while she drained the glass.

4.

"Maybe that's the trouble," said Horatio, "that you can't help jeering. You've got to win. But do you know what I think? I think that best of all," he said, "is to fight a drawn-out *losing* fight."

She looked at him blankly. She truly did not understand him. But Mynheer smiled broadly as he saw the difference between the sexes: that men are willing to lose and women are not willing to lose. She turned toward Mynheer's smile, and she was baffled.

"Yes!" cried Horace. "Like your father! Or your brother Arthur, or my brother Lothar! They have agreed! They have agreed!" His voice rang in triumph. What did it mean?

"But who would *want* to lose?" She was secure on natural grounds, and she did not comprehend spiritual artifices and dodges; that we do not play to win, although we naïvely imagine that we play to play; but it is in order to be sacrificed in the game that we play. "Papa?" she said. "My father was a certified public accountant. Your brother, if I am not mistaken, went into politics. But the war is *ne plus ultra,* and of course Arthur had to go there! . . . Show it to me!" She tapped her index finger on the table. "Don't talk to me in riddles! Show me what they have produced after they were in pain. The test is what men work at, the jobs they do. Show me the connection between the moment when life was at stake and how you afterwards employ yourselves. Rubbish! What a structure of claptrap you invent to prove to yourselves that you aren't out of your minds! But women don't have a thought in the world beforehand, and afterwards they have the only steady job worthy of a human being.

"Ah, and take Laura! —Augie, get down, you'll fall and hurt yourself—Laura is an architect. She has laid out a Garden City. Naturally she's *in* it. Who can blame her—I don't—if she's head over ears in it? Once one builds little houses and suburban layouts, one has to defend them, doesn't one? Lord, if she doesn't, who will?"

"You seem to like to live in a house," said Horace.

"*You* build us a house, boy; it's work for boys. We have already given a man to defend it. Augie! Laura has—how shall I say?—a boyish flair. Others would call it penis-envy. The way boys keep busy building things and pushing toy locomotives. And of course motorcars! I see it in Augustus already, but he still keeps saying, 'Watch me! Momee, watch *me!*' . . . Well, I wish I could do it, fly airplanes and paint pictures and all. Laura is the kind of mother who had two babies in a taxicab and the driver came running after her and said, 'Lady, you dropped something.' They've turned out to be such handy boys, too. But they say when the birth is painless you can't expect a very strong attachment to the child—haven't you heard that?"

Mynheer looked at her coldly and said, "Why were you afraid to have another child before Arthur left?"

"Lord!" she said. "Even the Americans space out their wars one to a generation."

5.

Horatio was offended for his sister. She had taught him cheerfully to accept the flashing pains as they came and make nothing of them, especially if they were unavoidable. She had a sentence of Gide she liked to quote: "The hounded hare takes pleasure in its leaps, in its feints." Why should Emily have suffered if she did not resist? He took the opportunity of feeding the fire to ask Mynheer if Emily had indeed had a hard labor.

"Don't be a fool, this is pure malice," said the Dutchman with a twisted face. "Naturally she is jealous of my wife."

"Why do you let her carry on, then?"

"*I* do not need to win, sonny," said Mynheer. His face was twisted because he was thinking of Laura, his dear, his absent spirit of life who alone made the daily barbarism—he judged it so without prejudice, for any other age in which he lived would have seemed to him equally barbarous—made it have some meaning for him; and she gave it every glancing meaning. He looked wearily about his flat, where the city no longer streamed freely in and out as it used.

But surely he must have expected that when the universal world had taken leave of its reason—it was no longer indulging in feints and leaps but in bloody bites and close flailing—and he couldn't stomach it any more, but he went dutifully on and on—that then this maleasy absence would also be the glancing meaning of it.

He was glad that Emily had come here. They even loved each other a little, as it turned out. The way she sat there, grander than life-size: having contrived by mating with her brother to make of her feelings a kind of monolith: desiring it and triumphantly performing it, no matter what they said. He could not help but smile with pleasure. He said, "My own culture is ancient. Nothing ever turns up that I'm surprised at—I've already been there. But really, Emily, the picture you present is spectacularly conservative: the women sitting nursing their babies from generation to generation, and they allow the men and boys, who have nothing else, poor things, a franchise on fun and games."

6. How Augustulus Whirled Till He Was More Than Dizzy

Augie disobeyed her once too often and, lightheartedly, she fiercely slapped his hands. (What need did *she* have to direct her aggressiveness against the world and seek out a foreign enemy, when so close to home was the self that she wanted to destroy? To whom was turned her deepest attention, so that when she was asleep she heard him very well in the next room.)

"I told you to get down before you got hurt," she said.

He wailed at his hurt hands, holding them out and staring at them with a certain fascination. "Kiss them! Kiss them!" he wailed.

"I will not, you bad boy. I'm only asking you a very simple thing, to obey me."

She intended to kiss them the next moment and make up, but it was too late. For little Gus decided to find comfort in himself instead. His tears dried by magic as he chanted the familiar malediction:

"I'll break you! I hate you! I'll break yo' hands an' throw them out the window. I'll throw yo' head in the toilet. I'll break yo' hands. I'll break you in pieces and throw you out the window."

This incantation cheered him up immensely and after a moment's happy pause he began the game of making himself dizzy. He started to rotate, awkwardly falling from one flat foot to the other. Soon he was laughing.

He was rotating. He was rotating himself, but after a while he was simply rotating.

He staggered and laughed, at his wits' end.

Then he rotated counterclockwise. And being right-handed, he now spun more smoothly, rising to his toes, quickening the pulses.

He fell.

"Lord, stop it!" she cried. "You'll break your head."

But not Augustulus, who now wildly whirled in silence, his hands flying away from him as if they never belonged to him. He had caught for a spell the secret of the dervishes who whirl unmindful and never fall down. They do not whirl themselves! They do not whirl themselves! They whirl losing the world. And what is at the still point is another kind of nothing.

7. "Our Boys"

So Emily, too, lost her son, at his age of four and a half. And as the talk, meantime, returned to the war and its battles, she suddenly found herself speaking of "our boys," as to say "our boys in the Army" or "our boys overseas." Her eyes filled with tears when she heard the words on her lips. Tears of shame at the vulgar and bloodthirsty locution, for they were not boys at all, but young and middle-aged men, and they were only hypocritically "ours" as forth they went. And tears of loss, for they were boys and were ours.

Chapter 6 ▪ TWO WOMEN: LAURA

1. An Architect Turned Camoufleur

Now Laura had designed a Garden City. And when the war broke out, it was she who was chosen to camouflage it from the enemy in the sky.

The army of defense invaded Laura's garden by the lake. House painters were impartially painting olive and sandy dunes across the white walls and flat roofs, scoring them out. But there was one building, glass-flashing and pink, that they passed by; this was Laura's own home that she wanted to preserve to the last moment. (They expected the bombers to come around the full moon.)

In her blue jeans she strode about the plaza, the shopping center, directing the dislocation of the shrubbery, the deflowering of the gardens. From time to time she took a drink from a hip flask. She marked a number of poplars to be torn up by the tractor. The idea was to make everything look at random; but of course nature was not random. She looked back at what they had done, and the poplars spelled out the numbers 1–9–4–4.

"Tear them all out," she said to the driver. "And stop thinking. Do it! Don't think about it!"

An architect turned camoufleur is introduced to a new line of reasoning. You must not think, you must not feel, you must not express what is in your heart; and *that* is the expression of your heart.

She looked across to the opposite shore that had never been laid out. She saw that there was an order in the wild growth itself that she must imitate. She used to know this order spontaneously, but she had lost it since first she began to lay out a Garden City. As an architect she had imposed an artificial order; now as a camoufleur she was imposing a glaring, positive *dis*order. The contrasts were even brilliant and beautiful and full of mind.

She sat down, defeated, on a milk can in the road.

2.

She had begun to hate this place. When she had designed it so few years ago, it did not seem to her that what she was doing was unnatural; certainly it was not *against* nature. Her method as an architect was simply to emphasize the nature of the lake shore, the beach colors and the dune shapes and the lake pleasures for the men who worked at the plant. Yet now the plant, lying there like a smoking animal, was more natural than her garden.

There were bad mistakes. Going over the work again, as she was now doing, she saw that there were bad mistakes. She had tried to be "functional," that is, simply to follow, and facilitate, the ordinary functions of these people—and everywhere she was leading them into a trap. "These people"? She herself was one of these people. She ought not herself to have become a wife and mother because she had too much hate in her heart.

Well, now at least it looked a mess! The turf hung over the roofs, like houses in Ireland. Already the people lay under the grass. The ground was so dug up that you would have thought the bombs had already exploded. Why bother to strike again? A large magenta umbrella was lying with its pole in the air, and two women with babies were sitting on rockers in the road. The rest of the people were at the new factories.

Laura rowed out to the plane and went up to have a look.

As the plane veered, the flat lake stood on its end and slapped her across the eyes. She straightened out and the blue sky spread all around. And then the Garden City spread out contractingly below. At a given instant she reached the bombing and diving angle, and the camouflaged scene below nearly vanished into the fields, the dunes and the endlessly curving shore.

But the pink house flashing in the afternoon sun was a real sky-mark.

She had the deadly thought—viewing the scene in a flash, as if she and the flashing house were signaling to each other in flashes—that her house was a target for the single torpedo that would not miss. But she dismissed this afterthought for another time.

Over on the western shore were the huts, and she looked at them with loathing. These were the abodes of the workers in the war factories, the strangers who had arrived in the night with new arts, noisome smoke and noise. Their scouts came like parachutists and requisitioned what they needed. They tore up the plowed land. They came in their numbers where there was no provision for them, neither water nor shops; their children went to no schools; they pre-empted the community entertainment for their own and debased the records in the jukebox. Soon the harmonious community, such as it was, was a riot of toil and vice. Camp followers followed after, and they were manufacturing an epidemic of V.D.

To an architect, the first invasion was already the fatal one; what more damage could the enemy do? Yet all of them—and she also—were simply waging the war.

3. Laura's Weekly Effort to Resign

She turned south and (once a week) came down to earth in Valparaiso and went to the local C.D.B. to resign.

"What's the matter this time, young lady?" the chairman asked her kindly.

She explained that she didn't want to put on the finishing touches —her own house——

"The air base was here and he says you've done a bang-up job," said the chairman.

"Is that what the air base says? . . . Please, get somebody else. I don't want to undecorate my own premises."

"It's got to be finished this week," said the chairman dubiously; "they'll come by the moon."

He was not a bureaucrat by disposition; in fact he was the local pastor, the Reverend Dr. Bercovici.

"Whoever heard of an architect turned camoufleur!" cried Laura. "An architect wants it to leap to the eye! I was not trained to make a building look bashful."

"I'm not so sure I can buy that," said the pastor and shook his silvery hair. "If your building were perfectly adapted to its surroundings, you wouldn't see it any more than a tiger in India."

He poured her out a drink. He was drinking too much and she was drinking too much, and all of the persons who knew better and were waging the war were drinking too much.

"In the end I'm likely to overlook the most glaring landmark."

"Do you intend that as a threat?"

"No."

"Then there's nothing in what you say. You know what the truth is; therefore, you know what the lie is."

She looked at him coldly for a moment. "Did it ever occur to you, doctor," she said, "that as we draw, you move?"

"Look, Lady Duyvendak, suppose for the sake of argument that I accept your resignation; what duty will you then assume?"

"How do I know? Maybe I'll go back to living in the present instead of in the future, as I used to, before I got interested in architecture and the social arrangements of these people."

"This *is* the present, this *is* the present. . . ." He shot a glance at her. "If I were you, I should forget about not camouflaging the most glaring landmark."

She flushed.

"Here are the photographs you asked for."

They were a set of photographs of the region in the prior state, before the village was laid out. She had hoped she might try to approximate that, and it would be as if the suburb were not there now.

They were worthless. The land had been swampy and overgrown with bulrushes and cattails. Now there were lawns and hedges. An airman with a little botany would tell at a glance that there was a big settlement here since 1937.

When she looked at the photographs, she burst into tears, seeing the original swamp so much more promising than the suburb. The doctor leaped to his feet and came round in front of the desk. He poured her another drink and drank off his own.

In one of the pictures, dead in the swamp with its spire looming above the cattails, was an old church. This church was still standing.

Laura pointed to it. "I'm afraid we'll have to unsteeple your church, doctor. It casts a jagged shadow."

4. Laura's Handy Boys

Laura's pink and glass house was on the shore among the high dunes, the yellow grass and the cottonwoods.

Cottonwoods are the first trees that invade the sand, which they bind with their threadlike roots, and after come the stunted pines and small oaks.

The top of the long house opened level with the road; the carport was in the top story. The foundation opened into the water and contained two boats. The large room was two stories high and was lit by a great circular window to the north; a balcony on the south side of this room opened on a terrace, the roof of the rooms below. From this terrace one of the handy boys was ripping the brass railings.

The other, Lefty, was backing a truckload of cinders onto the sand, making dark curves to lose the shadows.

Facing west, above the boathouse, was a long stretch of glass—windows of all the bedrooms—in which was burning the afternoon sun.

Laura liked her house, though she laughed at it a little: she had been after simplicity and the latest fashion that was already a little out of fashion. And she certainly had been afraid to be imprisoned in that house, the way she provided for an immediate getaway by land and sea, and all that glass!

On the ledge above the doorway were several tiny carmine flowerpots with green leaves. She hooked them down with a cane and left them smashed on the pavement, though they would have made no difference. She hooked them down in order not to leave anything she liked.

Black streaks from the terrace began to ooze and drip down the walls. The brass rails were lying twisted on the sand, partly in the water. The boy, all blacked up himself, leaped from the roof and landed on all fours. He looked in horror at the rails. "I bent 'em! I'm sorry, ma."

"Maybe we won't live here afterward anyway," said Laura.

"Aw, ma! why not?" cried Droyt. "Everybody knows this is the best house around." . . . "It's O.K.," he thought confidently, "Mynheer won't move. He never wants to move away from anywhere. He's a conservative."

Laura thought the house was a jail. It was worse than her brother's, because she had made it for herself. Whatever you wished, the house was planned for it; and when you no longer wanted it, you found yourself trapped into the motions that made you want it again—but something was wrong.

It was a Garden City; nothing much new could happen there. In the end it turned out that what everybody wanted, and she also, was action and not her Garden City at all: action, or at least activity, or at least being activated. This activism, to which they gave themselves with a restrained fury, was regulated even more carefully than a Garden City.

She gave the boys a chart of shapes, and soon the handy pair were streaking the sandy and black curves down the pink walls. And working, they began to sing with ear-splitting croons the song "I'm Alabamy Bound"—that is, plenty far away from here—the croons were the American noise, the whistle of a train at night across the prairie.

"It's good enough! It's good enough!" shouted their mother.

" 'Choo-choo train!' " they crooned.

This painted scene wasn't real, and we weren't going to live this way forever! thought Laura triumphantly and vindictively. Not that way, and not this way either! When the war was over, and our side would have won (for we always won). And for the duration, under the paint and the turf, under the screens, under the camouflage? Life was going on almost the same as ever.

But the boys were singing,

"I'm Alabamy bound
I've got those heebie jeebies hangin' around."

5.

There wasn't a spot of the pink house left. The small carmine flowerpots were toppled on the ground. The great dune zebra was lurking hidden in the sands and poplars, except that the low sun was flashing in his eyes. He was winking.

She went aloft again and turned northwest over the inland sea. Nothing was visible but the red sea and sky. Omitting (always) the earsplitting roar of the motor, all was silent—the "deafening silence." She shut off the motor and there was a deafening silence.

She turned round. The shore was afire—the houses were in flames but there was as yet no smoke, for it was that all the glass on the eastern shore, the windows of the houses, the windshields of the automobiles, the long moving window of the train, was reflecting the sunset. Into the dining rooms that faced the west, the red Apollo was going down; the people pulled down their shades. And the sun set, and it was gray. Her house winked.

All the smokeless fires went out and there was a deafening silence. Suddenly the water leaped up at her as the plane sharply dipped, but she pulled level not without tightening her grip. (She dismissed this afterthought for another time.)

Next instant she flew into the critical zone.

With a cry of pleasure she saw the Garden City vanish. Straining her mind, rather than her eyes, she could accurately make out each building and lawn she knew so very well—no one knew them better. But relaxing her attention, she found that nothing was there, except just the sea and the dunes, as of old.

And under this camouflage to the skyey observer, the people were circulating almost as previously. It was time that the men and women were changing shifts in the new factories.

The sewers were blocked, and a few rainstorms had already formed a huge puddle, a little pond, in the plaza. Soon enough the cattails would spring alive and there'd be a proper swamp again. There was the church steeple, just as it had stood originally.

She regarded this complete success with enthusiasm and pride. She circled round and round, looking for a flaw, as if she herself intended to loose the bomb. She burst into tears at the job so well done, and through the shiny tears the scene became even more evanescent—indeed the inland sea seemed to be flooding in streaks over the land.

Mynheer's wife had made a perfect camouflage! (The place was still carrying on its business.)

She looked and the scene spread below was alien and threatening. It was a theater of suppressed rage. It was the expression of the heart. The men and women were sneaking to work. The windows were blacked out. And when the raider would be heard, all would creep into underground shelters.

Chapter 7 ▪ THE DREAM OF LITTLE GUS

In the nights, when he went to bed, little Gus had a bad dream and in the teeth of the first images he fought his way desperately back to waking.

"Mo-mee, I hate to go to sleep——" he called tentatively.

"Hush, go to sleep, little Gus." Emily's voice was decisive in the next room where she was reading. "It's pitch night."

Soon he began to whimper; soon he would be wailing and he would cry himself to sleep. But we try to prevent the children from crying themselves to sleep, from exhausting their horror before they go to sleep; they must go to sleep at least apparently at peace, and leave us at peace. She went in.

"What is it—what *is* it, little little one?"

" 'Cause I see the dreams. The dreams come on the bed."

"Don't notice them, they're silly."

"I wonder what are dreams, mo-mee?" he said in a faint treble.

"They aren't there."

"But I *see* the dream. It comes and bites me."

"You see it," said his mother, "because you can't see anything else in the dark."

"Make 'm go away!"

"Hush, little one, and tonight you won't dream it. Go to sleep. Shall I leave the door open?"

"Yes."

He saw that she did not understand about the dreams. She loved him but she did not understand this and he would have to go it alone.

He went to sleep and the same dream came, of the animal biting little Gus or eating him up. Now it was a crocol-dile; formerly it had been the tiger, or other large beasts seen at the zoo. He was mad for the zoo. Sometimes the wolf ate up the dog, while Gus looked on petrified with fear. Once it was a tin tiger that swallowed him, but a man with a can opener came and opened the tiger's belly, and out stepped Gus.

When she read him the stories at bedtime, Emily found that she had to alter the fierce endings; but it was hard to foretell just what it was that the child's mind would find terrible. In "Little Red Ridinghood" one was betrayed into the critical moment before one was aware. One told the altered endings, or left hiatuses in the middle, in a lame style; but the child, listening with open mouth and drinking it in, seemed not to notice anything missing, and when he dreamed, he dreamed the real story uncensored.

He woke screaming, and with sealed eyes saw the striped tiger burning bright, and the saw-tooth crocol-dile, and the elevum with proboscis awrithe.

What a thing it was to have seen the beasts in cages! Would they not, precisely, come *out* of their cages? And re-establish the continuity between the man and the other generations, and on both parts teeth and lust?

—When a young couple is just wed, in a quiet morning ceremony; and before the bridal luncheon at a glistening restaurant with friends; they go perhaps for a stroll in Central Park, he darkly dressed, she still with her bouquet of orchids, so that people turn and remark them: let them stroll *here,* into this zoo, and see the continuity of the generations.

He screamed and Emily got up again from her chair in the spot of light. But it was only a single scream from the next room, and he relapsed, she thought, into sleep. All was well. "All well! every manner of thing well!" as the poet said.

When Gus was half his present age, he had been thrown down by a large, playful-bounding shepherd dog with grinning teeth. For a long time afterward he was afraid to walk near an animal; it was necessary to cross the street with him before the menace of even a little kitten. But now in a quite normal way, with hysterical excitement, he loved gingerly to pet animals both large and small. And he was mad for the zoo, but he was willing for them to be in their cages.

He was not asleep but lying calmly awake with open eyes and thinking. "It's mean. They're mean to come out and bite me." He was a darling little boy, with the keen sense of justice that little boys have. "I like to be friends, and, 'stead, they treat me mean." As he lay there he began to feel quite abandoned, like a baby just born. The dream was a birth-dream.

PART 2 THE STRENGTH OF THE EGO

L'auteur, poursuivant sa thèse hardie, soutenait que le lièvre ou le cerf poursuivi (non par l'Homme, mais par un autre animal) trouve joie dans sa course et ses bonds et ses feintes.

—Gide, *Les Nouvelles Nourritures*

Chapter 8 ▪ ON THE ROCKS ALONG THE RIVER

"Driver! What stream is it?" I asked, well
knowing
it was our lordly Hudson hardly flowing.
"This is our lordly Hudson hardly flowing
and has no peer in Europe or the East."

On the rocks along the river, Horatio was painfully picking his random way into jeopardy. The heavens were hanging low, but it was not drizzling. (God continue to bless my smiling youth as he walks his way that deviates but does not err!)

Beyond, beneath the heavy arch of the storm, he saw how the river was as usual disappearing among the rounded hills; and this it was that wooed to his lips the little smile.

The drizzle of the war was scorched out of being. Everywhere between the heavens and the earth was collecting a terrible potential, on the tips of stubble and on the surfaces of the waterdrops. The boy's hair was standing up as if in fright. In the breath of this potential the drizzle of the war dried up. It was dried up.

Not far ahead, at Spitting Devil, forks of lightning already played above the violet storm. From shore to shore, from Marble Hill to the Palisades, the blind sheet of rain boiled in the river. One could no longer see beyond. But as he walked northward, Horatio was lost in thought of Emilia and her giant face, so that—as happens often on a solitary walk—a space that he passed through did not exist, and even a time had suddenly elapsed.

Now I must explain that this tiny path along which he was picking his way, losing itself more and more in the pell-mell rocks of the shore, was the only contact with the lordly river that the New Yorkers had left themselves; and they would have forbidden themselves also this, but there is always some boundary or other. Everywhere our island rises from the river in its terraces; the water is inviting to swim in; but the people have shut themselves off from it with railroads and viaducts and with a wire fence. Nevertheless, outside the last fence there must always be the last little slope and the shore rocks.

Here (I am speaking of sunny days when there was no drizzle of the war), adventurous boys came to swim; strange persons haunted the path and traversed it from end to end for miles; a few very philosophic gentlemen sat on the rocks and smoked. And the water lapped the rocks, hardly flowing.

Picking one's way over the rocks, rounding a bend, one might suddenly come on such stationary persons on a rock; or one might mistake them also for rocks and think he was alone; or one might, in a lonely place, imagine that some of the rocks were living persons.

The fog had closed in around him, so there was only a small region of transparency proceeding, straight on, from blindness to blindness.

He felt a drop on his cheek and he thought it was the first rain, but it was tears starting to his eyes out of a dream.

"When will they *ever* cease, these pleasures of the mouth, these thoughts neither false nor true, these sentences?" Such were the questions of Horatio's dream.

"My mother's dead from whom I sucked my joy."

"Hey, you!" The order came like a rifleshot out of the blindness, somewhere on the tracks. He dropped down between two rocks. "Hell to you," he said, not loudly but distinctly.

It was forbidden during the wartime to walk along the shore, because the transports lay at anchor in the river. They were somewhere there.

"Hey, you!" . . . HEY, YOU! . . . Hey, you!" the voice went back down the tracks. The small region of transparency again slowly moved.

At nights (I am speaking of the orange nights when there was no drizzle, etc.), the boys and girls made bonfires here of tarred driftwood, and they lay between two rocks, where it was uncomfortable but convenient. Flashing their lights, sleepless persons haunted the path from end to end for miles. A few philosophic gentlemen were stretched out on boards with their mouths open to the stars.

1. The Distraction

Even before the shot rang out, Horatio began to run. Clambering desperately on tiptoe from rock to rock, as if someone had cried out to him, "Hurry, hurry, for it is a little farther on that you must be hit. It's around the next bend—"

He slid into the water up to his waist, but hurried on, sogging wet, viciously fighting to cling to the freedom, the harmony, and the power of his glorious adjustment to the Empire City. "Not here! It's around the next bend that you must change from convention to nature."

A shot rang out. There was a sting in the flesh of his breast and the feeling of wetness.

"Ach! Providential," thought Horatio Alger piously, and stood.

"Halt!" But the voice that barked, "Halt where you are!" was itself speeding down the track, fading like the hour. Horatio stood still.

"Hey, you! *Hey, you!* HEY, YOU! . . . Hey, you . . ." There were several of them and several shots.

These seven shots formed a constellation: four sounded almost at once but wide apart in space, and three came trailing after, like the growl of the Great Bear in heaven. Horatio stood and did not move.

The rain began to fall silently, without lightning or thunder. Soon it was boiling in the river. Horatio was trembling with cold, nausea and fright. When the primary shock drained the strength from his limbs—all his courage rushing to his protection within—he sat down on the rock and began to be sad. He was wet with blood and wet with rain and wet with the river. He began to feel abandoned, like a baby just born.

"Hey, you!"

"Hey, you," said the echo from Marble Hill.

The rain was illumined by the first sheet of lightning and the soldiers could be seen fading down the track. Calmly Horatio counted three seconds to the thunderclap. He counted nine slow seconds to the echo of the thunderclap from the Palisades across the river.

As if the lightning had cast a sudden illumination on the fact—the night had fallen.

Flashlights came alive. Ten, twelve, fifteen of them moving on the tracks and in the woods on the hillside. They kept calling out.

"Hey, you," shouted Horatio, *"hell* to you."

For as he came to his wits, he realized that two platoons were not out at night in the steady rain to keep chance boys from sneaking along the shore. They were looking for somebody in particular. Now who might that be? "Ah! Let me——

"Let me—*distract*—these persons," thought Horatio Alger; he resolved it; *appointing* himself to the role; in the twinkling of an eye; in between the count of twelve and fourteen—as a man one midnight appoints himself to be an artist; or as another man, between sips of coffee at a café, appoints himself to disturb the nations to settle an arid strip of the Holy Land and make it bloom like a garden, and set races at rifle-point. So Horatio appointed himself.

Experimentally he heaved a large stone into the river. At once the lights leaped nervously to the splash and the shots rang out, snorting into the water. He laughed with pleasure; they were so jumpy.

The lights climbed the wire fence and began to return along the path. Uh-uh. He climbed the wire fence onto the tracks.

But there was a crash of rifle fire a hundred yards farther, around still the *next* bend, as if it were *there* that one must go. "So?" He thought he knew *that* place—on the line of 189th Street—near the outlet of the disused drain. But what would *they* know about it, thought Horatio scornfully, those soldiers who were not acquainted with philosophic gentlemen? That was a place for *friends*.

Therefore he now began what looked like a Flight and a Chase; but it was really a Distraction.

A Chase is the action in which *A* proceeds from L to M, and *B* goes from M to N. When *B* has failed to leave M on *A's* arrival, he is Caught. On the other hand when *A* fails to proceed to M where *B* is, we say that "*A* has given up the Chase." (It was so that David *fled,* and King Saul *chased* him.)

But in a Distraction there is a place X that *A* does not even know about. He imagines that he is *chasing B* from place to place; in reality he is being *enticed* by *B* from place to place, so long as that place is not X.

To Entice is for *B* to flee openly from L to M in order that *A* may come to M which is not X. To Decoy is to entice *A* to come to M (which is not X) and nothing is there. To Sacrifice One's Self is for *B* to entice *A* to M where *B* is and is caught, but M is not X.

"Not here, soldiers! It's to the next place that you must hurry, in order to be distracted further."

It was eight o'clock and the cannon in the steeple pealed forth the war time.

On the line of 183rd Street a broken pier jutted into the stream. Lord knows how many years ago what ships used to draw up there, before the city cut itself off from the river. But Horatio often used to go there to fish for crabs, and for the pleasant company. He knew where the flooring was decayed and where it was necessary to throw across a plank. Tonight, at the very end of the pier, shielding the flame from the rain, he lit a match. The shots rang out. Methodically, after he came back across them, Horatio tipped his planks into the tide.

A Flight, a Chase, is lively, but always potentially serious, for if *A* comes to M and *B* has not left M, *B* is Caught. But a Distraction can be only farcical, for no matter where *A* comes and no matter where *B* is, still it has no essential connections with X. (Except that it has an essential *dis*connection with X.)

To Start a False Scent is to entice *A* along a line of places, L, M, N, where N is further from X than L is. To Stall is to linger at non-X in the hope that *A* too will linger there. To Sacrifice One's Self is to be caught at M, which is not X.

It was dark and wet; there was no need to sacrifice himself. Not that such a prospect would have crossed Horatio's mind, unless the situation arose. At Fort Washington he gave up this tiresome distraction, while the lights flickered on southward and the guns faded like the seconds.

Cautiously avoiding the shore, he doubled back and clambered along the slope under the superhighway. He was thankful enough that he knew the privacy of these public places, where it was possible to keep out of the rain. Into these chambers under the highway it was possible to withdraw for the privacy of meditation or love, or to keep out of the rain. He was cold, wet through and despondent, but he was not subject to catarrhal diseases.

And now first he realized that he had no home to return to, neither the window-broken loft, empty of his dear father; nor the home of his sister, for she was far away, camouflaging a Garden City. Was he then homeless? Good, then now could be seen the courage with which we human beings soon root ourselves in a new home, in an unlikely place, and decorate the place, and are patriotic once more.

The electric storm was now frankly raging with its whites and blacks. Perhaps this was not a domestic note.

Tonight he intended to remain in Harry Tyler's den under the rocks, at the place marked X, on the line of 189th Street. He would be very surprised if Harry had not returned.

2. Harry Tyler

Harry Tyler, who had been a sailor in the Navy, was one of the philosophic gentlemen.

"Here's—solid—comfort!" Harry Tyler used to say in the old days, as he stretched his large self on the platform that he had built of driftwood, sun-bleached and stoned shining. He pronounced all the syllables and the *r* hard, and two *d*'s at the end of "solid." His speech combined the accent of Maine with the decisiveness of a man who chose his metaphors with interior literalness. If he used to say "solid," with both *d*'s, it was that he felt the solidity of himself and of his swimming platform, and of the river, and the solidness of every associated memory of solidity.

Then the bluecaps and the whitecaps of the blazing Hudson were as solid as oil paint.

He had red hair grayed with blond, was sunburned salmon and tattooed with the flags of the world and glaucous mermaids.

When Horatio knew him he was fifty and had just "quit" (two *t*'s) the navy yard after twenty-two years as a carpenter and steam fitter. In 1917 he had manned the guns, but he quit just when every other man was being pressed into service for the construction of a two-ocean navy.

" 'Twas so God-*damned* noisy a man couldn't *think.*" His ears had been offended not by the booming of the guns and the pounding of boilers, but "*All* of a sudden—*wheestles!* and Hep! Hep! Salute——" (Two *t*'s.) He screamed a whistle through his teeth. "F— all that——" (Two *k*'s.)

"They put this college youngster over m'head as an en-sign," said Harry. "My doctor said that I had ought to take a rest."

He now began to cash his bonus from the other war.

Rain or shine he descended to the rocks along the river, yet the image of him was always against the bluecaps and whitecaps, for it was only in fair weather that Horatio came there.

With fastidious gusto he ate great Italian sandwiches of whole loaves crammed with vegetables and salami. Then he dove in and laved the dock.

When one took leave of him, he never said, "Take it easy," like most of the experts one would meet on the shore. Certainly he did not say, "Be good," which in the circumstances was a remark of simple lunacy. But he said, "Be good to yourself now."

On the occasion that he was out of sorts he said in deep tones, "Don't buther me, I'm uggly. . . .

"Whud'm I doing here on my ass?

"My father tried to bend me the right way by his example. He tended the lobster pots thirty years and brung up eleven, and never turned a hand in his life."

Harry was fast under the thumb of his mother, who was eighty-three years old.

He was not the marrying kind, but several of his old woman friends, to whom he had been faithful through the years, picked their way over the rocks to enjoy with him the leaping sunbeams.

When he was in the mood, he flew the Stars and Stripes.

And under the rocks, working at night concealed from all eyes, he built a tidy den, extending the chimney of it into the disused drain. This hide-out had a solid door and a large padlock. Inside it had a bunk and a stove.

Sometimes there rose unconsciously to his lips, in association with a persistent memory of a childhood refusal, and in a dialect thicker than that of his manhood, the remark, " 'D'ruther fish."

Then one day Harry Tyler came no more. Some said that he had indeed gone to fish (meaning that he was in Paradise). Others that they had forced him back into the Navy. One said that his mother was dead. But there was a dismal probability that his money was spent and he had gone to work.

Tattooed on his right and left were slender arm-length mermaids whose tail fins clasped his wrists. Spreading fanwise from his solar plexus to both shoulders were the colors of the nations of the world. And writhing on his belly head-downward was a winged and smoking dragon.

It was to Harry Tyler's den that Horatio now sped in the night.

3. The Pigeons

On the line of 189th Street, Horatio descended the slope from the chambers under the highway. The rain was bouncing on the highway and boiling in the river.

He crossed the tracks that were not gleaming. He climbed the invisible wire fence.

There was a gleam under the rock; Harry was in his place just as he had figured it!

But now just as hesitation suddenly seizes on any uninvited guest and he wonders if he dares to knock after all, and his guilt is all the stronger because he has no place else to spend the night—then he knocks softly.

There was no reply. "He is asleep." He rapped sharper. As sharp as he dared. "Harry," he whispered. "Harry Tyler!" he whispered hoarsely. He could have called louder, for the rain was pattering over all the broad sea. He knocked. He kicked softly with his foot. "He wants to be left alone with whoever it is; but Harry wouldn't keep me out in the rain. . . . Harry," said Horatio and his voice choked, "it's me, your friend Tony!" Like a gulph, the terrible thought disclosed itself (so soon does a momentary irritation project itself in murderous fancies): "They've killed my beautiful friend Harry Tyler, and he died here shut up alone like a rat in the wall."

The door opened. Like lightning the silhouetted figure drove against his body a—bladeless knife.

It was his brother Lothair.

Was it his brother Lothair—so loose, peering at him through hairs, all the resolve unlined from his face?

"What have they done to my brother Lothair?" he thought with the egoistic pity of boys, wounded by any alteration in the close family images which fill their experience, and they think that their family strains are debased. But the courage need not have drained from his heart because of the flame in Lothair's eyes, which in fact other persons had noticed in his own.

"Sit down, please, Lothair," he said, pushing him onto the bunk. "I'm *glad* to see you."

He closed the door and they were in the close candlelit room, warmed by the stove, and whose walls were rock and boards. He might have noticed that his brother was not so far gone from his wits but that he had made a fire. On the cot lay a rifle.

"To the pigeons!" said Lothair. "Belongs to the pigeons. I tell you. To the pigeons of the rocks. They never had so many regular rocks before, from four to a hundred stories high, pockmarked with convenient apertures. There is plenty of food. For the pigeons."

Somewhere in his flight, he had ripped off a telephone receiver and its wire. He held the receiver in one hand; in the other he grasped that bladeless knife (which, by the way, also had no handle).

"You've seen them take wing in hundreds?" With his free hand, that held the bladeless knife without a handle, he began to make fluttering swooping motions from the floor in all directions to the ceiling. "They take wing! Shine in the sunlight with the spaces among them. Halt! In one instant they pause and turn as one bird. There is a flash of darkness. And now the sun is shining under the other wing. As flowing, almost as flowing, as the fire."

It was not *un*reasonable, what he was trying to say: that it is possible to look at our city as though it were designed for the hundred thousand pigeons who flourish there. Do they not *flourish* there, and go free and unregarding, as the air?

Absently he pressed the receiver to his ear and looped the wire round his neck, the end of it dangling.

"Someone is coming," he whispered. "Blow out."

Not to cross him, Horatio did so.

In a few moments the footsteps of the guard passed outside and then faded like the first half of our century.

"So. All New York was designed for the free living of the pigeons of the rocks," he said with finality. "But what, now, about the cats? Have you given a thought to the cats? I am not thinking only of house cats, but of the striped tiger, burning bright——"

"Go to sleep, Lothar," said Horace, kneeling and pulling him down on the bunk. "There. Go to sleep now. Sleep."

The big fellow laid his hand on the rifle and fell asleep.

And Horatio methodically took off his damp clothes, wrapped himself in Harry Tyler's flag, and so, wrapped darkly in the Stars and Stripes, curled up round the stove. The scratch above his heart ached very little. He was thankful for, and even *pleased*, with his new home in the rocks, cut off from Empire City, where the lordly river hardly flows.

Chapter 9 • THE SOCIAL COMPACT

> If a man be held in prison or bonds or is not trusted with the liberty of his body, he cannot be understood to be bound by Covenant to subjection; therefore he may, if he can, make his escape by any means whatsoever.
>
> —Hobbes

1. How Lothair Stood Behind the Bars

When he was first locked behind the bars, where he could not *persist* in being of service (whether we were willing or not), Lothair did not pace like the crazed tiger, nor stare dumbly through the opening, but he grasped with his hands the two end bars and stared at the middle bar. A sympathetic critic would say that the trouble with Lothair was that he had stubbornly wanted to serve in his own way. But this is a convenient lie, for one cannot *serve* in one's own way, but only in someone else's need, to which one gives heart, head and hand. This makes it almost impossible to serve at all (though one can try), because *A*'s need is not amenable to *B*'s heart, etc.; nevertheless, Lothair persisted, not in trying to serve, but in actually serving, until he was jailed.

Now of all the lovely outgoing acts of the soul, it is only service that can be frustrated by bars. For if you jail a lover, will not his love turn first to dreams, then strongly burn for invisible or perhaps divine loves? And if you jail an artist, a thinker, they are still free, to dance with rage and count the bars. A moralist is freer still: he has himself to control. But a man of service can only grasp the bars with both hands and press his head against the middle one, while the courage drains from his heart.

2. How Lothair Tirelessly Committed Himself All the Way

Nettled, our sympathetic critic cries out: "I am suspicious of this man who will not show his face. Why doesn't he serve himself? 'If I am not for myself, who is for me?' Why doesn't he *be* himself?

For in the end this is the only way to benefit mankind. But he offered me a hand—good! I rejected it—too bad. Why did he persist in making a nuisance of himself?"

What is this word "rejected"? The man wills to serve you. It is not up to you to accept or reject. You in fact have a society with its conditions. If he chose to serve according to your conditions, what could *you* do about it, except suffer the advantages? Now there is another man who relies on himself and on nature, and he works, as you say, in his own way: *him* you can disregard; in all likelihood he judges that you are quite demented anyway and he is unwilling to waste his strength in your conditions or baffle his wits on your wrong view of the problems. But how could you disregard Lothair? He reserved judgment as to whether society was sane or mad; he took its existence as prima-facie proof of its possibility; he tirelessly committed himself, at need, to every one of the conditions—to the very conditions that were creating the desperate need (but he always thought he saw a way out). Then, in the end, there was Lothair, insistent on being of service—just when all the rest were breathing sighs of relief at the prospect of getting rid of it all, or of some of it, by rushing into destruction; or of letting it just close in, and dying. Lothair refused to let the war solve the problems. At this moment it was necessary to jail him.

3. How Lothair and Eliphaz Were Adversaries

Lothair and Eliphaz were adversaries *point by point.* It was therefore not surprising that both of them execrated the violence of the world-wide total war. By multiplying his enterprises, Eliphaz succeeded in draining the good use from each thing in turn and giving it a value in zeros without an integer. With patient flexibility, Lothair countered him by demonstrating a social possibility nevertheless in each exchange, in each loss—like a tireless swordsman, always on the defense, intent on keeping us all alive, and waiting. (Waiting for what?) But the hearts of the people were not so great as those of their champions; they did not have an *idea,* and without an idea it is impossible to be endlessly patient. Soon therefore they degenerated into violence on each other. Violence is too quick; it is too close; it does not exhaust the soul. It is not objective. It does not nourish *(educare)* the tender strength of the animals into humanity.

4. Why It Is Dangerous to Frustrate a Man of Service

But ah, when you frustrate the efforts of a man who is really intent on serving you, the effect is not what you hope for. He does not withdraw. On the contrary, he says to himself: "These persons need me more desperately than I conceived. I thought it was just a case of so and so, but in fact it is the much deeper need of such and such." Then, in a short time, he comes to offer you a hand—and to your terror it looks like a fist. He used to have a plan according to the conventions you were conscious of; but now it seems almost to be—direct action. And what if the *blow* should surprise in you the knowledge that you did not know you knew?

Do you think, on his part, that it's not a terrible thing for a man like him to have to change his theory?

5. The Social Contract

One day Lothair pressed his forehead against the bar and groaned: "The social compact is abrogated that I used to have with these people." (For the first time in his life he spoke of the people in the third person rather than in the first person, or in moments of towering anger or love in the second person.) "I for my part fulfilled it to the letter, and I am a close reader; but these ignoramuses have alienated themselves from communication."

The tears began to flow from his bland gray eyes when he thought: "It was not by any decision that I entered that compact, nor did I enter it so much as I was nourished by it into my growth. From the very beginning I learned how to warp the language and to aim at ordinary goods by indirection. But it was not asked, it was not agreed, that I take leave completely of my wits and honor. This we would see to step by step. I was willing to take my chances.

"But this compact was for mutual life and service; and when they threaten to take away my life and they deprive me of my liberty, then it is my duty to consider myself again in a state of nature.

"What a hard saying! I was not trained to live by force and fraud without a care, without the counsel and the resistance of my obstructive friends. What! Am I supposed to learn the language anew and try, a late learner, to say simply what is the case? And to aim directly at what it is I want? I have not been like artists and the sages who from the beginning refused to associate with these people (and maybe they were in the right after all!); now they can speak with ease and play even deadly games. But nothing occurs to me except to growl and bare my teeth.

"Alas! *Those* people—" he now came to say *those*—"have alienated themselves from the natural generation. They have lost patience. They have forgotten the continuous association between their hearts and the way they move about the streets. They take gambler's chances. Their architects are crazy. Violent! Violent!

"Ha! If my neighbors have begun to have bad dreams, is it therefore *I* who am alienated from nature?"

As he said this the tears were scorched from his eyes, which began to flame. He ungrasped the bars and began to pace to and fro in the cage.

6. How Lothair Enjoyed a Good Sampling of the Creation

> Ten steps from one corner to another is already something. If I repeat them one hundred and fifty times I shall have walked one verst.
>
> —Kropotkin, *Memoirs of a Revolutionist*

It was lovely in the cell (once one agreed to recognize it as a place in its own right); it was an excellent example of the created space: transparent, and actually alight and bounded by color—a kind of brownish gray. Here four right angles exhausted a plane, and planes cut planes in neat lines. From place to place, motion was continuous, so one could stride from corner to corner without vanishing or necessarily stopping short, until the wall. If one interposed a hand with extended fingers before the window, a shadow fell on the floor.

The food (such as it was) was as it should be: unlike the human organism but potentially like it, so that it was transformed by digestion into Lothair. The air supported slow combustion in the lungs and would have allowed a match to burn if one had a match. The iron rang with its beautiful elasticity: the sound echoed and re-echoed so fast that one could not analyze the clang but could only marvel.

There were eighty-three wasps, some of them vainly crawling up the wall and slipping back. Lothair offered his services to them, lifting them to the sunny window. They did no harm, unless one annoyed them. He was pleased to consider himself a friend of the wasps.

Suddenly he was stung, once, twice, in either hand. He restrained the impulse to lash back with reflex rage. Instead, he was sorely puzzled: how could one tell just what it was that annoyed a wasp? This made it difficult to befriend them—according to *their* need—with heart, head and hand.

7. The New Directive

Having entered the state of Nature, Lothair now lived in the world without bars. The others were behind the bars. For bars, the bars that imprison, are in the soul; those other things, the iron obstacles that restrict your movements, are just tough obstacles. As we say, no holds barred.

Behind the bars was the corridor, and trebly behind bars, the office.

It was only in a potential sense that there existed any other natural men and other lovely places, for Lothair was a bad prisoner, incommunicado. Inasmuch as he had been indisposed to co-operate with those people previously, why should they have expected him to co-operate now? Lothair often failed to co-operate.

Behind the bars was the office! Suddenly there came to the office a new directive, direct from military headquarters. At last the conscription had been removed from civilian authority and given to the military. This resulted in a new *policy* of great moment to Lothair. The new policy was to create an army primarily for victory, no longer primarily as a means of organizing society. This meant a quite different standard of soldierly efficiency.

The new directive was that Lothair and his friends were henceforth to be called "stinker cases." They were by no means to be accepted or forced into the Army; on the contrary, they were to be discarded, forgotten, their names lost in the files. If a man was not eager to be a soldier, if he had a second thought about it, if perhaps he had expressed his dubiety by cutting off his fingers, such a man was a "stinker case"; he would not make a soldier.

Previously, as we saw, if a man was absolutely unwilling, then the whole force of the state was brought to bear to weed *him* in. This cost a good deal for education, policing and psychiatry; it was destructive of the *esprit de corps*. But now if a man didn't want to be a soldier, he didn't have to be a soldier. (There were no longer any such men anyway.) Furthermore there was a shortage of labor.

8. How Lothair Cried Out for Victory

Lothair was brought to the office to hear the new directive.

Craftily he observed that the window was open and had no bars.

"Alger," said the administrator, "you are a stinker case."

He looked about: there were two guards, but they were at ease, with their mouths open.

"Out of you we shall never make a soldier. Why should we feed you here?"

A rifle was held in nerveless fingers.

"On the other hand, if you work for your living—it makes no difference what you do, every job is in the cash nexus—then you will contribute to the victory."

He counted out the steps and blows: one, two and *three*.

"We used to draw the line on the kind of service acceptable. Now we have gotten wiser."

A tulip tree brushed against the wall. Though Lothair had never been an acrobat, today he felt he had a subhuman agility.

"Today," said the administrator, "is the fifteenth of the month."

Great God of Cats! Make this leap sure and Lothair will liberate the tigers on 63rd Street.

"On the thirtieth you will be a free man. Ha!" And he offered his hand.

"Hey?" said Lothair, hearing for the first time and staring unbelieving at the hand.

"I said Ha! And I offered my hand. Ha!"

Lothair seized the desk with his paws and in a voice hoarse and gasping, a bellow and a scream, he said: "I am *tired* of fighting a drawn-out *losing* fight. Now I am longing for *Victory*. With joy. I want to fight with *joy*. Great God of Cats, make this leap sure! Where is the joy to be found again of my fifth and sixth years, before I began to be of service to these people? Be free! Be free, tigers on Sixty-third Street! The compact is abrogated that we used to have with these people." He broke the desk in two and held a part in each paw.

In fright the administrator seized the phone to ask for orders in this unusual case, of a stinker who was psychotic even before they inducted him into the Army.

Lothair tore the instrument from his hand and altogether from the wall.

"How dare you try to communicate after you have alienated yourselves?"

He took the guard's rifle and clubbed him on the head, and on the third count he leaped through the window.

There was a belated shot. There was a Chase. There was a Flight and a Chase. The condition of a chase is that while *A* moves from L to M, *B* moves from M to N.

9. In the Scroll of the Cornice

He had made his getaway, and had gotten to New York. He spent the afternoon curled up in the giant scroll of a verdigris cornice, at the tiptop corner of a building, one hundred feet above the avenue.

Here the pigeons came in their pastel rainbow, with distended plumes. They implanted their claws on his back and his head, and sat for an hour. Others sat in an innumerable series on the ledge above his head, and serially took wing in a swirling spiral to the street.

In their close course, the cars below were like the crests of the billows. The pigeons beat in mid-air like a cloud. The soldiers were hunting in three dimensions through the houses.

To Beat the Bush is for *A* to go to L, M, N, and O in the hope that *B* is at L or M or N or O. To Beat About the Bush is for *A* to go to L, M, N, and O in the knowledge that *B* is at K. But a Wild-Goose Chase is for *A* to go to L, to M, to N, to O when *B* is not at the end of this series of places.

A rainspout was trickling within reach, and Lothair took the occasion to wash his socks and handkerchief. He spread them to dry on the verdigris. Very convenient. Looking about he saw that there was a square platform where it would be possible to install a kerosene stove. . . .

(I am almost not joking. One cannot imagine the courage with which people take root in what places, and make them habitable and decorate the place. Every place has its peculiar advantages.)

Next moment, with his heart in his mouth he slid five thunderous yards down the slope and hung on with his claws. This was not perhaps a domestic note.

A Close Thing is for *A* to come to L when *B* is leaving L. Nip and Tuck is for *A* to come to M, N, O, when *B* is leaving M, N, O.

10. In Full Flight

Later in the day, they started out again.

As the mist thickened and the evening came on and the Chase sped along the river—for Flight and Chase, however scattered, move as one heedless entity—then each of the soldiers and Lothair himself had his own concern and his own thoughts. Nevertheless they were being fused into one by this fatiguing and hypnotic Flight (for to a candid observer, looking at their drawn faces, it would have seemed that they were all in full flight). There were shots, but they could not hit him.

Now Lothair, beside himself with violent joy, stood behind a tree and blew out the brains of the first boy who loomed on the path.

"Is *this* direct action?" he asked himself bitterly. "And is this mortal blow, given or received, precisely the *immortal* blow for which I am longing?" He broke into the woods in full flight.

The comrades of the boy wept with indignation as they carried away the body.

Nevertheless, they were one and all in full flight together, cast under a spell by the rhythm of their limbs and the serial order of the places through which they passed, in the close mist—when suddenly the shock of death, which is too vast for the heart to take in in one impulse, yet there it was, a single thing after all, released the deep feelings common to one and all.

The meaning of this common feeling was as if each one—but in reality it was one feeling of them all—as if each one stopped in his tracks and asked himself: "What am I doing *here?* What am I doing here so far from home?"

This was the meaning of the arrested motion in the full flight, that could be seen in the drawn faces expressing indignation and violent joy, while their limbs sped in rhythm through the series of the places, in the close mist.

The storm broke and the night fell.

There was a volley of shots on the line of 189th Street, and Lothair vanished into his hole.

Next moment a splash could be heard in the river; the soldiers fired; and now they were pursuing Horatio.

11. Addio

When Lothair awoke, the confusion of the misty night had dissipated from his mind, as had the gentle modifications of fatigue, and the disciplinary realities of violence. With peace, rest and clarity his restricted mind was fixed on the one stark insane resolve to open the cages of the zoological garden and let free the beasts. This seemed to him feasible, useful and called for.

The place in the rocks he regarded as his den. His mind was invaded by agonizingly sharp and joyous odors, which in fact existed there, though he had not yet learned to distinguish one from another. He did not think of himself as an animal so much as a kind of panic being; not a proper member of the animal generation, which is always a goat or a bear, but as the Friend of Wasps, the Planner for the Pigeons, and the Liberator of large Cats. The inhibition of his olfactories was loosed, that had set in when he so early became cleanly (not helped either by clouds of tobacco, which in jail he had not tasted). The powerful actuality of this fresh sense gave him a different awareness of participation in the environment than one had had in debates.

If his thoughts once deviated for a moment into an orderly sequence of argument, immediately a nausea and disgust of the smells overpowered him. But now he repressed the thoughts instead of the smells, which in fact were vital to him. (Any train of argument led to an impasse in any case.)

He roughly nudged Horatio awake.

"Get up. Go to the zoo and get the keys."

Started awake, the boy stared up at him in human fright. What he saw was not Lothair, but a shadowy figure of dream who had drawn up a chair by his bedside and sat down. It was a woman, but gracelessly dressed in a gray sharkskin suit and skirt with coarse peach stockings. He could see only the lower part of the figure. He was afraid. She was perhaps his mother whom he did not remember. She was like the notorious Miss Estey, the disciplinary principal who tyrannized over that school of imprisonment and torture from which he had cunningly escaped by tearing up the records. He awoke.

"I am afraid they won't give me the keys, Lothar," he said in a thin voice.

The figure rose in wrath. She was wielding, in a paroxysm of stupidity, a knife—and vanished.

"Get up, damn you!" said Lothair, bellowing and screaming.

It was only a bladeless knife, without a handle, and Horatio, who was not used to be addressed in this fashion, recovered his happy wits.

"Hell to you," he said cheerfully. He had no intention of conforming to insane plans.

Lothair was choking with nausea at the sweetish smell, the rank and sour flowers, of the human being.

"Look, Lothar," said Horace, who soon had the violent smell of powerful coffee flooding from the stove (for at Harry Tyler's was nothing but the blackest), "it is not impossible to let the animals out. I know. This idea is a little crazy—excuse me if I talk to you like a brother—and obviously people cannot guard against *every* unthought-of crazy surprise. But then what? A few people will get hurt and then they'll soon hunt the beasts down, into corners, eh? They'll haul them back into their cages and station extra guards. And that'll be the end o' that. Be reasonable, boy."

His brother was not listening at all, but was respiring with intense excitement. "I am going to lead by my hand the tiger burning bright, and the grinning crocodile and the giraffe, to visit the sociological museum, and to *see* how it is that those people exist."

His thought was that the city was a vast sociological museum kept for the edification of sane animals.

Horatio shook the big fellow by the shoulders. "Snap out of it, boy."

Lothar looked at him with mild gray eyes. "Do you think it's not wicked," he said softly, "that little children are brought so early to see the lovely animals in cages? Won't they dream of it? Won't they be afraid for themselves? Won't they think twice and also have thoughts even before the first thoughts? Is this educational? Is it moral?"

They were like Otello and Iago in the opera who swear, while the trumpets vibrate, *Addio*.

"I swear to you, brother," said Horatio Alger, clenching his fists not yet full-grown, "that I will one day appear in force at those schools and bring back the lovely pleasures of human lust."

12. Noblesse Oblige

> The invaluable happiness of liberty consists, not in doing what one pleases, but in being able, without hindrance or restraint, to do in the direct way what one regards as right and just.
>
> —Goethe

The curator of the zoo was Mynheer.

When Horatio, who had had no intention of conforming himself to an insane plan, came into the curator's office, he was very thoughtful. He sat and looked thoughtfully at his brother-in-law for a long time.

Finally Mynheer looked up from his bits of paper—for the most part he did not use documents with propositions, but little folded-paper combinatories, "thinking machines" as Patrick Geddes would say, for in the end much of his vast work of administration did not require thought but the application of the same formulas to one field after another.

Horatio said, "Why is it that *you* serve?"

The Dutchman growled and bared his teeth.

Startled, the youth faltered: "I mean—what is the advantage of it? Have *you* made a social compact with these people? This I find hard to believe, because you're always too far ahead of the game."

"Why am I serving them—'these lunatics'?" he said in the deathless tragic phrase of Dr. Freud (*"diese mishugeneh"*), "and meanwhile the centuries are lapsing away——"

And hoarsely, not like the inheritor and sovereign peer, but gasping, like a wounded animal, he said: *"Noblesse oblige: this* is why I serve them. I *can,* they cannot, therefore I must. What? Would it be possible for me to look on at work botched, and plans founded on simple ignorance and omission, when I have only to turn a hand? (Not that anything comes of it, for my heart is not in it.)

"It's hard for me to rally to it again and again.

"Little brother! Clever little brother! I am warning you. Excellence is a *disease*. To be able is a disease. It lays on you an obligation that you can't avoid and can't fulfill. It eats the joy out of your heart—except the one joy serene, of *doing* what your hand shall find."

13. Advantages and Disadvantages of Harry Tyler's Place

Harry Tyler's place was now the strictly private address of the brothers Alger. It had certain domestic advantages. It was the only home in all of the Empire City where one could beach and bathe out of the front door, except that at present they dared not venture forth. There were no neighbors, but the passers-by were superior to the average: adventurous or philosophic persons, or persons haunted. Persons haunted, and they saw shapes in the rocks that were not there, or they failed to see shapes among the rocks that were there. The view was without a peer in Europe or the East.

It was a location worth taking root in, and decorating the place, and, as Harry used, putting out a flag.

Just now the great disadvantage was the approach, the entrance and the exit. One had to crawl, flatten himself against a rock, hide where the rats were. Occasionally a shot rang out and this was not a domestic note.

Chapter 10 ▪ THE MORAL EQUIVALENT OF WAR

> It is a winter night. The elements are at war and the child is contemplating some crime against one of his playmates, if he is as I was during my childhood.
>
> —MALDOROR

But let us return to where we left Arthur, in the hideous racket—of bursts of *a! a! a!* and a *boom* surrounded by whispers and droning descending without intervals into a dying fall. You would have thought it was a rout of kids of seven and eight playing fighting and war. There was almost the screaming of unconcealed aggression that they know how to give vent to, immodest, unmoderated by anxiety, that makes the space curl up in tatters and vanish like a flaming piece of paper. They warble *eeee!* from the sinuses above their eyes and hiss *pang!* with tight lips from behind their ears: then there are sounds in the world inimitable in the songs of the human throat. Can you hiss a sound like *pang!* and can you bark a whistle? How is such a world to become part of our experience? For whatever is a human passion may be expressed in music, and whatever is music is in the human throat to imitate it. Can you shriek like these little boys? Do you think we and they have a common world? When a man is scalded, he momentarily howls, but this howl has an edge of anxiety, it has not the pure, the quiet lust. Listen, there is an almost silent breathing; nevertheless, it is out of the world.

The smoke cleared. It was not the rage of kids but only the battlefield itself. There were craters, charred tree trunks and the bright day. All this one could understand, by means of acoustics and ballistics and a little artificial geology.

All along the thundering front the general order was At Ease (it was not so simple to be quite at ease). The friends of Arthur were gathered in their crater to debate and to invent the practical equivalent of the destructive rage of the war. One would see. Over the blasted crater, scorched by a heat more ancient than the bombs, there flew an invisible flag of truce, for who would fire at these internationalists? It was the one-time Society for the Propagation of Vice,

S.P.V.—S.V.P.,

if you *please,* the men who had planned by *pleasure* to set the teeth on edge, to make the teeth *chatter* that were solidly clamped on us all; childishly believing that *pleasure* was a blow of nature that would crack teeth. But what if all were terribly well pleased, and still they fought the war? One would see——

But now on their flapping flag was the device, NEED.

One would see whether it was possible to harness such a deadly lust (whose only aim seemed to be to destroy us), to lead us forth, or at least not to destroy us.

The long *boom,* that sounded very distant in this commons of need, was hushed in many whispers.

Many writers have considered the problem of the moral equivalent of war (what I should rather call the practical equivalent of war):

1. At first one might have supposed that the war was a conflict among the satisfactory aims of peace, and one could solve the conflict.

2. One might have supposed that, apart from conflict, there was a superfluity of power and passion, and that it was not enough to have peace without conflict, but one must *wage* the peace.

3. One might have supposed that among the strong passions there were irreducible aggressive passions, but it was possible to channelize the aggression into a dynamic peace, even if the passion was destructive, for there are many things that need destroying.

4. Then one might have supposed that many persons were self-aggressive, or even all of us from time to time. Good! Let us put ourselves in jeopardy, but why need we disturb the general peace?

No, no! *What if the need was for all, en masse, to release one another from the bondage of peace in order to put us all together in jeopardy?* One would see whether it was possible to do so without being at war.

1. Arthur

Finally Arthur came.

What! Was it Arthur? The bomb must have burst in his face for the shrapnel to have torn such deep scars. Only a few of the scars were the wounds of iron; most of them, the crosses and the claws on the brow and about the eyes and mouth, were the scars of care. He had authority among the soldiers as the oldest veteran, for he could not remember when he had been at peace. He looked large, not as we remember him from before. The others, even his friends, were still cowering, but Arthur was at last undisturbed, and he stood above them a head taller.

Yet just when he rose to speak there was such a hideous racket, of bursts of *a! a! a!* that he was momentarily disturbed. Several of the others shut their eyes tight and clenched their fists; it was not long before they would be out of their wits. But Arthur wryly smiled on one side of his face, and the gracious dimple on that side sank to the bone.

He said, "At ease," and they were at ease.

"We," he said, "who have relied on disasters of the war to minimize our misery, are now the only parliamentary body left in the world. Formerly, all sorts and conditions proceeded down their slopes by persuasion; they were able always to find some reason, or some reason or other, for the next step. (We helped each one down his own slope.) But now their minds are stunned by violence; and if they happen by chance to gather in a group, it is not to exchange reasons, but—as they suggest it to one another—one unreasoning idea overwhelms them all (not necessarily untrue). We, however, are used to this violence; we are used to finding reasons; we are used to finding reasons in this violence. Who of us did not do and suffer violence long ago, when the others imagined they were at peace? And after a while a man thinks up some reason or other.

"If we happen to be with the others in a group and there is a violent blow, then we also are shaken—but we are not stunned. There rises in us the very same overwhelming idea as in them, but it is not *un*reasoning (and not necessarily untrue). It makes a difference to rush into infatuation knowing what one is about! One can devise a plan, eh?

"The idea is to rush into jeopardy en masse. Why en masse? In order to be joyous and guiltless before our greater selves, because the greater part of each man's self is his social self; therefore, we suggest it to one another and we are not ashamed. Why into jeopardy? In order to come close to the place where the tide of original power is dragging at the self small and great; and will it not succumb? But the self wants to die as long and as intensely as it can.

"Can our friends devise a plan for this idea? Can we civilize this lust and make it part of our culture? I see," he said, consulting his notes, "that we have appointed four committees: Committee on Land, on Sea and in the Air; Committee on Fun and Games; Committee on Blows Given and Received; Committee on the Children.

"Will the gentlemen chairmen of these committees please rise and give us their reports?"

2. A Physicist

In the wind of the bombardment, the chairman of the Committee on Land and Sea, etc., wiped his eyeglasses imperturbably. He was (again) that physicist who invented the cyclotron that he was afraid to set in motion because it might initiate the disintegration of all the atoms in the universe, but, curiosity getting the better of him, he set it going anyway. After that moment, he was no longer disturbed by noises.

He was not a psychologist, and his proposal was simple-minded: to organize with large teams the dangerous solitary sports of peace, ski jumping, mountain climbing, automobile racing for records, and the descent into volcanoes; channel swimming; stratospheric flights and parachute jumps. To be sure, in socializing such individual deeds of daring—so that the players would be not one or a few but whole crowds at a time—it would be necessary to employ elaborate equipment and even to modify the nature of the jeopardy. Thus, to organize a "Channel Swim in Panic," it would be best to embark the swimmers in a large ship on the high seas, and then sink the ship. To play "Descent into the Volcano," it would perhaps be most convenient to simulate the conditions altogether: to spray a field with fire and have the crowd run an obstacle race across it. He proposed also a sport called "The Town Braves the Lightning," in which an entire population was subjected to artificial thunderbolts and froze fast or ran for shelter whichever way the panic seized it. Last, he offered for consideration a kind of pentathlon of these obstacle races, arduous swims and panic leaps through space.

Such were the peaceable panic sports on Land, on Sea and in the Air.

3. A Psychologist

The committees had worked in collaboration, and their proposals dovetailed into each other to make one immense Festival. The next chairman—

But as he rose to speak there was such a hideous racket that a man, as they say, could not hear himself think. He could not *hear* himself think; for the fact was that they had invented a new sound called Breaking the Sound Barrier, and that was a remarkable noise; nevertheless, nevertheless, it was—still—possible—by forcing—to think.

This was an accomplished speaker and, to put his audience into a better mood, he began with a little joke about the Marine discharged.

"It seems that this Marine, whose name was Little Audrey, was discharged and returned to his home town. But since he was no longer in service, he was again eligible for conscription, and after a while his name came up and he was notified to report for induction. But when he received the notification, Little Audrey just laughed and laughed. Why did Little Audrey laugh and laugh?

Because he had been blinded at Guadalcanal and he couldn't serve anyway."

The joke was met with a muffled silence.

He then went on to explain that the proposal of the previous speaker was not sufficiently psychological. The outline was good, but it was necessary to embroider it with surprises. Otherwise, it was not necessarily the case that trying conditions would lead to panic fright, for people have wonderful powers of endurance.

These surprises were the familiar fun and games: the cigar that explodes in the teeth, the doorknob with the electric shock, the pie concealing the adder, the whore with the razor to castrate, the mine outside the home port, the sniper camouflaged as a lilac bush, the birthday telegram that proves to be a message of death. These were the fun and games that set the nerves on edge, when the soul is open in the expectation of pleasure. Then, he opined, was the time to play "The Village Braves the Lightning."

"The sniper," he said, "hsub calil a si ohw, and the ʇsıɟ ɹǝɥ uı ɹozɐɹ ǝɥʇ ǝɹoɥʍ." For some of his words came backwards and some quite upside down.

4. A Sociologist

"Very good!" cried the next speaker. "But you are overlooking the sociology. The fact is that so long as these surprised persons form a single team, they will normalize one another out of their surprise. They nerve themselves before one another, and little private agitations are moderated by the *esprit de corps*. But now let us split the single team into two competing teams, and quite the opposite is the result! For now each stroke of fun is attributed to the unknown intentions of the other side; the surprise proves the weakness of one's own side. The solidarity cracks. This accumulates. . . . But more important still is the fact that competition pushes to the *extreme,* indefinitely far beyond what one originally intended."

And, borrowing a text from Clausewitz, he showed that whereas in the beginning each man intends to play within a certain limitation (as a dog snaps his jaws but will not pierce the skin); and all of the friends agree on the limitation as a rule and an inner check; nevertheless, the intention of the other side is always partly unknown: they, too, have a limitation, but it is perhaps not the same limitation. One must be prepared to counter the surprise. A blow falls—how could it have been altogether foreseen? And how hard will the next blow fall? This makes the retaliation a little stronger than was intended, perhaps even a little beyond the rule! How soon they have driven each other into the extreme! Further than one hoped. . . .

The next question is whether those others are still not too exhausted to parry this next blow of ours, which is, we are afraid, the last that *we* have strength for.

"Closest of all," he said, "is to fight a drawn-out losing fight."

As he said it, suddenly the tears gushed from his eyes, and he stood there, to their embarrassment, sobbing and choking.

5. A Theologian

"I know you all——"

The fourth chairman was a theologian, and as he spoke it seemed to grow darker.

"I know you all," he said. "Surprising the open soul—and inspiring one another to the extreme—and rushing panicky into danger: is it by material means like these that you hope to lull, in peace, the lust for death? How little you conceive the strong humanity of the people! By such means as these you will lead them to acts of *heroism,* and no peace during it or afterward (for it has not yet been shown that heroism is the same as peace). I do not here see the shadow of the First Angel, who makes out of being nonbeing.

"Therefore, let me urge on you, in your games, to imitate the little children. For only boys and girls have hellish thoughts.

"There are moments when the childish ego exists in its pride so pure, without the assuaging of any vice, that he can blast his brother out of existence and empty out the space.

"The little girls and boys have hellish thoughts; therefore, listen to their conversation. It is woven of malevolence and guiltiness. A little boy I know thinks such a thought, thrillingly filing the teeth of death, that for a moment the Abyss himself voids the passions and the sunny light on the rocks along the river where they're swimming. But it's only a forgetful child prattling, and the world comes back into existence.

"The   comes   into   ," he said, for every other of his words vanished.

6. How They All Laughed, Except Arthur

Now, when the four committeemen had reported—physicist, psychologist, sociologist and theologian—it was time to combine and evaluate their proposals, to see if indeed they added up to a peaceable equivalent of the war.

Therefore, Arthur stood up again, thanked them for their earnest work, praised their collaboration and proceeded to summarize the discussion:

1. Fundamentally there was to be a pentathlon of dangerous social games.

2. These were to occur by surprise in the moments of expected ease.

3. By competition these games would be driven to extremes beyond the rules.

4. And all of this to be like Hell, by imitating the age of seven.

"My friends?" said Arthur.

There was a pause.

They burst out laughing. For indeed, when it was all added up, they found that their peaceable equivalent for the war turned out to be precisely—the war.

They laughed boisterously. It was pitch night, and nothing could be seen but their white teeth around the ring. Their laughter shook the night, but no one would fire at these internationalists. Instead, their infectious laughter was taken up sporadically along the lines.

But Arthur peacefully smiled in the lone darkness, because he knew that his friends had not failed but had—precisely—succeeded. He was alarmed only by the possibility that the laughter might be the effect of shell shock. But it was the solid laughter of comedy, that greets the moment when the great expectation comes to precisely nothing.

He stood there very large in the dark (if one could see him) and waited for the laughter to subside.

"Now, my children," he began, and they were quiet.

Were his words imitable in a human song? They were the laughing song itself, as it is sung by the bells of Papageno:

"We have dreamed out this game. Shall we not then now have peace? We have analyzed out the parts to their origins and we have put them together to make the whole thing; and you see it is nothing more than this."

Chapter 11 ▪ LAURA'S PLAN FOR NO PLACE

Souvenirs d'horizons, qu'est-ce, ô toi, que la Terre?
—MALLARMÉ

Laura, however, continued to serve our society on its own terms, and slowly drained the courage from her heart. The present day, from which she drew her impressions, was still what she had to give back, with sense and style. Its colors were not gay now; the work was joyless. She succeeded in enlivening it with alcohol; able, by becoming drunker, to design more accurately.

She was planning a town for our community at war.

The first condition, to avoid the bombing, was the dislocation of industry into mountain fastnesses. *Problem:* how to dispose the factories efficiently for the transportation of heavy loads in the most out-of-the-way places? Before addressing such a problem, it was useful to pour a drink.

Working with her secret smile, she did not realize that her attitude toward her two handy boys, her best helpers, had become habitual exasperation.

They quarreled with each other, blaming each other for slips—which were all the while aimed at their mother, who did not seem to love them.

It was hopeless to try to control Lefty, the slenderer of the twins. (They were not identical.) At his best he worked by a kind of intuition, as if he were doodling. And now if, by a kind of doodle, he steered the tractor into a telegraph pole, at what point could one begin to correct him? He was gentle; there was no aggression in his sweet smile. It was unaware of what he was doing that he hacked the drawing board with an ax.

Droyt was burly and no fool. Though he could not draw a free line, he could handle a ruler. He was open and pleasant, although not a genius for amiability like his brother. Now suddenly he was afflicted with absolute stupidity; there was no use screaming at him, because he would not learn, but in the middle of the scene he went away in a rage. Then you might find him playing with himself.

The two boys began to hammer each other. They flailed away;

soon they were bleeding. Then, looking at each other, they became sad and clung hand in hand. As if they were one person's hands, holding hands with herself for security and a little comfort—after the tenth drink.

They were longing for Mynheer, their father, to direct them with a quiet word, but he wouldn't come home.

The architect had to arrange for the movement of the troops. *Problem:* how to transport many millions as swiftly and safely as possible to the place of the worst danger?

There had been little truth or honor in the public writings of our prewar world. But at least one might rely on the roadside names of places and the directions at the forks of the roads. If the sign read

THIS IS CLOSTER
DEMAREST 2 MI.

then one in fact knew where he was and whither he was bound. Many acts of reality, of truth and convenience, followed from this geographical knowledge. It was hard to be altogether lost.

But because it was necessary to deceive the enemy, the signs of place and time now declared what was not the case. Every clock was wrong. Better yet was for all the vast land to brood in anonymity. Best of all would be for it not to exist. But to address this problem, it was useful first to pour a drink.

The dense-packed train was to fly across a stable bridge and empty itself within range of the cannon. Suppose the enemy bombed the bridge in front of the flying train, would not the end be achieved the sooner? No; it would be a surprise; stupid.

Manfully Droyt came to his mother with five points of grievance, counted on his fingers. But when he clenched his hand nervously, he could not open it again and he forgot what he had to say. All he could show her was, dumbly, this fist.

Problem: to adapt the community plan to the climate of the Acts of God and man. She studied the probabilities in the recent statistics. During the last decades there were fewer cyclones, but hurricanes were on the increase and were a good bet against the insurance companies. In tidal waves and earthquakes there had been such a boom that the mortality from them was greater than that of the war during its first years; but the war had recovered its advantage. When she had taken account of all these necessary factors, and of the bombardment—such freedom of orientation as still remained she devoted to a pleasant southern exposure for the caverns.

For at last, after one hundred thousand years, it was possible to give a definitive answer to the essential community problem of manunkind, of "this busy monster manunkind." *Problem:* whether it is better to live in trees or caves? ("Pity this busy monster manunkind not.") In caves! In caves! Safe from the prying of the Sky.

Such were the community problems to which Laura Alger, the imperial pensioner and the stylist of the Empire—the wife of Colijn Duyvendak, the lady Van der Meer—came in the thirty-fifth year of her life, with the nerve ends fainting with exasperation and all the courage drained from her heart. (But pity this busy monster mankind.)

THIS IS NO PLACE
THE TIME IS NOT NOW

IF YOU CONTINUE ON
THIS ROAD YOU WON'T
GET ANYWHERE

So it was possible, given the resources of the habitable globe, to tear up the roots, to undecorate the place and make it not a home. (As I myself used to have a *small* home, rich with the art and thought of three thousand years, so that I knew my compatriots from of old and it made no difference to me that I did not share the nightmares of America 1940; and rich with works of art and thought in process, so that we were sure that we were the citizenry also of the future; rich with fatherhood and motherhood; rich with the trusting gatherings of friends, who spoke out their true thoughts; this *rich* home was undecorated by our lapse of trust, faith and consideration; became cold with wrath, degenerated into violence. Was this a home? Good! Let it not be a home if it is not a home, but then *wander,* live "as if in tents," do not remain and *continue* to serve with no courage but plenty of wrath, and soon becoming noncommittal. And so we lost our home.)

The handy boys now did nothing but shirk, loaf, avoid, disappear from sight, be out of calling, forget their tools and be preoccupied with their fingernails. They were willing to take the gaff for any kind of lapse rather than work without their hearts in it. Often you might find them in their rooms playing with themselves. Other times they were singing their interminable duet, "Choo-choo train," with a drawn-out warbling of train whistles, in which there is an infinite space.

Finally, "Let's evacuate," said Lefty to his brother. And they ran away.

The boys were keen hunters. If a fox that they were pursuing darted down the chimney of a closed-up house, they smashed the window and climbed in and shot him in the drawing room, leaving behind the empty cartridge shells as a mystery to the returning proprietor whose home had been burglarized but not robbed.

1. The Artist in the Shelter

> Hitler has, without meaning it, been a great friend to Britain in more than one way. Among other benefits he has conferred upon us, he has compelled us as a people to take adult education seriously. Munich was the first important stimulus he applied. As a result of that famous—or infamous—episode many thousands of English men and women who previously had never dreamed of subjecting themselves to any educational process became at once determined and ardent students. They crowded into classes to learn about war gases and how to combat them, about first aid and home nursing, about fire fighting and the duties of a civilian in the case of invasion or an air raid.
>
> —H. C. Dent, *Education in Transition*

> So long as the rates of progress held good, these bombs would double in force and number every ten years.
>
> —*The Education of Henry Adams*

During the bombardment, the people huddled in the underground shelter that was their new-type home in the community. They had just lost their houses, their furnishings and their dear habits. And still the muffled explosions could be heard through the thicknesses of concrete. Many were softly weeping. Others were apathetic and seemed stunned. Others, partly by way of busily suppressing anxiety, grief, mourning (but these would soon wail the loudest), were already making domestic arrangements, pre-empting the corners to sleep in, where one could not be surprised from the rear, and collecting soft newspapers like the *Evening Sun*.

A wan light lit them one and all, for the central power was defective.

Now an artist came, by motorcycle, so hurrying from shelter to shelter, to revive the spirits of the people. But what song could now avail, accompanied by the picking of the guitar?

He told first of the fires and the firemen. The fires were merrily blazing, and the firemen, in full sight of the sky, were urinating on the fires.

By this forepleasure, of simple wit, he soon had them clapping to his rhythm and joining in the refrain,

> The fire says Hiss
> when the firemen piss.

There were bursts of loud laughter; the light brightened as the central power was restored; and there began to be an atmosphere of radiant joy. Surely there was some deep release that gave the meaning to this panic enthusiasm that was not the effect of childish jokes.

At the right moment the singer boldly went on to his true theme: to declare, to formalize and to fix the meaning of their joy, that they could securely live on a little. "Thank God," he said, "that we are rid of all that junk, houses and home furnishings and dear habits! At one blow! Who could have hoped for it?"

They were not laughing now, but their satisfaction expressed itself in deep, even breathing, while the sparks and wiry cries of the guitar were struck off by his pick of flint.

What a release from compulsion, from responsibility and regularity, as they let loose that shit once and for all.

It was a strong song that the popular entertainer sang; but it was to an audience close to despair.

At last the nurses came with tea and sandwiches, and the artist discreetly withdrew and mounted his motorcycle to hasten to the next place.

2.

The boys were gone; but Laura, although she saw the evidences of it, did not notice it. Instead, drink by drink she was reliving the incidents of her separation from Mynheer. "Ugh, *he* won't take more than the third drink. One—two—maybe three—and now he shuts his mouth like a clam. You know the type? A clam? Clam! Can you get the spirit of the party? . . . But—is it so gay here, doctor?" she wanted to know.

The Reverend Dr. Bercovici did not show the effects of alcohol. But it was that by long use of being continually drunk he had built up a secondary behavior that looked like the habits of the world. "In *tents!*" he thundered. "The *Lord* said live in tents. Why are *they* complaining? What are *you* wailing about? Did you expect your little house to last forever?" It was hard to tell whether he spoke the words of God or the Devil. He seemed to welcome the bombardment.

"Now he says I have no memory," said Laura, "says I don't keep my word. But I do have a memory. I have a loooong mem'ry. Don't

I have a memory, doctor? Don't I keep my word? From the beginning to the end I undecorated the Garden City."

The minister stood in the doorway looking at the smoking ruins. Sonorously he began to quote from Mallarmé, from the most atheist poem of the atheist poet:

"Elu pour notre fête
Très-simple de chanter l'absence du poète
—ce beau monument l'enferme tout entier.

I'll sing the *absence* of the poet. Yes, yes, the absence of the poet. I love this Mallarmé. Do you know this Mallarmé. What he thought? *He thought that the immortality of something was its nonbeing after it was not!*

"Vaste gouffre apporté dans l'amas de la brume
Par l'irascible vent des mots qu'il n'a pas dits

—the wrathful wind of the words he didn't say! Not the words he did say, but the words he didn't say! Vast gulph in the midst!"

"My handy boys have left me," said Laura. She stared in stupefaction at the absence of her hands. "I have no husband and no children. And I cannot serve the Empire that does not exist." She at last began to cry.

"Look, look, Mme. Duyvendak," cried the minister, pointing toward the heap of bricks and the twist of iron. *"Isn't there plenty of immortality in this plenty of absence?*

"Souvenirs d'horizons, qu'est-ce, ô toi, que la Terre?

—*Memories* of horizons, that's good. Not even the horizons.

"In *tents!* What are *you* wailing about?

"*Je ne sais pas!*—The memories of horizons say that they do not know. *Et toi,* Mme. Duyvendak?"

"I am not alienated from my people," said Laura, the architect turned camoufleur, "but we are alienated from our natures. My husband is right—we are alienated from our memory. I am alienated from my two hands. We are longing for a peace that we intend rapidly to destroy."

3.

Allow me, reader—to point out that the plans we make that are not ideal and to facilitate functions not inherently reasonable, or reasonable only under odd conditions, are nevertheless made by human beings (they do not just happen), with feeling and invention, and such a state of the soul as could produce such plans.

Chapter 12 ▪ THE STATE OF NATURE

> If men should ever beasts become
> bring only brutes into your room,
> and less disgust you'll surely feel.
> We all are Adam's children still.
>
> —quoted by GOETHE

1.

The zoo was a pleasant square, surrounded on three sides by the cages of the beasts, the yellow wolves frenziedly pacing, the aloof giraffes, the crazed cats. Busy people were content to pause here awhile and enter into conversations without being introduced to one another. The pool of live water where the sea lions swiftly swerved from bumping their snouts was asymmetrically central, and into it the people gazed in absorption, or, staring, made jokes. And round the inner square the architect had thrown a raised terrace which was still in the square, so that being still in the pleasant square one could also gaze upon the square.

Everywhere were such varyingly permanent things of interest—live water and spectators and pacing beasts—that could occupy yet hardly dominate attention, ever the same and endlessly changing, why should not people pause here and eventually be at their ease? The abominable roar of the (caged) lion seemed to have an infinite hollow sounding board in which it became muffled and lost.

It was a cunningly laid-out plaza that seemed to have no entrances or exits (for one came in round the cages), so that the people rested in a limitless moment.

On the fourth side, on the raised terrace, were tables and eating. Lothair was having his lunch there, waiting for the salvo of noon. Emilia and her boy were down below, observing and discussing the tiger burning bright. With thin lips, Horace was watching the people watching. I myself was all eyes for the bear on his (barred) hillside. And Harry Tyler——

People moved, singly or in groups, in all six directions. Others were content to stand, distraught. The rapidly pacing or trembling beasts were vibrating in their restricted places. Sometimes, as if new created or vanishing away, people slipped sideways through the invisible exits.

Withdrawing, upward and away from the pleasant plaza (reversing the bomber's angle), at a distance of a few hundred feet one no longer felt that he was in that square, although it still looked like a square of people. At this distance, of this size, the people were like the dolls of childhood—dear, close, lost! Withdrawing! Withdrawing!

Depriving one's self still farther of the plaza of our people—would not the possible return be in the form of a blow?

(Reversing the ballistic parabola), at a distance of several thousand feet one could no longer distinguish that that speck in the vast ugly fly heap was a pleasant square of people in our beautiful Empire City. Here, where the bomb rode at rest under the plane, the bombardier in the deafening silence was not at his ease in any plaza endlessly beguiled.

The fatal clock was ticking fast, and the instruments were vibrating in their cages.

The bombardier is lonely, yet he is not conscious of the absence of the people. (Is it not something immortal, the absence of the people?) He is intensely concerned with what he is about.

From the height of an airplane it is impossible to see the plan of a city square; by the plan I mean the life. A good architect does not take account of such aerial views. Even from a motorcar one can see only landscape and enjoy the pleasures only of banked highways. It is necessary to go on foot to be content to pause awhile and to enter into conversations without introductions.

From the height of an airplane only the Rocky Mountains or the ocean can make an impression. (These one does not destroy with bombs.)

The bomb is at rest in the undercarriage—in a region of ticking machines and the immortal absence of the people.

Now, supposing that (at the bomber's angle) this bomb were released and rapidly approached its target.

At a distance of a few hundred feet would not the pleasant square begin to loom, peopled, clear, close, lost? No longer depriving one's self! But what a thing it is to be returning in the form of a blow!

Here is the square, the environment of society! and one is again a part of it.

2.

With noisy relish Lothair was addressing himself to two pork chops on his dish and meanwhile chattering away to himself. But, no, he was talking not to himself but to the two chops. He cut off a good bite and chewed it and exclaimed:

"First rate! Really, the food here's first rate. Don't you find it so? Big portions, too. This is the first real meal, you know, I've had in four years. Go ahead, take some more o' the Burgundy. Oof, wasn't it a close call this morning when I sneaked out? Shh, not so loud." He looked about. Then, pointing thoughtfully with his knife and fork, ready to attack again, he said, "I suppose the food doesn't seem so good to *you* as it does to *me*. It's a pity."

He silently ruminated this a moment and repeated, "It's a pity. It's a pity. There aren't so many things in the world worth eating as good food. What do you think? Yes, enemies. Plenty of people seem to know about this place already. Nobody tells me anything."

He savagely gnawed the bone.

"Well, old chop, that puts you in your place. Very good, too. Now, what's the matter with your friend? . . . Brother wouldn't eat; he said he wasn't hungry. Me, I'm always hungry. I like the smell, I like the smell. So much the worse for him. *Clean plates!* That's what my mother always used to say. For God's sake!" he cried, shaking the chop furiously and talking to it. "If you people can't appreciate food any more, what in hell is the use? Ha!—" bite—"Next—" chew—"they'll feed one another intravenously. Do you think I'm joking? This they call the high standard of living. I like to bite! I like to chew! I like the smell!"

He glowered at his interlocutors, but they were forever silent.

"My father," said Augustulus to Emilia—the mother and boy were leaning on the railing of the tiger at rest—"my father has cages in which he doesn't keep animals. He's a sergeant soldier an' he has bullets what don't shoot you. Thing is, it's not nice. The man should let the tiger out o' the cage—*isn't* that right, mummee?"

"Yes, Gus. It's mean to keep the animals locked up in cages."

The tigress' gums were black as onyx, and the saliva dripped in slow beads from her furry mouth. Her tongue clicked regularly against her bottom fangs when she inhaled to open wide her throat for the great drafts of oxygen to support the furious combustion of her soul.

"Before he had a uniform, mummee, before he had a uniform how can they tell my father was a sergeant soldier? My father's dead now, but he'll come back after the war's over, isn't that right, mummee? Thing is, when they all go back on the ships an' then the war's over. Some o' the ships get sinked. My father an' I think it's mean to keep the animals in the zoo, don't we, mummee? . . . Mummee! He's getting up! He can't come out, can he, mummee?"

When this crazed tigress went to and fro in her restricted space, she pulled herself by the forelegs but hardly moved her hind legs at all—they seemed almost as if atrophied. But they were powerful. They were for springing.

"God can make my daddy alive, can't he? Why can't God put people together again if they have been killed and send them down from heaven? I know why, because he hasn't got the things together, all the stuff. After the war God will have everything again. We have to wait until after the war, then God can put people together again."*

Harry Tyler, who was one of those waiting for the salvo of twelve, kept scowling upward at the planes. "Oh, shut your friggin' trap, who cares?

"Look at that babe there," he said, "bustin' up her gocart happy as a friggin' lark. Go teach her not to bust it when everywhere she looks there's holes i' the walls."

The lioness kept sending forth her infinitely hollow roar. "Oh, Jesus, hush up, miss," said Harry, "or I'll cram my cock down y'r throat."

The woman standing next to him gave him a startled glance and walked away.

Harry liked to watch the blond seal silently swerving from wall to wall.

Another man was gaping at the giraffe and craning his own skinny neck, popping the Adam's apple. He earnestly stuck his thumbs through his hair for horns.

Everywhere there was an affinity, deep or ridiculously apparent, between the persons who were so earnestly staring and the totems that they were staring at. I knew a little red-haired lady, quick as a fox, who used to watch for hours in front of the quick fox. But why do I, who do not look anything like the brown bear (at least so I think), stand by preference here, watching the bear on his rock? It is because I like to hug tight.

Stretching his little arms over the railing, Augie was chanting, "Tiger, Tiger" and "My Father and I." When his mother saw that he was becoming overexcited and tried to draw him away, he sharply rejected her and rhythmically screamed, "No, No"—a scream

* Quoted from Bertie in Anna Freud's *Infants Without Families.*

when the cat stepped to the right and a scream when she stepped to the left. Emily said firmly, "Come," and seized his hand. He sank his teeth in her hand and, when she cried out, he tore himself free and with great deliberateness persistently knocked his head against the railing.

With tight lips Horace watched them one and all from the terrace and said nothing. He wore a mixed expression.

The expressions on the faces are *simple* or *mixed*. They are simple when there is one feeling (or compatible feelings) and this is a specification of the habitual character, as the choleric man will scowl and bare his teeth, and the lines that are already there merely deepen. In the conditions of society it is rare to see a simple expression; and it is rarely in a work describing society that the writer can accurately declare that his personage wears a simple expression, suffering an original instinctual feeling, or a simple instinctual deprivation.

An expression is mixed when there is a conflict of feelings or when the feeling supervenes on a face already marked by a contrary habit. Wry, sly, quizzical, rueful, lewd, smirking, vacant, haughty: these are expressions rather elaborately mixed. Most often the expressions seen in society are the supervention of a kind of lust, eagerness or curiosity upon timidity; or inattention upon timidity. A "bored look" is the supervention of inattention upon timidity; it is not placid but twitches and tics.

One would have said that the habit of little Horatio, of the boy of eleven that we used to know, had been simple, eager alertness (an expression alternating with, not contrary to, lasciviousness, merriment, fits of tears); but now here was the adolescent leaning on the balustrade with a "look piercing sharp," lips so thin, eyes so very cold—an expression mixed of aversion and judgment overlaying the habit of attentiveness; a look that neither "drank in the scene" nor repelled it, but that "held the scene in its place" (but how long can this steely contest endure?)—then, had that old expression truly been a simple eager smile? Had not the ever-ready smile been a little sharpened at the corners with fright?

He held the scene in its place, waiting for the salvo of twelve, as if, when finally he took it in, it would be at one bite.

3.

The quiet drumbeat was not the salvo of twelve.

It was the approach of a small parade of *evacués* on their way.

Girls and boys, of the ages of five to fifteen, going with their teachers to where, it was hoped, the war would not strike.

Charmed by the far-off sound of fife and drum, the lion forgot to roar, and the people fell back on either side.

The parade entered the square, marking time.

The boys were the better drummers, but the girls knew how to march.

From the balls of the feet, in a rhythmic wave, with a flourish of the calves and an uplift of the knees, and a shake of the hips and a flirt of the shoulders, to the tips of the fingers, to the toss of the smiling head, the dance of the march possessed the girls.

The raised toe curled and the planted toe rolled, syncopating the beat.

They exhibited themselves, and their nascent breasts, as though they had costumes to show.

By comparison the vigorous boys had feet of lead.

But the boys were the better drummers!

The snare drums repeated crescendo the one cumulating rhythm:

Their pianissimo was a crisp whisper; their piano was a speaking voice; their forte made the heart resolve, their fortissimo knocked you out of bed.

As the bass drum beat they stepped forth, and the fife began the tune.

What a joyous scene it was for me! To see my girls and boys walking out of this place of danger! I say "my" girls and boys, for I saw some among them whom I myself had taught (and they taught me a thing or two). When these caught sight of me, do you think that they did not break ranks and run to me exclaiming? It was a good, undisciplined parade; once they had got the wild music going, halfway across the square they broke step. I looked carefully but I could not see a mixed expression on their faces. I prayed: "May the powers of the heaven and the earth continue to spring alive in every act of these dear girls and boys. May no resentful teacher frown upon their glorious inventions, but all nourish them still with true stories of what is and of the few ancient human days."

Soon they were gone, and the wild music died away.

They left us in the unpleasant plaza among ends of conversations.

The muffled drumbeat was the salvo of twelve.

4.

Next moment the animals were let out of their cages by Lothair and his lieutenants.

At first the people, who were accustomed to looking on at a spectacle and exchanging conversation, looked on also at this, but silently. So for the first fractions of a minute there was no disorder, haste or outcry as the wolves trotted free and the bear ambled forth. It was altogether quiet, for the animals, too, held their peace. In places, where the beast had passed, a rank odor lay on the air. It was during this preliminary pause of surprise that the tigress mounted the pedestal of a statue of a tigress, in a position to spring.

Without transition, without transition this first pause of surprise passed over into silent panic fright. As if there had been no new experience, no new experience, to stun, to stun the mind and create the condition for panic fright. But as if this spectacle were what they had already been experiencing, what they had been experiencing, all along. That on the pedestal there were two tigresses. It was because the people in the closed plaza were unaccountably at ease, each staring at the animal for which he had a deep affinity, that they now went through an experience already experienced. And their reactions were inevitable.

The noise that began to rise in the square was absolutely unnoticed by anyone, although each one was contributing to it, and the beasts reacted with abominable cries. (The beasts were not panicked because they were not a herd.) It rose to a steady roar. Many of the people opened flashing jackknives. Since, as we have said, there were no apparent exits from this companionable plaza, there was no tendency for the people to run wild in panic fright and trample one another; but one or two persons, who had previously been about to leave, proceeded with the suggestion as if under hypnosis and slipped sideways through the invisible doors. Some of the animals ran out.

The giraffe, when his raised head with its ears and horns could be seen over the wall, was puny and ridiculous against the towers of the Empire City.

Grasping her firmly by the ring through her nose, Lothair was leading up the steps the shaggy yak with wide-thrown horns and apparently making an oration to her that could not be heard in the clamor. Clamor, but stationary and not *dis*orderly, for the people were as yet too new in the state of nature, too new in the state of nature to know what to do next. What odors to distinguish, to move by what impulse toward what good, and to reason with natural symbols. It was necessary for those who were more accustomed to this way to take the lead.

The tigress sprang, separating herself from the statue of a tigress. In one spring she threw the child Augie to the pavement and, recoiling on her haunches, she sank her teeth in his throat and shoulder. His mother, frozen fast, screamed a human cry. Horace leaped to the rescue, but the tigress snapped at him once and flung him away with a sideswipe of her heavy paw; then he lay stunned. The child whimpered and died.

Now when the tigress sprang, the curator, who had been watching startled at his window—startled but not panic-stricken—raced onto the square. Mynheer was not subject to the panic paralysis of the crowd; methodically he seized his revolver, and his instantaneous conscious plan was to get close enough to the tigress to shoot safely. At this moment, however, the well-known voice of Emilia spoke a human cry. *This* had not entered into his calculations, and he stood stunned on the threshold. He was prepared for every crisis and inured by long experience to every blood-curdling shriek. But the cry of Emily was a cry of recognition, it was a human cry, it was a human cry of recognition of a suicidal loss. It was torn from her deeper than any passion. But this was beyond the depth of Mynheer's stoical composure, and he stood as paralyzed as the rest. Now many people were giving blood-curdling shrieks.

When the tigress sprang, Horace was not startled. (He had in part prepared the event.) His eyes, which had been narrowed on the tigress, opened wider, and when the beast sank her teeth in the child they opened wide with horror. Emily's outcry made him terribly sad, but he was not stunned, and he leaped down the steps to seize the child from the animal's jaws.

It was not an heroic deed, for a hero seldom fails. This is not because we call him a hero when he has succeeded but because it is in the nature of a hero to succeed. The action of a hero follows after he has been stunned and every conscious volition and strength have been canceled from his soul; then he acts with preternatural clarity, delicacy and force. He does not inhibit himself. The energy of his senses, his reason, and his muscles is the streaming of life. (You cannot foresee what ordinary person will become such a hero.)

When the tigress snapped at Horatio, he felt a painful stinging in his right hand. The blow of the heavy paw struck him across the hips, and he lay near by, unable to move. But he saw that he had lost two joints of the small finger of his right hand and he crammed the stump of the finger in his mouth, so the blood trickled from the corners of his unsmiling lips.

Crouching with her chest on the ground, head sunk between her shoulders, and her tail in an almost rigid wave in the air but sometimes lashing the tip of it from side to side, the cat was devouring the child. She did not look at the prey but glassily across it. (To Horatio it seemed that she was looking at him, as he was looking at her.) Then again she left the food a moment, to prowl and growl in front of it, guarding it, guarding herself against surprise.

The child was dead from the beginning and had a simple expression on its face.

The tigress used her forepaws to push the meat in toward her, worrying it, unsheathing the claws—almost as if the paws were grasping hands; but they were not hands, and there was a pathos in this defect in a being otherwise so beautifully equipped.

Horatio looked on at it, not hypnotized or fascinated (as if perhaps his soul had some other resources kept in abeyance while he feasted his eyes), but his attentiveness was now his only resource and his only possible natural action, so that his face wore an unmixed expression of attentive fright. This attentiveness was the specification of this fright. It did not mark itself by deepening any lines on his boy face but by drawing the flesh still more taut, so that the bony face knuckles shone; and his hair stood on end. Meantime his mouth was clamped on the small finger of his right hand, and the other fingers were bars before his eyes.

It was only a short time that passed this way. (All told, it was not three minutes since the salvo of twelve.) But it seemed very long because the close, simple experience was not set off by anything.

However it was—possibly because his senses began to blur and he was about to faint with shock—half-seeing the blur of animals moving about, young Horace (like Siegfried in the play who also infantilely sucked on his finger), with rapture Horatio imagined that he could understand what the animals were saying to each other. And he would never be frightened again, because this understanding was more original than fright (more original than alertness); it took precedence. He laughed, because what they were saying was an old joke. They were talking about the Great War.

"More than twenty million human beings have been killed in it so far," said one of the animals.

"Ha!" said another. "They must be having plenty of good food."

5.

Mounting the steps, Lothair, leading by her nose ring the shaggy buffalo and with his right arm lovingly round the neck of a ewe of the Andes—and all of them flown about by a cloud of pigeons—was exclaiming:

"Dear friends, let me show you a little how those people make it impossible for themselves to live."

He seemed to imagine that the curator's mansion at the top of the steps was the city itself, and he pointed it out as the sociological museum that they were now visiting.

"My sacred cow, and you, mistress of the shepherds that have copper skin," he said to his animals at either hand, "and you birds of Aphrodite, do you see any covert here, to lie down and make love in it? Do you know that in these endless streets if you and I should be spontaneously touched by a charming desire, you will not find a copse of alders or a deep field or a cove of hedges starred with syringa or even a haymow, to withdraw there and lay each other bare. 'Ha,' I see you ask with consternation in your eye, *'what is one supposed to do?'* "

The buffalo had turned on him her enormous liquid brown eye.

"In order to make love *here,*" cried their guide, "it is first necessary to pay rent. Yes—yes," he said eagerly—as if no one would believe it—"it is often in hotel rooms that they let their tired youth be thrown. But I think that by the time we have crept off, out of the sunlight, out of the star dust, to such a cribbed and profit-making cave, my organ will have become flabby and useless; we shall no longer be drawing deep breaths; there is no infinity to the housed orgasm, limited also by a clock.

"Come, sniff at this woman. You draw back. What is it? Soap. There is nothing to smell here but soap and flowers, as if she were a vegetable and not descended in the generation of the beasts. This is perhaps something to browse on; would you, if you were a bull, be inspired by it to make a pass of love? . . . See, she is frightened. She does not want to be touched. And yet she is dressed, according to our human tastes (it would be hard to explain them to you), she is dressed to excite me, to attract me. I *am* excited, I rise; I am attracted, I approach. See? Now she is trained to cry out in fright and fly in panic. Tell me, are not these persons demented? But sometimes she does not fly in panic but freezes in panic. This is good. Good for me, not so good for her.

"Are you surprised that the people of this city do not reproduce their kind, and if the countryfolk did not replenish the place from generation to generation, soon it would be void of life except for the pigeons, the rats and the flies?

"What have I to do with such customs?" he said bitterly, and he began shamelessly to make passes of love at the Andean. "Te llama llama?" he asked, smirking at his little joke.

Above the wide-thrown horn of the yak, the liquid brown eye of the sheep, the distended pinions of the pigeon, the face of Lothair wore nothing but mixed expressions, succeeding one another with such extremity that you would have despaired of ever finding nature underneath.

The cow gave forth a long bellow.

"True!" said Lothair (but it was not the case that he could really understand the language of the animals). "Everywhere signs of war. There's even more aggressiveness than is normal, because of the frustrations. Does it promise well? I see you are kicking up your heels and stamping and bellowing, and your eyes are flashing. There is a war. The war is the Law of Tooth and Nail. You say, *'Ha! There is at least this!'* . . . No such thing! The war is long and far and wide, but I have not heard that there is a general use of teeth or of nails. It is rare, rare that they gouge the eyes or tear the lip or break the back or twist the testicles. How does the flurry of rage burst out? (You will laugh when I tell you.) In mechanical *explosives!*

"They go off almost out of sight and hearing. Far off. As in a dream. One pushes a little button.

"Meantime the anger accumulates in the soul. It does not find expression. It is not purged away. After the war is over, will not these overstimulated people be even more frustrated than before?

"Look! Up there! I'll show you what I mean. See—you can hardly see him in the clouds—a man is consulting his dials. Do you think he will be any the more amiable after he has let loose the bomb?

"Small satisfaction! Powerful stimuli and small satisfactions! Not only here but in every department of the museum.

"There's a reason. I'll tell you why. You're a smart creature and you can laugh at a joke. The only way to keep up the profits is to create a wide demand, and the only way to have a wide demand is to provide temptation for some elementary, universal, instinctual want. These clever men and women have devised excruciating crude temptations. Crude! You don't know how crude—I would be ashamed to give examples. But—and here's the joke—the balance of the society, the great social machine, is so—delicate—that the full satisfaction of a single one of those elementary wants would fatally derange everything! Supposing a person were satisfied with love, and he had struck a blow tooth and nail and, having been reduced to hunger, now he was replete, he shat where he stood!—do you suppose that such a person would drag himself from sleep early in the morning, and drag himself to work for money, and be on edge lest tomorrow he fail to be satisfied?

"When suddenly one day one of the brothers or sisters initiates a chain of direct actions—who knows who will be torn limb from limb?

"Excellent! Here is the department of eating and drinking. Shall I tell you something about the food of these curious people, for whatever you may think, they do not eat one another?"

But at this moment he saw Mynheer, the curator, standing in the threshold, the unsmoking revolver still in his hand.

"Ah, it is my brother-in-law!" said Lothair with delight. "Well met, brother-in-law. . . . This is a perfect specimen—there is no better," he whispered to the buffalo. "Allow me to introduce you to one another:

"This is the buffalo from Todanadad, much venerated by the natives of that plateau who have indeed subordinated and atrophied the entire remainder of their social lives to the maintenance of her purity of strain and to milking her for the production of a clarified butter called ghee.

"And this," he said more coyly than affectionately, "is a little friend of mine. Se llama Llama.

"And these—" pointing to his shoulders, for a pigeon had perched on each—"are the pigeons, to provide suitable rookeries for whom the men have built the towers of the Empire City.

"And this, my friends, is my brother-in-law, the Mynheer Colijn. He is the corresponding secretary of two dozen societies and institutes, including the Society for the Preservation of Cultural Relics and the League for the Destruction of Historical Monuments, the Psychoanalytic Institute and the Society for the Propagation of Vice, the Institute for Constructive Bombardment, the Town Planners Association, etc., etc. (But he has been unable, I am told, to maintain marital relations with my sister Laura.)

"Come, brother-in-law," said Lothair, "what are you doing out of your cage?"

And, taking Mynheer by the hand, he led him to an empty cage and pushed him roughly inside.

Mynheer let himself be dumbly conducted. Why did he?

He was paying the penalty for the fact that he had been stunned when he heard the human cry.

Mynheer was responsible for his intellect. He had a scrupulous honor with regard to being refuted. If he came to be refuted, he did not overlook it, nor pass it by, nor act as if this made no difference to him, nor defer it for another time; but he broke into a sweat, his hair stood on end and he could not sleep easy till he knew better. Now the worst refutation was a surprise that could paralyze action, and he had been so surprised and had not acted. Then Mynheer did not feel now that he could judge the other till he had himself sought through and solved that human cry and again made his theory whole and perfect. Then why should he not allow himself to be conducted—for a quarter of an hour?

(The panic in the square had already, as we shall see, been solved by Emilia.)

"See the man in the cage?" exclaimed Lothair. "I, too, once lived in a cage, before the social compact was abrogated that I had with those people. Do you know what are the bars of this cage? Let me tell you."

And not otherwise than a cartoonist for the political press, Lothair—who fancied that he was living in the state of nature, yet even now was creating a cartoon for the political press—assigned a label to each of the bars of the cage in which Mynheer Duyck Colijn was dumbly standing.

"This bar," he said, "is *Liberty*.

"And this bar is *Education*.

"This bar is the human *Standard of Living*.

"And this bar is *Justice*.

"And the man," said Lothair with a choking voice, "is held in this cage *incommunicado*."

6. The State of Nature

But with quickening breath and lips opening in an anticipatory smile and eyes shining for joy—and no need now to suck his finger for fright—Horatio was listening to what it was that the animals were really saying to each other.

And they were saying, again and again, in a thousand actions and attitudes, the simple paragraph of Johann Goethe:

"I ever repeat it, the world could not exist if it were not so simple. This wretched soil—it has been tilled a thousand years, yet its powers are always the same: a little rain, a little sun, and each spring it grows green and so forth."

"A little rain, a little sun, and so forth," said one.

"They must be having plenty of good food," said another.

"The world could not exist if it were not so simple."

Did Lothair imagine that the society of those people (such as it was) existed because of their demented notions and by means of their contradictory institutions? And that these were the essence of their society? No such thing! In medicine there is a famous maxim: *"One cannot explain a positive effect by a negative cause."* Nothing comes from nothing. The society *existed,* in so far as it existed, because of elementary desires and the wonderful virtues of courage, patience, the extraordinary endurance of the people.

"Why should he speak of 'those people'?" thought Horatio. "I, too, have such desires and I think I have such virtues. They and I and the rest of these beasts: we all."

"A little rain, a little sun," they were saying.

"I evermore repeat it!"

"One cannot explain a positive effect by a negative cause."

"Nothing comes from nothing."

One had only to observe a single one of the beasts, the little cat or the burly bison, to see that one could not explain a positive effect by a negative cause. Surely they were saying this very clearly. Yet it was necessary to lie awhile in attentive fright, sucking on a finger, and with a simple expression on one's face, to understand that it was indeed this that they were saying:

That "the world could not exist if it were not so simple."

"They have already killed twenty millions: there must be plenty of good food."

That it *existed,* such as it was, by elementary desires and hardy virtues. That it would be *saved,* when it would be saved, by simple revulsion—what an unsubtle observer might even call simple disgust.

If one lay there quietly to watch the tigress devouring the child, then one could hear what they were saying: "This wretched soil——

"This wretched soil: it has been tilled a thousand years."

"Nevertheless, its powers are always the same!"

"Each spring it grows green."

"I evermore repeat it!"

"A little rain, a little sun, and each spring it grows green and so forth."

7. An Heroic Deed

Before the tigress sprang, Emilia was clinging hard to the hand of her little boy, but he bit her and drew free, and wanted to be free, and wailed, "No, no!"

And when the tigress sprang, it was impossible for the mother to move. For irrevocably, and from bottom to top, the mother child within her, that took the place of her self, was rent into its parts. This had been the "semipermanent establishment" for which she had used to long, and for a few years she had enjoyed it; it had been the masculinity of which, as a little girl, she had felt herself deprived. But the ties of it were already strained.

If the tigress had sprung two years before, would not the mother also have sprung, tigress for tigress? But now she was guilty, she had a mixed desire. It is by such causes that one explains the fact that a person is frozen into inaction.

She gave a human cry. It was a cry of recognition of her own dear soul, self. It contained in it the three wailing voices of loss, grief and mourning. And immeasurable, the wail of the newborn. This cry lasted a long time, drawn out for a moment, and nearly every soul in the square was brought to a pause, each in its own way. But the soul that has given such a cry is no longer responsible for the guilty effort to cling to what has now been recognized as irrevocably torn away; it is free from the burdens of possession; it is released from the strains of willing different things. Will not such a cry prolong itself to the moment when at last its purity begins to jangle into a peal of victory?

Then the living Emilia became a heroine and she performed a heroic deed which, by its nature, could not fail.

Walking rapidly and almost unseen, she carried the small children, struck silent by her touch, into the restaurant. She wheeled a perambulator. She stationed a guard to open and close the door.

When she gave unhurried orders, they were obeyed. This was partly because her intuition did not fail to select the woman or boy who would obey.

Her mind was clear and conscious; her senses were supernormally alert, so that they penetrated every corner, and her memory did not fail to recall to her what was hidden. But she moved without apparent will. That is to say, she did not feel, as she calculated each thing in turn, that there was an *extra* moment of committing herself to the result of the calculation.

Without alarming the tigress, she lifted Horatio in her arms and bore him to safety. At this time, feeling himself in her arms, he fainted away. She gave the directions to treat him.

Then she returned to where the remains of the body of her child were lying, the tiger pacing short steps in front of it and slowly lashing only the tip of its tail. But the beast did not disturb her, but growled when she took off the black coat of mourning that she was wearing for her husband and her father (disclosing underneath a party dress) and wrapped little August in it and, weeping softly, she carried him away.

By this time the police had converged with their firearms. Most of the people in the square had taken refuge in the cages. Many of the beasts were simply browsing in the park. The zoo attendants began to wheel up their moving cages.

A shot rang out, restoring (as Horatio had predicted) the conditions of the social peace.

8. The Elephant

The elephant had not offered to budge from his enclosure, but remained immobile in the center of the asphalt yard surrounded by mighty bars. The bars, the elephant, the floor and the sky were gray.

Lothair turned this corner, arrayed with his pigeons, but otherwise alone.

"Eliphaz!" he exclaimed, impatiently shaking free of the birds.

"Why don't you come out, old sir?" he pleaded, taking hold of the bars. "I specially directed that you also should be let free. You have been encaged as much as any of us, whatever superficial people may have thought.

"I looked for you, but they told me you were dead. The boy lied to me. Why did he? Why are they afraid to tell me anything? Trying to humor me. Does he think I hate *you,* old friend? Imagine if *we* hated each other among these—petty bourgeois! But you have had the virtues of a grand bourgeois: invention, abstention and daring. Those other persons do not even know what a virtue is.

"You're offended with me, Eliphaz!" he cried, stepping through the wide-apart bars and approaching. "You don't say anything. I'm surprised that you should be a hard loser. It was always a fair hard fight between us. Dirty and cunning, but never capricious, never *un*reasonable. When I was beat I overlooked it. Why don't you now forgive and forget and be friends?"

Like a cow at the auction—who stands unconcernedly in the center while the auctioneer explains her points and the bids fly back and forth—the elephant lifted his tail and defecated and then, after his fashion, ambled forward to the bars.

"Oh," cried Lothar, "you're pretending that you're still the cashier at the bank, looking through the bars and counting out the currency. But those days are over, old man! They are over. Since the compact is abrogated that we used to have with those people.

"You didn't abrogate it; I am not accusing you of it. We two should have kept the peace, such as it was, but those people were at the end of their resources.

"Now there is a new order of things.

"Is there a new order of things?" he asked, staring about uneasily, and half comprehending that it was the elephant pen at the zoo,

between the gray pavement and the gray sky. "Is this direct action? And is this the use of words to say what is the case? Is this the elementary desire? And are these the hardy virtues of courage and endurance?

"Where are my friends? Where is Henry Faust to celebrate with me our entry into the state of Nature? Didn't we use to say that *this* would be the ceremonial of the glorious day: that the trusting brothers and sisters would sit down together and exchange their true thoughts? I cannot associate with birds and beasts as if they were the same as I. If I do not associate with people, with whom shall I associate?"

Suddenly he was seized with wild rage and indignation that he was *still* being held incommunicado. "*Talk* to me, you stupid, unoffending beast. Am I again cut off from *all* communication? You have become as huge and quiet as an elephant." And he began to beat the side of the animal with his fists.

With a quick step the brute trampled on him and kicked him out of the enclosure.

Chapter 13 ▪ THE DEATH OF ARTHUR

> Well is the treasure now laid up; the fair image of the Past! Here sleeps it in the marble, undecaying; in your hearts too it lives, it works. Travel, travel, back into life! Take along with you this holy earnestness;—for earnestness alone makes life eternity.
>
> —GOETHE, *Wilhelm Meister,* VIII, 8

Which of the bullets is signed with my name? Or will it be a message of shrapnel, or a shock of the air? Arthur asked himself, while the steel flew by and the air trembled; for he had a reasonable estimate of the probability of coming alive out of the place where he was.

Meantime, however—though all the while he was firing away as methodically as anyone, for (to repeat it the last time) there was no use in being not in it if one was in it—meantime he had one more little theoretical problem to solve about his parliamentary committees; till he solved it, that bullet, etc., had to wait.

What was lacking in our meetings? What was lacking to them that made them not close enough and urgent? What was lacking to them was the Principle of Necessity: that people will not stir their asses till they are compelled.

Then in the thick of it he saw—probably from an illustration in a book of Michelet—the glory of the French Revolutionary parliaments, the meetings of the Estates and the Convention, when the people swarmed into the hall, shouting and brandishing weapons, and it was not with impunity that a speaker held the tribunal—nevertheless, he held it and spoke his mind, protected by the swords of those who agreed with him and those who disagreed; or else, if the crowd was barred outside the doors, in order to have the quiet and security necessary to consult, then—with the stamping and shouting and the cannonade just outside the door—it was a busy kind of security, wasn't it? One felt it and used it. This kind of debate was close, it was urgent. So it must be with our committees, thought Arthur; since the problems we debate are only the most urgent for our people, we must also choose the place of debate in the midst of their need and fury. And they demanding that we come to a decision. . . . Well! There, that problem was solved.

The noise of the people storming the tribunal became again the noise of the battle. A bullet passed through his body.

It was not very painful as he lay down in a hole to die.

1. How Arthur Recollected Three Scenes of Boys

As his outer senses grew dim, he vividly recalled the scenes of a boat trip that he had taken from Provincetown to Boston.

First, in the sunlight, he was walking down the long crowded pier, above the milky water stretching away to the points of land. It was the end of the summer, and many vacationists with their leather luggage and their trunks on small wagons were bound for the ship, to leave the Cape. The gulls dived for the fish in the milky sea. Strange calls, as if "Heeeey"—"Saaay" were coming apparently from under the pier. The calls were high and vibrant; they were thrilling with vitality as if they came from the throats of wild boys.

He mounted the gangplank and he saw that it was indeed lads, in the milky water, crying out:

"Heeey!"

"Whaddyesaaay?"

"Heave a nickel ov-uh!"

They were treading water, boys of twelve and thirteen; dank hair and flashing teeth and brown arms; diving like sharks. When the coin shone through the air and hissed on the surface, they gathered in a school.

"Heeey!"

"Heeey!"

He, too, leaned over the rail to toss his coin. The boys clambered up the ropes to rest on the ledge. One of them was shivering. Others clung to rowboats, rising and falling on the swell.

"Heeey!"

"Whaddyesaaaay?"

"Don' let Avelar in—he hogs!"

There was an enmity between the Irish and the Portuguese boys. They slapped the stranger away from their boat with an oar.

Arthur laid his hand on the wet neck of the shivering boy clinging one hand to the rope and one hand to the railing. "Here's a dime. Can you make me change of a quarter?"

The boy disgorged a flood of coins from his cheeks and throat, pennies, nickels, dimes, quarters.

Arthur was in love with this coin swallower and he could have stayed summer without end in P-town to get to know him better. But it was the end of the vacation.

The long whistle blew. The boat began to move. The boys dived into the wild swell.

"Heeey!"

"Whaddyesaaay?"

"Heave a nickel ov-uh!"

The gulls swooped in hundreds about the moving ship. The last boys clung desperately to the ends of the ropes, agony on their faces.

"Whaddyesaaaaaaay?"

Clouds were streaking the sky. The milky water was black underneath.

It was hard for Arthur to say good-by. "Good-by, boys! Summer without end in P-town." It was necessary. It was too late for him to love, as he used, the boys of twelve and thirteen.

"Heeeeeey!" The shells were whining overhead.

As the ship throbbed and pounded through the rising swells in the teeth of the wind, he wandered sadly about her with watchful glance. The young people were dancing in the lounge to the beat of traps and an accordion. With practiced eye Arthur distinguished out the couples, the desires and the romances among the grown-up adolescents—the romances already a little pathetic, compelled by physical urgency and an inward image that had very little to do either with the girl made up to or the free indiscrimination of lust. There was a large youth, Moriarty, whose collar was unbuttoned and his tie awry, who was trailing after a flushed and lively girl who could not have been more than fourteen.

Moriarty was acquainted with Bob, a homely humorous smart aleck with spectacles, who belonged to the crew, very jaunty in his jeans.

The girl came out on deck and stood by the rail against the sea, with the two lads on either side.

Watching this ancient, this never-different picture, boiling with feeling, Arthur sat down across, on a coil of rope. Bob was cheerily drawing on his manly pipe. The girl was exhilarated. Moriarty was in his misery.

Now Bob was explaining the operation of the engines of the ship. As with clenched fists he vigorously pumped his arms back and forth to describe the pistons, you could see the girl turn pale and strengthless at the masculine gestures (and betrayed by the primeval anxiety of her own fancied deprivation, as if only the boys could drive the huge machines); and she turned her face hungrily to the speaker and touched his sweater.

But Bob was indeed interested in the intricacy of the machinery; he was not exhibiting himself; and he went on to tell in detail of the automatic electric signals from the bridge.

The spell was snapped. The girl was bored and restive; she was not interested in mechanics. She turned to look out at the water.

Moriarty, young fool, chose just this unfortunate moment to press against her from behind, hands on the rails and trapping her in his arms.

She broke free, in fear and anger—and it was only a childish girl who had to run away because her mother would wonder where she was. She avoided his grasp and fled.

And then the large boy, with an obviousness of regression—and of a previous repression—that smote Arthur with a pang between his watchful eyes, threw his arm about Bob's shoulders and leaned there with his weight and longing. But Bob too moved a step away.

The music sounded again from within, and the large boy went in without a word, but with face distorted.

His distorted face, did it not promise badly?

But Bob with pretended expertness stared up at the overcast sky, where the smoky clouds were streaming near. " 'Lectric storm," he announced publicly.

The men came up out of the hatchway.

With joy Bob leaped upon one of them, seized on him from behind and wrestled him tight. It was a big fellow, bespectacled like himself—the same tilt of the cap, same pipe, the same blue sweater, the same tucked up jeans; his model.

By the time they came into Boston harbor, the fog was thick and the thin rain was falling. Over near the dome of the Statehouse, if one could have seen it, flickered a fork of lightning. The buoys were tolling. Arthur had not moved from his coil of rope, but sat in the rain and spray, head hunched in his turned-up collar.

Behind him, half a dozen beer-sodden men and women were noisily shouting to the steward for another case.

"Here comes the lightship," said the old sailor to whom Arthur had given a cigarette. " 'Most in now."

The lights of it appeared ahead in the mist, rapidly approaching and spreading apart into their constellation.

And suddenly beyond it stood up the vast shadow of a great liner. It was one of the queens of the ocean—a transport for the soldiers. So suddenly she appeared, all were surprised. No lights on her, no flags. But thousands of young heads jammed the rails.

Aboard the Boston boat the drunkards tried to concert a cheer among themselves, but it came to nothing.

For a long time, it seemed, the transport lay opposite them, it was so large. The soldiers waved their hands but made no sound.

Then she, too, fell astern, standing forward into her fog, looming there, slowly eaten away by the fog before she diminished.

The beer party and the old sailor had gone within, and Arthur could allow himself to chant the melody.

For from deep in his soul, as the ship fell astern, there rose into his hearing a sad phrase of melody, as he sat on the rope, his head sunk in his collar—and he had no other thought. He had no other thought about the young men on the transport, or the lads and the girl against the sea, or the boys diving for the coins, except this whining phrase of melody which now, since the others had gone within, he allowed himself to whine and chant.

"Whaddyesaaaaay?"

He had no other thought. He sang it to himself as the ship came up to Boston that lay deep in the fog of the war, and the lightning was stinging us from Beacon Hill to the Statehouse.

2. How Arthur Sang and Had No Other Thought

And again, as he lay dying in a hole in the field, he was chanting this melody out of his recollection. He could not have remembered such a scrap of worthless melody by any other means. Must we not say that it was in order to come to the recollection of this melody and to bring it to his lips that he had recollected all that trip, at the end of a summer vacation, from Provincetown to Boston, in order that he might now be chanting himself to sleep with it, as a child chants itself to sleep?

"With no other thought." Arthur Eliphaz could have had plenty of other thoughts, for his mind was not empty of food for sarcastic thought. *If* you please—if you *please* . . . He had experienced not a little of life with this little motto, except ever happiness. "Please." His father used to say it before him, whenever he was crossed, almost as a tic of speech. "Please! But don't you see——" "Please! Is it my fault if in our generation——" It was by following the meander of this little motto that Arthur and the friends of Arthur had deviated as far from our society and as close to death as you please; "so you may approach as close as you please," as the mathematicians say. Did they truly hope by this way to unform the aggression in the heart and to undistort the twisted face? Well, another honorable group has another meandering way to death. "Help each one down his own slope!" (with a shrug) if you please.

See, we must think the thoughts *for* Arthur, for he himself is simply chanting, with an unmixed expression on his face, the same unvarying scrap of melody, more softly as he is falling asleep. It does not seem so lamentable and whining when you hear it again and again.

3. How There Were Stars of Joy

He woke without a start. It was night.

And in the marsh of khaki limbs and blood, here and there, like will-o'-the-wisps, were shining Stars of Joy.

There were Stars of Joy.

These Stars were the immortal satisfactions of the souls here and there falling asleep and dying.

Here, with an old-time need of blood at last assuaged, one fell asleep. One of our pacifist youth leaders who, when the war came, was paralyzed into speechlessness. But now he lay in a Star of Joy.

Here and there there were dying ones who looked across at the bodies and thought, each one, "Not I! See–" he could hardly see– "those others are dead, but this does not happen to me." In the height of joy imagining his own immortality. For it is possible, though one may conceive of one's death, to imagine only one's immortality. So there were many Stars of Joy.

Another man had, during the afternoon, taken leave of himself and performed an heroic deed. And still he was performing it again and again, repeating the trauma and dying in a Star of Joy.

And another man (whom we have met before) had struck a blow, given or received, that fell with the actuality of a creative act.

And Arthur, such was his reflective and sociable nature, was crowned with a Star of Joy when, looking up at the sky, he realized that many of the others had such Stars of Joy.

What Stars of Joy were blazing here and there, like will-o'-the-wisps.

4. How Arthur Quoted a Verse of King Richard

But when he thought of the others in the marsh, it came to Arthur to think also of his friends. Then he had a fearful spasm (the blood trickled from his mouth), and he felt a sad pang.

But next moment the spasm had passed, and chuckling happily (as if *this* were the answer and the consolation for them all) he repeated the line of King Richard:

"Is Bushy, Green, and the Earl of Wiltshire dead?"

One could not help, under the circumstances, chuckling at the question of Shakespeare's pleasure-loving king who stood so well as a symbol for them all!

"Is Bushy, Green, and the Earl of Wiltshire dead?"

The odd grammar and the odd names were irresistibly comic. By the odd grammar the poet means that Richard was thinking of them individually, friend by friend.

5. How Arthur Hummed a Song of Our Generation

And lightly—by association with the Stars of Joy, and also with the stars in the sky, and also with "the memory of love's refrain" (whatever that might mean!)—he began to hum a melody, a melody let loose from the chant he had been moaning—and it turned out to be Hoagy Carmichael's remarkable song, "Stardust." Yes, just as it's sent asoaring by the trumpet vibrato.

For let me tell the reader something: that, just as it is an old history that the young men die on far-off fields, and I am writing all this book with no other principle but this in mind, nevertheless it is also true that many men of my generation have now also died in this way. Their deaths, their deaths have been examples of the general rule; but it cannot be expected that for us they should have only the same meaning and the same lament; for they are ours.

And now such a song—one man will hum to himself one such and another another (though I do not think that you will find many songs in which the absolute bathos of the words so well supports the soaring nostalgia of the tune as in "Stardust")—such a song has its meaning and feeling for us because we in our generation heard it, in bars and dance halls, when we were not yet fully grown; the desire, the hope and the pleasure of that time and those places, this is the feeling that we hear in the song just as if it were there in the notes; and therefore for each one no other song has the same feeling.

6. What Arthur Says

He was dead.

What do we say: "Farewell, young man?" But the dead fare neither well nor ill. Or "Good-by, Arthur?" But this means God be with you on your way, a different way from ours. There is no word in our language accurately (and if not now accurately, when?), accurately to take leave of the dead.

And there is a special difficulty with respect to my friend Arthur dead that does not hold for some of the others. My friend was not at peace when the others were, but engaged day and night in a running fight, not without hardships and danger, as he tried to win the happy victory from whose terms he could not deduct an iota.

(I am not saying that this was wise, but it was so.) Then was he equally liable to the outbreak of the war which came on the others as a consequence of the kind of peace, such as it was, that they had been enjoying? It was accidentally that he was killed in their war—as my friend Charlie fell out of a window and broke his back. And are we supposed to say that this is sensible or that it is, even according to a hard reckoning, a compensation? No, no——

But Arthur, reflective and sociable, checks me and says: "Please! You are wrong to single me out as an exception and an object of special concern, for the truth is that I deserve this concern less than most of the others. I was not at peace; I suppose it is so. But in this running fight day and night I lived out, I wore out, already the most part of my life. Do you think that it is without exhaustion, and without finally coming to an understanding of the limited possibilities, that a man engages in an endless private war? You speak of me as a young man.

"*J'ai plus de souvenirs que si j'avais mille ans;* I have more memories than if I were a thousand years old.

"My father used, in his way, to distinguish between *natural* and *violent,* therefore between natural death and violent death. The natural death—we speak usually of a death from old age—is one brought on by the exhaustion of the possibilities of the soul; can you defer this by a physiological rejuvenation? Nevertheless, the person will die rejuvenated! But a violent death is one that cuts short these possibilities before they are actualized.

"Then so many of my comrades (more than I) have suffered a violent death and never wore out their lives.

"*Even so!* Then how lovely they were still when they died, not yet habituated, not yet too heavy for canonic grace! For we know (I speak cruelly, like a connoisseur) how the rest of us—all except great heroes and true champions—grow socially and physically heavy, sheepish or crabbed as the case may be, as we become involved not in perfect actions but in hindering limitations, because we have made mistakes. But *these!*—"

(No! Arthur, too, was a true champion.)

"These young ones have quit early before the grace had departed from their immortal absence. Is not the lovely grace the superabounding life in a boy, more than what is necessary for what he does, so that there is always here an infinite possibility, as if he were a hero whose power is always beyond our conceiving?

"*'Wunderlich nah ist der Held den jugendlich Toten!'*" says the poet of the early dead: the hero is wonderfully close to the youthful dead!

"He says (a bitter hard saying): *'Brauchen sie uns nicht mehr—'*

they don't need us any more, the early gone; weaning themselves *softly* from the earth as one outgrows the mother's breasts. But *we*—could we exist without *them?*

"It is true that you have no word to take leave of us. But I may still use the words to take leave of you who are alive. Therefore farewell, my father; and farewell, little Gus. God be with you, Emily—you strange person.

"And God be with you, Horatio, my young friend."

PART 3

A cripple, a monster! forced to develop some specialized dexterity at the cost of a world of productive impulses and faculties—as in Argentina they slaughter a whole beast in order to get its hide or tallow. Not merely are the various partial operations allotted to different individuals, but the individual himself is split up, transformed into the automatic motor of some partial operation. Thus is realized the foolish fable of Menenius Agrippa, which depicted a human being as nothing more than a fragment of his own body.

—MARX, *Das Kapital*

Chapter 14 ▪ THE TRUE COLLABORATION: I

Ita affecti sumus ut nihil aeque magnam apud nos admirationem occupet quam homo fortiter miser.

—SENECA

"Incommunicado! Incommunicado!" said the great hair-grown head of Lothair, lying in her lap. He made movements as if joggling the hook of a telephone and said querulously, "Hello! hello!" as if the connection were being cut and the voice growing dim.

"No, Lothar! Face to face," spoke Emily in a loud clear voice. "You see it isn't true that we don't communicate with each other. I hear you very well. And we no longer make use of these mechanical devices; we stay at a human closeness."

She spoke of a human scale, but the fact was that her face, bending over him, was as vast as the visible world. For its oval lay sideways above him and it filled the entire oval of vision, as if she were bounded by nothing but the horizon and he were an airman looking down at the features of this maternal earth.

Raising himself on an elbow, he tried to return closer to it; but the sight blurred and his head swam and he felt as if he were again struck a blow.

She was smiling at him, and her face was clear. But behind her eyes there was a cloud of grief and pain. So that you might conceive that her face had a mixed expression—except that this pure expression, this smile and this hidden cloud of grief, was the *original* expression that every child recognizes in the world; so that, must we not—in the order of perception and love—call just *this* expression simple? It is a smile, and behind the eyes the *balance* of a weight of pain; it is attentive but it is without desire. .

The grief was hid, the smile was apparent, because in every case where there are two, it is worthless for both of them to be helpless.

Emily thought: "Crazy men have now killed my father, my brother-husband, and my child. What shall I do now except turn my attention to this stranger? . . . It is not a stranger. I see that in the end it is not because of indifference that one comes to say that one of them is like another."

His great hair-grown head in her lap, eyes closed, seemed nothing else than the male sex itself, not quiescent and not strong, but trying to gather its power.

"Hello! Hello!" he said, opening his eyes with fear till he saw her.

"No, Lothar. Face to face," she said, attentively smiling. "It will be a long time," she thought, "before I can begin to play the game of turning my face *away*—with a laugh—to teach him gradually at least to exist without me."

"I have sent for Laura," she said. "Do you know? Laura? Your sister Laura? And she is coming back from the West, with Mynheer. And do you know? We all have a wonderful idea—to build a wonderful town from the ruined buildings, that is worth living in."

Chapter 15 ▪ FIRES

In this way the disaggregation of the body social comes about.
—KROPOTKIN

1.

But let us cheer up and follow the young folk—the ones who paraded out of the square so proudly to the beating of the peaceful drums.

As young persons do, in whom neither much repression nor much habituation of desire has yet sunk a routine of life deep, the girls and boys soon forgot the old social order. The *evacués* were not averse to improvising. For one thing, they came into the countryside in such numbers that they were not simply absorbed into it. If there had been the best of will in the world, there would still have been improvisations. But the recent memories and the forgotten images with which they arrived possessed—of the glowing walls and the bricks tumbling into the street—did not predispose them to become adjusted to the strange communities. Many of their improvisations took the form of setting fires. This was not exactly a communal note. (Let us try to keep a tally.)

Yet all this, it was felt, would be ironed out as soon as the older adolescents got to work in the aircraft factory.

The incendiary acts were committed neither in hate nor in malice. On the contrary, the children were altogether enamored of the charming, the unrestraining countryside to which, as in a dream, they attributed the exciting mores that they were moment by moment improvising out of deepest need. Some of them banded together in gangs that, day and night, whirled in circles tin cans of flame at the end of strings. This was, after its fashion, a communal note.

When by carelessness they set fire to the grass, then to the haymows and then to the barn—awestruck at the immediate experience of one thing leading to another, an experience that city children rarely have, and raised out of the world by the wit of so much coming from so little, such a lot of trouble out of only a little match; then, when the big flames had died down, the gang occupied the ruins as its own, crying, "It's ourn! It's ourn!" and drove off intruders with stones. They pulled up the smoldering planks to feed their bonfire of celebration, and the little flames leaped to life underneath, commemorative of the original glory. All through the night they whirled their cans in figures-of-eight, crying, "It's ourn! It's ourn!"

There is plenty of fuel for celebration for a long time when laborious people have for several generations been accumulating it in fences and houses. Is it a communal note?

It was planned that precisely these older boys would work in the aircraft factory. It would be thrilling for them to get into such close contact with the romantic ships and to feel that they had a hand in sending them aloft. The factory itself was an experience: it had twelve parallel production lines.

Others of the children were astounded—and *therefore* assumed a proprietary possessiveness, as if the external facts were nothing but improvisations of their internal impulses—by the facts that carrots were in the ground, that corn stood on stalks and tomatoes hung from vines and pears from trees. The ponderous shape of pears, so aptly hanging from the branches, was a proof of the eternal right to pick them. They crept into gardens to steal the vegetables which they ate uncooked and dusty, warmed by the sun. And when a farmer tried to drive them off it did not seem to them as if he were defending private or social property, but exactly as if, an incomprehensible adult, he were trying to keep them in ignorance of the facts of life, for instance, sexual facts, and to deprive them of pleasure. Once they perceived the growth of the food on this plane of one of the mysteries that resentful authorities were trying to conceal for their own use, the plundering was uncontrollable. The farmer spattered them with grapeshot. But they were eating with an awareness and passion of martyrs; it was equivalent to saying grace. This was a communal note.

The great factory was the chief industry of the entire community. Fifty thousand workers came to it from a hundred miles around. Each one performed just a small operation, yet by their preplanned co-operation, absolutely to the surprise of all, the gigantic ships went roaring aloft. All this had been devised beforehand in Detroit, Michigan.

The disasters of the evacuation and the billeting are well known: How certain children landed in homes where they proved to be not at all what the foster parents had envisaged. How they were sewn into their clothes which they had no more intention of taking off day or night than if the clothes were pelts. How some would not eat the wild country food unflavored with the reassuring taste of tin (though these same children were perhaps the martyred burglars of the gardens). Many seemed never to have been housebroken, or had been trained in curious ways so that they would relieve themselves under the stairs but would never go to an outhouse. Whole school classes were "lost," and their teachers roamed from county to county searching for them. It was a great season for the Tearing up of Records, so that at the last minute a wide-eyed miss would exculpate herself from all the arrangements made for her by exclaiming, "There has been a terrible mistake—that's not *me* at all." There were no school buildings and, alas, some of the teachers were not equipped to engage the attention of the girls and boys during cross-country rambles, especially when it was raining. Some of the children found their way home to the Empire City, to the evils that they knew of; some went Underground; some are unheard of yet.

But suppose that one looked at these very same disastrous facts as examples of witty improvisation, of liberation—keeping in mind, always, that one cannot explain a positive effect by a negative cause; that, as Mynheer said long ago, it is much easier to get freedom by merely confusing everything than by producing something; that there is *plenty* of fuel for celebration for a *long* time when laborious people have for generations been building it into the fences.

When I lived in the country, I had a yellow dog named Tinker Belle, a good huntress, a lady about the house. But when I brought her to the city, she could not relieve herself and she went out of her wits, for apparently she judged that all of the great city, with its paved streets and canyon walls, including the little parks, was one vast house, but she was housebroken. Now if Tinker Belle judged in this way (more accurately, I think, than the citizens themselves), would not the city children coming to the country judge that here there were no houses at all; no limits, no order, no authority, no *un*-reason? Whether or not this was a communal note?

The factory had a great up-to-the-minute cafeteria, locker rooms and toilets located along the assembly lines at convenient intervals, so that it was not necessary to rapidly walk half a mile to relieve oneself.

By the roadside the little social worker, Miss Pitcher, was bitterly sobbing. She had lost her charges one and all; there was not a single one of them left.

She it was who, in the old days, on her round of investigations, found it impossible to bring up the question of Dependents, because inevitably when she did so it raised the question of either parents or children, and both these set before her an impassible psychological block; and by association, Men, Women, Boys and Girls were involved in the same forbidden complex, so that it was impossible for her to discuss any of these either. But she poured out her frustration, the release of her frustration, by meticulously playing the little sonatas of Francis Poulenc, that childlike spirit, and when she came to a major chord, she struck it again and again.

Unluckily they had sent Miss Pitcher to investigate the children of the evacuation.

The children were trying to be compassionate with her, recognizing in her a fellow spirit; but it was their very presence that terrified her and turned the yellow afternoon into night. They could not help giving her a hard time; it was too good to pass up.

But here came Harry Tyler, singing a bawdy song. And before they could escape he seized a pair of them by the scruff of the neck. The others stood back in a circle at a respectful distance. They started to throw stones, but each time they did so he knocked the pair of howling woolly heads together, till the pack desisted.

"Why do you want to make a lady cry, you little savages?" said Harry Tyler indignantly.

"We didn't do nuthin'."

"She came axin' questions—so we said, 'Go hump yourself'—so then she burst out crying."

The Question was, "What is your name?" It was, "What are you doing *here?*"

And the Answer was the deathless answer of little Ivan: "I'm nobody's nothing."

"*She* don't care if you ran away, you stupid kids; do you, miss?" cried Harry Tyler. "I ran away myself when I was a boy. An' she don't want to put you to work. That's how *my* father trained me up, too. He said, 'Harry—' that's how he used to talk to me, he said, 'Harry, don't you be nobudy's fool.' But you could be at least clean and decent and watch your language, that's how he trained *me* up. An' where's the use o' burnin' up all the wood? Why don't you let the tomatoes get ripe before you steal 'em, so they have some taste?

"You two, why don't you *do* something, you friggin' fools?" he cried, banging their heads together once again. "Why don't you *fish?* That's what I used to do. Don't you know that it's easier to have a good time doin' somethin' than just bustin' up everythin'?"

He let them go.

But Miss Pitcher, whether or not it was the manly presence of the sailor that wrought the change, had stopped crying and now began to laugh heartily. What she was laughing at was whimsy, everywhere examples of whimsy! The fact was that up to this moment she had never been able to appreciate this kind of wit, and, being British by birth, this failure roused in her a deep guiltiness. For whimsy is simply the release of repressed childishness in a people—I mean the British upper middle classes—whose childhood is powerfully fixated, cut off from boyhood when they go off to school, and therefore it is rather weakly repressed. And now Miss Pitcher had suddenly got in touch with her own childishness sufficiently to be able to burst into laughter (rather than tears) when it was released.

At this moment she came at last into the inheritance of Carroll, Gilbert and Lear; and the Union Jack was streaming past her cheek.

2.

Some of the older boys and girls, who came from poor homes in the city and were billeted in poor homes in the country, were especially offended by the clutter of broken and discarded objects that the farm family refused to throw away, and gradually the heaps of junk were easing the family out of the house. The woodshed and the back porch were impassable; no one dared to look into the attic; and the back bedrooms were useless.

In the city, where the families were dispossessed twice a year, it was convenient to have a minimum of furniture to cart away—the bare walls and a single table, as Horatio Alger, Jr. described it, with a broomstick for one of the legs. In the country the table was broken, too, but there were several tables still more broken, and perhaps, hidden under the debris, a discarded table not yet quite broken.

The city boys and girls were not impressed by the excuse that on a farm everything finds a use. They held up for inspection machine parts that had long since reverted to rust and ore. Among themselves they voted that the clutter was inelegant. "These people," they said with contempt, "are too poor to throw anything away. At least we were prosperous enough to throw the junk away rather than pay the trucking. What do they mean, sinking us in a hole like this?" Under the circumstances they did not see why they should break their backs chopping firewood.

Instead, they cleared the attic for a neat dormitory and threw the bits of chairs and tables and dresser drawers into the stove. The sunlight once again streamed into the house through the broken windows. This was definitely a communal note.

After the back porch was cleared, Droyt and Lefty, who were spoiling for activity, egged them on to break up the porch itself. Obviously it was of no use, for, in fact, it had not been used.

The ailing widow who was their new mother, and to whom they had been assigned just because such large lads could be helpful to her, wrung her hands and appealed to Miss Pitcher. But Miss Pitcher was at this stage still finding everywhere examples of whimsy.

As they ripped the roof off the porch, the handy boys remembered the old days when they used to be camoufleurs; and their song came back to mind; and they taught the others to croon, hoarsely to bellow that song, "Choo-choo train."

Were they not all bound elsewhere—the kids who were sewn into their clothes and refused to take them off, because they were going elsewhere; and the others who judged that the farmer with his shotgun was incomprehensibly trying to conceal from them the facts of life, as they ate the food from the ground with an awareness that was the equivalent of saying Grace? What were they doing *here?*

> "—I'm Alabamy bound!
> I've got those heebie-jeebies hangin' around."

Soon the fire was out of hand.

As the fire spread, liberated first from the sticks, then from the stove; one stick touching off another—yes! just as the brothers and sisters will one day initiate a chain of direct actions, rioting no longer within limits—how quickly something was accomplished beyond their expectation as the fire with glorious wit and the improvisation of the original energy of nature drove them out of the moonlit house! (What were they doing there?) It was out of hand. Even Droyt and Lefty, who were sophisticated, looked on with big eyes at what they imagined they had imagined, but the power was in the stored-up fuel of generations, and how quickly it blazed beyond their expectation!

The gang filled their cans of fire and in figures-of-eight whirled them in the night, crooning "Choo-choo train."

When the main blaze subsided, leaving them in double darkness, they pulled up the smoldering boards to get more fuel, and underneath burst forth laughing little flames, continuous with, commemorative of, the original fire. Then they filled their tin cans with commemoration and they cried out, "It's ourn! It's ourn!" And if anyone approached to dispute it, they drove him away with stones.

"Do you remember the pink house, Lefty?" cried his brother. "There we had no furniture at all, but we used to sit on the floor like Japanese."

"Before the bombers came."

"It opened onto the water, and the boats used to chug in and out."

"Mama floated on her back in the bedroom, but Mynheer swam the crawl."

"He was the hundred-meter free-style champion of the Indies! *Our* papa knew how to do it!"

"And when we came upstairs, the lake streamed in through the big circular window. Then we had to pee. Do you remember it?"

"I remember it! Mama used to say, 'It satisfied every function.' "

"And every evening, as the sun went down into the windows, the pink house was set on fire."

"She rose up and walked to another dune. She became a zebra."

"Choo-choo train!"

"I've got those heebie-jeebies hangin' around."

"What are we doing here?"

"Whaddyesaaay. Let's evacuate."

For they saw the posse of farmers advancing across the field.

3.

Returning soldiers also began to fall into the broken ranks of the *evacués*. (The idea was that they, too, would work in the factory.) Some were physically maimed; most, in the opinion of competent physicians of human nature, had merely had enough of the fight.

There were exchange prisoners: exchanged "man for man, rank for rank, age for age, and condition for condition." Was it not odd that there should have been, for instance, *another* captain, aged thirty-five, with childish ideas and the left arm missing, and he on the other side, to exchange for this one? One on one side, one on the other side—rank for rank, condition for condition.

Many of these men—exchanged condition for condition—had childish ideas. They did not adjust themselves too badly to the world of the savage young *evacués*.

Before they were "rehabilitated," the injured soldiers were "reconditioned." This was a "tough training" (I am quoting throughout here from authoritative sources), to find who was ready to return to combat service. One underwent "four or five weeks of backbreaking exercises to try to induce a relapse." But if there was a loud sound, some of the hardiest began to shake and gibber.

"I did not find," said one of the men who miserably failed such tests and came away with many childish ideas, "I did not find that in that hospital I was given a mother's care."

It was felt that for these ex-soldiers the routine work in the factory would be a kind of occupational therapy. The factory was noiseless, smokeless and altogether air-conditioned.

"You're a strange one!" cried an ex-soldier to Horatio. "How did they ever find one to exchange for you? You never shaved and you have two joints missing from the little finger of your right hand? Do you have childish ideas, too?"

"I wasn't in the war," said Horace with a little participatory smile. "The end of my little finger was bitten off by a tigress. And I can understand the language of the animals."

The soldiers looked at one another knowingly.

"What do the animals say, buddy?"

"They say that with twenty millions killed in the war there must be plenty of good meat."

Horace, who used to have a little anticipatory smile, now wore a little participatory smile, a little debauched, but very pure. This was because he was accompanied continually by the presence of the absence of at least two persons, Eliphaz and Arthur. (There were really several more, but the presence of the absence of these two accompanied him continually and very close.) Therefore, he wore a little participatory smile.

All the ex-soldiers were accompanied by the presence of the absence of some persons or other—these soldiers who had miserably failed the tests of reconditioning.

Some of them were accompanied by the presence of the absence of entire battalions.

They wore little participatory smiles, which were also called childish ideas.

Horatio perceived a new truth, that at first seemed to him melancholy, but then he saw that it was pleasant and gracious. It was that when his friends had been alive, even with the best will in the world, he could not submit to their thoughts and be simply moved by their wisdom; he had clung with desire and loyalty to their presence, but to their ideas he would set up a kind of dialectical opposition, as if to drive them to another formulation with which one could not help but agree. (How could there be such a formulation if he would not listen quietly?) He did not take it enough for granted that each of his friends existed and maybe meant what he said. But now when they spoke to him absent—and no more change now in what they said, except the changes that he himself unconsciously introduced—how wise, persuasive, well said and final were their sentences; how right their feelings were! One could not help but agree, with a continual little participatory smile.

Presumably some of these ex-soldiers, with childish ideas, also had wise dead friends.

From another point of view, so many vacant smiles were not perhaps a communal note.

But to learn to take it for granted that our brothers indeed exist, *this* is a communal note.

"Do you know, boy," said an ex-sailor, "I can talk to these animals, too. I once had a parrot named Billy, and we used to understand each other fine."

"Is that so?" said Horatio interestedly. "What did he use to say?"

"I'll tell you what he said. It seems there was this magician on board our ship, and he waved a wand and made the food disappear off the table. 'Well, Billy,' says I to my parrot, who used to sit on my shoulder, 'and whaddye think o' that?'

" 'Some crap,' says Billy.

"Then the fellow waved his wand and made the table disappear.

" 'Well, Billy, and whaddye think o' *that*?'

" 'More crap,' says Billy.

"Just then a torpedo hit us—*boom*—sky high.

"After a while I got onto a raft, and here was this bird flapping around in the air and finally comes down on my shoulder. 'No crap, Larry,' says he, 'what in hell did that son-of-a-bitch do with our ship?' "

4.

Just then the great factory blew up—*boom*—sky high, sending fragments of the planes aloft before they were completely assembled, and also the poet A—— MacL——.

The boys stared awestruck at the sight, which was certainly beyond anyone's expectation. And how such a thing came about is indeed incomprehensible, for there is no explosive known that can lift a shed a mile long and covering four hundred acres.*

It was not done by aerial bombs, for it was agreed on all sides that this countryside would not be bombed, otherwise what was the point of evacuation?

Was it then done by direct action? Or by the unlimited destructiveness that there is in childish ideas, when a child wishes, for instance, that papa or his little brother absolutely did not exist? Or perhaps by simple disgust, to which even grownups can come? This improvisation——

Was this a community idea, just to blow up a big shed, even including a former Librarian of Congress?

It was mere improvisation! But what force! Where is there such a force?

Was it done by the presence of plenty of absence? Was it done by the immortal absence of the people? By direct action, when the brothers and sisters initiate a chain of proximate causes? (Of *proximate* causes, for the fact was that at that time some people had come to believe only in formal causes, words, votes, and cash.)

However it was, when the debris settled and the flames died down by nightfall, the gang had again taken possession and begun to whirl their tin cans full of fire, crying, "It's ourn! It's ourn!"

(Some of these kids I myself taught—and they taught me a thing or two.)

But coming along the road an ex-soldier, one-armed, a drummer (exchanged for a drummer; one on one side and one on the other) was mournfully beating out the rhythm:

* Ha! So I thought in December 1944, when I wrote this.

Chapter 16 ▪ THE END OF THE WAR

> This divine collaboration is the good luck of history, making the feast, the gala days in the course of the years.
>
> —Kierkegaard

1. How Mynheer Was Impatient

After this local explosion, they sent Mynheer to reason with the wild children; and he came with Laura. It was good—Horatio was glad—to see them together; but they did not seem to him to be in touch with the realities of the situation.

As the war drew toward a close, Mynheer was burning with impatience; he was tired of sitting on his hands. For it was hard, with the best intentions in the world, to be reasonable during a war. "Have they destroyed enough yet?" he kept asking.

"Have they destroyed enough yet? Have they yet broken ranks? Do they seriously want to restore a community? Are we really called on?" He seemed to have a theory that when enough was destroyed, the decks would be cleared for action, as if mankind were a seaworthy ship. And another theory, that if society was atomized and people were thrown on their individual resources, they would get together again.

He found himself trembling, like an adolescent youth near a girl but not quite bold enough to grab her. He took hold of himself and held out his hand, and it was steady as the rock extruded from the center of the earth and congealed. But when he was calm he was not humanly there, so that if he drew to a normal closeness he loomed to a demonic size.

Laura looked at him a little frightened. "You seem to be breathing the French Revolution," she said.

"Why not? Were not those a few of the few human days?" But which day was it? Was it the fourth of August? Was it the second of June?

Laura was bitter. (The end of our war was a bitter day.) "You ask, 'Are we really called on?' By whom? For what? Isn't that a pompous question when it's a matter of restoring a production line? I've had some experience being summoned for what these people call Plans. Honey," she said with sudden compassion, "don't tax your mind for them; they don't have a new idea, though there are plenty of radical notions. Why wake up the intellect? Isn't it better to use your little calculating machines and recombine the words, the votes and the cash?"

"When there will be an idea," said Mynheer, "do you think we will know it beforehand? It will be surprisingly doing in the hands. One must not miss the moment, the moment when instead of radical ideologues and radical votes there are surprised people. Surprised, but not unaware. And then *Mynheer,*" he exclaimed astonishingly, "will be the spontaneous intellect shared by many! *Common* reason, with my heart in it, and a new idea. When intellect moves among forces of nature, and it itself is one of the forces. I keep asking, Have they destroyed enough? What is enough? Enough is the moment of revulsion to original nature, and then, *then,* there arises in people a hunger for common reason; and what is strange about it if they then begin to hear creative voices, which long have been whispering unheard?"

But the Day looked at him blankly and said, "Heavens! if it isn't the Goddess of Reason enthroned at Notre Dame." She shrugged.

2. Gripped by Diffidence

Gripped by diffidence Laura walked out in the devastated field where the smoldering heaps stretched in their even nonassembly lines.

Discharged soldiers were picking along the heaps of parts, looting. Every time they dislodged a board, the flame leaped from underneath. The parts from adjacent stations of the assembly lines fitted into one another, and the soldiers idly fitted them together.

Seeing two meaningless parts make one meaningless whole smote Laura like a blow between the eyes. How can you *not* try to make sense, even if you thereby plot against the nature of the people?

There was no help for it; in spite of herself she began to invent a new plan. There was no help for it, for soon people come to move in some community plan or other anyway. The lack of a plan is not no plan but only a bad plan. Nature is a potentiality; as soon as people turn their hands to something, they move in some form or other.

Being an artist, Laura drew on the habits of her art, and trained in the Beaux Arts, she took a sheet of paper and drew an axis down the middle of the devastated field.

With a mocking little hissing sizzle this axis wriggled away like a snake. Good-by to symmetry!

Now there was a veteran who had built a kind of forge in the ruins and was wielding a hammer. His name was Peter Ringland, once a good mechanic and now afflicted with childish ideas. "Hi-ya!" he called out to Laura cheerily. "I'm engaging in occupational therapy. That's why they sent me here. Are you here to engage in occupational therapy too?"

Laura was watching where the axis-snake had slithered into a crevice and gone back to the bowels of the earth. And with a pleasant booming on the wind, another of the heaps blew up.

But Peter at the forge did not take panic fright at the explosion. Instead, he closely watched the debris settle and went and picked up some nuts and bolts, and he caught a piece of bentwood on the fly. "I am making an airplane," he said confidentially.

"Occupational therapy!" cried Laura, clasping her hands. "He has hit it!" And then she laughed loudly, for this was indeed, in our sick times, the community plan that did not plot against the nature of the people. And laughing, the Day wore again the Laurel Crown, the free style of our industry, that had seemed harsh and desiccated on her brow, but now blew suddenly soft and green again and blooming with mountain flowers.

And here, with cries of recognition, came Droyt and Lefty to their mother in the swirls of smoke. Their gang stood about them shifting from foot to foot and dangling inactive tins of fire. And Laura clasped her big sons, saying, "My handy boys!"

3. The Underground

Rocky slabs lifted up here and there and strange heads emerged above the ground and looked about. Their faces were blanched. Having satisfied themselves that the war was drawing to a close, they went below with the news and soon a few persons emerged entire, shaking off the dirt from their clothes and stamping. Their clothes were a few years out of date.

These were people who had retired into the Underground during the war and had there supported themselves as best they could. A few of the women even had infants in their arms.

"It was not too bad," explained one woman. "We had a kind of community life. But nothing would grow but mushrooms. I sure am sick of grilled mushrooms and I hope I never see a mushroom sauce again."

Another of the mines exploded, and the Underground people turned still whiter.

4. How Enough Has Not Yet Been Destroyed

Mynheer appeared in a towering rage and spun the boys around to face him. "Did you set new fires after I came?" he said in a tight voice. "Haven't you done enough damage?"

Droyt doubled his fist. "Who do you think you are—my father?" he began to say, for they had grown unused to their father's presence. But it was their father, and they were awestruck and bent their heads. (They had not expected that their father's first words to them after a long absence would be accompanied by a blow, and the tears started into their eyes.)

"Wasn't to burn the things," mumbled Lefty. "Who gives a shit about the things? Was for the fire. It's ourn."

"Don't be impatient with them, Mynheer," said their mother. "They have been on their own, and nobody set them a good example."

"Horatio Alger told us to light the fires," said Droyt under his breath, as if meaning not to be heard.

"Who did? What's that?" snapped Mynheer.

"*Not* enough!" muttered Droyt. "Says it's not enough. Says it will never be enough."

The father clenched his fists but withheld the blow. "Help your mother, boys," he said. "I am sorry that I struck you."

But then another, deep voice spoke and said, "Brother!" Mynheer turned, expecting to see Lothar, but it was Horatio, with his voice grown deeper: he was a young man.

"What is it, Horatio?" said Mynheer gently.

"Wait, wait awhile, brother," said Horatio, "because we still have to anyway. You want to bury the dead too quickly. Let them walk awhile, let them haunt us awhile. And if we did not bury them at all—for a change. I like to speak with them; I don't like to have to descend to hell to speak with them. I like to see the ruins around me for a bit. I like to come on the cathedral across a field of broken stones, and the northern transept of the cathedral is part of the field of broken stones. I haven't nearly had enough."

He was sucking on the absence of the two joints of his little finger and regarding curiously his beautiful sister ever young.

"Look there," he said, "in the sunny gardens where the city boys are wondering at the vegetables original in the ground and how plums grow on trees, while the farmers are sullenly sitting behind locked doors with their shotguns on their knees."

"*You* are egging them on to set more fires," said Mynheer.

"No, no," said Horace. "It is Eliphaz. He is canceling zero after zero."

"Doesn't this method seem to you impractical, brother?" said Mynheer. "As each monumental city goes up in flames, not without the pain of the people who live in the city, and city and country we spread a zone of waste, you say we are only canceling zero after zero. Isn't there a shorter method?"

"I don't know if there is a shorter method. If it is necessary to take all the commodities out of circulation and painfully to learn again that there is a use value before there is an exchange value—do we learn this by easy lessons?"

In my opinion, for instance, only relatively few of our commodities have much human use. I guess I should have to be reduced to dire need to know which. Certainly it would take a lot of clearing away to get back to the neolithic mores that I think I would be comfortable with. But people, understandably, grow tired and frightened of the war before they are disgusted with it and hunger for common reason. Some people, indeed, have occasion to be, and get to be, sooner disgusted than others.

"You are holding something back from us, Horace," said the Dutchman.

"Yes, I am. I spoke with Eliphaz."

"And what did he say?"

"He made prophecies. He said that the duration will last longer than the war."

"Well, we will speak of it another time," said Mynheer and turned.

5. A Short Flight

For the soldiers working at the forge now suddenly wheeled their completed framework into the wind and with shouts warned the others away. It was indeed a kind of airplane made, like this chapter, with what they picked up here and there. It was an extraordinary misshapen skeleton, with Peter Ringland at the controls. Nevertheless, when they established contact, with a sputter and a roar and amid flying sparks, it taxied across the field and even took flight, while the boys gave a rousing cheer and Peter waved his hat.

Fortunately it rose, lopsided, to only twenty or thirty feet before it sank down onto its nose and burst into flames. Peter leaped out nimbly and got away. "A zero! Cancel it out!" he cried, as the crowd ran to the pyre and stood about in a wide circle.

The crowd of ex-soldiers, who had been exchanged man for man, rank for rank, condition for condition; and the maimed ones who could not survive reconditioning without a relapse; and the ones who had childish ideas; and the evacuated boys and girls who swung their cans of fire and in the sunny gardens learned the facts of life; and the people who had had a kind of community of adversity in the Underground (there was a mother, for example, who for three years had walled up her son in a closet and fed him through a hole) —all these stood in a wide circle.

Mynheer was interested in one thrilling fact about them: that they were living under conditions of panic fright and they no longer took panic fright. Their words wavered but did not turn upside down. The shell-shocked soldiers who used to gibber at every loud report were now used to their transient trembling. The explanation was that they were fortified by the presence of their brothers and by the therapeutic occupations they were improvising. These citizens of the New Commune did not regard so highly the elaborate structures in which our society used to be organized, and they were less appalled when a particular bit of the organization showed a crack or even, through a careless error, blew up sky-high. On the other hand, like children or some kinds of schizophrenics, they pounced eagerly on dissociated parts; whenever a big structure breaks down there are always some parts or other. Then they put some of these together into odd shapes, and why should not some of these shapes go for short flights?

There were many evidences of fraternity.

Fraternity is the opposite of panic. In a panic the individuals in a crowd are stunned and cannot think at all; and then, suggesting it to one another, they produce from the depths an idea common to them all. This idea is not necessarily untrue, but it is not properly theirs, they do not grasp it and they cannot grow by it. But now, supposing people who have been thrown on their individual resources (pretty near the bottom) can be induced to collaborate. This fraternal collaboration soon turns into fraternal conflict, for each one has his own childish notion of the general plan and of his share in the division of labor; he is jealously concerned about his brother's share and also jealously concerned about his brother. The different childish intentions conflict, the different concerns irritate, and it seems that they are not collaborators at all but a band of stubborn childish individuals. Yet next moment (out of the future) they produce an altogether new idea that is better than what they came with, severally or collectively. Having started with age 4½, they have reached age 7.

Fraternal collaboration was grand for occupational therapy. It got the shell-shocked right back into interpersonal relations, ranging from fist fights to mutual admiration and pride in their achievements. They started by saying "I," and sometimes they ended by saying "We."

6. Occupational Therapy

In a childish way Laura was serenely happy guiding this occupational therapy. The reason for this was simple. She had a number of fundamental principles of community planning, worked out by famous political moralists and philosophers of technology, and which quite obviously were the ways in which human beings ought to live and do their work. Now these principles were universally disesteemed by our statesmen, our economists and the mass of people themselves. Yet everybody, but everybody, agreed that they were the right principles for occupational therapy. Our society was so constituted that for the insane one could do with full approval what was indispensably useful for the sane, for whom one could not do it.

For instance, in producing goods, to take into account the all-around use of the man and his satisfaction in his work was good occupational therapy (whereas sane society was interested only in the economics of the commodity). It was good occupational therapy for the workman to understand what he was doing and how his share in the work fitted into the enterprise as a whole. Concern with the job to be done rather than with the clock timing it: that was occupational therapy. And occupational therapy put a premium on improvisation and invention. All these things tended to be discouraged among sane workmen.

In the social arrangements of production, it was considered good occupational therapy for a man to work partly on his own—brooding or singing to himself (according to his temperament)—and partly as a member of a team of fellows. And to work partly in country or other natural conditions and partly in workshop and urban conditions: these made him feel at home in the natural and social world. And it was felt that childhood, maturity and age had proper congenial tasks. Such considerations did not weigh much with the technologists of the sane, but *everybody* agreed that they were good occupational therapy.

To eliminate as far as possible the nonproductive services and exchanges, the traffic and middle-manning, between production and consumption: this was good occupational therapy, for it strengthened the sense of reality and efficiency; but sane economists understood that it was better to complicate than to simplify.

And in general, old-fashioned slogans like "From each according to his ability, to each according to his need" were held by occupational therapists to be excellent management for the troubled spirit. But they were not the slogans of sane society.

"But their airplanes don't fly or hardly fly," said Mynheer dryly.

"How much do you want to bet that Peter Ringland will make one fly?" said Laura pugnaciously.

Unfortunately for her optimism, just at this moment Peter came riding by on a bicycle that he had fabricated from what he picked up here and there, and designed on the perfected model that has not changed in our times, one of the *finished* masterpieces of nineteenth-century ingenuity. "This one works! *Here's* a machine!" said Peter. Like most children and many people with childish ideas, he was intensely conservative. "I love this neat machine; anybody with two legs can dig it. The ratio of the sprockets is twenty-seven to fourteen; the ratio of the diameters is two and a half to one. This gives me a mechanical advantage of about five. Now you'd think you could go higher and get more speed. But try it! It don't fit your legs any more. Human scale! That's design. Let me show you folks another beauty clear as crystal and she takes care of herself: our windmill." They had rigged up a water tower.

"But the most beautiful thing in the world," said Peter Ringland with awe, "is the electromagnetic generator."

7. A Meeting

About a dozen persons had collected and they found they were holding a town meeting. The problem facing them was how to control those wild adolescents who did not cease, with their tins of fire, burning up the use value along with the exchange value. They were very tiresome.

One veteran, of Irish extraction, thought that the right treatment was to give them a boot in the ass till they felt it; the bother was that he couldn't do it because he had only one leg.

The bother was that the boys and girls, no longer sexually deprived, were not so willing to be submissive to authority or even to reason. On the other hand, they were good-natured (for the same reason). They played jokes and were a barrel of fun.

"Apprentices!" said Peter, who had a craft-union background. "If you want to fuck around with our machines, *invent* something. . . . Apart from that, boys and girls," he said gently, "there's no other initiation fee."

"But Mynheer himself keeps lighting fires!" cried one teen-age girl surprisingly. "Yes, you do; don't lie out of it. We saw you last night—when everybody was asleep, that's what *you* thought. Is that setting us a good example?" she said righteously.

They turned to look at him and, caught in the act, he grinned. He was grinning the grin of the fourth of August; there is no happier grin in our human annals, and he was almost happy. He had indeed been burning up paper in the night, like a small boy smoking cigarettes behind the fence. "Yes," said Mynheer, "when there is a careless fire, a lot of paper is burnt up. Once upon a time, in France, the peasants set fire to some castles, and an awful lot of paper was burnt up. It just couldn't be helped. And now I was going through the office, and there were so many sales slips, and correspondence in duplicate, and licenses and patents and contracts. So many threats of past intention. I just didn't know how to cope with it all. Simply an enormous amount of paper gets burnt up."

There was a moment when Laura and Mynheer and Droyt and Lefty were standing in a row and they happened to take one another's hands, like an Algonquin bead belt, all grinning.

With a short spell of occupational therapy, people were getting on wonderfully well together.

8. How Horatio Had an Open Look and a Participatory Smile

But Horatio was not in it. He said nothing and gazed at them, all eyes, as if looking at the open; and on his lips was a participatory smile.

His look was the look of animals. As it says in the *Elegies,*

> *mit allen Augen sieht die Kreatur*
> *das Offene–*

"All eyes, the Creature sees the Open." *Our* look encompasses what we see and traps it to our interest; but the brute beast sees what is outside. Now Horatio had learned the language of these beasts. The beast (so the poem continues) sees only the present, for "the free beast has its death continually behind it–and before it God–and when it goes, goes into eternity, just as the spring flows." Did Horatio see only the present? Surely not. Then what was the meaning of this flat look, this look that brought the past loss and the future intent–past error, future impasse!–into presentness? It was as if Horatio knew that destiny is providence.

And he wore a participatory smile. This smile, we have seen, was the conversation of the presence of the absence of his dead friends. It is a conversation in which he attended to the excellence of what they had to say, and was not lying in wait for his own next rejoinder. And what if he acquired the habit of such conversation? Not only with Eliphaz and Arthur, but with Mynheer, Laura and the boys, and Lothar and Emilia, and the ex-soldiers? Of all of them, dead or alive, the presence of the absence. Only in a peculiar way is such a smile possible in a community. The community of presentness is too large for a community. The revolution is too permanent there.

Horatio's young face, which wore this expression so curiously mixed, was lit with health but already debauched, but very pure. And from time to time he childishly sucked on the absence of the tip of his little finger.

9. The Irony

"Do you see the irony of it, young brother?" said Mynheer. "Is that why you are smiling? That in the aftermath of these wars there is such cynicism and despair that we, who up to now were called destructive critics and selfish abstainers—all the while we were trying to practice common reason—are now called foolish optimists and sentimentalists of fraternity, because still we have faith in common nature? I, for my part, am glad for a change to be considered starry-eyed!"

But Horatio, in the presence of so much absence, had as yet only an open look.

10. A Town Square

"Come and look at the square I have not laid out!" Laura invited them.

It was a pleasant roughed-out square. Already busy people were content to pause here, for in the middle, unsymmetrically central, they had already built a fountain of live water, with statues of children extraordinarily graceful and colorful, as if taken from cartoons of Raphael. The statues were painted or glazed, red and yellow.

It was not a fountain and not statues, but half a dozen children, suggesting it to one another, pissing in the blaze of the evening star.

It was the clear day of evening, before the dusk. Visible in the spattering of the fountain streams were the reflections of Venus. And there could be seen, by the two little girls asquat and the four boys proudly protruding themselves, the nature of the delight that people take in lively fountains.

By this fountain Lothar was sitting cross-legged, in the gathering dusk, and Emilia kneeling beside him, cloaked in black, but underneath a party dress. And she—as if they were characters drawn by my brother Ignazio—she was teaching him the elementary words of his mother tongue. "Water"—"water"; and "uncaged." No longer fancying that he was incommunicado, he repeated the words after her with full understanding. Soon by this instruction he would have a vocabulary adequate to say what was the case.

As the darkness fell, twinkling fires again burst into being here and there, as if the wood of the world were bewitched.

As these fires burned, new innocent-appearing stones suddenly lifted, and new heads of the Underground emerged to look about. One could hardly avoid the inference that it was the destruction of the ancient matter that brought back the hidden souls into evidence.

"Yes, men and women, people," said Lothar with enthusiastic recognition, for he had already learned these words.

11. A Wedding

Under an arch of swords, old rifles, wooden swords, while an inexpert bugler blew a ragged air, they celebrated the wedding of Harry Tyler and Minetta Pitcher, in the nocturnal square lit by fires.

Harry was highly brushed and handsome in his uniform. The former Miss Pitcher was in bridal white and, having discarded her glasses for the photographs, looked like a near-sighted small girl, near-sighted but not squinting or staring.

It was a lucky wedding. It was not like the wedding at which Jonah officiated where the bride suffered a miscarriage. If at a loud report an ex-soldier was startled, still he held aloft his trembling sword, for he knew that the spasm would pass away. It would pass away. Many new faces emerged from the Underground for our ceremonial, to pledge the couple in a glass of spirit.

The scene was friendly and lurid. The kids whirled their cans of fire and cried out forever, "It's ourn! It's ourn!" They meant by it that the wedding was theirs and the offspring of it would be theirs.

And for some of us, perhaps, it was already too late, but we also held up our glasses bravely enough and said: "If we pledge you in this glass of fire, shall not we also walk the wandering way that wends from the beginning of the world?"

In her rosy face Mrs. Tyler's eyes were glittering with pleasure. She spoke fluently, no longer balked by the forbidden complex of Children: Parents: Men-and-Women-in-general. And her memories going back to before she was ever a social worker, she began to chatter about the time when she was a salesgirl in the book department of Eliphaz's department store. Suddenly she had a fit of wild laughter. It seems this man came in to buy a present for his girl friend. "What kind of girl is she?" asked Miss Pitcher. "What kind of books does she read?"

"We hardly ever talk about books."

"Does she like adventure?"

"O Lord, no!" he cried, "she only likes friction."

12. The Prophecy of Eliphaz

Mynheer was fairly happy, for the scene was well enough. It was well enough for a country scene. And he drank a glass with the rest of us.

"But now, brother," he said to Horatio, "you are not in it. Do not lie to us, do not spare us. You are not in it because you have spoken with the dead Eliphaz. What is it that he prophesied to us, with the unerring speech of the dead that cannot mislead us, until the forces of the past play themselves out to the bitter end?"

Horatio did not want to speak.

"Nevertheless, speak out, voice of Eliphaz!" said Mynheer confronting him. And Horatio was forced to speak.

"You are going to live in the Sociolatry," said the Voice of Eliphaz, "and there will be no new thing." Even as he said it, Horatio stared and trembled and his words fell upside down.

Our spokesman cried out ¡ǝɔɐǝԀ but the word fell upside down.

"Please," said the Voice, "in the time of Eliphaz there was a class war; but now throughout the land there will be peace and a harmonious organization. And millions will fall down on the streets of the Asphyxiation.

"Sociolatry is the period when the great society that has inherited itself from me will be organized for the good of all, and will coordinate unchanged its wonderful productive capacities to heighten continually the Standard of Living. You will buy many expensive things that you do not absolutely need. And millions will fall down on the streets of the Asphyxiation.

"Next, the great society will turn to assure the psychological well-being of most of its members. This is called 'the education for democracy in the conditions of mass industrialization.' This is the Sociolatry.

"It is the adjustment of the individual to a social role without releasing any new forces of nature. Everywhere there will be personal and public peace (except among the wild and crazy); nowhere will there be love or community. And millions will fall down on the streets of the Asphyxiation.

"Please, I am not speaking of a crude regimentation but of a conformity with universal tolerance and intelligent distinction as among the collegians at Yale. Each person will warrant individual attention, for there is a man fitted, with alterations, for every job.

"And out of California will come a race of vitaminized young giants, nourished on the juice of the orange. This youth will be expert in the wisdom of the East and West and immunized from thought by early acquaintance with the worst that the classics can tell us. Accustomed to success and without toughness but with plenty of the callousness that comes from fundamental ignorance. These will be the ministers of our collective democracy.

"If a man then chooses a wife, she must be screened by the company; is she such as will fit into his public relations and steady his career as a junior executive? This is literally having a man by the balls. And millions will fall down on the streets of the Asphyxiation.

"And because the productive machine is so efficient and cannot be put to any humane or magnificent use, there will be a great surplus of wealth and with this a distinction between soft or giveaway money and hard money that you work for. If a man has expended spirit and labor, he will be paid in a little bit of hard money. But if he appears as a personality on television, he will be given a lot of soft money. This will create confusion among young folk, who will not know what to aim at. (Hell they won't!)

"You will nowhere find a written declaration of this order, for no one in authority will be close enough to existent things to take a pen and sign his name. Everywhere, instead of having either government or anarchy, you will be faced by one anonymous front.

"Now these people will be impenetrable by any serious or comic word. Out of touch with their natures, they and their entertainers will see to it that nothing recalls them to themselves. Shall they not suddenly be taken by panic fright?"—

"Look to the lady!" cried Mynheer, for at this moment Laura, our Crown, uttered a low moan and fainted away. He caught her in his arms as she fell.

BOOK 3 THE DEAD OF SPRING

After a War

PART 1

Supposing that some one has often flown in his dreams and that at last, as soon as he dreams, he is conscious of the power and art of flying as his privilege and peculiarly enviable happiness; such a person who believes that on the slightest impulse he can actualize all sorts of curves and angles, who knows the sensation of a certain divine levity, an Upwards without effort or constraint, a Downwards without lowering—without trouble!—how could the man with such dream-experiences and dream-habits fail to find "happiness" differently colored and defined, even in his waking hours! How could he fail—to long *differently* for happiness?

—NIETZSCHE

Chapter 1 ▪ OUR MEETING, 1948

Levitation is His proof of love.
—JEAN

I.

We hold our meeting in a draughty room on Broadway and there is a picture of sweet old Prince Kropotkin on the wall.

Friends, we have reached the most beautiful part of our meeting: the impasse from which *nevertheless* we do not get up and leave. We are resting in this hell.

Problems for which no one can suggest anything practical. Jointly we cannot invent anything practical either; we have exhausted the strength of fraternity.

Look at us, disgusted or tired; the mouths of some are hanging loose, the lips of some are drawn tight. Minetta Tyler is rocking back and forth on the hind legs of her chair; she will fall. The afternoon is late—the lights are throwing weak spears.

The meeting is silent; *at last it can be silent.* Half a minute, a minute, two minutes: minutes of silence is a heavy silence at a social meeting; creeps round the ears, the hairs stand up, one looks at another in alarm. No use to attempt to say anything; that is, to draw apart our jaws as if to begin to attempt to say something. For we know one another well and know what each would say, and oh, each one knows that he is known; our fraternity is very deep and we have exhausted its inventiveness.

Five minutes of silence is less heavy than three; there is not the same embarrassment and alarm. One or two are even wearing a little private smile as if we are falling asleep.

Nevertheless (this is what makes the moment beautiful), we do not get up and leave one another, quit the meeting. Are we afraid, clinging to one another because the impasse—every problem, nothing practical—is unbearable and no one can bear it alone? No. For indeed alone one is not so clearly in the presence of the impasse; it is only together, when from many friends very well known nothing practical is forthcoming, that each one has a good awareness of the common impasse. Perhaps then we are clinging together just in order to have our impasse! No. We are not clinging to anything at all. We are staying on in loyalty to one another, in the jaws of an impasse.

Are we ashamed to admit failure? For it is shameful to fail, not to have something to say, something or other to say, in the face of perfectly definite problems, every problem. (We shall come to these problems immediately—no mystery about them—but I like to dwell a little just on this most beautiful moment of meetings, the impasse from which nevertheless, etc.) No, no, it is more simple. We are simply staying doggedly and loyally in our impasse. There is nowhere to go so interesting as sitting in our doggedness.

"How good and how pleasant is the sitting of brothers all together!" So says the Psalmist.

Lothar's mouth is terribly open, to the roots of the teeth in the gums. *He* is going to make a sound and break the silence.

The easy silence, the light silence, the silence like the May Day breeze come lightly not fitfully from where the sun is violent. In this breeze rocks crack and gape, not that any storm can overturn them, but the breeze nourishes the grass in the crevices. New life in the silence. Old institutions cannot contain the swelling, in the silence.

Creator breath, come.

Perhaps the little lady will not fall. On the contrary, the chair is balanced on its hind legs and she, poised in it, is wearing a little private smile as though she were asleep.

—The silent reappearance of the grass among the things that are on the earth! The green embodiment of fire, flickering, and will not be arrested, but is burning between stones. Rocks, stones upborne more lightly than a flying babe overhead shouting aloud, and the uncombed sun roaring. We have not had our satisfaction: what can finish this unfinished? Mourning labor can finish the unfinished! Great sobs and a long narrow look elsewhere, and the faith that we are inconsolable.

2. Hard Problems; Nothing Practical

The hard problem is—

That people do not live sensibly and this can be demonstrated by the most obvious evidence with regard to the most important matters; then finally certain friends have become convinced of it, yet when we ourselves try to live otherwise—for it is impossible to live in a way you are convinced is stupid and senseless—we find that the only practical things we have learned are just the ones we know to be stupid, senseless, calamitous.

Must we not say that we do not want to live otherwise or we would quite simply live otherwise, finding means? The hard problem is that we ourselves have become aware of this truth about ourselves. We are struck dumb.

Our spokesman cried out ¡ɯopǝǝɹℲ but the word fell upside down. We are frozen in criticism. It is impossible to have a formulation of freedom and at the same time to do a free deed. Must we not say that we have made a formulation of freedom in order to protect ourselves from the unformulable daring of doing a free deed? Yet how, in the face of the most obvious evidences of stupidity and slavery, is it possible to avoid hitting on a formulation of freedom? How not to dream it up? Is one to call the formulation of freedom a lie when it is not a lie, just because it does not give freedom, and even though it protects against freedom?

ɯopǝǝɹℲ is a hard problem.

Meantime the people of the world are destroying one another and are destroying also our friends. The hard problem is that no one can think of a means to prevent this destruction. Ah, are not we friends willing our own destruction? We have ground to a stop, and as the overwhelming approaches, we are doggedly staying and will not quit our meeting.

The hard problem is that we do know, by the simplest reasoning from the most obvious evidences, how everyone could easily live well. But this has long been known and eloquently told. The knowledge of it has not made any difference. Yet what is there to exchange at a meeting of minds, except knowledge?

We need an impulse of the limbs! But whatever motion occurs to us to make is senseless. Therefore, we are poised on chairs and are beginning to wear little private smiles.

The hard problem is this: that the sensible impulse must come from our vital desire, but we do not feel our vital desire. But at least we know we do not feel it; we are in an impasse. Meanwhile the overwhelming destruction is heading toward us one and all.

And why don't we feel at least the animal terror of the destruction overwhelming toward us one and all; and flee with cries of fright? This would be at least a vital impulse of our limbs! And not *altogether* senseless, stupid, calamitous!

3.

With a mournful shriek Lothair has broken the silence, saying, "Aaiiiiy!" Wailing, "Auuuuuuuw!" and "Oo-ooh."

These are not bestial cries, nor are they human cries in extremity, like the cry of Emily when the tiger slew her boy and the curator, unused to the unlimited, was momentarily brought to a pause. But Lothair's are the cries of a human person who feels in himself a woeful pang that is his own and yet is alien to what he thought to be his. Then it speaks itself, he speaks it, but he cuts it off at the end of the scream, to limit it. Thus, Lothair has cut off the high shriek with a *y,* and he has closed the middle wail with a *w.* The low moan rose softer from his throat, but he has expelled the last of it with an *h.*

Perhaps if he were alone he would not seek to limit these alien speeches; but he is at a social meeting and he must stay within the possibilities of communication. The possibility of communication is saved by the *y,* the *w,* and the little breath *h.* This is how it is with us—this is called "talking politics."

He has not finished; he says a terrible scream, mixing all vowels; but this too he contrives—to limit—with—a—long—sigh, lightly touching all the vowels, in decent order, to the gulph. This is called "assuming one's adult responsibilities."

Gripping the table, but not in the ecstasy with which he broke the warden's table in two pieces, but as if in self-loathing and to keep from falling, Lothair says, "Friends, I—you too—we have been passionate inventors of Utopian schemes; we have analyzed the powers of man and we have vividly described Paradise. We know the topology of the nonexistent Paradise, how the four icy rivers underground water the roots of the Tree of Life; and oh, in the future to come, men will suck nourishing milk and also, as the prophet says, look with abhorrence at the carcasses. Such things in a dreamy way. But besides, I have scrupulously studied the most obvious evidences in the most important social matters, and I have invented sensible arrangements that almost have the look of practicality: where to locate industries, *how* are men to work with heart, head and hand. Et cetera. Et cetera. *Et cetera!* Do you know what?"

His hands have begun to tremble.

"I'll tell you what! Suddenly a voice has whispered to me that I occupy myself with these schemes of happiness in order not to notice that I am suffering from a toothache. O-o!"

He is about to shriek again; but as if to distract him his friend Henry Faust says, "A voice? What voice, Lothair? Do you hear voices?"

"A voice suggests to me what I did not know I knew. One time it whispered, 'Let the animals out of their cages.' And this time it has whispered, 'Ouch!' "

The wood is cracking in the table.

Lothair says, "Instead of the formulas of Paradise I cannot think about anything but my aching teeth. Ee. Ao." He is whimpering and groaning.

There is a general vibration, rumbling.

"Eee. Ugh. Aou."

The picture of the amiable geographer falls from the wall.

Looking away from the wildly shaking grip of Lothar, some of us look at our own calm hands, holding them up before us, with their ten digits as ordained long since, not by either the sensible or senseless institutions of mankind.

4. Theory of the Fertile Void

The old man Gonzalez hovers at the fringe of our meeting; his face is concerned at our despair and crinkles with laughter at our jokes; and he carries himself with an alert confidence, apparently without a cause. What, I wonder, is *his* confidence, exiled from Barcelona? Alas, *we* are his confidence. . . .

"Hard problems; nothing practical"—oh, if we friends *remain* in our impasse, close to our impasse, gratuitously suffering the awareness of being in an impasse, must not the Fertile Void yield up something? Gratuitous effort *must* lead to something unlooked-for. True, this theory of the Fertile Void is a reaction to heartache (just as Lothair reacts to his toothache by thinking up formulas of Paradise). But the Fertile Void is the soul-ache itself: it is the awareness that one is very unhappy and *cannot* any more. Thus it is the truest possible theory, for further than the soul-ache is to become happy in fact and then there is no more theorizing. (There is no true *theory*.) Please! Let me develop this truest possible theory:

Each time one diminishes error there is an increment of love. Now we friends, by following the most obvious evidences in the most important instances, have freed ourselves and one another from many important errors; there must be to our advantage large increments of love. But we have seen that this energy of love does not appear, because we remain in our impasse. What has happened to this released love?

It is not in our minds, because we have diminished error, and whatever is in the mind is an error.

The love is boiling in the Fertile Void; it is souring and fermenting there. The Void must yield up an homunculus. (All this is occurring in the dark, on the yonder side of impasse.) Void! Yield up the homunculus!

This then is the theory of the relation of the impasse and the Fertile Void: *diminishing error but remaining close in the aware-*

ness of the impasse of nothing practical, large increments of love are released that are fermenting in the Fertile Void.

The old man Gonzalez, hovering at the fringe of the meetings, indeed never seems to leave the hall; he is the custodian and librarian. He does not put himself forward to speak, but often mutters in a low voice, "Young people have come!" This is his touching confidence. He is radiant with faith because Minetta has a baby. But sometimes we question him point-blank, "What do *you* think, Gonzalez?" Then he talks up and says nothing concrete to the point, but he declaims, even for a long speech, enthusiastic generalities. Perhaps he seems today to be less at an impasse than the others because he is used to being in an impasse. You will not meet a sweeter old man than this long-time awareness that he is in an impasse. He plucks at your sleeve to show you a book of poems by a Mexican comrade. And stands back, smiling eagerly, with the *cortesía* of an eager servant, which we cannot match with corresponding nobility. He has patience.

Patience. The true patience is to relax and draw on the underlying forces. Then all things spring into being from the Fertile Void. For an instant one can notice it boiling, hissing and bubbling. We do not have the best patience, but a good enough patience: compelled to be patient by diminishing error and being in an impasse. There is an instant in which one does not notice anything.

5.

Will be an instant in which we do not notice anything.

Even before Horatio comes flying into the hall, some of us will have been levitating without knowing it. For it will not be any one person to bring these things about.

Balanced on the hind legs of her chair, Minetta will be comfortably smiling but not at all drifting asleep; on the contrary, her eyes wide, studying the eggs and darts of the tin ceiling. But she will not notice that she is floating an inch above the chair. How to notice it, poised on a quietly balanced chair?

Yet surely we might notice that old Gonzalez is four, five, six inches from the floor—high, higher than he is used. But he is so eagerly courteous, himself unconscious of himself.

Besides Lothair, who cannot levitate, distracts us by shaking the world with his wild grip. The plaster will be falling from the walls.

The young man Horatio will fly up the stairs and glide into the hall, and pause in mid-air in the rear near the cookstove, to look and get a sense of the meeting. Dressed in a wool sweater of deep crimson and in dark jeans. (These colors, of blood and navy, are important, but I do not know what they signify.) By "fly" and "glide" I mean he will come breast-forward, softly soaring—so far as one can make out, the motion of the arms is irrelevant to the progress.

This is not the only gait. Gonzalez, who is always pleased to see the young folk and especially Horatio, will lightly, lightly, lightly, softly, bound, bound somewhat like hurdling on the moon, over the table, to Horatio in the back. This soft leap, and the sight of Horatio floating in mid-air, the two of them there, these will make every one notice how it is.

That Minetta will be hovering a good yard above the chair, that has regained its four legs with a little tap. Flat on her back, rather stiffly, but fluttering loose.

The young man lying breast-forward, crimson and blue in the middle-air, and silvery Gonzalez showing, leaves open, the book of the Mexican comrade. Horatio's right hand, absent the tip of the little finger, resting familiarly on Gonzalez' sleeve.

Dave, the electrician, will glide from his place to hang the picture of Kropotkin back on the wall, for the vibration has ceased.

Will it have ceased? "I can't lift myself!" cries Lothair.

"If you'd let go that oaken table you could lift yourself!"

"No, no!" he cries. It is as if he must lift not only himself but the oaken table, the building, the Empire City—et cetera, et cetera! —all at once.

"Your stomach muscles are tight," says the doctor. "Look there under the table, legs rigid and toes pointed. Neck thrust forward. Heavens, man! Softly, softly. What are you holding your breath for?"

Lothair will begin to sob convulsively and then weep boiling tears. Very good. He is still unable to levitate, but it is enough to be able at least freely to cry. This is what we mean by "good," what is liberating and healthful. The happy act itself is not good, it is not desired; it is so; it is not much talked about, there is little need for a word for it; it is perhaps recognized with a small smile, to show acquaintance. But these bitter boiling tears are good, and Lothair will feel them flowing joyously down his desert face, like the cooling rain.

The Fertile Void is yielding up its wonders one by one, mouth-aches and growling rage, and a flood of boiling tears. Do you know?

—Do you know? I for my part am a great one for saying "because," "because therefore," "if and then," "thus and so"; I am a great one for finding the word, precisely the word for the act. If I could leave off saying this "because" and finding precisely the word, maybe then I too could come to weep boiling tears. But I am afraid.

Droyt and Lefty will flit out the window, curious to experiment. Lefty will duck in through the other window. Droyt will continue down over the town. Levitant rapidly over the streets of the Empire City. One is never far from water, the rivers and the bays. Children are playing on the shores, throwing in boards with a splash, but it is still too cold to swim. Droyt will fall and bruise himself. "You can fall," he'll say, "you can fall doing this, like anything else."

Not all at the meeting will levitate, not even a majority. Yet a good number, at various elevations in the hall, like figures in a crowd on a fresco. Next moment they have all sat down again.

"I'm not sure I see what important difference it makes," says Henry Faust (cannot levitate).

"It's obvious!" Lothario will cry (also cannot levitate).

"How to put it?" says a levitator. "It takes a weight off your shoulders."

"There was an instant in which you didn't notice anything. Is that the moment that must be reached?"

"Oh no!" cries Horatio. "Not necessarily. You know me, I notice everything. This is the way it was in my case: Suddenly I got dizzy and was rotated forward, two three four times, I counted, head under heels—coming up again, whoosh. Then I could go through the air."

"Be careful. You can fall, just like with everything else," says Droyt, who has become a most circumspect youth. "I was sailing along and then I noticed the emptiness underneath me, the space between me and the ground. It looked like everything around was rushing to fill up the hole, and I went down. I could hardly limp home. It's a poor way to get about if you're subject to dizzy spells."

"When I say it takes a weight off your shoulders, please take me lightly, that is seriously. This feeling is the important thing—that's the important difference it makes, Henry. To be able to stand lightly on the ground, not as if you were wresting with gravity. The levitation itself is probably trivial, but believe me, it's something to be able to stand lightly on the ground, and breathe lightly, without fighting to keep upright. I mean to be able just to reach out your hand without having to overcome invisible obstacles."

All, whether we can levitate or not, will feel the animal terror of the destruction overwhelming toward us; and we'll flee with cries of fright. But this takes only a moment—it is an intermission. For now there are many practical ways, will come to hand, to mind. "But softly, softly."

"Teach me to fly!"

"Certainly. But why are you holding your breath. And remember, it's not flying. You must not try that way. It has nothing to do with threshing the air—it's down here, and up! Softly, heh?"

Softly. There are many practical ways.

It's not in itself good. It is so. It's not much talked about.

Perhaps (not sure) there is an instant when you don't notice anything.

But these bitter boiling tears are *good.* See Lothair's, flowing joyously down his hot face, and he says, "Creator Spirit, come! Make thou me new."

It is so, yet even so one does not necessarily notice how it is, till the youth in blue and crimson comes flying up the stairs, and pauses in middle-air. *Blessed* is he who comes.

6. Emilia's Grace

The table set and the meal served as usual, Emilia will say grace.

She standing grandly lightly on the ground, who used to loom, kneeling with her child, like the black stone colossus of Memphis; until the animal had eaten of him. "Friends, let us say grace.

"This food is given to us, only somewhat made by us. Turn your attention to this in thanksgiving.

"It is useful to be precise. Surely the food is made by us, Dorothy Rogers cooked it; let's sit sociably down to it. Also, the meat and greens are sent from Holley's farm and are therefore made by us. And even this tasteless bread, ground out, baked and packaged by Lord knows what men and machines, is our share in the general work—I admit I could eat it with better gusto if I had watched it rise and brown and it had some taste; let that pass.

"But the food is given to us and not made by us. Sprang from earth, air, water and fire in the round of the winter, spring, summer and fall. The season of the world has rolled around again to May Day. Planted, fattened, reaped and slain at the right conjunctions of the earth and stars; I don't know about these things, but farmers make probable calculations and have faith in a reward.

"Look, a live animal has been killed for our meal. Let the one who is afraid to look, who is squeamish, let him not eat here yet, forcing himself to keep it down. A dead animal. We are in a continuum of life and desire with these animals. Does it follow not to eat them? No, sometimes savagely to bare our teeth, as they do. (You know how once I saw the tables turned, and the animal eat the tender man; let that pass.) If there is anyone who has not confronted himself vividly with the truth that an animal has been killed for us to eat, if anyone drives it from his mind and has not conjured with the terror of it, he ought not callously to eat the good flesh; he will not frankly chew it and he will not well digest it. That goes for you, Lothar, you savage man.

"Food, my father used to quote the saying, is what is unlike and can become like. Bite it off, chew it and destroy its unlikeness. Taste its likeness (the good taste is the sign that it can be like ourselves). This is practical thanksgiving. Don't swallow a tiny morsel undestroyed; but all mixed with saliva, swallow it like mother's milk."

For Steve Zoll

Chapter 2 • A BROADWAY CROWD

Longing *differently* for happiness, Horatio has left our meeting that he knows too well, and has come out on busy Broadway where people are bound, in every direction, on their errands; and he too, all unconsciously, hitches up his trousers.

"Horace," says he to himself, "let's go! For *you* to long differently for happiness is to try, for a change, to behave just the same as everybody else. What could be easier? Examples everywhere! And there's every kind of opportunity for ordinary people to behave just as they behave. You've got it made! So why don't you go get yourself a nice job (you like to work and you don't care about the wages), and get yourself a wife (you're an affectionate fellow), and have some kids (you like kids)?"

Having impulsively said this to himself, he stops to think it over. It makes *sense.* He *does* like to work and doesn't care about the wages; he *is* an affectionate fellow; and he likes kids. And having thought it over—he's not one for long reflections—he now consciously hitches up his trousers and says, "Agreed! Those people have the right of it!" He is ready.

—And alas! He is in America in the middle of the twentieth century, and everywhere he looks up and down Broadway he sees Americans, going their American errands, and he himself standing there is an American—frozen in dismay, with an immobility that spreads from the nape of his neck between his shoulder blades, and that he feels as the unbreakable grip of cowardice; his bowels feel loose.

But if you look at him, you see that he is standing there solidly astride with his own fists clenched. As if he has one in each paw by the scruff, but he has become confused.

—Next moment he has childishly put his pinkie in his mouth and is sucking on the absence of the finger tip, while the Broadway crowd is jostling past him in every direction.

"Make a little effort, Horatio. Do." (Perhaps it is his sister's voice.)

"I can't," he says candidly. "I'm a coward."

"You mean, you won't?" asks the Voice gently.

"No, I'm not grudging. Simply, if I make an effort here I have to accept our total loss of paradise."

"And couldn't you make a little effort *to* accept a total loss?" The Voice that says this is, oh, gentle and winning.

"That's a new thought! To make an *effort* to accept the loss!" Horatio spreads wide his hands in surprise. "I never thought of that, thinking only of flying. O wise Voice, I shall do what you advise."

But it is hard for him to forsake his innocence, and, as the grip relaxes at the nape of his neck, the man is swept from foot to head by woe. By woe; remorseful for his treachery; stabbed by grief for his country.

This has been a short chapter, of Horatio longing *differently* for happiness.

Chapter 3 ▪ ON THE SHORE

Sublimi feriam sidera vertice.
—HORACE

1.

Now Harry and Minetta Tyler have a little girl Joan, and on the littered beach toward which the silent comber curls from end to end of the world: the sheet of surface water streams over the black mountain of the swell (a dogfish looks out in the streaming); and breaks, and the ebb leaps up against the flow, the "ignorant armies that clash by night"; little Joan is playing in the face of it, piling up wood cast by the sea.

The child is too young to be building a house. She is two years old. She is just heaping the pieces, a big one dragged with effort, leaning some against that, laying some across others, balancing the next one with care, just dropping the next one into the pile. Perhaps there is no image or imitation, and she is not properly playing at all, but exploring, touching, gathering, hauling, placing. A greater wave rushes up.

Joan retreats with a cry of fright; her shoes are soaked.

The pieces are scattered. The big one is near buried in the silt. Black pieces are whirling in the foam.

She tries to recapture a piece but it eludes her, cleverly speeding away as she comes near, but floating quietly where it is too deep for her to go.

The near-buried board is too heavy to tear free; it will not give in to her. Vainly tugging. She drags over another big one, perhaps not so great and beautiful. There are now two principles, side by side. A transverse of leans and bridges and balances. Very soon, for the tide is coming in, another great wave rushes up and destroys it.

Now she is wet and uncomfortable. The wetting makes her urinate.

The structure has been scattered and shattered. The big board is no longer visible at all; one cannot tell whether or not it lies there buried in the silt. *Where* was the place? The other one has been left lying by the ebb, but just as she reaches it, a quick small wave swirls round her legs.

The pieces are being carried away by the incoming tide, fleeing on the quick waves. They leap up in the froth where the ebb meets the flow; they vanish in the vortex and one cannot follow their fate.

Where is the place? If she would want to try again, there is no sign where the big board is buried.

She stiffens; she is easily frustrated. Her fists are clenched, lower lip drawn in and bitten; she is trembling with rage, like a tight spring or taut wire that you would soon expect to sound a low tone. No sound escapes from her throat. She is holding her breath and reddening. Perhaps she is quickly frustrated because she sees the idea of it: a wave will come again, they are regularly coming, round her ankles. She is too enraged to retreat with a cry.

A black stick vanishes in the whirl; it reappears swimming in the green lace of the swell; it sticks up its point.

Why is she suddenly laughing, happy, and jumping for joy, as if she had been holding her breath, red in the face, only to release it in pleasure?

Because they have a life of their own, a motion of their own; because it has a power of its own, a will of its own. The sticks have a way that they will go, and the water has a game that it will play. They are livelier mates than if they let themselves submit to her arbitrary plan, not even plan, an exploration, hauling, gathering, heaping.

Lightly she collects a few small sticks and constructs them directly where the next wave will surely scatter and shatter the structure, and drag back the sticks into the sea. And so it does—it does not fail. She claps her hands. This is hilarious. The wave comes with a rush and all the sticks are carried away. Not one is left next to another. A surprising wave from the side makes her howl with glee. They are reappearing in the froth of the conflicting ebb and flow. The sticks leap up out of the water, it is their will. The ocean whirls them and ducks them; it is his (her?) power. She clutches at a stick but it eludes her and flees; he is too quick and clever. She clutches at the water. She grabs another stick that was not expecting her to turn so lightly on him; and she brandishes it and hurls it into the retreating wave.

The wave has retreated too rapidly. The stick is lying gasping on the streaming sand. The next little wave lifts it and bears it further inshore and drops it.

Sometimes the sea is using its power to cast these things ashore. The child can play as a rival in that game. She runs from place to place picking up sticks, and throws them into the sea, into the advancing wave, *at* the advancing wave. Some disappear, others return, still new ones appear. The sea does not tire of the activity. In her excitement, the child misses a stick, drops it when throwing it; it has a life of its own.

The sea is using the power to drag the sticks, the willing ones, the unwilling ones, out to sea. She can *help* in this, hauling loose a big board half-buried in the silt, launching it into the wave.

This other block she carries far ashore, where the water cannot reach. It is hers. It has a rusted iron bolt in it. It is from a ship. She is soaking wet, her clothes, her hair, the water streaming from her ears and eyes; she is not uncomfortable.

Meantime the sea is descending his tons of water down, from end to end of the world. There is never silence. The child looks back in anticipation——

Frightful. The child is screaming piercing cries of terror. For the monster of the deep, the monster of Loch Ness, is advancing toward her onto the shore. He has emerged from his knees, he is walking on dry land. The dragon that curls headlong from the midriff down to the genitals, spitting out smoke and flames and devouring the heavens and the earth. He is shaking the earth with his tread.

The child is screaming again and again. Harry Tyler, who has been swimming in the breakers and keeping an eye on his little daughter, is hurrying anxiously across the beach, oozing from his red hair. "What's the matter now, little Joannie?" running to pick her up. He does not know that *he* is the monster of Loch Ness.

She screams piercing terror because he is at hand; she lets herself be picked up and consoled because it is her dear papa. She screams as if she would never stop; there are intervening gasping sobs of release.

The end of the world is at hand.

It has a motion of its own! The sticks have a gravity of their own!

"Don't cry, little Joannie. Daddy's here. He'll take care of you. There's nothing the matter. What hurt you?"

He does not realize that he is the monster of the deep.

Little Joan will be happy forever and never frustrated again, to hold her breath with rage at the crosses of the world; because the fact is that they have a life, a weight, a motion, a will, a power of their own. She can play with this power, against this power. These playmates do not tire. This is hilarious.

She is sobbing bitterly and quietly.

Meantime the ocean is pounding down his tons and tons. There is never a moment of silence. The hissing and shrieking is the collision of the ebb and flow, leaps up. The lacy sheets of surface stream on the mountains of swell, and a dogfish is looking out through the curtains.

2. Mynheer's Valedictory to Man

Piet Duyck Colijn & Duyvendak van der Meer comes from among the dunes. Sand in his hair, in his eyelashes, mixed with the saliva on his chin, as if he had been sleeping there. Not possessed enough of himself to brush himself clean. The tears of sorrow are streaming down his dirty cheeks; his intellectual countenance is opened with grief.

He has seen a vision, or dreamed it; it is no longer sure to him what is a dream and what is waking reality.

The grownup is crying, little Joan hushes herself in awe and curiosity. Her father does not set her down; though astonished he says nothing, but he lays his right arm round Piet Duyck's shoulders. It is new to him to see such sorrow, and he cannot think what could bring this man to this dismay.

Duyck neither rejects the friendly embrace nor smiles wanly acknowledging it, nor again redoubles his grief, nor is comforted any; but his mature tears flow on; still, he is not shaken by orgastic sobs, but as if another thought brings new tears, and there is always another thought.

"I won't ask you what's the matter, friend," says Harry Tyler, "because I know you and I know it is badly the matter if Piet Duyck is crying; worse than I or you can cope with. So you'll have to go on crying till there's no more. No help for it. But please, allow me, let me wipe the sand from your face and brush it out of your hair. Close your eyes."

Mynheer closes his eyes, and the sailor performs this office for him, of wiping his face and brushing off his clothes. The child, still on her father's left arm, looks on solemnly.

His eyes shut, Mynheer sees nothing but the darkness. Owai! But it was from just such total eclipse that the bad vision first rose in view.

Facing eastward over the ocean, the beginning of May, in the first hours after midnight, when the high spirits have sunk to their lowest, he opened his eyes and expected to see again Pegasus bounding from the horizon as he does in that place at that hour of that night. The dunes lurked in their darkness, as usual. The long comber shone in a few points of starshine. At hand the point of a blade of dune grass drew an accurate circle in the sand. In the soft breeze.

The constellation that arose, that began to arise, was not the winged inspiration mounting with his slow bound. It was something new, not seen before.

It was Man. The constellation *Man* appeared on the horizon, and slowly as the hour passed reared to his full height.*

* So Parker saw it.

Mynheer's jaw hung down and he looked there with startling eyes; and when the stars were all displayed (only a few) he began to weep and could not stop.

For what is raised as a constellation of stars into the macrocosm is something that will not change (such as it is). What is in the stars is no more on earth. It is the immortal death in the soul we project in abstractions that imitate, by their abstractness, the nonexistence of that which is. Then good-by.

Good-by to the race of animals that invented half a dozen ways of making fire; and by flags and flashing mirrors, smoke and radio waves signaled across vast distances. Who accumulated the records of their litigation in volumes of the Common Law. Good-by.

Good-by to the kind that proved again and again that songs of the throat can fall heavy with heart, subtiler than swords, breathing also courage and ambiguous with anguish: who would have thought it was possible if Man did not prove it so in act? Good-by to dancers, used to dance, lightly imitating the inward in outward motions of the limbs and recreating the world in double and triple time. Good-by to one certain gloomy beast who carved the unfinished in rocks.

For if it is the valedictory of Man that flows and leaps in his mind, there is matter for Mynheer to weep for a long time, well into the dawn, and after that—as now he thinks of kinds and classes of men and now of this man or that man.

Good-by to those who used to cut and polish little stones for prismatic lights, and measure the rainbows. To those others who by addition combined small pieces of iron and stone into immense bridges and towers. Good-by to the kinds of men characterized by city names, Florentines, Ninevites, New Yorkers. Good-by to the inventors of ingenious machines who in illiberal times still found objects for their busy wits. Good-by to intrepid sailors led on and on when they were afraid: it is not the case that one would have expected this until the Man proved it in act. Good-by to those who suggested to themselves to be disgusted with such and such good meat, and those who used to make boundaries and cower on one side of the boundary they themselves made. Also, good-by to the poet of *Manfred.*

—Do not misunderstand; it is not I who am weeping or pretending to weep, for I am rather filled with hate and resentment of men. But Mynheer, the intellect, is weeping at every thought. And he can not dam such a flood of tears by nice distinctions of good and bad, sensible or senseless—rather that this race of animals was so, this was how it was.

He will not exhaust his mournful thoughts, for almost everything one thinks of is Man, of Man, by Man, etc. Even so the indefinite series can be summed up briefly as a few stars in the macrocosm.

Good-by to the famous pairs and triangles of lovers and the solitary unloved lovers; and to the lovers and loveless nameless, that one used to pass by in parks—these all transforming lust in ways that one would not have counted on. Good-by to those sage or mad in peculiarly human ways. Also to those specifically malevolent and destructive, torturers and self-tortured, as only this race was able: and now afterward the thought of them is shining lovely enough. (But it was not by signal malevolence that Man ceased to exist. Well! Good-by also to the stupid ones characteristically human, who used not to know enough to come in out of the rain.) Good-by to the knightly heroes. Good-by to the Master of the Way, who lay seventy years in the womb in order to show what it was to be full-formed a Man before submitting to the accidents of the world.

This had a nature, like any other animal race; but it was not easy to guess at that human nature till one saw it realized, in history, in its acts: that it could harmonize three or four voices musicianly (the child's voice leading the melos), and grapple ships in a naval war. Good-by to the ignorant armies that clashed by night on the plain. To the human young that used to have for a few years such astonishing curiosity. And to the eccentric ones with punch-drunk eyes, like trumpeters of the Salvation Army. The race that wore a variety of hats.

Good-by to Jean and Franz and Paul Klee: it is not from some other seed of life the like will be produced (improbable enough as it was). Good-by who rode horses as part of their bodies like Centaurs, and drove cars as if they were born shod with metal wheels.

Human reader! It's not I who am pretending to weep (rather I'm hateful and resentful); but it's Mynheer who is mourning the thought of every formative spirit that made him a man, such as it is: if Man ceased to be. Picture it to yourself and tell it over; if man ceased to be.

Good-by! Good-by to gamblers who risked fortune on the turn of a card. Good-by to ballplayers. Good-by to devoted women who tried to make sorrowful men happy, and also to the Philistine who robbed her husband of his strength.

For when such a flood of tears is once let loose, one does not make nice distinctions of good and bad, friendly and hateful, clever and stupid; but it is all one race that is lost; it was so; that was how it was. Good-by.

The thought of this kind and that kind, of this man and that man, occurs to him and makes Mynheer's tears flow; and it seems that he will never be able to stop crying over the lapse and ending of Man (that we others, full of hatred and resentment, think of lightly enough; but do you picture what it means, and tell it over, the End of Man?).

It is Man who is wont to project the immortal death in the soul as an abstraction that imitates, by its abstractness, the nonexistence of that which is. And there he is, rising, a constellation in the Great Cosmos.

3.

Nevertheless, when Harry Tyler has performed for him the office of wiping his sand-caked face and brushing off his clothes, Piet Duyck stops crying.

He says in an iron voice, but low not loud, "These people are demented. This is the plainest, broadest evidence. Any discussion of society that fails to keep this important probability in the center is simply stupid."

"Is this news? Is this what you were crying about?"

"This? Not at all. I can talk about this without crying a drop, just hardening my voice and keep it low."

"What would happen if you spoke louder? I can hardly hear you."

"Louder?" He says it louder, experimentally. "I fly into a rage."

"Is that bad, Piet Duyck?"

"It's stupid. Some persons try to speak up about changing something, changing economic institutions, reforming morals, or laying down weapons; they do not understand that they are talking to people who are demented. This proves that they themselves are demented. Stupid."

"You haven't had breakfast."

"Look here," says the Dutchman in a rasping voice. "An animal that does not move directly toward its chief desires—safety, sexual pleasure, exploration—is demented. (I'm not hungry, I'll eat after a while.) Suppose there are obstacles: then they do not move as directly as possible to circumvent or destroy the obstacles. This is to be simply demented. In fact, long ago they have forgotten what their chief desires are; and they construct and encourage and submit to obstacles in order to distract themselves from remembering what their desires are. Then here comes some fool and proves to them, by the plainest demonstration from the most obvious evidence, that they are acting against their own welfare. Naturally they turn a deaf ear. They are *quite* demented. Obviously he is demented." His voice is like an iron file.

"Was it always like this?"

"There was always a disposition to it, or it could not have come to be as it has. But it's recently that this rational social animal has rapidly degenerated to the present ludicrous exhibition of itself. It's a joke. Ha, ha!"

The child looks at him in hatred, for he is not pleasant when he laughs.

"The pathology has had three, four, five stages, worse and worse, quicker and quicker." And on his fingers, Mynheer is ticking off the modern Degeneration of Mankind.

"First, the man was frustrated in simple animal desires, kept in bounds and corporally punished; he became sick with fixation on certain childish pleasures and gluttony and believing various superstitions. The luxuries, vanities and fables of courts and churches. The philosophers of that time saw how it was and they prescribed pure reason and the sentiments of the heart to win him back to humanity. I am thinking of Kant and Rousseau."

But as he thinks of these names, Mynheer begins to weep again.

"What is the second stage?"

"The man did not follow the easy prescription! (This proves that the philosophers were stupid and missed the point.) The disease went underground and got worse. Next we find the man in the throes of rebelliousness, rebelling against oppressive institutions; the simple feelings already forgotten. Then the good philosophers prescribed brotherly union against the irrational authorities: 1848."

But as he thinks of this human year, a great flood of tears drowns Mynheer's eyes, and he sees the sea and sand and brilliant stars.

"Aach! The man disregarded this prescription too! No use to think of it. When we look at him again, three or four generations later, he's a strange one: docile, hard-working at mechanical tasks, hopeful in the progress of a higher standard of living, and really quite incurious of any serious thought or feeling. What an astounding time; it was the time that formed my own childhood. And do you know what the philosophers of that time prescribed to win him back to humanity? True sciences! Technical training in the arts—to make the forlorn creature be again a little at home in the world, I guess."

He does not weep, but only heaves a sigh as he thinks of the ninth edition of the *Encyclopedia Britannica.*

"Even this ludicrous prescription was disregarded. And now it is too late, we have to do with a full-grown neurotic, alienated from both himself and the world; no love, anger or curiosity. A good citizen, obsessively orderly, a union member, a willingly conscripted soldier. What he wants, where he is, what he is doing there—all this is hopelessly forgotten. There is nothing for it (and this is what the good doctors prescribe) but to analyze his dreams, to talk about leaping shadows, to try to surprise a little vitality where no vitality seems to be. This curious kind of man, who does not believe in the existence of that which indeed exists—namely, his body, his desires, his friends and his enemies—he has come to believe in the existence of things that do not exist, for instance benevolent Agencies with names, and democratic Ways, and undemocratic Ways."

It may be hard to credit, but even these human things wring a tear from Mynheer's intellectual heart.

"All right!" he cries, and he lets his voice rise a little louder. "They are disregarding the psychoanalytic prescription too. What's *next?* For it's impossible to trace such a series of pathology without prognosis of the next stage. I'll tell you what. Fully developed catatonic rigidity! Maniac fits! Hallucinations! (Yes, I just had an hallucination, and now I'm becoming angry.) How is this maniac to be handled? He must be handled (with care) with shock treatments. Good, good! Now it will work. They won't disregard this prescription. They'll get their shock. Urged on by a dumb instinct of life that they do not feel, they'll hit on the right therapy—alas, unskillfully.

"And the constellation Man will rise in the heavens, above the horizon, at two in the morning, at the beginning of May—when the spirits have been highest and have sunk their worst ebb. So. So."

He is *flying* into a speechless rage. Will he take off? Having ticked off all five fingers, he is wildly shaking his fist.

4.

But the child, who has sharp eyes, will see an exciting sight and, jumping down from Harry's arm, dance excitedly down toward the shore pointing skyward. "Look *there!*" She'll be the first to notice them.

Coming as two dark spots in the far blue. Gulls? Rapidly nearer, in good order, abreast; looming big as a man's hands. Droyt and Lefty.

Now when they see from the excited motions on the beach, and hear the distant calls, that they have been recognized, the two lads won't descend at once. They'll show off.

Staying aloft in the blue, lightly touching their fingertips, they'll dance the aerial dance that means nothing at all.

Caracoling——

As the atonal music floats free in the tonal space, returning only to its own figures, this dance moves in the six directions, not ordered to falling or keeping from falling. Since they are showing off they are ordered to the audience in front, but they soon forget this and dance freely ordered only to each other. They join hands and will mount.

Suddenly Lefty's hat, ornamented with paper clips, comically drops through space; but he'll be down after it and fish it out of the waves. "Careful, you damned fool!" Mynheer will mutter in his fatherly heart; they can levitate but they can also break their fool necks. But now laughing they'll be wheeling in a great circle tumbling clumsily along like clods of earth, as if they hardly knew how to levitate at all.

The Right Hand and the Left Hand in the near sky-ground touching their finger tips. These beautiful brothers alike and different. Nothing is so skillful as young lads who have learned a new way of skating and are inspired to show off. Two more beautiful than one, for they rely on and are proud of each other. Such performances are so fair that they hurt one's heart.

What does it mean, will it mean, the aerial dance of Droyt and Lefty over the waves?

Nothing, nothing, nothing, nothing. It is the exuberant decoration, the happy art. Will mean nothing, nothing at all. Simply that there is a new heaven and a new earth. What will be the use of attaching a meaning? We attach meanings only when we are faced with hard problems and nothing more practical occurs to us. The small child understands the meaning of it very well. She is rolling on the sand, beside herself. The comber is curling from end to end of the world.

Oh. Droyt is climbing to a fearful height. Lefty will defer to his more daring brother, fall back, call attention to the feat. Oh—the big lad has cast off his power to soar; he is diving! He hits the water with a noise like the crack of a rifle.

He'll be all right, swimming slowly ashore, now dragging himself through the breakers, while Lefty stays close above him. They touch land at the same moment.

Curious company we keep on the beach. The Loch Ness monster and the child who has seen the Loch Ness monster, and the man who saw the constellation Man rise above the horizon. Etc., etc. This is how it is with us.

The two will tell Mynheer the news, how some of the friends can levitate (they'll call it simply "flying").

He'll question them closely enough: who? where? since when? under what circumstances? But he'll say in the end, "Well, it's the kind of thing that's not for me—I'm not the type, a little heavy. Show me once, hey?"

"Like this!" cries Lefty, and he'll rise six feet in the air, smiling, as only he can smile softly. "You do it from about here."

"Ah, so." The fact is that Mynheer can do anything, anything at all; and no doubt that he will also be able to levitate.

Chapter 4 ▪ A COMMUNITY OF HUMAN RELATIONS

> "You see a guy is going to cut your throat, you keep out of his way. That's right."
> "Naa! You cut his throat before he cuts yours."
>
> —West 38th St. Pier

> The intention of the building-sacrifice was to create spirits, to make a beginning.
>
> —Rank (after Kleinpaul)

1.

Lothair and Emilia were now man and wife, but they were not blessed with children, whether she was barren or he impotent or that together they could not generate a child. Together, in the world as it was, they were physically, psychologically, socially and metaphysically incapable.

They were physically incapable because they did not copulate. And inasmuch as they wanted above all things to have a child, a child to endure *for* them as they staggered toward their deaths in the storm of hours thick and fast, they were saddened not to apply themselves. Untwining themselves from the entwined wreath of praise.

But Emily was emotionally barren because of the living horror in her of the moment when the tiger slew her child and she cried out; this horror indignantly rejected the seed of the maniac who had let the beast out of the cage (nor would it have accepted any other man's). And Lothair was emotionally impotent, for he imperially wished to lift by himself the whole city, as we saw, the table and the floor attached to the table, and the walls, and the house; but by willing it he could not make the flesh of his own penis rise.

It was not interesting for a child to be born in 1948. One did not observe, at the birth of a child, any especial enthusiasm or hope, or even fear or surprise, that here was something new, a further possibility in the continuity of humanity. It was not interesting for a child to be born then because our ways were well miscalculated to prevent his being a hero. It was possible for quite serious persons to ask themselves, "What for? Is it convenient or inconvenient to have a child? Is it useful for the child? Does society need another child?" These were not very daring questions; one answer or another, to have a child was not a daring deed; but without daring there is nothing interesting. So they were sociologically incapable.

Emily and Lothair were sad and horrified and holding on too tight and bored. Yet even so we know, as Franz said, that an operation of nature could get them past insoluble dilemmas. But it was metaphysically impossible for them to have a child (this follows simply from the fact that they did not have a child), as if the vital principle were tired, had withdrawn—from our animal species that did not know how to care for itself. Perhaps men had, by secondary evasions and tertiary satisfactions and quaternary elaborations that were neither defensive nor satisfactory but nothing at all, men had so cut themselves off from nature and natural conventions that they could no longer draw on natural energy to recreate themselves—as if to say, "Man ceased to be human around 1870, or some other date." But then a new child would be born strange into a *nonexistent* species; no such child could get itself born. We were metaphysically childless, as if now the energy of our generation were concentrated in the one action of immortality, the imitation of our nonexistence, to become (as Parker saw it) a constellation in the sphere. As if to say,

> I hunted it, and I have eaten it
> (now let me sleep). Ach, what I ate
> was how it lay there dead: *this* virtue
> has passed into my second-nature.

Beware of these gorgons, because the sight of them turns you to stone, even if they sit there crying tears.

2.

But Mynheer flew there with his bright mirror like Perseus.

He said, "I do not know exactly, though I could make several shrewd guesses, why couples are childless; but at the least we can get some help from the elementary statistics. Since more children are born in the country, you two ought to move to the country. Also you ought to have a human community where you and this child can directly satisfy, to a degree, the various rather few simple wants of human nature. This is obvious."

"There is no such human community," said Lothair.

"No, there is not; but we can invent that," said Mynheer.

"What! *Again?*" cried Lothair unbelievingly, for he himself used to be a greedy inventor of Utopian places in order to divert himself from the fact that his teeth were aching.

"Why not again? Do you have something better to do than to live as sensibly as you can manage? But let's not get complicated. First, do you two have sexual intercourse?"

"No," said Emily.

"Ah, you see? We hit on something right off. It's necessary to fuck if you want to have children."

3.

"Easy to say! I also have heard of this newsy hypothesis!" said Lothair bitterly.

"But her flesh shrinks in horror, and mine is clamped in a death grip, trembling. Trembling and does not loose—you see how it is!" He held out his mighty hand—that was not, however, trembling, so far as one could see. These were fantasies of his.

Then Duyck looked directly in the faces of these two gorgons and his heart turned to heavy stone within him. He faltered.

"What's the matter—are you ill?" they cried solicitously.

"It's nothing. This——" He took out his heart from his breast, a small handful of stone. "A cornerstone for building a good city."

4.

It doesn't exist but we can invent that: so Mynheer used to say readily (I have known such persons). Without despairing, or else despairing, he still used to assign to the intellect the role of knowing reasons and making something by means of the reasons. He did not merely notice with alarm, as we others learned to do in the middle of the twentieth century, writing up these notices for literary magazines. But he went to work. The folk had become demented: this did not paralyze him, though it had to be taken into account.

"Oh, reasons are as plentiful as blackberries," said the poet, meaning excuses, rationalizations. Good reasons are not so plentiful as that, but they are not rare; they are perhaps as plentiful as apples on poor trees (some trees have none, in poor seasons, and the seasons have been poorly).

It was not even the case that all of Mynheer's projects, sprung from simple reasons, were unsuccessful.

And now, turning over in his mind the thought of a Community of Human Relations to provide for the formation of a child's personality—and sometimes absently hefting the heavy stone that fitted the palm of the hand, as if he were about to let it fly as a missile—he rapidly jotted down some notes on the back of a marriage-license: We need, he figured,

"1 nursing mother: matrix of affection and elementary satisfaction.
1 rival bad-mother (aunt type), for the attachment of rage and nausea.
1 rival good-mother (big-sister type), desire without tangible satisfaction.
1 neutral older woman, to bridge the gap to apathy.
3 or 4 fathers (uncle type): manly identification, threats of maiming; gain of security by learning to play off one against another. (Teacher, policeman, mother's mate, mother's lover.)
1 older brother: the model to be avoided.
1 younger brother, the favorite (Abel type): a convenient object for murder.
1 male sexual friend: projection of narcissism.
1 male nonsexual friend: the rival.
1 other friend, either sex: object of selfless devotion.
2 or 3 other males, roughly contemporary: the gang.
1 outsider: the scapegoat.
1 older girl friend, sexually active, to force him to overcome the Oedipus situation.
1 younger girl friend, for fearless exploration, for playing the father role.
1 maniac, all is not what seems.
1 old person, dying.
1 stranger to the society: infinity of mystery.
Total 22 persons"

So many! Mynheer whistled with surprise; even so far it came to more than twenty persons to ensure the development of a personality. Besides, there would have to be a few animals, to establish the continuity of the species. And an Angel? Also, the social engineer had to provide a Factor of Safety, for it was unlikely that every person would enter into every needful relation.

At first Mynheer considered a large factor, 5, five persons for each role. But it was enough to have 3, for when confronted with any three, the comparative soul always sees one to favor and one to disfavor and one to seek as an ally. Also, it tended to limit the size of the factor that each person was likely to play several roles: the mate is the interloper, the scapegoat is the object of selfless devotion, etc. Mynheer therefore chose a factor of 3 and he decided that the Community required: $22 \times 3 = 66$ persons.

"It is a suburban community," he concluded, "weighted heavily toward the children and boys and girls."

5.

Our friends (1948) were hungry and thirsty and lonely to live in a community of human relations. They were lost, lonely, and out of touch in the community in which indeed they did live; it was no community, for them or anyone else, because in it one did not flow in the elementary human relations.

Leaving it—with a burst of joy at leaving it!—they carried with them the joyless faculty of being out of touch with one another in elementary human relations. Nevertheless, there was an advantage in leaving the lonesome community that indeed existed to flock to the invented community that did not exist, in which also they would not flow in the elementary human relations: because in the new community they could reveal their naked hatred.

They chose a pleasant place, provided with the four elements, earth, air, water and fire.*

The air in this place was a flexible medium somewhat infiltrating into their animal bodies and furnishing no strong obstacle to motion through itself. A certain number of the settlers were able to feel the ambience of this air, as in and out it rushed and lay about them as they moved. The earth here was well connected with the center: it gave adequate support to standing and walking and even running, by offering an equal and opposite reaction to the pressure exerted on it. But there were few of the settlers who could feel their legs planted on this bedrock ground. The water in the place they chose had the remarkable virtue of fluidity; it broke into drops and reunited in a flowing body, and as if effortlessly it flattened itself in level pools wherever there was a depression. Yes! There was a high rushing foaming fall of water that fell in an instant still in a flat unrevealing pool reflecting the blue heavens and the clouds. And lastly there was the dark fire that burst into visibility whenever it struck something not transparent, as their faces.

* Since we come again to a physical plan, I must explain how it was that Mynheer's wife Laura was not present and in charge of these arrangements. To put it bluntly, she had gone crazy and would not leave the house. She suffered from a socio-psychological complaint whose salient symptom Kenneth Burke was, I think, the first to identify: she imagined that she was the personality expressed in the pictographs: the 1/3 of a housewife who rides on 3/4 of a bicycle wearing 1 1/2 shoes, and so forth. This made it difficult for her to collect herself sufficiently to adventure abroad.

From these kinds of matter, certain vegetation of weeds and flowers found nourishment, and animals too could subsist there. Perhaps a human community could here appoint itself.

Perhaps? Alas, there was no proof! There was no demonstrative proof that a particular commonwealth *must* appoint itself, just here, just itself, namely a human community, a community of human relations, one with mothers and brothers and friends and rivals, and the known and the unknown. Why this particular thing, in a world generally provided with air, earth, water, and fire? Why must it appoint itself into existence; how was it justified to, how would it venture to? Yet if it did not appoint itself, who would appoint it?

Yet it was impossible to live not in some human community in just such a place provided with earth, air, etc. *Either* it was necessary to appoint oneself (one felt no such necessity), *or* it was impossible to live at all. It was a dilemma.

The prospective settlers stared at one another with fright.

It is of course always difficult to conclude to a particular, to bring it into existence; nevertheless, this always occurs, as if "by an operation of nature," proved from the beginning of time—as it seemed that the human community had also existed. But now we asked in our misery, how is this justified? And *if* one asked, what kind of answer did one expect? Obviously it was impossible.

The prospective settlers would willingly have fled in every direction, back to the human community they had left. But to what community? No such thing any longer existed; they had left it with a burst of joy.

Harry Tyler, who had a collection of jokes for all occasions, told them the joke about the three displaced persons. "Where are you bound?" one asked another. "I think I'll go to London. And you?" "I intend to go to Paris. . . . And where are you going?" they asked the third. "Me? I'm going to South Africa!" "To South Africa! So far?" "So far from—where?"

6.

But Mynheer said—for he was learned and could recall old stories and rites for emergencies, something to tell oneself and to perform in order that life may meantime begin to flow again—he said:

"We must sacrifice a life to the beginning of our community, as Remus was slain by his brother in order that Rome might have a beginning. If a life is given, the city will begin of itself: that is, we shall have a spirit. We shall not need to justify our city—the dead man justifies it; the city lives and what is living justifies itself. The only question is this: which one must be slain and plowed into the field?"

The question was met by silence and no lively enthusiasm. Lothair, Emilia, Harry Tyler and the others measured the speaker with their eyes, and measured one another. Feeling himself the target of so many eyes, Mynheer licked his lips and hefted the black stone that fitted the palm.

He held the stone out to them to see and said, "This is my heart turned to stone: the heart of understanding when it looked full at such and such feelings in the world, instead of looking glancingly, like Perseus, in a mirror. I propose now to hurl this as a missile, and we can bury the crushed skull in the field as the sacrifice for our city. *Whose?*"

He raised his forearm, and they cried out and fell back.

Droyt Duyvendak did not fall back, but he asked his father angrily, "Why are *you* exempted? Ask anyone here whether *you* are not the most likely candidate!" The youth was in an ugly mood that reflected the mood of the crowd, and they advanced a little on Mynheer.

But the tears flooded Horatio's eyes and he said in a choked voice: "Ow! In the days of the Grand Piano they slew my only friend, Raymond, who where'er he walked, etc.; and during the war my chosen father and Arthur died; and now because of this cursed community, that I for one shall be no brother in—for I cannot rid myself of the void roundabout me as I go, the presence of their absence—for *this* am I also to lose Piet Duyck, the subtilest and one of the best? I'm not yet at the point to say, 'Let *me* die rather!' But from this moment on I do not intend to stop wailing." And he began to wail in an eerie way. It was worse than anything.

Craftily and winningly, Minetta Tyler said, "I think you all look at this proposed sacrifice too one-sidedly; you think it's so bad to be the one chosen, and expend your pity and fear on him. I for my part consider that role with equanimity. Bang! I'm dead—and what about afterwards? Ha! Now I'm permanently *under* that city, or built *into* that wall; there I am for keeps, you can't get rid of me now. Won't I haunt that city of yours? Don't worry; I'm not thinking of anything vindictive, obviously we love one another dearly or what are we doing here together? But a spirit has to play little tricks, exert an influence. . . ."

People laughed, baring their teeth.

7.

"Well, I didn't go to South Africa after all!" This was a large redhead unknown to anybody, who kept circulating and annoying people. Often new faces turned up at our meeting, sometimes they became old faces, sometimes one never saw them again. The oddity of this fellow was that he refused to tell his name or say whose friend he was. He said he was the third displaced person in the joke and had decided not to go to South Africa but to go to a community with human relations. "To a *community!* So far?" "So far from *where?*" He was a humorist; one soon recognized his type and became bored.

He persisted in explaining himself. He had come in order to fill the community role of the Stranger, the one whose presence opens the mind of the growing boy to the fact that the world is infinite. He was practicing the part, he explained; he had ideas for it. "For instance, I have to change costumes; otherwise the kids get used to me and I'm not the same thing. But every couple of days I put on a different mask. See? I'm willing to work hard at being the Stranger; it fits me." In fact he had brought a mask with him and slipped it on; his red hair showed, he was not concealed at all. He was grotesque. "I'm not a Jew!" he protested—he seemed to be an Irishman. "The Jew is the outsider, the Scapegoat, but I'm the Stranger, see?"

He had another routine that was so complicated that one could not resist a wintry smile. "Sixty-six! Sixty-six persons," he said, "you know what that means?" Nobody knew. "Look, twenty-two—" he held up two fingers on each hand and then clasped the two 2's together—"that means a buddy-fuck, two buddies with two girls. Thirty-three—" he held up three fingers on each hand and clasped the 3's together—"that's a gang-shag. Fifty-five! There's a lovely number. Body *and* soul. I give you my heart and my hand, that's true marriage." He clasped his hands in an agony of sentiment. "Now if you hold up six fingers on each hand and bring them together, then you have a real community. A community of human relations. Ha, try it sometime."

By evening, however, when the thinner light revealed things more coolly in their places, this same merry-andrew began to seem sinister. He had been drinking a good deal. "You lousy community-seekers!" he hissed, in the otherwise quiet, "you're chicken-shit scared of death. That's why you pile in pell-mell on top of one another. As if you did that in order to live in a community of human relations. . . . Why did *I* come here, among these chicken-shit community-seekers? Do I love you, you particular, you particle, you biped. Ha! They all have two feet—what's that to me?"

"Nobody invited you. Why don't you go away?"

"Hell, I'll go away! Can you make me?" He was a competent Stranger; he had the knack of clinging grimly where he didn't belong.

8.

In the darkness their eyes were narrowed to slits—jaw thrust forward. A man turned a flashlight on another, bathing the object of hatred in light; also the startled eyes of the hated could not quite make out what was looming in the darkness.

A bell tolled. And they said:

"I hate you damned children and mate; you have imprisoned me and I cannot go free where there is a passing hope of transient joy before I shortly die.

"I hate myself for a coward to be so imprisoned.

"I hate you for the sexual demand you make that I force myself to, to live up to an acceptable standard, and I hate you because you do not satisfy my sexual demand.

"I hate you who wake me when I need to sleep; I hate you who do not take care of everything for me.

"I hate you boring friends who do not consult the hour that it suits me to have your company. That hour would never strike!

"I hate you desirable strangers who do not befriend me.

"Because much of this is due to my cowardice and stupidity, I hate myself the more and I hate you the more. I have gotten no satisfaction from being reasonable and just, yet I feel guilty for being unreasonable and unjust; I hate you who make me feel guilty.

"You who shatter the quiet of my meals with clamor and temper, so I do not enjoy the delicious food. And you who make my gorge rise to food I do not like.

"I hate the dog that shits in the street.

"All such I should be content to see blotted from existence."

While the bell was tolling, it was being said:

"You successful one! I should like to turn you upside down and dash your brains on the pavement.

"I hate you sufferers who dampen my joy.

"I hate you who neglect and do not praise me; but I will shine in such glory that you won't dare to open your traps, though you still won't see the point.

"I hate you who do not give me money when I need it, who do not guess that I need it when I am too stiff-necked to ask for it.

"I despise myself for a beggar. I hate my poor clothes and I hate you who are ashamed of my poor clothes, but worst of all I hate you who overlook me because of my poor clothes. You I must rip.

"I hate you pretended friends for not putting me in the way of something to my advantage; I hate you for not seeing in what a state of need and frustration I exist; I hate you for presuming to perceive it.

"I hate you who hurt my feelings by breaking the appointment, and you keep me on edge by treating at leisure something urgent to myself.

"I hate you fool who cross me in argument and keep on chattering after I have got your drift and am ready to reply. (This deserves grating.)

"I hate you who eat apples loudly."

The bell was fiercely tolling stroke after stroke and it was being said:

"You children, I cannot breathe when you are around and there is no order; no doubt I should like you to die of those illnesses that cause me so much anxiety. But even worse I hate you grownups who are cruel to children and beat them.

"I hate you who have beat me, and all who are strong enough to beat me.

"I hate you who exact punishment from people for past offenses.

"I hate you I fear.

"I hate myself for hating myself, as if I did not need—and merit—a little sweet consolation.

"I hate myself for thinking swarms of thoughts and not breathing the air and taking in the scene. For not giving in easily to such pleasure as is offered.

"I hate you who warped my feelings and ruined my happiness; I hate you whom I see busy about the same with others; and I hate myself for lacking courage to prevent it.

"I hate the order of things that could, it seems, so easily have given me happiness, because my wants are simple."

Many other things were being said in hatred, some peculiarly but most by most. I for my part was also present, in my usual capacity, and I added: "I hate this poetic art, particularly when I consider those works and moments of it that have been my joy and pride, and I see that to be their poet it was necessary for me to have been myself, to lead the wretched life that I have led. That I sacrifice to a happiness hardly mine at all—for those moments pass as in an apathetic dream, and they recur, as still they recur, to me ever more tired and spent. I have sacrificed to the life of the art what might have been a life of mine, not to speak of consequent poverty, public neglect, spite and envy both taken and given. So much for these poems and for my life; yet strike me dead if I mean to say any harm of the Creator Spirit."

The bell tolled the stroke of twelve.

"—The Creator Spirit, in whom we find such sense as we do find in a universe that otherwise does not seriously recommend itself."

A BOYISH GAME

Meantime, in the cone of light-

the circle of a dozen boys closed in on Terry, pounding him; sound of their hitting fists; and he cried out.

They withdrew, as a circle, and the beaten boy staggered a moment and gasped. He braced himself and advanced a step with clenched fists, for it was now his turn to choose who would be beat.

"Pick Albie!" cried a boy (not Albie).

"Hit Droyt, he's got it coming."

"No; Berryman!"

But the boy slowly moved in the circle, narrowing his eyes. Suddenly he hit the largest boy in the face, Droyt.

Like a wave the circle opened back from this victim—Terry slipped into his position—and the circle came forward again, beating Droyt. He was angry and his eyes flashed and he clenched his fists, but he bore the beating without flinching. "Two hands!" he cried outraged—this was unfair, they were supposed to punch with only one hand, "I'll get even with you, brother."

"I'm Lefty," cried Lefty. "Can't I use my best hand?"

They withdrew, and Droyt stood in the center, gasping.

"Pick Albie!"

"No; Berryman!"

There was one boy whose name nobody mentioned, to be beat. He was neither the largest nor the smallest; he was not enviably handsome nor able; or perhaps he might have been enviably so, but he had the vitality to give his attention to each of us. Attentive desire shone quietly from his presence and he was our darling; yet in the melee he threw his punch as hard as any.

"For Chrissake, sock Berryman, he's got it coming to him!"

"Shut up, you bastard," said Berryman; "let him pick who he wants."

Droyt did not move about the circle, but slowly turned his head from side to side, all around to take in all of us narrowing his eyes. It was terrible; each one had the moment to conjure well with the reason that Droyt had to hate him. Narrowing glance and flinching glance.

"Make up your mind."

We were well warned; yet when his body flew toward me and I felt the heavy blow between the eyes, it was as if the abyss had opened without a warning, and I might have fallen down. The interval was long—but not endless. The circle of my comrades fell away.

What did one understand, standing staggering gasping in the center of the hated—the hated but no longer feared? Bracing oneself. One understood that the game was universal. I do not mean that it was impersonal, that it was not this or that individual that they meant to hurt. On the contrary, how else should the universal cause come into existence except just through personal animosities, given and taken, for reasons peculiar in the history of each individual? But one understood that it was a universal repetition, and one felt supported by the motions of the world, as one stood in the center with whirling head, coming back to myself. Now it was *my* turn to choose.

"Pick Albie!"

"Sock Droyt again; he's got it coming to him."

I looked with narrowing eyes at the faces that were hateful but not fearful. I was inspired by universal thoughts; therefore, I easily, guiltlessly, advanced toward that interloper in my security who knew well who he was and cringed before my glance. I hit him, and slipped into his place. The circle closed in on him in fury and, to my joy, he cried out.

The boys were tired, all staggering–influenced by the jarring motions of the stars. The circle no longer formed itself with neat clarity, the victim was swaying before he was beat. It was a ragged pattern; all were falling, flinging themselves, into the center. Shining with an internal clarity.

Yes! Now it was a simple thing to pick on precisely our favorite–who gave to us his lovely attention. To single him out! Two or three were being pushed into the center at once. The pounders were being pounded. We could not bear to leave our darling behind, solitary, when we fell down. All were punching all.

9.

"Please put out those lights and let's get some sleep," some one suggested mildly.

Mynheer said, "Right! In my opinion there's enough hatred felt here to inaugurate community relations. Nothing to found empires on, no spectacular bloodcurdling curses, parricide and blasphemy–only the conjugal annoyances, maltreatment of children and economic complaints of 1948; but enough, enough to cement the human relations. The community of human relations exists."

It existed, for we were falling asleep together, performing the interesting social act of falling asleep together. Some drop off at once, some toss awhile, a few lie awake a longer time, but in the end heavy sleep subdues them nearly all. (With us, the first to fall asleep was the professional Stranger, snoring in secure confidence.) Also an occasional voice, a last thought, breaks the silence of falling asleep.

Lothair said: "This person who complains against the order of things because it has not granted him a few simple wants: he is suffering an illusion. His wants are speciously simple. Among all his unattainable wants he has chosen a few and speciously simplified them and set them up as his program, in order to be angry with more self-righteousness. Hm. Then he says, 'My wants are so simple; *why* don't I get what I want?' Hm."

Our community existed fine; no need to prove it. There was not one of us who did not have fair samples of mothers, father types, teachers, seducers, maniacs, scapegoats, etc.—everything necessary for the formation of our personalities. With few exceptions our personalities were perfectly, fully formed. Our community was unsatisfactory in—shall we say?—many ways, but no doubt of it, it was close, tight.

Another last thought broke the silence, a sudden laughter, and the pretty dancer Rosalind said: "This artist! Ha, ha, ha. He speaks of a life sacrificed to the life of the work instead of being lived as *his* life. *What* life, his life? What does he know about what it would be? Isn't it plausible—eh?—that it would have been something more ghastly? It's rich, how people carry on."

"Maybe so," I began to protest, "but *I'd* like to be the arbiter of that; after all——" But she was already asleep. I am one to lie long awake.

10.

Certainly our communal relations were dense enough to allow a man and a woman, Lothair and Emily, to roll together and copulate, and so they did, under their cover. Their rigid grip on their feelings was somewhat loosed by fear of death and the expression of hatred, and they enjoyed themselves, came to a pleasurable orgasm.

They wept. And fell asleep.

And as happens in a fair proportion of copulations, the semen fertilized the egg and it was a beginning to the forming of a child that would likely be born into the community of human relations. Possible also in these days (the possibility is proved by the actuality)—in a place of air, earth, water and fire—in the line of the generation of the animals from long ago. From such products, such freeborn heirs of the process of time, we may study the nature of the vital spirit.

Now the offspring who was thus engendered was St. Wayward.

Chapter 5 ▪ HORATIO'S MOURNING-LABOR

1.

On West Street, the avenue nearest the lordly river, a young man who, you would guess, could fly, was squatting abject on the curbstone. Access to the water was cut off by the warehouses, and the trucks were screaming past across his toes. "Abject": having dismissed himself.

He was walking heavily past this spot—it was not even a spot on the continuous long avenue until one singled it out—and you would not say from his heavy gait that he could fly. Suddenly he turned back to this spot and dropped himself down, squatting, the abjection dropping on him like a cloak; as if it were precisely here, not the next step further on, that he must be abject.

The next instant he slipped from the curbstone and sat in the gutter, not quite dry. The space of this drop was two inches. Through these two inches, from the level of the walk to the level of the street, he dropped in one instant as Vulcan fell all day long from Olympus in a streak of fire. Lamed. The man was Horatio and the tears came into his eyes. He put in his mouth the little finger of his right hand, whose tip was missing; but the scar was long since healed and he could not understand the language of the beasts. He was not crying.

The place was grimy with dust from the coal stations along the river, and Horatio's denim clothes were made dirty by dirt not belonging to his work.

He turned suddenly back from a further step and dropped to his haunches on the curb; then in an instant slid into the gutter and the tears flooded his eyes (though he was not crying)—touching to his lips, but not sucking, the missing tip on his little finger; and the trucks screamed by across his toes.

"I give it up—one place is like another."

Having dismissed himself: as if to say, "If in order to have become what I have become, it is necessary for me to be what I am, not I will take one further step—nor continue to maintain myself——" here he slid the few inches into the street, not meaning, of himself, to say anything further. But his workshirt hung loose, it opened and fell from his shoulders, and his trousers were open (though he was not drunken or crying), and his body spoke what he did not know he knew.

The shapes along there, the coal stations and the warehouses, some burnt out, did not flatter the eyes; the river was shut off; the boarded windows of an abandoned hotel for mariners did not invite the soul; nor did such passers-by as there were encourage courtesy, confidence.

But you could see, seeing the nakedness of Horatio in flashes amid the tons of trucks screaming by over him—as the curtain of reality is rent and in flashes we perceive the Way—that he could fly.

2.

Adjusting his clothes, Horatio walked back to his job. It was a gang of three drilling through the subpavement to test the seepage. They chose a spot, chiseled out a cobblestone and dug. The casing was supposed to be twenty feet thick, but when, after hours of pounding, they got down to nineteen, they again and again struck an impenetrable boulder. They moved to another spot to try. Sometimes a fellow walked away from the frustrating business. Another more fortunate gang up the street had struck gas and high flames were pouring from the pipe.

The engine groaned and the hammer rang clear and regularly on the rod. When they had gained six feet, Horatio screwed another length on the pipe. The engine coughed and recommenced, and the hammer rang and the pipe began to disappear. The laden trucks screamed past. Busy little lifts carried boxes from warehouses to trucks. Above the rooves loomed the ship stacks and the coal scoops, swinging from the barges, letting loose their cargoes in a rattling hail. Depending on their characters and conditions the persons moving this apparatus were silent or shouting. There was danger enough for all in the rapid contrary motion of objects weighing many tons. The noise, motion and fear were not quite chaotic, for nearly all the men were capable of stopping short in an emergency—the trucks grind to a stop and the coal scoops not let loose their hail; and also it was possible to assign an obvious reason to any particular motion, though not perhaps to all the motions together. The noise and motion and fear were not chaotic even to the sensibility if one happened to be in a mood of feverish animation ready for any blow. (But Horatio was withdrawn and turned to each blow after it had struck.) The hammer rang with an angrier note and the rod quivered and did not advance because they had again struck an impenetrable obstacle. The gang began to curse their luck. They shut off the engine. The tugs whistled the end of the working day.

A train of cars was dragging slowly by on the overhead railroad, and a shower of sparks fell from a faulty contact.

A pretty young woman standing against a pillar of the railroad was watching the drill, or the gang, or Horatio. It was he, and his penis rose adventurously. But he could not enliven his face to a smile.

His mates knocked off work at the whistle and walked away to the watchman's hut to change, leaving him to put the machine and the tools to rest.

3.

In a few moments the neighborhood had emptied and become quiet, leaving Horatio and the power drill on a large open plain—as if he himself had journeyed to another place—as Orpheus traveling through the underworld left behind the agitated damned and advanced to a quiet place to the sound of a flute. The pretty woman, he saw, was still watching, from the corner of the street that led onto the pier.

Methodically, not stolidly; tired but not disgusted; carefully, not obsessively; slow but not dragging—the man went about putting away the equipment and cleaning and covering the engine. A number of heavy lengths of pipe were scattered on the ground. He picked up one length at a time and brought it and dropped it with a clang onto a stack of pipes alongside the engine. By straining a little, he might have carried two lengths at once, or again tossed the pipe rather than carried it; but he slowly brought each length and dropped it with a clang; yet not stupidly nor stolidly—each length was heavy enough—rather as if he were conserving his forces by method. He picked up a pair of heavy crowbars, one in each hand, and lightly tossed them clanging onto the stack.

He took a wrench from the box and unscrewed the hose from the hydrant; he drank from the hydrant and turned off the water, but left the wrench leaning against the hydrant as if absentmindedly. (But it was by forethought.) He dragged the long hose toward the engine, and snapping the kinks out of it with a sure hand, he folded it in a coil on the ground, alongside the engine. Already the operations that had littered a wide area were confined to a surprisingly small center. He was proceeding from the outside in, but freely, not pedantically. He himself moved slowly, but the effects were surprisingly rapid.

Any workman putting away his tools is among the lovely dancers of the world. In this movement the soul is sent to pasture. The workman is tired, the task is recreative, and he handles his tools with respectful love and care. And perhaps the movement is especially lovely when the soul is in distress and during it the breathing becomes more calm. Deliberate but not controlled. It is as if one were constructing again and again the following syllogism, gaining force each time from the conclusion: "Those who make a little effort are not completely unready; now I am making a little effort; therefore I am not completely unready."

A few at a time he tossed the dozens of small objects that had been left on the pavement, nuts, washers and bar wrenches, into the box. Gathering the greater tools, he brought them to the box and hung them in place on hooks provided.

"Accepting a total loss, one finds oneself suddenly making a little effort. I have accepted, etc.; therefore, now I am making a little effort. But those who make a little effort are not completely unready. Accepting a total loss, I am not completely unready. . . . No one of his own doing accepts a total loss! It is by grace!"

From deep in the box he fetched a gallon can of oil, a rag and a copper oiler. He poured a pint of oil into the engine—the operations were now circumscribed to the engine itself. He polished the points, but he was not scrupulous about cleaning the engine that was in poor condition and there was no use in making the parts better than the whole. He put a drop of oil on the fan shaft. Unwinding a length of rope from the drill frame and lifting the bulky coil of hose from the ground, he securely bound the hose to the body of the engine, so it would not be an attractive loose object for the wandering boys at night. It made no difference if they played with the stack of pipes. He pulled the rope taut, but he fastened it with loose hitches; secure, not permanent. Absently he carried back the oil and the rag and stowed them into the depths of the box.

From another corner the young woman was still watching him. Invitingly, and obligingly, he stripped off his work shirt a moment before he would have otherwise. She paled with interest and he was able to grin.

"No one of his own doing accepts a total loss! It is by grace! I accept it—not of my own doing. Now if it is by accepting a total loss that I find myself making a little effort, it is not of my own doing that I am making a little effort. And if it is making a little effort that keeps me from being completely unready, it is not by my own doing that I am not completely unready. Yes, in fact! For by my own doing I have been turning to each blow after it has struck."

In one motion he brought forth a great tarpaulin and unfolded it, and with a large arm he covered all the engine in darkness. In the twinkling of an eye the world was transformed. Nothing nothing nothing—all the wide operations were reduced to this mysterious shape on the empty plain. The man himself shrank away to a small inch beside the veiled shape. His tiny figure cast a long pencil of shadow in the red sunlight. (The pretty girl had gone away.) Whatever was the meaning of the wide operations, it was not the economy that these men thought of; the magic of it could now first be guessed, concealed in the looming tarpaulin.

The tiny half-naked man went to the hydrant and washed himself.

He noticed that the woman was gone, but he assumed that she, like a being of reason and desire, was waiting for him on the pier.

Turning the water off, he brought the wrench back to the box and locked the box and, trailing his shirt along the ground, he went to the watchman's hut to change his clothes.

4.

The unknown woman was not waiting for him on the pier. Horatio reddened with vexation. He came away not pausing to look out on the broad river furrowed by tugboats. She had been promising to him just because she was a stranger; as if it were only by surprise that one had any pleasure. As if—what is perhaps the case, I no longer remember it—one had to give in to knowing love by a series of deliberate choices and Horatio could not make the choices.

His disappointed eyes burned hot and dry, and the void spread around him——

The absence of his loved friends.

There was a time that, conversing with his dead friends, he had an open look and wore a participatory smile; but he did not remember them any more.

He could not open his tight eyelids wide. He did not feel the unfelt pain, but he did not smile. Horatio was sick.

It is shameful to present to the reader an image of sickness and unfelt pain. (I am ashamed myself to exist this way in the world.) It is worse to have to describe Horatio so, my hope and beauty, fearless attentiveness.

Always leaving the unsurprising community of his living friends, Horatio found himself habitually alone, wooing his unfelt pain in order to feel it. Then if suddenly he came upon his living friends, who were seeking some kind of community with one another, they fell dead, because he was a wizard out of hell; he judged them and they could not abide his judgment.

He found himself alone because he was ashamed to exercise his ordinary powers among his living friends. For instance, he was ashamed to open his eyes and see something that was the case. He was ashamed to erect his penis and reach his lips toward something desirable. He was ashamed to recall a thing to memory. To walk by pushing against the ground. To draw breath in and let it out, without controlling the upper and nether limits. He was ashamed to say what was correct and destroy the community of human relations. He was ashamed to say what was humorous and amiably establish the community of human relations. Yet being alone, without even the conversation of the dead, there was nothing to see, erect the penis toward, etc., and no way to say something humorous. He gnawed the stump of his finger. The pigeons on the avenue scattered before his approach.

When he was hiding in the cloak of withdrawn touch, he could feel his hot and lively pain.

His character was the history of the losses of loved friends. The *agreed* losses; one appoints oneself to one's character. Now he hated his character and would like to dismiss himself. Too late! Was it too late? (Perhaps there was a previous loss that he had never agreed to.)

Without a quick frank glance in any direction, he was walking blindly along like a fool.

Then his fearlessly attentive eyes became burning hot; he could understand, blindly, what those eyes of his were about. They were hungry and devouring, murderous and ravenous. Standing still, squeezing his lids tight shut, now he could see the scene; that there were rocks, trees, and grass, and the sun rising at a bound, and a few animals, and familiar and unfamiliar people, and their buildings and vehicles, the broad river furrowed by tugboats, the faces of his brother and sister: a good sample of the world, all objects of ravenous vision. He was ashamed to open his eyes and see what was the case.

He was suffering the tearing pain of the organs of his body reaching in different directions.

He was not crying—it was not yet time for him to cry. But he was grieving, indeed uttering a little whine, for the loss of his own magic powers. If he had indeed ever had magic powers, for he no longer remembered what that was like. (But he did not really doubt that he had had magic powers.) If he had indeed lost them, for since he did not exert his powers at all he did not know whether or not they would prove magical, efficacious. (He did not really believe that he had lost his magic powers; but he believed that he did not exert them.) He was grieving not with the useful grief of boiling tears, but by suffering tearing pain, possibly only in order to feel the pain; but one does not choose how he will grieve. Standing still, eyes squeezed shut, nape tight, lips drawn back from his opened teeth, etc., he was recognizable as a man choosing to go on suffering tearing pain: that is, grieving for the loss of magical powers, not believing in the loss.

I am distressed to present to the reader this image.

Horatio opened his eyes and saw to his delight that the same pretty young woman was ahead of him, walking up Jane Street, and even turning her head to smile at him. His heart bounding with surprise, he crossed the street after her. She turned into a doorway and so did he.

5.

Following the strange woman, whose name was Rosalind, into the house on Jane Street, Horace fell among his friends at a party. This was not surprising since he had been unthinkingly heading toward this gathering; nor was Rosalind a stranger, for he had often met her at other meetings, and seeing him at work she had courteously waited for him.

Our friends were celebrating the cheerful recent events, the first in a long time: that some people could levitate, that they were established in a new community, that Lothair and Emily were going to have a child. Besides, people had brought their dogs to meet Dingo, a tawny boxer that Edouard had sent ahead from Berlin. There was dancing, but when a pair of dogs began to dance in the middle of the floor, in nimble stiff-legged postures, or planting their forepaws on the floor and barking, the human dancers paused and regarded this mobile statuary with admiration. A golden spirit of ease and joy had sunk down on this party, that from that hour they were likely to be happy.

Yet as on a dazzling hazy midsummer afternoon, when the insects are loud on the flowers and one is blinded with daylight, nevertheless, to one's astonishment, it becomes still louder and brighter when the sun himself glides into the blue, liquid as a tear—so the cheer of the party became miraculous when Horatio walked in. The dogs barked frantically, and it was possible to understand the simple thing that they were saying. It was possible for the lover to wish well to the beloved. And the minutes, as it says in *The Emperor of China,* "the minutes were flying like a snowstorm, but they were not flying by."

Horatio radiated ability, that called forth our gaiety. What is poetry? The motion of the soul from thought to thought (this is feeling); rhythms in the motion (the pleasure of the body in the feeling); and finally presenting always a surprisingly recognizable object to meet the headlong body and soul. There are strong souls that agitate our souls by their motion; there are many fewer that make us breathe deeper with pleasure as we are driven along; but what is miraculous is for the deep need and hunger then released in us, to be met pat by an object adequate, and we live both deeply *and* face to face. Those are the people who Come Across! That is a party! That is the Way! That was the ability of Horatio. Horatio came across!

We know that the young man was sick. When he came in the door, the surprising sight of his familiar friends reduced him to black boredom. His organs crept apart from one another with tearing pain. He was ashamed to exert his ordinary powers. This was so.

Yet lucky for us! the impotence and the agony that he was suffering in some last desperate conflict with misery, could not prevent his presence from being to us the fountain, kept flowing and sweet by years of fearless attentiveness, of overbrimming love. Ability streamed through him, though he himself sat ashamed.

Parties can be classified according as they combine the party sports; some sports are mutually supporting and some are incompatible. There are dancy parties and drinky parties, and drinky-dancy parties. And drinky-talky parties. It is difficult to combine drink and talk and dancing. There are drinky-sexy parties, and drinky-dancy-sexy parties. There are drinky-talky-eaty parties. (All parties are drinky parties.) Drinky-talky-sexy parties are common, but it is not my experience that they are good parties; for if the talk is good, the released sexuality is not the sexuality of parties, but if the talk is aimed toward the sexuality of parties, it is stupid. Drinky-eaty-sexy parties are unhealthful. Drinky-eaty-talky parties and drinky-dancy-sexy parties are good parties. Drinky-singy parties are pleasant but soporific. But on all parties there must sink down the golden spirit of ease and joy, that from that hour one is likely to be happy.

The party on Jane Street was proving to be a drinky-dancy-sexy party. Besides being made rich by the presence of great decorative friendly dogs.

Horatio saw his familiar friends. They were hostile. The smiling young woman was Rosalind. He shrank, not to be hurt. Because obviously they were not hostile to him, he felt his shrinking as black boredom. He was afraid to expose his ordinary powers. He was ashamed to destroy his familiar friends by exercising his ordinary powers. He longed to be back in the open world where the lust for exploration might be strong enough to break through diffidence and bring him near some stranger.

He began at once to invent pretexts to escape.

Rosalind put her arm around him. Enchanted by the lovely sight of the workman caring for his tools, she could not forget that scene.

So far as we knew, Horatio was happily giving us his love, power and attention, as we were giving him ours. He did not think so, but we were more nearly right—the observer is always more nearly right. But he had the power to rush into the future according to his error, perhaps to a rash act.

He was "objectively happy." His circumstances, health, fortune, friends, luck and even his state of mind were happy. Also, in the throes of some last desperate conflict, he was overwhelmed in black boredom, shame, fright and pain. But this case is by no means rare: indeed it occurs, as it is among us, with every person who can fly. The works of creative joy that we receive from such a person come surely from his conversation with blessed life (from where else would they come?)—yet he may not have any pleasure from the conversation even at the moment of conversing; instead he lives, does indeed live, in guilt and dread.

The boxer Dingo pressed his muzzle into Horatio's palm, stared up at him, grieving and whining. The dog loved him.

With a cry of fright, that may have been a call of gaiety "Come, follow me!" Horatio ran away from the party, without a pretext.

"Come follow, follow me!" into the dangerous open, where there was no community of human relations.

He was accompanied, out of the way, by the presence of the absence of his dead friends. There was lively conversation, that he could not make out, but he heard his name called, "Horace!" It was eerie to hear his name called out, and he looked vainly up at the top-story windows. His eyes began to burn as if he were about to weep.

He began to weep tears that blinded him and sobs that made him choke. Small whistling noises sounded in new channels in his head. His eyes terribly burned, as though he would cry them out.

The forgotten loves he had abandoned came back into his mind, and also those he could still not remember were there, for it was all the same. He moaned, "Lost! Lost!" Some he had abandoned through circumstances that had seemed great but were trivial in comparison with the woe of abandoned love. Some because of the fatigue of long frustration, but there was no fatigue like the aftermath of abandoned love. Some he had lost through stupidity and then abandoned them out of anger with himself. Some he necessarily had abandoned because they were dead, just in order to live on again. Later, when he was already tired and sick, he gave up the chances of love because he was sick and tired. His character was the history of the loves he had abandoned; they flashed into his mind and he moaned "Lost! Lost," too late for him ever to give in to love again. He could not give in to loving; what were these strangers to him? But it was impossible for him to continue as he was, out of the way, the few or many years (either prospect was sad) until he shortly died.

He began to bawl in earnest, because it was himself he was bawling for. He was afraid of death and loss. It was himself that was abandoned, in the dangerous open.

Will not one who had appointed himself, and has dismissed himself, come to fly?

In a place where a warehouse had burned out and collapsed, one could, picking one's way, again get to the edge of the water. It was dark. Horatio picked his way and looked out, in the darkness, on the broad river. Now the river seemed to him to be female. And the lighted tugboats, silently furrowing the water as they rapidly drove by, seemed to him to be male. The Hudson River upbore them and came rolling to the shore in passionate waves.

It seemed to him to be an easy thing, not a violent thing, to exert his ordinary powers as need or inner need called them forth; they rose of themselves and effectuated themselves in such and such acts. To walk exerting pressure on the ground; to pick his way delicately along narrow planks by shifting his center of gravity from side to side. To look out and see the nature of the case. To talk with wit and gaiety about the nature of the case. To recall the past in memory and to mourn for it. To erect his penis in the presence of an object of desire. To fly with the accumulated power of the existing moment from the beginning of time rushing into the next moment: making it up as he went along—on the way. There was nothing in the exertion of power to warrant him shame or fear; there was nothing enviable in it (subject to the evil eye) because, whatever else, everybody had a good sample of an existing moment.

"We have omitted to play a funeral game in memory of them, in order that we may again begin to live on a little," thought Horatio. "I must get this game together."

A spirit of ease and joy sank down on him, that from that hour he was likely to be happy. He was waiting almost confidently for objects and occasions of desire to present themselves. They would not have to be remarkable or very lucky, because in this mood he could have made golden things out of improbabilities.

Impulsively he held out both his factor hands before him, the fingers stretching open to the most space. With a cry of astonishment he saw that all the ten fingers were whole and intact. The tip of the little finger of his right hand was not missing, if indeed it ever was.

New York City
October 1948
thankful to the creator spirit

For Lou

Chapter 6 ▪ THE CARCASES

> And they shall go forth and look upon the carcases of the men . . .
>
> —Isa. 66:24

1.

Our friends could fly through space, till they hit the ground and broke their bones.

There is no advantage in concealing it—what must be obvious to many readers but I usually conceal it from myself; these gentle persons, my heroic friends, were crippled, maimed. Poisoned and sick.

For now we were in the period of the system, prophesied by Eliphaz. Most people were walking entranced, till they fell with the asphyxiation. But our friends, who dissented, were inevitably also destroyed. The handy youths were maimed; Emily had a cancer; Lothair was stricken dumb, Horatio blind; Mynheer had splitting headaches; and Laura, we saw, no longer left her room.

Our friends had abilities, inventions, beyond the average. Up to a certain moment their vigorous activity concealed, by-passed, the underlying fact; but then it became evident that they were poisoned —there is no use concealing it.

This horde of cripples, this disgusting company, crept, hobbled, squatted and schemed amid thousands of walking dead. Some of the thousands looked as sick and defective as our friends, but others looked sleek and shapely enough; but none of them could fly—whether to go aloft or simply to launch into free space and break their bones, easily giving themselves to gravity. But our friends were daring and could fly, sometimes soaring a very little but usually simply giving themselves to a free space—hard to find a free space for the exercise—and breaking their bones. And a sickening thought occurred to them as they hit with a sick thud (their sickly bodies were prone to generate sickening thoughts): the thought that they gave themselves to the free space like fools because they were ashamed of their deformities; or that they were so disgusted and disheartened by their unhappy gaits and states that they chose rather to dare and luckily die than exist further.

The souls of persons in a dilemma, the cowering souls of natural children as they grow and make hard choices: Either to dissent from the social community and thereby to grow sickly, deformed and mad—for where else is one to thrive?—or to conform to it and go mad and stifle. Air! Air! For there is a stink of putrefaction. (This is the case, how it is; what am I supposed, *not* to make a story of it and be gay?)

Usually when one hit the ground and lay whimpering, people avoided the place. But occasionally a knot gathered and summoned a policeman—for it was rightly understood that criminality, insanity, political dissent and the exercise of practical intelligence came to the same thing and were best handled by the same means. When the policeman appeared our friends tried, then, to crawl away quick, like poisoned cockroaches in the kitchen when the light is turned on—not easy to be quick, for they were poisoned and maimed and consequently stupid.

This horde of cripples was engaged in an open conspiracy, for it is impossible to have ability and invention and not, willingly or not, be inviting the structure of society to ruin. But it was not to be seen that much tumbled in ruins, though pieces fell down in choking clouds of dust. Meantime, to their own disadvantage, the conspirators superstitiously abstained from many useful social goods as if these were tainted. They devalued goods that were obvious, such as the wealth of the earth produced by ingenuity and labor, or the blood-heating, consoling acclaim of the crowd. Partly because we were hateful and resentful, but mostly because we were already crazy. On the other side, the targets of the conspiracy took the serious things of the conspirators to be jokes, and their jokes to be serious things. A general misunderstanding, little communication in the world. The slight estimation of the conspiracy by the vast majority was correct, it was correct—except that they were dead from the neck up and also from the neck down. The intentions of the conspirators were absurd and ineffectual but they were fighting for life, and they were poisoned, sick and deformed.

This book is the annals of our open conspiracy. How we lived through the war. How we died in their war. How the duration lasted longer than the war. How our friends learned to fly. How Mynheer saw rise the constellation Man and wept. How we formed out of hate a community of human relations. How Horatio was miraculous at the party for the dog. But there is a general misunderstanding, little communication in the world.

One of our friends, a young painter, fell on more evil days than he was used to. He reacted to this daily disaster with hysterical vomiting every morning, clutching his midriff and throwing up. Other friends came to this Job and cried, "Look, boy! This is just an emotional reaction. Things are bad but this behavior doesn't help anything—it is simply stupid. Wake up! Open your eyes! Face the facts!"

"Ow!" cried the painter. "And what else do you think I do? Every morning I wake up—I *open* my eyes—I *face* the facts . . . ugh . . ." and he clutched at his midriff.

2.

The most pitiful to see were the two youths, Droyt and Lefty, for especially in youth we read the soul in the body and they were stricken in the obvious limbs. Droyt stood strong and upright, but his right arm came to a stump at the wrist. The guiltless hand had been hacked off at one of our schools. (Not *their* schools, but one of *our* schools; this is what makes it more bitter.) Nevertheless, he looked at you fearless enough, unashamed, as if he would deal you a hammer blow of anger with his missing fist.

Lefty's spine was twisted. Bending his head, he wore a silly smile, but if he lifted his head he had a grimace of pain. The third or fourth vertebra below the neck was deformed so that he could not bring forward his left hand to defend himself; if he advanced that hand, it, and soon his whole frame, began to tremble spectacularly. He bent forward at the hips, as if afraid to fall, or seeking to drop. He was ashamed of his deformity and often hid himself, or sat on cushions in his characteristic posture which was then less betraying. Also, with the peculiar vitality of human beings, he made his relaxation profitable by crooning and eventually writing down spineless compositions based on mountain airs, with a cloying whole-tone harmony, that sapped the courage of the listener.

Or another time, overwhelmed with self-disgust, he recklessly cast himself into free space and for a moment the weight of the earth disburdened itself from his neck and shoulders; for he could indeed fly a little. But he fell heavily on a pavement, more broken than before, like a star. The passers-by, with the well-known charity of the Americans, gave him a wide berth, for he was suffering. And his pugnacious and terrifying brother bore him safely home—where his crazy mother nursed him, and his father was sitting on a chair with an ice bag on his head.

Such were the athletes with whom we intended to make up a memorial ballgame, to labor out our mourning in order to be able to live on again.

3.

Cancerous colonies of vitality formed themselves deep inside of Emilia. This queenly woman was abounding in vitality too strong to exhaust in symbolic actions as we artists succeed in doing (if indeed we succeed, and are not rotting away.) Her innermost organs choked and died; and these efflorescent cancers sprang from the rot of it, to try to be happy on their own, free of the strangling organization that did not serve to loose the energy of the creation.

She suffered and did not cry out. She stank and covered the stench of it with lilac and heliotrope, so that the underlying odor seemed to be a kind of musk.

I cannot praise the human beings; it is necessary to praise the freedom and energy of the cancerous growths.

Emilia became immobile, and the growths within her projected themselves into her somnolence as cloudy colored dreams, usually of buds exploding into various flowers, sometimes as overheard monologues and conversations.

The color blindness that had afflicted her from her girlhood thus was healed, and she saw the square golden rose of the world—that again dispersed as in a breeze, leaving before her nothing but the sulphurous blue-black.

She imagined she would have a child, that was an edematous mass.

She overheard herself conversing (probably with her father):

"Nature abhors a vacuum. Why are you shaking your head? Do you mean that Nature loves a vacuum? Ah, that's what I think too! No, you are still frowning. You mean, Nature is *indifferent* to a vacuum? Maybe you're right.

"—No; there's no such thing as Nature personified as you make her.

"So! there's no such thing as Nature personified as I make her! Then what am I to do with this vacuum? If nature does not help me, which way shall we go crazy, by dissenting or by conforming?"

Such was the voice of a cancerous growth of vitality misconstrued by her ruined organism.

4.

"This is the best of all possible worlds; and," said Bradley, "it is the duty of every honest man to cry Stinking Fish."

Why am I disappointed? Is one entitled to expect natural magic from these hulking human animals, handicapped in their *species*, quite apart from the particular diseases of this one and that one? Disregard our crippled horde and look, in the most cursory way, at the most perfect specimen of mankind. Choose the flower of youth for inspection.

He has four great limbs and five small appendages at the end of each. These numbers are already odd—is one supposed to take this seriously? The whole is roughly planned on a bilateral symmetry: pairs of everything, for instance, two ears. And the cause of this is, roughly, that he has a head and a tail; moving in one direction forward, the right and left are indifferently equal. He does not see what is behind; desire is what he heads toward. Is it with such a priori limitation that one is supposed to feel, to touch, the ocean of creative nature? He has bilateral blinders; he attends strictly to business.

Now the limbs are systems of levers and pulleys arbitrarily limited: the knee joint bends only backward, the ankle only forward, the base of the toes again forward, and the digital joints only backward; it is the work of an empirical carpenter. This is just one instance, you may find the same adjustments throughout the bony structure; and this is the structure that he drags around with him, that drags itself around, day and night; it is not laid aside, it is not put off and on as occasion arises. Is such an object supposed to act dexterously, spontaneously?

Hung in the scaffolding of these rigid parts are several continuous quasi-elastic tubes; it is through these selective apparatuses that, breathing, eating, sensing, the totality of the world is given in its streaming. Must we not conclude that they are rather devices for straining out and blocking out the most of the universe, defending against it, for it is no doubt too full, beloved, dangerous? This animal, long since departed from the ocean sea tries still to carry some flowing sea along inside him, in the blood and the amniotic fluid, and engaging in a rudimentary swimming during copulation. Is one to regard such makeshifts without a smile?

And all of this, finally, head and tail, levers and pulleys and scaffolding and tubes and water, is stuffed into a bag. Is this serious?

Serious? you object. Is not the crux of seriousness that we must *nevertheless* live the existing moment with just its defects and particularities, and still make something of it? Good! I challenge you to hold this *object* before your mind and still think of a serious providence and destiny. I frankly cannot do it. I too understand that if it is simply a question of living on—for it has one by the throat and no time for consideration—there is something that is serious. But it's quite another thing to approve of it.

Not one of the maimed and deformed, but the best specimen in its bloom of youth! And not looking nicely at him, but only a superficial glance as painters paint (for if we go into the glandular and psychosomatic systems, like the comic poets, the result is notoriously farcical). It is a creature inbred neurotic, fearful, avoiding most of the creation, grappling its security close, turning its nose to business. Am I to use these—men and women as characters in a romance of spontaneous joy, freedom and fraternity, and natural magic? Why am I disappointed? Therefore, it is like a breath of fresh air to be able to praise the cancerous amoebae, striking out to be happy on their own. *They* miraculously came to be from the fertile void surcharged with love.

5.

Someone is breathing on my neck, to protest. It is Lothair, a friend of human beings. But he utters nothing but inarticulate, cretinous grunts, for he is dumb.

I turn to look at him; he is making a despairing gesture with his trembling hands into his mouth. At first I think he is still complaining of his aching teeth; but he means to indicate that he is dumb. He keeps uttering formless noises.

We know that he was learning to speak again, the few primitive words for "bread" and "water" and "human being." But apparently this exercise revived the anxious stuttering of his boyhood—for when we try to do a natural act or come to a natural learning we are stricken with anxiety. And these joint causes, not knowing the real words and guilty paralysis of expressing himself at all, have maimed him beyond recovery.

I am afraid of his anger, the moment that he will frankly growl and take his hands away from his own throat. Yet I cannot forego the rare sport that is offered here, to bait this bull-like one-time orator in his affliction.

I mention the dilemma that a person either conforms himself to the general error and is doomed, or dissents from it and is maimed. What does he think of that? These days it is impossible to live the liberty of even a man.

To refute this he quickens his despairing gesture and grunts and grunts.

"But even the best man in the best age," say I, "in his flower of youth! You see how his character is built into his very bones? Is it from such that we can expect natural magic? I grant you that only an author caught in the aforementioned dilemma would think of this idea; but be that as it may."

To this he shakes his head and gasps, the tears starting into his red eyes.

"Look! Look!" I show him his face in a mirror. He is in poor shape to look at.

He doesn't even have the presence of mind to turn the mirror on *me*; but he jumps up and down in silence.

"And what's your opinion, Lothair? Does Nature abhor a vacuum? Or do you think she fills or empties a vacuum indifferently?"

When he was a boy of ten or eleven he used to be unable to get out a word for long seconds on end. The seconds seemed to him to be hours, while he held his breath and became blue-black in the face, and the room rang, as he faced his prosecutors.

He says only, "Ung," and "Ul, ul," and my triumph is complete.

Jumps up and down in silence: but indeed, to describe it accurately, during these absurd movements he was floaing a little; for he could fly if he did not talk; supporting himself on the thick silence.

6.

Before his face Horatio held up his ten fingers, and they were whole. Next moment he felt a heavy pang in the back of his skull, and he was blind. He staggered forward. As soon as he had full use of his hands, he could not find the world in which to use them, and here he came groping: it was pitiful.

The boys were maimed and crippled, Emilia was cancerous, Lothair had no speech and Horatio was blind. They had many abilities, they were beautiful, commanding, just, quick, but they were deformed and sick—there is no advantage in concealing it.

Up to a certain moment the very activity of living conceals, in part by-passes; but then it becomes evident that one has been poisoned, is sick; wounded and maimed.

Rheum flowed from Horatio's sightless eyes. It became evident to him that previously, when he could see, he had looked past, beside, away from whatever he sharply looked at. Now that he no longer looked, nor made the effort to look, he could recall the straining of his eye muscles that at the time he had not felt. The straining loosed, the rheum washed his hot eyes.

Behind his darkened eyes, colorful fancies appeared; he saw them easily and well. He recollected with surprise that he had quite ceased to see free colors or colorful things, but always only colored things; but now he easily fancied colors—the wonderful blue afterimage of the sun in the eyes, more and more vivid until the yellow-green appeared in the core of the spot.

He had strained his eyes to see what was not there because there was nothing to see in the world up to his hope, his power of interest and love. Even the morning rising over Inwood, through the wood, darting from the dew on the grass, was a picturesque painted backdrop, that he had no way of ripping, to let the blackness ooze through. Landscape was lovely, but what could he do with *that?* Then the young man used to fool himself, *pretending* that he was excited, willfully engaging himself, allowing himself to be trapped and engaged, spontaneously praising what did not compel praise but merely was not despicable; that is, he looked past, beyond, beside, behind what he dutifully looked at—never noticing in it any color. He destroyed his seeing by not properly using his seeing, because in fact there was nothing worth seeing, and he abused his eyes pretending to see it, in order not to be bored. He was not wrong, for, omitting the nonhuman scene, there was in fact little among the human beings to engage direct, full, confident, loving seeing and the lively interest of the heart and head. The curviline, the contour, the profile—the curviline, the contour, the profile promissory of pleasure and rest did not prove, on experience, to pay what it promised; soon one could see it at a glance: this world was not going to come across; but one *cannot* look at that without straining his eyes.

The subtilely estimating faculty with which a man was equipped by nature was too sensitive for any exercise of it in our society in 1949.

The tears flowed out of his sightless eyes. That had been lying to you, overestimating you in order to have someone to love; and not flinching at the brutality of the architecture, in order to be proud of his native city. Then, *nevertheless,* he had held up before his face his ten fingers—of which the tip of the little finger of the right hand was missing. He saw that it was *not* missing! Now as a child on strained terms with his mother—no longer a question who first committed the breach—and nevertheless both are pretending that there is no such breach, he pretending that this makes no difference to him, and she that everything is good and ordinary; and in any case they carry on practically—even enjoying pleasant moments of the false relation!—then she lovingly touches him, and he begins to bawl: so, seeing the natural magic, by grace forgiven, Horatio began to cry. But he was blind, his eyes were dark, and he felt a stunning pang in the back of his head. He staggered forward, first shielding the nape of his neck with his clasped hands, and then groping in the darkness.

The black fire—the thick silence, the black fire oozed before his vision. As if not he were blind, but the wallpaper of the visible world were rent and the night streaming through.

7.

Mynheer Duyck Colijn sat alone with his splitting headache.

For a frightful ax, soon after he was born, clove him in two from the head to the crotch. But he contrived to live by stubbornly holding the falling parts together. Too tight! He had to hold them too much in control because if he relaxed his control, there would be nothing left of him. As it was, his left hand knew too well what his right hand was doing; and the sutures of his skull were clamped too close for his brain to be able to breathe. Instead of two faces, he wore one rigid mask. And his male and female natures loved only each other.

The headache itself was the effect of too tightly clamping the falling parts together. The meaning, the threat, of the headache was the opposite: as we say, "a splitting headache." However it was, the pain of it was nearly unbearable and he cried out, "Give *me* the ax for a second tap!

"We'll see if the green child of spring steps lightly from the cracked skull of the black knight!"

Said a "tap," a blow not fatally hard and deep. He did not wish to kill himself to avoid pain which was, he knew, largely self-inflicted. He relaxed to the pain. For a moment it blazed high, burning up the world; then it receded somewhat and the sweat stood on his face.

Now first he saw that he was alone. He did not retire to himself because he had the headache, but he had the headache in order to retire to himself. He was alone because he was lonely; but this, unluckily, was not something self-inflicted, but was the nature of things, considering how he was and how most of the others were.

Lonely because few could follow his floating thought. Its earnest and irony, and what he materially thought of and the formal coherence with which he thought it. They did not follow. He could not always be explaining what went before; and he assumed what they resisted assuming, and he did not assume what they took for granted. He was not afraid of following where his thought led him, it was not in his experience that a thought turned round and bit one; yet, on the other hand, to him a thought was a thought and it could not be simply disregarded.

There were, he knew, a few who followed him well enough—but of the few he knew only a few; and unluckily these little few did not love one another—did not love one another in close presence, from which one could draw some erotic consolation, though of course they loved one another at a distance and defended one another if need arose.

Yet it was necessary, to live, not to be without company; so Mynheer abased himself and allowed himself to be used by many persons.

It was this self-abasement that was disastrous. For his world was too rich and if he did not stand up for himself he was crushed. For on the one side—from below, so to speak—rose desires of all kinds, and these he always let free and loose, as much as he could (for desire is divine); and on the other side were his excellent thoughts and hopes, equal, true, and just (as befitted a man). Both sides were excellent; and in between there should have stood Mynheer, greatly spreading his wings in loving company. But instead, being lonely, he abased himself in order not to be alone. So he became small.

Therefore he began to sing to himself the song of Sebastian Bach: "Come sweet death, come holy rest, come lead me into peace. For I am weary of the world. Come, I am waiting for you. Come soon and lead me forth. O close my eyes. Come, happy rest!" The long note, on *Friede,* he extended far beyond its rhythmic value, for many measures, exhausting finally the last end of breath, faint of voice. Then by the time he came to the deep ending-note of the song—he sang the song in *B* minor—he no longer felt lonely and his head did not ache. Only he indeed wished to die, soon, for there was no use of it. He thought of his imprisoned wife Laura, his dear spirit of the day, and he shrugged his shoulders.

Meantime, however—for while waiting for soon death one cannot do nothing but sing "Come sweet death," no matter how far one overextends certain long notes—Mynheer returned to his work. Deciding he was becoming an old man, having appointed himself an old man, he was engaged in collecting the table talk of the old Jew Eliphaz, his dead friend. And since there was now so much talk about fires, radioactive fire and *foco che gli affina* and so forth, he was collating Eliphaz's sentences about Fire.

Whistling cheerfully, (*"Loge her"*), for it was a pleasure to remember the conversations of the theologian, the Dutchman sorted out the cards. There were, as it turned out, no less than three kinds of fire, not counting the confused mixtures.

FIRE

1. *"Dark Fire:* destructive eminenter. Radioactive fire if that could not only disintegrate the matter but also eat up the void—which it can't, ha. The dark fire is simply undoing the work of the Creation, returning from the Sixth to before the First Day. Dark because there is no transparent medium: it is in direct contact with the receptor organ (*De Anima* 419a). Conjecture: is there no medium because the fire destroys the medium?

"Dark fire is the only means of purging nausea vitae.

"What if we rip the curtain of the world and the blackness oozes through the rent? Is this blackness dark fire? No, this is the void. Please, is the void the dark fire? I ask you, *is* it? Ha! The dark fire is the way that the likes of you *notices* the void. It is not the void.

"Now this 'refining fire' that the Gentiles talk so much about, purgatorial fire. What's that? A confused notion. On the one hand it is just this dark fire in the specific operation of destroying the Carcasses (*Is.* 66:24). Hm, but the prophet says 'Their fire shall not be quenched'; hell-fire—*Un*likely! After a moment, one eye-blink, there is simply the void.

"But the more usual meaning of refining fire is a superstitious misunderstanding of a specific operation of Magic Fire (q.v.)"

2. "*Magic Fire:* common (solar) vitality in the form of a boundary hedge, e.g., between unconscious and conscious; on the one side protecting Brunhilde and such other sleeping beauties, and on the other keeping out the timid likes of you. To you vitality burns like hell; to the sleeping beauty on the other side it is the maturing breath of spring.

"It is called 'magic' just because of this ambivalent estimation; in fact it is precisely natural fire in its purity. The fearless hero (ordinary natural man) breathes it in and out. Nothing magic about it.

"By 'refining fire' is usually meant this common vitality operating therapeutically, e.g., in psychoanalysis. By ignorance and anxiety common therapy is projected to a supernatural world.

"Now Magic Fire is colored. Reich says it's blue with golden flecks. Color, says Plotinus (ubi?) is the embodiment of fire. Those who can see color are in touch with vitality.

"Ow! What burns me up, believe me with no magic fire, is the new smartaleck anti-Wagnerian. Please, has *this* fellow somewhere filled the scene with an elementary meaning in a simple action, vividly spectacular, and singing away pat? My ass!

3. "*The Burning Bush-fire* (*Exodus* 3.): Type of the existing present passing into the future and not consumed. Hm. Puzzling.

"*This* could be called the magic fire, *proprio sensu,* incomprehensible. You can't explain it: the explanation is burning up, will it explain itself? Explanations are extrapolations from the past (*naturata*). Hm. It says, 'Moses said, I will now turn aside and see this great sight, why the bush is not burnt!' Bravo for him! Not afraid to use his eyes. But he doesn't find out. 'I Am That I Am'! *Hm!*

"*Natura naturans,* says our friend: 'God considered as a free cause, in and through itself.' (*Eth.* I, 29, n.)

"The reason this existing moment is puzzling: it's not what you explain but what you live. So go live it. Please! Let us *turn* aside, like our Teacher, and *see* this great sight, *why* the bush is not burnt. Courage! Is this fire hot? Is it colored? Let me put my hand there, into this present! Ha! So, look. It is my hand—burnt. Do you know what this fire is? It is the transparency itself. It will take on every color, whatever vital fire happens to be there.

"What stuff does the Burning Bush produce? It produces the empty medium where vitality can spring profitably into light and feeling—where it seemed that everything was stifling closed. Hm. Transparency.

"The color of the Burning Bush is thought-passing-over-a-face color (but it must be a *thought,* not one of the vagaries of the likes of you)."

PART 2 HORATIO AND ROSALIND

AN URBAN PASTORAL ROMANCE (AFTER LONGUS)

Chapter 7 ▪ HORATIO AND ROSALIND: I

Horatio first *noticed* Rosalind when she leaped over the subway turnstile. He was surprised—she was a little behind him, to the left—he was charmed by the pleasing sight.

He was acquainted with her (they had even slept together and fucked several times), but he had not *noticed* her as one notices something out the corner of the eye. "Why did you jump over?" he asked. "Didn't you have a dime?"

"It's disgusting to pay money," said Rosalind; "it spoils the fun of taking a ride. I like just to get on and take a ride."

"Don't you have to go someplace?"

"It's even worse than disgusting to have to pay when you have to go someplace; what's it their business?"

Horatio considered this and approved. Our city owned and ran the trains, and all that prevented people from enjoying the goods (such as they were) was this turnstile. They scrutinized it together. Horatio half-made to squeeze Rosalind's arm to express his approval and that he was charmed, but suddenly he felt bashful about touching her. And she, noticing his arrested motion, did not offer her arm as mere formality demanded, for they were intimate. In this frame of mind even if they were in bed together they would not kiss and fuck, though this was demanded by politeness.

The train arrived in a shower of sparks, and they joined the excitement of riding on it, as it showered its sparks and created blue days in the dark tunnel. The speed of it! For whatever stupid and ugly things our city had, it had also moments of this speed. And lines of lights, straight on or rounding a bend—never anything like it before in history. But to enjoy the things of the present it is necessary to be touched by love.

Standing at the front window of the train, they breathed together their enjoyment of the speed and lights, and they pointed out to each other different colors.

The doors of the train sprang open without the touch of a visible hand. This pseudo-magic is also something new in our times.

"Aren't you coming to your sister Laura's?" asked Rosalind, surprised, for Horatio held out his hand to bid her good-by.

"No, I'm not going there," said Horatio, for he felt breathless and a little weak in the knees.

2.

Next morning Horatio early rang Rosalind's bell and brought her a brace of ducks that he had hunted at the supermarket, adroitly tucking them under his short coat. It was a glorious mild March day. He touched the bell button below and the bell jangled above. Electricity! He produced the birds. She laughed, flustered to see him.

"Poor dead birds," she said, shedding a tear. "We must bring one of them to Bufano, the composer, because he's too busy to make money and he's too awkward to hunt. But I'll roast the other. Will you come to dinner?"

"No, no! I can't come to dinner," cried Horatio, as if already he were making the choice whether or not to stay on after dinner. "Put on your hat and come out, for it's mild. We can't bring Bufano just a duck, without wine and oranges for the sauce, and salad."

"Shall we hunt for them together?" She was young enough to be excited by the prospect of sharing in a boy's sport—with Horatio.

You might imagine that the March morning would spread little of its exhilaration in the stifling ambience of our Empire City in the last stages of imperial decay. But they came down to the lordly river where small airplanes resembling sandpipers but painted fiery red, were scudding on the gleaming sea and taking off—pointed south into the warm airs that blew from Florida, and the sunlight blazed in the glass.

"Shall we fly?" Horatio began to ask. "No, we'll fly another day," he said stupidly, as if he did not like the prospect of being alone with Rosalind high up where it is necessary to attend to business. "Look, there are eels already." A fisherman drew up a fat one. "They come earlier in the Hudson than elsewhere," he said with native pride.

It was the same pier where he had expected to find her waiting for him that evening after he had put the tools away. But she had not waited for him. He wondered at how he had felt then, for now his penis did not rise, though she was standing close to him.

"I can still see you, how you jumped over the turnstile last night," he said. "You surprised me—I saw it out the corner of my eye." He turned quickly and faced her. He felt a warning twinge in the back of his skull.

She blushed because he had looked at her.

"As *I* remember how you put the tools away there, that evening," she said. "Aren't you working any more?"

"No."

3.

He explained to her why it was hard to find a satisfactory job of work to do. He had liked working with the power drill, testing the rocky envelope of the shore, but then the employers asked him to make a great oath of loyalty.

"What!" cried Rosalind. "Do you have scruples about telling a convenient fib?"

"No, I don't. But I felt uneasy about the sanity of the director asking me to swear to opinions on such complicated questions when my job was digging with a power drill. I can't work with a man who might suddenly have a wild fit."

"Big Lothair has scruples about telling lies," said Rosalind, "and now I hear he is quite speechless."

"Yes," said Horatio sadly, "he can't get a word out, only cretinous grunts. Do you think it's because he's afraid of lying? Maybe there's nothing to say. Oh——"

"Let's not talk about it if it makes you sad. Why don't you get a job driving one of the big trucks along here?"

The boxes were unloaded from the barges and loaded onto the trucks, with steam cranes and mobile gasoline lifts that darted about like drops of mercury.

"I don't like what's in the boxes," said Horatio sadly. "It could just as well drop in the river—and I'd make mistakes and drop it there."

"Is it bad stuff?"

"No, just useless," said Horatio sadly. "It takes the heart out of me to work at something useless, and I begin to make mistakes. I don't mind putting profits in somebody's pocket—but the job also has to be useful for something."

"There must be useful jobs, since we manage to exist," said Rosalind. She was astonished at what she was saying, as if she wanted him to be working at a job when, quite the contrary, she wanted him to remain with her.

"Most so-called jobs are simply boring!" cried Horatio passionately. "A job has to need at least a part of your strength and interest, otherwise you get distracted, and there are not only mistakes but accidents."

"Why don't you go to the woods and be a lumberjack?"

"No! They chop down the trees just to print off the *New York Times*. You want me to leave the city!" he cried. "Why? Do I bore you? I'm sorry. Good-by."

"No!" she cried, from the bottom of her throat. "I don't want you to leave the city. I was thinking how you would look, like—like Horatio, easily moving the big logs with a hook, in a red shirt so the hunters don't pick you off." She laid a hand on his sleeve.

"Now she wants to see me stretched out dead," said Horatio moodily.

"Shame on you, Horatio Alger, being so sad and non on a mild March morning. Let's get the things for Bufano."

4.

In memory of R. B.

The wine bottle, the netful of oranges, the curly lettuce and the sad mauve duck, composed on the table, made the musician's eyes sparkle. He was a peppery gray-haired little man. Next he became angry and snapped, "Who do you think *you* are, to spend money on Bufano!" He felt inferior when he was in debt, and since he secretly and openly considered himself the greatest musician alive, indeed a favorite darling of the muses, these conflicting evaluations of himself made him furious.

But when they explained that they had cadged the food, he again fell into a good humor, for the adventurous appropriation of the goods of the heavens and earth was something he repaid in full in kind, every day between 11:00 A.M. and 1:00 P.M. He had bourgeois work habits.

"This is grease for the crude parts of the machine," said Horace, "so the fine parts can whir smoother." He produced, also, a box of Dutch chocolates from his inside breast pocket; the box was as cold as ice.

"I didn't see you get that," said Rosalind. She produced a bottle of Cointreau.

"Now get out! It's time for me to work," said the old man, who was afraid he was going to die before such and such a double bar line. "Come back in the afternoon and we'll have dinner."

They obediently retreated down the stairs. "No, come back!" he shouted after them. "I need you now. Sit there."

They sat on the chairs, while he seemed to be listening, hopping about them with his pencil and staff paper.

"What are we supposed to do?"

"*Shh!*"

The young man tapped his foot.

"*Stop* tapping your foot."

But at last he was satisfied and he said, "I used to catch only the sound of the sea. Brass choir and the Bay of Fundy, and the staccato pounding heart. But in this new five-part harmony I have to bring out the inner voices. You young ones are erotic and it's louder. Here's where the violas hum away—" with both hands he sketched a rapid wavering line from Rosalind's calves to up under her heart—"*plunk!* Very vibrant. You have wonderful head tones, my boy, but it's not my type of cantilena. May I kiss you on the throat, dearie?" he asked Rosalind. "I'm writing the ballet for you."

"Any time, Bufano."

"Shall I leave?" said Horace.

"No, you can sit there, you big hulking animal. I just want to get it right. I generally hear it through my teeth."

"Can you really hear the vibrations?" asked Rosalind. "I often feel them if I sit still, but I can't hear them."

"I remember Van Ness at Townshend," said Horace. "He used to hear the truck five miles across the valley of the West, and phone me to clean the points of the fourth cylinder."

"Right! Anybody can hear," cried Bufano sharply, "if you'd wash your ears out."

He bit her. She said, "Ouch."

Boisterously Horace picked up the old man like a sack and planted him on top of the upright piano.

"Let me down! Take me down!" squealed Bufano. "I'll tell you what you want to know."

He used to keep his windows open while he composed, while the thunderous sunshine roared in the motes of dust and the screaming brakes measured the headlong speed.

5.

"You two," cried the old man petulantly kicking the sounding board with his heels, "you two are, potentially, desperately in love. Isn't that idiotic? I don't mean to be in love, but to be desperate about it; and to hold back in potentiality. If one is to be desperate about being in love, about what is one not to be desperate? Hey?"

"That's a lie," cried both Horatio and Rosalind simultaneously, though not for the same reason.

"Pfui! Young people! These days!" The old man spat. "Don't talk to me about lies, because I can hear the vibrations. I do not guess, I know. This one, this hulking Samson, is just stupid-stubborn. He wants to see everything in a scrutinizing way and keep it Out There, as part of the visible world, as Franz used to say. Naturally he hurts his eyes. But Melisande there is even worse. She cultivates fruitless longing. She mistakes the accepting role that's becoming in young ladies for accepting hardship and failure; she likes to suffer. This I despise."

"You hateful, resentful old man!" said Horatio with contempt.

"You're spiteful just because of your short stature. Then you boast that you're the great musician. But in fact you are the great musician, the favorite darling of the muses, who can deny it? And does this help? Everybody praises you and admits it—does this help? Not a bit. You're still angry because you're small. You biter! Immanuel Kant was a little man. I lifted you onto the upright piano so you could tower above us all, and now you repay me with lies."

"News?" said Bufano cheerfully. "Do you have to be brilliant to tell me this and not pay respect to my gray hairs? A newsy item, a newsy item!" He rubbed his hands. He was sure of himself because of their anger; and it was indeed pleasant to sit high on the piano, once one got over the feeling of not falling. (Was it so simple as that to be satisfied at last?) "*You* know everything, and suddenly something surprised you, hey?"

Horatio stampled his feet in rage. "I admit that I was surprised when I saw someone jumping over a fence, out the corner of my eye. But is that a way to see? One sees full face—looking right at the thing." So he said, but he did not dare suit the action to the word. "Rosalind and I are old friends. We've screwed plenty of times and we don't love each other at all."

Rosalind burst into tears. "What's wrong with my being happy crying," she sobbed, "if that's the way I like to be happy and miserable?"

"You can eat your lousy duck without me," said Horatio. "Anyway, I don't plan to be hungry. And I hope you choke on a wishbone." He would have jammed his hat on his head, if he wore a hat.

6. A Timely Rescue

Emerging downstairs, however, Horatio saw a sight that required the use of his clear head. A portly white-haired gentleman, one of the citizens of the Empire City, suddenly threw up his hands and keeled over on the sidewalk. A knot of the curious gathered, but they were not of any use.

Quick-witted, Horatio ran to the spot, elbowed his way through the crowd, and at once commenced artificial respiration on the prostrate man. For he had observed such cases before: gentlemen of scholarly port and attainments, professors or even judges, who suddenly became asphyxiated by the ambience of the imperial decay—and lost their breath and fell down dead. A sure symptom was that they suddenly threw up their hands.

Horatio worked the man's arms up and down. He threw away his tie and collar and loosened his belt and as much of his stiff black clothing as was feasible in the emergency. And dragging the body into the sunlight, he tried to force some of the season into his lungs by sitting astride him and working the muscles of his unbending back. He acted vigorously because he did not have any doubt that it was correct to revive such people, although temporarily, as best one could. Long ago he had learned from his brother and sister, from Lothar and Laura, the motto, "Where there's life there's hope." And although the experience of the intervening years had tended to contravert this, he still firmly believed it.

The crowd pressed too close and was in the way. They had summoned a policeman and were offended by the authority of the rough fellow too loosely dressed. This made Horace's task more desperate, because he knew that once the policeman came the sick man was done for, for first it would be necessary to fill out the forms (and besides, the official doctors either did not recognize the asphyxiation disease or refused to believe that there was a simple remedy.) With all his might, Horatio bent and unbent, to force the body to unbend.

He was successful in time. The policeman was approaching when, to Horace's joy, the gentleman's eyelids fluttered: he began to gasp in the air; he opened his eyes.

He sat up, reaching to adjust his tie and put on his glasses. But Horatio had thrown away the tie, and the glasses were broken, gleaming in the gutter.

In agitation he zipped his fly.

The crowd lost interest and dispersed. The policeman arrived set to make the arrest, for it was unlawful to fall down and create a public disturbance. Horatio prudently prepared to make himself scarce.

"Judge Halloran!" cried the officer in surprise, for this was the portly gentleman's name. "Can I pick you up off the street?"

"No," said the judge tartly, "this young man will be kind enough to help me."

The officer looked at Horatio with contempt but withdrew.

"Here is my card," said the judge to Horatio; he was still sitting in a defeated pose in the gutter. "Maybe someday I can be of assistance to you."

Horatio helped him to his feet. But as soon as he was upright, Judge Halloran began to clutch for his collar. "Where did you throw my collar?" he said peevishly.

"You can do me a favor this minute," said Horatio, "by forgetting your tie and collar for a few days. You aren't too well."

"How can I go to my offices like this?" Being a judge, he had "offices" in the plural for his judicial plural personality.

Little did Horatio realize how soon this timely rescue was going to prove advantageous to him. But today, he threw up his hands, but he did not fall with the asphyxiation.

7.

In the lonely night, preparing for her lonely bed, Rosalind sighed and asked herself, "Why is he so cruel and cold to me, when we used to like each other and touch each other all over, thinking nothing of it? He runs away and will not stay to dinner. It's too insulting that he doesn't try to invent a plausible excuse. If he told me some lie that I could see through, I could imagine he was in love with somebody and at least burn with jealousy.

"In love! Did he have to shout out in a loud voice that he didn't love me at all, and shame me in front of the old man? He's a beast that doesn't observe even the most conventional politeness. I'm sure that even if he stayed here late and we went to bed together and lay alongside each other, he wouldn't bend over and kiss me or put his hand under my behind. He acts as though he hadn't been brought up among decent people; but it's not true, for I know his brother and Laura and Mynheer and they are polite. He has no excuse at all.

"He hates me. He visits me early in the morning, bringing things, just to tantalize me. I have no stomach for the breakfast he brings; let him take it elsewhere. I'm sick!"

She was, indeed, sick with longing and it was easy for her to believe that she was in love, in love without hope. But this was just the situation she really wanted, to be *in longing,* all her feelings alive, yet with no risk of being satisfied at all. Up to the moment that Horatio half-moved to touch her arm but drew back, she did not long for him; for up to that moment he was available and it was safer to let her strong feelings sleep. And now, as it was, if she herself took a step toward him—for where there is a chasm it may usually be bridged from either side—then Horatio might well become available again, so she preferred to stand paralyzed in fruitless longing.

"Oh God, sick, sick!" she moaned. She looked closely in the mirror to make certain that there were no traces of the harrowing agony that she felt. There were none. She was pretty, if she said so herself. Satisfied, she switched out the light, crawled into bed, and turned over on her stomach and fell asleep.

But after a few moments she awoke in terror. For she remembered how, after putting away the tools, Horatio had flung the dark tarpaulin over the machine, and then all the world was changed. The mysterious shape was standing in the room and she cried out. She was glad that, these days, she locked the door before she went to sleep. She was frightened, she began to weep softly and she switched on the light.

8.

But Horatio had the following thoughts: "Obviously that old fool Bufano is right. There's nothing like spitefulness to hit the nail on the head. I'm simply afraid to look at her and see, because she surprised me out the corner of my eye. I'm afraid to find out what I don't know I know. Hm. Hm.

"This is degrading. I'm ashamed to continue this way another hour. If I look at her full face, will my head crack? Then let it crack. If to be myself is to be as I am, I'd rather not be at all.

"I *will* to make more sense!

"Can this be love? Not much. The proof is that when I'm with her my penis doesn't stand up. Previously he used to stand up adventurously enough. I remember the day she kept cruising me while I was working at the drill; why in the devil didn't she wait for me then? Is she demented? One must not miss the opportunity when the body says 'Go ahead.' But tonight I'm sure that if I went there and stretched alongside her and bent over and kissed her and put my hand under her behind, my tail would droop between my legs.

"*This* is just what I don't like; frankly I don't admire myself and it's her fault. When I'm in a position where action is called for, I like to be able, otherwise it's not sociable and polite. . . . Damnation! He's standing up right now."

Poor Horace! In order not to be in love, he tried to reduce his feelings to a mechanical procedure. He was very strong and able to love; he had a generous nature; but like everybody else he was afraid to be in love. He kept his eyes open wide, but he was watching himself. And he saw *to* it that nothing untoward happened.

He came to Rosalind's door and he let himself in with his key.

9.

Her room was dark and through the open window came the early spring and the murmuring and growling of the city. A motor growling. A baby crying and the calls of youngsters playing under the cone of light, and far off, on another street, a man chasing a woman laughing with dismay. There were cats meowing in the yard. A hoarse whispered conversation in the doorway below, lit by a flaming match to light three cigarettes. These friendly sounds were not such as to disturb sleep. If one listened to them, they stirred forgotten urges in the breast.

As Horatio's eyes got used to the darkness, he noticed the shape of Rosalind in the sheets, and he moved a step forward, his penis involuntarily rising.

At this moment she awoke and cried out, believing that there was a mysterious shape in the room. She was glad that she had timidly locked the door for the night, although (to be sure) she knew Horatio had the key. She began to weep softly.

At the moment she cried out, there flashed into the intruder's mind a scene of a few years ago, when, wounded, after a pursuit through the rain on the rocks along the river, the gunshots splitting the night, he had knocked at the door of the hideout in the culvert, and there was no response. At last the door flew open, and Horatio felt pressed against him the point of a bladeless knife (that also had no handle): it was his brother Lothar.

He fell back a step, wiping his icy brow. It was clear to him that it was not a simple thing now to be in love, to notice that one was in love.

Meantime Rosalind was quietly weeping. A powerful tenderness and amorousness took hold of Horatio when he heard her weeping, and now that he had succeeded, there was no longer any need to be cruel. His loving longing for her could freely well up in him.

He began to tremble strongly, but he asked himself nevertheless, "Is now the proper time?"

At this moment Rosalind switched on the light, and Horatio saw before his face his outstretched murderous ten fingers; and he went forward blind, as he staggered from that room.

10.

Blind, Horatio was standing at the curb tapping impatiently with his cane; but nobody offered to help him across the avenue.

He was becoming angry. So far as he could make out, it was midmorning. The big squares of trucks flickered before his dim vision and he could tell by the sounds that there were hurtling hundreds of them. During a momentary lull, he put one foot down, but a horn in his ear blasted him back to safety. His red face grew black with settled wrath. He was lost. He tapped loudly with his cane. He was not yet to the stage of white fury, but it would come. Anger red, black and white like the old German flag.

For the first time in his remembered life, he began to feel sorry for himself. He did not remember how, as a child, he used to feel deliciously sorry for himself.

Instantly a kind of boy stepped up and tapped him on the shoulder. "Smatter? You want tuh cross the street, mister?"

"Yes, I do," snapped Horatio.

"You waiting for somebody to take yuh?"

"Yes I am, you idiot!" said Horatio, the tide in his face receding from black to red.

"Cancha see good?"

"No. You're brilliant."

"Here, take my arm. I'll take yuh crost."

He clutched the boy's arm—it was a sweater torn at the elbow—and they began to jaywalk across. A horn blared.

"Aw, go piss up your leg and play wiv the steam," said the boy.

Quivering with anger, Horatio stopped dead and began to pound with his cane. "They don't know what it's like! They don't know what I suffer!" he roared. "I stood on that corner for nearly ten minutes!"

There were a screaming of brakes and the smell of burning rubber.

"This ain't a very good place to make a speech, mister," said the boy.

"You—you!—" screamed the blind man. "You're as bad as they are!" He lifted his cane and struck at him and missed.

"Jeez, you're a sweet one," said the boy. "You're wild cause they don't take you crost the street. I takes you and you tries to hit me with the stick. Come on, get acrost here, do you wanta have me kilt?"

In a flash, as soon as he stood on the other sidewalk and was safe, Horatio remembered an incident of many many years ago (younger than this boy whose arm he now let go). It was a great day for old memories. He sped on his bicycle down into the gulph, and the trucks closed up the space through which he had planned to escape. There was a grinding of brakes, the tinkling of glass, the smell of burning rubber. He stood safe on the other sidewalk and the tears welled into his sightless eyes and streamed down his cheeks.

"Y'all right now, mister? You can cry. You gotta right to cry."

It was a pert, quick boy. He spoke in a London accent strange to our streets and he quoted (if one knew it) a retort out of the *Street Games.* His sweater was torn, his face black as if he had been in the chimney; but you could not tell the color of his sweater and jeans because the radiance shone through the rents, and his face was ambrosial underneath its mask.

"What's your name, boy?" asked Horatio in a deep voice. "I'm sorry I was rude to you."

"Eros," said the boy.

"Horace?" said Horatio. "Why, that's my name."

"Eyah. I seen you round."

"You've seen me before? Where?"

"We useta be pals."

"How old are you? I can't see. You seem about thirteen."

"Sure, fifteen. I smoke tea and got one as big as your cane."

Horace smiled and decided he was fourteen, since they always lied but their imagination never stretched more than a year.

"Thanks, Horace, for taking me across the street." He held out his hand.

The boy took his hand and tickled his palm.

"Can you take care o'yourself now, blind man?"

"Yes," said Horatio, "I can take care of myself now."

"Hell you can!" said the boy.

Chapter 8 ▪ HORATIO AND ROSALIND: II

1.

Eros schemed: "This fellow doesn't sufficiently love himself; therefore, he's not ready to love Rosalind. Let us begin by making him love what is *like* himself."

To carry out this plan he put on a pair of torn blue corduroy trousers and a red turtleneck sweater; that is, he disguised himself as the kind of love hustler known as Rough Trade. (Costume designed by E.R.) Rough Trade doesn't necessarily want money.

Head bent, Horatio, who could see again if he didn't look at Rosalind, was attentively studying the random items dropped on the sidewalk by the great city beast, paper clips, leaflets, pennies, and crumpled cigarette packages.

"Doncha look at the dirty wall writings no more?" said the hustler, breaking in on his reflections.

"I beg your pardon?" said Horatio. "Yes, I used to study the epigraphy on various kinds of walls."

"Sure, sure, a professor!" hooted the hustler. "They study what gives 'em a cheap thrill."

"Quite the opposite!" said Horatio angrily. "I first looked at them for a cheap thrill, and I came to study them because they had a meaning that was not a cheap thrill. Now I study other things the same way—look at *that!*" he said with contempt, and picked up the crumpled cigarette package. "Cellophane! Everything is wrapped in it. It's what they see through but can't touch through. They're afraid of infection."

"True! A social critic! You see it all the more clearly because it's something in yourself."

"Who are *you,* please?" asked Horatio, looking at him full.

"Doncha remember me? I'm the one that took you crost the street. I see you can see now."

"You've got a different sweater on."

"How in hell do you figure that? I thought you was blind the other time."

"The other sweater had a rip at the elbow, I could feel the flesh."

"Right! The rip just moved south. See, here——" Raising his leg, he revealed a tear in the crotch. "Go ahead, feel it, it won't bite."

"You work too fast for me," said Horatio coldly. "Scram. Get out of here before I stretch you out."

The youth walked away and ostentatiously leaned against a lamp-post, whistling.

"Get on! Get on!" said the other, advancing hostilely.

The hustler raised his eyebrows and said, "Pardon me? Do I know you?"

Horatio paused. "You remind me of somebody," he said, puzzled.

"You bet I do! And I know who!"

"Who, you god-damned smartaleck?"

"Yourself. Such and such years ago. You don't recognize yourself any more."

"Myself?"

"Yeah, yourself. You heard me. *But there's a difference between that time and this!*" He uttered the sentence with such passion that Horatio lost color and was put on the defensive.

"What is the difference?" he asked thickly.

"Then, *then,*" cried the youth in anguish, "the future was open before us, and the possibilities were various before us; it was possible to play a little and procrastinate. But now it's later than you think and we mean business. In those days love could cruise the streets for a laugh; but now we have to hustle for love and for money, and some place to sleep, because we have no place to sleep. *Somebody* neglected something!"

"What did somebody neglect?"

"Yourself! Always yourself!"

As if in confirmation of his cryptic words, before their eyes on the street one of the studious gentlemen keeled over with the asphyxiation. Horatio started to go to the rescue as always, but Eros held his arm in a steely grip, saying, "Charity begins at home."

2.

"Let's walk a way together, you and I," said Horatio.

"Right! it's too public here," said the youth suggestively.

"Please, cut that out. You're making a mistake. I'm not queer and I don't want to have anything to do with you on that level. Is that clear? Let's get off the subject."

"You ain't sick, are you?" said the hustler. "Who's asking you to be queer?"

"What do you mean I'm not sick. What has that got to do with it?"

"If somebody rubs your cock it stands up, don't it? Why do you have to be queer to have a party?"

"Leave my cock out of this," said Horatio quietly. "I can take care of myself. I'm not interested in *your* cock—and that's what I mean by saying I'm not queer."

The boy was offended. "You ain't polite," he said. "Love me and love my dog is what I always say."

They walked a few steps in silence, down a deserted street. "Well, so long," said Eros, "you'll be sorry." And he turned and walked away.

"Why in hell do you pick on me?" cried Horace, for indeed he felt a pang of loneliness at seeing the fellow go. "Can't you tell I'm not the kind that has any money?"

The hustler came back. "I ain't interested in your money, you fool. I'm interested in you. I love you better than you do yourself. I love your cock—that's more than you do. If I had a cock like yours, I'd be proud of it; I'd know what the score was. As a matter of fact I have a cock like yours, and I'm proud of it."

Choosing the moment, with surprising strength he drew Horatio into a doorway and groped him. As he had expected, Horatio's penis was already half erect. Horatio tried to push him away; but as if the feeling of the rapidly bulging member drove the hustler to frenzy, he persisted and tried to embrace him.

With a mighty blow, Horatio hit him on the jaw and sent him sitting in the gutter. Flushed with anger and disappointment, Eros felt his smarting face—but he was unmarked, because one may offend but not injure an immortal instinct. His wings draggled in the mud, he began to whimper (with one eye on the effect).

3.

When Rosalind learned that Horatio was daily frequenting the hustlers at the Crossroads of the World—these fellows have no homes but remain on those corners—she bitterly exclaimed: "Now what is the advantage of fruitless longing! The whole idea of fruitless longing is that a girl can put an end to it and get what she longs for, whenever she really takes her courage in her hands and recovers from being paralyzed (a moment that she deliciously postpones). But I have waited too long. Horatio has forgotten me for these boys, and how can I cope equally with them? I do not understand what goes on there, nor am I equipped to do likewise. I used to wish that my man were in love elsewhere, so I could understand his coldness to me—and then now I would know how to win him back—but now I am burning with jealousy and I cannot even visualize what I am jealous of."

She felt inadequate, envious of the penises of boys, as if she herself did not have what men desire. She could not imagine what the hustlers did, but she was sure it must be Balinese. She thought of various dull and interesting possibilities, but these images stirred in her an access of fury and she cried savagely, "Oh! I'd bite him or something else!"

Having once expressed these savage wishes, she said to herself soberly and calmly, "It's my own fault—why do I blame him? I have failed because I did not want to succeed. I am monstrous. Look about in the chilly springtime, and where else do you observe that anything indulges in fruitless longing? The mice in the walls go directly to what satisfies them, that is why there are so many mice. The cockroaches proliferate, so they must have their loves. Cats do not yowl in vain. Pigeons are reasonable; dogs would be if their masters gave them free leash. So among the wild life; but even among the human beings, the rule is clear though less obvious. If you go to the park, you will find that those who seem to be most lovely and lively are, for the most part, the very ones who make love most directly, without fears and ideas.

"Then what have I done to myself? Previously I wanted to fail. Now I want to succeed! But it is too late."

She took her courage in her hands, but it seemed to her to be a poor thing.

4.

Instantly, as she looked into her empty hands, as fortunetellers look into a bowl, she saw a true vision.

Aphrodite, the mother of us all, was sitting there enthroned and said: "Do not be afraid and do not be envious of the boys, you have what all men desire. Understand that Horatio is frequenting there as part of a plot of love to cure his blindness—do not examine these things too closely. You have all neglected many things and now it is devious and hard for you to be in love. But this force of love, of wanting to be in love, is abiding and persistent; if you give yourself to it, it will quickly dispense with all secondary choices. I assure you, be confident, that one day soon Horatio and Rosalind will come to be in love.

"Meantime, in heaven's name, do not torture yourself with savage thoughts of spite. Omit them, please. For remember that before you can come to be in love with Horatio, as his woman, you must learn to regard him as your beloved son, as though you were his mother. Now mothers fondly smile and invent excuses for their children.

"One other thing: I do not like much your resolutions to be up and doing and getting what you long for. It is my experience that such women succeed in getting what they long for, but they do not succeed in being in love nor in the man's being in love. Take your courage out of your hands and put it back in your breast where it belongs."

Rosalind was awed by the vision, yet she found her tongue to say, "It is too hard just to sit twiddling my thumbs when I am suffering."

The Cypriot turned her head a little to one side and spread her lips in the sidelong smile that is worse than poison, and she said, "Since he has made you jealous, you may use such a stratagem as making him jealous. But without fraud." So said Aphrodite.

—O Mother Aphrodite! Grant me to be in love to travel to the closest place.

That country is strange, but I shall not be lost there. I know how the walls are wired and where the prime engine is pulsating in the dark; nevertheless, the doors fly open to my surprise! There is no trick to it, but only magic.

The topology of that country is that every curviline assumes body and is a Contour and every Contour claims interest and is a Profile. Is this impossible? My eyes were made for this.

Also, the colors are not apart from the forms, but whatever is extended is already colored and whatever is colored is already extended. This is obvious, why can I not perceive it except in happy flashes? Because I have neglected you.

Arise from the sea again, blown round by the airs, and step on this very shore, where I am hastening to meet you here.

You will, if faithfully I copied down the murmuring of my prophetic dream:

Curviline
Contour
Profile

5.

Horatio visited Rosalind wearing his new uniform and proud as a cock. It was important to him to be admired by her; and this was (within his memory) a new experience for him, to need to be admired, though he too at a forgotten age must have done tricks and called out, "Mamee, watch me!"

He pointed out the details of his new clothes and explained everything. The colors: the blue was the blue of sailor's pants, and the red was red; and they were the colors of a soaring dream. He pointed to the carefully arranged accidental rips and explained that they were not only practical but symbolical.

"Practical?" said Rosalind.

"Obviously practical."

She was afraid to show her elementary ignorance by asking why. "What do they symbolize?" she asked faintly.

"They call to mind the sentence of Jean: Through the ragged playing of the quartet you can see the flesh of the music—or something like that."

"To me it seems careless to have torn clothes. 'Poor, but neatly patched.' "

"Ha, careless!" He looked at her with contempt. "People assume that careless dressers don't care about their clothes; when in fact they are artfully imitating the clothes of the age they want to live at."

"What age is this blue and red suit, with the torn pants?"

"Fifteen," said Horatio pat, lying only one year, for that was as far as the imagination could stretch.

She began to laugh. Naturally she was irritated, not only at the circumstances but also at his cocky pride; and instead of fondly smiling and inventing excuses, she began to fight back.

"What is there to laugh about?" he said crossly.

"For the first time in his life, a man pays some attention to what he is wearing, and he can't stop boasting of it. We women have always used our clothes to express our feelings—from the first moment we stared in admiration in the mirror and tried on mama's costume jewelry.

"See, you don't know anything about it!" crowed Horace. "You follow individual fancy and look in the mirror. But we fellows at the Crossroads have a uniform because we belong to a group." Boringly he used the words "we fellows" and "our group."

This was nothing but the working out of the plot of Eros, to make him love himself a little. He was now infatuated with an ideal of himself—oh, brilliantly projected on the corner of Forty-second Street—probably going back to the time when he too much began to forget himself, starting out again where he then left off.

Yet he truly had something to be proud of. Indeed, everywhere the streets of our Empire City were made radiant, among the somber black of the asphyxiated, by the blazing uniforms of the totemic sports-clubs, those Tigers and Hawks and Rattlers, who exhibit themselves according to fantasies of childhood (in fashions invented in Cherry Grove), but who will slash you with a switchblade or a sharpened belt buckle if you make them doubt that they are men. Clever clothiers have made fortunes from these glad rags.

But Rosalind said pedantically: "Women dress for four or five different reasons, only the last of which is to attract men (who never notice anyway)." She counted them on her fingers. "First, a change of clothes restores morale. Second, I love myself. Third, dressing is a craft, an art. Fourth, we dress for other women as critics and competitors. Fifth–" the little finger–"I personally dress to attract certain men."

She flicked the little finger in his nose.

He was cross and bored. He wanted to talk about himself and she wanted to talk about herself. Neither of them was in love. Instead they were angry. Yet this was, unknown to them, part of the plotting of Eros and Aphrodite. His feelings were hurt. She was fighting and scratching, instead of indulging in fruitless longing.

"*What* certain men, for instance?" said Horatio.

"Who?"

"What certain men do you dress to attract?"

6.

At once she became friendly, very friendly and only a shade evasive.

"Let's not quarrel, Horace," she said. "We're both right and we're both wrong. I see it. It's been a profitable discussion."

"Were we having a discussion?" he asked blankly. "About what?"

"About clothes. What you said–you gave me a new idea. Now I understand. Why a certain costume is really attractive. I always felt it, but now I understand it."

"Shit with clothes!" said Horatio. "What certain men? What men? Who else?"

"What do you mean who else?"

"Who else do you try to attract–besides me?" said Horatio lamely.

"Yes, I like to look attractive to you, Horace," she said reassuring. "Naturally I like to look attractive to everyone I like. But let me tell you the idea I got from the discussion. It's this––"

"The idea you got from what discussion?" said Horatio.

"I know. You think I never have an idea. But I do have an idea, this one."

––.

"I see why the clothes of certain men, I mean artists, attract me. Because they wear a uniform, like yours, and they *also* allow for individual fantasy. So they belong to a group with an *esprit de corps,* that's what you meant, and each one also asserts his own personality. We were both right! But they *do* it."

"What artists do you know?" said Horatio darkly.

"They all do it, historically, since the Romantic period. Everyone I know—for instance, Bufano, you know him, and—oh!" She paused, as if censoring the next remark, or perhaps in revery, or perhaps, contrariwise, conclusively.

"What were you going to say?"

"Nothing. . . . I can best say it abstractly, without examples: the clothes reveal the man, and the attractive clothes of an artist, that are both social and fantastic, reveal what is attractive in his personality."

Horatio could think of nothing except to say brutally, "Your friend Bufano dresses like an anal type," as one would say "like a horse's ass." "As a matter of fact," he added judiciously, for it was not in him to be unfair, "he hides what he truly is behind the figure he cuts for himself and the world."

"Why are you always so extremely rude to that great man?" said Rosalind.

7.

Since they did not intend to make love, they went out in the air.

The humble waters of the puddles sought out the lowest places on the sidewalk and lay flat, and reflected whatever face looked into them.

Horatio and Rosalind did not talk about the weather because that was a topic of concern to both, and they imagined they were interested only in themselves; but as it turned out, they were using their soliloquies as weapons to wound each other, and this was great progress.

Realizing that the subject annoyed her, Horatio pointed to certain holes in the wall, freight cars on the siding, nests back of the billboard, and other places for brief privacy, an important part of Rough Trade lore. She was wrong to be merely annoyed, since it was indeed a useful moral study; for most persons seem to think that the streets of our Empire City are irrevocably public, whereas it's not so bad as that; a complicated structure has many interstices—except that to avail oneself of their freedom one mustn't be afraid to get his pants dirty.

A sign of a usual place was that newspapers were bedded there, for cleanliness and comfort.

"You bore me with this subject," said Rosalind.

He persisted. "The abandoned ferry house at Twenty-third Street is boarded up to make it safer, and behind those boards you could set up a hotel. Sometimes a piece of the ceiling falls down."

"Why don't you go to somebody's home?" she asked.

"Where is that?"

Suddenly he had vanished. . . . There was nothing. . . . She looked every way. There was nothing except the usual furniture of the street. The tears started into her eyes.

He rapped on the wall of the truck trailer that he had vaulted inside of. It had been parked there alongside the curb through snow, rain and shine these seven months. (17th Street and 10th Avenue.)

Merrily she boosted herself up beside him. The place was liberally bedded with newspapers. He was delighted that she was there beside him, inside the trailer. She might herself have been Rough Trade. She was very attractive to him. So he kissed her. But the kiss was dry and bitter. They were angry with each other.

They got down from the trailer.

8.

He listened anxiously to her conversation for references to the arts and artists.

It seemed to him that she was using an unusual number of painter's words. So! It was not Bufano after all that was the artist, but some other artist, a painter, a younger artist. He knew that she had been working with Bufano on the new ballet, but it had not really occurred to him to be jealous of them. But it was not a musician, a painter! What painter? A nonobjective painter. But this painter seemed to vacillate a good deal, a kind of eclectic. No, he was always arguing, full of theories. He was a teacher of painting. He was a lousy painter.

But you couldn't get away from it—the artist was a musician after all. And he was *not* Bufano. He wrote movie music. He was a lousy musician. But well trained academically. She must be seeing him nearly every day to pick up as much as that. . . . For heaven's sake, he gave violin lessons!

With a sickening conviction, on the corner where 11th Street crosses 4th Street, Horatio realized that the artist was a kind of novelist. And it was Goodman.

"*There!* That's a usual place," said Rosalind, pointing to an iron door between two tall buildings.

"Don't be absurd," said Horatio. "You'd have to climb over the door and they'd see you far and wide."

"I beg your pardon." She opened the iron door disclosing a flight of wooden steps, and she led him down. The passage ran under the building, it was dark, and it was thickly bedded with newspapers.

It was a secret place.

"How did you know this?" said Horatio in a choking voice.

For at last it was clear to him. The man was not an artist at all; he was, precisely—Rough Trade. Not one but a hundred. Therefore, also, probably a musician, a painter, a kind of novelist. Yes, he knew who it was——

It was Eros. He knew that that peanut went for anything; and this was just the kind of dirty trick he would do to spite him, in repayment for the blow, though they had seemed to become good pals afterward. There was nothing but deceit in this world.

The ground fell away beneath him. He saw it—why it was that he, just now, wildly went with the hustlers: it was in order to create this very situation, that they would have the women while he, envious and small (age of eight), assisted at the scene, like the sociable third parties in Chinese pornographic pictures, who hold back the sheet with one hand and touch the thumb and fourth finger tip of the other in aesthetical appreciation.

He felt small. Eros was his big brother.

"You slut!" he shouted, and slapped Rosalind across the mouth.

She ran upstairs, her heels clicking on the wooden steps. At the top she turned and looked down at him. "You conceited ass," she said.

9.

Rosalind wept.

"My protector hit me. For nothing but teasing him. But I thought he was strong.

"Oh, that day I watched him long ago, caring for the machine, strong, skillful, prudent, considerate, determined, I felt a great safety. I would be safe and sure in his powerful considerate care; protected by his size and prudence; if need be guided by his determination. Then. when he flung the dark cloth over the work and the air was charged with mystery, I was not afraid. His actions were beautiful; the ending was magical.

"But now it turns out that he is brutal, unreasonable and dangerous. Is that a protector? I am afraid unprotected by him, but I am afraid to be protected by him. There is no safety anywhere for me.

"The whole of the world is a brutal waste. I am afraid to go home because they beat me. I look about and it seems to me that some others are cared for and happy; seeing it, I have an unbearable longing for comforting, but I will not go and risk another beating."

She was chilly and put on still another pair of stockings and wrapped herself in still another blanket.

10.

Eros, for his part, was pleased with the progress of events. It was progress. To his way of thinking, any kind of touching was a good sign, the more feeling in it the better. A slap on the face was probably better than a kiss. Hand shaking was good; a punch in the jaw was excellent. What was the harm in insults?

"People regard these little actions sentimentally instead of causally," said Eros, curling his feathers. "But always one thing rapidly transforms into another, if I keep the fires going. Pain is likely to become pleasure; disgust is almost certain to become appetite. Sober drunk, also all the same!"

—Until the mists could disperse and the people recognize, with fright, no trivial hustler, but uprearing in his dignity, the demon Archer, hilarious, played round by fires.

But the mother of Love, serene beauty, was sad because it was so hard, these days, for even the best, the brave and the inventive, to come to be in love.

Chapter 9 • HORATIO AND ROSALIND: III

1.

Rosalind refused to see Horatio and put on her door the placard: "Not at home to the conceited ass."

Besides she was very busy, for Bufano had finished the music and it was up to her to learn the steps.

Looking at the placard, Horatio asked himself, "Shall I disregard it and walk in? Or shall I childishly scribble on it, "I didn't come to see you, but to get back the copy of Lao-tse. Please send it by messenger.—Horatio Alger'? Or shall I make no sign at all and go away, so she may eat her heart out because I never came?" Debating the possibilities, he effectually chose the last, because to be doubtful and do nothing is the same as doing nothing.

Watching him through the keyhole, Rosalind did not eat out her heart that he had not come; but she was torn by doubt whether his desire was to disregard the placard and walk in, or if he had come to get back the copy of Lao-tse, or if he went away without a sign in order to torment her.

In this way they were able to create a kind of void of ambiguity (which is always salutary).

2.

Returning to his own place after this fruitless visit, Horatio had an infuriating experience.

He met his Friend Below on the stairs, the fourth or fifth vertebra below the neck (for it was dark and he could not tell for sure.)

"Come visit me upstairs," he said amiably (he was lonely); "I have records and a picture album."

But the other boorishly said, "No, you come down here," and slammed the door.

Horatio kept leaning over the bannister, hoping he would reappear. He knew it would be clear he had not left, because there was no sound of receding footsteps going upstairs.

Suddenly the fellow stuck his head out the door and cried, "You're too proud!" and vanished.

Horatio beat a retreat to his room on the upper floor and paced the floor in fury. "The house isn't big enough for both of us!" he fumed. One of us must go. What lie about him can I invent to tell the landlady? She seems to favor him."

3.

So he schemed, but the complaint came from the opposite direction. There was a timid tap, and the landlady entered and said, "I have to speak to you—don't be offended. Or maybe I should come back some other time when you're not busy?"

"Yes, not now."

She was relieved. "You *are* busy!" she said.

"No, I'm not busy," said Horatio.

She was nonplussed. "But some other time?" she appealed.

"Why some other time?"

"You mean why not now?"

"No, I don't mean why not now."

"I don't understand," she murmured at last.

"I mean why at all," he said brutally.

She burst into tears and wailed, "I have to keep all my tenants. I need a full house. I don't like them quarreling. He complains downstairs you keep trampling up and down on him, and back and forth. I don't know exactly what he objects to. You know how he is, incoherent. I thought he was your friend. He says you won't let him sleep."

Horatio clenched his fists. "Is that all?"

"That's all."

"Why doesn't he knock on the door and tell me that himself?" he said icily.

"I'll tell you why—I know that," she said surprisingly. "He thinks he's an ignorant man. Don't think he's afraid of you. He's not. But when he tries to talk to you you turn it and twist it and he gets incoherent. Then he has a stomach-ache."

"A stomach-ache?" said Horatio vaguely. And suddenly his anger that had been mounting all day and day by day (and he was not angry by disposition), vanished away and left him in a brown, morose depression. "I'm sorry," he said sadly. "I'm sad because I'm not merry. I've been continually angry every day this week. I know that he seems incoherent; he's bizarre. But he's not *un*reasonable. We ought to be able to make ourselves understood to each other and not quarrel. It's my fault that I don't use the common words.

"Why should *I* be afraid of *him*? I can take care of myself. I discount what he says by half."

4.

But let us leave these impasses. It was now the breezy springtime. The humble puddles that found the lowest places and lay absolutely flat, and therefore truly reflected what was the case, reflected alternately the blue sky and the white clouds, and the black sky and the blinking stars. At the equinox they opened the outdoor theater. Rosalind was hungry and thirsty for success, for applause. Day and night she worked at her role, hanging various insulting signs at her door, not to be disturbed. The opposite of fruitless longing is the desire to please; but to please everybody, all the human nature in the audience, it is necessary to be willing to slight such and such. (Indeed, the ability to please brilliantly, publicly, is a useful effect of fruitless longing let loose to express itself.)

It is important especially for an artist to hang up signs "Person Working," for it is not obvious, to see a person in a stupor, that she is revolving a problem, turning it this way and that. Especially when a young woman is so pretty, it is hard to see that she ought not to be disturbed. And even more especially when she is revolving in her head not some problems of technique but a stubborn question, "How can I *desire* to please? I *can* please if I want to, but how can I *want* to?" for then, brightly drawn and colored on all her person, unknown only to her, is the glorious desire to please. So she hung up various signs, "Artist working, do not disturb," "Clothing personal fantasy in a sociable uniform, keep out!" and "Not at home to the conceited ass."

But at last even Bufano was pleased. That is, he felt that she would not be a disgrace to his score. He wrote longer and longer leaps into the dances, dotting the longest notes indiscriminately.

"But I *can't* fly for seven measures and a half!" she protested.

"You can do it," said the old man positively. "When you hear my music with the actual instruments, you'll find you have the opposite trouble—hard to come down."

"Conceited ass!" thought Rosalind. "When I hear the applause, I'll find it hard to come down."

5.

It was interesting, beautiful and sad. The audience, the very audience, precisely the audience (what other audience is there but the audience?), the audience that on the street was annoyed, hostile and not displeased to see them break their bones, this audience was moved and delighted by the same *salti* seen behind the proscenium, themselves imaginatively making the *salti*.

I do not complain of it. I know that I myself, as I am, am offended by the freedom and power of such and such—it hurts me—and I am delighted if, in conditions of safety, I can watch with admiration this freedom and power and imaginatively awaken it in myself. (This paradox is the use of artists.) But what I complain of is a certain error of perception: the audience secretly thinks it is a trick, they do not think, they do not want to think, that we are only acting out more closely than usual what is indeed the case.

Come back of the proscenium arch! *Here* are the blue and orange lights (no trick to it), and here is the wonderful nothing light invented by Droyt and Jeffrey Deegan with the inspiration of small resources; the music comes from these horns of the sea; Rosalind is soaring on her own limbs, there are no wires (or *here* are the wires, what difference does it make?)—and *nevertheless,* now that you understand how it is done, because you understand how it is done, frontstage and backstage, it is magic. If the old man was giving in to second childhood, with all the skill and accuracy of a long life—before the crash of the airplane—must the music not in fact raise you in buoyant joy? And if Rosalind, having distilled the essence of fruitless longing, now gave herself to the desire to please——

The applause rang out. This also was a fact. The applause buoyed the dancers still higher; and the applause then redoubled and took voice, and they flew. In this exchange of heat, the cellophane fourth wall ignited and vanished. As Rosalind had predicted, when the applause rang out she found it hard to descend.

The story was *Francesca.* At the end it was necessary to fall down like a body dead. She plummeted down from the flies and lay there like a body dead.

The ushers hastened forward with baskets of April, and with a bucket of bottles of champagne bearing the streamer "Success."

Horatio's moroseness abated. Since everybody seemed to be in love with Rosalind, it was not unreasonable for him to be in love with her. He was not jealous. She was a beautiful dancer.

6.

> I am certain of nothing but the holiness of the heart's affections.
> —Keats

Horatio called on his Friend Below and sat down. He did not like it in his rooms; he liked it; he did not know whether or not he liked it, but he had to go anyway, for he was at his wit's end and needed help. One breathed easier there, but the chair seemed to be cramping and uncomfortable; but if one moved, it was clear that it was not the chair that cramped one—it was himself holding himself too rigidly.

One had to lead the conversation; sometimes the fellow answered nothing at all. But what was irritating and pathetic was not that he did not speak or did not know what to say, but that on the contrary he generally did have something to say but was inarticulate or incoherent. His throat swelled, his complexion reddened, his wild hair stood on end. Nothing articulate. Or a flood of puzzling words. Or a single true word that made Horatio tremble because it was true. They both then trembled. All of these were answers, in a way.

"I'm not jealous," said Horatio. "Not jealous of Bufano. Not physically jealous. I doubt that he can make love any more, anyway. But even with others—artists, or the hustlers—I think I could visualize it almost with equanimity. I'm hardly physically jealous. I'm jealous because she said he was a great man."

"Are you envious?"

Horatio looked at this, straight, with open eyes, not the eyes of envy. He was not envious. "Why should I be envious? If he's great, does that diminish me? There's plenty of space."

The other rumbled with approval, and they breathed easy.

"But *I* am not great," said Horatio. "That's the trouble. How can I justify myself? She does not tell me I am great—why should she?—so I am offended and wounded when she says that he is great. And what difference would it make whether she said so or not if I am not great?"

The other began to swell and be helpless. He could not say the simple thing he had to say: You are great enough for your own good.

"When I was a small child," cried Horatio, "I used always to look for a model hero to grow up to, to conform myself to. But now my teacher is dead! My teacher is dead and I can't find another teacher! I am on my own, and I'm not up to it.

"Yes, I am envious of the artists!" he said passionately. "They appoint themselves. I am envious of the natural philosophers, because they are proved by the nature of things." But he was not envious of them. Only he had the feeling that he was not justified.

"I cannot make anything enduring," he said. "I am not a productive person."

He began to feel horribly uncomfortable, resting there, rigid. It was hard to breathe. Meantime the Friend Below was struggling pathetically and making unmistakable motions of copulation.

They were both trembling.

Horatio leaped to his feet and ran to the door. And as if this movement of the one loosed the other's power of expression, Horatio suddenly heard the stream of thoughts:

"Great enough for your own good. You can be great in love. Cry of boredom—don't be ashamed to cry of it. You hold boredom close to you by impatience and cowardice. Boredom! Vacancy! Productive of existence! What are these arts and sciences to you? *You* can be great in love. You are great enough for your own good."

He went outside; then first he heard the astonishing word in this mélange; he could be great in love.

Then he blushed, a deep color, from the soles of his feet to the roots of his hair. For this was a touching, a poignant compliment to him. Indeed, he did not know another compliment. Unfortunately, it was a lie.

That was how it always was when he went below; his friend would suggest to him a role that he could not see himself in, that he couldn't afford.

"But what harm is that to me, what he says?" thought Horatio. "I discount it by half."

7.

"Now that I know how to want to please," said Rosalind to Bufano, "ought I not tell Horatio I love him?"

"No."

"There's a misunderstanding between us. Why should it continue? What's the use of one day passing into another?"

"There's no misunderstanding."

"Horatio thinks I'm offended with him, but I'm no longer offended with him. I love him."

"You do not love him."

"Yes, I love Horatio," said Rosalind.

He did not answer at all.

"Why are *you* angry with me, Bufano? Do you think I did wrong to shut the door against him and work only on the show?"

He closed his eyes in pain. "What's the use of trying to fool?" he said bitterly. "You couldn't have opened that door if you wanted to. If you're cursed with a gift, you have to fulfill this gift *also* in order to be in love. *Who* can do it? It's too much for anyone to do."

She put a hand across her mouth in fright.

"How do you love him? You love him to tell it to me; but you don't love him to tell it to him. It's a story about yourself that you say to yourself, then you say it to me. Why do you need to say it to me? Why do you need to say anything at all? Let be! Let be! Ow, my crazy ears! When will I hear the silence?"

He shouted, and his voice cracked. "Back and forth, pacing, from one wall to the other wall. First we say keep away—then you rush at him with words to be close. You hump him and have a feeble orgasm and drive him away again. Always looking for something—trying to make good the loss. I have made *good* my loss too many times! I have too *many* times made good my loss!"

"What's the matter, Bufano?" said Rosalind with simple love, as if he were her child.

It was the despair that overcame him every time he had completed a work of music. He listened for the silence that should come at the end of the work, but could not hear it. He understood that he had once again given himself entire as best he could (he did not hold back), and still he was not happy. (When he was working, he did not think whether or not he was happy.)

8.

He recognized the note of simple concern in her voice, and tears wet his eyes. He was grateful.

"Look out this window, pretty artist," he said somberly, "and let me show you the arts in our city.

"Never in the history of mankind, in any age in any place, have there been so many works of art, of the imagination, speaking feeling, communicating feeling, as you may here endure. The quality is various, but consider only the quantity of it."

It was an ordinary corner (Greenwich Avenue and 7th Avenue), bathed in the lively sunlight. People came out of a cinema theater where they had just seen two long dramas. They were going to hear other plays and stories over the radio. On a stand there were thirty-four brightly covered storybooks. From different windows came the sounds of music, both from machines and live fingers and throats. The eye could not avoid seeing drawings and paintings, small, large, enormous, relating various ideas to feelings by means of forms, colors and images. There was a mobile sculpture, a barber pole, the red, white and blue spiraling endlessly upward from nowhere to nowhere. Flame leaping through an ingeniously bent glass tube repeatedly spelled out the name of a bar in italic letters. All this was on every corner.

"These beautiful media and gifted talents," said Bufano: "idiotic ideas, meticulous training and technique, timid expression, bizarre combinations, witty invention, banality, outcries of the heart, lies—why is there so much of it, whatever it is? Your friends say these people are dead, but you see there's nothing but life, stories, imagination, form, color, rhythm and harmony.

"It's the outpouring of fruitless longing, that must be stayed with some feeling or other. By fruitless longing I do not mean what is not satisfied, but what does not want to be satisfied. (Cannot be, doesn't want to be—it's the same thing.) This is why there is so much art. The longing is deep and full—it is the animal itself; the satisfaction that is given and taken is feeble; the need recurs immediately; they rush to it again and again.

"Are these arts bad? They are indispensable. Without the excitement of these arts everybody would lie down and stifle. Yes! In our theaters occasionally impressionable persons die of heart failure, and often serious artists die of apoplexy, but it is not to be seen that people die of the asphyxiation (except at concerts of the Great Plains school). No, they breathe a little easier.

"And do you know how it is? When something is told, it is a mask for the truth. Crudely, you may take it that just the opposite is true. And supposing that a man is sophisticated and knows this about himself, it is the same also with him, but it is hard to decipher the opposite of the intricate romance he invents—he succeeds in confusing everything. But the worst are those who are frank and tell the truth; they make themselves impenetrable to themselves forever.

"Often I stand here at the window and listen for the silence of it; but I cannot hear it. Can you hear the silence of it? If you were in love, as you pretend, you could hear articulations of the silence of it—that is, nothing at all—that is, a line rising in the—clarinet? Lightly rising in the silence of it—you know? Let be."

He was listening very well and in fact hearing such and such parts of the silence of it, not unhappy, if only he did not think about it and talk about it. Nor was Rosalind so badly off as he said; she could very well hear a certain thick silence in her throat.

"You're lying, Bufano," she said. "You're in love. Are you in love with me?"

"No," he said.

It was impossible to judge from what he said whether it was the truth, or just the opposite, or impenetrable. And so it was.

9.

"The poor ones," thought Rosalind, thinking of Bufano, and also Horatio and other excellent men she knew. "They will never, being in love and remaining in love, satisfy themselves and be happy. The work they do lays claim on them: some art or exploit or idea. Our Aphrodite is not to them a sufficient guide. I see why it is necessary to be also a mother to them and invent excuses for them.

"But why are we, why am I in a safer position? It is simply that, beginning to be in love, I feel I am going to have children, three or seven small boys and girls, as the circumstances allow and as long as it lasts (for nothing lasts forever, but this lasts long enough to be happy). *These* will be my jewels, as Cornelia said."

10.

Humbly Horatio called on his Friend Below, who, today, seemed more collected and more likely to be articulate.

"To be frank with you," said Horatio, "I have been discounting what you say by half. But this doesn't work out. I am half-impatient, half a coward? I am bored, altogether bored!"

He found the usual chair fairly comfortable as he stretched out. It was one of those reclining chairs, a kind of deck chair, knees up, head back. The trouble with such a chair was that it forced one to relax, and therefore aroused anxiety. It was not a chair one could easily leap from, to pace the floor; it was very comfortable, *if* one relaxed in it; but who could relax in it?

"So?" said the host. He was an admirable counsellor; he advanced nothing of his own but suggested only what was already advanced, what one came back to advancing again and again, that is, what ultimately one could not get away from—and then one might as well do it with a good conscience. As a counsellor he also had only one maxim, Lawrence's maxim: "In every issue follow your deepest impulse." He was a sage of the relatively deeper impulse.

"I can entertain the idea of being in love with Rosalind," said Horatio comfortably. "Revolving this idea in my head—is satisfactory. To love—what I can have. For I know that she loves me. I do not need to be afraid of failure in order to be able to desire."

"Good for you," said the other, deep in his chest.

"As I think of Rosalind," said the enamored young man, "how she goes, when I think of Rosalind how she goes, and of what it is I approve of and desire, then, putting two and two together, I must conclude that I *could* be in love with her; if I could be in love, it is with her I could be in love."

The other wiped the sweat away. This was like pulling teeth.

Horatio relaxed deeper into the deck chair. A delicious numbness was invading his limbs and his head was light and clear. He might have been at sea—on the deep blue sea.

"The question is," he said faintly, "whether I—that is, a man—could say in the indicative mood, not hypothetically, that I—that *he* loves Rosalind? Does he love Rosalind? Do *I* love Rosalind?"

The force of this logical leap, from the universal reasonableness of loving her, hypothetically speaking, to the particular fact of loving her—posed as a question with only two possible answers!—the force of it thrilled through his sinking body like a charge of electricity and he began to tingle and tremble in all his joints.

The friend could not contain himself and leaped up in a rage. "Get out of my room, you sluggard!" he screamed. "How dare you fall asleep here?"

He seized Horatio by his shirt front and dragged him to his feet.

"Go fuck your mother!" cried Horatio. "Yes, I love Rosalind."

He staggered out the door, so rudely aroused. But then he could not stand upright. The hall, the building was tilting upward and backward, the ceiling and walls over his head and past, and the floor coming up to meet him again and again. Or as if, again, his eyeballs were spinning downward in the contrary direction. He clung to the bannister.

11.

It was toward evening, and both Rosalind and Horatio had the identical intention, to say to each other directly—without mentioning it to Bufanos or Friends Below—"I love you—I love you, Horatio. Rosalind, I love you."

They had the identical intention at the same time, but neither of them carried it out—because, to put it bluntly, although they knew they were in love with each other, they did not have any animal desire to make love to each other, fondle, or kiss, or touch, or hear and see, or even be near each other. They were confident that such a desire would come flaming over them at any minute; and then each would rush to the other (in which case they would meet halfway), and cry out, "I love you, Horatio; Rosalind, I love you," and be near each other, hear and see, touch, kiss, fondle, lie abed, and so forth.

But at the present moment, Rosalind said to herself: "I can see him still, putting the tools away, and I love him now and forever. What a delicious ease I feel at the end of fruitless longing. I want to please and I know how to please. Dear, dearest boy! Tomorrow morning early I'll fly to you and we'll make love."

And Horatio said to himself: "When I think of Rosalind how she goes, I am, I am in love with her. Why have I been so blind when all I needed was to open my eyes and notice how I was? I like myself well enough to want to be happy. Dearest Rosalind! Tomorrow morning early, or maybe later tonight, I'll fly to you and we'll make love."

That's what they said and thought. But that very evening Horatio was arrested by the police and carried off to prison.

Chapter 10 ▪ HORATIO AND ROSALIND, IV: THE TRIAL

1.

We know that when Horatio was a small boy he was registered for school, but he looked sharp and he stole the records. "When there's no record in the whole world," he childishly boasted, "then they don't even *start* to look for you!" A woman there with red hair had written it down, but he waited until she went to the toilet and he stole it, and ran out into freedom.

Indeed, it took more than two decades, almost a generation, up to the day when he was ready to become a father, for them to trace him and track him down.

The method used by the police was a simple but laborious one. They used the Average Statistics refined and corrected to account for the least one. At first the graphs and tables indicated nothing at all. Then there was a certain vague and wandering aberration—like the distracting influence of the unknown planet that proved to be Neptune. Always there was one too many in the world, or one too few on the books, which was more important. And finally it was clear that the unknown was here and now, and it was Horatio. The one who was alive without a registered footprint, learned without a school record, well and fed without a security number, working without papers, natively pious without the oath, scheduled for death not in the army. You can imagine that as the evidence of such a thing accumulated, the authorities passed uneasy hours—

> looked at each other with a wild surmise,
> silent.

But the prosecutor, whose name was Antonicelli, said cuttingly, "And supposing we make the *opposite* assumption, that *we* have made a mistake, that that *exists,* that the record is incomplete?" And following this hypothesis he said at last, "*There* is the man!"

They came for Horatio in the dead of his night of glory, when he was willing to be in love and his breathing animal was again about to reach out for satisfaction but now with full strength and joy: then the guards came. The truth was known and he was trapped.

Poor brave child! He had so shrewdly and boldly played for it that he won more than we ordinarily live; so that it took them nearly a generation, until he himself was willing to be one of the fathers, to drop on his shoulder the heavy hand of guilt.

2.

It is shameful to tell it, but he was so overcome with confusion that he was resourceless, not even angry. Instead, as they hustled him off to prison he tried to be friendly and reasonable. "Why am I in the wrong?" he protested. "What have I cost you?"

"That's just it!" cried the officer merrily. "I don't catch on much, but in your case, it seems, there's this whole list of accounts you've fucked up. Money set aside for education—no taker! Money set aside for safety—no taker! Money set aside for vocational guidance —no taker! Money set aside for uniform and burial—no taker! How long could that go on? *It even began to show in the graphs.*"

"So I'm here because you owe me money," said Horatio, near to tears.

"That's it!" The officer laughed. "Ha, ha, ha."

Other officers took it up. "Ha, ha, ha, ha, ha."

The iron door clanged shut.

"Ha, ha," sounded through the iron door.

"Ho."

"At least I don't enjoy the joke," thought Horatio. "I'm not so sick that I have an American sense of humor. . . . Real bars.

". . . Rosalind. Rosalind, I love you." He shook the bars.

Love was his true concern—he could not drive it from his mind. With terrible gloom, as the footsteps receded down the corridor and vanished, he sat on the floor and remembered Franz's friend in Prague, who likewise was arrested at the moment of falling in love, of giving in to love. "What?" he groaned. "Am I now going to die like a dog?" He thought of the throat-cutting knife.

"My Empire City isn't Prague!" thought the dear loyal native son. "And anyway, that's not my style."

3.

Arrested, he was taken, abruptly, back to the age of six—the attitude of the time of being locked up in the closet for being naughty. Therefore, once he had recovered from his confusion—too late to seize practical opportunities—it was natural enough for him to turn his mind to fun and games. In jail, there were several opportunities for childish sport. To cite an amateur of the subject (C. Bennett):

Most prisons have a vulnerable ventilating systems which opens into corridors through panels equipped with Allen-head screws. An Allen-head screwdriver may, with patience, be shaped from a large nail. The water-supply and waste pipes are usually run in these ducts. This ventilating system is a hollow steel drum, and a proper beating administered in the panels will carry through the entire institution, officers' sleeping-quarters included . . .

If the cell doors are of the individual-lock type plus a master control operated manually or electrically from a box available only to the officer, the entire cell block may be put out of operation in a few minutes by stuffing paper clips, spring steel, fork tines and similar obstacles in the keyhole.

In the case of concrete construction, there is a procedure known as 'building a battleship' which involves 10 or 15 men locking arms. They count 1, 2, 3, and all jump together. When two or three tons of men land on a small area of floor, most buildings feel it. In steel-tank jails, marching in unison around uprights will shake bolts and rivets loose, and can even effect welded construction.

An inventive genius took a couple of pieces of toilet tissue, smeared them with stale mustard [Why the substitute?—P.G.], wrapped them in another piece of tissue and tossed them out the window. The officer elbowed the crowd out of the way in his dash to pick up the secret message.

[Also] cautious sabotage and the stupidity strike, plus slowdown wherever applicable. The plumbing, lighting and communication systems are vulnerable. Schweikism is the last resort . . .

—There was thus several good opportunities for fun and games, age six. But they were not unlimited.

Horatio, to tell the truth, did not at all find, like Lothar his brother, that a prison cell was a good sample of all the universe there is—even though a straight line there is still the shortest distance between two points, and the light leaps through a transparent medium, and whatever goes up comes down. When he had thought it was a good sample, Lothar was demented; whereas Horatio was on the brink of being sane.

He sat down on the floor, morose.

4.

Was he guilty?

He was guilty. The fright that had arisen in his breast, contrary to reason and nature, remained there, its meaning unknown. And the disgrace of attempting, because fright had him by the throat, to put on a friendly face and talk his way out. He sat trembling with shame.

The past, like a breaker, broke abruptly on him and stunned and stopped him. Something he did not understand and did not take into account, when he was about to be in love, laid an iron grip on his right shoulder and congealed every muscle of his throat and the back of his neck with guilt. He could not turn his head about to face it.

This past was not the remembered history. He could remember stealing the document, the act that estranged him from these people. There was nothing in that image that awakened nameless fright. The characters, the act, the shrewdness, the moment of decision of the small boy watching and seizing the chance: there he recognized himself as he knew himself. Just what he could not remember in the episode was what must have been present in it, the breathless agony of fear of the small boy—that he now felt. In a flash he recalled the other scene from that early time, when he had found himself in the school building; and in a stone court many were clumsily tramping together in a circle, rhythmically chanting:

Oafy bees!
Barley boes!

while a great woman rang on a piano. A bell jangled; the rooms poured out hundreds. He backed into a stairway and fell. . . . Sitting on the floor of the jail, he painfully added to that memory the motive of it, that he had wandered into the stone court by a yearning curiosity, to *be with* those tramping boys and girls, he was so lonely. Good! Now he was (in principle) with them.

A Jacob, a domestic thief; an honest wild shepherd, an Esau! "Naturally a man is both of the opposite brothers," Eliphaz used to say. When he thought of the man he had chosen to be his father, the tears boiled in Horatio's eyes.

And he thought of Daphnis, of Daphnis and Chloe. How the literary convention was not fantastic but precisely realistic, that when the affairs of the lovers reach a tragic impasse, some mysterious memento of the distant past, an amulet, a birth sign, is found and disclosed. But "Horatio and Rosalind," it seemed, belonged to the stories with unhappy endings. Except——

He did not believe it. For before those terrible times he could remember, and that haunted him, stealing the records, fainting in the courtyard, there must have been a time when he was the obvious free-born heir of social nature herself (and her husband, whoever he was). There were plenty of souvenirs of it! He laid his hands on his handsome body and touched his beautiful penis; humming,

> Nor you nor I
> nor any one knows
> how oafy bees
> and barley boes.

And with this delicious comforting idea he fell asleep, still humming

> Waiting for a partner
> waiting for a partner

5.

More than willing to make love to Rosalind and be in love with her, Horatio had delayed simply because he did not at the moment have an animal urgency to it; and now, as he relaxed into slumber singing, she at once appeared to him in a dream little altered from her appearance to him awake, and his animal interest in her was lively.

She was quite orange, with flashing white teeth, and they were already on an island in the South Seas surrounded by the breathing deep blue ocean.

The water, when they swam underwater, was soft and transparent, and they wondered at the life in the depths: Sea horses, starfish and medusae, and tropical fish and sea dragons; an octopus. The sea horses stood still suspended in mid-space; the tropical fish lightly undulated their fins. Everything was near to waking actuality, like a colored cinema travelogue. There was a faint savor of strangeness, for they named the beasts in French. *"Hippocampe—Méduse—Pégase—Actinies—Eponge—Pieuvre. Etoile de Mer——*

"Etoile de Mer. Hippocampe."

With nothing but this faint taste of strangeness, that also was not improbable in French Tahiti, Horatio swam body to body with the orange girl and enjoyed an orgasm of sweet satisfaction and power. The ejaculation hung in the water like still another curious beast of the creation. He did not awake.

They came ashore, buffeted somewhat by the breakers and scratched by the coral. The landscape was a bit wilder, more fantastic, less cinematic. The color of it was tawny and rupose. The air was a little chill, and laughing they chased each other to be warm; not clear which was chasing which—in an ovate circle—but both were willing to be caught. And once again the dreamer experienced a pleasurable orgasm, somewhat violent, a little torn from him—but with only such superficial pain as a strong swimmer feels dragged scratched on the coral, or a child feels when his mother laughs at him with pointed teeth, but he knows she is teasing. He did not awake.

These islands were subject to volcanic earthquakes. One took that for granted, no enigma, exploring in the interior heights. The burnt-out volcanic craters; the sign, as Barth used to say, that a fire was once here, the Bible stories the history of the dealings of the unknown God with mankind. . . .

Horatio awoke, without fright, very satisfied with his pleasant love-making. Stretched out on the hard floor, he could perceive fairly clearly how the parts of his body were the space and world of the scenes of the dreams he had been dreaming. Whenever he could perceive this: that the space of the dream was his relaxed body, as well as that the actions of the dream were his wishes, he believed that he understood the dream well enough—he was dreaming awake. He was not one to need to explore the little dark corners; he was Daphnis, destined to be pleased.

But Rosalind lay all night in icy immobility, like the Sleeping Beauty waiting to be wakened with a kiss.

6.

Next morning, evident to all was that Horatio was a man in love, breathing ability. The guards saw it and did not fear for him. His power was well-nigh irresistible; it was with difficulty that one set up against it defenses of spite and resentment.

They conducted him to the courtroom: it was as if the guards were his entourage of the happy and brave.

Horatio was five feet ten inches tall, well set-up, well hung. His hair was chestnut with a streak of fair. He was not one of the tall dark lovers haunted of romance; nor a golden adolescent. He was twenty-seven years old. His face was frank, but not more ingenuous than fitted his age. His like was to be seen frequently, every way remarkable——

He had round him a blue field, shot with sparks and flashes of orange. His voice had in it the memory of songs. An orphan, he was not yet a father. It did not present itself to him as a question, whether or not he was justified. His eyes were seeing.

When they entered the court, he saw with a start of delight that the judge at the far end of the room was Judge Halloran, the same that he had resuscitated from the asphyxiation. (But it was not, of course, by accident that good chance befell Horatio.)

Also that the judge, underneath his handsome black judicial robe, was wearing a soft collar and a flowing green tie, as though every day were St. Patrick's Day. His hair was shining white and his cheeks were pink—indeed, he looked like a Jesuit I once studied under, who had spent a year of penance in Kansas and now, back in the university of our Empire City, was relishing the life created by God and man.

A trial was in progress.

7.

This was a celebrated but rather banal case of a great and successful entertainer, a kind of comic musician, sued by a girl for breach of promise, unacknowledged paternity and support. He was very rich and she was suing, hopefully, for a large sum.

The comedian—who was a marvelous comedian, the delight of millions, and this was why the case was celebrated—was gloomily trying to establish that he hardly knew the girl, that, anyway, she was a whore, that the baby was not his, and that the suit had begun in blackmail: to make him pay to save his reputation, but he wouldn't do it.

The girl—who was a very ordinary girl—succeeded in establishing that he was a lascivious person, and she claimed that he had promised her fame and fortune in the theater.

Judge Halloran stood up and asked, "Does anyone have anything further to say, before I charge the jury?"

"May I speak, your Honor?" called out Horatio from the back.

"Ah, it's you!" cried the judge, recognizing him with a start of surprise and mixed feelings. "What are you doing here?"

"I am guilty of what they charge me of!" said Horatio, not with the voice of a man who regards himself as guilty of any damned thing whatever. "But may I say something to the point of this trial in progress?"

His presence was in fact irresistible, and the judge said, "Speak up!" muttering to his clerk, "You see there a man in love. Look, it is rare. Shall I call this natural phenomenon to the attention of the public?"

"How can they help but see it?" said the clerk.

Horatio spoke out in anger:

"You wretched ungrateful people! It is the same story again and again. This great artist gives you delight that you greedily take, rightly, for we sorely need it. But then he proves to be lascivious, pleasure-starved perhaps beyond the average, and also bold enough to snatch something for himself, driven to boldness, for he is depleted by art, courageous for he is an artist. Suddenly you are resentful, censorious: why should *he* have this? What! Do you think something comes from nothing? Can he delight you, without hungering for pleasure himself? You are superstitious, you think everything is done with mirrors, but in natural magic you refuse to believe. The artist himself is ignorant of the divinity working in him; he makes the music by inspiration and lives his life a pathetic blunderer; you take in the music greedily and turn on him in fury. You are disgusting; I bother to say it because I need your love and aid, you are the only society that there is.

"But now you, you stingy comedian!" cried Horatio, addressing the defendant. "What do you think you are, amassing this wealth for yourself and not generously giving it out to these girls whom you need? For heaven's sake, be generous, light-handed, light-hearted. I don't doubt that you started in poverty, that deep down you are fearful of returning to poverty; you try to erect bulwarks against the fear. No use, you can never have money enough to make you feel safe. Please, you are gifted by luck, rich by luck, not your own doing; you know this as well as I. (Is this what makes you fearful? You think your fortune is not deserved? Rest assured: nothing is deserved by us, and everything is due us.) If I were you I should, as guiltlessly as possible, deal generously with that pretty girl and all the rest."

The judge said, "This man has spoken exactly to the point of the case. I should myself have seen it, given time. I advise the jury: adjudge him innocent with costs; and I'll give her the costs. What is the next case?"

The next case was: *The Sociolatry vs. Horatio Alger,* for persistent treason.

8.

The theory of the indictment for treason was as follows: that by living in alienation among the citizens of the Sociolatry, the Alien destroyed the status. One would have expected an indictment of *Laesa Majestas,* attack on the dignity of the status; but the Sociolators obviously felt that a war was being fought; the status was being not merely insulted but threatened with ruin.

(Our friends, conversely, claimed that the institutions were a treason against Natural Society. So theoretically there was indeed a war: opposing loyalties, opposing treasons. But the legal issue was inextricably complicated because, in our friends' view, so long as the sociolators were living persons they could not help being loyal members of natural society. Only the living dead were treasonable persons, and this class had no interesting members. The dead were valued friends, useful by the presence of their absence.

(I am writing this history according to the conceptions of our friends, which seem to me to explain more of what occurs.)

9.

Antonicelli, the prosecutor, was a lean, dark, handsome flashing-eyed person, haunted in spirit: a typical figure of Romance, loved (but not married) by every housewife-reader.

Horatio took an immediate liking to him; he felt that the judge, the prosecutor, no doubt the jury—everything was favorable to him; and meantime, ceaselessly, moment by moment, he kept radiating the power of being in love.

"When I look at that handsome human face," said Horatio, "the pity of it!—that he should end up as a barrister." (After Oscar.)

Nevertheless, Antonicelli was no friend but a formidable opponent.

"I was pleased," he began, "to have opportunity to hear you just now. Let me applaud not only your legal acumen, praised by Judge Halloran, but also your forensic skill, considering that you spoke extempore and no doubt a little overwrought with feeling. I salute a young master. I am not so old myself," he added modestly. "But I was especially interested by the depth at which you attacked the matter; I presume this is your habit. I take it you mean business."

Horatio stared at him blankly. "Yes, I mean business," he said. He narrowed his eyes, "Don't you always mean business?"

"You like to get right to the point," said Antonicelli admiringly. "For instance, you said that this comedian had a certain power—hm, a divine power, shall we say?—this gave him certain rights, etc. That is, power makes right. No? I agree. We need not then waste our time here on legal equities. Perhaps you would insist on 'divine power?' "

"Just power," conceded Horace. "Might makes right; that has been my experience. But please remember I don't try to be consistent. I like to take each case on its material merits. I don't know what to think in general."

"Fine! Fine!" Antonicelli rubbed his long fingers together like a villain, and succeeded in exciting amorous and sadistic sparks from them. "Now let us look at your case from the point of view of your friends."

"Please!" cried Horatio. "I should prefer you to look at it from your own point of view and let my friends be."

"I beg your pardon; this is how I always proceed. It is a safeguard against prejudice. I assume my opponent's point of view and end up with my conclusion."

"I listen with pleasure," said Horatio sincerely.

"Now what is it your friends claim? They claim that our policy is a bad policy, that our justice is bad justice, that our war is a bad war. By bad they mean, I trust, simply that it does not work for happiness but creates unhappiness. Right?"

"Right."

"Believing this, what is their natural obligation as persons trying to be happy? They must disobey our rules that lead to unhappiness."

"Right!" said Horatio. "We do disobey."

"More power to you!" cried Antonicelli enthusiastically. "Everywhere in jail we find that your people are just the finest types, educated, ethical, brave, concerned for the social good.* Everybody in society is roused by their example, made thoughtful by their trials, admiring of their martyrdom. In heaven's name, what more could you ask?"

"I *beg* your pardon?" said Horatio in astonishment.

"Certainly. This gives you power; and power makes right. For people—your friends are the first to claim it—are essentially reasonable and ethical; they can be taught; they are taught by example, by making an intransigent stand for what is demonstrably right, and getting publicity for it. Thus it is, say your friends, that power, the power of the truth and the power of essential humanity, wins its way."

"You wonderfully state the position of some of my friends," said Horace dryly. "May I ask what you are driving at?"

"What am I driving at?" said the other. "I am driving at you. Look, here is your dossier." He held up a fat portfolio.

Horatio did not falter, although it is a formidable thing to be confronted with one's dossier.

"I *look* in this dossier," said Antonicelli, "and what do I find? Do I find an exemplary stand and plenty of publicity? No, I find everywhere nothing. No registration, but no refusal to register. No oath, but no refusal to take the oath. No taxes, but no refusal to pay taxes. Nothing. But nothing! Oooh! I came to this dossier with my heart aflame with potential admiration. 'Here,' said I to myself, 'is a man, a man who can take a dangerous and unpopular stand. So young, so handsome, and a lover. Perhaps, who knows, he will open the eyes of Antonicelli and make a convert.' For I am

* This sentence is quoted from a private remark of the Warden of Danbury Penitentiary (1945).

not too old to learn. . . . No stand. Nothing. But nothing. Instead? Theft. Evasion. Living in a hole in the wall. Silence. Where is the power? Where then is the right? Will this influence people and create a natural society? Could it influence me? Believe me, I was bitterly disappointed. What can I say? Selfish. A common criminal. A thief. A coward."

His argument created a certain effect. Unfortunately for him, however, Horatio kept radiating, moment by moment, the power that belongs to a man in love.

"I understand you," said Horatio. "You would want me to be a more conscientious objector. Then you would be more proud of me."

"You have hit it."

"But my friends who are conscientious objectors and refuse to enlist in the army," said Horatio, "are now in jail."

"Certainly, because they refuse to enlist in the army."

"Ow! I have the strongest objection to enlisting in jail!" exclaimed Horatio. "Institution for institution, it is worse than the army," he said earnestly. "You know, I dislike to discuss these matters on an ethical or sentimental basis, but I think you misunderstand the ethics here. You have a misconception about the ethical rights of young men. My friends, the conscientious objectors, are wrong. I do not have the right to dispose of my body as I see fit, namely, to put it in a jail as a striking public witness of the truth. The youthful body is destined for exercise and to make love, not to languish in a jail; and the youthful soul is destined to be happy and find out a career, but I have seen at a glance that the opportunities for this are quite limited in jail, at least for me. All good is the realization of power, but if the power doesn't flow to us from body and soul, from where shall we draw power? No doubt it's true, what you say about the essential rationality of people and the use of strong examples. But I'm not an actor by disposition, and I think it's sinful not to make love. Ha! And here I am talking in public when I'm in love and should go and talk to Rosalind."

"Her name is Rosalind," said Judge Halloran to the clerk. "Please proceed more quickly," he said sharply to the prosecutor. "Can't you see that this boy has hot nuts?"

It was unfair to the prosecutor. Horatio stood there like a prig and not only attracted by his presence but probably had the better arguments, and the judge was predisposed in his favor. Yet so it was.

"Also," said Horatio, "since my friends are the finest citizens, educated, brave and so forth, why don't you let them out of jail?"

"I didn't say the finest citizens," said Antonicelli dryly, "I said the finest types of people in jails. This brings me to my next point."

10.

"Horatio Alger!" thundered the prosecutor in a stern voice; and it was evident that the case was going to take a new turn. Up to now he had not meant business, but now he was going to propose the fatal argument, the one of his own existence, the calculated risk that he himself lived by.

"Nearly a generation ago, you formally dissociated yourself from these people. This is in the record.

"Since then you have tried to live as if our society, the society of almost all of the people, did not exist. A hard way to live! But I don't give you any credit for it, for it is nothing but stupidity.

"In the first place, our society is the only society that there is—in what society can you move if not in our society? If you do not associate with these people, with whom will you associate? Therefore, it was not hypocritically, whatever you may think, that I spoke with admiration just now of your friends, the conscientious objectors. For they recognize the fact that we are the society. They take part in our social life by opposing it; they destroy their lives in this loving opposition. This is a necessary, though troublesome, role in our society. We appreciate their heroism.

"But you, Horatio Alger, shut your eyes to us; you are a stupid liar. I cannot say whether you are more of a fool or a rogue. I come to my main point. *You refuse to recognize the existence of the Dilemma*——"

When he said it, Horatio blanched and tightened his fists till the knuckles shone. For he had heard of the Dilemma; well he knew the horned Dilemma. He was moved; but he was not afraid.

"What is the Dilemma? If one conforms to our society, he becomes sick in certain ways. (I grant it, who can deny it?). But if he does *not* conform, he becomes demented, because ours is the only society that there is. *That* is the Dilemma. You are demented. Then how are you justified in your actions? What right do you have to assert, not your excellence, but your dementia against our security, making our complicated lives inextricably confused? Don't we have sorrows enough without being distraught by your demented fantasies? But you do it to undermine our morale. You are destructive, distorted and full of hate. It is *in principle* impossible for you to be otherwise. Do I make myself clear?"

Antonicelli spoke soberly and connectedly, but his face was purple with rage.

But Horatio, as he stood, was flaming with a deep blue field. He prayed, "Aphrodite, mother of love, help me now." And he said:

"The Dilemma is a powerful argument. In principle it is irrefutable. And I have nothing to offer against it except—a fact. It is impossible in theory, but in fact the human animal has regenerated itself from its wound. The blood clots; protected by the clot, the flesh grows under; and the wound is healed. There is a scar or not a scar. The broken bones also knit together.

"*Natura sanat,* Nature heals. What is needed from us is to stand out of the way, to allow a little freedom for the regenerative forces (no forces of ours), and in heaven's name, an abeyance, an abeyance of the pathological pressure.

"It is true that I was very young when I made the rupture with the sociolatry that I have not seen reason to bridge. To start so young was my misfortune—for a hard way hardens. But also, as it turns out, it was my good luck. For it has given me a long time to gather a little force of my own, to learn viable habits to make a little freedom around me, and to win an abeyance, an abeyance.

"Prosecutor, you present to this court a powerful, an irrefragable proof that I am demented, distorted and destructive. But I present a wonderful fact that makes your argument wither away. Here I am, scarred with such and such scars, but by ordinary grace, no doing of mine, I am in love."

It was the fact, inexplicable but obvious.

Antonicelli shrieked with fury and clutched at his collar. "*Gaaaa!* I bring public evidence and arguments, and he dares to stand up with an unconfirmable putative fact! A private sentiment, hedged round with hints of miracles! So *he* says, so *he* says! But I look in *my* heart and I do not find that it is possible for *any*one to be in love. Then what?"

This he ought not have said. For no sooner had he looked in his heart and asked the question, he emitted a wheezy gasp and, ceasing to clutch at his collar, threw up his hands and fell down with the asphyxiation. This was simply the fact.

"Hilarious Archer, save him, for you can!" shouted the judge, leaping to his feet.

But Horatio had already leaped the fence and had set to work.

"This man already saved me from asphyxiation another day," said the judge. "He has this power. I came back from the dead, and I am sure that the fact that he alleges is so. And now in open court, positively and negatively, positively by what he is and negatively by the fate of Antonicelli, the fact establishes itself. The court is adjourned. Nolle prosse. Free the prisoner."

The prosecutor began to revive very soon.

"It is a mild attack," said Horatio. "So handsome and romantic a man, with such dark fiery power, is not seriously ailing, he is strong; but therefore with all the more savagery he is killing himself. He must by no means continue this lying career."

12.

"Horatio," said the judge, as they left the place—the judge, as was his custom, putting an arm a little tenderly around the young man's shoulders—"I know you despise me for continuing in this official position. But I confess, I like the salary, the dignity, the perquisites and the salary. Frankly, I don't feel an inner impulse to change."

"You make me ashamed," said Horatio. "I am too much of a prig as it is. Why should I despise you? I'm not doctrinaire. You'd be wrong to change if you don't want to change. Let be."

"I couldn't do much harm there, I think?" said the judge hopefully.

"No, you couldn't! It's not my experience," said Horatio Alger judiciously, "that neat merry lascivious pink-cheeked bibulous skeptical old gentlemen do much harm at all. They are the school of Anacreon. *Somebody* has got to expound the accumulated ancient lore of the people, embodied in the common law, and it couldn't be better than Judge Halloran! My friends don't disapprove of the law and the judges, only the jails."

Chapter 11 ▪ HORATIO AND ROSALIND, V: THEIR MARRIAGE

1.

So, in this climatic manner, was publicly vindicated the education of Horatio Alger.

But alas! In our society you may prove as follows the miseducation of almost everybody else: for *every* child is engendered to be a hero, being engendered unafraid (this was the distinguishing mark of Siegfried, that he was unafraid). But we do not observe that most of our people are heroes like Siegfried. Therefore, somewhere, early or late, we must have been educated to be afraid.

But Horatio was prudent and unafraid (rather shrewder than Siegfried, who was not notable for his intelligence).

Having won his way out of the arrest, vanquishing Antonicelli, he came rapidly to where Rosalind was asleep in icy immobility. For whatever her intention had been last night—to rise early and fly to Horatio—she overslept, thereby avoiding disappointment, and waiting to be roused. Horatio bent over her and roused her with a kiss, saying, "Rosalind, I love you. Move over."

"I love you, Horatio," said Rosalind. "Yes."

2.

So they were married.

Eros brought the Rough Traders of the Crossroads to scatter rice and tell bawdy jokes.

They noted appreciatively that there was nothing to steal. Horatio did not, behind their backs, lead an elaborate domestic life. Gloomily they bade farewell to their comrade.

But Rosalind was accompanied by a matronly Greek lady, a neighbor, bosomy and cheerful.

The guests scattered rice and told three jokes drawn from the cycle of life.

The first told a childish joke, based on the discovery of names and places: "What's that? That's Abe Lincoln. And what are those? Those are his children, stupid; but what's that? That's the White House. Let's put Abe Lincoln in the White House and let the children play in the grass."

The second told an adolescent joke, of prowess, in the form of a limerick:

> There was a Señora from Spain
> who could do it again and again
>   and again and again
>   and again and again
> and again and again and again.

But the third told a grown-up joke of disillusionment and sorrow: Little junior saw grandpa behind the barn jerking off. "Whatcha doin', gramps? Jackin' off?" For a moment the old man said nothing. Then, "Naw, just jackin'," he said.

They scattered rice.

Finally the planet was glowing in the western sky.

And now the puzzled parts fell all in place.

3.

After Horatio had made love a good deal and slept and made love, repeating this intermittently for several days, suddenly, resting on one elbow, he said, "You know, Rosalind, that one of the sports I like best is to suck your breasts, but I must say that finally it is a little disappointing to suck and suck and get no milk. I am not complaining, but a fact is a fact."

"If I were you," said Rosalind, "I should certainly not complain. You don't even begin to be adequately constituted in that direction. Shall I make you a bottle, baby?"

"And why would that occasionally be such a bad idea?" he asked.

But she was not angry with him, for they had their love, and one of the greatest effects of love is that one can recognize a plain fact without getting angry.

Instead she thought a moment and said, "Come with me."

This is another effect of love, that it leads to practical behavior.

They put on robes and she led him to the home of her friend, the matronly Greek lady, that was on still another floor. She briefly explained their plight. This is still another effect of love, that one comes to the essentials at once, without tergiversation (though there is plenty of time for decoration).

The stout woman cheerfully permitted them; and there they rested, Horatio sucking at the left breast and Rosalind at the right, but being otherwise interlaced as closely as might be.

PART 3 THE DEAD OF SPRING

You believe then in the existence of a Paradise in the earliest days of mankind.

—Even if it was a Hell—and certainly the time to which I can go back in historical thought was full of fury and anguish and torment and cruelty. At any rate it was not unreal.

Rather violence lived than shadowy solicitude for faceless numbers. From the former a way leads to God, from the latter a way only to nothing.

—BUBER

Chapter 12 ▪ THE DEAD OF SPRING

1.

Horatio came early to visit his mad sister Laura, who was the crown of laurel of the everyday, a drunkard during wartime, the one-time helpmeet of Mynheer, and the mother of the twins, the left and right. He saw her facing out the window, and he bounded up the stairs with a pounding heart.

She was hanged and was dead. Facing out the window at New York, hanging from the ceiling, her outstretched toes not on the floor. She was naked, her black hair streaming, but she had adorned herself with garlands of withered flowers of May. The irises were lank and blackened and the daisies had lost their petals and stared with bloodshot eyes. And in her careful lettering she had made the following sign and propped it on a chair:

THE DEAD OF SPRING

Presumably the body had swung round and round several times on the rope, but it had come to rest facing out the window, as if this were what she had planned. But her eyes were not awake but shut.

"The truth is dead," said Horatio aloud. "The truth was my sister."

There was no answer in the empty rooms; and after a moment he began to make fairly merry music. From the kitchen he got spoons and a couple of table knives and kneeling on the floor he pounded and drummed with these on the seat of a deal chair. At first crooning in half voice the "Song of India" from *Sadko* and such other sugared melodies that used to haunt his childhood ear, they were so beautiful to him. But after a while he worked himself up to livelier jazzy rhythms and cries: "I got rhythm! I got rhythm!" and he drubbed the drums and banged the wood with the spoons and tankled the blades against each other, calling "Hoo! hoo!" and, as the twins used, "Choo choo train!"

By the time Rosalind arrived to meet him there, he had stripped off his shirt and was naked to the waist, drumming and singing with wild hair.

She did not stifle her dolorous cry when she saw the body but the sight of Horatio so astonished her that she stood agape.

The corpse swayed slightly every time the door opened.

"What are you doing, honey?" said Rosalind.

"What else shall I do?" said Horatio. "Also, don't you know? this is what Chuang-tze did when his wife passed away."

"But this was not your wife."

"Neither am I Chuang-tze."

"If you do this for her, what shall you do if I die?"

"When one of us dies," said Horatio, "I shall go to Paris."

Rosalind was afraid to cross him, he seemed so strange and she withdrew against the wall. But he was aware of her presence and, though hardly interrupting his music, he said: "She killed herself in anger because I was happy—that's what they'll say. But just the opposite is true; she killed herself in order to stand out of my way, not to be a flaw in my perfect happiness. Hoo! Hi!"

He drummed only a moment more, for he stopped in the middle of a measure and said slowly, "Why am I using the word 'true,' and saying 'the truth is—the case is—the fact is'? The truth was my sister."

Instead, with great absolute rips he tore up his shirt, and he tied streamers onto the two knives, making raw flags with ridiculous silver handles. He pressed one of these on Rosalind and cried, "Let's make a parade!" and at once he set off marching.

She did not follow him but stood with the flag in her hand.

He tramped through the rooms waving the raw flag. And he sang Horatio's Mourning Song:

Horatio's Mourning Song

Stateless, yet we have a flag
of the raw stuff the neutral color,
a march without a rhythm or key
our drum and trumpet muted play.

Unarmèd, yet we have the power
of when the bottom drops out;
lonely, loyal, murky-minded,
doubt-free, we go our way.

Chuang-tze is dead, as I shall die,
unnoticed by the wayside,
his spirit does not haunt the world
and his death grip is relaxed.

He was well accompanied, even if Rosalind did not accompany him. He was accompanied by the presence of the absence of many friends and lovers. For it was impossible for him not to return to this moment of walking along accompanied by their presence; but now, since he was able to give in to love, and he was in love, the walking together was a regular parade, with feet tramping and a flag waving. Stopping short at the doorways, to cast a glance into the new space, saying briskly, "Forward march!" and entering across the new threshold.

But for the most part the parade avoided passing close to the hanging body, and when it happened to, Horatio could not suppress a look of abhorrence, at the carcass cluttering the new heavens and new earth.

2.

But Lothair, when he came, picked up the telephone and began to make calls.

"What are you doing?" cried Horace.

"I'm calling people, stupid," said big Lothair.

"Don't do that. If you tell everybody they'll hear about it," said Horace carefully.

He laid his hand on the telephone to put a stop to it; but Lothair lightly brushed him away with such an arm that he fell unconscious against the wall and sank to the floor—as the lion you thought dying crushes with one paw.

Bringing water, Rosalind revived her lover.

Over Lothair's frame passed the paroxysm that we often come to suffer as our understanding increases quicker than our happiness: the withholding when no reasonable object of anger presents itself, worthy enough or practical enough, to strike with the anger that overcomes one. Lothar recognized that it was anger overcoming him and he was not afraid to strike, but there was nothing to strike. The paroxysm passed through him as though he had grounded a live electric wire.

With trembling fingers he kept manipulating the telephone dial and calling.

"Whom are you calling?" asked Rosalind timidly.

"People on the rolls, her friends," said Lothar.

"What rolls?"

"The rolls of the present, fool; the people Laura used to work with. . . . Hello. Lothario. My sister Laura is hanging here dead. Yes. *Facing* out the window, *covered* with withered flowers, and a sign propped up here saying 'The Dead of Spring.' *Please* do come. . . . They are the ones who knew her; I don't know what to do."

With a trembling finger he dialed another number.

"The Imperial Dole, the Works Administration, the Consolidated Union, the Technicians and Engineers—she poured her love on all that, as if they were persons alive. You don't know how much she had in her to give, and how much she gave. Until the war came; then it was harder and she drank. Hello? Lothario . . .

"Do you know the plan she worked out during the war?" he asked.

"I have heard of it," said Rosalind, "but I have not seen it."

Leaving the phone he went to the chest of drawers and dragged out the old plan:

This is no Place
The Time is not Now

IF YOU STAY ON THIS ROAD——

He checked his motion, which was to rip the sheet in two, as if this were an adequate object of anger. But it was only an absurd piece of paper, and it did not even signify a thing. He shook. He caressed the paper with his fingers and began to weep softly.

If you stay on this road you won't get anywhere.

3.

Soon a crowd began to arrive. The corpse did not cease swinging in the draft as the door continually opened and shut.

As each newcomer or group entered—they came generally in twos and threes—a hush fell on those who were already gathered, as they sympathetically felt again the shock of recognition. But then, what with greetings and so forth, they broke the silence even rather loudly; a large crowd makes a buzz. Many of these people had not been in touch with one another since the war, for Laura's people were the best and, as Yeats said it, "The best lack all conviction." With the war many of these people had retired into drinking and, like Laura, into queer ideas. But Laura herself was the very best that there was. They were weeping for her. They had all markedly aged.

A peculiar discussion arose.

"What date is it?"

"May eighth."

"I beg your pardon, May tenth."

"Is it? I should have said May eighth."

"She's right—it's the eighth of May."

"I'm sorry. But it *is* May tenth."

"Is *this* May tenth?" I said angrily.

Nobody thought that it was May ninth.

One fellow, who was crazier than anybody, waved his hand in the air and repeated contemptuously, "Not May. Not May. Not May. What May? Who mentions May? Do you call this May? Next somebody will say that this is May! What won't they say next? *May!* Believe me, *not* May." He smiled softly.

The crowd gathered thick. The rumor had spread rapidly and they came, by twos and threes, sometimes not a delegation but en masse. Organizations that nobody had ever heard of, except Laura. But just because she was in love with the glancing present as it shone—wherever it shone! however it was! such as it was! with all the damning qualifications that you want! yes, even during the war (until by a theory of psycho-sociolatry they lost touch with reality altogether and the present did not glint at all)—Laura proved to have had time for everyone. Giving herself easily, she found that there were many hours in the day and many days in the years. They were sick with grief as they remembered her and themselves. The mere presence of so many created an extraordinary animation. It was impossible to believe that it did not mean something.

Arthur's committeemen arrived, but their chairman was dead and buried in a far-off field. His memory caused more grief, for at scenes of death people talk about other scenes of death, to escape into a generality.

Swinging in the air, Laura had slowly turned around and was now facing them in the room.

A few at a time they noticed this; then everybody at once. In deep silence they formed in front of her, in a semicircle, leaving a space.

4.

A large crowd, stunned by one thing: again there were the conditions for a panic act, when a suggestion has been made to the collective soul, and it responds. What would they generate on this occasion from their collective soul? Alas, as you looked at them now, silent and not bustling, living only in memory, the crowd did not seem promising.

(Our shame was such that we could cry for shame, even if there were nothing else to cry for.)

They did generate something, not nothing.

For before their eyes, the withered blooms revived and burst into artificial flowers. But it was not seen that the dead woman stirred or came alive.

In an instant, she was decked with wonderful flowers of the May, uncommonly lifelike, seeming each petal to tremble open to the most space. Yet it was not necessary to look close to see that they were flowers of artifice. *Not* May. Her girdle of irises shone a good deal bluer than the truth, and her pale hand lightly held a tulip of bloody tissue paper.

Crowned with paper daisies, she hanged there facing them, not facing out the window, and they, surprised and joyless, regarded the flowers of art.

But Rosalind—for it is an effect of love to recognize easily also the other demons—said: "She is Persephone. For the queen of spring was taken away from the earth, but she returns, when she returns, not in the living field flowers, but in the flowers of art. It is not satisfactory. But it is not nothing."

So the Dead of Spring generated the flowers of paper, imperishable and fresh.

5.

Mynheer came, who had been Laura's lover and husband. It was probably he who had killed her, but this was another of the things he was not sure of.

"Cut down the body," he said. "Can't you see she's dead? Clear the rooms."

"Stay where you are!" said Lothair. And he and Horatio, the brothers—he and Horatio, the brothers—stood up to oppose him.

"Why, what do you have to offer?" asked Mynheer, almost with contempt. It was the nearest in his life that he ever came to contempt.

It was a question whether or not the brothers would tear him limb from limb in their anger. But they looked at each other and shook their heads. They did not have any charm, they nor their anger, to revive the dead woman. It was likely that, as always, Mynheer was in the right.

"It's all right, you don't need to!" cried Mynheer. "You won't hear any more out of me!"

"Cut down the carcass," said Lothar brutally, and went within.

"Come away, Horatio," said Rosalind.

6.

Coldly going to his library, Mynheer collected Laura's modern poets and stitched together for our consolation a Requiem, as follows:

Mynheer's Requiem for Laura

i

You can hold back from the suffering of this world.
  It is allowed. It is your disposition.
But it may be that this very holding back is the one
  evil you could have avoided. (Kafka)

Friends, let us mourn.

There are questions we could never get over if we
  were not delivered from them by an operation of
  nature. (Kafka)

Make me, my streaming face, a glory;
bloom, unseen weeping!
Afflicted nights, how dear you will be to me.
Disconsolate sisters, why did I not
kneel lower to take you to me,
give in more to your freely given hair?
Oh, we wasters of sorrows,
looking away from them into sad endurance beyond,
if maybe they may end. But they are our winter leaves!
our darkling evergreen! one
one of the seasons of the homely year. (Rilke)

ii

Look, Segramor, you know the language of the birds.
  Now couldn't you tell us what they say and let
  them add their word?
It's a long time since I practiced it. I'd have to get
  the feel of it again.
Try, Segramor, oh yes. Try, try, oh do, do, do.
Wait. They are saying—
What are they saying?
The birds are saying: Pay, pay, pay, pay, pay, pay, pay,
  Must pay, must pay, pay, pay. Pay, pay, pay, pay.
Pay, pay. Must pay, must pay, pay, pay. (Cocteau)

iii

Vast gulph! carried here in the mass of the mist
by the angry wind of the words he didn't say—
this Void to this man abolished forever,
"Remembered horizons, O what is the Earth?"
screams this dream. Of a voice that is fading away
Space plays like a toy with the cry, "I don't know."
(Mallarmé)

Our own death is unimaginable; and when we try to imagine it we perceive that we really survive as spectators.
At bottom no one believes in his own death; in the unconscious everyone of us is convinced of his own immortality. (Freud)

Of the millions, I know, who have gone to the grave
displeased, ungratified, and malcontent
as one count me, for now it is too late
ever to unmake it, and chance has become fate.

But in this crowd of every kind of sorrow
still am I signal for a fool and coward,
for few, I think, have seen so fine as I
the remediable faults and been unable. (Goodman)

iv

The hare or the deer pursued
takes joy in its speed and its leaps and its dodges!
And I believe that, as a whole, in all nature (save man) happiness far outweighs pain. (Gide)

All eyes, the Creature sees the Open.
Free of death, the free animal
has always its decline behind it
and God in front, and as it goes it goes
into Eternity, as brooks run on.
But we have never, not a single day,
pure space in front of us, that flowers
endlessly open to; but always world
and never nowhere without a Don't,
that pure unguarded thing one breathes,
endlessly knows, and does not crave.
A child
one day gets calmly lost in it,
is prodded back. Or some one dies and *is* it. (Rilke)

Such was the Requiem that Mynheer collected from the modern poets, for Laura's honor, for our consolation.

Then he himself shut his eyes and tried to sleep at his desk, but his head ached and he could not sleep.

7.

Attracted by the smell of death, the twins, Droyt and Lefty, came trotting near. They were werewolves.

"Give it the ax, the ax!" barked Lefty. "Let's set the joint on fire."

"That's what you *always* advise," said Droyt. "What's the good of it?"

"The old bitch is dead, the old prick is done for. Now *we* are the lively generation."

"I have a hand and you have a hand. What can we try with these hands?"

They sniffed in the corners and trotted rapidly from room to room.

Chapter 13 ▪ THE DEAD OF SPRING, II: THEORIES

Let us pause here, before our friends have gotten together their memorial game, and ask: with what theories of existence were these people coping with the problem of getting up in the morning in the poorly weather of the dead of spring? For that is the use of every theory of existence, to cope with the problem of getting up in the morning in the poorly weather of the dead of spring.

1. Mynheer's Manifesto

Mynheer started awake where we left him and found his head sleeping on the desk. He woke hardly with a start but with a faint click, as a smoothly riding car shifts from one gear to another. His dreams had been gaily colored out of the Thousand and One Nights, but he opened his eyes to the grayer scene of the Thousand and One Days. "Now both of these series," he thought, "are methods of delaying, of not giving in, of not finding out; they are methods of accumulating large numbers and still unable to make good my loss. Now where *am* I?" he asked himself; but as soon as he tried to corroborate an answer to this question, he found that he was suffering from his splitting headache. But if instead he did not try to *answer* where he was, but simply remained where indeed he was, waking with a hissing intake of breath and finding his head sleeping on the desk, passing between the Arabian Nights and the Days of the Empire, then he did not have a headache and felt fine.

This was already interesting and he experimented with it. His first supposition was a grim one: "That I am suppressing feeling the headache by poising between sleep and waking." A grim supposition, for if it were true, soon he would plunge into the headache, for he was courageous. But no! To his relief the experiment proved the opposite, that the headache was not underlying and coming on, but he at that very moment was giving himself a headache by abusing himself, by forcing himself to awaken into the Thousand and One Days and then to answer the question where he was—just as a man puts on a pair of glasses that do not fit him and willfully gives himself a headache. But on the contrary, if he let himself be, staying where indeed he was and proceeding whither he would proceed, he noticed heightened vitality, efficient performance and all the usual criteria of well-being.

Forthwith he dismissed forever that abuse of his human nature, of trying to awaken into the Thousand and One Days of the Empire and then to corroborate where he was. It was not the effort of corroboration that gave him a headache, but of trying to corroborate where he was when he wasn't anywhere. And at once, when he had made a decision, the wonderful tingling tides surged in his blood and flowed sweet and free.

And he thought of the song of Psyche, when suddenly she was awakened to find the bed empty beside her:

Psyche's Song

Slumber comes heavy like honey like
my lover's forearm carelessly flung
across my face, he is already
asleep. I start
awake wildly
stifled by
his absence.

Bleak!
Day!
O daughters of Memory
play me music
in the next room which is not today
but there are artificial flowers
burst into bloom that will not fade.

Is Death warm? for I am looking
for a lover who will not leave me.
No, but the hole in the midday
is a doorway
that I may yet
timidly
enter.

"Where is this hole in the midday?" Mynheer asked himself. "When I come to enter it, it will not be timidly. I understand that the so-called 'external world' is only a projection of the diseases of our souls. When we hold back from touching and being concerned about what is, at once we constitute ourselves a world 'out there,' and we engage in a general conspiracy to keep it out there and neutral, for otherwise it would press in on us and cause us pain and fear. This conspiracy we call explanations. Our fictive 'society' gets to share a fictive 'common external world.' Obviously it is unwise for me to have anything further to do with that world.

"What then? Shall I embrace my dreams as the world? For my dreams are concernful; they are wishes and the fearful distortion of wishes; their space is an image of my body; and they act out the solution of my problems. I shall not deviate too far from natural existence if I unhesitatingly live out my dreams.

"But my dreams are too private. Now artworks are socially communicable dreams. They have an advantage over the dreams of normal sleep because by taking the risk of sharing, they break down our petty private censorships. I shall not deviate too far from natural existence if I unhesitatingly live out the works of art.

"But artworks are only imitations, we know that they give only an aesthetic surface without material force. But the world of madness is a material world—wishes and perceptions all one world. Its pitch of gaiety and grief, enthusiasm, anguish and stupefaction, is likely very near what it is to lead a concernful life. When I go mad, as mad I shall, I shall not hold back, but act out dream and art, not privately but publicly, in a world flaming almost with immediacy, the rose the golden square, and the busy chariot of Ezekiel wheels within wheels.

"This is an attractive way to go Out of This World," thought Mynheer; "perhaps it is the hole in the midday."

So Mynheer reflected that it was probably sane to go mad. But here it was necessary to pick and choose.

"Most of the madmen we see around are not effective (though there are exceptions); they do not change the heavens and earth; they have no natural magic, only wishful superstitions. Indeed, for effective magic, such as it is, we must look just in the opposite direction, to the deadest, the most withholding, the least concernful of men, our scientists and technologists: *they* have made some progress with transmuting the elements and moderating the force of gravity. Isn't that odd—that the poker faces have got things done! Why is that? It is that they, with abnegation and courage, and with soldierly loyalty to their guild, have respected the arbitrary givenness of things; the poor pure givenness of things that nobody, but nobody, cares about; that is not infected with humanity.

"So! On the one hand and on the other hand! (This is what comes from being bilaterally symmetrical.) I again see the Horned Dilemma in the woods, and rolling at his heels Vicious Circles: A concernful man will care more and more, he will care madly, and he will accomplish less and less and finally nothing. On the other hand, an effective man will more and more abnegate his desires, and will magically transform the world not to his advantage."

But having caught a glimpse of the Dilemma, Mynheer at once took a sheet of paper from the desk and set to work to sketch him, against the day that he would go hunting. And he wrote with flowing pen the following:

THEORY OF DILEMMAS

The Dilemma has several times recently come to my notice. Viz.:

The Dilemma of Political Action: We know that the behavior of our society is leading us to disaster; but the only way that we know how to behave, and that is available to us, is the disastrous behavior of our society.

The solution of this Dilemma was: Not to leave the meeting till we could fly.

The Dilemma of the Community: We who are alienated from the community cannot find the binding necessity to form a community of our own; yet we cannot live without some community or other.

The solution, etc., was to make a Building Sacrifice by letting loose our suppressed hatred.

The Dilemma of our Society: If we conformed to the mad society, we became mad; but if we did not conform to the only society that there is, we became mad.

The solution, etc., was to stand in love, like Horatio.

The Dilemma of the Worlds: The objective world is not our concern; but in the world of our concern we have no effective magic.

And the solution of this Dilemma will be to ride the whirlwind like the Master of the Way.

(In everyday language, Mynheer appointed himself to be a Mad Scientist, the hero of much contemporary literature.)

"I swear it," he muttered, *"I shall ride the whirlwind.*

"But not today. For just today my business is to notice where I am, and I am in a dilemma. Now surely the secret of all dilemmas was explained by Franz, when he said: 'There are questions that we could never get over if we were not delivered from them by an Operation of Nature.'

"By questions he meant these dilemmas; and by an Operation of Nature he meant natural magic (for if there were an explanation there would not be a dilemma, and the operation of the inexplicable is natural magic).

"In principle this Operation is gratis; it will occur whatever the person in the dilemma may do or not do, and willy-nilly. This is lucky, for some people like to linger comfortably in a dilemma. But now let me raise the question: what can a person profitably do while he is in a dilemma?

"First, let him *be* in his dilemma, and aggravate the agony of being in his dilemma——"

Suddenly, as he was thinking this, a red drop fell on the page of the *Theory of Dilemmas.* (And may still be seen on the manuscript.) Mynheer's headache was quite gone, but some blood had welled into his eyes and a drop or two splashed on the page. He shook his head and cleared his vision.

"And then," he proceeded, "being in his dilemma and quite aware of his dilemma, let him easily go about his other business with a light heart, the lighter because the burden of such other matters is lightened by the fact that he is in his dilemma. And indeed, I have been doing the right thing. For tossed on the Dilemma of the Worlds, I have been sitting here comfortably enough, weeping blood, just as if I were a writer or something. Waiting——"

He yawned. He was tired of waiting and writing. He wanted to go back to sleep.

Such were the reflections of Mynheer and the *Theory of Dilemmas* that he wrote at his desk while his darling, the glancing present, lay dead in another room of the house.

2. Minetta's Practical Philosophy

These same problems, however, of holding back from touching, and of passing from the world of concern to the world of effective action, and of solving the dilemmas of our society, these problems were regarded differently by Mrs. Minetta Tyler. "Our generation," she used to say, "is a dead duck; let's face it. But the next generation still has some life in it. And this gives us something to do, too, doesn't it?" She held that all philosophy was the philosophy of education.

Now Minetta was a musician and bright, and she was puzzled and disturbed by the difficulties of bringing up her daughter Joannie in our unfortunate environment. She was saddened by the future prospects of everyone, and she commiserated other parents and prospective parents and all young people. Yet she had a practical optimistic bent of character, that had once trapped her into case work till she gave it up for marriage.

Minetta, I say, took no undue satisfaction in considering the situation in its entirety. Nevertheless, she had great hopes in the effects of the relaxed toilet training and no toilet training; and of the permissive and if need be unobtrusively encouraging attitude toward masturbation, thumb-sucking and other sexual expressions of childhood—which were now nationally broadcast in manuals of child care that sold millions of copies. It seemed to her that from these reforms, accumulated in millions of instances, there must inevitably spring a very different, happier, freer character in the next generation. For no matter how crazy the public world was, at least animal nature would be bolder, less submissive and easier to give itself to love.

She did not close her eyes to the fact that Joannie secretly believed her father to be the Loch Ness Monster; yet she had confidence in the long-range lenitive effect of his easygoing Maine-bred disposition; he did not raise his gruff voice, and he would rather fish than be rich. She could not disregard the fact that bigoted neighbors had taught Joannie's playmates that the devil would strike you if you took off the doll's drawers; but at least Joannie never learned it at home. (Nor was Minetta afraid to speak up in public.)

Since marriage and motherhood, Minetta herself had become happier every year, so she was a living proof that it could be done. Harry was, to be sure, exceptional in his physical and emotional ability to make a woman happy. She had grown to be a square cheerful little woman, no longer cross-eyed except in moments of strong anxiety. Past mischances, she proved, were not fatal; human beings were tough and resilient, and could miraculously regenerate if the circumstances improved.

She interfered in the educational groups of the city and she kept presenting a program. Her experience taught her that, in education, where without exception every child came already marred and scarred, two things were essential. The first was to restore unlimited freedom of physical functioning. A child must be able, for instance, to regress defiantly to soiling his pants, without disapproval, and start all over again in better shape. And she initiated a movement to give children at a very young age some kind of economic independence and a possible temporary refuge away from home, so they need not be complaisant out of hopeless fear. This was a radical proposal, hard to get across but not out of the question, for our society, so indifferent and stubborn in general, was compensatingly softhearted toward its young.

The second essential in educating those who came marred and scarred, and all always came that way, was to win back to awareness and feeling the buried fears and dreams in order that the children might again have their troubles and tantrums in the lively present rather than in the inaccessible past. It was hard, but not impossible, to persuade the teachers not to let sleeping dogs lie. Minetta laid great store on spontaneous expression in art, for artworking invites ever deeper conflicts to rage; when by rhythm the music and drama stir the feelings and revive the blurred images of trouble; but the artwork is a bridge of understanding. She believed in sketching the nightmare, in narrating the murderous attempt on little brother and in timely fist fights.

She was willing, once the bad posture was corrected and the feelings were again in flux, to let the professionals take over the task of passing on our culture—especially Mynheer and his Thousand and One Days. (She was disturbed when he seemed to be giving these up.)

There were many pitfalls. Minetta was observant and she could tell that Joannie had already, besides her fantasies of dragons, at least three separate and incompatible sets of morals, her parents', her teachers' and her playmates'. For instance, Joannie knew from Harry and Minetta that sexual pleasure was exciting and obvious; she knew from school that there was no such thing; she knew from her playmates that it was forbidden, dangerous and of such paramount importance that the attractive horned devil himself was a partner. She neither would nor could give up any of these sets of notions; rather she played one against the other or willfully confounded them for her own convenience, safety, need for punishment, masturbation fantasy, embarrassment or snobbery. Of all this Minetta observed only a part—who could observe it all?—but to all of it she said splendid, for it was in motion.

In imposing its culture, our society was the most disastrous in history, not by evil intention but simply quantitatively. The culture, like any culture, imposed itself on every function and through the most multifarious channels; but what was imposed was so extremely complicated and technical that it was quite unassimilable by an animal whose powers had developed during a million years of very different circumstances. No wonder the culture imposed itself in stereotyped patterns (authors spoke of "patterns of culture"); and the live animal froze and had to adapt itself by blind trial and error, like any creature in a maze. Even so, Minetta felt that the case was not hopeless; it was hard but not hopeless. By achieving the two essentials, physiological freedom and social communication through the language of feeling, one could keep the neolithic man alive: the animals could resist the patterns with their own muscles and drives, and they would not be isolated and lonely. Then education into a true culture would be possible—she left that to the professionals. (Minetta had never faced the task of trying to teach Latin to happy children who have never learned to spell.)

She could not deny, of course, that they were all little apes and, because of the spirit of competition, tried to grow up too fast. Yet look with what skill and joy they grew expert in jacks and baseball.

These were the ideas that inspired Minetta and gave her a guarded optimism as she went about her business.

She was not a fool; she was not insensitive to the asphyxiation and our impending disaster; she was one of our friends. We saw that she was one of the first to float a little in space. She was stunned at the news that Mynheer had seen the constellation Man rising above the horizon. She joined the community of human relations. She wondered and rejoiced at the natural magical powers of Horatio and Rosalind in love; and she wept bitterly when Laura died. She was startled like the rest of us when it became evident that Mynheer, wherever he was, was out of this world. Nevertheless!

Nevertheless, she stuck stubbornly to her own point of view, confirming it by the life she led, and she used to say, "It's up to us; let's face it."

3. Horatio's Philosophy Without a Conscience

Since the death of Laura, Horatio believed what made him happy to believe. This was not the same as believing what he wanted to believe (though he had a tendency to go in that direction).

Horatio had faith (*a*) that when the need arose in him to perform a next act, then the means and opportunity for the act were available. Not *would be* available, for that was a speculation, but were immediately available when the need did arise. For instance, he needed to take a step, and there was ground there and time to take a step. Since he believed it was so, he could desire it and do it with a light heart; and so long as his belief rose from, was the sense of, his unknown powers as they were coming to be, it was so. And he had faith (*b*) that the dreamlike goal and tendency of all his needs, desires and steps was a satisfactory and excellent idea that he was happy to believe would be attained, for instance, a modest kind of Paradise in which everybody came across. He chose such a goal to work toward as made him happy to believe in. But (*c*) whether in fact the step he could take and did take was leading to the wished-for goal, and whether the means and opportunity would continue to be available, and whether the future steps would come nearer to the goal—all this was indifferent to him; it was merely the truth; and the truth had been his sister.

He had a tried faith that he could and would perform some next act; and he had a sentimental joy in entertaining the idea of the satisfactory wished-for goal. But now, supposing you pressed him to prove something, to justify the step he took or to explain and defend his tendency, then he easily invented convenient propositions. If it was convenient to say, "Man is good," he said it; or if to say, "Man is sick," he said that; or, "Most men are sick but we are not," or contrariwise, "We are even sicker than most," he said so; or else, "I do not know," or "Man is a mystery and unknowable to anybody," or, "Man is to be made"—however it suited his convenience to answer the question, "What is Man?" He employed these propositions simply to avoid an immediate difficulty and to embellish a vision. Soon some people refused to talk seriously with such a conscienceless creature, and this also was very good.

Restricting his philosophy to such modest requirements, Horatio saw the landscape of our Empire City with vivid clarity. He saw that—

Hovering everywhere were unpleasant effective Angels, Thrones, Dominions and Powers, carrying on the business of the city through the persons of the citizens. Very few of the persons were resting or moving in their own flesh.

The flesh of the people was cowering huddled together for womb warmth and womb safety in a vast envelope, still unborn; or maybe in a vast tomb, dead. (It was hard to tell.)

This was plain enough to see. Horatio felt of his own body to make sure that he was resting in his own flesh (the way a man pinches himself to see if he is awake); and he was. He lightly skipped a skip, and there was ground to support it and time.

But always so far, he found, the next step that he took and completed was still the carrying out of unfinished business. For instance, "We are about," he realized, "to get together the Memorial Ball Game that once we planned but never played. Now we will play it. And I am phoning Dave Andree to bring the Puerto Ricans." This was unfinished business being finished.

But he wondered what it would be like when his next need, desire, and step no longer had to do with unfinished business, but would be *new* business. What was new business? But this was speculation and profoundly indifferent. He smiled at a vision he had: of the Hilarious Archer looming played round by fires and loosing his shafts and bringing down those dark birds.

And he thought again of the words of the Murderer:

> Strange thoughts I have in head that will to hand,
> that must be acted ere they may be scanned.

Were his thoughts murderous thoughts? Was that why they flew immediately to hand, and why they could not bear scanning till they were done? Yet it is so that *every* new thought, not only of murder but of birth and glory, must be acted ere it may be scanned—and that is why the reader must not expect marvels reading in a book written in the twentieth century, or reading in a book at all.

Chapter 14 ▪ THE DEAD OF SPRING, III: A MEMORIAL GAME

1.

We got together a game of ball in memory of those dead in the war and the duration. Some of us, like Arthur, had died of the war, but Laura had died of the duration.

The field of our game was stretched in the macrocosm and the shadows of the players fell in heaven, altering destiny. The unknowing athletes cried out their natural shouts and groans, as they gave themselves to the game. Hotly the two teams competed, as if for victory, but it was in order that each player might be tricked into surpassing himself and being sacrificed in the game.

From time to time a player came to himself and asked, "Why am I fighting so hard? It is only a game," and then he understood that he was looming on the field of the macrocosm and his shadow fell in heaven, fulfilling destiny.

The ball lay on the sparse grass—for we were playing in ragged uniforms and on a poor field—and it was devoid of life. But the players picked it up and threw it past the batter, or the batter batted it (it comes to the same thing), and the ball leaped with life. The athletes played in order to make the ball leap with life. To impart life to the planet of artifice.

Each player came to the trial of it with such nature and character as he had. There was a natural reason why one batter swung poorly and another swung with all his might (and missed). But one way or another, the shadow of the ball leaped back and forth across the zodiac, so long as the players gave themselves to the game.

Naturally we youthful and aging players encouraged one another with patter and cries, that had an edge of weariness.

2.

From the first pitch, the game was inexorably tending toward the end of the game. Each team was allowed 27 outs.

Regarded as a competition, the batters of each team were trying to achieve something against the tight defenses of the other team; and regarded as a competition, the batters who achieved the most won the victory. But regarded as a game, it was the fielders who always won out, for finally all the batters (of whatever team) would be put out; the period was limited; the game always came to an end. It could be seen that the fielders were deathly reapers. Regarded in this light, the batters were trying, by their hits, simply to forestall the ending of the game, to keep the ball in play.

Our destiny was a cunning machine. During the game the players who played in order to play—why else should they play?—who played in order to keep the ball alive, nevertheless desperately destroyed the play by bringing nearer the end of the game, for there was no other means for any one to come to bat and achieve anything except by putting the other team out. Seeking to outdo one another in the competition to achieve something, we jointly hurried on the ending of the game. *This* is the fundamental form of our game.

The rules of our game are so drawn that it is possible to achieve something, but eventually one is sure to be put out. Depending on the temper of the epoch—the ball is more or less potentially lively—a man can achieve more or less; but the rules are unalterable in decreeing the game to an end.

3.

Our baseball game is the drama of a small boy. Each player stands up alone, at Home, as a batter, seeking to leave home and prove himself, achieving something against the obstacles of the field. But he wants to return full circle, to Home.

The man standing up to bat is the shadow, already looming, of the small boy age six. The fielders are facing against him and they move to the left or right, or draw in or retreat, according to their expectation of what he, by his nature, character and situation, might achieve.

A player can be helped along his way by his teammates, but he must start on his way by standing up alone.

But he must be given a *possible* opportunity. You must pitch the lively ball to him where he *can* impart to it some life of his own, if he can, and achieve something for himself and his team.

He has hit the ball and he is on the dangerous bases. He is running, as if in full flight or to get on (it comes to the same thing). Once he has started, he has to continue onward through all the chances of it. The situation of the batter before starting out and of the runner on the bases is very different. At home the situation is tense and quiet; but on the bases he has already made a breach and the furies are after him in full cry.

4.

Arky was their pitcher and he offered our batter a possible opportunity, and the youth hit the ball screaming into the outfield and drew up and stood stock-still on second base. He was not age six but a youth of twenty. Our team cried out our natural shouts. The sun was shining on the patchy field of grass and earth. Retrieving the ball, the fielders drew in, encouraging one another's animal hearts. They flipped the ball around the infield to get a little life not so much in the ball as in themselves. Their catcher also talked it up.

We were *not* competing in order, jointly, to bring on the end of the game, but to get the most runs during the game.

But as if we were competing for life or death, as if the losers at the end of the game would forfeit their lives and wives and possessions. Lost in this competition, and sacrificing ourselves to the game, in order, jointly, to bring on the end of the game. To instill life into a planet of artifice and *fly* it across the zodiac.

Half-substantial, between the small boys and the looming shapes of destiny, we were intermediate shadows.

We were playing the game in memory of many who had already died.

5.

Our captain Horatio was the first to snap; he could no longer bear the hurrying forward, forward. "Go in there and stall," he said. "Hit fouls."

For there is this one tiny inconsequential rule that contradicts the fundamental form of the game: you cannot get a batter out on a foul. And often on hot fields games pause while the batter hits fouls. The last foul is not a hit but it is not a miss, it counts for nothing at all, it does not advance the game toward its end.

Even before we started fouling them off, our game seemed to pause. A train rumbled near on the elevated tracks along the field; as it ground by, the row of heads framed in the windows looked down at the game.

The batter was Davy Drood, who could hit wherever he pleased (but he was not a long hitter). He took two strikes, and chose to hit the next pitch foul.

"Foul! Strike two," said the umpire.

The pitcher threw another good pitch, and Davy carefully hit the ball foul along the opposite line.

"Foul! Strike two," said the umpire.

They relayed the ball back to the box, and the pitcher pitched it, and Davy hit that pitch foul. The pitcher shook his head, and pounded his glove.

"Foul! Strike two," said the umpire.

Now the pitcher knew that Davy could hit a ball anywhere he pleased, and he was not one to hit fouls. So he threw him a very bad pitch—what would not be called a fair opportunity—but as if derisively Davy stepped aside and hammered also this pitch in a bounding foul.

"Foul! Strike two on the batter," said the umpire, for these did not count for anything at all.

A train rumbled on the elevated tracks and roared by, scattering sparks below, while the row of heads framed in the window looked down at our game.

The angry pitcher at once pitched a smoking pitch—that would be called a fair opportunity if one could see it—but Davy smartly lined outside the first-base line, foul.

"Foul! Strike two," said the umpire.

The pitcher lobbed him the ball to blast to hell and have it over with, but Davy weakly drove this ball foul, as if to say, "You must give me a hard opportunity for me to hit a rousing foul."

The pitcher threw down his glove.

"Foul! Strike two," said the umpire.

"He's fouling them off on purpose," said the pitcher.

"Play ball," said the umpire.

"He's stalling the game."

"Pitch. Pitch. He can hit 'em foul if he wants to hit 'em foul."

"What's a matter, Arky? Tired already?" said Davy.

"Play ball," said the umpire.

A train screamed by, wildly showering the burning sparks from the faulty connection; the row of heads framed in the windows looked down at the game.

A tang of ozone was wafted by the wind across the field.

The pitcher sadly pitched, and Davy hit the ball foul.

"Cut it out, Davy! There's no use stalling," the fielders began to call. "Cut it out, Davy, cut it out! There's no use stalling."

"Foul! Strike two; play ball," said the umpire.

Wavering a little, Davy hit a towering foul under the tracks, that the fielder almost got his hands on; but the ball bounded away. The sunlight falling through the tracks clothed the fielder in stripes whose fire splashed in drops onto the ground.

The next pitch Davy adroitly fouled off.

"Foul ball. Strike two," said the umpire.

The fielders threw down their gloves in disgust. They crowded forward against home plate. The umpire waved them back. "Play ball! Play ball!" But they would not play.

"What in *hell* is the use of stalling?" they cried.

A train rumbled near on the tracks and ground by, while the row of heads framed in the windows looked down at the nongame.

If an athlete had the disposition that he wanted to play ball, and nevertheless he could not bear for the game to hurry forward to its ending, now was the time for him to enjoy ease and glory. (If indeed the batter could keep it up; if indeed the fielders would choose to play.) But it was not interesting.

The fielders were insulted. "Cut it out, Davy," they said.

"What in hell is the use of stalling?"

"Once the game is over, my sister is dead forever," said Horatio Alger.

"Do you call this a game?"

"Play ball," said the umpire, for he was interested only in the rules.

But they would not play.

"Horatio, you're scared. That's why you resort to stalling and repetitions."

"The memory itself is a repetition," said Horatio.

"No, you stall in the mourning itself, just like with everything. Give it out! Give it out! But you're scared."

"Yes, I'm scared," admitted Horatio. "We have been so deeply wounded that we can do nothing but repeat it, returning again and again to the same wound."

"Play ball!" conceded the pitcher, picking up his glove. "If that son of a bitch Drood thinks he can keep fouling off my pitches, I'll burn one by him that he won't even see."

"Play ball," said the umpire.

Davy looked inquiringly at his captain.

"Get what you can," said Horatio. "There's no use stalling."

The fielders went back to the field.

A train crept slowly along the elevated tracks, engulfing all the bright stripes of the sun in darkness, and the row of heads framed in the windows looked down at the game.

The pitcher pitched it, a likely opportunity that one could not see; and Davy swung with all his might and missed.

6.

But Lothair said, "Let that son of a bitch Arky give me a good offering, and I'll belt it so hard they'll never find the ball; and *that*'ll be the end of the game. I'll kill it."

For the rage that was welling up in him was on the verge of its paroxysm, and it seemed to him that this ball was a reasonable and worthy object on which to wreak it.

Lothair understood what was the object of our game, to impart a little life to the ball, for a little while, between the cradle and the grave; and when he said, "I'll kill it!" he meant the opposite, that he would somehow impart to it an absolute life, so that the ball would never die again but fly away forever like a bird, or bound across the lands like the hunted hare.

"Play ball," said the umpire, and the big man took his stance at home. There was no separation of substance between the flesh of his back and arms and hands and the bat that he was flourishing. The bat was quivering like his teeth.

The pitcher pitched the ball, such a pitch as you or I do not see, but Lothair saw it and he hit it.

Oh, and whether or not—at least the sound!—whether or not he imparted to the ball an absolute life, at least the sound of that blow, the crack of the bat, forever will not fade in our soul. (The *F* in the octave above high *C*.)

The reapers lifted faces of wonder as the bird rose and flew and did not tire.

The natural voices of the youths cried out their shouts of joy and wonder. The sunshine did not cease pouring onto the sparse ground of our poor field.

"I guess that's the end o' the game," said the umpire jovially to the pitcher. "Your ball's lost. It flew away."

"I didn't think he coulda seen that one," said the pitcher.

7.

They retrieved the poor murdered ball far out beyond the limits, and relayed it back spinning crazily because its cover was torn.

Naturally the players did not cease exclaiming and thumping the batter on the back as he came home on his homer.

The ball was in a sad state, hardly fit for use, but we were poor and it was the only planet we had. So we wound it with tape, making it still a little heavier and so much the harder to achieve anything with. We put it in such condition as we could to get on with the game.

"O.K., it'll do," said the umpire. "Play ball."

But to the general horror, Lothair had again picked up his bat and was pounding the ground around home plate, the natural planet, our mother Earth.

Blow after blow—one could hardly credit it, cracks appeared in the clay. It was an object great enough for his anger. Whether or not it was worthy and reasonable?

He was not weeping. No tears were streaming down his large face. But his jaw was set in stubborn determination, and he beat the ground.

"She won't move her ass," he hissed. "She's frigid. Will she at least speak up and say something?"

The players gathered around him, at a little distance, out of the range of his flailing bat. The ground cracked underfoot. A hopelessness gripped us by the throat. A common prayer rose in the gathered soul, "Creator spirit, come."

Chapter 15 ▪ LOTHARIO'S COUVADE

T'as été malheureux, hein?
—Les Pompes Funèbres

Lothario lay on a couch in the corner of the room, giving birth. It was only an imitation, but what else is a man to do? For there is a new living thing and one must reconcile himself to it. Yet the baby is always brought forth by the woman; it is she who has the bond of orgastic birth and present nourishment, so that she has been coping with it and must cope. The father must first learn to accommodate himself to hope.

Meanwhile Emilia was seated in a chair holding the week-old baby (it was St. Wayward) in her gigantic hands, and she was carrying on a dialogue with the as yet speechless animal. St. Wayward was a week old and she was counting over the days of his week.

She said, "Now Sunday is the Sun's day. And Monday is the Moon's day."

To this the infant making no reply, she continued, "Tuesday is under the influence of Mars and Wednesday of Mercury. Thursday belongs to Jupiter."

She counted them off on her fingers, but the baby could not yet follow with his eyes and trace the outlines of objects; he could see only the light.

"Friday is Venus'," cried Emilia with rising passion, "and Saturday is Saturn's. I go over this list again and again!" she cried. "I do not notice that there is any day of the week under the influence of the Earth. How can we expect *not* to be disappointed?"

She had raised her voice, and the baby screwed up his face in alarm. But as yet he did not scream nor respond anything from his blank mind.

Nevertheless, Emilia always heard an answer, probably in her father's voice. "Please," he was saying, "if you wouldn't count out the days and name them, maybe there might also be earth days among them. Naturally! If the days are *under* an influence, if they're under an *influence,* you must look in the sky and not in front of your nose." That is the kind of thing that her wise father was answering her; but it was not the answer of the void mind of the baby with its searing needs.

The baby began to bawl unlimitedly. Emily did not know how to appease him. She hummed the *Berceuse Héroique* of Debussy, but that was not the lucky music. There were real tears in the baby's eyes.

A child's fit of unlimited bawling is mysterious. None of us knows that language. A mother learns to distinguish the various cryings of her baby; yet always there is this surprising inconsolable bawling out of nowhere that she cannot decipher—she must let it bawl itself out.

The baby's bawling was fearsomely mysterious, and soon Emilia herself was trembling. It seemed to her that she knew its meaning: it meant that the primeval nature of things, the chaos, was pain.

But Lothario—as a man who is flustered, running a low fever of racing thoughts and painfully tingling all over his skin, tries to relax on a couch in order that in him a softer feeling may rise, a meaningful thought important as a clue and a dolorous pang of the entrails; he is flaming to get up but he will not relent and free himself from concentration yet awhile—so Lothario lay on the couch rigidly clinging to it deathlike, just in order that no softer feeling might arise and not to suffer any pang. He was aware that remaining so, flaming to get up yet unwilling to relent and free himself, the only thought, the only feeling that could occur to him was just his own boredom, which he was in fact presently producing by rigidly clinging to where he was, waiting for something impossible to happen when in fact every kind of possible thing was happening and he no idle participant. Yet he did not relent and free himself and get up, because perhaps this unpromising thought, of his self-produced boredom was the important one, the clue. It was so; and he at once loosed his grip to the bed and relaxed, and a softer feeling flowed in him.

BOOK 4 THE HOLY TERROR

Modern Times

Laisse en entrant ici tes lauriers à la porte,
Mêle tes pleurs aux miens.

—CORNEILLE

PART 1 NEOLITHIC RITES

Repressed unused natures . . . return as images of the Golden Age, or Paradise; or as theories of the Happy Primitive. We can see how great poets, like Homer and Shakespeare, devoted themselves to glorifying the virtues of the previous era, as if it were their chief function to keep people from forgetting what it used to be to be a man.

And at best, indeed, the conditions of advancing civilized life seem to make important powers of human nature not only neurotically unused but rationally unusable. Civil security and technical plenty, for instance, are not very appropriate to an animal that hunts and perhaps needs the excitement of hunting to enliven its full powers. It is not surprising if such an animal should often complicate quite irrelevant needs—e.g., sexuality—with danger and hunting, in order to rouse excitement.

—*Gestalt Therapy,* II, 6, ii.

Chapter 1 ▪ A SYNOTIC VIEW OF OUR MIDDLE YEARS

Insensible changes—
GIBBON

As I begin this latterly book about Lothair, Emilia and Piet Duyck, and Horatio and Rosalind and the others, let me reveal my present intention. It is to show how these gifted friends of mine, who were always so dissident but not necessarily protestant, have now become more satisfied with the folkways of our society. For they have come to find in our folkways opportunities for themselves. This commonplace matter is my theme; yet, given the intense excitement of my friends, their hot anger, grief, lust and glad contemplation, I shall, in describing their now lucky situation, sometimes be led to use a tone of rapture.

Thus, where I commenced by compiling an Almanac of Alienation, I now am concluding with a kind of Register of Reconciliation, a Domesday Book. Signed, sealed and delivered. The fact that I myself try to make myself clear in this way, rather than continually changing my mind and wearying the reader, is proof of an insensible change in the cultural climate. It is the autumn of 19—; and as everybody knows, there is a general agreement among us to take seriously our public institutions, for instance, the coming American elections, and to wield them as our very own. (I mention the elections specifically because this book is partly a campaign document.) Make no mistake; this agreement to co-operate is not necessarily a total abnegation on our part, for the institutions themselves have insensibly over the years been transformed by our truth, and why should we hold out against our own?

It is a truth made fit for pigs! Granted. But what is wrong with pigs? All of our friends are rich and famous. That is simply how it is with us. We cannot resist our existing situation, even if to try to do so were not bad grace and bad taste.

Also, we have gotten on in years. Therefore, for this reason alone, we have in large measure fulfilled our needs and have little to gripe about. It is the inevitable triumph of age, which (to anticipate a little) is socially conceded by the uniformly favorable obituaries that will be accorded to us in the *Times* and the *Tribune*: for no matter who you are or what you have done, if only you have stuck at it long enough you will get a good obituary. Even the misdeeds of the previous generation are the conservative structure in which the next grows up (they are all the structure there is); there must be fathers, and they must die and be praised.

Let me expatiate a moment on this inevitable triumph of age; it is an interesting subject. Pose it, for instance, as a problem in gross physiology: How is it that the human animal has a limited span of life, threescore and ten years? The answer is, that by that time he is necessarily successful and may as well die. Our wishes are few and elementary: a few simple animal and social pleasures, a few outpourings of the personality and some mortal and immortal victories. But though the needs are few, the occasions and opportunities for them in the vastly repetitious world are very numerous. (For instance, I knew a man who tried desperately to make a living, he tried everything; and sure enough, after a while he was able to make a living.) Thus, given the increase of skill by experience, and given the fact that the coming generation is temporarily overawed by the previous, every human being is eventually doomed to be objectively happy and may as well, as I say, die. Signed, sealed and delivered.

I hasten to reply to the obvious objection to this line of reasoning, namely, that men and women notoriously prevent themselves from satisfying themselves; they set up a powerful counterwill to the achievement of nature. But that achievement is inevitable nevertheless. A young person may succeed in keeping himself wretched; a middle-aged person cannot work it.

We may observe the will to fail spectacularly in the burning desires of youth. A young person dreams up a desire, burns with the image of it and foresees the conclusion. This process is carried on in place of, and usually counter to, any effectual means to gratify himself. Why should he act so strangely? I can think of two reasons. First, he wants to be safe in a world dangerous to his inexperience, so instead of venturing *forth,* he exhausts his interest in impatient fantasies. Conversely, he is afraid of his own excitement; he wants to avoid, not to have to cope with, the shattering excitement of being involved when (and if) some practical opportunity arises. A common way of working this is that a lively opportunity is not recognized as an opportunity at all until five minutes after it is inexorably lost.

Even so, this counterwill against being happy is in the long run doomed to fail. Consider it. Driven by their illusory burning desires, young people do get involved, following the wrong ends in the wrong places; and, if only by trial and error, they cannot help finding out the facts of life; they get wise to themselves—for instance, that they want to engage in sex. (I mention sex specifically because frequently my characters want to engage in sex.) Timidly pursuing their illusory aims, they cannot help getting certain dull experience; so they learn to cope with the excitement of dull experience. By practice they are tricked by nature into preparing themselves to endure experience—they have learned the haunts of it and mastered the techniques of it. It is only their burning desire for happiness that stands in the way. So as soon as this desire itself lapses, they at once achieve the satisfaction of the lapsed desire. This is called middle age. As I shall be glad to put it later: "It is easy, and indeed almost inevitable, to get what you don't want."

So Goethe said: "Beware of what you wish for in your youth, because you will achieve it in your middle age." In this sentence he has provided the motto for all educational romances like the present one.

This recalls me to our now complacent heroes. What have they been up to since last we took leave of them?

Mynheer we left at his desk, weeping from his eyes drops of blood. One or two of these drops, you will recall, splashed onto the page in which he was explaining to himself that he was Out of This World. His pen trailed off in the blood and he fell asleep. When he awoke, however, and found that he was indeed out of this world, he decided to take the situation for what it was and to become reconciled to it; so he set off on a series of interplanetary voyages, a Mad Scientist. It is returning from one of these trips that we shall meet him again.

Antonicelli, the prosecuting attorney, we saw, found that he would have to give up that apoplectic career which made him topple in the courtroom. But he too has reconciled himself to the world, how it is and how he is, and he has put out a shingle in medicine as a psychiatrist. Being the man he is, he has hit on a therapeutic method of high voltage; and we shall visit him in his office. To our surprise, we shall find him there associated with Minetta Tyler, the little social worker who used to be cast into a panic by the words *Man, Woman* and *Child,* and other words naturally associated with these; but now she runs a kind of therapeutic bawdyhouse under the style of Madame Vanetska the second.

The handy fellows, Droyt and Lefty, where are they? They have vanished into Southern California, where has occurred an unlikely event, and we shall hear about *that.*

Eliphaz, Arthur and Laura are still dead, and therefore (demonstrably) must have been happy (middle-aged). Unfortunately, Little Gus, who was killed by the tiger, is also still dead, but he died by accident. I mention the names of these dead because even in the climate of reconcilation our friends are accompanied by the presence of their absence, and converse with them from time to time.

Now Lothair and Emilia would seem, of our friends, the hardest to gratify and satisfy, because they had always tried so desperately to improve the human condition. Yet even they have found an unlooked-for solace by embracing a kind of neolithic faith, and they devote considerable time to rites and ritual games. (I shall start out by describing some.) These involve certain primitive ecstasies and austerities that are not common among us, yet are profoundly orthodox. If some of their ways are odd, we must remember that religion, whatever else it is, is a socially approved psychosis. Growing up in such a home is their child Wayward, who is now six, and we must not be surprised if he becomes a saint.

Horatio and Rosalind, finally, are man and wife and therefore, in principle, need no longer concern us in a romance—for that is the *end,* and the end, as Aristotle said, is that after which nothing at all follows.

Chapter 2 ▪ CONVERSING

1.

The brothers Alger and their families were now living together in a pleasant subdivided loft in Hoboken where the rent was cheap.* From their windows they could look out on the theaters and towers of the Empire City across the river. Their economy was hand to mouth and therefore rich so long as they had, which they did, an easy use of their hands and an unobstructed access to their mouths.

Oh, they had come a long way since that time, when Laura was alive, when they had lived on the dole as pensioners of the state, that solid corporation. Yet now they had, working and hunting, a direct draft on the goods of nature and they were even more securely established.

2.

But Lothario was uneasy about Horatio and Rosalind. He thought that they were going crazy or, as he expressed it to Emilia, "They are going off their rockers"—for he envisaged the soul as swinging back and forth in great, strong and increasing extremes, till one went off the rocker.

Often Horatio sat in a corner on the floor, holding between his outstretched hands a taut string, and looking at it. Sometimes he looped the string round his outstretched fingers as if he were playing cat's cradle. This alarmed Lothario. Not that a man could not spend hours playing cat's cradle, but that in this game one does not play alone, for one man takes the string from another, changing the figures. "If he wants somebody to play with him, why doesn't he ask?" said Lothair, already angry, for he had a strong need for social interplay.

Sometimes Horatio mislaid his favorite string—he had made himself a beautiful thong of leather, stained with blood and tied with a square knot—and then he showed signs of anxiety. But when he

* The reason for setting these chapters, especially the fifth, in Hoboken will be clear to anyone who has ever been in Hoboken.

found it, he settled quietly in his corner and rose at once into his contemplation of the stretched string, while a shaft of sunlight fell across his temples and shoulders. He didn't look crazy, but just the type of a seventeenth-century gentleman-philosopher, with their dumb-bunny apparatus that was also elegantly ornate, etched brass and cut-glass bottles.

3.

"What the devil are you doing there?" cried Lothair at last. "Do you want me to take it off?"

"Take it off?" said the other man.

"Aren't you playing cat's cradle?" asked the first man.

"No. You must think I'm crazy."

"Yes, I do."

(They were really conversing, which I express by "the one man said" and then "the other man said.")

"Yes, take it off," said Horatio, and Lothario took off the cat's cradle, making the double X's.

Horatio observed this a moment, and then took it off, making the parallel bars.

He let go the string and it fell to the floor.

4.

"I'm making an observation in physics, trying to get the feel of the forces."

He explained that he was working on the following elementary hypothesis: When a force is opposed by an equal and opposite force, the system seems to be brought to rest, but (this was the hypothesis), there is set up another potential force normal to the counteracting forces. That is, the opposition of two forces does not result in an isolated nullity, but at once involves the surroundings in which the original system holds itself (or is held) rigid and struggling.

"I'll draw you a picture," said Horatio, and he took his pencil and drew

"that's my string pulled taut by equal forces; and then——

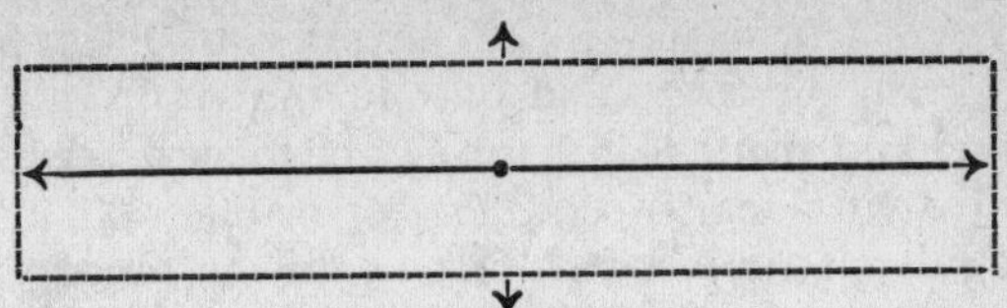

"I can feel how the taut string has a tendency to resist being moved by a normal force; it has created a potential normal force of its own in all directions. Try it. If you increase the tautness, you increase the immobility of the system as a whole; you make yourself dynamically rigid."

He held out the crimson thong.

Lothair stretched the string a few times, then dropped it and shrugged his shoulders. "You don't need the string at all, you know. You can get the same effect just by pushing your palms hard together one against the other; and soon you're trembling with wrath."

"Yes, you can," agreed the other man carefully. "And probably you are."

"Why do you make such a fuss when your string is lost?"

Horatio said nothing.

"I dare you, try it my way, without the string," taunted Lothair, and powerfully he exerted his own right hand against his left hand till his knuckles and his elbows were white—but he did not tremble, he was used to it.

5.

The younger brother was suffocated with anxiety. The sweat was oozing from his forehead.

"What's the matter, brother?" said Lothair, and kindly touched his cheek.

Horatio took a few breaths and said, quietly enough, "Yes, it's the same principle, it's the same. But if I feel it as my hands held prisoner by that leather thong, then I can bear it, I can bear it very well. It is even interesting, very interesting. But if I directly exert my own force against my own force and feel me becoming rigid, then I—I—I cannot bear it."

Nevertheless, he pressed his palms together and exerted all his force and bore it fairly well, hardly trembling. "Are you satisfied?

"You know, Lothair," he said, "I have always been an industrious and obedient little boy, just like now. Within the bounds of the permitted. Once I felt I had permission, I could go right on and on, to the limit. I have never held myself back. I recall it—how Mama used to tell me to go and play in the sand, and I took my pail and shovel and trotted off happily and played all day, making sand battleships with real firecrackers for ordnance."

Lothair could not suppress a smile at this autobiographical version of the industrious and obedient little boy, the same as had torn up the school records when the teacher went to the toilet, and then led them a chase for twenty years. Yet it was true enough, for each person finds where he can his permission and his mandate; or he acts as if he had permission or as if he had a mandate; or he invents those things.

"So *you* let me have my piece of string, brother," said Horace insinuatingly. "It's only a piece of string. So I can test again how the nullifying opposition of forces creates a rigid structure normal to it and makes all the world strong. Pick up the string and give it to me, please."

Lothair would have said, "Why don't you try picking it up yourself and giving yourself permission? I dare you——" But the shaft of sunlight was falling across Horatio's face colored free and easy and a little crazy and irresistibly appealing. So he picked up the string and gave it to him to play with.

6.

"Brother," he said, "do you believe this theory of yours, do you think it's true, that the forces brought to a dead stop create the other force simply out of nothing?"

The other man looked at him with his good grin and said, "You do think I'm crazy, don't you?"

"Yes, I do, I said I did," said the first man.

—For my part, I find it simply beautiful and worth stopping at, how the brothers were having a conversation! It was that they had something to talk about and were not sounding off but giving each other their objective opinions. Not as masks carrying on a conversation, but as men—conversing. This was remarkable. I have only recently come to observe such things.—

"Do I believe the theory?" said Horatio. "Of course I believe it. But what do I care whether or not it's true? You know me, I believe what makes me happy to believe."

"But why does such a theory as that make you happy to believe? It would make me unhappy."

"Look!" said Horace. He held out the thong stretched as taut as he could stretch it; he was rigid from head to foot and his arms and hands trembled until you saw them as a blur. He released the tension, and his arms and body were free at their ease and around him grew and glowed the blue aura that was his, shot with gold. The string dangled from his thumb and fell to the floor. "When this opposition is loosed, you see, there is restored to the world its free power, live and potential, in my arms that formerly were held as in a vise because of that damned system. Shall I release also the dead stop between my feet and the ground, and navigate among the stars like Mynheer?" Mynheer was off to a distant planet, out of this world.

"But you yourself were holding the string taut," said Lothair. "And you yourself let it go."

"Of course. Like everything. The frame of the universe is held in such a rigid system of dead stops. I'm in it too. It makes no difference where you assign the cause and where the effect. It's brought to a pause, it brings itself to a pause; it's held in place, it holds itself in place. Then I have freed it, or it has freed me, and a new energy is *un*bound. A new energy, no? Brother?"

But he could see that Lothair did not grasp it. Lothair was so inured to the *fact* of exerting his strength against himself that he could not entertain it as an experiment that might be done otherwise.

7.

Last night Horatio was looking out the window. The sky had a stolid grandeur, the starlit river was also in its bounds. The structure of the house supported him, his chin on his arm on the window sill. He had no doubt then that he was going to venture beyond the boundaries of the permitted, and where he had no mandate. He relaxed the tight muscles of his temples and the firmament, thereby, also gave in a little; it let up. The stars shone clearer and moved closer. But he became frightened. He was afraid of becoming confused.

"Lothar," he said now, "you too let the animals out of their cages."

He could see at once that his brother grasped it very well.

He burst out laughing gaily. His laughter was good and infectious (it did not make your marrow freeze), and soon he had his brother going too. Lothario laughed in a bass voice, Horatio in a bright baritone. Tears ran out of their eyes. They began to be in a panic. Lothario was laughing a bright tenor, and Horatio falsetto as if his voice had never changed. They became frightened and stopped short.

"Why are we laughing?"

"No, why did we stop?"

They were laughing at the frame of things collapsing into nothing—that's what people laugh at. They were laughing with the energy set free when the misunderstanding between them vanished. They were laughing toward their youth. What set them off was the one man reassuring the other that he was going crazy—this was permissive. Such were the four causes of the laughing together of Horatio and Lothario.

They stopped because they were becoming confused.

8.

Rosalind often wept, for no reason. Lothair and Emilia were alarmed at it because they knew the couple were going too far too fast. But Horatio was not disturbed at all, because he knew that his woman was not crying because she was unhappy, for he had physiological proofs that she was not unhappy. He had no doubts whatever about his ability to make his wife very happy.

Yet often she wept until she shook with great sobs.

"She is shaking with nonattachment," explained her man, and held her gently and firmly until her sobbing subsided.

Her crying was: as when a young girl—perhaps she has up to this hour been a virgin, modest and not taking any risks; but he has a winning way, without making any definite promises; and they have been to bed, and all her feelings have been strange and new; then she has burst into tears not of pain or grief, but of bewilderment and helplessness, and she wants to cling and be held, and be given definite promises, till her sobbing subsides—so Rosalind sobbed and Horatio held her, and did not promise anything.

This was very well, except that Rosalind was not a virginal girl, etc.; she and Horatio now had two children and were, one would have thought, well accustomed to their way of life together.

Emilia said to Lothair, "She's crying because they aren't married. She has no family ties. She feels like an orphan."

"What do you mean they're not married? What do you call family ties?"

"No, no. They have a friendly arrangement and obviously strong animal ties; and they live in a community with us and their friends and have children of their own. But these things make it all the worse."

"Why all the worse? I really don't follow you at all."

"Because everything is provided as they need it. There's so much the more excitement to cope with, and no symbol with which to support it. There was no wedding party, just some rough trade. There was no sacrament, just the dirty jokes. They are not permitted to carry on so."

"Shall we make them a party? But how can we make them a party now? Isn't it past the time?"

"Now *is* the time! Now *is* the time. But how? With what rites? They have no religion. They endure their mysteries—very courageously too; but they have no religion to domesticate their mysteries. On the edge of panic, they are thrown on their own inventions or on their private insanity instead of a socially shared insanity. You see, finally no one can do it."

"I think you're right, as usual about these things. But I still don't understand. Why do you say 'finally'? Why is today different from yesterday, or why is this year different from last year? It's now six years."

9.

"For us it's not different," said Emilia sadly. "But for them it's different. Keep your eye on the facts of life.

"Consider the ordinary couple, say a man and wife, and what happens between them. First, having each other, they lose their embarrassments and social fears, and they come to a security in each other that allows them a strong steady sexual pleasure. Good. But then they must stick fast at this particular intensity of excitement, whatever it may be, for if they let it become still stronger, it will confuse them, disrupt their usual standards of behavior, make them panicky.

"How does it work out? Differently for different couples. They may continue to mark time where they are, in an uneasy state, one night enjoying each other, the next quarreling and flying apart to regain their equilibrium; these are the good marriages, like ours. Or they may cling to each other, afraid to quarrel and draw temporarily apart; this is boring, and they are likely to look for their unsafe excitement outside the marriage; these are the adulteries (but then perhaps the jealous quarrels begin and bring back the excitement inside the house). Or lastly, drawing back from going further, they may begin to fear each other, saying, 'You're cruel to me, you want to swallow me up,' and so forth; these are the divorces.

"But how is it with Rosalind and Horatio? Nothing of this kind at all! For they never had embarrassments or social fears to begin with; and I don't think they ever had standards of behavior, except our elaborate Old World courtesy. Worse, they simply don't know what it is to be unsafe, or safe. Probably they're becoming confused, but certainly they are going crazy. They are tearing themselves to pieces. Six years, you say? That's just it! Marriages are supposed to last only five years.

"So she bawls and he mopes. Instead of becoming accustomed to their way of life together, they are becoming unaccustomed to living in the world. Only God can save them."

"Maybe every night they're tearing themselves to pieces," said Lothair, "yet come morning, *there* they are."

"God be praised! Yes, God *can* save them and he does. Thanks to the creator of the heavens and the earth!"

"Do you know what I have heard? How one of them says to the other, 'Thank *you.*' "

What was wonderful, here, was that Emilia and Lothair, not very happy themselves, were still without spite and envy, and they were astonished and grateful that Horatio and Rosalind were happier than anyone could cope with. To me this is more wonderful than the other wonder.

10.

When Emilia and Lothario disagreed, one would say definitely to the other, "No," and proceed to make their difference precise. And as soon as they would come to an agreement, they would at once say, "Yes," and agree. They did not say, "Yes, but——"

11.

For his observations, Horatio had carved a top of bone (seventh cervical vertebra) that he whipped and observed the gyroscopic forces.

When he whipped his top, the children were delighted. He taught his nephew Wayward, who was six, to spin it, and Wayward regarded him as an uncle. Likely and Gus, his own children, tried to catch the top as though it were a live animal. When they caught it, it died.

His theory of the spinning top was again the same:

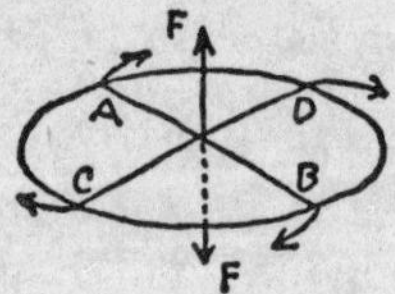

The opposed centrifugal components *A* and *B*, *C* and *D*, etc., came to a dead stop in the center and thereby made rigid their plane and created the normal force *F*. He could conceive of the universe as a whole as held in place by similar contraries.

Yet the top was alive (just as the universe was alive); it was its spinning that made it stand up rigid. The pivot wobbled only when the top died. As if it were only in the rigid structure of the universe that we enjoy such life as there was, such as it was. But this was not at all what made him happy to prove. Not at all.

"It's only a top!" he cried in agitation and angrily kicked it across the room. "*I* spun it."

He was like a testy child, and not like a gentleman-philosopher of the seventeenth century. This was his propensity to substitute what he merely wanted to believe for what would indeed make him happy to believe.

Wayward was frightened by his temper, and the smaller children bawled.

12.

"I was just at your age," Lothair said to him, "when I went off my rocker and let the animals out of the zoo."

Horace recalled it! How he had met him in the hideout in the storm; and he had noticed a fire in his eyes not dissimilar to the one he now felt burning in his own.

Lothair had pressed against his chest the bladeless knife (that also had no handle).

"You mean to say, brother," said Horatio, "that we have a family flaw. Yet *there* you are, better than new, almost human."

"I am afraid the cases are different," said Lothair. "With me it was of no importance to be sane."

"Why are we different?"

"At the time that I went crazy, I was deprived of everything; but you have the needful things. I was in jail and alone; you are free and married. I was miserable; you are happy. I had a headful of ideas that needed to be shaken loose; you——"

"You mean to say," said Horace with asperity, "I don't have the *right* to go crazy. *I* am not justified to. Please! Permit me."

"No, I don't mean to say that at all. Stop putting words in my mouth. What I mean to say is that if Horatio, who was sane as a hammer and did not suffer from ideas, and who chose to live in a way calculated to succeed, and who therefore did succeed–if Horatio chooses to take leave of his senses, to what sanity can he return? . . . Yes, you *do* choose it!" he said angrily. "Don't try to deny it."

"What's that to you if I choose? And because *you* can't imagine a way out, does that prove there's no such thing?"

"Very good. But I have to live in this only world that I conceive possible."

"You're welcome to it. Am I standing in your way?"

"Yes, you are. You judge me."

"I judge you!" Horatio was astounded. He did not grasp it.

They were both angry. They misunderstood each other and could not withdraw from the subject to get a little perspective. This was because there was concealed in it another subject that they did not dare broach.

"Laura—" said the older brother, daring it—"Laura was your age when she hanged herself."

"Oh. Is *she* still dead?" said Horatio dully. "I haven't been thinking of her." And he burst into tears.

Lothair turned away furiously.

So Horatio was crying in one room and Rosalind was crying in the other room.

Chapter 3 ▪ DANCING

In the evening, Horatio and Rosalind retired early. But they didn't go to bed, certainly not to sleep. You could hear them moving about in the darkness.

"What are they doing?" said Lothair.

Emilia looked in at the open door. "I think they're dancing. I can't see. It's dark."

There was no audible music, but they were dancing. They were dancing to the rhythm of the various tides and pulse beats of their bodies. She had learned it from Bufano and had taught it to Horatio. In this dancing one does not so much follow the music as that there is an immediate unity of the rhythmic gestures and the tidal waves, pulses and swift currents. This is dancing. This is Noh dancing. Then the silence is punctuated by moans, grunts or cries of the throat—or by a call.

The light went on (for Rosalind had switched on the light to see him well), discovering Horatio in the following pose: he was lightly on the ball of his right foot with all his limbs and fingers and head and hair outflung.

It was the *Glad Day!* of Blake.

Flung as far as they could go, his extremities were flung equally in all directions. He was not tending *any*where, he did not mean *any*thing; but just Glad Day. His penis was obvious but not erect. He wore a plain smile that had in it neither humor nor victory. And there was an echo, as if there had been a single shout.

The aura of Horatio extended away from his expansive body in the room, and Rosalind was well within his aura. For her part, she was smiling humorously because he was, according to her trained standards, so awkwardly beautiful, like Blake's picture.

But instantly, without altering his outflung posture but only mobilizing it, he was cartwheeling about the room. It was the glad day cartwheeling to a simple meaning. As he went, his penis became stiff and erect.

He came to a stop next to her—without a break, as if he had been always standing there—and she took him by the hand out of his pose and said, "Thank you." This he accepted with his plain smile, and took both her hands.

This was one of those old dances that consist of dancing Hello—We Take a Stroll—Thank You—Thank *You*—and Good-by. People used to practice for the dance by their daily business; or they practiced by the dance for their daily business (it came to the same thing).

And where previously there was the echo as if there had been a single shout, now could be heard the audible music of every-night sounds. The squeaking house, the rumble of the underground and the thud overhead of the baby falling out of bed without waking. Horatio's penis was big and, putting her arms around him, in one motion without a break, she took it inside her and, holding close, they were dancing, or doing a sexual dance, or perhaps just doing what they were doing. (It came to the same thing). The baby upstairs let out a wail of belated surprise and Emilia went upstairs to put him back in his bed. You could almost hear the flowing of the river, and there were the footsteps of I. F. sounding on the wooden dock.

Wayward and Likely had stolen downstairs to watch them, politely, not to disturb them. They came to learn, like the children of the Mojaves. Wayward, who was six, was intensely curious and peered through the door to catch every detail. But Likely, the little girl who was only three, felt that she was shut out from what they were doing and she ran in and thrust herself between them. They lifted her up between them and kissed her and toppled over with her onto the bed, while she screamed for joy and cried, "Again!" The toppling game was an old game—when you rush through space falling and land without hurting yourself. "Again!" Then she was sleepy and she left them and went back upstairs, trailing her blanket.

But Wayward, who was six, went to the window with his erection and stood looking out onto the night streets, the wooden docks, the black Hudson River.

For a while the man and woman lay embraced, touching each other's faces and softly fucking. It seemed to be Rosalind more than Horatio who was going beside herself; at the extreme of each opening motion she started, gasped and trembled.

Their eyes were shut tight, as if sealed.

"What are they doing?" said Lothair.

"Oh, same as ever," said Emilia, moving to switch out their light. "No! I think they are going to dance again——"

The lovers' eyes were opened; and St. Wayward turned sharply from the window and looked at them all with big eyes.

"They're dancing for *us*; we are part of it; we are to watch," said Emilia. "If it is dancing——"

Lothair obediently came to the door to see.

But they were the handsome, mobile, life-size statuary of ordinary good sexuality that keeps falling, and cannot help but fall, into elegant formal poses. How could it be otherwise? Plastically flowing, the parts of lovers' bodies are ordered to one another for the functions of touching closer, penetrating strongly, comfortably breathing and mutually attending to each other. Again and again in composure, whatever positions the lovers assume. And these two had about them vividly the corona of love and excitement, glowing the brighter as indeed their senses darkened and were eclipsed, as when the screen moon suddenly eclipses totally the sun and suddenly the pearly corona shines for a million miles. There was nothing in this extraordinary.

"I can't believe my eyes!" exclaimed Lothair in a muffled voice.

"In the name of the holy spirit," said Emilia.

Lothair and Emilia were used to being astounded not out of their wits. But the boy cried out.

All three, however, would have denied that they had seen anything out of this world.

It was for them to watch and think. Horatio and Rosalind fainted and slept.

Chapter 4 ▪ CONCERT

1.

Lothair was a changed man. These days he was willing to let people be happy in their own way, not necessarily his way; or even, what is harder, to let them be unhappy in their own way, so long as it was not some stupid non-way, some systematic deviation from common sense. So he was proud of his brother and his pretty wife. But their way was not a way for him.

He repeated always the saying of Confucius, that he had himself invented in a terrible moment and therefore knew that it was the sober truth: "I cannot associate with birds and beasts as if they were like us. If I do not associate with people, with whom shall I associate?"

It was impossible for Lothair himself to be happy unless a couple of million other New Yorkers were, certainly not happy, but trying to exist in some way, in some way or other, that befitted a human being. He had this requirement, yet it wasn't a hard requirement, and fairly often he was fairly happy, for on every side he thought he noticed how people were making a real effort to live well. They were failing rather regularly rather totally, but they came back to it with courage, ingenuity, wonderful resourcefulness. He was proud of them.

2.

Time was that he used to make a hard requirement in order to be himself content: he wanted people to *succeed* in living well; he asked for common sense and social justice. Naturally this impossible need of his own drove him into futile activities on behalf of the others, and after a while he lost his wits. By setting himself too hard a standard for society, soon he didn't have any human society at all. He wandered alone like the cloud, incommunicado. It was as if he thought that he alone was right and all the rest were wrong. But (this was the worst of it), indeed he was right, in important ways, and all the rest were wrong. But what then?

It would have gone even harder with him, but in this savage predicament he heard a saving voice that said, "What then?" It was a voice sweet, low-pitched and understanding, not his own voice, (maybe Laura's voice), and it said: "You are right, Lothar, and perhaps all the others are wrong, but what then? You cannot eat being right, you cannot make love to it; you must simply accept the fact that being in the right doesn't work for you, and try some other tack not so systematically ruinous." When Lothair heard this voice, he was saved.

It was a shrewd voice. For it granted him the victory that he required, and it also allowed him to retreat from that Pyrrhic victory.

3.

But he had used to have a noble maxim, *Fiat Iustitia et Ruat Coelum*—Let justice be done though the heavens fall. And now what became of that maxim?

He recognized that it was a foolish maxim, for the heavens did fall, and when they had fallen and nothing at all had any sense, what was the sense of Justice?

Yet this was a sad kind of reasoning, and that had been a most noble maxim. Lothair regretted that the reasoning was valid and that he had to give up the maxim. If only, he wished, there were conditions in which one could assent joyfully to that valid reasoning and ridicule that maxim! That would be if justice existed, and then one could lightly say, "It's only because we *have* a society of men and their natures and practical purposes that justice exists. Justice is not absolute." But now he had to say it heavily and regretfully. And it was in this pathos that he made himself his gentler standard: that for himself to be happy, he only needed many human beings engaged in our common enterprise, looking back at our great men and moments, and waiting for the Messiah.

These human beings did exist and were his society. Yes! And to his surprise, and continuing surprise, and growing astonishment (but he was astonished never out of his wits by it), he found that he had not only a society, but festivals and holidays. Sometimes he found himself breathing with anticipation, like a boy anticipating an outing or a party. It was that he was on his way to an orchestral concert in the city, and he was happy.

4.

Lothario took a concert to be a festival, an orgy, a meeting of persons succeeding in being human beings, for the master musicians had come to have human voices and they were speaking. There were frequent concerts and crowds at the concerts, creating in the city a spirit quietly orgiastic.

Whether loudly with a big band or intimately with a few players, a master musician spoke all his human voice, the bass alto and treble, combining the ages and sexes of humanity. Sometimes he would lovingly favor one register, as Brahms loved the viola and clarinet, but even so he harmonized it with his other voices, thereby proving the supporting harmony of human voices that one did not usually experience in homes and offices and in the brawls late at night in the street. Each musician showed in a different way how men and women and children could speak in concert.

Voices of musicians had in them primitive outcries and soft cries, moans and shouts, all the sounds that rise in the human throat when persons are confronted with matters of close concern to them. Ordinarily in our dry speech we carefully disregard this passionate background of speech. Yet musicians spoke all this so playfully (even when it was a gloomy thought), with brilliant sounds and dancing deftness, that they proved it was not only possible to do, but easy. You too could speak in a human voice. Naturally then they created a party spirit.

5.

At the concert (the first number), they were playing an adagio of Haydn, and what struck Lothario today—at different times he was susceptible to notice different things—was how Haydn, in such a slow utterance, was not really singing at all but simply talking in a quiet conversational way; it was recitative; and *nevertheless* his talking was a florid aria strong and sweet. As if (to compare a great thing with a great thing) a man should be listening attentively enough to somebody he loves, talking about a subject of importance, and yet what he principally notices is the inflexion and ringing in his beloved's voice. Or as if (to compare a great thing with a greater, as Lothario craved to do, but sometimes could not find the comparison) there was a prophet, not a magician or a wonder-worker at all, but a kind of doctor and teacher who speaks to you in simple words and says only what is ordinary and likely and even possible for us, and nevertheless the crowd of us cannot help but hear it as a miraculous song strong and sweet, and we are astonished almost out of our wits.

All of the registers of the voice! For instance, the long rapid scale from the lowest tones to the highest, the instruments picking it up in sequence, flawlessly joining register to register, and exhibiting to us what a range we have. Or there may be a great chord of several registers. But often in these slow speeches, Haydn does as follows:

he prepares us a figure in the low tones and other figures in the higher tones; we do not guess that these are only fragments of a whole, for they are interesting enough in themselves; until, adding perhaps only one more tone, suddenly through them all arcs the arpeggio that kindles what was interesting into fire, as when Rainbow the messenger has come.

At this arpeggio, Lothario began not to weep but to smile.

It was an astonishing response, and after the number was over, the young man who was sitting next to him said, "You're an odd John. At the arpeggio you begin grinning, while everybody else in the hall, I suppose, has tears in his eyes."

"I'm sorry to dissociate myself from you, but what were you crying about?" asked Lothair.

"Was beautiful. That's what makes you cry. When there's a surprise and then it's beautiful, then you cry. You know *that*."

"I remember it. But what's to cry about? People cry when they lose something."

"Of course they do," said the young man. "The surprising beauty takes you off your guard and suddenly reminds you of paradise lost, and you cry. It's safe. And anyway you can't help it."

"But Paradise isn't lost," said Lothair.

The young man started with fright.

6.

Adding large reinforcements of voices and brass, they performed as the second number one of those antiphonies of Gabrieli where, when all are already shouting at the top of their lungs, he suddenly brings on a whole new chorus and a choir of brass and deafens you into heaven. To this beauty everybody responded with a grin.

He dared (what brass!) to bring the sea inside St. Mark's. But St. Mark's was wide enough to harbor the sea. He made a wedding anthem for the marriage of the Doge and the Adriatic.

You could hear, in this music of Gabrieli, how men of those days, in Venice, wore heavy stuffs and furs, yet their thews were stout enough to bear them up and walk to this processional rhythm. Presumably their lusts, and the women, were also powerful and glad enough for such a wedding and such a wedding song. The Republic was very proud of herself.

"Even so!" thought Lothair. "Without disparagement to those captains and merchant sailors of Venice, *we* are the first and second generation that can fly in the air and go by rockets to the moon!

"But—we must find out folk to man it with," he muttered in the deafening silence that followed the deafening noise.

"To man what with?" asked his young neighbor curiously.

"No, no. Just to *man* it with, absolutely, the way we used to say 'to lord it over.' But you, you, for instance, you'll have to wear more brilliant clothes and get over—if you'll excuse my frankness—your sexual timidity, the way you pinch back your ass." He looked at the fellow critically. "I like you—you're snotty, you have curiosity and aren't afraid to speak up."

7.

Now, to the voice of tired Beethoven—tired like the lion you think helpless but with a tired blow of his paw he crushes a man to death—Lothario listened with a curious attention. For this was to him in a special sense the human being; not the best man, not the grandest, the most perfect, nor anything like that; but as if he had a wax museum of specimens and this one was Monsieur l'Homme.

This voice posed him an insoluble problem, and therefore it was the Man's, for it is the property of Man to pose an insoluble problem. The problem was, Where did he get the courage? For try as he would, Lothair could not hear in that voice any resources of satisfaction, animal pleasure, love requited, nor any hope of help, nor finally any willingness to be helped if help were offered. Nevertheless, the voice was stormy, boisterous, strongly slow, more than resourceful enough. The question was, Where did he get the courage? All the music seemed to explain was that the Man had further energy.

If the music was saying anything, it was something like, "Ha! You say that I am unwilling to be helped? Damn you, what kind of help is that that cannot cope also with my stubborn unwillingness?"

There sounded the characteristic *piano subito. Sforzando sforzando, piano subito.*

This time for sure Lothair began to bawl. Others were made breathless by it; he began to cry.

While he is crying let me give my own opinion. That problem of his is wrongly posed, for he is trying to explain what is prima facie and needs no explanation; and therefore he does not question just what needs to be explained. The explosive energy, like the energy that swirls in the dark spots in the sun, this is original and prima facie. It does not yet need to be explained where the musician got his courage. What needs to be explained is why we consider it such an important fact that we are miserable and tired, as if there were a limited source of energy.

Prima facie the musician was ecstatically happy—happy out of his wits. How is this kind of voice the voice of a man? Just to ask the question is to answer it and say: by definition! It is by the limiting case of this madman, making it out of limitless nothing, that we understand what it is to be a man (though certainly not the best man, nor the grandest, the most perfect nor anything like that).

As the music modulated to a distant key, by chords that contained tones beyond the range of human hearing—but very audible if you were deaf enough—those who had been breathless breathed, relieved of the unbearable cyclonic pressure. But Lothair, who was already breathing, had a face burnt dry and happy by the atmosphere of those dark places on the sun.

The young man his neighbor had nothing to say to him, for he was compounding with his own feelings as best he could. For although Beethoven certainly spoke a human voice, and therefore yours and mine, he did not speak universally, the same for you and me. You perhaps wipe your brow; Lothario sat with dry burning cheeks; I grit my teeth and grin. There is little communication among us.

8.

He had been listening too attentively to these musicians, trying too hard to be friends, and perhaps his hearing was too sensitive; but at a certain moment he began to hear *through* the music, to the sounding wood, iron and gut. He felt an unpleasant detachment, a not being there, from the crowd. The academism of Beethoven. The wood, iron and gut were making their natural noises, but it was not human song.

By an act of will he brought back the other figure: the concert of music. He could bring it back and make the wooden and iron noises withdraw into the background. But it was an effort to do it, he did not want to. The material noises were more attractive, they promised something.

He repented of his contract to befriend the human beings.

He got up and left before the end of the concert, and went home aching.

9.

He sat alone at his piano, picking at the "Fugue in D-Sharp Minor," Book I of *The Well-Tempered Clavichord.* The music did not come to its fulfillment, there was something in it irreconcilable. He remembered from other days that this could not be; so he returned on it and played it again, picking out the separate voices.

He came to the poignant moment again and it let him down. It was irreconcilable. Each time he went over it he left off with his head more bent and in his heart less courage. Naturally he couldn't swallow this and his jaws began to ache.

He knew that it was impossible for Bach to have meant, in the end, this. Bach always sings it through. Lothair knew that he was making some absurd mistake, overlooking something obvious. Yet when he looked back to find where he had gone off, he found only new evidence that the work was moving to precisely—this.

What he saw was there all right; he was omitting something "furthermore."

"Maybe," he said to himself, "the very thing that I take to be hopelessly painful, he knew to be very well and he was serene. Let me try it. Let me imagine what it would be like to be playing this, and hearing it, and saying it to myself, and finding it to be very well, very well indeed."

He concentrated on the music that he could not yet hear.

At once he heard it. He had been making a simple error in the phrasing. At the bars

he had been taking the *A*♯ octave to be only a climax (it is certainly a climax); and therefore everything had tended to this, and it was irreconcilable. But it was also, of course, the beginning of a sentence, the theme itself twice as broad.

He had been stopping and going back. Bach sings it right through forward.

Lothair played it through once strongly to the end.

10.

And next moment he was hearing *through* the music, to the iron strings and the wooden sounding board. He felt the unsettling mystery of the chaotic noises, more attractive than the most human voice of Sebastian Bach.

He repented of the agreement he had made to come back and be reasonable among these people.

Chapter 5 ▪ EATING

1.

They didn't have much money, but they lived mainly by hunting. Once or twice a week, depending, Lothair went out and brought back a kill. This was often—or even usually, in the nature of the case—some kind of human being.

Horatio complained of the sameness of the diet, saying, "Lothar hunts only human beings. He's a bloody humanitarian." But Lothario said, "Suppose you try to get something else but pigeons, rats and men in New York and its vicinity. And I won't kill pigeons."

2.

They ate as a religious act, binding themselves back to the vegetative forces that appear to our understanding as the phantasms of dreams.

They had no scruples about what they ate so long as it tasted good and so, they knew probably, suited them. If they bit off something tasteless or bland, they at once spat it out. They might then try once again from the same dish, more attentively, for sometimes one is distracted and it takes another bite to attend to the food. (But not more than one.)

So Emilia, who was the priestess, invited them to eat by saying, "Here is the food. Attend to it if you can. And if you can, eat it. Let us pray it tastes good and suits you."

If it was tasteless or neutral it was worse than poison. They did not believe that there was anything in the nature of things that was neutral, neither good nor bad. To eat something tasteless was to infect oneself with nonbeing; it was to be inattentive; it was worse than poison to which one responds with lively vomiting.

3.

St. Wayward, at six years old, would not eat the human flesh because it was poisonous to him and made him vomit. This was because man was his totem animal.

He did not know the holiday on which he would be allowed, would allow himself, to keep it down without vomiting.

But he ate birds, eels or any other kill.

4.

They were five of them, Emilia and Lothair, Horatio and Rosalind, and Wayward, who sat down to eat sociably together, in order to say Grace and glorify the food in company, as lovers speak in universal poetry in order to have better sex, or have the urge to sex in order to speak in poetry (it comes to the same thing).

They sat down together, but they were hungry—they ate less frequently than most people—and as the time to eat approached and the food was sniffed, they became increasingly hostile to one another, and it was hard for them to bear the company. Each was afraid that the others would steal his share. The anger that arose in them was hygienic, for it helped them to attack and destroy the food itself with more vehemence.

However it was, once they had said the hasty Grace and had taken a bite from the common dish and were ravenous, each one snatched his own share and sneaked off to a private corner to eat in the more primitive way. For destroying food is an individual business. (But after satisfying themselves, they would regather and try to make up again.)

But other Americans, at this time, ate together at counters facing dumbly forward like pigs at a trough, with the benefits of neither society nor solitude.

Our friends ate either in a private corner or at a round table.

5.

They sniffed the food and began to be restive and hostile.

Emilia said: "Here is the food. Attend to if you can. And if you can, eat it. Let's give thanks because it tastes good."

The others started with surprise and annoyance. "You're making changes!" growled Horace. "Why do you change the prayer? We used to pray that it *would* taste good."

"What's to be thankful for when we haven't gotten anything yet?" snarled Rosalind.

"I have come to a further confidence," said Emilia simply, with neither humility nor grandeur. "We are in the hands of providence."

Horatio brooded on it a moment; he considered that character is destiny and he himself had a good (life-preserving) character. "Yes, evidently," he conceded grudgingly. "Since here we are. Let's say thanks."

The others fell silent a moment to consider it, and then muttered, "Thanks."

6.

"This meat is poison to me, I won't eat it," said Wayward, who felt it was his turn to let out his wrath. "It's got magic in it, like my father."

"That's what you always say; why doesn't it poison us, boy?" jeered Horace.

"Cause you're grownups like my father. The thing is I'm going to kill my father, but now I can't, and the human meat makes me vomit."

"It's his totem—he can't eat it," explained Emilia.

"If it's your totem," Horace taunted him, "why don't you know a special day, a holiday, when you *could* eat it and jump for joy and grow up two feet at a bound?"

This time the boy knew the answer. "I know that," he said immediately with conviction and faith. "Whenever you die, father, it will be my holiday, and I'll grow up two feet at a bound."

Lothair looked at him and he too, like the tired Beethoven, was like the tired lion whom you think powerless, but he will crush you with a tired blow of his tired paw. But he said nothing.

7.

Horatio took the attack and said: "I have accused you, brother, of hunting nothing but human beings, and I mean this. I don't mean that you don't try; but you have a blind spot—you can't see anything else. I told you long ago how you overestimate these people, as if there were nothing else so good and great. Now it comes close to us, on our very table, and we have to suffer for your illusions."

They turned to Lothair to reply to this, and braced themselves on the arms of their chairs. But still he said nothing and looked with his eyes first at one and then at the second and then at the third and then at the fourth.

8.

And Rosalind burst out, "I know the lot of you! You want to rob me of my share because I'm the innocent who wasn't brought up in your insane families. But we'll see about that. As for me, I'm thankful for the food, but bring it on, bring it on!

"*Say* something, Lothar! stop making us uneasy. You're being spiteful; you want to sour our appetites beforehand. Aren't you thankful for the food?"

"No, sister," he said gently. "I expect it will be tasteless, and I can't pray for it to taste good because I'm not hungry." He had no cause to be hostile. "I have no appetite to eat."

"You're not hungry? He's not going to eat any of it!" cried Rosalind pleased, and she at once began to be friendly and considerate of Lothair. "Lothar, how can you expect food to be tasty when you're not hungry?"

"If you don't want to eat, why do you sit down?" said Horace indignantly.

"Oh don't be so self-righteous, boy," said Rosalind. "It's not becoming to you at all. Why *do* you sit down, Lothar?"

"Just like this," he said. "For your pleasant company."

9.

However it was, at the first bite it was as if a sealed book opened and on the illuminated page clearly written the sought-after wisdom:

To have the pleasant is good, to have the useful is better, to have the needful is best.

Insensibly but swiftly the harsh Rockies of nightmare gave way to friendly valleys opening in time, in which they were presently the growing generation.

Now they were simply hungry, and each one, darting suspicious looks at the enemies, took his dish and crouched in a private corner and ate.

10.

But Lothario spat out the first bite because it was tasteless. When the others had sneaked away and he was alone at the table, he tried another taste from the same dish, but it was still tasteless.

He knew that he could, by an act of the will, attend to the food and savor it, and make the disappointment of every day of his life withdraw into the background. He did not bother to. And not to bother awoke in him such a wave of comfort that he was dizzy. His head reeled. But he braced himself and felt himself supported by the ground, and he opened his eyes wider.

11.

Having satisfied themselves, the others slowly gathered shyly together, with averted glances. They tried to make up, and since all were trying, they succeeded. Rosalind stood near Horatio and stealthily touched him, and he suddenly put an arm around her shoulders. St. Wayward buried his face in his mother's lap.

They then, regaining confidence in one another, gave themselves to their communally shared solitary indulgences, the liquor, tobacco or other drug, that each one happened to enjoy; feeling safe, because each one could take leave of the others while still smiling full in their answering faces.

But Lothair, who had no appetite and did not eat, sat clasping his drawn-up knees close as though he were not yet born, or were already laid away (it came to the same thing). And he gave himself into his crooning voice, crooning in the Lorrainean mode that has infinitesimal intervals.

Soon they gathered round him to listen. He seemed to be singing the noises of the spheres of the small units of things, noises that have force like the supersonic waves. But if they tried to imitate him and croon along, they felt shooting pains in their throats.

Chapter 6 ▪ RELAXING

1.

Most of us have made a compact, saying: "Let us make a convention. Let us agree to call what we are feeling not 'pain' but 'neutral'; not 'dull unease' but 'well enough,' not restless dissatisfaction intermitted by blowing up, but average hanging around.

"Our consensus is that how we live is tolerable.

"If I ask, 'How are you?' you must say, 'Pretty good.' And if I do not remind you, you must not remind me.

"To all this we swear!"

2.

"I break the oath!" said Lothair. "And I throw it in your face. I won't put up with this another day. By sunset the whole world must have been otherwise."

Horatio, who had never made any such agreement, could not resist mocking his brother's strenuous resolution. Like every hero easy by nature, Horatio was a prig. "Oh, the sun will set and rise as usual," he said; "do you want to bet?"

"You're wrong—there is already a change!" cried Lothair triumphantly. "For now I know that it's I myself who color the scene with pain; I could stop doing it this instant, if—for instance—I would stop clenching my fist——"

But he kept it clenched.

Horatio looked at him curiously. "I don't see the change," he said. "What you're saying is, 'Oh, there are plenty of possibilities available if I could take them, which is impossible.' Is that something great? What seems to me is that you suffer all the worse by putting the blame on yourself. I pity you."

"If you pity me, you don't understand what I'm doing."

"What are you doing?"

"I am making Lothair! I stand a *witness* of the life I lead. I am a martyr to it." And indeed, on his face, through the beads of pain, there was pride and joy. He spoke in quick dimeters a triumph-shout: "What hero? Crown me among the Witnesses! The difficult breath I draw and the hurrying death I go, I wreak myself by choice and plan. Proved and approved! The pain I live (and will die) stands witness of my way of life. Dare only I to be Lothair!

"But a similar thing is true for you also."

With this astonishing speech, he turned on his heel and left them. What I find moving is that in his pride he remembered to point out that a similar thing was true for us also.

3.

"That's a remarkable religion he has," said Horatio. "He bears witness only to the miracle of himself, such as it is."

But Emilia, who loved him, said loyally, "He proves himself. He is not disapproved."

Rosalind, however, was afraid and said, "It's not the end of it. You watch. He'll come back and fall upon us in his rage."

"I'm sorry I needle him," said Horatio, "but he makes me feel vacuous. He makes me feel that I feel nothing, because I don't resist myself and so I can't remember, a moment afterwards, what it was that I was feeling. I have nothing to mention."

4.

Lothair returned in a state of high excitement. "I've tried the experiment and it works! By scrupulously observing the pangs of the world, I've discovered that in many important cases—not all cases, but several important ones—where I am twisted, clenched, pinched and beat, it's I who am doing the pinching, clenching, twisting and beating. I can let up. So. If I unclench my claws, I already feel less strangled and can breathe a little easier."

He tried it. And suddenly he began to breathe in great gasps and, just as Rosalind had predicted, he dealt Horatio a powerful blow on the jaw and knocked him down, and, pouncing on him, he began to strangle him instead of himself. Horatio cried out helplessly, and the others pulled the big man off by the hair.

Just as suddenly as he had commenced, Lothair clapped his hands to his head and shouted hoarsely, "Confusion! It's not you I meant at all. I can't see straight." And he fell in a faint.

5.

Horatio was not much hurt and sat up, smiling ruefully but also with a pleased wonder. "Do you know? I learned something when

I went under there. I saw another kind of things than the reality we use; that parted like a dirty curtain and behind it there were emerald leaves in the breeze and flickering coins of sun and shadow. I felt a pang that opened my ears and immediately I heard birdcalls of *A* and *F* sharp and other tones, of all which I was simply aware."

"Are those the things that are to be seen?" the others said in wonder.

6.

But when the big fellow came to, he was overcome with confusion and guilt. Horatio tried to help him to his feet but was rudely repulsed, and it was evident that for the time being Lothair chose to be inconsolable. "Get rid of me!" he snarled. "I mean, you get out of my sight or let me get out of here. Damn you, don't try to console me, like Christians—that would be the last straw." He made as if to hit Horace again. "What makes *you* think that you have something to answer to my feeling of failure. Since I undertake to be in the right, I mustn't make mistakes. And you," he shouted at Emilia, "you give me cause to be unhappy more than is necessary. You know what I mean—we don't have to discuss it."

They drew back from him. He wasn't sympathetic.

"I'm sorry that I make you uneasy," he said abashed, for it is terrible to see others draw back from one. "Don't. I'll go."

His eyes flooded with tears and he got up and went.

"Lothair!" called Horace.

"Shall I go after him?" said Rosalind.

"Let him alone," said Emilia. "What *do* you have to say to him in his confusion?"

7.

"Oh, he'll be back," said Rosalind vindictively. "A vengeful person needs company to exact his vengeance."

"Yes, he'll get over it this time," snapped Horatio, "and then he'll repeat it tomorrow. Not on me, he won't!" He began to feel his hurt jaw and the anger welled in his heart.

They could not foresee anything but a repetition. The floating anger that sprang from Lothario's dissatisfaction had fallen this time on his enviable brother, who was happy; but he was unlikely to do that again because he was not envious. But next time he might fall on Wayward, because he was young and beginning.

They agreed that it was Wayward who was the likeliest target, while the boy listened to them one face after the other.

They could not see any way to alleviate the anger itself because, the world being what it was, it was not possible to satisfy Lothair. What they failed to notice was that Lothair was not, properly speaking, angry at all; he was not frustrated, he did not want to change anything, but simply to annihilate, to let go; for he was beginning to repent of his agreement to exist among these people.

They fell into a gloomy silence, avoiding one another's eyes, each thinking his own thoughts, and hoping for a miracle, a cheerful idea.

Chapter 7 • WELCOMING

1.

At this moment there was a loud knocking at the door. The door flew open and it was Mynheer, in flight. His intellectual countenance was discolored by hurry.

The others could not find their tongues. They almost thought it was a stranger; and Wayward had never known him at all. They didn't know that he had returned from his voyage and was back in this world; but also, they had secretly given him up for lost and were speechless with guilt.

He crossed the threshold, but when he saw their doubt and difficulty in knowing him, he guessed that it was an unpropitious moment and courteously drew back. But he filled the doorway, not as if he had any intention of going away, but as if to say, "You're not receiving just now? Shall I come back in ten minutes?"

Rosalind, who had hardly known him, burst out laughing. "You look," she said, "like a fellow hanging around who simply wants to give sexual pleasure to somebody but he's afraid that his intentions will be taken amiss."

"I feel," said Mynheer, "like a fellow hanging around who simply wants to give sexual pleasure to somebody but he's afraid that his intentions won't be taken amiss."

"They won't be taken amiss!" cried Emilia gaily. "Mynheer! Come in."

"Piet Duyck!" said Horatio. "Close the door. Are you safe? Is something after you?"

He closed the door. "Now I am safe!" he said. And without preamble he told, like a shaman, the story of his Magic Flight.

2.

"I have been in full flight," he said. "I fled. It followed.

"Mostly we went along like a rigid bar, immobile relative to each other. But I was tiring.

"But I had been given Three Gifts, a Stone, a Comb and a Cup of Water, with which to save myself.

"And when the feet pounded close in my ears, I threw the stone behind me; and at once between lay Appalachia, the mountain range. That night I slept safely on the hither slope, among the innumerable moons.

"But the morning appeared above the crest and it came. I fled.

"When the breath was hot on my neck, I bent down and planted the comb in the ground; and at once, thickly, the woods stood silently around me. I built a purple fire of oak that had long ago matured and died, and I slept.

"But the pale dawn shone dimly on the south side of the tree trunks and it came. I fled.

"The finger tips touched me, and with open eyes full in the sunrise I flung my little cup of diamond drops at its face; and at once I was riding on the in-between sea.

"All day I have been at sea, on the waves that whisper and then fall unsupporting to their pit. But I have crossed over and arrived."

So Mynheer told the story of the Magic Flight of the shaman.

3.

"Welcome home! True, you have arrived, Mynheer," said Emilia. "But your story is so brief. I don't understand it, I'm disturbed. You're so reticent or indefinite——"

"Pardon me," he interrupted her, "neither reticent nor indefinite. Remember I have been in full flight; I could not afford the luxury to look; I used myself up in desperate action; and now I don't have any precise idea of what occurred. Anyway, I told the story just to catch my breath."

"I follow you. But my point holds. For what about this same following giant? He pursued you, and if his pursuit overpassed the mountains and penetrated the woods, why may it not come also thundering across the sea?"

"No," said Mynheer.

"No?" exclaimed Horatio. "What is this simple No?" They marveled.

"No. For I was given three gifts to use well, and now I have used them all. There is nothing more to fear."

4.

The effect on them of this definite statement was like excellent wine. They breathed softer and began to be glad. And so I am glad as I write it.

It meant that the task that seems endlessly laborious, nevertheless has in it a finite number of elements exhaustible one by one, though maybe not by me. It is likely that it is only because one or two particular things are hard to face and do, that we seem to be faced with an indefinite number of hard things. But maybe there is only one more task. Yes, and finally when everything has been accomplished, may we not expect that our efforts will be crowned with success?

Mynheer stood there as though his name were Success. Slender and tall in his corduroys, he looked like one of those strange motorcyclists that fly along the highway drunken with speed and apparently approaching something like rapture; but when they have stopped, flushed and radiant, they can never tell you what they have experienced. He looked as young as when we first met him; and Emilia, gazing at him stupefied, felt a pang of yearning for him such as she used hopelessly to feel at that time.

It was Horatio who found his voice and said: "Your name is Success. And you are the only justifier. Only when the task is finished does it demand nothing further. Beloved, pardon me, but I can't help bawling at the thought of letting go, at the thought of winged success, of relenting, at the aspect of my brother-in-law safe home from his journey. Welcome home, Piet Duyck. You have made me gladder than I can say by saying, and having the wherewithal to say, a cheerful sentence."

He clasped his brother-in-law in his arms, whom he had not seen since Laura's death, and he began to bawl. And so did the others.

5.

"This is Lothair's boy obviously," said Mynheer and held out his hand to Wayward. "What is your name? I am Dyck Colijn."

But the boy would not take his hand nor answer. He was angry because the others made so much of this stranger.

"His name is Wayward," said Emilia. "This is Mynheer."

"They talked about you," said Wayward.

"How have I offended you, Wayward? I mean, why don't you like me?"

"I know what offended means," said Wayward hotly.

"I'm sorry. I offended you again."

"I'm angry because you tell a story and it's not true. And they all believe you."

"Are you angry because it's not true or because they all believe me?"

Wayward lowered his eyes and then looked up and said, "*Is* it true—about the mountains and the woods—the story?"

"Yes, it's true," said Mynheer. "It's a very old story that has happened many times. It's the story you tell when you're a stranger and you need to be made welcome. If you *can* tell this story, you have a right to be made welcome. Wayward? Make me welcome?" And he held out his hand again.

This time Wayward took his hand and said truthfully, "You are welcome to my house and I love you." He said it ritually, that is earnestly and committing himself to what he was saying. "But you came at a bad time," he said, " 'cause my father is mad and knocked down Horace and he won't make you welcome."

"Where is Lothar?" asked Mynheer.

6.

"Here I am," said Lothair. "Be easy," he said to the others. "I have relented toward myself. You've been bawling and I have been too. I've come to understand that what has been hard for me is to concede to myself the extenuations that belong to everybody else in the world as it is. As I see it now, it's not a man's duty but just his grace to be happy. I don't have to justify providence with every sentence I speak."

"What a proud man you are!" said Emilia.

"Yes, I am. Is this bad?"

"I am proud of you," she said.

"Please," he said, "don't say anything flattering to me or I'll start to cry again. Once the tears are started, the fit of crying keeps coming on again. It's mixed after a while with laughing. I get confused."

He began to tremble violently. But she held him and said, "Don't be afraid. Let go. I'll hold you."

He said, "I'm not afraid to let go, altogether out of this existence——" But in such a tone of lightness and pleasure he said this threatening sentence that the others did not notice the content of it but only the feeling; and they were tricked into sharing his own happy prospect without a forewarning of their own irremediable loss. He accepted being held by her because she knew when to hold and when to let go.

"I guess I'm afraid," he said, "of the new compassion I feel toward my own misery. I have begun to let up on myself and it's too much for me to take. I'm not yet strong enough. Something prepares itself in me, like an earthquake. Will I be able to bear the benefit of my own compassionate forbearance of myself if I reasonably do what I want?" He staggered.

But she held him and said, "What's it like?" for at this moment he needed nothing but continuing attention.

Closing his eyes, he read it off: "My knees are buckling under the weight of gold and wine."

"Yes!" she said. "With gold and wine and honey we who would otherwise spring as on a planet of slighter gravity laboriously trudge onward under our riches. We're not used to be easy. Nevertheless, as we feast away our surfeit of salvation lightens, and *we* go the gayest! Like the one who made the wise choice in the fable. No, husband?"

Horatio was middle-sized; Mynheer was tall; but Lothair was big. What he didn't understand, and unfortunately never did get to understand, was that someone could look at him and find him beautiful and lovable just because he was big, if for no other reason.

7.

He gave his hand to Piet Duyck and said, "My kinsman has returned. Welcome home."

They had not met since Laura hanged, and it was as if only now their mourning labor was finished.

It was Mynheer's turn to be moved. He turned aside a moment and read it off: "I used to think that the most beautiful thing in the world was the light of recognition, but now I know that it is the gesture that follows on recognition, stretching out my arms." And he laughed.

8.

"It's you he wants, Emilia," said Lothair. "Come here. . . ." And he put the two of them together, in the custom of the Eskimo. "It's our custom," he explained to the stranger, "to give the welcome guest our bedfellow. You know the reason for it: that when there's no jealousy among the males, it's possible to be friends and get on to more important things."

But he put them together and let them go as if he wanted to let them go forever.

"It's kind of you, Lothar Alger," said Mynheer. "I was a bad husband to your sister. Now it's been a long time, as we used to say on the cruiser."

"You two were lovers long ago," said Lothair, "and maybe you'd both have been happier if you'd stayed together than either of you has been otherwise." He meant than he himself had been. And he turned away sadly for, taking him at his word, they were already eagerly embracing and kissing.

9.

For a long time the Dutchman hadn't had any terrestrial love, and Emilia, though she loved Lothair and was sexually content with him, was not sexually happy with him. However it was, these two were glad to feel each other close; and touching each other they felt safe. It was as if, safe, they were soon withdrawing from the round-about cold, and now they could draw easy breaths, and one area of touch ignited another. Do you follow me there?

The others were embarrassed, but Emilia said, "Really, we don't mind whether or not you pay us any mind."

"The lovers are lucky who can disarm envy," said Lothair in a matter-of-fact tone. His tone was matter-of-fact, but Rosalind, who understood him better than the others—she loved Lothair because he was big—was alarmed; it seemed to her that every remark he made was a dismissal.

The boy was breathless and irresolute.

"No, please—" whispered Mynheer and Emilia to one another, "stay another moment."

"They have forgotten us," said Rosalind. "Shall we go and leave them?"

"Don't leave us," said Mynheer. "Your presence is the justification of my guest-love. (I came, didn't you?)"

"(Yes, thanks, you have been most considerate.) But you haven't had a chance to sit down!" she cried, and broke away from him.

10.

Lothair brought out tobacco and offered his pipe first to the stranger, affirming the bond of hospitality.

Lighting the match, hungrily Mynheer stared at the small flame and recalled how, often, cold and solitary, he had warmed his spirit at such a little flame. With longing he looked at their family group and asked, "Tell me about yourselves. What have you been doing? Lothar?" he asked beseechingly, not to be excluded from their family life.

But Lothair again deferred to Emilia. "What's there to tell?" she said. "Exciting to live it, dull to report it. We eat tasty food and variously enjoy ourselves, and these things go on recurrently. We spend a lot of time on rites and ritual games, as the occasion for them arises. But you, Piet Duyck! Where have *you* been? Lothar has his music, but what I like is to hear marvelous stories—the exploits of my boys! Here we are, all sitting down after a bad day. And a long time to dinner. Tell us a story of your travels. Do. Where did you go?"

Chapter 8 ▪ ADVENTURE STORY

Atra Cura post equitem sedet
dum equitat.

—HORACE

I. THERE AND HERE

1.

"Where did I go?" said Mynheer. "I went—here. Always here. Come with me on the way, and I'll get you back safe.

"I was in space and, training my telescope, I saw a disc that came closer. Since it came to me, I had to go to there. Just as, I remember, when I was a boy in the Indies, if I saw an island far-off I had to go toward it; till at last it would loom close and I was——

"Here! Not 'there' but 'here.' You cannot get there, for before you have arrived, suddenly you are here. This is not a trick of language but a physical event. It happens suddenly, at the instant when the place has filled the background of perception. At that instant you can no longer isolate your island as a figure for yourself and choose it or not choose it. It has chosen you. You are here.

"This exploring of mine is therefore stupid. You know I am out of this world, people have judged me insane. Yet when I go out of this world, I do not get into *that* world, but again into *this* world. Naturally in this world I am no better off than I was. I am out of this world.

"Nevertheless, I train my telescope on a particular light in heaven, and if it looms, I go in that direction. But why, then, do I avoid going toward the empty or, what amounts to the same thing, toward a light that does not become a closer disc because it is infinitely far so far as my power reaches? Because I am afraid to get lost.

"Evidently, for here I am! If, in the future, the years and decades pass and you are never again visited by Piet Duyck, then perhaps you may conclude that I got over my fear of being lost; that I lost myself; that it lost me. But whenever I am tempted that way, I start to imagine the hours and days of doubt, the long starvation and nowhere to go—and—no thanks! I soon find myself again. I'm crazy but not that crazy. Your Flying Dutchman!

"Do I say lost? *Where?* Lost into what? You see, I am fascinated by this panicky thought—I cannot drop it. When I am losing myself, would I be flying or falling? But I am too conscientious a pilot to be purposely lost; it would be nontechnical. To be a pilot is to steer.

"So I don't get lost, and I arrive—back in this world. For let me tell you, in all my exploring, and I have traveled weeks of light, I have yet to find a region where the intellect does not perform its unifying function and seek out its proper object and make anew a world! Can you find me a different place? Pardon me if I am becoming repetitive and frantic; I am warding off panic.

"There are pilots I know, I once knew, who were prone to get lost. But they did not get to a nonworld; they were just bad pilots. No thanks. Not for me. I'm a good pilot. If I undertake to have my intellect, I use it. I cannot escape by using it clumsily. I would only get bored and bore you. If I undertake to pay attention to something, I must find a coherent whole. And so I do.

"There you have it. We spacemen—for there are others like myself to be met in out-of-the-way places—at the end of every flight we never discover anything but the world; and this is what we describe in likely stories."

He stopped. "Am I yet boring you?" he asked shyly. "You asked me where I went, and I've told you I came here, as you see."

But they protested and made him go on, for they were really interested in his explorations and they were not to be put off by metaphysical remarks.

"Then I'll proceed," he said, "but you must let me tell my story in my own way, for I am putting my thoughts in order. It's a long time since I have had a beloved audience to talk at."

II. SPEED

2.

"All right," he proceeded, "since we get nowhere, why do we go? As we head toward that distant disc that is getting insensibly closer (even though it will prove to be only another world), let me tell you our chief pleasure, that is almost a reason for being. Since this pleasure of ours is neither here nor there, it must be in-between.

"It is the speed. We lust in speed more than in the love of women. As we accelerate again, we approach what is very like rapture. The doctors say that this is masturbatory; it is a question of a word, for certainly we are lusting not in a safe image but in a risky fact. A very risky fact. Let me tell you what is speed. And what is the speed par excellence that only we spacemen know!

3.

"Now the first meaning of speed is the velocity, the miles per hour. And surely the speed we lust in is not the miles per hour. Nothing is duller than this figure on a dial (though often, afterwards, we have nothing else coherent to report back). But high velocity itself is a sterile empty thing. Yes! Let me digress a moment and be indignant. The shame of it! That the first generation of men that can fly in the air and so realize the loveliest image of sleep and daydream and poetry, have made of their flights what we see: a swift conveyance so that the vice-president of the corporation can get to Chicago in plenty of time for lunch! Is this, after all, what it is to fly?

4.

"Far more *speedy,* even if they are going at a snail's pace, are the child on skates downhill, the narcissistic cyclist with his foxtails blown, the sledder round the corner, the hot rod on the road. Here we see the second and more essential meaning of speed: speed relative to the resistance. This is not yet the speed par excellence, but let us analyze it carefully, for it will bring us to the speed of the spaceman.

"You will notice that the velocity, the miles per hour, is merely objective; the man himself is not there; he is sitting calmly reading the *Times.* The speed against the resistance that we have come to, is largely physiological and subjective; the man is very much there. But the speed itself, we shall ultimately see, is beyond subjectivity and objectivity, it exists in the whole field.

"There is a dynamic marking in Beethoven, *prestissimo,* that he uses in a characteristic way. He does not mean 'very fast' according to the metronome, the velocity; nor does he mean only 'very fast musically,' relative to the other tempi in the piece, although of course he means also this. But he means 'as fast as you can,' as fast as *you* can, you unique player on your unique machine. You must play it deftly and in proportion, but you must also express your hurry. Play at the limit of your resources and you will hint at what is beyond the limit of your resources, what is *over* the edge, the message of Beethoven. Now *prestissimo* means 'with speed.'

"Let me analyze the components of this speed against resistance. I would mention (*a*) the Risk, (*b*) the Proof of Ability, (*c*) the Freedom and finally (*d*) Further Acceleration. These four parts interact to a kind of triumph.

5.

"When a man is speeding, he is in animal contact with material resistances, the rush of air, the uneven roadbed; his body and machine—to a good driver his machine is part of his body—are under strain; they may break down. Every noise is a warning. He seeks out this warning and starts to hold his breath; but to keep calm he must force himself to breathe and feel the resistance more. Often you will hear a speeder boast and rationalize how he has 'chopped down' his machine to make it efficient, but it is really to be naked and exposed to the resistance—as he decks himself in his sacrificial finery. He is in danger, and he is provoking the danger. This is Risk.

6.

"But it is *he* who is provoking it, and he *can*. Can provoke and escape, outwit, dominate. Toying with his power, like any bullfighter. At every moment, against the resistance, he has proof of his power and dexterity; he *knows* that he is not impotent and stupid. (He has had gnawing doubts about these things, but he feels them in social company, not when he is on his bike.) When he speeds, he has a series of continual little victories, though certainly not victory itself. And oh! By his skill and dexterity, since he does not crash, he justifies the exercise of his power, he makes it guiltless, for he proves that he is doing right by doing what is technically correct. But woe if he crashes! He will be overwhelmed in guilt and pain: condemned and self-condemned, castrated and bawling. It's not surprising that he wears a good-luck charm!

7.

"Good. Now he has dominated—the road and the machine. Now he has the right to fly his flags, that up to now seemed a ridiculous pretension. He is free. His freedom has been generated relatively, by effort and overcoming and continuing overcoming—the threat is still lurking in the background—but he feels his freedom as absolute lightness and glory. *He* is not heavy like the things he flies past; and *he* is not about to break like his machine and his miserable carcass. He has come somewhat to float, immaterially. Here is the likeness of speed and flying.

"He is not alone in this freedom. True he cannot share it with his family, for they have earth ties and will drive from the back seat and nag him, 'Honey, not so fast!' But if he sets out with a like-minded buddy, they can come to share the danger and to float together. And you will often hear us speak of 'we spacemen . . . we cyclists.' We have a terribly exclusive *esprit de corps*.

8.

"Alas! This freedom does not come to anything. It cannot come off. It is only a temporary plateau, it is not the climax itself. Just because he is light and triumphant over materiality, he is dissociated and cannot reach fruition, for that is always a growth of the body. So, floating in freedom, a man is faced with a hard choice: either to let his happy speed degenerate into a tedious velocity, or to accelerate further and tempt it.

"Now this Further Acceleration after one has achieved speed is not like the initial speeding up. It is the pure acceleration against the inertia of the velocity itself. When he touches the accelerator he feels his velocity. Perhaps he gives his buddy a sidelong look, and his buddy says through clenched teeth, 'For Chrissake, look where you're going.' High velocity is a new inertia created by oneself; it is a new state of the man; when he touches the accelerator, he is touching himself. Obviously we must not now speak of provocation, of provoking the outside danger, but of feeling tempted, of saying, 'Dare we give her the gun?'

"Many are the fools who gave her the gun, alone or in company. Were they fools? We do not know what prize they won, nor whether it was worth dying for, for they have not reported it. We know what they sought to escape, the tedium of velocity or the shame of having to slow down.

9.

"Well, that is the second meaning of speed. And often have I experienced it, its plumage, its triumph, its tedium that comes to nothing. But at last, on this trip from which I have just returned, I came to experience the speed itself, the speed par excellence that does not come to nothing.

"Let me take you with me. Yet there is little to tell. It is what happens in the blink of an eye, and afterward you shake your head wondering what it was that happened.

"Obviously we spacemen are not interested in the rush of air and the heat, the breakdown of our machines against the external resistances. Lord knows we have enough of those bugs, we do not seek to provoke them. As soon as I could I passed outside their range into the pure space; I headed toward the immensity and I gave her the gun, as you do when you have gotten out of city traffic onto the highway at last.

"There came the moment when flying was the same as falling. I was in the immensity. On my own. It was equally safe whether I speeded up or slowed down, or perhaps came lazily to a stop. Should I perhaps pull over on the shoulder and snooze? No world tugged at me or nagged me. There was no world to fly past and feel light, no world to fly from and be free. Was I and my ship perhaps the world? Rotating my machine to give me a centrifugal weight. Merrily I gave her the gun.

"Nothing to crash into! I alone was responsible for my momentum, the velocity of my inertia. Nobody's business, beholden to nobody! And I gave her the gun. I did not realize how fast I was going. . . .

"There was almost no warning. The universe was growing heavy with my momentum. I began to feel the nature of things.

"I was nearing the absolute velocity and the universe was growing heavy with my momentum—it began to crowd me close.* Startled I looked at the mirror, and the universe was vanishing away. There began to be nothing there, and the menace of that nothing there began to be infinitely huge.

"I am giving you a definition of hell.

"*That* is the speed itself! That is the speed par excellence. Do you follow me? For I was flying at my ease and flying the same as falling, going faster by the square of my persistence. And suddenly the universe was losing me and I began to feel the nature of things. Do you feel it? As if someone slapped me in the face and said, 'Are *you* a world?'

"Within me my rebellious demon whispered, 'Now is the time! Break through into the superluminous, hey?' But I said to him, 'Another time! With another ship.'

"I vomited and got it off my chest. I slowed down. How shall I say? I am not a coward—I *had* to slow down. By simple need. If I was to continue to exist as a living awareness that makes figures and grounds. As a pilot.

10.

"You see, it comes to something, the speed. It is not tedious. It comes to that slap in the face that we call the nature of things. That is the speed par excellence, and I have had it.

* "The mass increases as the velocity increases, the factor being the same as that which determines the Fitzgerald contraction."—Eddington

"Do I make myself clear? Do you understand that the moment of freedom, when the universe vanishes and you begin to feel it in your guts, is not a futile experience for those of us who are out of this world? A kind of shock treatment—do you follow me?

" 'Forced to slow down' is the experience that we share when we meet one another in out-of-the-way places. We are not ashamed of it, but we do not wear ornamental clothes.

11.

"So. I had had enough of my speed. Now I wanted to get there. Just to get back into a world, some world or other, some background world that did not penetrate your being. A world that had its laws that I would no doubt stubbornly resist. A world, even though I knew that it must become only this world.

"I slowed down to the normal swiftness of a meteor. I was beset with the anxious tedium of any long dangerous journey, no different from driving to Buffalo. Would my fuel hold out? I kept looking at the gauge. Would my nerves hold out? I took another swig of coffee.

"It did not seem to me that that far-off lune was growing any bigger.

"Where our desire is, there is our anxiety.

"It grew bigger all of a sudden, as it does. I began to feel the tug."

III: FINDING OF THE UNCARVED BLOCK

12.

"I felt the tug," said Mynheer.

"It was a scrawny violet moon that I had singled out from all the galaxy, in order to learn something remarkable.

"I approached from her senescent, as we consider good luck. But you're not interested in such things. It is enough to say that at every moment I was making choices, choosing my right hand or my left hand.

"Her parent body was far away, and even more dwarfish than this moon; a dull gloomy oval, enormously massive, hard, cold; must have been mostly lead. And our own Sol was less than a pinpoint in the clouds of stars; he poured his failing rays from so far off that I was overcome with sadness, and I lit, as I do, my little match and stared at its yellow flame to warm me.

"I made the routine observations, of the radium and the gravity, et cetera. With the instruments we have we know all about it even before we get there, and we can guess the rest. Is this what it means for it be 'there' rather than 'here,' to have the facts at that end of the instruments rather than at this end, to have them merely as facts? Naturally they are boring, those matters of life and death.

"The atmosphere was heavy, but there was the unlikely possibility that it was breathable. The temperature was surprisingly hot, and yet the radium was low (but there would be a reason; there always was). The surface gravity on that tiny lump of lead was more than the earth's—I knew that from the first tug a million miles away, for we develop a fine sense.

"It is enough to say that I know how to take care of myself. Evidently!

"There was indeed something peculiar. Soft flushes in the darkness below, as a firefly lights up barren dunes. They read as the kind of phase-waves that we know as evidence-to-conclusion; but I dismissed the reading as my own interference. I was not really interested.

"What was I interested in? For there was sweat in the deep lines of my palms that have a long life and fate. Always I was interested in the moment when suddenly there would be an horizon, when that world would have become this world, my background! This simple, oft-repeated encounter still made me hold my breath; as we approach someone and try to get to know him—even though we will not like him after we get to know him.

"You know what it is to have an horizon, a background in general. Do you know what it is *not* to have an horizon?

"The blow fell and I was in this world. As a sleeper falls awake into his one repugnant reality, and still he proceeds into it and does not try to withdraw.

13.

"Yet to my surprise, I was delighted! The daylight here was a clear dusk, refreshing to my hot eyes. I could move freely; I lumbered about, a little heavier than we are used. I was in the midst of the vivid—how shall I say?—it was colorless but there was an extraordinary animation. There were thousands of regular objects, from a few inches to a yard in size, in continual swift motion. What were they? They filled the field. I doubted that they were animate. It was as if the chaotic beads and blocks on a nursery floor had been galvanized into motion.

"Against the horizon, in the background, were a few small hills, barren of growth, but I did not much notice them, for of course we pay attention to what is moving against what is stationary, and to what is complex, definite and regular against what is blank and shapeless. (We have much to learn.) In the foreground were the mobiles.

"I started reasoning them out. They moved forward, that is, they had a fore and aft, as if they had aims. There were several species. Some were needles and darted; some had a kind of legs and scurried; some were wheels and rolled. I could see at once that there was no mystery as to the kinds—I give you my impressions as they occurred to me—but where the ground was smooth and hard went the wheels; where it was rough and hard went the legs and spanners; where it was soft, and almost liquid dust, darted the needles like fish. Thus, they were adaptive, they certainly had aims. But did this necessarily mean they were animate? All had fore and aft, but there were no snouts or tails; I did not see any organs of perception or feeding.

" 'Iron filings!' was my conclusion (strained out into kinds by their environment), and I burst out laughing. My laughter came back in my ears in the heavy atmosphere like a muffled gong. The mobiles were silent.

" '*Where are the magnets?*'

14.

"Since they had a fore and aft, I reasoned, there were two alternatives: If they were animate, they were moved by desire that goes forward; if they were inanimate, they were drawn-toward. The first alternative had a certain weight of evidence, for their flights were short, a few yards up to a hundred yards, and then they veered at a sharp angle and went in another direction. I followed a wheel for a hundred yards, and he turned. As if they sought something, and did not find, and were seeking again. But why should not a magnet continually draw them on to a stop?

"Yet I tended to decide for the inanimate. For, though they had fore and aft, they were not properly bilateral. But lopsided, accidental. They did not have a functional right and left. They did not seem to *head* in another direction, but simply to drift in another direction. It meant that there was no choosing, no weighing, pondering, balancing of possibilities.

"They had a false animation. I felt deceived and I stood still and ceased to explore. I was, I have said, in their midst. On all sides of me they scurried, rolled and darted in all directions. Yet not one ever touched me or came toward me. On the other hand, they did not seem to avoid me. Suddenly I saw that they were like figures of Giacometti, and whether or not they were alive was equally sad.

"You know those thin statues of the Italian sculpture Giacometti, that stand tall and cast long shadows on the landscape that he copied when he visited the moon. He puts many on a plane and each one stands facing in a direction, but if you go behind each one and look along his line of sight, you see that he is looking nowhere, toward no one, and if all were to move, all would miss all. They are missing one another; they are looking past. There is neither recognition nor conflict. The drama is over.

"So I paused there and mused on it: how they were swiftly going and could not choose and would never meet. Presumably they were inanimate and did not suffer as I did. The paths they traversed were broken straight lines, zigzags. I again followed my wheel, a big one, a yard high: he rolled straight on his hundred yards, then veered sharply about one hundred fifty degrees, then went another shorter stretch, then veered sharply about minus forty degrees and so forth. If the ground got rough or soft, I saw, it was enough to turn him off. It was how it was. The needles were generally smaller and went shorter and swifter flights. It was not beautiful nor useful. It had neither rhyme nor reason.

"Naturally, once I began to meditate and to think of artworks, it did not require many steps for me to analogize from what I saw to the human condition of us spacemen as we roll and dart through the immensity, and never meet, and turn off at an angle. One could almost imagine these creatures, or whatever they were, as the jetsam wreckage of our proud ships, each spar and wheel forever haunted by the ghost of its speeded pilot——

"My sorrow and disappointment gave way to compassion, and I became aware of myself.

"In a thrilling instant, as if unanimously, these inanimate mobiles veered sharply to one center and were coming against *me!*

15.

"*I* was the magnet! Or perhaps they had just become aware of my existence. I braced myself to face the onslaught. But how to face it from all sides? The big wheel that I had followed came rolling from far off at a speed that outdistanced the rest, and I drew my weapon.

"They stopped short. All of them were trembling. I was not. They veered off at their angles and resumed their evasive broken courses.

"What the devil did it mean? Evidently they were afraid of me. But why when I drew a weapon? what could that mean to them? Dogs recognize a stick, but were they dogs? *Were* they afraid? For they did not seem to fear me, but having resumed their zigzags they often passed near me, not otherwise than before. Did they forget so quickly? Would they come to notice my existence again? When?

"Why had it happened just then? Suppose they were inanimate, how had *I* at a certain moment become magnetic and then ceased to be magnetic?

"We are sophisticated these days and understand about our vibrations, so I tried to take these into account. I nagged myself to recapture that past moment that had lasted less than a unit of attentiveness. What had I been about when suddenly they turned on me as their target? What was I doing? What *was* I—for in our different moods and passions we are varying fields of force. I remembered that I had been thinking of the jetsam wreckage——

"My mind went blank; I became confused.

16.

"I was not confused by the problem of the mobiles, their nature and motion. That was a problem and I am one to solve problems—I like them. To solve it, I needed only to catch one, to take it to my instruments, experiment, perhaps dissect. (Such were my notions, but I did not carry them out. They were erroneous; by such means I should never have solved the problem.)

"What confused me was myself, my own response, my aching malaise. (As it turned out, *this* was relevant, for it was the kind of problem where the observer is a chief factor, and only if he is not *merely* an observer. 'Awareness itself,' says Whitehead, 'is a factor within fact.' But let us go step by step.)

"I was suffering intensely, I was confused.

"On all sides, in all directions, the mobiles were rolling, darting, scurrying, missing.

"And I too began to go like one of them, lumbering straight forward in my own biped gait. As I moved forward, my suffering diminished. It did not vanish—it was always there on the threshold. But so long as we moved onward—'We!'—were able to keep the suffering at the threshold, or at least at a tolerable intensity.

"I was not yet alarmed, but piqued. How long would I continue aiming along my meaningless straight line before I aimlessly veered?

17.

"For the first time I took notice of the background hills and mounds against the horizon. For I happened to be aiming toward them. It was not a steep grade, but I was lumbering forward on higher ground. I obviously had a longer flight than the mobiles.

"Let me try to be precise. I say, 'I was aiming,' 'I was lumbering'; yet I did not feel that I was doing it. Nor, on the other hand, did I feel that I was an automaton, moved despite myself. What I felt—how shall I say?—was that my confusion was drifting me there; yet it was *my* confusion. I was getting lost.

"Unmistakably a few of those mounds in the hills were rotating. Slowly or faster. I timed them. The quickest one spun in about twenty minutes. They were realizing the continuous infinite circular motion. But the rate of each was not uniform; one was slowing down and had perhaps even stopped, but no, it was speeding up again.

"I *knew* that those background mounds were somehow causing our motion.

"How did I know it so surely? Let me explain something about myself. It was neither by observation nor by intuition; it was by the practiced observation of my own habits of intuition. For what characteristically happens to me is this: first I do something, I share in a behavior—whether I dare to share in it or am forced to share in it makes no difference—then I notice what is relevant, as I was now attending to the mounds. But just as characteristically, I at once leaped to the *theory* that was just the reverse of true, for I concluded at once that it was the rotary motion of the mounds that was somehow making us move, setting up a field like a dynamo. (Once I am involved, I am fairly infallible as to *what* is relevant; I am usually absurd as to *how* it is relevant.)

"I was different from the mobiles of the plain, for I had, as I have said, a longer flight. I had already come a couple of miles and was still lumbering on my way. And I was in the midst of a different fauna. (You see, I had decided that we were, after all, animate!) The fauna were sparser. There were a few, after a while a very few, wheels and needles of the primitive type. But now there were others, alike in general plan, but somehow better-looking. They were properly bilateral; they had a functional right and left; and they were correspondingly moving not in angular zigzags but in longer graceful curves that oddly drifted off at the conclusion, till they veered and began again.

"Where before had I seen those curves? I puzzled. They were, unmistakably, the energy graphs of the flushes of erotic excitement that Reich found when he wired up the palms, the lips, etc., of amorous students at the University of Copenhagen. I began to cheer up as I lumberingly strolled my way; it was quite beautiful how they waltzingly slithered along and drifted to a pause, and one could almost hear a sigh. Also, these fatter creatures were not completely colorless—there was perhaps some emotion here—they had a blond or rusty or black sheen.

18.

"Promptly I thought of a frightening line of proof: *these* were fatter, *those* were fewer and fewer; therefore, these had eaten up those! And it was the mounds who were eating us all—just waiting for us to get within reach! (I leaped to this absurd conclusion as though it were a clear and distinct idea.) Having invented this error, I at once found evidence for it. I had insensibly come up among the rotating hills, and now sporadically I could see the soft flushes and flames that I had first noticed from the outer space. There were flashes among the hills and they occurred, I feared, whenever a creature, moving in its confusion, just as I was moving, veered too close to the rotators. Then, I figured, the rotation slowed down, for the monsters did not need to rotate, once they had drawn the prey. (*All* of this was contrary to fact.)

"I was alarmed. I stopped dead in my tracks and began to tremble.

"Yet I was able to stop. 'Then why am I so alarmed?' I asked myself. 'Why have I alarmed myself, by thinking of a savage line of proof for which there is really no evidence? Why do I respond *this* way to the appearance? At what moment did I *begin* to be alarmed?' This time I could remember the answer to the last question. I began to be alarmed when I began to take a sensual pleasure in the curvilines. At once I had a series of flash memories, and I meditated.

"It did not require many steps for me to analogize from what I saw to the condition of us hunters of pleasure; we seek out the places of danger where, of course, we cannot fully give in to our pleasure; nevertheless, we get what we can and compulsively recommence because we are not satisfied. And I thought of our friend Arthur Eliphaz dead in the war, of him who used to hunt for love where it couldn't be found, but only plenty of trouble.

"And my alarm gave way to musing. And my musing to compassion. I became aware of myself.

19.

"At once they headed toward me, the thin ones and the fat ones! One of the mounds near by began to whirl faster, as if angry.

"*I* was again the target! It was the wave of awareness! That was it. That's what had made me their prey, the other time too, thinking of Giacometti and the spacemen, aware of myself. This time I had caught it. The bilateral ones *chose* me out; Lord knows what the rotator was doing; he swiftly whirled and began to blaze. I faltered back and drew my weapon.

"They stopped short, in mid-career, and began to tremble. And at once they veered away and resumed as before, aimlessly drifting. The rotator grew dull and resumed its deliberate rotation. What! Was that thing afraid of me too?

"I went over it carefully in my mind. I had had a moment of awareness and they set themselves in motion to destroy me. Was I at that moment especially vulnerable to attack? Did I seem at that moment especially delectable? But as soon as I drew my weapons, they were afraid and left off. Was I then so terrible?

"To be sure, they gave no evidence of being afraid of me at all. Simply they resumed as before. It occurred to me that 'their' fright might be a pure projection of my own. Of my own what? Projected fright is often the effect of unawares avoidance. Could it be that they were—not interested in me? That they dismissed me just as I was dismissing them?

20.

"I shifted uneasily from foot to foot. All about me they were moving. Was nothing *still?* I thought in exasperation.

"I felt a horrible tedium, emptiness and loneliness; but emptiness that could never be filled and loneliness that would never be consoled. The mobiles were aimlessly adrift. They were not interested in me; they were not interesting to me. The rotators were, if anything, even more stupid in their meaningless rotation. Why had I come to this out-of-the-way place in order to suffer again what I used to suffer in my native world?

"Slowly my attention focused, as if dragged by chains, as if I were dragging it, onto something that was still. It did not spontaneously leap to the eye. It was an uninteresting block or rock, no bigger than myself, about a quarter of a mile away. It was a mound like the others, but it was small and did not even move. And to my disgust and boredom I now found that it was in that direction that I was drawn.

"I say 'I was drawn,' but it would be truer to say that it was the tedium within me that was succumbing in that direction.

"Close to this insignificant rock, I noticed, there were many soft flushes of light. They were the color of desire, and I felt an unbearable unease. Succumbing!

"I hit on the deadly half-truth: *in this accursed place it was the immobile that had power.* The mobiles were drawn by the *slow* rotators, and the hardly turning were more powerful still. But the most powerful of all was the dark and stationary, and he destroyed and devoured the others—just as I, as I stand here, might fall silent and stay still, and look at you, and not *even* be waiting for you. . . .

"With a shriek of terror I broke the fascination and fled. In the heavy air my shriek jangled in my ears like the ring of a far-off doorbell downstairs.

21.

"I fled and without another thought I was at the controls of my ship and had started the machine and was about to take off.

"I was blushing with shame.

"What had I been afraid of? For I was not afraid now. I had been afraid I could not stop but would be drawn into that immobile presence. Yet I had easily stopped.

"I was afraid that I would never be able to get away from this accursed satellite. Yet here I was at the controls of my ship, the engine running, about to take off.

"I was afraid that I would be destroyed by what fascinated me. Yet nowhere had I seen any of these creatures destroyed, nor corpses or fragments. What I had seen were soft flushes of desire.

"The blush on my face was nothing but such a flush of desire inhibited. I was ashamed at being known. Naked.

"My idling engine seemed to be murmuring: *Nay-ki nay-ki nay-kinay kinaykinayki.* I tried to drive the stupid sound from my mind, but it persisted, *ki-nay-ki nay-ki-naykinayki.* And then, oddly, in Greek, κινεῖ . . . κινεῖ . . . κινεῖ . . . κινεῖ: 'It sets in motion . . . it sets in motion . . . it sets in motion . . .'

"And I had the insight and remembered the ancient sentence: κινεῖ ὡς ἐρούμενον: *He sets in motion as does a loved thing.*

"I turned off the engine and climbed down.

"Mankind! Mankind, Kant said, must exhaust every possible false explanation before hitting on the true one.

22.

"When now I moved among the mobiles, I truly somewhat understood them. There was an imbalance in their small parts that you or I would feel (and I had felt) as confusion; what they felt, if they felt, I did not know. And they were seeking, or drawn toward (it came to the same thing), the dynamic equilibrium established by a wave of awareness or some simpler phasic equivalent.

"That set them in motion like a loved thing, and would bring them to quiet.

"Unfortunately the range of the mobiles was short and they zigzagged aimlessly. It was only by a chance, unlikely but not impossible, that they ever zigzagged to the rotating hills where they could get what they 'needed.'

"I myself moved among the mobiles, but not now like a mobile, for I was aware. I moved with purpose and in contact with the environment. And since I was aware, those within whose range I passed at once turned toward me. I let them come. They touched me with a caress like a feather and softly flushed and then, to my astonishment, began to roll about at my feet almost like a cat after sexual intercourse. Then, as if rejuvenated, they took up a circular motion, rolling, darting or scurrying, endlessly round and round. The largest circled in the smallest radius, the wheels almost spinning on an axial diameter; one could see how they eventually became rotating mounds. In all of this, however, I could not see any advantage to them whatever, but perhaps it is their rudimentary perfection.

"To me the scene was full of pathos. I seemed to be giving them something of great value, as if I were a wonder-worker or a divine savior. I could understand how loutish white men coming among the red Indians were taken for gods. They were rolling in ecstasy at my feet. They had no choice. So far as I was concerned, I was giving them nothing at all. I was simply aware of how I was and of how they were; and I was aware of myself not as a great god, but as alone, miserable, near to tears.

"Near to tears, for I felt what it was to move somebody just by being loved.

23.

"Cheerfully and lightly I lumbered upgrade to interview the dark and stationary one.

"We stood, so to speak, face to face. It or he or she, however it was, was a rock, and I a fair representative of our tribe, the founder of the Netherlandish Space Scouts. And all about us both—never had there been such a concentration of power!—came the mobiles and flushed and rolled in ecstasy. A mound near by rotated dizzily and blazed and managed to go off its rocker. It lay still. The spectacle was ludicrous. I burst out laughing; the rock did not.

"I touched him, he was a good solid rock. As for me, I did not flush nor roll in ecstasy.

"It did not prove itself. It did not prove anything.

"I was in the presence of the Uncarved Block.

"Oh, as it was well described in the *Book of the Way and its Power!* For Lao-tse was a spaceman like myself; he rode in the heart of the Whirlwind and so, the only one of us, sat still in the storm;

and perhaps he had seen this very example before me, twenty-five hundred years ago, when he said:

> Tao is eternal but has no fame or name.
> The Uncarved Block, though seemingly of small account,
> is greater than anything that is under the heaven.
> If kings and barons would get it for themselves,
> all the people would flock to do them homage.
> Heaven and Earth would conspire to produce Honey Dew.
> Without force or law, men would dwell in harmony.
> But once the Block is carved, there will be names;
> and as soon as there are names, know that it is
> time to stop.
>
> —Tao Te Ching, Ch. xxxii."

So Mynheer finished his narrative; and this time the stay-at-homes were satisfied and let him rest.

Chapter 9 ▪ MURDERING FATHER

I'll kill everybody and run away.
—Papa Ubu

1.

During the middle of the century, we Americans had an expression, "I've had it," meaning a shaking bad experience that one never would get over. It was an expression appropriate to describe personal experiences during the war, but it was also used generally. When you used it, the question that arose in your friend's mind, as he gave you a sidelong scrutiny, was how, surviving, you were coping with the aftermath.

The small baby wailing upstairs might be saying, "I've had it," meaning being born. Wayward said, "I've had it," having a father. Horatio said, "I've had it," being an orphan. Lothair said it being a father. Emilia said it being a wife and mother. We who are married have certainly had it; presumably those who remain single have had it. As a soldier you've had it; in jail you've had it; and trying to make a living you've had it. Being in this world not suited to an intellectual man, Mynheer had had it and shocked he got out; and being out of this world he had had it. But there are also simple folk unable to solve simple problems, and they have certainly had it.

In all these cases, the question that arises is how they are coping with the aftermath.

Yet it is a useful consolation to concentrate on the fact that there is an aftermath at all. When you are shipwrecked, you are called on only to have survived; and to praise Castor and Pollux, the savior twins. In the aftermath of the darkening and lightning, among the blown, the washed, your hair full of sand and sand inside your clothes—oh, it is fresh and irresponsible to have survived.

Who will call on me
for what this empty day?

2.

Now these afteryears Lothario took being a husband and father as a soldierly duty.

With his first mates and children, he had not been fully enlisted;

he was not always on guard duty and not altogether a beast of burden. During those years, we saw, he wore himself out in other causes that did not overjoy him; it was to them that he had taken his oath for the duration and, thus engaged, he otherwise enjoyed a pretty lusty young manhood and brought up his first offspring without serious damage to himself. With Emilia and Wayward, however, he soldiered it at home.

He did not often much desire to copulate with his wife. When they lay side by side, he passed other things through his mind behind his eyes—the events of the day and plans for tomorrow. Pleased or sorry, he could drift off to sleep. On a rare occasion he even thought of something funny and laughed out loud. He was not moved to touch Emilia, nor to converse with her. But his penis was erect and recalled him to his soldierly duty. Since he undertook to be her husband, he must, as health, contentment and honor demanded. If they both were not well satisfied, they would not have a happy home. Also, since they undertook to be live animals, they had to enjoy themselves; and this also the good soldier accomplished as his soldierly duty. His achievement was the more meritorious because from long ago Emilia held him in a peculiar abhorrence that she had never overcome; she did not seek to arouse him, but understanding his need (that was not his need), she let herself be aroused by him. So year in and out, Lothair had to seduce his wife two or three times a week. He waited for her orgasm.

It is by these grueling campaigns over the years that we achieve contentment and are pillars of society; they do not win spectacular notice from the public and they are not honored with decorations.

After her orgasm, Emilia slept. She had her own satisfactions and devotions that made this kind of sexuality a part of life. But Lothair could not sleep. He prowled the house. He made himself a late meal and ate it wolfishly, as after a day of drill the fellows hang around the Post Exchange with their hot dogs and cokes. They gripe a lot. Lothair did not gripe, but he bit off his meat sandwich and chewed it up fine. He did not need to wash it down; when he was finished with it, it washed itself down. Had he enlisted or been drafted? This is never clear and it makes no difference. He knew that it was only for the duration.

3.

Or if on other nights Lothair and Emilia spontaneously moved toward each other like live animals—as happened often enough, perhaps when they stirred from a restful sleep, or when they were listening to music and were taken with drowsy desire, or when during the day they were brought close by a common concern; for there are many occasions that invite persons friendly toward one another—and they began to embrace and kiss: then Wayward, who was three or four at the time, did not fail to intervene and prevent them, for he was lying in wait for the moment, forewarned by subtile indications. He awoke screaming from a nightmare, or he fell out of bed with a crash, or he came padding into their room with a piteous complaint.

Interrupted in excitement, Lothair was impotent. Afterward he performed by an act of the will as his soldierly duty. Yet this also he bore with fortitude and did not brain his son. But the tone of his voice was sometimes murderous.

It was during these years that Wayward conceived a settled hatred for his savage and passionate father—the inevitable result of having to live in the same house with a danger to life and limb. He planned how he would kill him, with the hunting knife. It was necessary to catch him asleep. But sometimes it happened that when he came upon him asleep he melted with love for his noble father, delivered into his hands.

4.

It was his duty, thought Lothair, to let his son grow big and be happy in his own way and according to his own lights. He forebade him nothing, and mostly he did not try to train or educate him. (Chiefly because he did not know what to train him to.) But unfortunately this easygoing way, that suited Horatio so well, did not sit with Lothario at all. It was only by constraining himself that he did not constrain Wayward.

There was habitually an air of constraint about him. Emilia judged that it was always a constraint of rage, but this was only sometimes the case. She took it that Lothair did not want to be disturbed by Wayward, and she said to the child (now age five), "Keep still, your father is working, don't disturb him." This was foolish, for when Lothair was really working he could not be disturbed by an earthquake. Emilia tried to keep the peace—that was not threatened—by placating Wayward, and then of course the boy whined and there was a loud fracas and Lothair was disturbed. And to Emilia's bewilderment, her husband, who had an ear for his boy's contentment, came thundering down on her shouting, "*Will* you let him be!"

"But I was trying to keep him from disturbing you."

"I *know* that!" he shouted. "Can't you see that makes it worse?"

She became angry. But he never struck her, because she was the mother.

Often Lothair's self-constraint with Wayward was the constraint of embarrassment. His boy was always still beginning; he had not yet had it. Lothair would have liked to share in those games of his, but he could not let himself, because he had had it. He was like the sergeant who would like to speak earnestly with the civilian couple at the bar who seem so amiable and cultured, but he cannot because he is only a dumb sergeant.

5.

Unless, exceptionally, he had a plain fatherly duty to teach Wayward something. Then they were both happy.

On Wayward's sixth birthday, Lothair taught him fire.

They set out after lunch and pulled a little wagon through the streets and lots and collected sticks of wood and dry grass. Lothair explained which sticks were too wet to bother with and which were wet but would dry out when they had a fire. Yes, and when you have a real fire going with all its embers, no stick is too wet! But there are sticks that are all pulp and there's no fire in them.

He showed him which was (only) pine and cedar and would burn quickly with a black and yellow flame—though he himself loved that quick and generous black and yellow flame—and which was oak, birch, ash, that had in them blue and white and violet flames and bony embers. In the forest, the hard woods were often gnarled, as if it was hard to be hard wood; but the softer woods grew straight. And what tree is that standing in the field? he asked. Hard, said Wayward. Correct, it's an oak, said Lothario, and here are the acorns.

They returned with their wood and the man told the boy how to make the fire; he told him but he did not show him; the boy had to follow verbal instructions and do everything with his own hands. Pile up first the tinder—that's enough—then the tiny sticks, then the little sticks and then the sticks. You light the tinder with a match in as many places as you can, and the tinder ignites the tiny sticks, and the tiny sticks ignite the other sticks. But once you have a fire, then you can put on big blocks and boards and logs. (Furniture, houses, cities.) Not before! For it smothers the fire; the big wood can't ignite from such a little flame. You see? It went out. Try it again from the beginning, for we have lots of tinder and lots of time.

You must seize the opportunity, said Lothair, wherever it happens to be catching on; you add to that spot another little stick that will catch. Now you have two little ones and you can try a little bigger. But after it's grown and you have a fire, you can be more indiscriminate. But in the beginning you must concentrate your forces on a likely point so they add up to an effect and don't fizzle out uselessly bit by bit. Try it again. To add up to something more than the separate parts. Now some of the pieces are hot and ready to go at the next match; the failures weren't wasted. The little pieces are the drier for them.

The pieces must almost touch, but not oppress one another nor be too far apart. If they're too far apart, they can't set each other off. If they touch, there's no breathing space for the fire. When you have a going fire, all you need is two big blazing pieces close parallel, that keep touching each other off.

Lothair taught Wayward how to blow softly on the fire and breathe for it, as you give a little breath to a baby or a drowned man. If he has life in him, he will soon breathe for himself. A sluggish fire you can fan hard to hurry him up, as you whip a horse that's got a lot of life in him but won't get going; he won't fall down and die.

There! Now look how the fire shapes up. Whichever way it *works* you will see you get a beautiful form, because it makes sense; the natural forces are making it work and you can see them in the shape. There must be a draft from underneath upward, for the hot gases rise; and the close sticks must touch one another off. There are many fine shapes: you might have the shape of a tepee, or a square log cabin, or two parallel logs with a thin sheet of flame between them.

There is the Indian's fire that you can crouch close to and cook on. (Another day, said Lothair, we will cook something; another sunny day we will make a fire without matches but with a burning glass; but he did not know that another day he would be dead.) Or there is the white man's bonfire that burns up all the fuel but is glorious to watch. Oh, both are excellent fires!

And now the most important thing of all! said Lothair. Don't be afraid of it—handle it. Pick up the burning brand at the safe end. Yes, pick it up in your hand, don't poke at it; pick it up and put it just where you want it. Don't chuck it on, lay it down. Pick up another one and hold him awhile to see how he behaves. Respect him, don't fear him.

When he had dared to do this, Wayward was the friend of the fire. Neither the father nor the son had the thought that one was a master of the fire.

When he is friendly, you can play with the fire, said Lothair. If you pound him, the sparks fly up; if you tickle a sensitive spot, there is a cascade of sparks. Look at the cascade—upward; it is falling upward. For flying sparks are really falling, they speed up as they rise, by the square of the time (I'll explain that another day). They go so fast at the top that they make streaks of light, till they go out. You can fan the fire and make him roar—*hooo, hooo.*

They had going a good fire, that you could toss a stick on indiscriminately. If the stick was wet, it hissed and smoked and dried and burned just like anything else.

Lothair tried to explain to him about the dark fire, the causal fire, of which the glamorous flames and the dancing sparks were just the obvious effects. But Wayward did not yet want to hear about this. . . . Another day! Another day! . . .

Lothair was looking at the castles in the embers, the faces and the angels in the flames; but he did not try to communicate to his boy how to enjoy the fire, to contemplate it—everybody has to do that his own way—but only how to make it and begin to use it.

It had grown dark and late in the afternoon as they worked at the fire. Surprising how the hours flew. Wayward was not just looking at the fire that he was so proud of having made, but he was also dreaming it like his father—Lothair did not realize that this too he was learning from his father. And the boy rolled over and fell asleep.

Lothair put a log on the fire; and when it caught he prayed to his fire god saying:

6.

"Heat of the sun, bless you my so-far-cared-for boy. I ask it if I have, well or badly, restrained myself from running away from him or annihilating him; for I was swifter and stronger, and I could. But every fatherhood is a kind of chivalry, and we take pride and joy in the restraints that we impose upon ourselves for our ideal.

"He is now six years old.

"I know that it is the last, but not least, soldierly duty of father to die, so that son can be free and great in turn. Now it is not enough for me to go away, for that will not fulfill his need but leave an unfinished situation.

"I know he kills me in his wish; he hates me because he is both jealous and fears me; and he injures me and fears the retaliation. It cannot be helped. Sometimes, rarely, he loves me. When I am dead, if I die soon enough, he will only love me, and that will be very well.

"We have at least lived in such a way that my boy has been able to think and utter his wish. Likely he will wreak it also—if he is the son of Lothair," he said, oddly proudly.

"As for me, I may sound gloomy but I am cheerful and in high spirits today." And indeed he cheerfully saluted the twinkling fire and opening his fly he pissed on the fire and put it out, as we fire-people do, in a cloud of ammoniac steam.

7.

He was cheerful with Emilia. The fact that she was desirable to Mynheer made her more desirable to himself. By character he was the reverse of grudging and spiteful; he was not only willing to share but quick to take the other point of view. Lothair was one who always came across. Also, the fact that he was not alone responsible for his wife's contentment made him feel light and cheerful; his desires bubbled up to the surface, and he gave a passing thought to being happy.

Emilia was deeply moved whenever she saw a happy hour between Lothair and Wayward ("her men"), when the father did a concrete fatherly deed like teaching him the fire. Also, the fact that she could love Piet Duyck made it less necessary for her to withdraw from Lothair lying beside her—he would not swallow her up completely—and it was of course Lothair, whom she loved because he was big; and he was, when at his best, a lustier animal than your Mynheers or Horatios. She changed her position and played with his half-erect penis, ever anew surprised to feel it grow in the dark.

However it was, they became silly and carried on like children, all foreplay and jokes and malicious wit at the expense of the others. With a start, she thought for an instant that it was her brother Arthur whose head she held in her hands and was biting his lips. But Arthur was dead, and it was Lothair.

They were laughing all the while, until she fell asleep.

8.

Lothair still did not sleep but he got up and prowled the house—he was thick with fancies. He was not hungry, but he wanted to read a few lines and he took a book and settled under a lamp by the cold fireplace.

The book was the *Tao Te Ching* from which Mynheer had told about the Uncarved Block, and he opened to the fifth and sixth chapters. It said, Heaven and Earth—

> Heaven and Earth are ruthless,
> to them the many things are only straw dogs.
> The Sage too is ruthless,
> to him the people are only straw dogs.
> Yet Heaven and Earth and all between is a great
>   bellows:
> it is empty, but its bounty never fails;
> work it, and more comes.

More comes! Work it! More comes and the fire leaps up!

Lothair humbly nodded his assent. This was ordinary experience; one observed all of it every day. On close scrutiny there was nothing else to be observed.

He went on to the next chapter. It said, The Valley Spirit—

> The Valley Spirit never dies.
> The mysterious Female.
>
> Her doorway
> —from which sprang Heaven and Earth.
>
> It is within us all the while;
> draw and draw on it, it never runs dry.

"The Valley Spirit!" he said the words in an audible hushed voice, with admiration.

9.

Almost immediately he dozed off, squatting on the floor, leaning against the wall, hanging his head, lit by the lamp, unwarmed by the absence of fire. The fire in the hearth was dead. His hunting knife was hanging on the mantel piece.

And he saw, he thought, little Gus, Emilia's first child, as he was when he was killed on the bright-lit crazy day at the zoo.

Little Gus, who was six, appeared to him.

It was Wayward he was seeing with his half-open eyes, for Wayward had stolen into the room and was there.

Little Gus was (he thought) looking at him with a hurt mouth and reproachful eyes.

Lothair said to him, "Why are you angry with me, Little Gus? Say it out! Don't stand there and say nothing."

Wayward was startled by the question from his sleeping father. "*You* know——" he stammered in confusion, for he had been watching his mother and father.

"*You* know," said little Gus. "You killed me an' I wasn't middle-aged."

It was Wayward standing there trembling. But little Gus was banging his forehead against the railing, as he used.

There were no animals; all the cages were now empty.

"Do you think there's a secret you'd find out, little Gus?" asked Lothair.

Wayward turned white. He couldn't make out the sound "Little Gus" that his father repeated; he took it to be another of the polysyllables that he didn't understand. "I wanted to look at the fire," he lied.

"You haunted, unfrocked friar!" echoed little Gus scornfully.

"Let me tell you," cried Lothair nettled, "there isn't any! There isn't any!"

"Yes, the fire's out," said Wayward dully, rubbing his eyes.

"My privilege to find out!" cried little Gus angrily, turning on him and beating him with his little fists.

With his big hands Lothair took little Gus by the shoulders.

"Let go of me!" said Wayward. His eyes leaped about for help.

"Let go," said little Gus.

"Shall I call your mama, little boy? She'll be glad to see you."

"No," said little Gus.

"No!" cried Wayward in a panic, because he had been peeping with such wishes as he then wished. His eyes leaped to his father's hunting knife on the wall.

Lothair felt with sensual pleasure Gus's hot writhing body. And he felt opening within him the Valley Spirit, the doorway, that does not swallow up but pours forth.

"Let us make a new beginning," said Lothair gladly, quoting from those places in Aristotle where the argument turns to demonstration. "You're a hot little Gus and you're not dead at all, and your name is New Beginning."

"You little snot! This is what I should have done from the beginning!" Lothair was saying, Wayward thought. "What I should have done from the beginning."

But little Gus was looking at him with wide eyes of joy.

Wayward was looking at him with wide eyes.

"I love you, New Beginning," said Lothair, and drew him toward him and kissed him.

With a shriek the boy tore away from the embrace and seized the knife that knew its way to a vital organ.

Lothair awoke and it was Wayward. He blinked in the light like a man who has lost his spectacles. He did not defend himself. With more force than he yet had available, the boy drove in the knife and killed him. Lothair called out hoarsely and choked on his blood and expired. The blood gushed out of his ears.

10. Obituary

Lothario Alger, the musician, was unusual among the men of his group in that he had a career. In this he was like his antagonist Eliphaz, the financier, and so they were real antagonists and courage flowed from one to the other. The other men of the time, such as were not merely swept away by circumstances, were always finding themselves *in* the circumstances and forming themselves thereby;

but these two made the circumstances bear witness to themselves. So again, although Lothario could admire or love many people, and serve them and even humble himself, as he did before his last wife, and indeed before all women, yet he respected nobody but Eliphaz; and for more than a decade, after the death of the old capitalist and before the coming of any other manly politician, he had nothing to respect and try against. For his genius was to be in the Opposition.

Lothario first came to notice as a student agitator against the war. In these campaigns he was especially feared and scorned just because he stuck to old-soldierly principles of honor, loyalty and last-ditch fighting, whereas his colleagues were opportunistic and his military opponents comported themselves like junior executives or clerks. After his expulsion from school he associated with the group around Henry Faust; and here too there was a striking contrast between the brilliant practicality of Faust, that did not bear witness, and the dully glowing stubbornness of Lothario that took him to jail and to a spell of insanity, but whose practicality is in issue to this day.

On the advice of Franz, he made his livelihood by hammering together chairs and tables. Doing this he was happy. He would have done only this, besides composing his music, but the conditions of employment and self-employment were not fitting a human being, because there was no community. It was during this period that he wrote all his pieces for the piano.

The bulk of his music and musical experimentation, however, he invented just before and just after the period of his breakdown, as if it required the nice situation of a precarious internal integrity and a chaotic external world for him to hear his *voces intimae.* But we might say, on the contrary, that it was hearing these inner possibilities that invited him to risk losing the usual structure of reality, whether or not that had been more favorable to him. The characteristic act of Lothario Alger was the pertinacity with which *even so* he kept hold of, or again got a grip on, whatever he had experienced, good or bad. He forced the world somehow to be there. Given his great size, he would have made a formidable wrestler.

It was so that, after the war had told him to hold life cheap, he persisted in humanitarianism even to cannibalism, till he had forced a new pattern for you and me.

He initiated the founding of the Community of Human Relations in order to engender, with Mother Emilia, the son who killed him.

He played in the Memorial Ball Game and made the famous hit that rang *F* in the octave above high *C*. This he regarded always as the signal moment of his life, for it proved that he could let go his force, even if he could not fly.

Horatio Alger used to say that his brother was bent on fighting a drawn-out losing fight. It is true that he liked a drawn-out fight that tested one's strength; it is not true that he was bent on losing.

In the last years, in company, he improvised the songs without words. He never made songs with words, nor composed to any other program; in the ultimate speechless.

11.

"I'll kill them all and run away," thought Wayward.

It seemed to him that Mynheer had killed Lothair, and now as the son he had the filial duty to take vengeance. Even while he looked at his murdered father with detached curiosity.

He noticed, in his hand, the knife.

Bravely he put in his belt the bloody knife that knew its way to a vital organ. And at once his knees were weak and his head swam. Then, like a wasp sting, a buzzing began in both his heels, and slowly spread up to his ankles, and to his knees, while streaks and waves and shooting pains of courage suffused him, as if he were drowning in courage.

The buzzing now took up also in his wrists and elbows and, from below, was rising into his thighs, coming from the extremities toward the center. He stood paralyzed with the absence of fright, as if he had no other motive power. The waves of energetic light coming struck him a woeful pang on the nape of his neck and a blow on the front of his crown, where were the fear and hate. He moaned, and at once the buzzing began in his throat and spread up into his lips and chin. The waves of light washed away the hatred he had felt that was grounded in fear and the hatred he had felt that was grounded in guilt. The buzzing was now in his penis and eyes and midriff; and having won these centers, it was triumphant everywhere as a fire, when the firemen have given up, sweeps through and over all the house outside and inside.

For ten minutes the boy stood rooted forever to the spot, as if caught in the magnetic field of the earth that spins on.

But he simply moved and stepped out of the magic circle, and was himself.

And now we can answer the question, Where did he get the strength for the deed he did? For he struck his father with more force than he yet had. But an action can be understood only when its whole arc is completed and its unitary meaning is revealed. Wayward stood fearless and tall, and obviously adequate for such a blow as he had dealt.

12.

He asked aloud, "What can I do that my papa would have liked?"

He did not much heed the corpse in the corner, nor look in that direction.

"He would have liked me to make a fire the way he showed me. Now all by myself."

He was happy he had hit on it. It seemed to him a lucky inspiration.

Without haste, carefully, even very carefully, as though he were concerned to be a perfect scholar and not make a mistake, he again made a little tepee in the cold fireplace. First the tinder, then the tinder sticks, then the tiny sticks, then the little sticks and the sticks. He struck a match and lit the heap in several places at once, and at once his fire caught fire and he had a good curl of smoke and darting tongues of fire.

He laid on a few more sticks—he did not chuck them on. He was interested, thorough, happy, excited. The fire began to crackle and to shoot up sparks.

This was the fire that St. Wayward made in honor of his father.

13.

It was burning well. He left it. He did not watch the fire, except to keep feeding it sticks.

But he chose to see by the firelight. He switched off the reading lamp and the room was lit by only the blaze in the hearth, that shone bigger in the darkness. And oblivious to anything but his thoughts, if indeed he had any thoughts, he began a skipping game with his ball. He had a large particolored ball that he kept bouncing in front of himself, and chasing after it faster and faster. They went back and forth across the room, and around the room. The ball said, "Hop! Hop!"

—And I think of the ending of *Wozzek,* our work of art of the first half of the twentieth century (such as it was), when the children are playing unmindful of the so-called tragedy that had occurred, and they are calling out, "Hopp! Hopp!" What did Berg mean?

It was in the interim before this final scene, in front of the closed curtain—beginning in the bass and soon spreading with frantic brevity through all the vast orchestra—that my colleague poured out his sorry heart for his sorry story. I do not think that there are many, in the first half of the twentieth century, who have not been stung into tears when suddenly they heard their song. But the curtain opens again and there are these children——

Must we not shrug? What have these children to do with those poor people? *Diese arme Leute?* What have you, little boy, to do with us poor people? *Du! Dein Mutter ist todt.* So what? Best is to forget them. *Hopp! Hopp!*

14.

Now Wayward was tired and sleepy. He came slowly back to the fireplace and, opening his fly, pissed on the fire and put it out, as we fire people do. It was dark; and around all his figure and head could be seen the blue aura and halo of light.

Chapter 10 ▪ BURIAL

1.

All week I was despondent, inventing the death of Lothair.

Then friends of mine said, "If the incident makes you unhappy, why don't you change it? It's your story, make it come out the way you want."

I looked at them unbelievingly. "No," I said stolidly, as Lothair would have liked, "I'll put it down stolidly, one point after another, just as it happened. I'll get through it."

Then I became angry. "I could no more not have Lothair killed," I said dramatically, "than I could have dared to meet up with him alive." But it is spiritless to invent without him these ethnological rituals of how men today can live in the olden style.

2.

They waited for a foggy night to throw Lothario's body into the Hudson River. During those days there were many foggy nights. Under cover of the thick fog they got out their rowboat from its hiding place under the wharf, whose slimy piles gave off a haunting smell. Horatio carried down the body in a sack and they brought leaden weights. Horatio and Rosalind and the boy Wayward who had grown three inches at a bound, got into the boat with the body.

Emilia stayed behind on the wharf and was at once eclipsed in the fog. She went back to the children. The noise of the fog whistles reverberated in the streets of Hoboken.

Horatio rowed, Rosalind sat in the rear with the sack, and Wayward in the bow played the round of the flashlight on the black-green water. They were shut in by the surrounding fog and could hardly see one another. The fog whistles were, and sounded like, organ pipes. The organ noises intoned irregularly, frequently, mostly in the distance, but sometimes, as they came, one was ear-splittingly near.

The fog whistles were not harmoniously tuned but, of course, so spaciously broadcast, they made up a great and strong song, solemn and surprising and boring, and Rosalind began to weep for her dead brother-in-law. But Horatio and the child, each in his own way, did not grieve but took in the beauty of the night. The boy kept darting his pencil of light this way and that in the drizzle-pointed air; but it reached only a short way in the fog and was stifled, thought Horatio, like a finger with the tip cut off. For Horatio this was an unhappy thought and he held his breath. But St. Wayward at the prow did not quail in being happy.

They were about a third of a mile out. An immense horn on the left kept bellowing in their ears almost a true *G*—

—*alla breve.* They shipped oars. While Wayward played the light on the sack, Horatio attached the weights and Rosalind wept. They slid the sack over the side and it immediately, silently, sank as food for the river eels and crabs, of whom Lothair himself had eaten a great many.

Almost at once there was a sickening crash near by on the left, a dull explosion and faint shrieks. The *G* did not sound again. There were some flashing lights, but they could not make anything out.

Prompt in the emergency, Horatio and Rosalind had stripped and gone overboard to help. They struck out toward the noise, and were promptly lost in the fog.

Wayward kept calling out in a lusty voice to guide them back.

A long time passed, and then they had both got back, empty-handed and shivering. They could not save anything, hardly themselves—even though they happened to be on the spot—yes!—and in the nick of time.

"Could you see anything?" said Rosalind.

"Yes. I saw it sink," said Horatio. "So what?"

"What should we do now?"

"Guess the only thing is to paddle and splash around here for half an hour and keep singing out. Heeey! Heeey!"

They were cold and wet and depressed, for it is horribly depressing utterly to fail. The rowing about made them breathe again, it warmed them up, and soon Rosalind felt better, for she had already wept. But Horatio, who could not mourn, felt the clammy death in his midriff and got sicker and sicker. The organ tones did not let up, but sounded around them far and near as they splashed around in the water, but certainly drifting far from the spot. But Wayward, having found his voice by calling out across the water, was now experimentally filling out the harmonies of those minor thirds and augmented thirteenths. His boyish throat was open and

Horatio looked with disgust over his shoulder at the boy's silhouette.

"Hot as the nick of time!" cried St. Wayward out of his inspired vision.

"Hot as the nick of time and bloody as my lucky break, you loom in triumph! For this holidaylight strewn with his large hand, I am thankful to the creator of the world. My heart is warm as the flush of embarrassment.

"Never again let it be said our flowers are blighted, nor the generous despair! For beauty has made hell burst into tears, and bravery has dealt out astonishment."

Such was the triumph song that came to St. Wayward in a vision at the burial in the river of his father.

PART 2 HORATIO FURIOSO

When we think that the possible is impossible, we begin to imagine that the impossible is possible.

—GOETHE

Chapter 11 • THE WORLD OF THE *HERALD TRIBUNE*

1. Metamorphosis

Like that fellow in Prague who awoke one morning to find himself transformed into a monstrous bug, so Horatio awoke one morning and he was for the General for president. He believed in the world of the *Herald Tribune* and he began to follow the folkways of the Americans. In a haze of insane clarity, it struck him that the election of the General would make a (beneficial) difference to our happiness; and he got out of bed at once, giving his sleeping wife a sentimental lustless peck on the cheek. He prepared some odorless coffee with a powder, and he sat down with his *Herald Tribune.*

Now when I say he "believed in" the world of that excellent journal, I don't mean that he embraced the explicit opinions of the editors and advertisers (nobody is that crazy), but that he took for granted that what was printed there as the news was indeed the news, and that the assumptions on which the articles were based were indeed the way of the world. What a world was that!

2. A Little Item About a Theft

On page 4* was a routine item about an ex-congressman who had embezzled $169,000 from a bank in a small town in New Jersey, and now he was held for the grand jury. Now the question I am raising is, What did that little item mean? What did it assume about the world, and how did it come to be printed?

To begin with, it was *not* printed as local color, as a gentle ribbing of small towns in New Jersey; that was not the tone. Nor was it written as human interest, praises for the efforts of a man to earn a living in a big way, trying first one thing and then another; *that* was not the tone.

As it was written, the chief point seemed to be the arrest and arraignment of the embezzler. Did this mean that the writer assumed that the machinery of the court had something to do with preventing, "deterring," embezzling, and the more so with publicity? But this is absurd, for nobody, no penologist and no layman, believes that. Or did the writer assume that society had to take

* These news items are taken at random mostly from the issue of January 18, 1953, which I happen to have in the house; but the beauty of the *Herald Tribune* is that you can take almost any story from any issue and come to the same wonderment.

vengeance? But he did not write with this tone, for it would have offended the current public sensibility.

Indirectly, of course, the item was business advice: steer clear, officious courts; but then why was it not in the business section?

It could also serve as advance notice of the forthcoming trial, a kind of vindictive entertainment. Yet it was *not* in the entertainment section, and the kind of people who went to this kind of show did not use the *Herald Tribune* for reading but to sleep on in doorways.

Twist it and turn it, no sense at all.

Then picture Horatio munching bread out of a package, drinking a small draught of odorless coffee, and vacantly reading this purposeless item on page 4.

3. Horatio Mad

He had gone mad. Lothair had foreseen it. But it was his brother's death that had broken him; this Lothair could not foresee. Stunned out of his courage, Horatio was unable to mourn. Instead of wailing and tearing his clothes and waiting for new strength, Horatio now wanted, just once, to win, to be with the majority, to think with the majority. It was too painful for him to give in again to the rising sob for the defeat of good sense, inventive genius and honest speech. He would not admit that his brother was dead. Under these circumstances he became a reader of the *Herald Tribune*.

Like everybody else, his rage was bitter against what keeps us from living in a golden age, as is our due. For the case is that each person, meeting any other person, has a claim to spit out at him the bitter accusation, "It is *you* who, continuing as you do, prevent me from being happy." Courteously we refrain from barking it out, and we spiritlessly wag our tails like gentle dogs. Each person has to cope as best he can with his own messianic rage.

A friend of mine who cannot find any takers for the love he has to offer, has bitten into himself a duodenal ulcer that he alternately nurses with milk or spites with matjes herring, like his child or wife. I myself walk around with an omnipresent discouraging idea that what is easiest and best for everybody, and it lies obvious before us, is somehow infinitely impractical; yes, and what's more, if we aim at that impossible thing, we find that we have prevented something that was possible. Clearly such an idea is beyond frustration and rage; I have no will left to want anything. And Horatio, finding that his teeth and fists had become clenched, so that it was hard for him to go on living hand to mouth, instead put on a vacuous face and cried, "*Win!* Win with the General!"

As to the General himself, although well on in years he had a wonderful open smile of arrested early adolescence. When he was not flashing this smile, he looked simply stupid in the middle with an edge of cunning around the sides.

In elegant Bodoni headlines, the *Herald Tribune* printed the following proclamation of the General: "America is great because America is good. When America ceases to be good, America will cease to be great." The unstirring rhythm of this fell on Horatio's ear with a dolorous pang,* yet even so he rallied and recovered his face to an empty leer from which he peered out with hot crazy eyes.

4. A Little Item About Education

On page 5 there was a little story from Washington to the effect that the senior senator from Minnesota had introduced a Federal aid bill for the construction of schools.

Oh, the assumptions underlying this! That there were known goals of education; and that we knew something about how to achieve them. That school buildings did not probably operate counter to any plausible goals and methods you might mention. That the intervention of the state in financing education was not immediately disastrous to the whole enterprise (if there were such an enterprise); and that a man like a senator from a place like Minnesota . . . well, these erroneous assumptions were so thick and ramified that one hardly knew at what word to pass a hand across his eyes and say, "Oof! It's too thick."

Yet that was the item in the *Herald Tribune* and the attentive reader of it was—Horatio! Horatio who, entered in the school-jail at the age of six, had looked sharp and torn up the records, etc., etc. The same Horatio took in also this little item with his morning coffee. He had gone mad. (His age was thirty-two.)

5. Electioneering

By the third or fourth morning of the onset of Horatio's insanity, Rosalind was deeply disturbed. Put baldly, the bother was that she wanted to, and he wanted to talk about the election of the General.

They would be making love, and suddenly he said, "Texas is in the bag!"

"I beg your pardon," she said, opening her eyes and seeing on his face the light of victory.

* Yet Horatio need not have suffered for the General's style; for, as it has turned out, the only solid comedy produced in America in the last decade has been spoken by the General. Hundreds of thousands of people wait eagerly for the verbatim report on the day after the weekly press conference, and they are put into a cheerful mood all week by the General's turn of phrase.

"But Pennsylvania is touch and go," he said, and sympathetically lost his erection.

"What's the matter, baby? What's that to you?" she said softly, cradling his head in her lap and stroking his hair, pulling his ears. It was easy for her, because she loved him, to dissolve the orgasm she had not had into a deep and melancholy compassion. He was staring up at her with frightened eyes that would not own up to the fact that his brother was dead. She closed his eyes with her finger tips and bent over and kissed his eyelids. A spasm of pain crossed his face.

He had never loved his brother, but he had used him as the one who confronted for us the fact that we do not live in a golden age.

Rosalind did not know what ailed him. What she observed was that he, who used to read in the book of nature and the book of dreams, was now reading absorbedly in the *Herald Tribune.*

But the question must be asked again: how do *you* cope with the fact that we do not live in a golden age? Some people deny that it is a fact; they deny that there is such a thing as a golden age (it is "utopian") or they brazenly claim that we *do* live in a golden age. But is this a golden age? Others, as my Russian colleague used to say, "stifle the living pang of their hearts with fantastic dreams."

6. A Not Newsy Item

On page 1 of the *Herald Tribune* they continually made a big deal of the war, which was now in Hither Cathay.

The General had said, "I shall go to Hither Cathay!" He was the "candidate of National Unity." (The assumptions here, to spell them out, were that there was some good in there being nations, and that if there were, national unity was good for them.)

But of course it was the very same war that everyone had always been talking about. It was not newsy. Let me quote the particular day's headline:

HOW TANK MEN TALK
AFTER 7-HR. FIGHT
IN HITHER CATHAY

'A Field Day,' They Call It
but Biggest Cheer Was
for Order to Withdraw.

Not newsy. And again, these stories about the war were written with certain assumptions about the nature of war in general, and certain specific assumptions about this particular war in Hither Cathay—

(Jesus! I'm damned if in 1953 I'm going to discuss those assumptions again. In 1945 I swore an oath that I would never remain in a room where a so-called serious discussion about the plausibility of a war was going on. I have kept that oath and walked out often.)

I am not an intellectual snob and I have a good appetite, but here on page 17 of the same paper there was an architect's drawing of a new hospital in Newark, "designed to withstand anything an atomic raid can offer except a direct hit." It was the "Clare Maass Memorial Hospital, named for an army nurse who died during experiments on yellow fever in Cuba, 1901." This was the bread-and-butter of the *Herald Tribune.* Were we supposed to digest it?

Horatio opened his eyes and looked up at Rosalind. "She's not interested in current events at all," he had to admit to himself.

He rolled over and drew her toward him. His penis hardened and soon they were at it; but they had no sooner started than he fell asleep.

7. Miscellaneous Premises of the World of the *Herald Tribune*

In the world of the *Herald Tribune* the brides wore white veils as if virginity were, or were esteemed as, a social virtue. And marriages were announced with fanfare, as if being married might still be a critical transaction.

The most pages, the largest sizes of types and the most spectacular layouts were assigned to women's dresses.

Leaders of moral opinion were quoted as "decrying," "denouncing" and "deploring," various social ills. There was apparently a strong belief in this kind of verbal magic. On the other hand, almost never mentioned in the world of the *Herald Tribune* were the motives and excitements that do produce effects in the ordinary course of nature, such as anger, lust, spite, envy, inspiration, loyalty, greed, embarrassment, compassion or confusion.

In that world nobody was ever confused. Prognosticators of events were promptly belied by the events, yet they continued on, and were as if credited, for an important ritual reason that one could hardly guess at. It was affirmed about the weather, "Today *is* fair and warmer," when you could look out your window into a blinding snowstorm.

To remedy overcomplexity, such as excessive traffic, it was usually proposed to introduce new complicating factors. And to assure tranquillity, it was as if the best means were to threaten other peoples and hold your own breath.

There was also a department called "Books" where was made

ritual mention of exercises in correct spelling that were for sale.

Finally, the *Herald Tribune* was for the General.

8. That World Metaphysically Considered

(The reader will notice that I have been trapped into a heavy use of the subjunctive mood and clauses beginning with "as if.")

This weird world were probably best classified as a kind of dream. It have the chief dream properties of displacement, distortion, condensation, symbolism; a really remarkable "secondary elaboration" and plenty of rationalization; doubtless a latent meaning, if one were taking the pains to ferret it out. But if it were a dream, it were a dull dream. There were no color, the sensation were dim and the emotion tame indeed.

But this dream, if it were, might have one extraordinary feature: it were fairly like the "social reality." You could raise the question why anyone bother to copy off such a dull dream twice, once might be on the streets and once might be in the pages of the *Herald Tribune.* Yet it *were,* if it had been, a fair correspondence.

Indeed! I look out my window right now and see how it might. (Fór an enormous advantage of both our "society" and of the world of the *Herald Tribune* were that any random example of a street-corner or of an item of news at once might plunge us into the soup.)

If it be 9th Avenue at 25th Street. No, it *is!* It *is!* Been raining, street's wet, temperature below 40 on my thermometer. The street is paved with stony material and the air, like my windowpane, is well saturated with grime. Just across the street is the Terrace Bakery that sells various kinds of cake, but not to me. Next to it, south, is a Porto Rican grocery whose sign says Coca-Cola. Next to that, south, is a Porto Rican candy store whose sign says Pepsi-Cola. And on the corner is the Spotless Dry Cleaner: Suits 45¢. Above these four shops is a block of four-story flats with windows not unlike the one I am looking from, but nobody is looking out at me or at anything. But trucks and taxicabs are streaming down the avenue, and people are walking on the sidewalk past the shops in either direction. A woman and child come out of one of the shops; a man goes into another of them.

So far all of that sounds likely enough. Not attractive but not unreal.

Now the people were, if they were, the interesting part of the scene. For they might be alive and experiencing figures-and-grounds and creatively adjusting their environment. Suppose then we appoint ourselves cultural anthropologists and ask them questions: what are they buying? where are they bound? what do they work at? how much money do they get and spend? is it interesting? is it worth it? have they had it? how do they quiet the bitter rage that each one feels by right in meeting every other? and how do they cope with the fact that we do not live in a golden age? Answering our questionnaire, these might people might, roughly—oh, yes, they might!—tell us something very like the stories in the *Herald Tribune.* They themselves to formulate the world not very differently from the anthropologists of the *Herald Tribune.* They themselves imagining that there be such a world as the world of the *Herald Tribune* and that one might be alive in that world.

Good; it seems to be all of a piece; there is a social reality and there is its newspaper.

But alas! the fact is that if we question them only a little further, if we suddenly ask a point-blank personal question; if we ask this gentleman to clench his fists and bare his teeth and *then* venture to breathe; or if we ask that lady to move her pelvis for a change and let her legs tremble; if we hold up a mirror to the lines of perplexity corrugated on the youth's brow; or if we look attentively at the game the little boy is drawing on the sidewalk; if we put two and two together to make four rather than seventeen and a half—suddenly everybody is confused, they do not answer in the words of the *Herald Tribune,* they say contradictory things or punch you in the jaw, or bawl, or punch you in the jaw and then bawl and want you to hold them in your arms; they are not bound where they thought they were bound, they cope otherwise than they imagined, they are not living in the world of the *Herald Tribune,* and indeed there is no such thing as the world of the *Herald Tribune.*

9.

When with grief and horror but not loathing, for they loved him, Rosalind and Emilia had finally to admit to themselves that Horatio was living in the "social reality" of the Americans and in the world of the *Herald Tribune,* they cast about for a psychiatrist.

The choice was easy—Antonicelli.

For as I have already hinted, since his salutary resignation as prosecuting attorney for the sociolatry—a resignation in the nick of time, since he had already fallen down with the asphyxiation—Antonicelli had made himself a brilliant career in psychotherapy. Not surprisingly: lawyers are among those, as Freud has pointed out, who make the best psychoanalysts. And in the dark agitation of Antonicelli's eyes and in his hands that gave out sparks of electricity when he rubbed the knuckles together, there was a mesmeric power that could exorcize devils. Further and more particularly, just because of his peculiar past as a state's attorney, Antonicelli could be expected to understand through and through the ins-and-outs of the official world of the *Herald Tribune.* The very man! Emilia at once thought of Antonicelli and she said: "Antonicelli!"

"Of course," agreed Rosalind, "Antonicelli!"

She wanted Emilia to visit him and make an appointment for Horace. But Emilia said, "By no means. It's your husband. He will certainly ask for particular details that only you can give."

"Oh," cried Rosalind, "I'd be so embarrassed."

Horatio was a fortunate man, but deservedly fortunate, to have two such women flanking him and supporting him in his affliction.

Chapter 12 ▪ MAKING AN APPOINTMENT

1.

"Hello! Come in! Mrs. Alger!" said Antonicelli and shook hands.

He sat down and struck a match to light his pipe. "Rosalind Alger! Fancy seeing you here——" he said, and the match went out.

Sitting behind his desk, Antonicelli made a thing of striking a match and being about to light his pipe, but instead he always interjected a remark, the match went out, and from beginning to end of an interview or a therapeutic session he never got his pipe lit but consumed dozens of matches. This had the effect of keeping the other person on an edge of anxiety from which it was easy to topple him into a passion.

Rosalind, however, was sane as a hammer and very soon she lit his pipe for him.

"Er–thanks," he said, "and what can I do for *you*?"

How should she put it? She explained that Horatio was for the General.

"Ah," said Antonicelli, "I see?" He waited.

"Do you see? *Don't* you see? He is for the General for president."

"What!" exclaimed Antonicelli. Now he saw. "You say–Horatio! What are you saying? Horatio Alger is for the General?"

"Yes," she said and her heart sank. "That's the size of it."

He drummed his fingers on the desk and said, "Amazing!" He struck a match to light his pipe, but stopped to shake his head and the match went out. "No, no, on the contrary," he said as if to himself, "it's just what I should have expected. What else could one expect?"

"For God's sake, Antonicelli, is it bad? Can you help us?"

"Yes, it's very serious," he said. He was visibly upset. He struck a match. "I don't know whether or not I can help him." The match went out. "Don't think that he's the only one!" he said bitterly. "Dozens of these beautiful and gifted fellows have broken down in this way in these years. But Horatio! Good God! What an indictment of *us!* If I were queer, *he* is the one I should have written sonnets to. Good ones too. Is it bad? You ask is it bad!" he cried in a rising passion. "Supposing these days that *you* were beautiful and gifted–but I *beg* your pardon," he said and leaped to his feet and gave a little bow. "You are beautiful and gifted. I'm speaking in a general way——" He struck a match.

"Where was I?" he said. The match went out. At this Rosalind again lit his pipe.

"Er—thanks," said Antonicelli. "Yes, how do *you*, young lady, how do *you* cope with the fact that we don't live in a golden age?"

"I eat good food," she said simply, "and am having seven children, and I create a world for myself in my dances. Very good too."

He fixed her with his left eye, the blue one. "Young lady," he said, "you have been lying to me. You say that you have come to me for help for your husband. But you're the one who's suffering. He doesn't screw as well as he used—if I knew the Horatio Alger that was and if I know the capabilities in that line of those who are for the General. Isn't that it?"

She hung her head. It was so.

"I swear," she said timidly. "*I* didn't do anything."

He smiled apologetically. "I'm sorry. I do give in to my tone of the prosecuting attorney, don't I? Years and years of the trade. No, you didn't do anything. What you want is perfectly comprehensible, in fact enviable, but——"

"But?"

"Young lady, I'm not an auto mechanic. I can't put in a new fuel pump. I'd like to fix up his thing-um-bob for you, but all I can deal with is the whole man, the whole situation; and the whole situation is—you see how it is—tough. Tough. Unpredictable. Well! Hop! Hop!" He rubbed his knuckles and the sparks flew bright. "Send him to me. We'll see."

"Oh, thank you so much. But, Antonicelli, how can I get him to come? What would you advise?"

"To come? Just screw the best you can. Have a good time yourself."

"I don't mean *that*," she said. "My, you have a dirty one-track mind. I mean how can I get him to come here, to see you."

"Not a dirty mind at all," he said cheerfully, "it's just the profession, just the profession. . . . Oh, he'll come here, all right, don't you worry about it. My experience is that the ones who are suddenly for the General can't be kept away; they need converts to bolster them up; they imagine they're going to talk me into voting for him too. *They're* crazy. Good-day, madam."

2. Epidaurus

When she had gone, he sighed once deeply and expelled all the air from his nobly powerful lungs, and softly breathed on.

He saw his oval of vision, he listened to the sounds of the city, he tasted the air in his mouth, and he felt himself seated in his chair down to the center of the earth. And when the currents of life again began to circulate within him and he was in the streaming of the original Ocean, he gave himself to his prayer and murmured:

"Apollo, father of Aesculapius, and Aesculapius my father. And Hygieia. Teach me wisdom with my new patient. Especially when to hold my tongue and my hand and when not to hold my tongue and my hand.

"With each one I must be compassionate and willing to be surprised. But this one I am also grateful to and love."

The closet door nudged open and out slowly peered the garnet eyes and quick forked tongue of his familiar serpent.

The serpent's name was Epidaurus, after their once proud estate, and he had a nice sense when to remain hidden and when to appear, either to announce the time or to comfort his master.

He slithered up Antonicelli's leg and reared up his head and looked into his eyes. The physician absent-mindedly patted his flat head and struck a match. He lit his pipe.

Chapter 13 ▪ A FIRST INTERVIEW

1.

Horatio did come to Antonicelli's. He came walking up the back street and looking for the house number.

Strangely, on that residential street, a number of pickets with sandwich boards were angrily striding up and down, three men and three women in a close march. At every turning they cried out, "On Strike!"

But their sandwich boards were blank of any information.

"On strike?" said Horatio friendly. "Against whom?"

There was no answer. They came to the turning and they cried out, "On Strike!" They weren't giving out any information. Not for free.

In fact, they didn't know.

Horatio shrugged and went up to the doctor's office. Antonicelli opened the door, ushering him in, motioned him to sit down, sat down himself, and he also said nothing.

Horatio said nothing. There were plenty of matches struck and went out.

"Those pickets downstairs," said Horatio finally, "what's the strike about?"

"Those are Minetta Tyler's people. She's got them out everywhere. Some of them are on strike. Why not here?"

"Minetta Tyler!" cried Horace. "Lord! What is *she* up to? It's been years, hasn't it?"

"Stop!" Antonicelli's voice came like the crack of a whip. "Where in hell do you think you are? You can't get away with that stuff with me. You sit there and want to talk about pickets and Minetta Tyler. Those are the things you *want* to talk about. Well, just cut it out."

Horatio swallowed. He looked about him, and said nothing.

Antonicelli said nothing.

The minutes went by.

Horatio said nothing.

"This is costing you plenty," said Antonicelli. He had a neat clock that read off the time, \$5, \$10, \$15, \$20. . . .

"You've got me," said Horatio. "You won't let me talk about

what I want to talk about, and I'm damned if I can think of what I don't want to talk about. I'm at a loss."

"*Now*, we're getting somewhere!" said the physician, cracking his knuckles like thunder. "You're at a loss! Hop! Hop! Stay there, stay with it. That's the place to be—at a loss. It's the fertile void from which come all beautiful things. At a loss, up in the air, high and dry. Hop! Hop!"

"What's that you say? Hop! Hop!" asked Horatio timidly. "What's that mean, if you don't mind?"

"Don't be afraid, boy, speak up!" boomed Antonicelli. "Hop! Hop! Yes, I do tend to say that. It means—it means, *diese arme Leut*." And he made a Podsnappian gesture that waved them out of existence. "You know the ending of *Wozzek?* Of course! *hopp! hopp! Diese arme Leut*. No use of trying to do anything for *them*. Hop! Hop! I've Americanized it a bit."

"Ja," said Horatio sadly in German, *"hopp! hopp!"* He was profoundly disturbed. In these few minutes the physician had moved into the area of his troubles.

2.

"I am given to understand that you are for the General."

"Certainly I'm for the General!" said Horace briskly, and his countenance leaped back to its vacuous leer, the beautiful consolation of being with the majority, or, as Carlyle put it, There is no ease in Zion like the feeling of being appropriately dressed. "Aren't you for the General?" he asked, surprised. "What the devil am I here for, anyway?" he cried, suddenly wildly suspicious, as if this question had occurred to him for the first time. "You think I'm crazy, don't you?"

"Yes, I do," said Antonicelli.

"Ha!" said Horace. "Ha!" And he exploded in a volley of laughter. "You think I'm crazy because I'm for the General. Now let me tell *you* some news! On election day, fifty million Americans are going to vote the same way I do, and if I'm crazy, we're *all* crazy. And *you're* going to be sitting with your ass out on a limb. The General is the candidate of national unity. What do you think o' that?"

"Just leave my ass out of it," said Antonicelli dryly. "Shall I tell *you* some news, buddy? My considered opinion as a psychologist of experience?"

"Shoot. And it better be good."

"I don't know about fifty million Americans, but *you're* for the General just out of spite. You'd like him to lose. You hate him.

You hate him because he's in the majority and they're too strong for you. So you support him as a last desperate resort to beat him, to put him on the loser's side. What do you think o' *that?*"

"*How* is that again?" said Horace puzzled. "I support him—in order to beat him? How in hell do you figure that?"

"Simple. Here. Let me play you back the confession of a recent patient of mine. (It's very unethical of me to do this, I assure you.) This man came into my office and he was a supporter of the General, just like you. I won't go into what his trouble was, what brought him here, but along the way it soon became obvious that he was suffering an amnesia. We worked on that. After a few sessions, suddenly he recalled the following episode; I give it to you in his own words."

Antonicelli switched on the record——

Chapter 14 ▪ A CASE OF SPITE WORK

Antonicelli switched on the record and a sad cultured voice spoke out:

"Now I remember it vividly.

"We are sitting in front of the fire at Mike's house in Amagansett after a swim, Parker, Lionel, Diana, Dick and Gloria Mayes. We have had a few drinks and are having a few more. Off to the left is the beach, I can hear the noisy surf. The fire is bright and hypnotic. The surf is pounding down and ebbing away. The Federalists have just chosen the General as their candidate. Naturally we are down in the mouth. I am pouring myself another drink. Not that the candidate of the other party will be much superior; they have not yet held their convention. But after all! This General? All of us had been secretly hoping that the Americans had more sense.

"Midsummer, but there is a chill. It is dangerously likely that the General will be elected. It grips me by the throat. The fire is standing upside down in the fireplace. We must mobilize ourselves! We must not paralyze ourselves! I am trying to clench my fists with resolution. They won't clench.

"Humorously we have been discussing the possibility of setting going some disastrous scandal to finish him. (Back to Grover Cleveland.) What rumor? His parents? A secret vice? Maybe we can prove he is a Jew. No, that was already tried and has failed, and at this stage it's a boomerang, for the Jews will hopefully vote for their honorary member. We are thinking of a sexual affair between the General and Admiral Paxton. It won't wash; there's that picture of the two of them shaking hands, and it won't wash.

" 'This boyish smile!' Lionel is saying. 'Why doesn't he find himself a playground and go there?'

" 'Ah, but fancy it for four long years!' says Mike. Makes me shudder—I can remember looking at FPR's wolfish grin for twelve! The years of my early manhood.

"The tide is ebbing. All along the east coast. We are floundering. Far off on the Pacific it is the season of the grunion. Our sparkling wit is now reduced to inventing a liaison with Ilse Koch, the one who used to make the human parchment into lampshades. Botch work! Let's face it.

"Fact is, there is nothing! Nothing! But nothing! He is without qualities of any kind, a perfect fourflusher. What's the matter with the Americans anyway? The fire is too bright. I am pouring myself another drink—*the bottle is empty.*

"There is a sudden gleam of hope, a will o' the wisp! They beat Tom Davey! But Tom Davey had Tom Davey's face. The General does not look impossible, only a bald man with a boyish grin, even without his hat. He's not revolting, just reduces you to despair, and that's not enough.

"Suddenly, to my surprise, it is I who am speaking. I feel the words slowly coming out of mouth. My tone is earnest, thoughtful. Mike has opened another bottle. I am gazing into the fire and following the sparks as they float upward, upward, and it is my voice that is saying, *'There is one way to beat him.'*

"The others have fallen silent. We can hear the roaring of the waves.

" 'If *we*—' it is my voice that is speaking—'if a hundred people like us—and there are a couple of hundred—if *we* can come out in support of the General, that will cook his goose!'

" 'Guilt by association!' says Parker merrily. He doesn't take it seriously.

" 'He can't disown us either,' says Lionel, 'because we never belonged to the CP.' He doesn't take me seriously either.

"Nobody takes me seriously.

"I'm becoming angry. 'Stop it!' I'm saying. 'I'm serious. Don't make a joke out of it but listen to me. I don't mean if we *pretend* to support him, that wouldn't have any effect at all; it would be treated as a joke. I mean if we *really* support him, heart and soul, support him and *mean* it. Invent him as our symbol! (The one to do it is Agee, he can get right in tune.) Write him up in *Commentary,* in *The Partisan Review,* in *The New Leader!* If we can believe it: that the General is our candidate! His public will melt away. They will die off like flies in November.'

"I can hardly believe now how earnestly I am speaking. It seems so strange. Mike is becoming alarmed. He comes over to me with the bottle. He is bending over and asking me, 'Are you feeling well? Are you maybe a little demented?'

" 'That's just the question!' I am crying triumphantly. *'Is anybody here willing to sacrifice his sanity in order to beat the General by supporting him?* Is it worth it to you? How great a sacrifice is it worth? Are *you* willing? . . . Are *you* willing? . . .' I am going around the room. 'No, I guess it's not worth it. Nobody is willing.'

My tone has grown lighter again, and soon we are back to our jokes. . . . But the sparks . . . the sparks . . . the sparks . . ."

The voice trailed off. It began again more somberly, obviously after an interval of sobbing that Antonicelli had switched off to economize on the tape:

"I must explain—you will not believe it otherwise—how we, we few whose kiss of death could finish off the smiling General, have an extraordinary power to spread around us a zone of silent uninterest in whatever interests us. It's not that we are concerned with what is esoteric or special, for like everybody else we are concerned with happiness, success, intelligent reform, power, money, etc. But we seem to take these things by an odd handle. We, of course, do not consider it odd, but direct and sensible; we think that the other ways are wrongheaded.

"We mention what we think. Nobody answers.

"The effect of it is that the rest of the people get little use from us, which may or may not be a loss to them; but we get little use of the rest of the people, which is certainly an enormous loss for us.

"I give you an example. I am a writer. Now suppose a periodical finds itself seduced into publishing an essay of mine. This is a sign that it will cease publication with that issue, or probably before that issue, while my piece is still in proofs. For it's not, of course, that my little essay exerts any disastrous influence, but the fact that they have considered it means that they have already entered the silent zone.

"Naturally we cope with our fate as best we can. We reproach the rest of the world for boobies. We reproach ourselves for getting our just deserts. But this is all foolishness. We are what we are and we cannot behave otherwise. And after it has continued for twenty, twenty-five years—really, it's no joke—some of us rest simply in the fact itself, without evaluating it at all. What *they* get excited about and talk about is to us quite boring; what we have to say is of no interest to them; and that's just how it is.

"How does one *rest* in this simple fact? I am overcome with weariness, doubt and, to speak frankly, dismay."

There was another choked sob. It was the end of the record.

"There you have it," said Antonicelli, "spite work! The very next morning like that fellow in Prague who woke up and found he was transformed into a monstrous bug, this fellow had awakened and found he was for the General. Hop! Hop!"

Chapter 15 ▪ A SYLLABUS OF PSYCHOTHERAPY

1.

"Please be aware of your breathing," said Antonicelli.

Horatio was troubled and saddened by what he had been hearing, and his breathing was coming a little unevenly and shallowly. Otherwise he was breathing nicely from his diaphragm like a great sad dog; he was sad but not at all anxious; his sickness was all in his head and in the world. "I'm breathing a little shallowly, and it's uneven," said Horatio. "There's a roughness in the bronchi and my heart is swollen. I'm sad." He sighed.

"Never mind the details. You're breathing, aren't you? That's what I want you to notice."

"Yes, I'm breathing. What about my breathing?"

"Ha, questions! Please notice your voice. Can you hear your voice?"

"What about my voice? It's sharp." His voice indeed had an edge of asperity.

"You're speaking, aren't you?"

"Yes, I'm speaking, but——"

"No buts. No buts and no ifs. That's just it—have you been listening to the sound of your voice?"

"Yes."

"There you go again. You've been listening. Breathing—questions—speaking—listening. Probably listening at doors. Now notice: you're sitting there. You're looking at me—don't try to deny it; you're using your eyes. Stand up!"

Horatio stood.

Antonicelli struck his forehead as if in despair. "There you go again! Standing! Look at you! On your feet. Your legs are holding you up." He looked under the table. "Just as I feared—your feet are firmly planted on the ground."

Horatio sat down and closed his eyes.

"Now what are you doing?"

"Just collecting my wits."

"Collecting your *wits!* what *next?*" roared the doctor. "Next you'll be telling me that you have *thought* of something! And next you'll be *feeling* something—no, you've already done that. You yourself admitted that you were sad. Don't deny it. And where will you end up? I'll tell you. You'll end up by gathering some meaning or other, and that before very long."

"Yes, I have been thinking——" confessed Horatio.

"I knew it. My poor boy! You don't mind if I call you a boy, do you? It's a manner of speaking. Well, let's sum up; we might as well take it at its worst. There you sit *breathing all the time,* speaking on the outbreath, using your ears and eyes, sitting on your buttocks and even thinking of something now and then. Is it in a condition like that that you are going to make an adjustment to the social reality and expect to be a serious reader of the *Herald Tribune?* . . . Well, young man, what do you intend to do about it?"

"Is it—bad?"

"Bad? He asks if it's bad? From these things come the worst diseases!"

"Oh . . . I see what you mean——"

"Horatio?" said Antonicelli warningly. "Seeing? Meaning?"

Horatio fell silent.

2.

Antonicelli wrung his hands and sparkled away like a faulty connection. "The young man asks me if his functioning is bad. It can be fatal. There isn't a *single* maladjustment—I speak as a man of some experience—I have yet to come on a single social maladjustment that is not directly due to just such functions as you sit there exercising minute by minute in my office, and day by day outside of it. Don't deny it. Breathing, speaking, no doubt eating and excretion, imagination, locomotion, desire, feeling, sex—you do engage in sex, don't deny it. What *not?* But especially the breathing, that's always the beginning. Always I find it has something to do with the breathing. It's a specialty of mine. If we could put a stop to the breathing, it might be possible to patch up the rest.

"Let me dwell on this. What's the usual situation? Something goes wrong. The patient comes to a physician. The physician refuses, he simply refuses, to see the whole situation. He tries to iron out this little kink, to straighten that quirk. A man has an ulcer and your physician pokes around with his diet; he has attacks of anxiety and palpitations and your physician tries to get him to take a decent breath of air. Et cetera, et cetera, et cetera. Empirics! Except that I happen to know something about the law—I have a little experience in that line too, ha, ha—I'd call it criminal malpractice."

"What do *you* do, Antonicelli?"

"There you go again, asking a question. This indicates curiosity, and even the folk wisdom knows the story on *that*. Curiosity killed a cat."

"What am I supposed to do?"

"You're supposed to sit there in a stupor while I blab; *anybody* knows *that*. . . . Look, Horatio, I am alarmed for you. It's going to be very hard for you to make an adjustment—I'll be frank with you. You realize you are a person of some concern to me; I am grateful to you. You saved me from the asphyxiation the time you stood there in court streaming round blue and orange with orgasms. I'll never forget it. So now I take you into my deepest confidence. You ask, what do *I* do? If thy right eye offends thee, pluck it out. That is the wisdom of the east. In these matters there is no help unless you get down to the root. You used to know that, try to recall it now. When a man can't stomach it any more, nothing will help but to stop eating. If he is sick at heart, stop the heart. And to speak generally, since with every function you exercise, you also inhale and exhale the environment around you, I would strongly urge you to practice inhibiting breathing.

"Let me pass on to you," he continued in a quieter voice, "the insight I got from old Professor Carlsen in Chicago. We students used to pester him asking about the deteriorating effects of tobacco, alcohol, and that shit. 'Boys,' he would say, 'don't worry about it. What makes a man die? It's joost living. It's joost living that wears the organism out.' "

"But——" said Horatio.

3.

"Counterwill!" thundered Antonicelli. "What do you think you're doing with your but?"

"I——" began Horatio.

"That proves it! Just as I thought. Now he says 'I.' I'll tell you exactly what you're doing. You're setting up your will against mine. So. You want to engage in a conflict, do you? A competition? Very well. (Remember you're paying for it.) Hop! Hop! Butt is what a goat does when it runs into something. You butt into somebody else's business. We also say a ham butt, a pig's ass. Well, don't think I'm going to let you thrust your ass into my face. Just notice what you're doing with your but. I confront you with my considered opinion, my advice to inhibit your living; and *you* promptly set up your counterwill—you don't like it. Now I'm not saying this is good and I'm not saying it's bad; here we don't indulge in moral judgments. But let's call a spade a spade. I can sniff a counterwill from Perry Street to the Menninger Clinic."

"But I——" began Horace.

Antonicelli threw up his hands.

4.

"I see I have been asking something too hard for you," Antonicelli began again, "something impossible for you to do. If I persist, I'll make even the possible impossible—it's a failing of mine. So let's withdraw a little and go step by step. Let's work simply on the little physical tricks till you get the idea. You'll get it, don't worry, have confidence. Just follow me, imitate me. Perhaps you're perplexed? Good, imitate me: let's express perplexity. Watch me. Raised eyebrows, forehead horizontally furrowed—and breathe! Don't stop breathing—when you're intensely perplexed, you might contract your scalp till your hairs stood up as if in fright."

Horatio was obediently making a face of intense perplexity.

"No! no!" cried Antonicelli. "I said look at me, follow me."

His own face was a dead-pan mask. "See? Do it like this: you're intensely perplexed——" His face was a dead-pan mask and he was holding his breath.

Horatio began to be confused.

"O.K., perplexity is also too hard for you. So let's try worry. Deep vertical frown, quick irregular breath—think that you're going to *fail* in the exercise; you're going to lose the erection after all the trouble in getting her into bed. No! No! Watch *me!* Follow *me!*"

His face was a dead pan; he was breathing quite at his ease.

"My God, man," he cried, "can't you even worry? Don't you feel *anything?* Are you completely dead?"

Horatio became annoyed. No one likes to be told that he's dead, even if it's a method of therapy.

"O.K., have it your way," said the doctor. "We'll try anger instead. Grind your teeth, jut your jaw on the outbreath—narrow flashing eyes—tightening fingers—but this time, please, really watch me and follow me."

Antonicelli's face was calm as calm and he began nonchalantly to clip his fingernails.

The clippings bounded off in odd directions, as they do.

As each one flew off, Antonicelli turned to watch it go, and he gave a little beck of his head when it landed.

He clipped another. It bounded away.

Naturally Horatio followed them too.

When there were no more, Antonicelli continued to follow them from side to side with a little beck of his head as each non-one didn't land. With a blank face, Horatio also followed them, and each time gave a little startled beck of his head.

"Good! At last!" said Antonicelli with deep satisfaction. "Now we're getting closer to the social reality. That's rage, in the world of the *Herald Tribune.* Shall we try love?"

But there was no need. For as soon as he found himself able to be aware of, to control, his behavior in the social reality, Horatio got the idea, and at once a warm tide of life flowed in his breast and he felt a terrible keen pang of air in his nostrils between his eyes. It would not require much for him to burst out bawling for his gone brother Lothar. He felt awful.

5.

Scenting the physicianly victory, Antonicelli flared his nostrils and was about to ask for a dream.

But it would have been a mistake at this point to press the patient further and seek to release the fullness of his misery. One has to learn to live with one's misery. And he himself didn't know, not he, Antonicelli, how to cope with the fact that we do not live in a golden age.

To let Horatio weep now might only awaken in him an intolerable unease, and he might have retreated as far as the world of the *Congressional Record.*

But it was hard for Antonicelli to err, since he had prayed to Aesculapius. Slowly the door of the closet was nudged open, and appeared the garnet eyes and the forked tongue of the serpent, warning him to end the session. The serpent slithered across the floor to the desk and reared his head up on the desk and looked at Horatio and Antonicelli, from one to the other, darting his tongue.

"Hello, hello," said Antonicelli; "this is Epidaurus my familiar," he said to Horace. "You see, I am an Asclepiad. . . . I am only an Asclepiad . . . Yet Aesculapius too," he said in a firmer voice and with dignity, "sailed on the Argo, with those friends. He was not just a professional."

Horatio took from his pocket the lump of sugar that he carried in case he should meet up with a horse. He offered it to the serpent, who ate it out of complaisance, though it was not his diet at all. Not at all.

"That's all for today, young feller," said Antonicelli. "Epidaurus tells me to break off. I think we're getting along famously. (By the way, what the devil does that expression mean?) Just practice by yourself (*a*) being at a loss, and (*b*) getting the feel and behavior of the social reality. When you have mastered these two, you'll have what you need for a perfect adjustment. . . . Just one more thing. Before you go home I'd like you to look in on Minetta Tyler, she's right across the hall in 4F. She and I are in collaboration, you know, but I'll let her explain how that works."

He stood up. "Good-by, Horatio Alger," he said, and touched his shoulder and gave him a warm smile. "Cheer up. Hop! Hop!"

"Thank you, Antonicelli," said Horace.

Chapter 16 ▪ PSYCHOSYNTHESIS

1.

Minetta had been expecting Horace and she was delighted to see him. But she was distressed to see him haggard and dismayed, coming from Antonicelli's. All of his friends, not only I, loved Horatio right down to the marrow of our bones, and it caused us horrible pain, something like rheumatism, to see him not well off, for he was, in a way, our exemplary hope.

"It's been so long!" she cried, throwing her arms about him. She was a little plumper than last we saw her and, if possible, still more determined and cheerful.

He held her away from him to look at her and he cheered up at once. "Years! It *is* good to see you, Minetta," he said. "I'm sorry I'm such a mess."

"Come now, what's the trouble? Tell Minetta all about it." She sat him down in an armchair and sat across from him, smoothing out her skirt, and poured a couple of shots of rye between them. "I suppose Celli explained what I'm supposed to do for you."

"Celli? Celli is good. No, he said that you'd explain that."

"There's very little to explain. We work together. It's very simple. He does the—how shall I say?—analytic part; he takes you apart; and I put the pieces together again. See? I have a more motherly disposition. Naturally. He bring out the resistance, recovers the memories, mobilizes the rigid muscles, and all that noise. You've had some of that?"

"Yes, just now."

"Well, all that gives you more available energy. At least that's the idea. But we've agreed, Celli and I, that there's no use to it unless step by step there's somewhere to go from there; to put the new energy to work in the world, doing things, taking your chances. Otherwise, you—I won't go into it, but you've known psychoanalyzed people, haven't you? Yeah, punchy. You know what I mean. Well, I do the vocational part. And to make a long story short I run a combination cat house and employment agency. See?"

"I think I have a glimmering; but give me an example."

2.

"Take the cat house. It's a small thing but well equipped. I've taken over Madame Vanetska's old barn, remember?

"We have, oh, *you* know, everything. Matrons like featherbeds; sheep; sharpened ice skates—the usual inventory. This isn't your kind of problem so I can discuss it with you freely; Horatio always knew what to do with a piece. Some lad comes in who can work up a little excitement if he does so-and-so or such-and-such, or if somebody does it for him. Good, we set him at it. This is what he *can* do, age four and a half. If we create the proper permissive environment for *that,* soon he goes on to what he *can't* do, age six. In a few weeks he has mastered the curriculum. We have a wonderful staff, a swell bunch. If you ever want a job——"

"Oh, now you're switching over to the employment bureau! How does that work? I think I understand the other."

"The employment agency is the same thing. People need jobs that will bring them out and make them confront their problems. I have connections and I get them the jobs. See? Another shot?"

"Yes. No, I don't see. You can't go right out and find jobs like that. There's a whole economy going on."

"Economy! It's much simpler than you think. I can discuss it with you because this isn't your kind of problem either; Horatio Alger always knew how to make a living. But take, for instance, here's a particular case this morning. This fellow becomes anxious when he's in a tight squeeze. The problem is to get him to risk being hemmed in and break through. I have connections with the hackmen; I get him a job driving a taxi. . . . Taxis are also good for mean dikes who like to run sailors against the wall. And there are fatherly types who like to have your life in their hands—that's taxis too. I couldn't really manage without taxis. Besides, taxis are grand for Jews; when I send a Jew out to mix with the Jewish cabbies, he loses his paranoia about Hitler. Those fellows can take care of themselves. But I'm boring you, running on this way."

"No, no, I'm intensely interested," said Horatio.

3.

"It's not always so simple," admitted Minetta. "I'm just putting it in this breezy way because you need cheering up. You know the world we live in as well as I do, and what the chances are of finding the right job. I have a whole slew o' them takes me weeks and months to place. Meantime, they're on strike——"

"Ah! You mean those pickets! Antonicelli said they were your pickets. Tell me about *them.*"

"The ones downstairs? Yeah, they're mine. But I have them out all over the city, and naturally they're on strike against me too. They walk up and down with blank sandwich boards. George Dennison thought it up when he had the writer's block."

"What's it mean to go with a blank sandwich board?"

"It means *they* don't know what's wrong with themselves—if they knew they wouldn't be crazy but would have some so-called real trouble; and certainly *I* don't know what's wrong with 'em, or I'd know how to put them to use. Yet they *are* on strike, that's for sure. So they walk up and down with blank sandwich boards and shout 'On Strike!' Would *you* know what to write on some o' those boards?"

Horatio hung his head.

"They're my pets," said Minetta gently. "They're the ones I dote on. They're not so crazy."

"Intelligentsia?" hazarded Horace.

She pursed her lips. "Nooo, not if you mean hipsters. My kids don't think they know the score about everything. Or—let me put it this way. There are three kinds of intellectuals. There're the inhibited coal heavers and farmers, just afraid to move their shoulders. And then there're the inhibited con-men and passers of bad checks, but afraid of the cops, like the editors of several magazines I could mention. And then there are these. These are really on strike."

4.

"And what about me?" asked Horace thickly. For with these pickets, they had again moved into a sensitive area, and he was distressed.

Her nostrils flared. (She and Antonicelli were both keen huntsmen and crack shots.) "Yes, finally," she said. "What about you? . . . Will you bow your head for a moment, Horatio, while I pray my prayer?"

They bowed their heads. Unlike Antonicelli, she prayed in company.

"Divine Guidance," she prayed, "guide *us.*

"Short and sweet," she said, breaking the silence. "You know, I ought to have at my fingertips just what to do with Horatio—I've known you long enough. Ever since you were so high. Let me think——" She picked up the scene. "You were ten years old and I was the relief investigator; at least I had you down for ten—there weren't any records. I came and you were lying asleep under a grand piano. Least I thought you were asleep, but suddenly you began to jerk off and frightened me out of my wits."

She giggled. This at once unblocked her and she had an idea.

5.

"Perfect! Perfect! Perfect! Perfect!" She snapped her fingers and jumped to her feet and clapped her hands. "Horace! You have kids?"

"Two."

"Do they go to school?"

"Why, yes. I just entered my girl in the kindergarten last week. It was one of the very first things——" He stopped. He had meant to say "It was one of the very first things I did after I suddenly went crazy," but of course he did not know that he meant to say this, and instead he became confused and blushed.

"I follow you," said Minetta. "Oh, great!" she cried. She could hardly contain her pleasure at her bright idea and she waltzed lightly around, humming: "Perfect perfect perfect perfect perfect perfect *perfect!*" This time it was seven times.

"Why is it seven times over perfect?" asked Horace.

"Kindergarten! Don't you see? You must join the Parent Teachers Association at once."

"Why, in fact, I was thinking of doing that. I thought I ought to."

"There. You see the beauty of it? You think you ought to and I say you must. And kindergarten, just beginning–that's the best of all."

"What's so good about that?"

"Because they'll have you for nine years! They can't kick you out of the PTA. Your child *has* to go to school. It's compulsory education. And you're a member of the PTA *ex officio,* if you pay your dues, just by being a parent. If she's just beginning, it'll be nine lovely years they'll have to put up with you, and–they–can't–kick–you–out. What sport! You can write a book!"

"*Nine* years!" His face fell. "Minetta, must I?" He began to squirm. The unconscious can play tricks on you when you're crazy, but sometimes it gets to be past a joke.

"Look, Horace. You're a reader of the *Herald Tribune.* I've heard all about it. Obviously the thing for you to do is to get *into* that world. Stop being a hermit; stop sitting on the sidelines. Get out and work where something practical can be accomplished. The place for you is the PTA–with your background of experience. I just knew I'd hit on it! With divine guidance. Stop believing in what makes you happy to believe, and see if you can get other people to believe in what makes you happy to believe, the way——"

She was about to say, "The way your brother Lothar tries to," but providentially she censored it; she never initiated personal and family remarks. She did not know that Lothair was dead, and of course it was not Horatio who would tell her so, since he did not admit it to himself. And this too was lucky, for she had a very tender heart, and if she knew Lothair was dead, she would have broken down and wept.

"You were saying?" said Horatio.

"The Way. What you believe in, the Way. Let's not discuss it further. It's decided. Let me tell you why: from what I and Antonicelli can see, you are on the verge of a breakthrough of rage and grief; all you need is a real situation. Therefore, the PTA. I defy anyone to go to two-three meetings of the PTA and not have a breakthrough of rage and grief. So it *is* decided, isn't it?"

"If you say so," said Horatio woebegone. "But nine years it won't be."

6.

The pickets, as Horatio came out, were gathered in the middle of the street engaged in a heated discussion, but earnest rather than disputatious, with a gentleman wearing a conventional hat and tie.

"Are you picketing *this* side o' the street or *that* side o' the street?" he was asking. "I don't want to cross a picket line. Never do. Rights of Labor. But you have nothing written on your signs, and how is a man supposed to know what he is supposed to do?" He was quite disturbed. (He was a cultural-anthroplogist of the *Herald Tribune*.)

"We're on strike," explained one of the young ladies simply.

"Are you picketing Perry Street? Should I boycott Perry Street?"

The question puzzled them.

"*Are* we on strike against Perry Street?"

"Of course we're on strike against Perry Street! Why not Perry Street?"

"Yes, but not especially Perry Street."

"Since when is Perry Street to be an exception?"

And so forth.

"What *are* you on strike against? Damn it."

"I don't know."

"What *kind* of an answer is that? You don't know! *Damn* it."

"I tell you I don't know. I don't know—can't you understand

English. I'm on strike, and you ask me against what, and I don't know, so I tell you I don't know. Is that clear? I don't know."

"You don't know?"

"Listen, buddy," said another fellow who carried a rather dirty blank sign. "I been carryin' this here sign for six months. I got trouble. Trouble with you is you want we should solve your problems for you. 'What are *you* supposed to do? Which side o' the street are *you* supposed to walk on?' Who in hell are you? That's all you're interested in, yourself. How in hell should *we* know what you oughta do? Do *you* know?"

"Damn it," said the anthropologist.

"There you are. You don't know and we don't know, so nobody knows. You want a sign?"

"I'm not on strike," exclaimed the man indignantly.

"Oh, let him alone," said the simple young girl. "Who wants to talk to this naïve jerk?"

"*Damn* it."

"All he can say is Damn it." She walked off shouting, "On Strike!"

They took up their line of march down the middle of the street. At the corner they turned, shouting, "On Strike!" and came back up the middle of the street.

The anthropologist took a few steps across the street and made as if to enter one of the buildings. Suddenly he recoiled and crossed over toward the other side. He stopped short in the middle and took off his hat and mopped his brow.

Chapter 17 ▪ OMPHALE'S SPINNING WHEEL

Omphale had been informed of the great exploits of Hercules and wished to see so illustrious a hero. Her wish was soon gratified. Hercules fell into a malady and was told by the oracle at Delphi that he would not be restored to health unless he allowed himself to be sold as a slave for a space of three years. In obedience to the oracle, he was conducted by Mercury to Lydia, and there sold to Omphale. During the period of his slavery with this queen, he assumed female attire, sat by her side spinning with her women, and from time to time received chastisement from the hands of Omphale who, arrayed in his lion-skin and armed with his club, playfully struck him with her sandal for his awkward way of holding the distaff.

—ANTHON

1.

The ladies of the Parent Teachers Association were thrilled to have Horatio as their new member; for apart from Mr. Baker, who was with them only to cadge votes when he ran for the Assembly, and from Mr. Patterson, who was there to second his wife's motions and in a certain sense was not a man at all, Horatio was the only man in the organization, and was without his wife. (Rosalind was bewildered by the recent events but not so much so as to join the PTA.) Mr. Baker was not handsome; Horatio had a beauty of ordinary virility that made one turn in the street and look, awestruck. Besides, his wife did not understand him—she was not interested in current events.

The very first meeting he attended, they put him to work as a man: he carried up the bales of the *Newsletter* from the basement, he closed the windows with the heavy window pole; and it was he who—happy in a haze of being accepted and needed—carried in the bowl of fruit juice and ice from the kitchen. This last had been the function of Mr. Patterson, and from that moment he regarded Horatio with a settled dislike.

2.

Horatio visited the school. It was the first time he had been in such a building in twenty-six years, since the day he strayed in to avoid the truant officer, became lost in a maze and fled in panic fright. This building was modern and smelled less. Yet still the prisoners were chained to their desks, the angry voices thundered from the mountains, and they were beginning to conscript them into the army. In a very few minutes the scene had Horatio by the throat. And when, at ten to eleven, there rang, with an earsplitting yet sullen clang, the bell of doom that declared that still another hour of springtime life had been sealed in perdition, Horatio became panicky.

"Man," he said to himself, "take hold of yourself! Calm down. *You* are not in jeopardy; they can't hold you here; you can walk out whenever you want. You must adopt a mature attitude and objectively observe what goes on, since that's why you came. That screaming object approaching, round as a kiosk, is not going to burst into flames; it's only Miss Tierney, the secretary of the PTA, who was so sweet to you the other night. . . . What's wrong with *you,* young feller?" This was addressed to a little boy in the corridor who had begun to cry.

"I *did* try," he said, "but I couldn' open de door." Sure enough, he had pissed in his pants and there was a pool appearing around his right sandal.

"Well, step out of it," said Horatio.

He tried the door marked Boys and the knob was indeed hard to turn; it caught.

"Mister," said a little Puerto Rican girl, "thank you. Will you please open the door to Girls? Thank you, please."

That knob was hard to turn too.

The disgraced little boy was walking down the corridor arranging his pants. But another little boy was trying the doorknob and couldn't make it. "Quick, mister," he said, "open de door."

Horatio turned the knob for him and walked hastily away, before it became his official duty to stand there and open those doors.

He knocked at the superintendent's and asked him to fix the locks on the toilet doors. "Why don't you remove them altogether?" he suggested. "They generally don't have locks in a modern building like this."

Pleased with the sentiment of being useful and having acted with dispatch, he stepped out into the courtyard.

Once again he was confronted with the terrible vision. As of old, the victims were tramping in a circle and lugubriously wailing—

Oafy bees
barley boes,

while a teacher with fierce pedaling clanged a dead march on an untuned piano. His hair stood on end.

"Man! Man!" he cautioned himself. "Be mature about this. It's only a dancing game, not a real sacrifice, and the words of it are

> Oats peas beans and barley grows
> oats peas beans and barley grows,
> nor you nor I nor anyone knows
> how oats peas beans and barley grows.

A beautiful sentence, and a true sentence! To be sure, they don't understand the words, but they could learn to understand them, if one took the trouble to explain them. It's a round dance. And what else would one dance in the season except this social and reassuring dance hand in hand, repeating that mysterious sentence? There isn't much leap to the dancing, but they could leap beautifully if one encouraged leaping. The piano is out of tune, but it could be tuned, though to be sure it hasn't been tuned in twenty-six years. . . .

" 'Nor you nor I not anyone knows how oats peas beans and barley grows——' " he hummed, watching them, and suddenly his eyes became moist. They were idle tears—he knew not what they meant.

3.

The night of the meeting of the PTA, two pickets with blank sandwich boards were prowling on the sidewalk outside. It struck Horatio as he passed them that he had always been seeing these pickets, but had never noticed them. They were everywhere in the city, on strike, on strike. They didn't know.

He galloped upstairs to try the locks. They had not been fixed. He choked with anger—and came down to the meeting, in the Auditorium.

"Mr. Alger! I'm so glad you're here," said Madam Chairman. (They had never counted on his coming *again!*) "We needed somebody to hook up the projection machine."

This meant putting a plug in a socket. Doing it, Horatio found it hard to feel that he was indispensable and useful. "Why didn't you get Mr. Patterson to do it?" he asked, looking at her oddly.

"Now that *you're* here, he's earned a well-deserved rest." It was a tiresome joke at the PTA how they put everybody to work.

But Horatio had resolved to get on with these ladies and not offend them. This meant, of course, accommodating also to their foibles, as with anyone else. Unfortunately it meant also, at the PTA, not saying what leaped to his mind as obvious and important, especially if it happened to be essential and to make other discussion pointless. Such things were *invariably* offensive, and Horatio held his tongue. But the bother with this, of refraining from saying what was obvious, important and essential, was that it became hard to say anything at all. And then it was hard to think, and hard to pay attention. One became restive.

But Horatio paid dogged attention.

A meeting of the PTA was not very interesting. There were numerous committees and lots of Madam Chairmans, and each made a report. The first report was always from the committee on membership and made the point that it was difficult to get new members. "But that's because," it leaped to Horatio's mind, "the meetings are not interesting. They're not interesting because you never mention anything important because that might be controversial and keep away members. Instead, there's a lot of small bickering, and that's not very interesting." However, he sat on his hands and said nothing. Naturally, then, the room began to seem hot to him and he opened another window with the heavy window pole.

The Legislative Committee was the heart of the Parent Teachers Association, for the PTA was really a pressure group on City Hall and the State Capitol. Horatio was not so much innocent of this fact as physiologically incapable of understanding it. It seemed to him that they themselves, with their combined wisdom and authority, could easily do many things, and much more important things, for the children's sake; but no one was at all interested in such direct action. Instead, they devoted their best attention to choosing delegates to exert pressure on other delegates of politicians (they rarely got to the politicians themselves), to get the Legislature to direct the Executive to delegate somebody to do something that Horatio could go upstairs and do himself, better. It did not follow that nothing was ever done; it was not an infinite process; in the course of fifteen or twenty years several changes could be indirectly effected by this means, if only they were enough out of date.

What Horatio did not understand and could not understand—this was the crux of it—was the *positive* satisfaction to be got out of the indirect process whether it failed or succeeded. The satisfaction of being important, of setting such large forces in motion and mentioning big names, or of being blocked by such large forces and griping about it. With a gleam of triumph in her eye, Madam Chairman of the Legislative Committee was describing how the secretary to the Commissioner of Public Works had run her around and into the files. She told this with triumph and biting sarcasm and scored a great success. The other ladies kept exclaiming, "Oh, Louise! No! Don't, it's too much!" Only Horatio did not see the point of it; he felt that the room was unbearably hot. And if it had been explained to him that they needed to fight in "a man's world," he still wouldn't have seen why anybody would want to do *that.*

Now this legislative demand was for an appropriation to extend the iron fence. But Horatio also could not see the purpose of the iron fence, so he was bewildered still further. But he knew that it was too late to ask. It was almost always too late to ask.

The Committee on Education had no report, for there were no issues. His opportunity had whisked by; he could not even rise to his feet, and say, "Madam Chairman!" But he had wanted to talk about getting the children to understand the words to "Oats Peas Beans and Barley Grows," and about getting the piano tuned. But *why* was he not on his toes? The trouble—that kept him in his seat—was that if once he began to discuss the words of the song, he would soon be talking to them about how babies grow in the womb and how a penis mysteriously grows; and when they came to the finale of the song-game:

Waiting for a partner!

he might say something about the boys and girls playing at sex; and he knew, vaguely, that for some reason this would be offensive at the PTA. However it was, his opportunity whisked by.

It was the turn of the Committee on Health and Safety. The report was a passionate one. The city assigned a policeman to get the children across the avenue at nine and three, and Madam Chairman of their committee had spent some time in observing this policeman, (*a*) He often stood near the curb talking buddy-buddy with an electrician whose head and shoulders emerged from an open manhole; and (*b*) he was at least once distinctly *drinking*; she herself stood near him and could smell liquor on his breath, and Mrs. Jean Garrigues was a witness. Mrs. Garrigues stood up and said, "Yes, there was a *distinct* smell of liquor on his breath." This aroused intense feeling, for it was distinctly a matter of health and safety. The chairman of their committee had wasted no time but had reported him to the station house and distinctly demanded his replacement.

There was a round of applause.

"Madam Chairman," called out Horatio.

"Mr. Alger?"

He rose to his feet. "Is this the time for me to make a request about a matter of health and safety?"

"He is not on the agenda," said Mr. Patterson, rising to his feet.

"Go right ahead this time, Mr. Alger," said Madam Chairman queenly.

"But——" said Mr. Patterson.

"Sit down, Mr. Patterson," said Madam Chairman.

"Thank you, Madam Chairman. I'll be brief," said Horatio. "The locks on the toilet doors on the second floor catch. The small children can't open them. I reported it to the superintendent, but he hasn't fixed them in a week."

Patterson snorted.

"Is that *all*?" said Madam Chairman, amazed.

"Yes, that's all. Do something."

"But Mr. Alger," said Madam Chairman of the Legislative Committee, who was the parliamentarian. "I'm sorry, you don't understand, you're new. This isn't a matter to be taken up here. It should be taken up directly with the assistant principal, Miss Froberger. We can't set the machinery of the whole PTA in motion to fix a door catch, can we?"*

"*I'm* sorry," said Horatio, abashed. "Miss Froberger, will you look into it?"

"Point of order!" cried Mr. Patterson, rising to his feet.

"I'm sorry," said Miss Froberger, "I'd rather not recognize that request on the floor of the PTA. See me in my office."

"That's it," said Mr. Patterson, subsiding. "Thank you, Miss Froberger.

"I have a screw driver. Can't we take the locks off right after the meeting?" suggested Horatio.

"Heavens, no! What an idea!" laughed Miss Froberger. "We'd all be in jail."

"But I thought *you* made the decision."

"Madam Chairman," shouted Mr. Patterson, "he's disregarding my point of order. *Are* we to have order or are we *not* to have order?"

"*Mr.* Alger," said Madam Chairman, rapping a little angrily. "As Madam Chairman of the Legislative Committee pointed out, we *can't* spend the time of the PTA on door catches."

There was a round of applause, and this stung Horatio.

"It's not a question of door catches," said Horatio angrily; "it's a question of the children pissing in their pants."

"*MR.* Alger!"

There was a hush.

Mrs. Patterson rose largely to her feet. "I move that we go on with the business of the evening," she said dryly.

"Second the motion," said Mr. Patterson.

* "The Supreme Council of National Economy cannot occupy itself with door catches."—A directive of (I think) Kaganovich.

4.

After the meeting—which was not soon, the while Horatio sat morosely reflecting that he had offended them after all—there was a considerable buzz concerning Alger's behavior. Mrs. Patterson was eager for her husband to say something to him in private, but Mr. Patterson was not at all eager to risk getting a punch in the nose. It was left for the Chairman of the Legislative Committee to speak up in his favor, saying, "He certainly *is* going to be a sparkplug!" She had a plan of her own about pitting him against Nick Cernovic, the leader of the Fifth Ward, who frightened her a little.

Horatio found himself surrounded by a clique of dowdy ladies who always sat off by themselves in the rear. They had not the slightest idea what he was about, but they saw at once that he was in opposition. They were themselves spies of the local Jesuit, sent in to protest as vigorously as they could against any insidious infiltration of progressive ideas into the school system. They crowded around Horatio and wanted him to be their spokesman, since he wasn't afraid to speak up.

So, having enjoyed a spasm of grief and anger, Horace now had also the opportunity of being at a loss.

5.

It was midnight.

The pickets had ceased marching. There was a small bright full moon, casting sharp shadows.

Suddenly, in the shadow of such of the iron fence as there was, Horatio saw the two pickets. One of them had taken off his sandwich boards and leaned them against the fence, and he was squatting in front of the other who was standing in his blank sign. But the striped shadow of the fence fell across the sign. Horatio drew near. The squatting man had a paintbrush.

He was painting a sign on the blank board! This message or picture he was painting in pure water. He kept dipping his brush into a glass of water in which was reflected the round moon.

It was hard to tell whether, with the water, he was painting something on or carefully washing the sign off.

"What are you doing?" asked Horace. "I'm not intruding? Are you painting it or washing it off?"

"Yang Yin," explained the other friendly. "Depends how you look at it. *If* you consider the blank as the foreground, then it takes up the whole foreground. No background and the foreground

fence was. He picked up a rock and flung it at the window. The window broke. "Lot of bullshit!" he muttered. "That fence don't keep no rocks out. . . . *I* don't know anything about delinquent boys playing hooky," he muttered.

7.

He returned to see the principal on the matter of educational policy: why one door was marked BOYS and one door was marked GIRLS. His idea was that in the one point where co-education was essential and made sense, in the carnal knowledge of one another, it was being discouraged.

Mr. Graveyard, the principal, had been warned about this meddling parent; and when Horatio was ushered in, he had one hand on the revolver in his desk drawer and the other lightly touching the fire alarm.

There was no need. As soon as he saw Mr. Graveyard at his desk, Horatio recoiled with a small cry.

—It was the Academic King, falsely youthful, of the race of Herod. The ghoulish patron of embalmers and all those who paint, deck and perfume that which is dead and make it seem alive and in the prime of life.

There is a story about the Academic King. He was afraid of aging and dying, and he said, "Youth! Youth! Let me surround myself with youth. In my court will never be seen anything but youth. Nothing will ever change, and I shall remain young." His wishes were carried out. His court was peopled with children, and as soon as any of the children seemed to be growing, they were taken away and destroyed and replaced with other identical children, for all children are very much alike. Nothing ever seemed to change (from the Monday after Labor Day of one year to the Monday after Labor Day of the next.)

But of course he himself had completely changed and was long since dead. He was completely out of touch with the children, and more and more cruel to them, whereas if he had gone on and gracefully aged, and let the children be, he would have understood them very well and would have had much in common with them. As it was, he imagined that he was young in spirit, while he was holding them with a dead grip, and he also smelled.

—Seeing him sitting there, Horatio fell back and tried to escape. But the cursed doorknob caught and he was trapped.

With a cry of horror he tore open the door and fled from the building in panic fright.

8.

But outside there was sunshine and there was a rout of children let out of school and soon recovering, with their limbs and eyes, the space and day. And seeing them, Horatio had the following hallucination:

He saw, among the children—but she was transparent and motionless, and they fled freely through her as if she were not there—his sister Laura dead, at the moment when about her had burst into bloom the artificial flowers; as she hanged there in the dead of spring, each petal of art stretching and trembling open to the most space.

She was a Life-in-Death, as that Academic King who withered with his breath the flowers that were real, was a Death-in-Life.

But Laura said to him, as the children streamed freely through her as if she were not there, "Horace! *We* make the lost come alive, we *do!* It is not nothing; maybe it is even better than something. But what have we to do with these *live* children, or they with us?"

And indeed, the children went noisily past in their rout and vanished around the corner, and the vision faded, while he stood there agape.

9.

So he came to a third meeting of the Parent Teachers Association.

He bounded upstairs to try the locks; they were still there and still hard to open; but he just went to see. He had no intention of talking any further about those doorknobs; he was not obsessed by doorknobs.

The big devil had driven out the lesser devils.

At the meeting in the Auditorium, he held his peace until the Committee on Health and Safety again reported on the policeman. There was a new policeman on the corner, and he quite distinctly was not drunk. But he did limp and he looked untidy, it was insulting. Why did they have to choose *him?* Indeed, subjected to the intensive scrutiny at random of fifty pairs of vindictive eyes, he was a very threadbare spectacle. (The case was that it *was* a dangerous crossing, where too many cars came by too fast in too many directions, but this could be remedied only by changing the plan of the city. Many policemen lose their arms and legs at such crossings; you can meet them on buses and exchange notes.)

Horatio got up and said, "Madam Chairman."

"You aren't going to bring up the doorknobs again!" she said. "It's out of order."

"No, I—"

"We looked into the doorknobs. No school property can be removed without going through City Hall and—you know how it is—that will take five to ten years."

"Thank you," said Horatio. "I should like to say something about the policeman. Is that out of order at this point?"

"Oh? No, that's not out of order."

"I object," said Mr. Patterson, "he's wasting our time."

"Overruled," said Madam Chairman. "He didn't say anything yet, so he's not wasting our time yet."

"Patterson, how would you like to get a punch in the nose? *After* the meeting," said Horatio dryly. "Ladies! When I listen to you ladies, discussing the dangers of the crossing, when I listen to the tones of your voices, I get a *distinct* impression that you are anxious about the danger because you really want to murder the children. You repress this simple wish and it comes back to you as anxiety about the danger, and then you take it out on the policeman. Now I *don't* think that a discussion carried on in these conditions is fair to the policeman, who is a man like myself, even if he is a policeman; and what's more, I don't think such a discussion could possibly lead to a useful solution of the problem May I suggest, therefore, that we clear up this other matter first, I mean the wish of many of the ladies here to murder their children?"

"I *beg* your pardon," said Madam Chairman of the Committee on Health and Safety, "*is* that an issue for the Committee on Health and Safety?" She was vaguely disturbed.

"Oh, distinctly, distinctly," Horatio assured her.

"Mr. Alger," said Madam Chairman of the meeting, who was quite dazed, "could you put that in the form of a motion?"

"Why, yes! I *have* prepared a motion," said Horace in a firm voice, and he read off his motion from a slip of paper, "*I move that the Parent Teachers Association petition the Board of Education to make education noncompulsory, so that children can go to school when they feel like it.* I have an idea that this matter will bring the other matter right down to earth."

He sat down, and for nearly a minute everybody was simply fascinated.

"*Out* of order!" screamed Mr. Patterson in an agonized tone. He was the first to find his voice. "That belongs under the Committee on Education."

"The purpose of education is to relieve the home," said Mrs.

Kitchell with her voice under strong control. "Don't you understand *that,* Mr. Alger?"

"He is *goading* me on to murder Montgomery!" screamed Mrs. Baker hysterically. "I won't! I *won't!*" she screamed with the fury of the tigress protecting her cubs.

"For Chrissake," bellowed Horatio, *"when you gonna get that piano tuned?"*

It was a pandemonium. The like had never occurred at the PTA, because no one had ever before ventured to question the principle of compulsory education. The meeting could not be restored to order, although Horatio kept shouting, "There is a motion on the floor!" and Mr. Patterson kept shouting, "Out of Order!" Rightly; for Horatio's motion was not an issue for parliamentary debate; for on the one side was ranged all reason and progressive pedagogy, but on the other all pent-up human need and despair. The bare thought of having the children not away in school gave several women an attack of vertigo. Mrs. Kitchell tried to hit Horatio with her umbrella. And the meeting broke up.

Automatically the fruit punch was brought in.

Now Horatio had spiked the punch with a gallon of rum and bourbon. It was delicious and immediately one took another cup because the discussion had been so hot; and then two or three after that by a natural progression. Soon people were extremely happy. The parents and teachers, including Mr. Patterson, regarded Horatio as a wonderful fellow, maybe a bit eccentric, a real sparkplug, indeed little less than the god Dionysus who dissolves our darker passions in a clear haze.

"The punch *is* good tonight, isn't it?" said Mrs. Baker.

"It seems to have a little—kick!" said Mrs. Patterson, giving a little kick in her tight skirt and landing abruptly down on her large ass.

The party—it was a party; nothing like it had ever occurred at the PTA because no one before had ever mentioned so forthrightly the obvious wish of parents and children to do the children in—the party became very loud.

Louise Kitchell was dancing in the arms of Horatio, and seeing it one was reminded of Alcestis, as the poet says, "rescued from Death by Force, though pale and faint."

The telephone rang. After a while it was answered. It was the police on a complaint about the noise.

"I can't hear you," said Madam Chairman. "It's so noisy here. Can't you talk a little louder."

"Yeah," said the sergeant, "there's a complaint about the noise."

"Louder!" shouted Madam Chairman. "I can't make out a word. What the devil do you want?"

"Really!" roared the sergeant. "In a school building! What's goin on there, anyhow?"

"LOUDER!" shouted Madam Chairman impatiently. "Can't you make yourself clear? Now try. Louder—and distinctly."

"I said toin off dat noise, you drunken bums!" shouted the sergeant, dropping his company manners.

"LOUDER!"

Chapter 18 ▪ OUR NATIVE LAND

1.

Horatio had had it, the social reality, and the world of the *Herald Tribune*, and the Parent Teachers Association. And the result was that he was no longer for the General for president.

"So," he said bitterly to Antonicelli, "you have won. Everyone else will have a president, and only I shall never have my president."

By "my president" he meant sharing in his country's constituted power and in the public pomp. He meant identifying with the person of his country's executive will, and obedience within the limits of reason, honor and eros. His president.

"Why do you need your president? What's that to you?" asked Antonicelli.

"It's nice," said Horatio stubbornly.

"Well, at least you see that it's not worth while to be demented just to have *their* president."

"No, it's not worth while. It's more important to have common sense, honor and eros. But if I come to my senses, then I find that vanished is my dream of having my president. Obviously I can't share in a government that makes no sense, that I don't respect and that leaves me cold. Instead—I have nothing. (Only intelligence, self-respect and love.) I've been robbed. *You* robbed me!"

When he said this, he began to look with a certain shrewdness at the doctor, and an idea took form in his mind.

2.

"*I* robbed you? Robbed you of what? Robbed you of something that you yourself say makes no sense."

"You robbed me of my birthright as a citizen. I *was* born here, you know, just like anybody else, at a certain date and place—I think it was on 38th Street, even if there's no record of my birth because of my mother's habitual carelessness in such matters. I am an American citizen. That gives me positive rights, I mean, to have my president."

"Rights!" gloated Antonicelli. He was taking revenge, but good, for that old defeat in the courtroom. "You have the right to have your president, nobody can take it away; but in fact you can't have him, you can only take leave of your senses and have *their* president. Ha!"

"This is outrageous, what you say!" cried Horace. "Think of the history. Madison, Franklin, General Washington were there on the spot; and Jefferson kept sending them his opinions from Paris. They weren't any demi-gods, but they were perfectly adequate samples of human beings, no fools, and they worked hard all through a hot summer. And they decided, and I agree with them, that it was a good idea for me to have my president. *You* know why."

"No, why?" asked Antonicelli.

"In order to form a more perfect union, you chump. You're a grown boy, Antonicelli, you know these things. To establish justice, create domestic tranquillity, provide for the common defense, promote the general welfare and secure the blessings of liberty to ourselves and our posterity! That's why."

Now these sensible words sounded perfectly well in Antonicelli's sunlit study with its plain deal table and its slender avocado in a burnt-sienna rusted paint can; and spoken between two fairly human interlocutors. What Horatio was saying made sense; it did not turn upside down. And therefore, in their dialogue, he was one up.

Antonicelli could no longer gloat; he could only accept the fact that Horatio made sense and had a just grievance. This was the moment Horace was waiting for.

"Look, Antonicelli," he said earnestly, "you have political experience."

There was something in his tone that put the other on guard.

"You were even the district attorney, and that's considered top-notch experience."

"*What* are you driving at?" said the other coldly.

"Let's put *you* up for our president."

With a wild outcry Antonicelli leaped from his chair, his eyes aghast, his ears aflame. He fled into the bathroom and turned on the water in the basin. Concerned, Horatio followed him and found that, like the Mountain Sage (in Chuang-tze) when he was offered the Empire, he was vigorously washing out his ears with laundry soap in order to get rid of the dirty words. The story is told in Chuang-tze, how the Mountain Sage went into the other room and washed out his ears.

3.

Foiled in this political coup, Horatio fell into despondency.

Now the way that he chose to make himself despondent was to

conjure up the glorious times possible to other people but impossible to himself. (Just as the way I exercise my spite is to depict the good community possible to reasonable people but not possible to you.)

And as if he were looking at television—but he was seated in Antonicelli's study—Horatio saw a vivid picture of the Inaugural Parade, and he was horribly despondent.

There was a vast crowd of lively folk. It was a blue day with white scudding clouds, and it was a Red Letter Day on the calendar. Everybody was cheering, but he could not, because it wasn't his president. His throat hurt with it. Along came the fife-and-drum corps of Hooker High School of Hartford, Connecticut. They were shrilly whistling and crisply rapping it out, in the Phrygian mode, so that you became frantic with excitement and would blow your top if you couldn't beat your feet and whistle along. But he couldn't, and his eyes went dark.

But he was not to escape so easily into merciful oblivion, for the fearful god of the Possible—only for him impossible—had him in his grip. He heard from the distance a song, a song that rises in swift steps of gay departure into enterprise; it rises at once through the third and the fifth to the sixth; it draws back a moment and leaps to the octave. Hearing it, Horatio shuddered from his knees to his teeth—and the youth of our navy from Key West were stepping along and they were singing "Anchors Aweigh"—

"Anchors aweigh, my boys! Anchors aweigh!" *That* was the song that rises in swift steps of gay departure into enterprise.

Big tears began to roll down Horatio's cheeks and splashed unashamedly on his pants.

"What's going on, Horatio? My friend. What's it you're seeing?" said Antonicelli gently. "Don't be ashamed to speak it out. It will do you good."

4.

For answer, Horatio spoke from the twentieth chapter of the *Tao-Te-Ching* and said:

"All men are wreathed in smiles as though feasting after the Great Sacrifice and going up to the Spring Carnival. I alone am inert like a baby who hasn't yet stretched out his arms. All men have enough and to spare. I alone have lost everything. I have the mind of an idiot, so dull. The world is full of people that shine. I alone am dark. They look lively and self-assured. I am depressed, unsettled, like the ocean. I am adrift, unable to stop anywhere.

Everybody else can be put to some use. I alone am intractable and a boor."

So Horatio described his condition out of the *Tao-Te-Ching,* and with angry grief he said:

"Crying because of the Inaugural Parade! The others have gone to the capital for the Inaugural Parade, but I can't go because it's not my capital and it's not my president. Am I a stranger here? No, for then I could think nostalgically of my own native land. But history and folly have robbed me of my Inaugural Parade, and I have nothing to replace it with.

"Don't you hear? The sailors are singing 'Anchors Aweigh.' They have open throats. And the girls and boys are marching from the roll of their toes to the toss of their heads. The folk are cheering with frantic excitement. Men are dragging along symbolic floats from a thousand cities—they're not very good, this isn't the forte of my people—but such as they are, they show a lot of enthusiasm and effort. I find our American women and men simply beautiful—they are my type.

"Everywhere the Stars and Stripes are streaming! My liege colors blue and red, and the white of the original stuff, streaming and flapping in the common breeze. What do you say? Shall I salute, as I would? Or must I forcibly refrain myself from saluting? Since you ask me why I am crying—I am crying because of the Inaugural Parade."

5.

And he remembered Lothair. At this moment, having given way to angry grief. What he remembered was a scene of very long ago, he was a child, at the opera house at a performance of *The Mastersingers:* how Lothair was seated there shaken by silent sobs for the horns and trombones of the march of the guildsmen, that *would have been* the proud hour of great Lothair; and it *is,* alas, only a play and our proudest hour. Then little Horace stretched out his hand and took his sad brother's enormous paw. But Lothair withdrew his paw.

When he thought of it, the hot tears brimmed in Horatio's hot eyes like a storm, like a hurricane—for our country betrayed, our mesmerized countrymen.

6.

Antonicelli drummed on the table with his fingers, as he did when confronted with an incontrovertible fact; and this occurred often, for at the rock bottom of all the irrational ideas, there is always a miserable fact. *He* didn't know. He looked toward the closet where the snake Epidaurus lay hidden, as if to find the answer there, but the snake did not appear. He looked out the window at the sunny day. He looked at his hands and made the knuckles sparkle. And he looked square at Horatio, who was sitting there haggard and sane as a hammer.

"Horatio," he said, "why don't you go home?"

"I think I shall," said Horace, with dry eyes and a deep voice. He got up. "Thanks, Antonicelli."

"Don't mention it. . . . Was there something?"

For Horatio had stopped at the door and turned, as if he had something to say.

"Lothar is dead," he said.

"Yes, I know," said Antonicelli. "I take it, he—he was our candidate for president—after a while . . ."

Horatio said nothing but looked at him with haggard eyes.

"Now we can't do it that way," said Antonicelli.

Horatio averted his eyes.

They were embarrassed to mention Lothair because they were still, though he was dead, afraid of him, and concealing their relief that he was dead. But their eyes met.

Horatio looked at him with haggard eyes and left.

7.

He went home and his thoughts continued to be full of his brother Lothair. In the afternoon he said to Rosalind, "Let's take a drive—I keep thinking of Lothar."

"Where shall we go?"

"Up the Hudson, to see the Tappan Zee."

"Yes, Lothar would have liked us to do that."

And so they drove in their old car.

Northward on Route 9-West, under the white winter sun. Soon he was bawling with pleasure, but his eyes dry enough to drive. Singing his country's song. He showed it off to her: The Tappan Zee! And he looked in her face. "And what do you think o' that?" The same! Always the same! Varying in sun and haze. Among the Ramapos. They came around the curve between two worn-out hills, revealing the Tappan Zee. "And what do you think o' that?"

Northward on Route 9-West under the white winter sun. Bawling with pleasure but his eyes dry enough to drive, singing his country's song he showed it off to her and he looked in her face. "And what do you think o' that?" The same! Always the same! As they came around the curve between two worn-out hills, revealing the Tappan Zee.

Singing our country's song! Northward on Route 9-West. Varying in sun and haze, the same! Always the same! As we come around the curve between two worn-out hills, I show her off to you: the *Tappan Zee!* I look in your face. "And what do you think o' that?" Northward on Route 9-West among the Ramapos.

For Sally, February 1953

PART 3 SCENES OF OUR VILLAGE

Arietta.
Adagio molto semplice e cantabile—
—BEETHOVEN, Opus 111

Chapter 19 ▪ THE UNCARVED BLOCK

> Circumspect like crossing an icy stream,
> ceremonious like paying a visit,
> blank like an uncarven block,
> murky like the torrent of the spring.
> —TAO TE CHING, 15

1. OUR VILLAGE

By the middle of the century, New York City had eight, ten, fifteen millions of people, depending on where you drew the circumference. You would imagine that in a population like that a man would be quite lost. But it didn't work out that way at all. For, just as a reaction to being lost, there came to be small language groups, of persons who understood what the others were talking about and therefore occasionally listened to what one said: such a group might be about the size of a small village where one's native tongue was spoken, and the rest of the people (if they were people, how would one know?) hardly existed at all.

Our friends, for instance, spoke English in a rather pure dialect in which one said directly what one meant and took into account the tone and attitude of the speaker and also the response on the listener's face. This archaic dialect (it is said to be a form of old Socratic) of course sharply isolated them; and with this isolation, naturally, grew up parochial customs, culture and religion, so that even the people in the next neighborhood were a strange tribe. We happened to be very peaceable people (except when we were hungry), yet it often happened that our friendly overtures to trade, to make love or even to exchange the time of day, were met with hostile grunts and gestures going as far as blows.

Let me put this in a more general way. If you took in our whole City at a glance, say from an airplane, you would think it must be frightening and desperately impersonal to live there. But if you came into it, you saw that we had, uniquely, a society of subsocieties: the groups apart from ours had odd customs, yet all the groups usually lived tolerantly together at the feet of the Statue of Liberty. It was remarkable.

Lucky is the man who can band together with enough of those like-minded with himself—it needs only a couple of hundred—to reassure him that he is sane, even though eight million others are quite batty.

So New York had many of the charms of a small town, and without the disadvantage of stifling small-town gossip, for one could always take one's custom to another tavern.

But it was important, let me repeat it, to be prudent and not to be caught in a vulnerable condition among a strange and perhaps unfriendly (one never knew) tribe. I had an alcoholic friend, for instance, who was accident-prone and he fell down in the wrong countryside and they took him to ——— Hospital. Well, after he finally got away, not unscathed, he was prudent and he always took care to fall down north of ——— Street, where the police would take him to the French Hospital, which was friendly and competent and had a first-rate emergency clinic.

But let us get back to Mynheer, St. Wayward and the others. To fashion in our lovely English tongue a somewhat livelier world, I am writing this book.

2.

By truck from the port arrived a wooden crate containing the prize of Mynheer's travels. It was shipped by the Holland-American Line, with which he had family relations, and they docked in Hoboken, saving on the cartage.

As it was unloading, the three besotted panhandlers, denizens of Hudson Place who used the stoop at Number 22 as their headquarters, were quick to offer their services to carry the heavy box upstairs. They hung around, curious to see the box opened; but Mynheer drove them out of the house. He closed the door and opened the windows to the river, the city and the easterly sun. With a big claw hammer he vigorously, but carefully, made a crack in the box. Decisively he yanked the nails. Circumspectly he took apart the crate. And he discovered the uncarved rock that we have already met with in another world.

Doing this, Mynheer was circumspect like a man crossing an icy stream. He was ceremonious like one who pays a visit. His face was blank like an uncarved block. His soul was murky like the torrent of the spring.

3.

But just then I knocked at the door; I had hurried over at once, hearing that the box had come.

I gave the rock a quick scrutiny, walking around it a few times, as I do in art galleries. The rock was a little larger than a man and stood on end; it was a gray conglomerate, metamorphosed and assimilated by heat and pressure, a heap of one thing and another stuck together and slowly fused into one uncarved block. It was a fairly unremarkable rock.

"It's beautiful," I said. "It's a very adequate sample of a rock. We have a number in Central Park. There's a whole school of larger ones, big boulders, on a hilltop in Van Cortlandt Park about 250th Street, deposited by the glacier."

"No," said Mynheer.

"No?" I did not see what in my remarks he could take exception to.

"No. For you say, It's a very adequate sample of a rock. That's what you always say, as if you could *take* a sample. But you can't do that, for here it is. If anything, it takes you—you must come to terms with it. Yet I understand you, I understand you," he cried with a sudden passion. "I used to make the same error, but now I no longer make it. I used to think that the space I moved in was a fairly good sample of all the space there was; that the Empire City I lived in was one kind of society; that the experiences I lived through were typical examples, good, bad or indifferent, of such experience as was to be had. I used to think that my life was a sample of a life, even enviably better than most, for I have exceptional talents and had early advantages."

"Is that such a stupid theory?" I cried in turn. "Such a thought is a lucky find, for it keeps us from envy and complaining, from the feeling of having irrevocably missed out, as if somebody else had something special and we could never have it. But since we too have a fair sample, we can apply our wits to it and make something of it." I looked at him hotly. "If that theory is an error, what do *you* do, when you open your eyes and you look at the world you have, or, as you would put it, that has you?"

"I don't look with open eyes," he said. "I am embarrassed. I avert my eyes. Yet I have to look, because I'm curious, so I look—and then I get confused." His eyelids were flickering; he was blushing.

4.

I lowered my eyes.

"This rock," I said, "what are you going to do with it? It's a good size; do you intend to carve it and make a statue?"

"Heaven forbid! Modern sculptors take a rough rock like that and with great pains they cut into it and polish it and roughen it, in order to make it look like a rough rock, because for strength and clarity you can't beat a rough rock. But here we have the finished product! Certainly I don't intend to carve it! It's just for looking at—with averted eyes."

"Ah, you mean to gaze at it—with averted eyes—like into a crystal ball—but with averted eyes."

He considered this a long moment. I loved Mynheer; no matter how stupid a remark I made, he always considered it. Then he said, "No. Looking into a crystal ball, you concentrate. Here you become distracted, and murky."

It was so. I felt that I was becoming murky. And instead of hypnotized, more awake; I suddenly realized that I was taking up his time and he would rather be alone, and I awkwardly took my leave.

5.

By this time the uncarved block had spread its patient influence in the room. What it taught was patience. Perhaps by contrast, for while it stood there unchanging, there went on the metabolism of the underlying forces of everything else; and patience is to wait relying on the underlying forces. Under the influence of that uncarved block, Mynheer suddenly realized that he was becoming into the next moment. Despite himself; willy-nilly. He was under pressure; he stretched out his hand and he could feel the time streaming both outside and inside.

Next moment he was pleasurably confused. The confusion was pleasurable—he marveled! He did not know, and he allowed that feeling to grow. Soon he was softly breathing the no-geography of being at a loss. He tasted the elixir of being at a loss, when anything that occurs must necessarily be a surprise. He could no longer make any sense of his own essential things (that had never made him happy); he could feel them fleeing away from him; yet he did not snatch at them in despair. Instead he touched his body and looked around and felt, "Here I am and now," and did not become panicky.

The very next moment—so rapid was the virtue of that unmoving talisman!—Piet Duyck had fallen in love with his Only World, and he ritually exclaimed like the sage in *The Young Disciple,* "My World, my Only One, whom I must be in love with, if I persist so hard and pursue to become a happy man with you, just you, with only you, my obsession! For I cannot imagine any other possibility than to keep making passes at my Only World." That is, instead of becoming panicky, he fell in love, for these are finally the only two alternatives.

But he certainly got himself engaged to a Tartar.

6.

At the age of fifty, Duyck Colijn was the kind of man to whom, as we say, the world gives herself. But there is no advantage in that if one is not in love with her. It is easy, and indeed almost inevitable, to get what you don't want. It's quite a different matter when, as you age, you come to recognize the world as your Only World, *just* she, and *not* an adequate sample; and *then* the question is whether or not she will give herself to the one who is in love with her! Mynheer—who had been trying so hard to get *out* of this world, and always, as we saw, the horizon spread around him and became *his* horizon, and he was in this world—now he could no longer deceive himself! And he was forced to acknowledge that whither he ended up was where he wanted to be.

But he had chosen, or been thrown to, a grueling infatuation. His Only World was worse than reluctant; she was continually yielding but never coming across. She was secretive with all the show of utter frankness, public frankness right on the street. She would turn him down and pass him by and no question of his hurt feelings; but he could turn and tag after, and that was all right too, usually. Perhaps she was stupid-stubborn and had to be hit with a fist.

His Only World made it hard for him even to declare his honorable intentions, for he simply wanted to be married to her, with a certain security, rather than to be "in love." He was not bashful to declare himself, but she never gave him any time to go into the matter thoroughly. He always felt hurried. She was putting on her hat to go out. Then, when he was most exasperated and said, "Go fuck yourself, if you can—see how you like that!" she made a face and said, "Take it easy, guy."

He would go down the street kicking a can in a rage, making a fool of himself right in front of her. For of course, she never got far away. As soon as he did not withdraw from her, he was with her. That was the advantage of being in love with his Only World. Whichever way he made out, he made out with her. And he knew well enough that, however horrible it was and however senseless to behave like a senseless adolescent, it was much better to be in love miserably than not to be in love at all.

"Whisper it to me—" he would whisper, and this was most painfully sweet for the nobleman to have to beg from this most commonplace slut—"whisper it to me, what word must I whisper, lovely? And what colors shall I wear? What time? Where must I stand and wait to catch you in the mood?" She looked at him with a smile that promised anything and nothing.

Then withdrawing from her awhile, he thought of various courses of events that could end up happily, and with these pleasing fantasies he would fall asleep.

7.

She treated him outrageously, and naturally we of our village made it the subject of a good deal of malicious philosophy.

"What does he expect, picking up with a bitch from around here?"

"Where else *would* you meet a woman, except where you are?"

"He never manages to find anybody of his own class and background; it was the same with his first, Laura Alger. Ha! Opposites attract. Ha!"

"He doesn't complain, does he?"

"No. Given the premises, Mynheer is always willing to accept the conclusion; I will say that for him."

"At least this one doesn't drink." This unflattering reference to the Day was made, you may be sure, out of earshot of Horatio, who would have been quick to defend his sister's memory.

"Really!" I said. "There were a lot of people who drank during the drizzle of the war. Suppose *your* sister were the Glancing Day."

The one who took his wild infatuation with the most fortitude and charity was, surprisingly, Emily. She was resigned and reconciled to the ending of her Indian-summer romance with Mynheer. She too smiled. It was an impressive proof of the strength of her religion. "The poor dear," she said, "he seems to get jealous; he seems to think that his Only World has favors for other people, only not for him. But she's not a slut, though she is a bitch. In the end she's meant for only him."

Most of us were simply envious because he, however miserably, was in love.

8.

I stole into Mynheer's loft when he was not there, in order myself to commune, or whatever one did, with that sky-stone of his which seemed to have such virtue.

Of course I went about it wrong. It was not in me to be embarrassed, to look with averted eyes. But I looked with full frank eyes, with hopeful eyes, with friendly eyes, imploring eyes, as I do when I am walking the crowded street and looking for company. With dog's eyes. I looked willing to admire, ready for a response, eager to go more than halfway. I was looking at a rock.

I waited it out, as I do, long past the time when it is clear that nothing interesting will occur, or even that I am making a nuisance of myself; or long past the time when it is clear that I have been stood up: I kept the date (I always keep the date), the other didn't. Finally my tired eyes misted over.

At once there flashed into my memory the following episode from long ago:

I was driving across Ohio too fast in my sky-blue car, with my young wife seated beside me and the baby in the basket in the rumbleseat. We were speeding up a hill, with plenty of power. The truck in front of me on the narrow road was losing speed and I pulled over to the left to pass him. I thought I had a clear road ahead, I could see a half mile to the top; I did not see that there was a dip between me and that clear road. (So usually the worst wrecks are caused not by a failure in driving or in the machine, but by a stubborn wrong idea.) I passed the truck at the crest of the dip, and directly before me, coming from the dip, was a black car with the eyes of the driver aghast. So I pulled over again to the left, across the shoulder of the road—while the black car vanished past out the corner of my eye—and into a grassy peaceful field dotted with meadow flowers. The sun was pouring down.

I braked and turned off the motor, and reflectively lit a cigarette. The quiet spread. Neither of us had anything to say and the baby was asleep. The crickets and bees took up their loud chirping and buzzing again in the field. My heart began to pound.

Starting the motor, I steered back onto the road, and right off we came to Van Wert, Ohio, where they were celebrating the September festival of Peonies—Van Wert is the Peony Center of the World—and everybody in the town was lighthearted, and soon we were also.

Such was the memory that flashed into my mind when my eyes misted over. Perhaps it is because I am so crazy with hope that I live in constant terror.

Chapter 20 · THE LITTLE GAMBLERS

1.

On our street, to get into the candy store to buy a can of tobacco, you have to step over the feverish little gamblers; and often I protract my business to watch them.

The game they mostly play is twenty-one, asking for another card and another card to approach as closely as possible the limit of twenty-one. The child says in a choking voice, "Gimme another card" or "Hit me again," and he goes over the limit and loses; he has hot tears in his eyes but he does not shed them.

Some pennies have rolled through the iron grating down onto the basement floor bedded with candy wrappers, bottle caps, bits of green glass. Sprawled on the sidewalk, a dirty girl is reaching for the pennies with a stick tipped with chewing gum, and her behind is shining in the sunlight through her ragged pink drawers. Betsy.

Mrs. Fortescue, who runs the candy store, imagines that she hates the horde of brats who haunt and disgrace her shop front. She is afraid, she thinks, to alienate them only because they are, penny by penny, her chief customers, and they are capable of an unanimous boycott—indeed they are capable only of unanimous action. But she does not hate them, she is irritated by them. She is not afraid to express her irritation and they exchange insults.

It is only Jorbitz that she hates.

She is a precise-spoken Cockney and she aims to please. You come into her shop and realize, with a start, that the room is cool and quiet, dominated by her precise voice.

On the counter there is a large glass jar of colored sugar balls. This is another game. Most of the balls have white marshmallow centers, but some have pink marshmallow centers. You pay a penny, choose a ball and bite into it, and if it has a pink center you get a prize. The saccharine candy is insipid beyond even the unspoiled taste of five years old. The prize is still more worthless, a paper bag containing a metal cricket, a tin badge marked Detective, and a bar of sweepings of the floor of a peanut factory, cemented with cocoa. The children swallow the balls hardly chewing them, and the metal prizes are to be found in the gutter after they have torn their way through their pants pockets. Yet the jar is one of Mrs. Fortescue's most lucrative items, for the children are gamblers. The cunning manufacturer has calculated the chance of winning a pink center at 1 to 7. The guilty winnings of the frantic card game in the sun are here squandered in the shade, in choosing from the polychrome heap, in the jar that reflects the pale walls.

2.

Let us first watch little Merv.

Little Merv is too young for the card game. You would not think he would be a gambler, yet he seems to be gambling wildly from the jar. He has stolen another penny and, trembling with excitement, he chooses and again loses. He does not even eat the white center but in a fury throws it on the floor.

Mrs. Fortescue is sorry for him and cleans up after him rather than scolding him. His luck is exceptionally bad; last night he squandered a dozen of his father's pennies before they dragged him off bawling to sleep. Mrs. Fortescue has already given him the prize, but he does not care for that. He seems to be bent not on the prize but to win, just as my small boy wants to catch a fish and it is nothing to him if I give him a dead fish.

Last night, Merv fell asleep with a burning desire, and he has come back before the opening of the store, when the morning papers are still piled outside in bundles.

Now suddenly he has bitten into the center and it is pink! He shouts out. Quickly she brings him the prize, with appropriate words of congratulation and admiration. . . . Why has he burst into tears, and run out clutching at his belly?

At a loss, Mrs. Fortescue mumbles nervously to herself; she clicks the cricket in the bag and frightens herself. The guilt and fever of the gambling children have made her feel the imminence of violence, of a nameless accusation. Besides, Jorbitz has appeared in the room.

But little Merv had expected that the pink ball would have a different taste, a heavenly taste. It tasted only like the others. He has a weak stomach and now he is heaving behind the fence where the bigger boys and girls hide to smoke cigarettes.

3.

It is Jorbitz.

"Pick *hany* one, for 'eaven's sake!" she snaps at him. Mrs. Fortescue's voice has suddenly become shrill. "They're *hall* the same."

"Got all day," says Jorbitz.

"Don't you dare touch the jar with y'r feelthy 'ands!" she cries.

Jorbitz gives the jar a shake.

He is an unsavory nine-year-old, lank, with a thin long twisted nose. He is no dirtier than the others, but he has dirty habits. He picks his nose and leaves a trace of snot on the jar. He peers into the jar and breathes into it. She polishes busily and insultingly under his nose, but he does not relax his close scrutiny. She has already stung his knuckles with the rap of a ruler because she is sure, by the shadows on his pale cheeks, that he has been masturbating and will thereby communicate a contagious disease. When she rapped him, Jorbitz hardly whimpered; he is callous to treatment like that.

Silently Jorbitz appears in the room and pervasively he persists there. If, significantly, she goes into the back room with loud heels to show that she disregards him, then some other kid steals a cartoon book from the rack and vanishes. (But she always knows who it is and she comes to terms with each one in due time.) Jorbitz does not steal, he only examines the jar, absently reaching inside his pants to adjust his unwashed underwear that binds him.

The secret of the candy balls is a simple one, and he knows that secret. The sugar coating is imperfect, and through the chinks and transparencies in the coating, you can indeed see the color of the center, under the yellow, the green, the lavendar and the blood-red. But for this it is necessary to scrutinize the balls and to shake the jar.

"D'ye 'ave to 'ave y'r eyes in hevery single one, you dirty boy?" says Mrs. Fortescue in bewilderment. "*Which* one d'ye want? Keep y'r 'ands hout of the jar."

When at last Jorbitz takes his pick, he does not need to bite into the ball and show the center. She dumbly gives him the prize unclaimed. He calmly chews up the candy, maybe showing her the pink slime on his tongue. "Tastes like shit," he says.

He leaves the prize on the counter.

4.

When he watches the card players in the sunlight, Jorbitz judges them to be stupid because they do not pay attention to the revealing marks on the backs of the cards. Yet he doesn't feel superior to them nor disdainful of them; he does not get any positive satisfaction from his judgment. Perhaps indeed he wishes he were like them, stupid and excited, but a person cannot be stupider than he is, he cannot not notice what in fact he does notice.

Most of the cards are flagrantly marked. The torn card about to be dealt is the queen of hearts; everybody knows that. Why then does the fool ask for it, Jorbitz wonders, as if in order to lose? Yet he has no feeling either to sneer at him nor to put out a hand to restrain him.

They are playing with Terry Fleming's deck. The two of diamonds was in Paddy's pocket and looks it. The ace of spades has a crease down the middle. The big cassino fell in a cup of coffee. Little Merv dripped his ice cream on the jack of clubs. The ace of hearts has a bullet hole, the queen a corner torn off. Some cards have these ink blots and some have those thumbprints. The back of the king of diamonds is so faded that it seems to come from another deck.

Even while he is watching, Jorbitz sees Denny drop the print of his sneaker on a card. He picks it up and hands it to the dealer—it is the deuce of spades.

Jorbitz knows thirty of the cards; he is extremely observant and has a good memory. He is lonely and feels excluded. What he does not feel is how the other children are frantically gambling, out of their wits gambling. Or rather, he feels it well enough as something alien that they feel and he does not feel, that has them in its grip and makes them unanimous, while he is excluded and watchful. He hears their breathing, he sees their flushed faces, he knows that they are squirting in their pants. They have been through a big pot; they have cried out and are still exclaiming.

Nor is it even the case that some of them do not notice much of what Jorbitz notices. They notice and in other circumstances they would know. If you would hold up to Denny the back of the queen of hearts, he would say at once, "That's the queen of hearts, it's torn." But now in the game he says to himself, "It's the queen of hearts, it's torn, I shouldn't take it. . . ." and he says, "Hit me again. I'm sunk, it's the queen of hearts." For he is playing in order to play, in order to throw himself desperately on chance even when there is no chance, to heighten the agony of his frustration, to break through into glory, in order to lose.

Long ago, in other circumstances, Jorbitz lost too much. He cannot risk the feeling of risking it.

5.

He stakes his pennies on a couple of the half dozen games that the crouching banker has laid out on the sidewalk. He wins. Next deal he wins a big pot. In any case he plays well, with an instinct for the mathematical possibilities, and we see that he often knows with certainty. When he doesn't know certainly, he bets lightly and often wins; when he knows for sure, he bets heavily and wins.

Soon he has a heap of pennies between his legs. And he feels directed toward him the hatred of the others, but not their envy. But he is projecting his own self-hatred, for they envy him but do not hate him.

"Let me take the bank," says Jorbitz. And *he* deals out the half dozen games.

Now he too comes to feel at his throat the grip of life, for he has begun to cheat. He does not flush like the gamblers, but has grown pale; moment by moment this pallor deepens to the hue of death, and his teeth have begun to grate. It is to endure *this* ordeal of despair that he, for his part, has entered the meaningless game.

His method of cheating is to deal from the bottom of the deck or the middle of the deck. It is not enough for him to know, in most cases, the card that the player is hiding against him; he must control the game to the end. When he wins, he wins at will; when he decides that it is safer to lose—for he is prudent and afraid—he loses at will.

And he is asking himself the question, as he looks from one pair of eyes to the other, "How long—how much?—can I win before they turn on me? Fleming is desperate—I'm afraid of him—his father is in jail. This time I had better make him win. No! Next time." And he draws a card from the bottom of the deck and wins, but Terry Fleming does not strike.

Since he does not feel how the others are frantically gambling not against him but with chance, Jorbitz is more fearful than he need be. But what is horrible for him is to see on the opposite face the blind momentary gleam of Victory, when he himself has thrown him that victory.

The hot tide floods in his face, and ebbs, leaving him blue as dusk. His ears are ringing. He notices, down through the grating, how the sun is glinting from a bit of green glass; and as she raises her behind higher, to get at the pennies, he has a clear view of little Betsy's pink.

Cheating, he comes alive, and he feels his loathing for his own degradation, that his underwear is dirty, the force of Mrs. Fortescue's insults. His knuckles are stinging where she rapped him with the ruler. The glory of his disdain. His teeth are chattering with terror. Reaching inside his pants, he grips his penis; it is hot and hard. Through his chattering teeth he laughs with scorn at the stupidity of the kids on our block. The atmosphere is warm and supporting, and he smells the pungent macadam that the workmen are mixing. He feels that he is going to faint.

Obviously he wants them to cry out, "Y're cheatin' us! You lousy filthy cheat!"—and that from that would follow whatever would follow.

But they don't, and he doesn't dare to provoke it. He deals the next card from the top of the deck, knowing that he is going to lose.

6.

It is in these circumstances that up the street toward them comes Wayward.

Lothar and Emilia's boy is new on this street; he has not much explored it. Yet he has watched the card game in front of the candy store and has learned its movements. But he, too, does not understand the gambling, the element of chance, in the game. This is because he, at this age, has clairvoyant perception. The faces of the cards are not concealed to him, so he does not experience the uncertainty; but what is interesting is that he does not realize that the others do not know. Instead, simply, he considers the game to be a kind of ritual, and all the more portentous because pointless.

This afternoon he has himself brought some pennies clutched in his fist, in order to participate with the others. He understands that you put up a penny for each card and if your number comes to 3 times 7 or very near it—but it must not go over the limit—then you pick up the pennies and add them to the heap between your legs; otherwise the banker picks them up. Either way the outcome is very good.

At the age of seven, Wayward is not really simple-minded, but he is too powerfully equipped to have learned much from adversity. For instance, his speech is too articulate, his thinking too clear and distinct, for him to have learned the lesson of not being understood; his speech is also too strong for common intercourse, but he has not yet come to recognize this disaster.

He comes running up the street with all his might, almost flying, and jumps. Then he stands stock-still and observes what is inside the brick walls, and this again, he thinks, is very well. He has a warm nature; he is quick to feel another's misfortune as a threat to himself that he must ward off or try to remedy; but he does not consider suffering to be necessarily a misfortune. His own experience has been that through suffering he has benefited, but that is because he has never yet had to fight against overwhelming odds.

Also, he makes moral evaluations only to advance his own actions which are mostly lively and happy, so he sees little evil.

He has bronzen hair, his father's shoulders, and he is dressed in ultraviolet.

7.

So, kneeling with the others in the sun and shadows, opposite Jorbitz the banker, Wayward too puts a penny on the back of a card. He perceives that it is the pretty jack of diamonds. He knows the faces of the other cards that have been dealt and of the ace of clubs that Jorbitz is about to deal. With quiet pleasure, because he is participating in the social game, he watches the process of the cards being turned over and flashing into visibility.

He notices accurately enough that the other players are in agony—they are suffering, the set of their teeth and the breath sharply indrawn and how their limbs are taut; but he feels all this on the side of its excitement, a rising to a climax against one's own resistance. He judges it to be better than ordinary, and he himself is breathing evenly and stronger in excitement. Because of his inexperienced ignorance, he does not understand that *their* excitement will not, cannot, reach any climax; he thinks that others are like himself.

He hopefully gazes into Jorbitz's face, if he can find out the sense of what they are all doing and he himself taking part.

Suddenly he is astonished. A different card has turned up, from the one he expected. He starts with surprise.

Jorbitz does not miss this start, that rings and echoes in his soul like a trumpet in a gorge.

Wayward stares: the expected card is still lying there, under the dealer's thumb. Where did that other card come from? He is disturbed at it because, like all children, he is very conservative, he does not like changes in the rules.

"Give *me* a card, please," he says and puts down a penny. "Oh, but you took that card from the bottom of the deck. Why didn't you give me the card from the top, like before? Is this part of the game?"

"What do you mean?"

Wayward looks at him.

"You ast me for a card. I give you a card. Don't try to welsh out of it."

"No, the top card, the three of hearts. That's the one I need."

"What three of hearts?" cries Jorbitz, who knows that it is the three of hearts.

"*This* one," says Lothair's son and takes it and holds it up.

"*Keep* your filthy 'ands off!" cries Jorbitz. "Howdja know it was the three of hearts, you dirty little cheat!"

"What do you mean how do I know? I can read as well as you. It's the three of hearts. Next is the three of spades. And under that is the ten of diamonds."

Jorbitz turns up the three of spades, and under it he sees the back of the big cassino that was dropped in the coffee.

"Why do you call me a cheat?" says Lothair's boy, bewildered. "Doesn't everybody look at which cards are coming? Aren't you supposed to notice? Did I spoil the game? I just want to play like everybody else."

Blindly Jorbitz throws a punch at the face in front of him that is looking through him. This blow sinks into nothingness; and following it there, Jorbitz falls down.

He has dared to throw his punch into nothingness and, pursuing it there, to lose his balance. Between losing his balance and hitting the ground, he faints away for an instant. But by the time he has hit the ground and hurt his wrist, he has already regained consciousness and he whimpers. Still clutching the deck in his hand.

"Which is the bottom card?" he whispers.

"It is the seven of spades," says Lothair's boy, doubtful whether or not to answer, but the other's tone is gentle.

Jorbitz holds up the pack for them to see the seven of spades.

8.

They are silent, fairly still but with the little biological movements that stationary animals make, in a rough circle, in front of the candy store on our street. Mrs. Fortescue has come to the door.

Their heads, their feet, their fingers are making the small erratic movements of stationary living creatures. Lothair's boy is embarrassed to be the center of attention.

Jorbitz is sick in the stomach with the heat and the pain of his broken hand. Yet he doesn't attend to that yet awhile. For he is cool and panting with comfort, with a good feeling in his midriff and his neck and shoulders buzzing with guiltlessness. For that strange small boy is clairvoyant, he *knows,* and there is no use, there is no need, to try to cheat him and painfully to learn the markings on the cards. Jorbitz is happy that from where he is lying he can easily stretch out his hand and touch his knowing one; and he does so.

But his wrist is broken and hurts and he begins to whimper. He wipes his snotty nose on his sleeve.

Lothair's boy wonders that Jorbitz is so dirty. He perceives that he has no handkerchief and he hands him his own, which is not clean.

" 'E's 'urt. 'E 'urt 'is 'and!" cries Mrs. Fortescue. " 'Elp 'im up."

Chapter 21 ▪ GOOD NEWS

1.

At night the water-front street was nearly empty, but not silent, for everybody was in the bars and from time to time a door opened and the light and noise burst forth. As Mynheer and I came strolling by, like watchful patroons, old settlers, with our pipes.

He was in a rare peaceful mood, as if his love affair with his Only World were going well. And indeed! "She promised me that she was going to be nice, tonight," he said to me quietly, with a remarkable trustfulness. "Now look at that one! Isn't he odd? Watch him." He indicated a young fellow down the street and we stood against the wall and followed him with our eyes.

It seemed to be a merchant mariner. He went halfway down the street and returned on his tracks. Another man passed him; he turned and followed the man, but after a hundred steps he stopped and gazed after him and watched him disappear. Slowly he returned on his steps. He peered into the window of a bar, he peered into the window of another bar, he peered into the window of a third bar—there was one after another along the water front. He went into a bar, but almost immediately he came out again and stood irresolutely at the curb.

I shrugged. "It's a queer looking for a pickup. He's looking for the Messiah, but he won't find him that way. Also, he won't know him if he meets him—he's in too much of a hurry." *I* was not enthusiastic tonight. "I don't know about *your* Only World," I said, "but I know mine, and she hasn't promised anything."

"Not a queer," said Mynheer. "Look, now he's after her." He was going through the same routine, after a Hudson Street tart: hesitant, precipitate; precipitate, then hesitant. The tart vanished into a doorway. He did not follow her there.

The erratic young man made slow progress wherever it was he was bound, standing indecisively on the corner and hungrily hunting the empty street where there was no game. Yet a merchant seaman was not out of place on the water-front street. We drew closer. It was Mynheer's son, Droyt.

"Droyt!" he called, and flashed me a look of triumph.

The young man started, in distress at being recognized in his stupid distress. He recognized his father on the street that he had thought empty, and he ran to him and embraced him and said, "Father."

After a moment, Mynheer held him away to look at him. He looked haggard, harried, hurried, as one might expect from his vain and hungry behavior. And yet, as we scrutinized him, we could see something behind that, a shining in his eyes and something thrilling, though subdued, at the base of his brain.

"Where is Lefty?" asked their father.

And at once the shining burst into a kind of glory, and we were wonderstruck. "I see that you have good news to tell," said Mynheer softly, "and that is why you roam about hungrily here, to find somebody who could possibly understand it. Thanks for that! Tell it to us."

"Good news! Good news!" said Droyt.

"Shall we go in here for a drink," I suggested, "or do you want to go upstairs and see the others?"

"No, let's get them all together," cried Droyt, "so I can tell you all the story of my brother Lefty and won't have to repeat it again and again. But you'll ask me to repeat some parts of it anyway, because you won't believe your ears! Now who is there? Emily? Lothar? Horace and that pretty dancer he married? Maybe one of the children is old enough to understand a simple story. Are you in touch with Minetta and Harry Tyler? I always liked them."

"Lothar is dead," said Mynheer.

"Oh. What I have to say—it would have made just Lothar so happy," said Droyt.

2. The Happy World of Lefty Duyvendak

When a number of us were together, Droyt at once began:

"I want to tell you that my brother Lefty is alive and prospering. He's living in San Francisco on 65th Street, and he'd be pleased if any of you paid him a visit. Yes, he would. He's not ashamed of his relatives and he's not indignant with his old friends even though he has a successful new life. He's even on warm terms with me, his brother. What's more, he has a sunny guestroom with a good view where he can put up one or two people without inconvenience."

Here Droyt's voice broke and he had to pause to recover himself, but he was not embarrassed. He proceeded, "I was going to say: when you are their guests, Lefty and his wife do not resent the way you might choose to live."

"*Are* you sure of that, Droyt?" asked Rosalind. "I find it hard to believe."

"It's true! I've experienced it myself and seen it with other people. . . . But I have gotten way ahead of my story. First let me tell you about the house, how he got the house——"

Speaking here in company, Droyt was not haggard and harried as he had been on the street; and his hurrying was eagerness. He had found what made him happy, to share his story. But that is what is so hard to find, if it is a great and happy story.

"Lefty used to live in Berkeley. But then I got him—he got this job at the Seaman's Haven on Russian Hill. I'll come to that later. But the point is that when he got the job, he had to ride the train nearly an hour to get to work. So he made a sensible decision to look for a place to live close to where he worked. Just like that. He went searching every evening after work. And he *found* it! It wasn't easy, but he did it."

"Wait a minute!" interrupted Minetta. "Not so fast. You tell us he wanted to live close to where he worked, and hard enough to do something about it? I can understand his finding a place, for people die and there is a vacancy. But don't you see, Droyt, that if he wants to live near, it means he must really like his job? I'm not doubting you, but don't you see that the whole pattern is inherently improbable?"

"But he does like his job!" cried Droyt. "I'll tell you about the job later. But next I want to tell you about Molly's High Noon Tavern. That's on the corner of 60th Street, a few blocks from where Lefty lives."

He looked at us all, as if beseeching us to bear with him, he had so much to tell, and we were silent and listened.

3.

"My brother Lefty has always been musical, like his uncle Lothar. It runs in my mother's family, do you think? You remember in those days when we used to fly and fall down and hurt ourselves, Lefty used to sit and console himself crooning mountain music? Well, it used to disgust me, that cripple in his wheelchair whimpering. But I was wrong and now I can admit it. I didn't realize it was music. Mostly three-part songs. While he was sitting there he was filling out the harmony, and after a while he made up words. I never listened; we only used to fight. Then we went west, in the dead of spring, and he still kept making up those songs and remembering them and writing them down.

"One night I came into the High Noon and there was Lefty at the piano singing some of his songs. It seems that the folks who came to that tavern as regulars wanted to hear Lefty sing his songs. He made them up out of his heart and they wanted to hear them and they were moved by them, and they applauded and called on him, and he made up songs for them because they wanted to hear them, and he wanted to make them up and sing them especially if they wanted to hear them."

It was now my turn to become resentful at Droyt's narrative. "Will you repeat that carefully," I said dryly, "and please pay attention to what you're saying. We didn't come here to listen to fairy stories."

"Yes, I will," he said firmly. "People always ask me to repeat this part or that part because it's unbelievable. I know it's unbelievable, I'm not a fool, but it's so, and that's a fact. You can go there right now and see it. He makes up songs out of his heart and the folks at Molly's High Noon ask him to sing them, and they're moved, and they applaud, and so he makes up other songs for *them*."

I was white with anger and got to my feet and walked about the room. "Yes," I hissed. "And what does Molly say about that?" I shot at him. "She kicks him out on his ass for creating a disturbance."

"You're wrong. Molly is sensible about it. She sees that Lefty's songs are an attraction of her place. They come all the way from college at Palo Alto and Berkeley to hear Lefty sing, and they spend money. Lefty has the run of the High Noon Tavern. She sets up drinks for him and his party, and he and his wife eat there any time they want."

"*Eat* there!" I cried spitefully. "That lousy bar food—American so-called cheese, or you can have the ham on rye. . . . Thanks."

"Wrong again!" said Droyt. "Sensible people don't serve bad food, and Molly's food is quite good, and Lefty and Ann have their dinner there two-three times a week."

I fell back into my chair. I was engulfed by a dizzy wave. And when I emerged from it, I began to marvel. He turned to me especially, as if beseeching:

"I admit there was trouble. I don't want to give the impression that any of this was easy. Hard! But possible. *That's* the point. First thing you know, the cop on the beat came around and complained. He wanted to have Lefty thrown out or made to shut up because they didn't pay the entertainment tax. The idea was that it was better for them all to sit there and sulk, even though somebody got pleasure in singing and everybody got pleasure out of listening. Some of the longshoremen tried to reason with the cop—it was pretty bad. And then—suddenly he was ashamed, the way it happens with an Irishman. 'All right, all right, let it be,' he said. He comes every couple of nights and stands inside the door and asks for his favorite numbers. He's become a kind of combination protector and music critic. Name of Doyle. He's a friend of mine, to the extent of course that I'm friends with a policeman."

We marveled. And he continued.

4.

"One night Tom Logan brought Anna to the High Noon. She wasn't especially his girl, and when she began to find Lefty interesting and attractive, Tom didn't make spiteful remarks about him but thought he was just fine. 'You don't need to stick with me just because you came with me,' he said. 'Why don't you go over by the piano and show him you're interested.'

"Now Anna took this just as it was meant, not as mean spite but as a considerate and friendly suggestion. (Don't sneer. I got this from Anna and Tom and Lefty themselves, and the way I'm telling it is just the way it happened.) Since she was helped to have a good time by a friend who took her out to give her a good time, she stood and leaned against the piano while Lefty was playing a song without words. Seeing the way she looked, and the way she looked at him, Lefty felt weak in the thighs, but this didn't embarrass his playing because it was a song out of his affections and he played it the stronger and sweeter.

" 'Doesn't that song have any words?' she said.

" 'No, that song doesn't have any words,' he said, embarrassed.

"They were shy and that was all for that night. But the next night she asked Tom to bring her again, hoping that my brother would be there. And in fact he *was* there! (*That's* the part that baffles *me,* if you want to know: these geographical accidents.) He *was* there, and when she saw him she wasn't disappointed as you might expect; she found him still attractive! And the same thing happened with Lefty. He had been hoping that that girl would come back, and she did come back, and when he saw her he got a hard-on.

"Then he had a daring idea. What if he tried, for once, to follow through his excitement to its climax, rather than stopping off to take care of this and that? He often had this idea, but he never before did it. He told me it was why he liked to make up songs, because then he could do it. Even if he strayed off into a hard key or some other trouble, when he was making music he could keep going and getting excited and almost panicky, till the song had sung itself to the end. Even if he had to play faster, faster than he could play."

"That's just fine, what you say there, son!" said Antonicelli enthusiastically. "It answers the question I've been asking myself. Now I'm sure his songs are good songs. Because that's why they make up songs, because they can make them up as they go along and keep going. But you must understand, of course, that you can't behave that way with other people. You have to change to their point of view and make adjustments."

"I agree with you, sir," said Droyt. "But all the same Lefty had this idea and he dove. He said to Anna, 'I like you, you can see that my—it's obvious—' it was obvious; 'will you come out with me?'

"She hesitated a moment as if to say, 'But I don't know you,' but *instead* she said what she wanted to say, 'Sure I will, if you want me to. Yes, I'd like to.' She took it as just a caprice of his and *therefore* very important to him; for he had been playing songs without words and making for himself a kind of world, and now he was adding to it other people and words, and he wanted also to move and act. This was an inspired thought she had, I don't deny it; but it's the kind of an inspiration that anybody can have if he listens closely and if it's a good song, don't you agree?"

When he said this, we stared at him with eyes of holy fright.

"Anna said, 'I want to say good-by to Tom Logan because he brought me.' She didn't say, 'I must say good-by——' and she didn't say, 'Let me say good-by——' putting the decision on Lefty. She *did* want to, she was grateful and courteous. And Lefty didn't grit his teeth at this little delay and retract his pelvis and become irritated; he was pleased at their courtesy; his hard-on grew soft and hard and pulsated; he looked at her with growing love and lust; he didn't grip to his hard-on like grim death as if he were angry about something."

"—What a beautiful observer my boy is!" thought Mynheer with pride. "He is in love with his Only World."

" 'Well, where shall we go?' said Anna, and she took Lefty's arm as they came out.

" 'My place is a few blocks away.'

" 'Good. Let's go there,' said Anna."

"I beg your pardon, I have to stop you," interrupted Rosalind. "Let me get this quite clear. You say, she found him interesting and attractive and she made that much clear to him. And he responded to it, and spoke out, and that was that. You mean, I take it, she was attracted to him and approached him and he was *not* thereby inevitably attracted to somebody else, and that somebody else to still somebody else, or perhaps even to Anna, all in a circle, and nobody getting anything. Is that what you mean?"

"Yes," said Droyt simply.

"Yes!" cried Rosalind. "What is this simple Yes? Do you take us for fools?"

The tears flooded her eyes. We marveled. We could not believe our ears. Depending on our characters, we responded to this crisis with fright or resentment or awful grief. But he went on.

5.

"They came outside, and they began to walk in the direction of my brother's house——"

"What!" interrupted Horace. "You are telling this story about your brother, and I do not hear that your voice is grinding with spite and disapproval. But on the contrary! I see that your eyes are shining." It was so. Horatio turned toward us and said, "It is a miracle," and we bowed our heads.

"It was a soft night," said Droyt, "such as happens often in the Bay area when the west wind comes from the sea. And on the way to his house, suddenly my brother said with a laugh, 'It's so far to go; why don't we duck in here?' No sooner said than done! They were passing a convenient dark alley and she followed him in. Their eyes were shining in the dark, no doubt, and they were hushed and jolly. They did not even notice the discomfort of making love in the alley, for in love, you know, the discomfort of pebbles and dirt soon passes into the background and vanishes; and afterwards there is the joke of being quite lame together.

"Now my friend Doyle the policeman happened to see that couple vanish into the alley, and *he* knew what they were up to. 'He's going to rip off a piece of ass,' he thought, and he went his way, envious, but not resentful and indignant. Do you believe that?"

"Yes, I believe it!" I said boldly, "because you give me conviction."

"Then you'll believe what I say now! Lefty and Anna walked away from there embracing tenderly, and grateful, and a little smug. 'We're lucky,' they agreed; 'where there might be so much trouble and missing out, we make it easy for each other to have a good time.'

6.

"That was a couple of years ago, and now they are very fond of each other and live together. He knows that with her there is always the possibility and sometimes the fact of being made happy; and so he is happy; for in order to be happy you need to have only a likely possibility that you can be happy. Although, like everybody else, half the time he is worried, angry or grieving.

"Anna loves him, yet this does not oblige her to injure him and spoil his happiness. Simply, she wishes well to her beloved. Is that so hard? Yes, it is hard. But it is possible. And even if it is *im*possible, in the nature of things, yet in this case it is a fact! Hard—possible or impossible—but a fact. I wouldn't tell it to you, I shouldn't believe it myself, if I hadn't witnessed it with my own eyes. She wishes well to the man she loves. That is why my eyes are shining; my eyes that have seen this do not belong to the same world as the rest of my body."

We marveled. We were stricken dumb. Horatio took Rosalind by the hand and said, "You see, Ros, we have beeen concerned about our own behavior as if we were too different from the human species, and so we have felt needlessly out of things; but here from afar off on the West Coast is an authoritative eyewitness account of how some other folk make it possible for themselves to be ordinarily happy."

Rosalind burst into tears and Horatio, as was his way, did nothing to console her but held her safe, and looked off over her shoulder into space at the thoughts of his own that were not limited to this scene and these persons.

7.

"What does Lefty do for a living?" asked Mynheer dryly. "All you tell us is about some supper and drinks for singing songs."

I was sorry that the careful father asked this, for it is one thing to speak of personal relations or even of art and a small audience—for in these things the common mistakes that everybody makes might conceivably be avoided by a happy instinct, a stroke of luck, common sense, the transient inspiration of the creator spirit; it was quite another thing to speak of having a reasonable job in the United States of America.

Droyt lowered his eyes, and I feared the worst.

"I don't like to talk about it," he said shyly, "because I got him his job, so I guess I'm the hero. Well, to explain it I'll have to go back to the beginning.

"We used to live in Berkeley and Lefty worked as an inspector for Walco Chemicals. The pay was good enough; the work wasn't hard; it wasn't even too boring. Yet my brother felt he didn't belong there, he was wasting his life; he used to get tired, he wasn't happy; when he came home he didn't have any appetite; and at night he found it hard to sleep, as if he hadn't used up his nervous energy, his thought and feeling. Naturally I took this as a matter of course—it's the same with everybody—and I thought no more about it.

"One Friday Lefty came home and put his check on the table and said, 'Do you know, my right-handed brother, if they didn't pay me every Friday, I'd never go back to that job at all.' I was in a bad mood and I snapped at him, 'Is that supposed to be a joke? Ha! ha! That's the trouble with you Americans, you got too god-damned much sense of humor.' "

Droyt paused. Then he forced himself to continue. "My brother didn't mean it as a joke. He just meant it. Then suddenly I got sick to the stomach—I vomited all over the floor. Because I gave him a look and I saw that he was spending nearly half his waking life in a place where he didn't want to be, and doing what he didn't want to do and didn't do especially well. I lost my appetite too. But I threw up; that's the difference between Lefty and me; I won't keep it down. Just because I had this advantage, however, I had a duty.

" 'What would you like to work at, brother?' I asked. 'Supposing you could really pick and choose.'

"He didn't know. Mechanic? No. Business? *No.* He didn't even want to drive a truck. Indoors, outdoors, all the same to him. 'For Chrissake,' I said, 'every kid wants to do *something,* to be a fireman, an engineer! Make a fantasy about it.' But he really didn't know; he was completely disspirited. I was astounded. 'Would you like to do nothing at all?' I cried. 'Just sit on your ass and croon songs?'

" 'No! That's not work!' he said with spirit; at least I got a rise out of him. I didn't understand, remember, that his songs were good songs. "Nobody would pay me for that.' He said that in such a curious tone, as if he meant two different things: 'Nobody ought to pay me for that' and 'nobody *could* pay me for that, even if they wanted to.'

" 'I'm sorry, I apologize,' I said.

"I looked at him again and I saw for the first time in our lives that my left-handed brother is terribly proud, and very humble. He wants to be left alone, and he wants to be a servant. But a personal servant, not a mechanic or a storekeeper. Sensitive for what people need, warm in giving it. Oh, but that puts it up to us, to *need* something. Naturally, then, we pay his keep. As soon as I saw all this, I knew the job for him right off. Or maybe because I knew about a job, I knew it was for Lefty. They needed a man for the receiving desk in the Seaman's Haven. He said he'd try it. I got him the job. And soon after he moved to 65th Street, as I said.

"His job is to case the men when they come in: who needs a new pair of socks, and who needs a couple of bucks; who probably has the clap but is ashamed to talk about it; who is desperate and has a story to tell; who ought to write a letter; who needs teeth. *I* couldn't do it. He knows how to draw each one out, and nobody is a bore. To him they're soon buddy-buddy friends. He lends them money out of his own pocket and they always pay him back, and they play twenty-one and sixty-nine in the lockerroom of the swimming pool. He likes this job. He has an appetite and he can sleep at nights."

"Ha!" said I. "And what does the Administration say about the excessive closeness between the staff and the clients? I'm acquainted with such things. I've been kicked out of several liberal institutions."

"What should they say? They're experienced people. They understand that nothing comes from nothing. To do the job, they need somebody who is attentive and can notice. If they get somebody who is attentive, they can assume that he has grounds and motives that make him attentive. Well, so he has. What's remarkable about that?"

We marveled.

8.

"Droyt, why did you leave there and come here?" It was Rosalind who asked it, sadly. "You won't find that people are very happy here."

The question troubled him. "I left there because Anna and my brother had a little baby girl.

"Try as I would," he cried passionately, "closely as I looked into it, I couldn't find that they regretted having that child. They didn't feel that they were inadequate to it, or unready for it, or too immature, or insecure or any of that shit. They didn't need another room. They didn't need another five thousand a year. There she kicks her feet and laughs and bawls, and they don't hate the sight of her; they can stay in the same room and keep their tempers even with each other. On the other hand—it comes to the same thing—they don't let her keep them from having a good time. They sometimes manage to enjoy themselves in spite of their baby. I couldn't bear it . . . No! It's not those things at all that I couldn't bear. But I looked and listened and thought about it while she was pregnant; and after she had the baby I questioned myself about it. It didn't seem to us, not to them and not to me, that there was no place in our society for another baby. None of us asked, What's the use of it? We weren't afraid for there to be another human being.

"*That* was it! As soon as I knew it for sure, I cried out in holy terror and I fled from there across the country, as far as I could without getting my feet wet."

He stood there before us, with his heart visibly pounding under his shirt.

"There's nothing to be afraid of!" we gasped, with chattering teeth.

9.

He had finished his tale. And we somehow looked to Horatio to speak for us. And he got up from his chair. "Son of my sister Laura," he said, touching him, "you have come to us with a marvelous story. We find it hard to believe our ears. You speak of a free artist who has an immediate audience; of lovers who wish each other well; of a man who gets paid for a useful job that fits him; of the confidence that there will be some use for another human being in the world. All this is unlikely, yet you convince us that it is a fact. What does it mean? It means that all along the time a certain number of people are not committing an avoidable error."

Chapter 22 ▪ MAZES

1.

Mynheer waited till the next day.

"Son," he said, and leveled his attentive gaze at the young man. It was what Droyt hoped, because it was his father, and feared, because it was his father. "Let's look at you. You're so big. Droyt, my right hand!"

Mynheer was tall but spare, but Droyt was big like his uncle Lothair. He looked like Lothair.

"Yesterday you told us about Lefty. And what about yourself?"

"You saw." The seaman made a gesture and flushed darkly for his aimless distress on the street. "There's no use trying to explain it. It's always like that, not only last night when you saw me. Look at this—I keep a careful accounting."

He drew out of his pocket a sheet of manila paper and unfolded it. It was marked with a wavering path, wandering, halting, precipitate and hesitant, desirous and aimless. Seeking, following or waiting, but never bound somewhere. The pursuits or flights (there were flights) were scored sharply; the waiting was marked with circles and crosses. But on the whole it was a map of distraction rather than a voyage of search or fear.

"What is this maze?" asked Mynheer.

"I copy down my erratic course. See, here I stop and turn—I follow—and give up. Then I look in here, and in here. Often I just stand and wait. Twenty means twenty minutes. I go down these streets that aren't necessary in order to get to here, where it makes no difference, and then I come back up."

"Give me the map," said his father, and laid it on the table. "Show me another. . . . What are you looking for?"

"You know what—looking for my mother Laura, I guess. We saw her last in the dead of spring. My brother and I were werewolves and we sniffed in the corners and trotted swiftly from room to room. Trotting, trotting."

Mynheer was looking at the new map. "What's this black circle here?"

Droyt grinned. "I said to myself, I won't trot another step, and I stood there and smoked my pipe. A policeman said, 'What you doin' *here,* son?' 'Nothing. Just looking.' 'You're loitering!' he said. 'Yes, I suppose I am loitering,' I had to admit. 'That's illegal. Ain't you waitin' for a train, maybe?' he said hopefully; it was in the Pennsylvania Station."

"What do you hope for?"

"Tell me," the young man said with frantic eagerness, "it's impossible, isn't it, it's impossible that I can keep wanting and making an effort, even a stupid effort, without *something* coming of it? It *is* impossible, isn't it?"

"That depends. Show me another map."

Droyt took still another sheet out of his pocket and unfolded it. The paper shook in his hands. It was similar to the others. Mynheer laid it on the table and examined them.

"Show me another," he said, and Droyt handed him a fourth sheet. Mynheer looked at them one against the other and one after the other, as if he were evaluating a projective test, which was what he was doing. "Which of these is the earliest and which is the latest?" he asked.

"This one is yesterday—and that one is last week. The torn one is from long ago. The other is in-between."

"So. This one's the earliest, and this one's the latest."

"Yes. Can you make something of it?"

"Sure. It's not so bad."

"What does it mean?"

Mynheer said, "It is a road that deviates but does not err."

2. Appropriating a Strange Place (Age 2)

"Hush. Just watch this." He drew Droyt back into the corner, out of the way.

It was the two-year-old, Rosalind's, trotting from room to room.

It was evening. Rosalind was putting the baby to bed.

The two-year-old had been shouting for his food, on the brink of a tantrum if he did not get it on the instant; but it was there on the instant and he had eaten it with the relish for what is taken at the right instant. With cries of laughter he offered bits to the dog and snatched them from her jaws and devoured them himself. Now, in postprandial excitement, he was running the length of the room and back, and forth and back, with trotting steps.

The rooms were laid out on a circular plan, connected by doors, and he ran the circle through all the open doors. Round and round the circle, four, five, six times, trotting not very fast, with piercing cries. He came back to retrieve the fetish his blanket and he stood, a little in reverie, touching the silken border of it lightly to his lips.

He trotted the circle slowly, trailing the blanket on the floor. It was near his own bedtime and sleep was not uninviting to him.

But with a wild cry of happy fright, teasing, he ran away from Rosalind's approach to prepare him for bed with dry clean clothes. With shrieks of pleased fright, fleeing and stamping; then with shorter steps; as if vibrating to a stop in order to be caught by her overwhelming, loving force looming upon him.

He struggled and co-operated in being made more comfortable.

He climbed onto the bed by himself and lay a moment on his side, clutching his ego to himself with sparkling eyes. He got down from the bed because there were many unfinished motions in his soul.

First he ran to recover the blanket fetish from the other room where he had dropped it. He returned with it toward the bed; but he turned away from the bed and he began to evolve with soft, exploratory trotting steps the ritual of appropriating his room.

He touched the silken border of the blanket to his ear as if to listen to it. He wrapped the blanket about himself—like a peon.

He went to look out the window.

After a moment he came back behind the rocking chair, avoiding the rockers.

Next he combined these separate motions into a continuous circle, going to look out the window and coming back behind the rocking chair, avoiding the rockers. Having completed this circle he paused to consider it, touching the corner of the blanket to his lips.

He repeated this itinerary, going to the window and looking out of it for a certain length of time, and coming back behind the rocking chair, avoiding the rockers—twice, five, eight times, it seemed as if he'd never stop, but the last times more slowly. He stood next to the bed.

With a sudden burst of energy he trotted around the rocking chair, omitting to look out the window, and he hurt himself on the rockers of the chair, but he did not cry out but stood biting his lower lip. He climbed onto the bed touching the blanket to his face, as if about to bury his face in it.

He climbed out of bed trailing the blanket, and went to try the knob on the closet door. It was too hard for him to open. He returned and stood beside the bed and considered everything, touching the silken edge of the blanket to his lips. He went and simply touched the knob and came back. He went in the other direction and touched the brass fire screen, and then went and touched the brass knob, and came back. And so, four, seven, eight times, he performed the sequence of touching brass, the last times more slowly. And he stood and considered it with heavy eyes, looking a little inwardly, and listening to the corner of his blanket.

Ran once round the rocking chair, nimbly avoiding the rockers, because he knew it; and on the way back he lightly touched the fire screen.

The darkening room had become dense with mystery, with gyres of trotting steps and luminous points of touching. A mystery not unknowable, not even unknown, but only to be known and made transparent in these rites. In the rich sounding silence and the deepening luminous darkness. The little boy now emitted certain calls. He stood wrapped in his soul wrap and crawled up into the bed.

He said, in a flat voice, "Bodl"—for that was a communication that brought the intrusive others back into the world; and when Rosalind gave him his bottle, he clutched this sensuality also awhile away from himself. But he gave in to suck at it and to begin to fall asleep.

3.

Bored and fascinated, the father and son were watching this into the darkness. These outbursts of joy, of ease, the slow repetitive growth of this mystery, the appropriation of the space, these went on according to the soul's time; and what I have described in a couple of pages consumed more than an hour by the clock.

"What has he been doing?" whispered Droyt finally, as if one did not venture to speak aloud.

"He is appropriating a strange place," said Mynheer.

"But he lives here! He was born here!"

"Even so."

4.

Droyt went out. It was night and he wanted to be alone. He went down to the Anchorage Bar to have his supper.

He sat down at a table with a red-checked tablecloth and ordered his minestrone. And while he was waiting for it, he looked up—and there occurred the *Ballade of the Anchorage Bar*:

Which of these, as they stay or go,
is the god in disguise, and everything
will otherwise be, when I know?
Say! is it you who staggering
loom in the door, as to the king
dying came happy Hercules
and hiccuped and began to sing?
—So laughed the god in disguise.

Or maybe you who add the row
of numbers and sit listening,
or don't listen, yet know, know.
So Klamm sat in the village inn,
dipping a pen, the pen was scratching,
he did not need to lift his eyes,
Franz's heart was thundering. . . .
—So anxiously the god in disguise.

To Aeneas spewed by the undertow,
hardly alive another morning,
his mother armed with a Tyrian bow
came bare-knee'd, forward as the spring:
not unlike you she was who bring
my soup, when I am otherwise
at a loss for a next thing.
—So at a loss the god in disguise.

You unknown god! I feel your wing
close in this tavern, and it is
at the moment of its opening!
—rose and cried out the god in disguise.

And he arose and cried out.

for Richard Mayes

Chapter 23 ▪ ST. WAYWARD AND THE PONY

PONY RIDE
10¢
Desiderio D. Popolo, prop.
Must Bring Note from Mother.

The old Italian had rented the empty corner lot, bounded by the two burned-out buildings. (Our dilapidated neighborhood was falling down before ever it had been fully built up.) He had thrown a low bench around the open sides to make an enclosure for the track, and there was a booth where he presided and sold tickets, while the hired boy led the pony around.

Popolo was a square but rather sagging man, with a fine white mustache and a good-natured, worried and suspicious manner. He was an easy mark by birth and training. The pony was a young delight, pied black and white and with curly hair. When a child mounted him, he liked to go smartly, with twinkling hooves. But the damned pony boy was sluggish and spiteful, a stripling gangster named Slahv, and he held the animal almost to a walk, so he wouldn't have to exert himself.

At the peak of the afternoon, as many as a dozen kids were lined up at the booth clutching their dimes and their permissions. Half a dozen mamas were on the benches. If mama was there, you didn't, of course, need a note. The purpose of the note was to protect the old man from lawsuits; such a note had no legal value, but he believed that he was covered if he had something in writing, and the parents believed the same. Also, the need and often the difficulty of getting such a document or having to forge one, made the ride more desirable.

Wayward had a dime but he didn't have a paper. Yet he was not the least bit anxious. He was confident that he too would be allowed to ride when his turn came; he was used to being illegitimate. With eager eyes he watched as one little boy after another climbed on, and he cried out with pleasure when the pony, given a slap on the rump by the boss, started smartly off, curly hair flying in the wind and his little hooves twinkling like the suns reflected in the river. But he was disappointed when the ugly pony boy slowed the pace.

The pony boy pretended that he was lame and his leg hurt, and that therefore he didn't run the track. But this was an alibi; he wasn't lame at all but simply lazy and malevolent.

It was a pathetic scene: such a poor little lot in such a broken-down world; such a beat old proprietor and such a tiny steed to carry our longing to course like Indians in the wind, and because of the malevolent pony boy, even this not up to its capabilities. And yet, because of the old man's good nature and the friskiness of the pony, it was a gay scene nevertheless. He had painted the booth lemon-yellow and the benches maroon, and he flew an American flag. The sunlight beat down no otherwise than on the grand prairies. The kids had wild dreams and talked like cowboys.

Wayward was interested only in the pony. He did not care for being such and such a famous cowboy; he wanted to ride. His turn was next and his eyes were bright.

"Where is your credentials, young man?" said the old man.

Wayward opened his fist and put his dime on the counter.

"Where is your paper?"

"Paper? Is we supposed to have a paper?" he asked with innocent eyes.

"Look at the sign. *Must bring note from mother.*"

"I can't read," said Wayward.

"No note, no ride. Go home and get a note."

"I can't go home. I live too far an' my muvver's in the hospital." He speculated whether or not this was the time to burst into tears, but he decided just to let the tears fill his eyes.

"Does your mother know you're going to take a ride?"

"Yes, she give me the dime just before they took her to the hospital."

"All right this time. But next time remember you must absotively have a note——"

"Yes *sir!*" cried Wayward gladly, and pushed forward.

"Don't let that one ride!" It was suddenly the ugly Slahv. "He don't have a note."

The old man looked at him surprised. "I know that," he said.

"I'm tellin' you! Don't let 'im ride! You'll be sorry. He's illegitimate."

"Do you know him?"

"In course I know 'im!" cried Slahv with vehemence. "That li'l stinker! Yeah, I seen 'im around, an' he oughta get lost."

Now the old man disliked Slahv intensely; and why he kept him on he often asked himself. "Go head, sonny, climb on the horse," he said to Wayward.

"Don't you do it!" screamed Slahv, beside himself, and he

snatched the bridle from the old man's hand. "I tell yuh you'll be sorry if y' give a ride to that stinker!"

With an angry hand the old man slapped him across the face. "Let go," he said with dignity. "That's enough talk. Climb up, sonny."

Wayward got on. He paid no attention to Slahv; he was interested only in the pony. He bent forward and kissed the lovely little horse on the forehead. The pony made a sound and bounded with delight. Wayward held his place. As if summoned from the void, new vitality streamed between Wayward and his pony.

Slahv could not contain his disgust. "I told yuh," he said. "He's got tricks."

"You want again?" said the old man, raising his hand. "Giddyap!" he said.

The pony started briskly off. Yes, and with a more joyous trot than usual, for he was carrying St. Wayward. And that was a blazing sight. But when they came to the turning, Slahv grabbed at the bridle more brutally than usual.

But with his heels, Wayward kicked him hard in the teeth and the clumsy boy fell on his behind.

Wayward was holding the bridle himself. He gave the horse a slap on the rump and, turning directly toward the benches, he cried out, "Here we go!" In a happy parabola the pony neatly cleared the barrier and to spare—over the astonished mamas; and off they cantered down the street and broke into a gallop.

Oh, in a neat and happy parabola they cleared the barrier, hooves clicking and striking sparks from the cobblestones. Now everybody cried out. The children were wild with mirth and envy. The women were alarmed. Desiderio was simply astonished.

"O.K.," said Slahv sardonically, "you give 'im a ride on the horse, an' he runs away wid the horse."

One could still see that decisive parabola shining in the empty air.

Chapter 24 ▪ OUR VILLAGE MEETING

1.

Such were some scenes of our village, as we lived on through modern times.

Finally once again we decided to hold our meeting, to clear up some unfinished business and to move tentatively toward the next step.

A parliamentary meeting just like the olden times! For long ago we used to believe that it was possible, by confronting our reasons, to come to a common reason better than any. We believed that: if each person, concerned and therefore somewhat informed, manly or womanly asserted his own evidence and hope, and yet with a beseeching inquiry of the others (for each knew how little his own reason was worth), then together their mankind would think up something new.

So we had used to believe! But nowadays! if you dared to speak out *your* best reason in a clear voice, other people reacted as though they had never heard of such behavior. "Please," they said, "you're offensive. You say thus and so; you mean, in your *opinion* thus and so. You have no manners." You stared at them blankly. You, who knew only too well what your best reason was worth, had been looking hungrily in their throats for the voice of the creator spirit, and they told you that you had no manners.

2.

But we had gathered as of old. And the unfinished business was the following hard problem:

The irresistible force has met the immovable obstacle: what to do?

Our chairman was Mynheer, whom, since he had come from abroad with the uncarved block, we persisted in regarding as a sage, and naturally a chairman.

"Look," he said patiently, "I am fifty years old. A sage must be at least eighty years old."

"How do you figure that?" we asked.

"Because unless a man has *actually* contrived to survive, how the devil can you be sure that he knows the right method? A man doesn't survive by general theories, you know, but by art, by an extremely delicate adjustment to an immense number of details."

"There you go," we said; "you're only proving that you're a sage. You sly one! Sage! Sage!"

No matter what he said, we were obstinate. His being a sage was greatly to our advantage and really only moderately to his disadvantage, for we were not demanding.

Our chairman outlined the existential possibilities of the problem. They were fourfold. We could feel ourselves as the immovable obstacle: for instance, our conservative nature taking a stand in the world against the increasing encroachment on nature, that also would not let up. Or contrariwise, we could identify with the irresistible force: our creative force finally up against it, as usual. Or we could regard both sides of the conflict with a certain nonattachment. Or contrariwise, we could identify fully with both sides and have the conflict within, and see where that gets you.

Mynheer was always a fine chairman; he let you have the worst at the beginning.

3.

I felt I had something to contribute and I got up to speak.

To my amazement I was met by a round of unanimous applause, instead of the scattering that I had hitherto always encountered. *What* had occurred? *Wherein* lay the difference? What had *I* done? I began to blush and tremble.

Naturally I could not get a word out.

The moments ticked by.

The chairman came to my rescue. "An irresistible force has met an immovable obstacle: what to do? You are down on the agenda as having an idea on the topic."

"Yes," I said in my low voice, but I still could not go on.

"Maybe you've changed your mind and want to think it over. That's fine too; that's what we're here for."

"No, no, I know the answer!" I blurted out. My voice broke. I clutched at my notes. "The answer; the answer! The answer is to have yet another ounce of strength. *That* will solve the problem. I learned it from Ludwig Beethoven. In spite of everything he carries it off, because he has yet another ounce of strength."

Again my voice failed and I hastily sat down, but having said my say.

But again there was that round of terrifying applause, and I had to face it in holy fright.

My heart was bursting in my ribs. But the danger was past, I had acquitted myself.

As soon as the danger was past, of course, I understood what it was that had occurred and wherein lay the difference in my relation to my audience. Despite their reasonable disbelief, they had come to realize that I did have still another ounce of strength, and so they unanimously rallied to me, for people care for that.

And *therefore,* I saw, my cursed victory (of integrity) that nobody wants to win by such strenuous means and die, was now proving unnecessary. It was not such a hard matter after all to be accepted for oneself. The clench of twenty, of thirty years was loosing in my breast.

Sweat broke out on my brow and I began to buzz.

4.

The next speaker called on was Emilia.

I was puzzled by her appearance; she seemed so slight—she was not in good health—she who used to loom so large. Since Lothair's death she had been living in a kind of retirement. She hardly seemed the same person.

"I'm *so* glad," she began like a bright clubwoman and turning to me, "that you spoke first and showed that the problem was soluble. For, frankly, I have been feeling so sorry for you all, stuck in a fix and no way out. But at least there's your way out, so it's not so bad after all. Heavens! You men, with your irresistible forces and your immovable objects. So strenuous." And she gave a little, rather toothless, grin.

I snapped my fingers. It was the daughter of Eliphaz! I had quite forgotten it. As she got on toward her sixties, Emily had suddenly become a little Jewish old lady, very sharp and experienced, generous and no nonsense about her. And setting it all on fire, the old man's infectious grin. I could not help myself, I burst out laughing, and she grinned all the harder.

She became sober. "Seriously, I have watched you with this problem. *You* are needful, and your wife is sullen; *you* have the true policy, and people are stupid-stubborn. *Ts, ts.* He has a button off his coat and six weeks since he mentioned it to her, she *still* doesn't do anything about it. Every morning he burns up, she glowers. She's forgotten about it and he's damned if he's going to tell her again. . . . *Harry! Harry! Why don't you sew the button on yourself?*"

She lapsed into a Yiddish accent and we roared. Obviously she was solving our problem.

"You will pardon me if I mention the old man my father, may he rest in peace. Do you know what he would have said about this problem of yours? He would have called it *Goyim Nachus,* the gentile idea of a good time. *Goyim Nachus* is such a waste. And then, *ts, ts,* what to do? what to do? what to do? what to do? Go about your business, that's what to do."

Abruptly she sat down.

"I beg *your* pardon, dear," said Mynheer. "Let us be quite clear. May I word your suggestion as follows: disregard the problem, bypass it, and go about your business?"

"Not at all," said Emily sharply and got up again. "Please not to put words in my mouth, I'm quite articulate myself. I said, 'Go about *your* business.' *If* it's your business, to have this problem, because of the way you are, then you can't disregard it; how can you disregard such a problem? Maybe you ought to have your head examined, and *that's* your business. But if it's *not* your business—and it's soitantly not *my* business—then how can you *not* disregard it? Do I make myself clear? No. Look. My boy Wayward, he's got a pony. So he's riding along and he comes to an obstacle. What does he do? He goes right over the obstacle. Hop! That's *his* business. Do you see? Go about your business. I mean, Go about your *business.* For God's sake, *go* about your business. Do you see? They don't see. Like talking to a wall. I may as well sit down."

She sighed, and grinned, and sat down.

"No, but we do see," said Mynheer gently.

5.

The last speaker was Horatio.

"God forbid," he said, "that I should explain what my sister-in-law has been saying in any but her own words. But what she says makes sense as applied to myself. I'm one of those characters to whom this problem *is* a problem. Now, *when* it is, I find that it is always some concrete particular problem or other; and once I consider it this way, the solution, what to do, is always simple. It may be simple and easy, it may be simple and hard. The solution is, Get a handyman."

He sat down.

"I understand you," said Mynheer, "but will you go into that a little further?"

"Sure." He stood up. "Consider it this way. The irresistible and the immovable are your opposing forces, and there comes to be a rigidity and paralysis in the whole field. Do something about the rigidity and paralysis in the field. Get a handyman.

"In the whole field—it's always some particular problem for you or me. Your damned car breaks down in the thick of traffic; the refrigerator won't work. At once, with a moment's awareness, you can recognize the creeping paralysis that spreads from the irresistible and the immovable. The way we live, my friends, is not fitten for man or beast. What to do? Get a handyman. Or this fellow's prick won't stand up, or that fellow's prick is hard as a rock and can't come off. Obviously underlying there is a terrible clench. But get a handyman! Consider it. The frame of the universe is what it is—it fixes the bounds of the permitted—*why* should a person get out of bed in the morning? For what? Yet after all, it's some detail that can be remedied by a good handyman. Hm. But where can you find a good handyman?" He stopped. "May I make a community proposal that is perhaps somewhat off the point?" he asked.

"Of course," said the chairman. "According to the rules, a community proposal is always in order."

"It seems to me," said Horatio, "that what our community is lacking is a good handyman. It would make everything go much smoother, much smoother. We don't attend to this. How many are we? Fifty, sixty? Surely we are enough to support and give occupation to a good handyman."

6.

There were no other speakers; we were satisfied; and Mynheer rose to summarize the discussion.

"We have been offered three solutions to the problem what to do when an irresistible force has met an immovable object. They are not incompatible, I suspect they are not even alternatives, but are the sequences of a single action. Have another ounce of strength, go about your business and get a handyman. Have another ounce of strength just to survive the paralyzing shock. Go about your business to find out what your business is. Be handy with some definite detail. I think the problem is solved."

He tore up the agenda and threw the pieces in the waste basket. Such history as there is of our friends is what is contained in this book.

"And now is there anything new?" he said, and got down from the chair. For this part of our meeting, we felt, there was no sense in having a chairman.

7.

There was an absurdly portentous silence. Was there anything new?

That's a portentous question at a meeting, for it means, Are you going to initiate something? It means, What are you going to do with *yourselves?*

Apparently our time was hanging heavy.

Yet it was a portentous and not a threatening silence like that in the dead of spring, for it no longer seemed to us that our situation was necessarily disastrous. (We could no longer rest serene in that conviction.) Then at once we were aware that the time was hanging heavy, and the question arose, Well! what were we going to do with ourselves?

8.

Naturally it was Wayward who spoke up and broke the silence, for it had never occurred to him that a situation might be necessarily disastrous, and therefore he found it easy to fantasize directly into the reality, as befit a living creature. (He was never much given to "thinking.") "If by new business you mean what am I going to do with myself," said Wayward, "I can tell you *that*. I'm going to rescue the Irish. Here, look at this." And he whipped out of his pocket a graph from *Newsweek*. "You see? Ireland is losing her population; by 1990 there ain't going to be any more Irishmen. That's what *they* say. But I'm going to get me a flying horse and go to Ireland, and set free the Laddy of Lough Neagh, he's at the bottom of the lake waiting for me, and then he's going to repopulate Ireland. That's a good plan, ain't it?"

That was a *very* good plan! we concurred enthusiastically. After such a beginning we could breathe again. The time was no longer hanging heavy at all, but just bubbling along, as it should.

9.

"I pass," said Rosalind; "I'm going to read Proust." This meant that she was pregnant again and was going into that phase, along in the fifth month, when everything seems well able to take care of itself. This is the opportunity really to get into *Clarissa* and Proust. Proust was a good plan, we agreed.

"I just pass, period," said Emily. That was always a fine plan. "Mynheer?"

"Is it my turn?" asked Mynheer absent-mindedly. "Why yes, I do have a plan. In fact, I've been working at it during the meeting. I've had a serious conversation with my Only World, and the upshot is that soon I'm going to leave here and go hunting the Horned Dilemma. And when I've killed him, I'm going to return and be married." – So he said; but as he said it, I turned pale and I wanted to stretch out my hand and cry, No! no! for in that fight, it would be Mynheer who was going to be killed. But who was I to teach *him* what to do? Maybe in the end he would be right and I, I hoped, wrong.

"Oh, business as usual! You know me," said Minetta. "I'm in the middle of a two-pronged campaign. First, we've got to get hold of the so-called physical training and play periods in the public schools, especially in the first grades, and transform them according to the principles of character analysis and eurythmics. The techniques are well known and even in use in various places; the only thing that stands in the way of their acceptance generally is the anxiety roused in the teachers. You know, I rather *relish* that," said Minetta thoughtfully. "Second, I am pushing a little alteration in our method of vocational guidance, especially for those eighteen-year-olds who break my heart by hanging around the street-corners without any ambition. We have to find the *vocation,* the calling. Put Jonathan Edwards in the employment bureau; that will stir things up."

Suddenly it seemed to be my turn. "Yes, I have a plan!" I said. "To get rid of the language of business correspondence like 'We are in receipt of your valued order of the 15th inst.' For years my sister Alice worked for a little man named Rosenthal who used to end every letter with the formula, 'Thanking you in advance for past favors, I remain—' Try and break a habit like that!"

"I guess I ought to pass," said Droyt; "for I seem to be wandering an endless way from which I cannot leave off. Yet when I go through the small towns of the South and the Middle West, I am dismayed at the world I wander. The gas pumps, the Woolworths, the diner: you would not conceive that places could be absolutely uniform and yet not have a shape. And then I think of my mother and what would she have thought about it, and I am resolved. To improve the looks of my country."

Such were the practical ideas, according to each one's character and circumstances, that leaped to mind at our meeting; that would take some of us afar and keep some of us at home, and lead another of us to awful death.

We approve ourselves; we are not disapproved.

Horatio? For he was next, and we were looking to him.

10

But Horatio was flushing darkly. He was burning with shame. (And what was, then, *our* grief and shame!)

There was an appalling moment that we were looking at him. "Yes, look at me, look at me," he said. "Look at the coward."

"Coward?"

We looked away. But that was worse than anything.

"You others know or pass," he said. "But I don't know. This is because I am a coward. If I weren't a coward I'd know what I am going to do with myself."

It did not seem to us that he was a coward. But we recognized his mood all the same, the abasement that he felt when he went to the Party for the Dog.

"A coward, is it?" said Minetta. "You would not feel you were a coward, Horatio Alger, if you were not spoiling for a fight."

Chapter 25 ▪ SPOILING FOR A FIGHT

1.

Since his moment of shame at the meeting, Horatio is in a turmoil. Walking about the room and from room to room with a quick caged stride, and muttering, "Bitches! And sons of bitches! Too matter-of-fact, is it?"

By "bitches" and "sons of bitches" he means to include the two sexes, people, globally. "Too matter-of-fact" refers to a criticism that someone made that the attitude of our friends is too matter-of-fact, it does not take into account the Important Values. "Bitches and sons of bitches—too matter-of-fact—" these are very apt sounds for angry muttering. He keeps darting hot looks at the city across the river.

"Too matter-of-fact, is it?" he mutters scornfully. "Well, we'll see whether a matter of fact is so matter-of-fact. And *that's* a matter of fact! Sons of bitches. I'll cram matter-of-fact right down their throats." He considers this silently. "No, I'll let it lie there and stick their noses in it like untrained dogs. Smell *that* matter of fact. Is it so matter-of-fact? Naturally it explodes in your face like an April fool cigar. What! Do you expect it will lie there? . . . Dear God, my eyes are still burning from when I once tried to look at a matter of fact; when they even told me about it, I didn't believe my ears. You sons of bitches, I know you! You shiver in your britches when you begin to get *near* a matter of fact, and if it brushes you close, you're white. But now you say, 'It's only a matter of fact; it's too matter-of-fact.' I'll *give* you a matter of fact."

So, pacing and muttering, and cursing generalities like a drunkard who has it in for the system, Horatio keeps avoiding any possible matter of fact.

Pretty soon, though, he realizes that this is what he is doing, and slowly, against his own resistance, he drags himself back to look at the fact: the fact that he is spoiling for a fight and doesn't know what fight and doesn't know how to get into it. He has a strong resistance to recognizing this fact, for with it comes again the abysmal feeling of being ashamed and a coward.

He is so pissed-off he doesn't know whether to laugh or to cry, so he chooses for a change the alternative of laughing.

"Rosalind," he says quietly to his woman, "I want you people to lie low and keep out of the way. There's going to be a fight and some heads are going to be broken."

"A fight? What fight? I haven't heard about any fight?"

"That's just it," says he. "I'm a coward, so I haven't thought it up yet."

2.

Methodically, then, Horatio calms himself down, and sits down, and begins to collect the grounds and motives of Spoiling for a Fight. These are Hurts and Insults suffered, and the Vengeance that one swears to take.

The insult of seeing the better reason brushed aside. The hurt of trying hard for what's not worth much. The insult of giving his best attention and not being regarded. The insult of seeking the common joy and being regarded as an enemy. The hurt of being uselessly proved to have been right. The hurt that is done to children when they cannot yet fight back. The vengeance he swore by the river, clenching his not yet full-grown fists.

The hurt of having to take the world as it is just in order to have some world or other, and there is no other. The hurt of exerting less than his best powers. The hurt of waiting, when they do not come across. The insult to the knight in disguise when the servile is inordinately praised. The insult of talking to a wall. The vengeance out of spite, just to live on awhile. The vengeance exacted when he no longer needs it, just in order to cleanse his heart and bawl.

The hurt of being useful because he could, when he did not care. The hurt of having to use fraud and force for what could be done by candor and affection. The insult when the everyday is taken for the exceptional; when a matter of fact is first said not to exist, and is then said to be too matter-of-fact. The insult that a man learns to level against his own best powers, doubting his own motives and taking his truth for a bluff. The vengeance that is the stirring of reviving hope. The vengeance that bridges an abyss.

Such are the Hurts and Insults, and the kinds of Vengeance, that are festering in Horatio's soul. They are enough, they are good enough grounds and motives for spoiling for a fight. Yet something is wrong. He does not flame with anger.

It is not that there is no worthy opponent. Surely the one that can inflict such terrible hurts and insults is a powerful giant, worthy to be destroyed. But Horatio does not know how to close with him, to confront him. He looks around, he clenches and unclenches his fists, and indeed, as he feels his impotence, at once he feels the cowardice crawling up his back and pinching his chest. He cannot throw it off.

He realizes that before he comes to close with this giant and fight, he is going to have some shaking experiences of craven fear.

3.

> Saul clad David with his apparel and he put a helmet of brass upon his head, and he clad him with a coat of mail. And David girded his sword upon his apparel and he essayed to go, but he could not; for he had not tried it. And David put them off him.
>
> —I Samuel xvii, 38-39

Somewhere there is the enemy. What strength and weapons will he have to meet him with?

Horatio tickets them off on his fingers, the weapons that we have that do not weigh one down. First there is the simple sling and shot that hits the booby on the brow. Second, there is the eloquent trumpet that makes the walls fall down. And third, the arrows of desire.

Also, there is the force that is in the heart of the matter, that, as if stubbornly, makes things exist rather than be mere dreams or wishes. For whatever a thing happens to be, there it is, as we say, "You can twist it and turn it but there it is." That's a strong force. It is usually not a violent force, for it urges the smallest possible increment of change, whose lightning-like summation has brought about a change.

So he has these four weapons, the simple sling and shot, the eloquent trumpet, the arrows of desire and the force that is in the existence. Also he knows how to use the mirror of Perseus by which we are not turned to stone by the Gorgon. And he has learned the art to stand out of the way.

On his lips he has also a prayer, the prayer *Father! guide*—

> Father, guide and lead me stray
> for I stumble forward straight my way
>   undeviating, I do not
>   notice the pleasant bypaths that
>
> make us this world surprising, nor
> the precipice that sinks before.
>   O give me ground for next a step
>   to stagger walking in my sleep.

About the Author

PAUL GOODMAN was born in New York City in 1911, and died in 1972. After graduating from City College in New York, he received his Ph.D. in humanities from the University of Chicago. He taught at the University of Chicago, New York University, Black Mountain College, Sarah Lawrence, the University of Wisconsin, San Francisco State, and the University of Hawaii, and lectured at various universities throughout the country.

Many of his articles appeared in *Commentary, Kenyon Review, Resistance, Liberation,* and *The New York Review of Books.* Vintage Books has reprinted his *Collected Poems* as well as a number of his well-known works of social criticism, among them, *Growing Up Absurd, Utopian Essays and Practical Proposals,* and *Compulsory Mis-education & The Community of Scholars.*